ROSS MACDONALD

ROSS MACDONALD

FOUR NOVELS OF THE 1950s

The Way Some People Die
The Barbarous Coast
The Doomsters
The Galton Case

Tom Nolan, *editor*

THE LIBRARY OF AMERICA

Contents

THE WAY SOME PEOPLE DIE

To Roddy and Zella

Chapter 1

THE HOUSE was in Santa Monica on a cross street between the boulevards, within earshot of the coast highway and rifleshot of the sea. The street was the kind that people had once been proud to live on, but in the last few years it had lost its claim to pride. The houses had too many stories, too few windows, not enough paint. Their history was easy to guess: they were one-family residences broken up into apartments and light-housekeeping rooms, or converted into tourist homes. Even the palms that lined the street looked as if they had seen their best days and were starting to lose their hair.

I parked in front of the number I had been given and leaned sideways in the seat to have a look at the house. The numerals, 1348, were made of rusted metal and tacked diagonally across one of the round porch pillars. A showcard above, printed black on white, offered ROOMS FOR TOURISTS. There were several rattan chairs and a faded green glider on the porch, which covered the width of the house. A second-story porch, with more rattan, was surrounded by a wooden railing that looked unsafe. The third story had Gothic-looking towers at each corner, fake battlements that time had taken and made ridiculous. The roller blinds were low over the windows on all three levels, so they stared at me sleepy-eyed.

The house didn't look as if it had money in it, or ever would have again. I went in anyway, because I'd liked the woman's voice on the telephone.

She came to the door in a hurry when I knocked. A tall woman in her fifties with worried vague dark eyes in a worried long face, a black crepe dress over a thick corseted body. A detective was an occasion in her life. Her iron-gray hair was set in a sharp new wave that smelt of the curling-iron, her nose and cheeks and chin were stark with powder. The light fell through the purple glass in the fanlight over the door and made her complexion livid.

The woman's voice was her best feature, gentle and carefully modulated, in a low register: "I'm Mrs. Samuel Lawrence. You're Mr. Archer, of course? You got here in no time at all."

"The traffic's not so bad between nine and ten."

"Come in, Mr. Archer. Let me make you a cup of tea. I'm just having a midmorning snack myself. Since I've been doing all my own work, I find I need a bite between meals to sustain me."

I stepped inside, and the screen door swung to languidly behind me. The hall was still and cool and smelt of wax. The floor was old parquetry, and its polished patterns glowed like jewels. A carpeted stairway climbed to the high dim ceiling. An ancient oak hatstand with polished brass hangers stood at the foot of the stairs. The contrast with the traffic I'd been fighting gave me a queer feeling, as if I'd stepped backward in time, or out of it entirely.

She led me to an open door at the rear. "This is my own little sitting-room, if you please. I reserve the front parlor for guests, though I must say they haven't been using it lately. Of course it's the off-season, I only have the three just now, my regular, and a lovely young couple from Oregon, honeymooners! If only Galley had married a man like that—but sit down, Mr. Archer."

She pulled out a chair from the heavy refectory table in the middle of the room. It was a small room, and it was as crowded with coffee- and end-tables, chairs and hassocks and bookcases, as a second-hand furniture store. The horizontal surfaces were littered with gewgaws, shells and framed photographs, vases and pincushions and doilies. If the lady had come down in the world, she'd brought a lot down with her. My sensation of stepping into the past was getting too strong for comfort. The half-armed chair closed on me like a hand.

I took the present by the tail and dragged it into the room: "Galley," I said. "Is she the daughter you mentioned?"

The question struck her like an accusation, disorganizing her charm. She didn't like the look of the present at all. She faced it when she had to, with a face clouded by bewilderment and shame. "Yes. My daughter Galatea. It's why I phoned you, as I said." Her gaze wandered, and lighted on the teapot that stood on the table. "You must let me pour you some tea before we get down to business. It's freshly made."

Her hand on the teapot was cracked and grained by dirty work, but she poured with an air. I said I took mine straight. The tea tasted like a clear dark dripping from the past. My grandmother came back with it, in crisp black funeral silks, and I looked out of the window to dispel her. I could see the Santa Monica pier from where I sat, and beyond it the sea and the sky like the two curved halves of a blue Easter egg.

"Nice view you have from here."

She smiled over her teacup. "Yes. I bought it for the view. I shouldn't really say I've bought it. It's mortgaged, after all."

I finished my tea and set the thin white cup in the thin white saucer. "Well, Mrs. Lawrence, let's have it. What happened to your daughter?"

"I don't know," she said. "That's what upsets me so. She simply disappeared a couple of months ago—"

"From here?"

"No, not from here. Galley hasn't lived at home in recent years, though she always came to visit me at least once a month. She was working in Pacific Point, a special-duty nurse in the hospital there. I always hoped for something better for Galley—my husband Dr. Lawrence was a medical man, and a very well respected one, too—but she wanted to be a nurse and she seemed to be very happy in the work—"

She was veering away from the present fact again. "When did she disappear?"

"Last December, a few days before Christmas." This was the middle of March, which made it about three months. "Galley *always* came home for Christmas. We never failed to decorate a tree. Last Christmas for the first time I spent Christmas by myself. Even her card came a day late." And the vague eyes swam with self-pity.

"If you've heard from her, I wouldn't call it a disappearance. Can I have a look at the card?"

"Of course." She took a black leather volume of Swedenborg out of the bookcase, opened it, and drew out a large square envelope which she handed to me as if it contained a check. "But she *has* disappeared, Mr. Archer. I haven't seen her since early in December. None of her friends has seen her since the first of the year."

"How old is she?"

"Twenty-four. She'll be twenty-five next month, April the 9th, if she's alive." She bowed her face in her hands, having brought herself to tears.

"She'll probably have many happy returns," I said. "A twenty-five-year-old registered nurse can look after herself."

"You don't know Galley," the damp voice said from the hidden face. "She's always been so fascinating to men, and she's never realized how evil men can be. I've tried to unknow the error, but it does no good. I keep thinking of the Black Dahlia, all the young girls that have been stolen away and destroyed by evil men." The wide gold wedding band on the hand over her face gleamed dully like a despairing hope.

I took out the card, which was large and expensive, decorated with a sparkling mica snow scene. Inside it said:

TO MOTHER ON CHRISTMAS DAY

Though my boat has left the harbor
In the sea of life so wide,
I think with cheer of Mother Dear
Each joyous Christmastide.

It was subscribed in green ink by a bold and passionate hand: "Much love, Galley." The envelope had been mailed in San Francisco on December 24.

"Did—does your daughter have friends in San Francisco?"

"Not that I know of." The woman showed me her face, with tear-tracks in the powder. She blew her nose discreetly in a piece of pink Kleenex. "The last few years, since she graduated, I didn't really know her friends."

"Do you think she's in San Francisco?"

"I don't know. She came back from there, you see. She didn't come to me, but the man who runs the apartments down there, a Mr. Raisch, saw her. She had a small furnished apartment in Pacific Point, and about the end of December she turned up there and moved out, took away all her things. There was a man with her."

"What sort of a man?"

"Mr. Raisch didn't say. There seemed to be some kind of secret about the man—something sinister."

"Is that a fact, or only your impression?"

"My impression. I suppose I've been too open to impression, lately. I can't tell you what my life has been these last few weeks. I've gone down to Pacific Point on the bus half a dozen times, whenever I could get away. I've talked to the nurses that knew her at the hospital. She hasn't been near the hospital since before Christmas, when she finished her last case. It was a man named Speed who had been shot in the stomach. The police came to question him, and he nearly died. The people at the hospital seemed to think that this Speed person was a gangster. That's one of the things that frightens me. I've hardly slept a wink for weeks and weeks." There were deep bluish hollows under her eyes, pitiable and ugly in the morning light from the window.

"Actually, though," I said, "you've got nothing concrete to be afraid about."

"My only daughter is gone—"

"Girls leave home all the time. It tears the hearts out of their mothers, but they don't know it. They don't find out till their own kids grow up and do it to them. She probably ran off and married this man that was with her at the apartment."

"That's what Mr. Raisch thought. Still Galley wouldn't marry without letting me know. Besides, I've checked the registrations in Pacific Point, and Los Angeles as well, and there is no record of a marriage."

"That doesn't prove a thing. You can fly to New York or Hawaii in a day." I took a cigarette from a pack in my pocket and automatically asked her: "Mind if I smoke?"

Her face froze, as if I had suggested an obscenity. "Smoke if you must, sir. I know what a hold the nicotine habit has on its victims. Dr. Lawrence was a smoker for years, until he finally broke free, with God's help."

I replaced the cigarette in my pocket and stood up to leave. Even with a million dollars, she wouldn't have been the kind of woman I wanted to work for. And she probably didn't have two nickels to rub against each other. As for the daughter, ten to one she'd simply decided to have a life of her own.

I put it less bluntly to her: "I think you should take it to Missing Persons, Mrs. Lawrence. I don't think you have anything to worry about, but if you have, they can do more for you than I can. It would be a waste of money to hire me. I charge fifty a day and expenses. The police do everything free."

Her answer surprised me: "I expected to pay you well. And I am not going to go to the police."

"Why not? Missing daughters are their specialty. They've got a national system set up to find them."

Grim bony lines came out in her face, and her eyes weren't vague any more. "If Galley is living in sin with some man, it's nobody's business but my own."

"Aren't you jumping to conclusions?"

"I tell you you don't know Galley. Men have been after her since high school, like flies to honey. She's a good girl, Mr. Archer, I know how good. But I was a handsome girl myself when I was young, and I've seen the pitfalls of the flesh. I want to know what has happened to my daughter."

I stood by the table and lit my cigarette and dropped the match on the tea tray. She didn't say a word. After a stretching moment of silence, she reached from her chair and took a framed photograph from the top of the bookcase. "Look at her, you'll understand what I mean."

I took the picture from her hand. There was something slightly shady about the transaction, a faint implication that she was offering her daughter's beauty as part payment on my services. Or maybe I was having impressions. I had one when I looked at the girl's face. It was passionate and bold like her handwriting. Even in a white nurse's cap and a high chaste collar she was a girl you saw once and never forgot.

"It was her graduation picture, taken three years ago, but she still looks exactly the same. Isn't she pretty?"

Pretty was hardly the word. With her fierce curled lips, black eyes and clean angry bones she must have stood out in her graduating class like a chicken hawk in a flock of pullets.

"If you want to spend fifty dollars," I said, "I'll go down to Pacific Point today and see what I can find out. Write down her last address and the name of whoever you talked to at the hospital."

With the caution of a pheasant hen returning to her nest, she went to an old-fashioned sewing machine by the window, lifted the closed top and removed a worn black purse from its hiding place. Opening the tarnished clasp, she rummaged in the purse and counted five reluctant tens onto the table.

Dropping my ashes in my empty teacup, I noticed the arrangement of the leaves. My grandmother would have said it meant money and a dark stranger. The stranger could have been male or female, vertical or horizontal, depending on how you looked at the bottom of the cup.

Chapter 2

I DROVE south through Long Beach to Pacific Point. Crossing the mesa that flanked it to the northwest, you could see the town spread out, from the natural harbor half-enclosed by the curving finger of land that gave the place its name, to the houses on the ridge above the fogline. It rose from sea level in a gentle slope, divided neatly into social tiers, like something a sociologist had built to prove a theory. Tourists and transients lived in hotels and motels along the waterfront. Behind them a belt of slums lay ten blocks deep, where the darker half of the population lived and died. On the other side of the tracks—the tracks were there—the business section wore its old Spanish façades like icing on a stale cake. The people who worked in the stores and offices inhabited the grid of fifty-foot lots that covered the next ten blocks. On the slopes above them the owners and managers enjoyed their patios and barbecue pits. And along the top of the ridge lived the really wealthy, who had bought their *pieds-à-terre* in Pacific Point because it reminded them of Juan-les-Pins.

The wife of a client of mine had taken an overdose of sleeping pills in a Pacific Point hotel, so I knew where the hospital was. I made a left turn off the highway and drove through empty afternoon streets to the hospital building. It was a rambling place of bilious yellow plaster, and the sight of it depressed me. My client's wife had died of the sleeping pills. All that he really wanted was a divorce.

After a good deal of palaver I found myself in the basement waiting-room of the hospital's X-ray department, talking to a plump young thing in white nylon. Her arms and shoulders glowed a pleasant pink through this progressive fabric, and her straw-blond hair was cut sleek and short. Her name was Audrey Graham, and she didn't mind talking at all. I told her the truth—that I was a detective looking for Galley Lawrence because her mother was worried—which was a refreshing change from my usual approach.

"I never did know Galley really well," she said. "Sure, we were in the same class at Los Angeles General and graduated together and all. But you know how some girls are, introverted like. I'm more of an extrovert myself. I like meeting people, in a nice way, you know what I mean. Are you really a detective? I never met a *private* detective before."

"Yeah," I said. "The introverted kind. Mrs. Lawrence said you were Galley's roommate."

"Just for a while, last year. She got a chance at this apartment and I went in on the rent, but after a couple of months I found a place of my own. We agreed to disagree, you know what I mean."

"Not exactly."

She perched on the edge of the receptionist's desk and swung one round silk leg. "Well, I mean we got along all right but we didn't live the same. She ran around a lot and came in all hours of the day and night and it wasn't so happy-making, me with a regular job, I mean, and a steady boy friend. When Galley was on a case she was spit-and-polish but in between she liked to break loose a bit, and she was crazy for men—I've never been myself. I mean, a girl has a right to her own life and she can do what she pleases as far as I'm concerned, only she shouldn't try to attract a boy that's going with somebody else."

She colored slowly, aware that she'd given herself away. The round eyes in the rosy face were ice-blue, cold with memory. If Audrey Graham was Galley's best friend, Galley had no friends.

"Where did you live with her, and when?"

"August and September, I guess it was—I had my vacation in July. Galley found this little place in Acacia Court, one bedroom. It had twin beds, but that didn't work out either." She'd embarrassed herself again, and the flush rose higher, to the roots of the straw-colored hair.

"What kind of men did she run around with?"

"All kinds. She had no discrimination, you know what I mean." The refrain was getting on my nerves. "My boy friend is going to college under the G.I. and you'd think a girl who thinks she's something special because her father was a doctor, or so she claimed—you'd think she'd watch out who she went out with. Of course she had a couple of doctors on the string but that was married stuff and I never could see it myself. She had boys from the Safeway, a law clerk, a fellow that said he was a writer but *I* never heard of him, even one that looked like a Mexican once. Italian, anyway."

"Know any of their names?"

"I mostly knew them by their first names, when I knew them. I wouldn't want to tell you the doctors' names. If you want my honest opinion, Galley just got sick of this town and ran off with one of her men. Las Vegas or someplace. She was always talking about seeing the world. She set a high opinion on herself. She blew her money on clothes she couldn't afford and half the time she was eating off of me."

There were footsteps in the hall, and the girl slid off the desk. A tall man in a white tunic looked in at the door. His eyes were masked by wide red spectacles. "The pyelogram's on the table, Audrey, be ready in five minutes." He turned to me. "Are you the barium enema for tomorrow?" I told him that I wasn't, and he went away.

"You can be glad you're not," the girl said. "I'm afraid I have to go now."

"He said five minutes. What about this man Speed, the bullet in the stomach Galley nursed?"

"Oh, that was Herman Speed. He had peritonitis from lead poisoning or something, she didn't go out with him. He was on Ward C for three weeks last December, and then he left town. I heard he was run out of town. He promoted the wrestling down at the Arena and there was an editorial in the paper about how he was shot in a gang war or something. I wouldn't know. I didn't read it myself, one of the doctors told me."

"She didn't leave town with him?"

"No, she was still in town after he left. I saw her one night with this Mexican-looking guy, I forget his name. Turpentine or something. I think he worked for Speed. He came to see him a couple of times when he was on Ward C. Tarantula, or something?"

"That's a kind of spider."

"Yeah. Well, Galley was no fly. Anybody she went with, she had a darn good reason. I'll say one thing for her, she knew how to have a good time. But what she saw in this guy that worked for Speed—I wouldn't trust a Mexican or Italian, they have no respect for women."

I was getting a little tired of her opinions, and she was repeating herself. I got out of my chair and stood up. "Thanks very much, Miss Graham."

"Don't mention it. If you need any more information, I get off here at half past four."

"I may see you then. By the way, did you tell Mrs. Lawrence what you told me?"

"No, of course I didn't. I wouldn't ruin a girl's reputation with her own mother. I don't mean that Galley had a *really* bad reputation or I wouldn't of lived with her. But you know what I mean."

Chapter 3

A CACIA COURT was within easy walking distance of the hospital, on a quiet middle-class street across from a school-ground. It probably wasn't so quiet when school was out. The court consisted of ten small stucco bungalows ranged five on each side of a gravel driveway that led to the garages at the rear. The first bungalow had a wooden office sign over the door, with a cardboard NO VACANCY sign attached to it. There were two acacia trees in the front yard, blanketed with yellow chenille-like blossoms.

When I got out of my car a mockingbird swooped from one of the trees and dived for my head. I gave him a hard look and he flew up to a telephone wire and sat there swinging back and forth and laughing at me. The laughter actually came from a red-faced man in dungarees who was sitting in a deck-chair under the tree. His mirth brought on some sort of an attack, probably asthmatic. He coughed and choked and wheezed, and the chair creaked under his weight and his face got redder. When it was over he removed a dirty straw hat and wiped his bare red pate with a handkerchief.

"Excuse me. The little devil does it all the time. He's my aerial defense. I think it's your hair they want, to build a nest. He drives the nurses crazy."

I stepped in under the shade of the tree. "Are you Mr. Raisch?"

"That's my name. I told them they better wear hats but they never do. Back where I was brought up, in Little Egypt, a lady never went out without a hat, and some of these girls don't even own one. You wanted to see me? I got no vacancy." He jerked a large gray thumb at the sign over the door. "Anyway I just take mostly girls from the hospital and a few married couples."

I told him I wasn't a prospective tenant, but that was all I had a chance to tell him.

"I can afford to pick and choose," he said. "My place doesn't look like much from the outside, maybe, but she's in absolutely tiptop shape. Redecorated the whole thing with my own two hands last year, put in new linoleum, fixed up the plumbing. And I didn't raise the rents a red cent. No wonder they come to me. What did you want to see me about? I don't need a thing if you're selling."

"I'm looking for Galley Lawrence. Remember her?"

"I should say I do." His blue eyes had narrowed and were appraising me. "I'm not so old and dried up that I'd forget a pretty girl like that one. Even if she had a hump on her back and one glass eye I wouldn't disremember her. I don't get the chance; seems that every few days somebody comes around asking after Galley. What do you want with her?"

"I want to talk with her. What did the others want?"

"Well, her mother was here a couple of times. You'd think I was in the white-slave traffic the way that biddy talked to me, and all I did was rent her daughter a home. Then there was all her young men calling up—I practically had to have my phone disconnected back around the first of the year. You one of her young men?"

"No." But I was grateful for the adjective.

"Let's see, you're from L.A., ain't you?" The eyes were still appraising me. "You got an L.A. license on your car. These other customers were from L.A., the ones from the pinball company. You work for the pinball company?"

"Not me."

"You're carrying a gun. Or maybe you got a tumor under your armpit."

I told him I was a private detective, and why I was looking for Galley. "Do you carry a gun if you work for the pinball company?"

"These customers did, the thin one anyway. He let me know he had a gun, he thought he'd throw a scare into me. I didn't tell him I was handling firearms before his dam dropped him on the curb and kicked him into the gutter. He wanted to think he was smooth and sharp and I let him go on thinking it."

"You're fairly sharp yourself."

The flattery pleased him, and his big red face relaxed into smiles again. He felt the need to express himself some more. "I didn't get where I am by sitting on my rump waiting for the cash to grow on trees. No sir, I been in every one of the forty-eight states and I watered every one of them with my good sweat. I lost a fortune in Florida and that's the last time anybody put anything over on me."

I sat down tentatively in the canvas camp-chair beside his, and offered him a cigarette.

He waved it away. "Not for me. Asthma and heart condition. But you go right ahead. The old biddy must be really anxious, hiring detectives and all."

I was beginning to think she had reason to be anxious. "You said the pinball boys tried to scare you. Any particular reason?"

"They thought I might know where Galley Lawrence was. Her and this slob she went away with, some kind of a dago or wop. They said his name was Tarantine, and I told them it sounded like something you put on your hair. The lean one wanted to make something out of that, but the short one thought it was funny. He said this Tarantine was *in* his hair."

"Did he explain what he meant?"

"He didn't say very much. Seems that this Tarantine ran off with the collection money, something like that. They wanted to know if Galley left a forwarding address, but she didn't. I told them try the police and that was another laugh for the little short one. The lean one said they'd handle it themselves. That's when he showed me the gun, a little black automatic. I told them maybe *I* should try the police, and the short one made him put it away again."

"Who were they?"

"Pinball merchants, they said. They looked like thugs to me. They didn't leave their calling cards but I wouldn't forget them if I saw them again. The one with the automatic, the one that worked for the other one, he was as thin as a rake. When he turned sideways he cast no shadow. Front-ways he had his shoulders built out so his jacket hung on him like a scarecrow. He had a jail complexion, or a lunger's, and little pinhead eyes and he talked like he thought he was tough. Take his gun away and I could break him in two, even at my age. And I'm old enough to qualify for the pension, if I needed it."

"But you don't."

"No sir. I'm a product of individual enterprise. The other one, the boss, was really tough. He walked into my office like he owned it, only when he saw he couldn't push me around he tried to be friendly-like. I'd just as soon make friends with a scorpion. One of these poolroom cowboys that made his way in the rackets and was trying to dress like a gentleman. Panama hat, cream gabardine double-breasted suit, hand-painted tie, waxy yellow shoes, and he rode up here in a car as long as a fire truck. A black limousine, and I thought the undertaker was coming for me for sure."

"You expecting the undertaker?"

"Any day now, son." He started to laugh, and then decided against it. "But it'll take more than an L.A. thief with a inner-tube on his waistline to kiss me off, I can tell you. The little man was hard, though. He had his own shoulders and you could see on his face that he'd taken his share of beatings. He had a way of looking at you, soft and steady-like, that chilled you off some. And the way he talked about this Tarantine, the man was as good as dead."

"What about Galley Lawrence?"

He shrugged his heavy collapsing shoulders. "I don't know. I guess the idea was if they found her this Tarantine would be tagging along. I didn't even tell them I knew him by sight."

"You didn't tell Mrs. Lawrence either. Did you?"

"Sure I did. Twice. I didn't like the lady but she had a right to know. I told her when Galley moved out this Tarantine carted her stuff away in his automobile. That was on December the 30th. She was away for a week or ten days and when she came back she said she wanted out. I could have soaked her thirty days' notice but I thought what the hell, I had people waiting. She drove away with Tarantine and I haven't seen her since. Didn't even tell me where she was going—"

"Mrs. Lawrence didn't know Tarantine's name."

"Neither did I, till the pinball merchants told me. They only came here two days ago, Saturday it was, and Mrs. Lawrence hasn't been here for weeks. I thought she gave up."

"She didn't. Can you tell me anything else about Tarantine?"

"I can tell you his fortune, maybe, and I don't need a Ouija board. Folsom or San Quentin, if the long and the short of it don't catch him first. He's one of these pretty-boy wops, curly black hair that the women want to run their fingers through. Hollywood clothes, fast roadster, poolroom brains. You know the type. You'd think a girl like Galley would show better taste."

"Think she married him?"

"How the hell would I know? I've seen pretty young girls like her take up with coyotes and live on carrion for the rest of their lives. I hope she didn't."

"You said he drove a roadster."

"That's right. Prewar Packard with bronze paint and white sidewalls. She hopped into the front seat and tooted away and that was the last of Galley Lawrence. If you find her, you let me know. I liked the girl."

"Why?"

"She was full of vim and vigor. I like a girl with personality. I've got a lot of personality myself and when I see somebody else that has it my heart goes out to them."

Thanking him, I retreated to the sidewalk. His loud optimistic voice followed me: "But you can't get by on personality alone, I learned that in the depression. They say there's another one coming but I don't worry. I'm sitting pretty, ready for anything."

I called back: "You forgot the hydrogen bomb."

"The hell I did," he yelled triumphantly. "I got the bomb outwitted. The doctor says my heart won't last two years."

Chapter 4

IT TOOK me half an hour to find the Point Arena, though I had a hazy notion where it was. It stood in the lower depths of town, near the railroad tracks. Beyond the tracks the packing-case shanties of a small hobo jungle leaned in the corner of a dusty field. One of the huts had a roof of beaten gas-tins which gleamed like fish scales in the sun. A man lay still as a lizard in its dooryard.

From the outside the arena looked like an old freight warehouse, except for a kind of box-office at the street entrance, the size of a telephone booth. A dingy yellow billboard over the closed box-office window announced: WRESTLING EVERY TUES., GENERAL .80, RESERVED 1.20, RINGSIDE 1.50, CHILDREN .25. A door to the right of the window was standing open, and I went in.

The corridor was so dark, after the bright sun, that I could barely see. The only light came from a window high in the left wall. At least it served as a window; it was a square hole cut in the unpainted boards and covered with heavy chicken-wire. Stretching up on my toes I could see into the cubicle on the other side. It contained two straight chairs, a scarred desk bare of everything but a telephone, and an heirloom brass spittoon. The walls were decorated with calendar nudes, telephone numbers scrawled in pencil, publicity photographs of Lord Albert Trompington-Whist the Pride of the British Empire, Basher Baron Flores from the Azores, and other scions of the European aristocracy.

Somewhere out of sight a punching-bag was rat-tat-tatting on a board. I stepped through a doorless aperture opposite the door I'd come in by, and found myself in the main hall. It was comparatively small, with seats for maybe a thousand rising on four sides to the girders that held up the roof. An ingot of lead-gray light from a skylight fell through the moted air onto the empty roped square on the central platform. Still no people, but you could tell that people had been there. The same air had hung for months in the windowless building, absorbing the smells of human sweat and breath, roasted peanuts and beer, white and brown cigarettes, Ben Hur perfume and bay rum and hair oil and tired feet. A social researcher with a good nose could have written a Ph.D. thesis about that air.

The punching-bag kept up an underbeat to the symphony of odors, tum-tee-tum, tum-tee-tum, tum-tee-tum-tee-tum-tee-tum. I moved toward a door with a push-bar marked EXIT, and the beat sounded louder. The door opened into an alley that led to the rear of the building. A colored boy was working on a bag fastened to the corner of the wall. On the other side of the alley a Negro woman was watching him across a board fence. Her black arms rested on the top of the fence and her chin was laid on her arms. Her great dark eyes had swallowed the rest of her face, and looked as if they were ready to swallow the boy.

"Who runs this place?"

He went on beating the bag with his left, his back to me and the woman. He was naked to the waist; the rest of him was covered by a pair of faded khakis, and pitiful canvas sneakers that showed half his bare black toes. He switched to his right without breaking the drumming rhythm. The full sun was on him, and the sweat stood out on his back and made it glisten.

He was light-heavy, I guessed, but he didn't look more than eighteen, in spite of the G.I. pants. With his height and heavy bone-structure, he'd grow up into a heavyweight. The woman looked as if she could hardly wait.

After a while she called to him: "The gentleman asked something, Simmie." All gentlemen were white; all whites were gentlemen.

He dropped his arms and turned slowly. The taut muscles of his chest and stomach stood out in detailed relief like moulded iron sculpture. The head was narrow and long, with a slanting forehead, small eyes, broad nose, thick mouth. He breathed through the nose. "You want me?"

"I wondered who runs this place."

"I'm the janitor. You want something?"

"I'd like to talk to the boss. Is he around?"

"Not today. Mr. Tarantine is out of town."

"What about Mr. Speed? Isn't Herman Speed the boss around here?"

"Not any more he isn't. Mr. Tarantine been running things since the beginning of the year. Before that."

"What happened to Herman?" The surprise in my voice sounded hollow. "He leave town?"

"Yeah. Mr. Speed left town." He wasted no words.

"He got shot," the woman said. "Somebody riddled his guts. It broke his health. It was a crying shame, too, he was a fine big man."

"Shut up, Violet," the boy said. "You don't know nothing about it."

"Shut up yourself," she answered in ready repartee.

"Who shot him?" I asked her.

"Nobody knows. Maybe he knows, but he wouldn't tell the police, he was real tight-mouthed."

"I said shut up," the boy repeated. "You're wasting the gentleman's time."

I said: "Where's Tarantine?"

"Nobody knows that either," the woman said. "He left town last week and nobody seen him since. Looks as if they left young Simmie here to put on the shows all by himself." She laughed throatily. "Maybe if you talked to Mrs. Tarantine, she might know where he is. She just lives down the road a few blocks from here."

The boy jumped for the fence on silent feet, but the woman was already out of his reach. "Stay on your own side, Simmie, I given you fair warning. Trim's in his room."

"You're trying to get me in trouble, been trying to get me in trouble all winter long. Ain't you? Why don't you get out of my sight and stay out of my sight?"

She wiggled her heavy body disdainfully, and disappeared around the corner of the buildings: warped plyboard cubicles laid end to end like miniature ten-foot boxcars and fronting on another alley. There were dark faces at some of the windows in the row and after a while the woman appeared at one of them.

The boy was talking by then. I'd broken through his reserve by praising his muscles and asking about his fights. He had beaten the local talent, he said, and was grooming himself for his professional debut. He called it that. Unfortunately they hadn't had fights in Pacific Point since he started to get his growth. Mr. Tarantine was going to try and get him on a card at San Diego one of these weeks. I suggested that Mr. Tarantine was a pretty good friend of his, and he agreed.

"I hear he married a beautiful wife."

"Mr. Tarantine got no wife."

"I thought Violet said something about a Mrs. Tarantine."

"That's the old lady. Violet don't know nothing." He cast a wicked glance across the fence at the woman in the window.

"What does she think about the trouble he's in?"

"There isn't any trouble," the boy said. "Mr. Tarantine is a smart man. He doesn't get into trouble."

"I heard there was some trouble about the pinball collections."

"That's crap. He doesn't collect on the pinball machines anymore. That was last year, when Mr. Speed was here. Are you a policeman, mister?" His face had closed up hard.

"I'm opening a place on the south side. I want a machine put in."

"Look it up in the phone book, mister. It's under Western Variety."

I thanked him. The drumming of the bag began again before I was out of earshot. After a while he'd be a fighting machine hired out for twenty or twenty-five dollars to take it and dish it out. If he was really good, he might be airborne for ten years, sleeping with yellower flesh than Violet, eating thick steaks for breakfast, dishing it out. Then drop back onto a ghetto street-corner with the brains scrambled in his skull.

Chapter 5

I STOPPED for gas at a service station near the arena and looked up Tarantine in the phone book attached to its pay phone. There was only one entry under the name, a Mrs. Sylvia Tarantine of 1401 Sanedres Street. I tried the number on the telephone and got no answer.

Sanedres Street was the one I was on. It ran crosstown through the center of the Negro and Mexican district, a street of rundown cottages and crowded shacks interspersed with liquor stores and pawnshops, poolroom-bars and flyblown lunchrooms and storefront tabernacles. As the street approached the hills on the other side of the ball park, it gradually improved. The houses were larger and better kept. They had bigger yards, and the children playing in the yards were white under their dirt.

The house I was looking for stood on a corner at the foot of the slope. It was a one-story frame cottage with a flat roof, almost hidden behind a tangle of untended laurel and cypress. The front door was paned with glass and opened directly into a dingy living-room. I knocked on the door and again I got no answer.

There was a British racing motorcycle, almost new, under a tarpaulin at the side of the house. Moving over to look at it, I noticed a woman hanging sheets on a line in the yard next door. She took a couple of clothespins out of her mouth and called:

"You looking for something?"

"Mrs. Tarantine," I said. "Does she live here?"

"Sure thing, only she ain't at home just now. She went to see her boy in the hospital."

"Is he sick?"

"He got mugged down on the dock the other night. He was beat up something terrible. The doctor thought he might of fractured his skull." She disposed of the sheets in her arms and pushed the graying hair back from her face.

"What was Tarantine doing down at the dock at night?"

"He lives there. I thought you knew him."

I said I didn't know him.

"Well, if you stick around she should be back before long. They don't let visitors stay after four o'clock."

"I'll try the hospital, thanks." It was a quarter of four by my watch.

At five to four I was back where I had begun. The nurse at the information desk told me that Mr. Tarantine was in room 204, straight up the stairs and down the hall to the right, and warned me that I only had a minute.

The door of 204 was standing open. Inside the room a huge old woman in a black and red dotted dress stood with her back to me so that I couldn't see the occupant of the bed. She was arguing in a heavy Italian accent:

"No, you must not, Mario. You must stay in bed until the doctor says. Doctor knows best."

A grumbling masculine bass answered her: "To hell with the doctor." He had an incongruous lisp.

"Swear at your old mother if you want to, but you stay in bed now, Mario. Promise me."

"I'll stay in bed today," the man said. "I don't promise for tomorrow."

"Well, tomorrow we see what the doctor says." The woman leaned over the bed and made a loud smacking noise. *"Addio, figlio mio. Ci vediamo domàni."*

"Arivederci. Don't worry, Mama."

I stepped aside as she came out, and became interested in a framed list of regulations on the wall. If her hips had been six inches wider she'd have had to take the door sideways. She gave me a black look of suspicion, and bore her huge flesh away on slow waddling legs. Varicose veins crawled like fat blue worms under her stockings.

I went into the room and saw that it contained two beds. A sleeping man lay on the far one by the window, an ice-bag around his throat. On the near one the man I was looking for was sitting up against the raised end, with two pillows behind his head. Most of the head was hidden by a helmet of white bandage which came down under the chin. The visible part of it looked more like a smashed ripe eggplant than a face. It was swollen blue, with tints of green and yellow, and darker marks where the skin had been abraded. Someone who liked hurting people had used his face for a punching-bag or a football.

The puffed mouth lisped: "What do *you* want, bud?"

"What happened to you?"

"I'll tell you how it is," he said laboriously. "The other day I took a damn good look at my face in the mirror. I didn't like it. It didn't suit me. So I picked up a ball-peen hammer and gave it a working over. Is there anything else you want to know?"

"The pinball merchants find you, Tarantine?"

He watched me in silence for a moment. His dark eyes looked melancholy in their puffed blue sockets. He rubbed a black-haired hand across the heavy black beard that was sprouting on his chin. There were scabs on his knuckles where they had been skinned. "Get out of my room."

"You'll wake up your friend."

"Beat it. If you're working for him, you can tell him I said so. If you're a friggin' cop you can beat it anyway. I don't have to talk, see."

"I'm not on anybody's payroll. I'm a private detective, not a cop. I'm looking for Galley Lawrence. Her mother thinks something happened to her."

"Let's see your license then."

I opened my wallet and showed him the photostat. "I heard you drove her away when she left her apartment in town."

"Me?" His surprise sounded genuine.

"You drive a bronze-colored Packard roadster?"

"Not me," he said. "You're looking for my brother. You're not the only one. My name's Mario. It's Joe you want."

"Where is Joe?"

"I wish I knew. He blew three days ago, the dirty bum. Left me holding—" The sentence was left unfinished. His mouth sagged open, showing broken teeth.

"Was Galley Lawrence with him?"

"Probably. They were shacked up. You want to find them, huh?"

I acknowledged that I did.

He sat up straight, clear of the pillows. Now that he was upright his face looked even worse. "I'll make a deal with you. I know where they lived in L.A. You let me know if you find them, is it a deal?"

"What do *you* want him for?"

"I'll tell Joe why I want him. When I tell him he won't forget it."

"All right," I said. "If I find him I pass you the word. Where does he live?"

"Casa Loma. It's a ritz joint off of Sunset in the Hills. You might be able to trace him from there."

"Where do you live?"

"On my boat. It's the *Aztec Queen*, moored down in the yacht basin."

"Who are the others that want him?"

"Don't ask me." He lay back in the pillows again.

A cool trained voice said behind me: "Visiting hours are over, sir. How are you feeling, Mr. Tarantine?"

"Dandy," he said. "How do I look?"

"Why, you look cute in your bandage, Mr. Tarantine." The nurse glanced at the other bed. "How's our tonsillectomy?"

"He feels dandy too, he thinks he's dying."

"He'll be up and around tomorrow." She laughed professionally and turned away.

I caught her up in the hall: "What happened to Mario's face? He wouldn't tell me."

She was a big-boned girl with a long earnest nose. "He wouldn't tell us, either. A friend of mine was on emergency when he came in. He walked in all by himself, in the middle of the night. He was in terrible shape, his face streaming blood, and he's got a slight concussion, you know. He said he fell down and hurt himself on his boat, but it was obvious that he'd taken a beating. She called the police, of course, but he wouldn't talk to them, either. He's very reticent, isn't he?"

"Very."

"Are you a friend of his?"

"Just an acquaintance."

"Some of the girls said it was gang trouble, that he was in a gang and fell out with the other members. You think there's anything in that?"

I said that hospitals were full of rumors.

Chapter 6

I ATE dinner at Musso's in Hollywood. While I was waiting for my steak, I phoned Joseph Tarantine's apartment and got my nickel back. The steak came the way I liked it, medium rare, garnished with mushrooms, with a pile of fried onion rings on the side. I had a pint of Black Horse ale for dessert, and when I was finished I felt good. So far I was getting nowhere, but I felt good. I had the kind of excitement, more prophetic than tea-leaves, that lifts you when anything may happen and probably will.

I switched on my headlights as I wheeled out of the parking lot. The gray dusk in the air was almost tangible. Under its film the city lay distinct but dimensionless, as transient as a cloud. The stores and theaters and office buildings had lost their daytime perspectives with the sun, and were waiting for night to give them bulk and meaning. The double stream of traffic into which I turned continued the theme of change. Half of the lemmings were rushing down to the sea and the other half had been there and decided not to get wet. The wild slopes of the mountains overshadowed the slanting streets to the northwest and reduced their neons and headlights to firefly sparks.

The Casa Loma was on a side street a block from Sunset where the boulevard rose towards the hills. It was a four-story white frame building with cheerful lights shining from nearly half of the windows. Not quite the ritz, as Mario Tarantine thought, but it would do. The cars in the parking lot behind the building were nearly all new, and a Pontiac 8 was the cheapest one I saw. The people who lived there spent their money on front.

No doorman, though, which suited me. No desk clerk or hall attendant. I crossed the small carpeted lobby to the brass mailboxes banked on the wall by the plate-glass inner door. Joseph Tarantine was the name on number 7. His card was handwritten in green ink, apparently by the girl who had left the harbor on the sea of life so wide. Most of the other cards were printed, and one or two were engraved. Number 8 was very beautifully engraved with the name of Keith Dalling, whoever he was.

I pressed the electric-bell button under his name and got no answer.

Number 12, a Mrs. Kingsley Soper, was more alert. Probably she was expecting company. When I heard her answering buzz I pushed the plate-glass door open and inserted a doubled-up matchbook in the crack. An ancient ruse, but it worked sometimes. I walked to the corner and back, and found my matchbook where I had left it.

There were fifteen apartments in the building, so that number 7 was on the second floor. I went up in the halting automatic elevator and found it easily, a locked door at the end of a narrow corridor. I stood and looked at the grain of the wood for a minute, but there wasn't much sense in that. I could break the door open, or I could go away. The door of number 8 was directly across the hall, but there was nobody in it. I took the heavy screwdriver from my car out of my inside breast pocket. Number 7 had a Yale-type spring lock, and they were easy.

This one was very easy. The door fell open when I leaned my shoulder against it. Someone had got there before me. There were jimmy marks on the door-jamb, and the socket was loose. I put my screwdriver away and took out my gun instead. The room beyond the door was full of darkness, cut by a thin shaft of light from the hallway.

Facing inward, I closed the door and found the wall switch beside it. Even in the dark there seemed to be something queer about the room. There was a faint light from the large window opposite me, enough to see the vague shapes of furniture which didn't look right. I switched the light on, and saw that nothing was right. The four plaster walls and ceiling were there, but everything inside of them had been destroyed.

The upholstered chairs and the davenport had been slashed and disemboweled. Their stuffing covered the floor in handfuls like dirty snow. The glass coffee-table had its legs unscrewed. Torn reproductions of paintings lay by their empty frames. The metal insides of the radio-phonograph had been ripped out and thrown on the floor. Even the window drapes had been torn down, and the lampshades removed from the lamps. The pottery bases of two table-lamps had been shattered.

The kitchen looked worse. Cans of food had been opened and dumped in the sink. The refrigerator had been literally torn apart, its insulating material scattered on the floor. The linoleum had been torn up in great jagged sheets. In the midst of this chaos, a half-eaten meal, steak and potatoes and asparagus tips, lay on the dinette table. It was the sort of thing you might expect to find in a house that had been struck by a natural disaster, cyclone or flood or earthquake.

I entered the bedroom. The mattress and covered springs of the Hollywood bed lay in shreds, and even the skeleton of the bed had been taken apart. Men's jackets and women's dresses had been slashed and thrown in a heap on the closet floor. The rags of some white nurses' uniforms lay among them. The dresser drawers had been pulled out and dropped, and the mirror taken out of its frame. There was hardly a whole object left in the room, and nothing personal at all. No letter, no address-book, not even a book of matches. A gray fuzz of duck down from a ripped comforter lay over everything like mold.

The bathroom was off a tiny hallway between the bedroom and the living-room. I stood in the bathroom doorway for an instant, feeling the inside wall for the light. I pressed the switch but no light went on. A man's voice spoke instead:

"I got you lined up and you can't see me. Drop the gun."

I strained my eyes into the dark bathroom. There was a glint of light on metal but it could have been the plumbing. Nothing moved. I let my revolver clatter on the floor.

"That's my boy," the voice said. "Now back up against the wall and keep your hands up high."

I did as I was told. A tall man in a wide-brimmed black hat emerged from the dark room. He was as thin as death. His face had a coffin look, skin drawn over high sharp cheekbones, blue down-dragging mouth. His pale glistening eyes were on me, and so was his black gun.

"What's the pitch?" He had yellow teeth.

"I should be asking you."

"Only you're doing the answering." The gun nodded in agreement.

"Joe asked me up for a drink. When I knocked on the door it flew open. Where is Joe, anyway?"

"Come on, boy, you can do better than that. Joe never asked anybody up for a drink. Joe's been gone three days. And you don't drop into a friend's place with iron showing." He kicked my gun towards me. "Don't pick it up."

"All right," I said in tones of boyish candor. "Tarantine ran out on me. He owes me money."

Interest flickered wanly in the pale eyes. "That's better. What kind of money?"

"I manage a young fighter in Pacific Point. Tarantine bought a piece of him. He didn't pay up."

"You're doing better, eh? But you'll have to do better yet. You come along with me."

To the land of shades, I thought, the other side of the river. "Where do you stay, the morgue?" His temples were clean and hollowed like a death's-head under the black hat. The paper-thin wings of his nose were snowbird white.

"Be still if you want to walk. I can have you carried." He stooped quickly, scooped up my gun and dropped it in his pocket. I had no chance to move on him.

He made me walk ahead through the living-room. "You did a nice thorough shakedown on it," I said. "You should apply for a job in an asylum tearing hemp."

"I've seen it done to people," he told me dryly. "People that talked too much." And he jabbed his automatic hard in my kidneys.

We went down in the upended casket of an elevator, as close as Siamese twins, across the deserted lobby, into the street. The buildings had grown thick into nighttime shapes, and the lights had lost their hominess. The man at my side and one pace to my rear had a car with a driver waiting halfway down the block.

Chapter 7

THE MAN behind the wheel was a run-of-the-mine thug with a carbuncular swelling on the back of his neck. He gave me one dull look as I stepped into the back seat and paid no more attention to me. When he switched on his lights I saw that the thick windshield had the greenish yellow tinge of bulletproof glass.

"Dowser's?" the driver grunted.

"You guessed it."

The long black car rode heavily and fast. My companion sat in one corner of the back seat with his gun on his knee. I sat in the other corner and thought of a brigadier I'd known in Colón during the war. His hobby was hunting sharks in the open sea, with no equipment but a mask and a knife. I used to run his speedboat for him sometimes. Nobody on his staff could figure out why he did it. I asked him about it one day when he nearly got himself killed and I had to go in after him. He said that it gave him background for dealing with human beings. He was a very shy man for a general.

They took me to a hilltop between Santa Monica and Pacific Palisades. A one-car private road turned off the highway to the left and spiraled up the steep slope. At the top a green iron gate barred the entrance to the driveway. The driver honked his horn. As if in automatic response two arc-lights on telephone poles on either side of the gate came on and lit up the front of the house. It was a wide low ranch-style bungalow painted adobe gray. In spite of the red tile roof, it looked a little like a concrete strong point. The man who came out of the gatehouse completed the illusion by strolling sentry-like with a shotgun under his arm. He leaned it against the gatepost, opened the gate, waved us through.

The front door had a Judas window shaped like a mail slot, above a brass knocker that represented copulating horses for some reason. Judas himself opened the door. He was a curly-headed man with a kind of second-hand Irish good looks. He was wearing headwaiter black for the occasion, with a dingy black bow-tie that could have been made of leather.

Paleface lagged behind me and Judas walked ahead, down a hallway decorated with red, black, and gold striped wallpaper. It looked as if the decorator had been influenced by the Fun House at a carnival. The hallway ended in a door that opened into a bright high-ceilinged room. Judas stood aside to let us pass.

"Watch your lip with Dowser," the man behind me said, and reminded my right kidney of his gun.

A man in a midnight-blue suit was standing with one foot on the brass rail of a twenty-foot bar that took up most of the other side of the room. He made a point of waiting and turning very slowly, as if he could easily take me or leave me alone. Behind the bar a great mirror with an old-fashioned gold-scrolled frame hung on the oak wall. It repeated all the contents of the room: the television set built into a grandfather's clock, the silver-dollar slot machines, the full-size snooker table, the illuminated juke box, the row of French windows in the left-hand wall and the swimming pool beyond them, everything a gentleman needed to entertain his friends if he had any friends. I could see myself, in sports clothes and hatless, with a gunman on either side of me, and the gunmen's boss approaching across the polished floor. It made me angry. A Channel Island boar's-head sneered from the wall above the Mauve Age mirror. I sneered back.

"Trouble, Blaney?"

"I picked him up in Tarantine's flat," Paleface said respectfully. "He claims Joe owes him money."

"Him and everybody else. Was it smart to bring him here?"

"I did what you told me, Mr. Dowser, if anybody showed."

"All right," Dowser answered softly.

We sized each other up. He was a head shorter than I was, almost as wide in the shoulders, wider in the hips. His double-breasted blue suit made him look almost cubical. His head was a smaller cube topped by straight sandy hair that was trimmed too short in a brush cut. He was forty, perhaps, trying to feel like thirty and almost succeeding. His skin was fresh and boyish, but there was something the matter with his eyes. They were brown and wet and protuberant, as if they had been dipped in muddy water and stuck on his face to dry.

"Who are you?" he said.

Having nothing to lose by telling it, I told the truth.

"That isn't what he said to me," Blaney complained. "He said he managed fighters in Pacific Point."

"You caught me with my veracity down. When you cock a gun at me it breaks up my conversation."

"Talkative," Dowser said. "You from Pacific Point?" He took a sip from a pewter mug he was holding in his right hand. The liquid it contained looked like buttermilk. He made a buttermilk face. "I'll have a look at your wallet."

I took it out, removed the currency from it to insult him, and handed him the limp sharkskin folder. His dirty-brown eyes bulged over my identification, and his lips moved silently. I noticed that one of his ears curled inward on itself like a misshaped mushroom.

"You want me to read it to you, Mr. Dowser?"

His fresh skin turned a shade darker, but he held his anger. He had an actor's dignity, controlled by some idea of his own importance. His face and body had an evil swollen look as if they had grown stout on rotten meat.

"So you're looking for Joey Tarantine. Who you working for, Archer? Or you working for yourself?" He tossed the wallet at me unexpectedly. His motions were fast and trained.

I caught it, tucked the bills back in, put it away in my pocket. "I'm working for a certain Mrs. Lawrence. Her daughter seems to be traveling with Joe. She's worried about her daughter."

Dowser laughed without showing his teeth. "Now why should she be worried about her daughter? Joe's a sweet kid. Everybody likes Joe."

"I like Joe," Blaney said. "I like Joe," Judas repeated. Dowser had made a joke, so they made the same joke over again.

"And what are you going to do with the girl if you find her?"

"Take her home to mother."

"That will be fun."

"What girl is that?" a woman's voice demanded.

I had been watching Dowser so closely that I hadn't noticed her. He had a quality of unacted violence that held the attention. Now I saw her through the mirror standing in a doorway to my right, like somebody's conception of a Greek goddess painted in a frame. Probably her own. She moved into the room with white silk evening pajamas tossing about her ankles, a girl so colorless in hair and skin that she might have been albino. Except for the dark blue eyes.

They passed me over coolly. "What girl, Danny?"

"Mind your own business."

I said: "Galley Lawrence. Know her?"

"Shut up, you."

The girl took up a cheesecake pose on the edge of the snooker table. "Cert'ny I know her." The voice was flat and rasping, as incongruous from those fine lips as a peacock's screech from a peacock. "I heard she was in Palm Springs. How come I never get to go to Palm Springs, Danny?"

He walked towards her quietly, speaking more softly than before: "What was that, Irene? You heard about Galley Lawrence someplace, huh?"

"Sandra down at the Beach Club. She said she saw Galley in Palm Springs last night."

"Where?"

"Some bar, she didn't say."

"Who with?" His right arm was straight at his side, the fingers opening and closing at the end of it.

"Not Joey. I know you're looking for Joey so I asked her. Some other male, she thought it was some actor. Sandra said he was cute."

"Cute, huh? *You're* cute. Why didn't you tell me, 'Rene?" He reached up suddenly and took her chin in his hand, clenching it hard.

She struck his arm down. "Don't handle me, you monkey. I was minding my own business, like you said."

His fingers kept on working. "So you bust out with your business in front of this jerk."

"He's cute," she said in a bored deadly whine, and shifted her look to me. "Danny can't get away with rough stuff on account of he isn't cute."

"I think he's cute." I was getting bored myself.

The bulged eyes swiveled to me and back to the girl on the green table. She was hugging her knees as if she found them lovable. Her blue eyes met him levelly.

His left hand jerked up with the pewter mug, and the buttermilk spattered her face.

"All right," she said, dripping white from the point of her chin. "You'll buy me a whole new outfit, *two* new outfits. Tonight you take me to Ciro's. Tomorrow I go to Westmore's for the works."

"I'll give you the works," he said slowly. "I'll drop you off the Santa Monica pier."

But he stood back as she swung her legs down. Her high-heeled gilt slippers hammered across the room. He followed her at a distance, shorter and much older and not nearly so beautiful.

"We might as well sit down," Blaney said. "It goes on like this all the time." The girl had given us something in common, though I didn't know exactly what it was.

Judas went away. Blaney and I sat at the bar, one empty stool and the gun in the space between us. He wouldn't talk, so I amused myself reading the labels on the bottles in the racks. Dowser had everything, including Danziger Goldwasser and pre-World-War Green River.

He came back ten minutes later, wearing a different suit. His mouth was red and slightly swollen, as if somebody had been chewing on it.

"Nice-looking girl," I said, hoping to needle him.

He was feeling too good to be needled. "I got a proposition for you, Archer." He even laid an arm across my shoulders. "A business proposition."

I stood up, placing my shoulders out of his reach. "You have a very peculiar business approach."

"Forget it." As if I had apologized to him. "Put the gun away, Blaney. You're working for old lady Lawrence, you said. You do a job for me instead, what do you say."

"Churning buttermilk?"

He took it without a word. "Doing what you're doing. You want to contack Galley Lawrence. Go to Palm Springs and con-tack her. I'll pay you one grand for her, five for Joey."

"Why?"

"I like them so much. I want to invite them over to look at my television."

"Why don't you go yourself?"

He paused, then decided to tell me: "It's out of my territory. I don't like crossing over out of my territory. Anyway I got you to go for me, isn't that right?"

"If you say so." It was an easy out.

"That's the old esprit de corpse," he said surprisingly. "You bring me Joey and I'll slip you a quick five G's." He showed me a thick pack of bills in a gold clip shaped like a dollar sign.

"Joey alive or dead?"

"Alive if you can handle it. Dead, the deal's still on. What could be fairer?" He turned to Blaney: "You got our friend's gun here?"

"Yeah." Blaney stood up to answer the boss.

"Okay, give it to him outside." Dowser turned back to me, smiling with a kind of canine charm: "No hard feelings, old man. Everybody's got to look out for himself, that's my philosophy, isn't that right?"

"Speaking of looking out for yourself, I usually get a retainer." I didn't want Dowser's money, but I had to ask him for it. The giving and receiving of money, its demand and its refusal, were Dowser's basic form of communication with other people. That and the threat, the blow, the infliction of fear and pain.

He grunted, and gave me a hundred-dollar bill. A piece of money takes its feeling from the people that have handled it. This money twisted in my hand like a fat green tomato-worm.

Chapter 8

By ten I was in Palm Springs, making the rounds of the bars. I worked up one side of the main street, a miniature Wilshire with horsy trimmings, and down the other side. Old or young, fat or thin, the bartenders gave me the same cool pitying smile. They looked at me and down at the photograph and back at me again.—Nice little beast, eh, nope I never see her.—What's the matter bud your wife run out on you?—If she was here last night I'd know it but she wasn't.—She wouldn't be your daughter would she? That was the most unkindest cut of all.

I had spent about six dollars on drinks that I left untouched or anyway unfinished, when I finally got my lead. It was in a little side-street place called the Lariat. A knotty-pine box of a place with longhorns over the bar, seats and stools upholstered with riveted saddle-leather, a color-retouched photomural of Palm Springs in the days when it was a desert outpost, which weren't so long ago that I couldn't remember them. A great deal had been done to fill the Lariat with old western tradition, but it was so contemporary that it barely existed yet. A pair of fugitives from a Los Angeles wolfpack were playing shuffleboard in the rear. The bartender, who was watching the game, came forward when I took a seat at the bar. He was a youngish man in a Hopalong Cassidy shirt and a wide carved cowhide belt.

I asked for a Scotch and soda. When he brought it, I showed him the photograph and made my little speech. He looked at me and down at the photograph and back at me again, but without the pitying smile. His eyes were large and brown, and they slanted downward from the middle of his face, so that he looked like a cocker spaniel. They had the earnest look of one who sincerely wished to help.

"Yeah, I know the face," he said. "She was in here last night. The joint was jumping last night, you wouldn't believe it. It always slows down on Mondays, after the week-end and all."

"What was her name?" It seemed to have come too easily, or maybe too much bar Scotch was making me uneasy.

"I didn't catch the name. They weren't at the bar, they sat down in the back booth there, by the shuffleboard. I just took them their drinks. Daiquiris, they were drinking."

"Who was the other half of the they?"

"Some guy," he told me cautiously after a while.

"You know him?"

"I wouldn't say I know him. He's been in here a few times, off and on."

"Maybe you know his name."

"I should. I thought I did. I guess it slipped my mind, though." He lit a cigarette and tried to look inscrutable and failed.

My change from a ten-dollar bill was on the bar between us. I pushed it towards him. "You can tell me what he looks like."

"Maybe I can and maybe I can't." He squirmed in his cowboy shirt, eying the money wistfully. "I don't know what the setup is, mister. If this is a deevorce rap or something like that, I wouldn't want to shoot my mouth off too free."

"If divorce comes into it, it's news to me." I told him it was a prodigal daughter case. But with Dowser and Tarantine in it, it was growing much bigger than that. I left them out, and tried to forget them myself.

The bartender was still worried. The bills and silver lay untouched on the black Lucite, nearer him than me. "I got to think about it," he said in pain. "I mean I'll try and remember his name for you."

With a great appearance of casualness he went to the other end of the bar and took a telephone out from under it. Leaning over the bar and hunching his shoulders around the instrument so I couldn't see him dial, he made a call. It took him a long time to get his party. When he finally did, he spoke low and close into the mouthpiece.

He came back briskly and took my empty glass. "Something more to drink, sir?"

I looked at my wrist watch, nearly midnight. "All right."

He set the second glass on the bar beside the money. "Do I take it out of this, sir?"

"It's up to you. It's eating into your profits, isn't it?"

"I don't get you," he said. But he waited for me to produce another bill.

I handed him a single from my wallet. "What did your friend tell you on the phone?"

"My girl friend, you mean?" he asked brightly. "She's coming over to meet me when I close."

"What time do you close?"

"Two o'clock."

"I guess I'll stick around."

He seemed relieved. He flicked a dish towel out from under the bar and began to polish a row of cocktail glasses, humming *Red River Valley* to himself. I moved to the back booth. I sat and wondered if that was as close as I'd get to Galley Lawrence, and watched the coatless boys at the shuffleboard. Red beat blue, which meant that blue paid for the drinks. They were drinking vodka, and they were all of eighteen.

Shortly after midnight a pair of short fat men came in, ridiculous in ten-gallon hats and jeans. They were very very particular about their drinks, and filled the room with name-dropping accounts of their recent social triumphs, related in high loud tenors. They didn't interest me.

A few minutes later a man came in who did. He was tall and graceful in a light flannel suit and an off-white snap-brim hat. His face was incredible. A Greek sculptor could have used him as a model for a Hermes or Apollo. Standing at the door with one hand on the knob, he exchanged a quick glance with the bartender, and looked at me. The tenors at the bar gave him a long slow once-over.

He ordered a bottle of beer and carried it to my booth. "Mind if I sit down? I know you from somewhere, don't I?" His voice was beautiful, too, rich and soft and full with deep manly overtones.

"I don't place you. But sit down."

He removed his hat and exhibited the wavy auburn hair that went with the long dark eyelashes. Everything was so perfect, it made me a little sick. He slid into the leather seat across the table from me.

"On second thought, maybe I do," I said. "Haven't I seen you in pictures?"

"Not unless you get to look at screen tests. I never got past them."

"Why?"

"Women don't do the hiring. Men don't like me. Even the pansies hate me because I won't give them a tumble. You don't like me, do you?"

"Not very much. Handsome is as handsome does, I always say. Does it matter if I like you?"

He came to the point then, though it cost him an effort. His purple eyes were shadowed by anxiety. "You could be working for Dowser."

"I could be, but I'm not. Whoever Dowser is."

He waited for me to say more, leaning gracefully in the corner of the booth with one arm on the table. He was tense, though. There were wet dark blotches under both arms of the flannel jacket.

I said: "You're scared stiff, aren't you?"

He tried to smile. The effect reminded me of a device I read about once for making insane people feel happy. It consisted of a couple of hooks that raised the corners of the mouth into smiling position. Its beneficiaries were forced to smile, and this made them feel like smiling, at least that was the theory.

"Okay," he said. "I'm scared stiff."

"You want to tell me about it? I'm wearing my hearing aid tonight."

"That won't be necessary," with the forced wry smile again. "You might explain how you come into the picture, Mr.——?"

"Archer. Lew Archer."

"My name's Keith Dalling."

"I'm a private detective," I said. "A Mrs. Lawrence employed me to look for her daughter." I was getting pretty tired of that pitch. It sounded too simple and corny to be true, especially in the Palm Springs atmosphere.

"Why?"

"Maternal anxiety, I guess. She hadn't heard from her for a couple of months. Nothing to be afraid of, Mr. Dalling."

"If I could be sure of that." There was a beaded row of sweat along his peaked hairline. He wiped it away with the back of his hand. "I heard from a friend in L.A. that Dowser was looking for Galley. It puts me in a spot—"

"Who's he?"

"You must have heard of Dowser." He watched me carefully. "He isn't the kind of person you want on your trail."

"You were saying, it puts you in a spot."

Once he had begun, he was eager to talk. Dalling was big and strong-looking but he wasn't built for strain. He had bad nerves, and admitted it. He hadn't slept the night before, and he was the kind of fellow who needed his sleep.

"What happened last night?"

"I'll tell you from the beginning." He took out a briar pipe and filled it, as he talked, with English-cut tobacco. He was such a perfect artistic example of his type that I began to like him, almost as if he were a creature of my own imagination. "I own this little place in the desert, you see. The place was standing empty, and I had a chance to rent it to Joe Tarantine. He approached me about it week before last, and his offer was good so I took it."

"How do you happen to know him?"

"He's a neighbor of mine. We live across the hall from each other in the Casa Loma apartments." I remembered the engraved card on the mailbox, with his name on it. "I'd told him about the house, and he knew I wasn't planning to use it myself. He said he and his wife wanted to get away for a while, someplace where the pressure would be off."

"Galley is married to him, then."

"So far as I know. They've been living in that apartment as man and wife since the first of the year. I think he mentioned they were married in Las Vegas."

"What does he do?"

He lit his pipe with a wooden match and puffed out a cloud of smoke. "I didn't know until yesterday, when this friend of mine phoned me. Tarantine is a mobster, or something pretty close to it. He handles Dowser's interests in Pacific Point. Dowser has half a dozen towns on the coast sewed up, from Long Beach on down. But that's not the worst of it. Tarantine has stolen something of Dowser's and skipped out. Apparently he planned it ahead of time, and he's using my place as a hideout. I *wondered* why he asked me not to tell anyone. He said if it leaked out the deal was off."

"This friend of yours," I said, "how does he know all this?"

"I don't exactly know. He's a radio producer and he does a crime show based on police files. I suppose he hears inside information."

"But he didn't hear what Tarantine lifted from Dowser?"

"No. Money, perhaps. He seems to have plenty of it. I rented my house to him in all innocence, and now it's made me look as if I'm an accomplice." He gulped the beer that had been growing stale in his glass.

I signaled for more drinks, but he refused another. "I've got to keep my wits about me."

"I don't think it's so bad," I said. "If you're afraid of Dowser, why don't you go and talk to him?"

"I daren't show myself. Besides, if I talked to Dowser, I'd have Tarantine to worry about."

"Not for long."

"I can't be sure of that, either. Frankly, I'm in a mess. I phoned up Galley, Mrs. Tarantine, yesterday after I talked to my friend. She agreed to meet me here. She didn't realize what a chance she was taking, until I told her about her husband. She was shocked. She said she was practically a prisoner out there. She had to slip away last night while he was sleeping, and God knows what he did to her when she got back."

"You like her pretty well."

"Frankly, I do. She's a lovely kid, and she's got herself mixed up with an awfully nasty crew." Not all of his anxiety was for himself.

"I'd like to meet her," I said. "I never have."

He stood up suddenly. "I was hoping you'd say that. I have a normal amount of physical courage, I think, but I'm not up to dealing with gangsters, all by myself, I mean."

I said that that was natural enough.

Chapter 9

M Y CAR was parked six blocks away, where I had begun my rounds. Dalling's was waiting at the curb. If I had been asked to guess what kind of car he had, I would have said a red or yellow convertible, Chrysler or Buick or De Soto. It was a yellow Buick with red leather seats.

As we drove out of town, slowing down occasionally for a stop sign, I asked him what he did. He had been and done a number of things, he said, chorus boy in musicals before he grew too big, photographic model for advertising agencies, car and yacht salesman, navigator on a PBY during the war. He was proud of that. After the war he had married a rich wife, but it hadn't lasted. More recently he had been a radio actor but that hadn't lasted either because he drank too much. Dalling was frank almost to the point of fruitiness. Starting with the assumption that no man could like him in any case, he said, he figured he might just as well be himself. He had nothing to lose.

When we got on the highway he accelerated to eighty or so and concentrated on his driving, which interrupted our one-sided conversation. After a while I asked him where we were going. "At this rate we'll be in Mexico before long."

He chuckled. Surely I'd heard that chuckle on the radio. People didn't chuckle in real life. "It's just a few miles from here," he said. "A place they call Oasis. I suppose it's not exactly a place yet, but it will be. This country is filling up. Don't you love it?"

I watched the dim arid tundra sweeping by, dotted with cactus and gray sage like the ghosts of vegetation. "It looks like a sea floor. I like a sea floor with water over it, it's more interesting."

"It's funny you should say that. The Gulf of California reached almost to here at one time."

We turned right off the highway and followed an asphalt road across the lightless desert. A dozen miles to our right the town lights sparkled, a handful of white and colored stones thrown down carelessly. A few lights gleamed ahead of us, lost and little in the great nocturnal spaces. Dalling said they were the lights of Oasis.

We entered a maze of gravel roads crisscrossing like city streets, but practically uninhabited. A handful of houses scattered here and there, street-lights at most of the corners, that was Oasis. It reminded me of an army camp I had seen at a staging point in the far west Pacific, after its division had left for bloodier pastures.

"What is this, a ghost town?" I asked him.

"It almost looks like one, doesn't it? Actually it's the opposite of a ghost town, a town waiting to be born. It's a fairly new development, you see. I got in at the beginning, and it's growing by leaps and bounds." But he didn't sound too happy about his real estate investment.

He took a series of turns on tires that screeched and skittered in the gravel. I kept my sense of direction straight by watching the high escarpment that blotted out the horizon to the southeast. On the far edge of the skeleton town he slowed to a crawl.

"That's my house up ahead."

There was only one house ahead, a white frame shoebox with projecting eaves, lengthened by the garage appended to the rear. As we passed it I saw light in the front windows, leaking faintly around the edges of closed Venetian blinds.

"I thought we were going to stop and pay a visit." The Buick had kept on rolling, on to the next intersection and beyond. He finally brought it to a stop at the side of the road.

"I've been thinking," he said uneasily. "Tarantine knows me, and he doesn't know you. Wouldn't it be more strategic if you went in alone? I'll stand by, of course. I'll keep the car here with the motor running." His voice, trying to be charming, was pretty dreary.

If Dalling had a normal amount of physical courage, he must have used it up on me when he first came into the Lariat. I pitied him a little. "Whatever you say, Dalling."

The pity, or the contempt that went with it, must have showed: "After all," and the deep manly overtones had departed, "you've been hired to find Galley Lawrence, haven't you? I'm doing what I can to help you, man. And if Joseph Tarantine knows I've given him away, you know what will happen to me."

He made sense, in a way. If I had had an equal amount of sense of a similar kind, I might have stayed in the car and gone to work on Dalling. Two would get you twenty there was a soft spot in his story to go with the soft spot in his spine. The one thing real and certain was his fear. It hung around him like a damp contagion. It was Dalling's fear, or my reaction against it, that made me foolhardy. That and the whisky I had drunk in line of business. Without its fading glow in my insides I might have reacted in a different way. I might even have saved a life or two if I'd gone to work on Dalling.

But I contented myself with a smiling threat: "Don't stand me up or you won't be pretty any more. *Or* popular."

The invisible hooks worked on his mouth. "Don't worry." He switched off his headlights. "I really appreciate this, your attitude, I mean—" He gave it up and settled down for a wait.

There were more stars over Oasis than I'd seen since I left that island in the Pacific. The unbuilt street was still and peaceful as the desert was supposed to be. But I felt a hot prickling at the nape of my neck as I approached the stucco house. I transferred my gun from shoulder holster to pocket, and leaned my moral weight on it.

I circled the house at a distance. There was no fence, and the house stood by itself on the bare ground. The doors were closed, including the garage doors at the back, and all the windows were blinded. A bronze-painted Packard roadster shone dimly in the starlight at the rear of the gravel driveway. I passed it close enough to make sure there was no one in it, and circled around to the front of the house again.

The lights were still on behind the two front windows. The blinds fitted too well to let me see past them. Holding the gun in my pocket with the safety off, I mounted the low concrete porch and knocked on the screen door. My knocking wasn't loud, but it sounded loud to me.

Quick footsteps crossed the room on the other side of the door. The porch light flashed on over my head. Somebody pulled aside the blind in the near window, and I caught the gleam of an eyeball in the opening. The blind fell back into place, and there was a waiting silence. I knocked again.

Someone fumbled the inside knob. The lock clicked. Slowly the door opened to the width of a brass chain that held it secure.

I saw a four-inch segment of a woman's face and the muzzle of an automatic gun.

"Go away," she said.

"I would if I knew how." The obvious story was the best I could think of. "My car broke down up the road, and I've lost my way."

"Oh." Her voice relaxed a little, but her gun was steady. "Where are you going?"

"Indio."

"You're way off the track."

"I know that well enough. I hope you've got the safety on that automatic."

"If it bothers you, you can go away," she said. "As I suggested." But something told me, probably my ego, that she was glad to see me. Me or anybody.

"I guess it makes people very inhospitable living all by themselves on the desert like this. Are you a spinster?"

"No. Why?"

"You're acting like one. I wish you'd call your husband if you can't help me out. He probably has a road map of this place."

"Be quiet. You'll wake him." It was a natural thing for her to say, but she said it much too vehemently.

I wondered where Tarantine was sleeping, but I wasn't interested enough to want to disturb him. I kept my voice down. "Why don't you put up the gun and let me relax? I'm completely harmless to women."

To my surprise, she lowered the gun. Then, to my greater surprise, she unchained the door and opened it.

"You might as well come in, but please be quiet. I'll see if I can find a map."

I couldn't understand it. It had been some years since my boyish charm had been able to work minor miracles. "Why the sudden reversal? Not that it isn't pleasant."

"You don't look much like a holdup man, I guess." She unhooked the screen door and held it open for me. "Come in if you like."

I had my first good chance to look at her face. She was the girl in the picture I was carrying, a few years older, no less striking, I thought. The straight nose, curled lips, round chin, were the same, the boldness enhanced by the short black hair molded to her head. She was wearing a blue skirt and white blouse. The gun hanging low in her left hand completed the costume, and didn't seem wholly out of place.

As I passed her in the doorway I reached fast for the gun and twisted it out of her hand. She backed away from me in the confined space until she was flat against the wall of the little hallway. "Give it back to me."

"After we have a talk."

"There's nothing to talk about. Get out of here." But all the time she kept her voice quite low.

I dropped her gun in my left-hand pocket, to balance the one in my right. A faint cool breeze from an air-conditioning system was blowing past me. I shut the door behind me, quietly. "Why don't you go home to your mother, Galley? Joe isn't going to live long, and neither are you if you stick."

"Who are you? How do you know my name?" In the half-light from the open door of the living-room her dark eyes shone with an amber gleam.

"The name is Archer. Your mother sent me to find you. She's been worried about you. With reason."

"You're a liar. My mother doesn't know about Joe. She never sent you here."

"She gave me your graduation picture, I have it here."

"You stole it from her."

"Nonsense. You're just trying to unknow the error, Galley."

She recognized the phrase. Slowly she straightened up clear of the wall. In high heels, she was almost as tall as I was. "Please go away. If Mother sent you, tell her I'm all right. Tell her anything."

"I think you should come along."

"Be quiet," she whispered.

From somewhere at the back of the house, I heard a faint dull sound. It could have been a man's boot drawn softly across the floor.

"Please." She was almost whimpering. "You've wakened Joe. He'll kill me if he finds you."

I opened the door. "Come along with me. Dalling's waiting in his car."

"I can't. I daren't." She was breathing quickly, her sharp breasts rising and falling under the blouse.

"Will you be all right?"

"If you go now, please." She leaned towards me, one hand on my shoulder pressing me backwards.

I reached for the screen door behind me, but it was already open. Galley cried: "Look out!"

The warning came too late. I was a sitting duck for the soft explosion of the sandbag against the back of my head.

Chapter 10

THE ARGUMENT began in my head before I was fully conscious. Had Galley tried to save me, or set me up for Tarantine? In any case, I'd been a pushover. I was ashamed to open my eyes. I lay in my own darkness, face down on something hard, and endured the thudding pain at the base of my skull. The odor of some heavy mantrap perfume invaded my nostrils. After a while I began to wonder where it was coming from.

Something furry or feathery tickled my ear. I lifted one hand to brush it away, and the furry or feathery thing let out a small female yelp. I rolled over and sat up. Through ripples of pain distorting my vision like heat waves, I saw a woman standing above me, dimly silhouetted against the starlight.

"You startled me," she said. "Thank heaven you've come to. Who are you, anyway?"

"Skip the questions, eh?" My head felt like an old tired baseball after batting practice. I braced one hand against the wall beside me, and got to my feet. The woman extended a gloved hand to help me, but I disregarded it. I felt for my gun, which was gone, and my wallet, which wasn't.

"I only asked you who you were," she said in a hurt tone. "What happened to you?"

"I was sapped." I leaned my back against the wall and tried to fix her faintly shimmering outline. After a while it came to rest. She was a large hippy woman in a dark suit. A dead fox crouched on her neck, its feathery tail hanging down.

"Sapped?" she repeated blankly.

"Sandbagged. Hit over the head." My voice sounded nasty even to me, thin and dry and querulous.

"Goodness gracious, should I call the police?"

"No. Leave them out of it."

"The hospital, then? Don't you need some kind of first aid? Was it a robber?"

I felt the swelling at the base of my skull. "Forget it. Just go away and forget it."

"Whoever you are, you're not very nice." She was a spoiled little girl, twenty years later. "I've a good mind to go away and leave you to your own devices."

"I'll try to bear up under it. Wait a minute, though. How did you get here?" There was no car in the road.

"I was driving past and I saw you lying here and I wasn't going to come back and then I thought I should. I left my car and walked back. Now I'm sorry I did, so there."

But she didn't mean it. Spoiled child or not, there was something I liked about the big dim woman. She had a nice warm prewar middle-western voice.

"I didn't mean to be rude."

"That's all right. I imagine you don't feel very good, poor man." She was starting to mother me.

I turned to the door. The screen door was unhooked but the inner door was locked. I wrenched at the knob and got nowhere with it.

"Nobody answers," she said behind me. "I tried knocking when you were unconscious. Did you lose your key?"

She seemed to think I lived there, and I let her go on thinking it. "I'll be all right now," I said. "I can get in the back door. Good night and thanks."

"You're welcome." But she was unwilling to go.

I left her lingering hippily on the porch and went to the back of the house. The Packard was gone from the driveway. There were no lights behind any of the windows. The back door was locked, but it was equipped with a half-length window. I took off one of my shoes and used it to punch a hole in the glass. I was pretty certain that Tarantine had gone. He wouldn't have left me lying on the threshold if he was still inside.

I turned the inside knob and let myself into the kitchen. Hoping the woman would take it as a signal to go away, I switched on the kitchen light. Monel metal and porcelain and brand-new off-white paint dazzled my eyes. The kitchen had everything: dishwasher, garbage disposal unit, electric range, even a big deep-freezer in the corner by the refrigerator. There was a little food in the refrigerator, milk and butter and ham and a head of lettuce, but nothing at all in the freezer. It looked as if Tarantine hadn't intended to stay long.

I went through the small dark dinette into the living-room and found a table-lamp, which I turned on. It cast a parchment-yellowed light on a couple of overstuffed chairs and a davenport to match, a white oak radio cabinet, a tan-colored rug of cheap frieze, a small brick fireplace. The room was so similar to a hundred thousand others that it might have been stamped out by a die. There was nothing there to give me a clue to the people who had used it, except for a *Daily Racing Form* crumpled on one of the chairs. Even the ashtrays were empty.

The bedroom was equally anonymous. It contained twin beds, one of which had been slept in, from the middle-income floor of a department store, a dressing-table, and a chest of drawers with nothing in the drawers. The only trace of Galley was a spilling of suntan powder on the dressing-table. Tarantine had left no trace at all, if you didn't count the bump on the back of my head.

Going back into the living-room, I heard a tapping on the front door. I went to the door and opened it. "What do you want?"

"Why, nothing. I only wondered, are you quite sure you're going to be all right here by yourself?"

She was overdoing her Good Samaritan act. I switched on the porch light above her and looked hard into her face. It wasn't a bad sort of face, though you might have called it moon-shaped. It had a fine mouth, wide and full and generous. The eyes were blue, slightly damaged by recent grief; the lids were puffed. She looked like a soft and easygoing woman who had come up against something hard and unexpected. Her carefully curled red hair was too bright to be natural. The fox was blue and expensive.

"What are you looking at me like that for? Have I got a smut on my nose?"

"I'm trying to figure out why you're so persistent."

She could have taken offense, but she decided to smile instead. Her smile, complete with nose wrinkling, was in a nice old-fashioned idiom like her speech. "It isn't every night I stumble over unconscious men, you know."

"All right," I said. "I'll lie down and you can stumble over me again. Then will you go away?"

"I will not." She stuck out her lower lip in an impressive pout. "I want to talk to you. What's your name?"

"Archer."

"Then you don't really live here. It belongs to a man named Dalling. I made inquiries this afternoon."

I had forgotten the man with the memorable face. I pushed past her out the door and beyond the circle of light from the porch. The road was bare on the other side of the intersection, and as far as I could see. Dalling had run out long ago.

She followed me like an embarrassing bulky shadow. "You didn't answer my question." Her voice was sibilant with suspicion.

"Dalling's my landlord," I said.

"What's his first name?" Her cross-questioning technique reminded me of a grade-school teacher conducting a spelling bee.

"Keith."

"I guess you really do live here, Mr. Archer. Excuse me."

While we were standing there on the unseeded lawn, lighting up the sky with our repartee, a pair of headlights swept up out of nowhere and slid along the road in our direction. The car passed us without stopping or even slackening speed, but my overworked glands spurted adrenalin. If Tarantine came back to inquire after my health, I didn't want to be available.

"You better go home," I said. "Where do you live?"

"I'm staying at the Oasis Inn, with my husband."

"Can I get transportation to Palm Springs?"

"There's a taxi stand at the Inn. I'll be glad to drive you over."

"Good. I'll be with you in a minute."

I went through the house turning off the lights, closed the doors, and rejoined her in the road. Her car, a new Cadillac, was parked on the shoulder a couple of hundred yards from the house. She had to use a key to open it. Another thing that puzzled me was the fact that the Cadillac was turned towards the house.

"Let me get this straight," I said as she started the engine. "You were driving past the house when you saw me lying on the porch. So you backed up two hundred yards in the dark, locked your car, and then went back to investigate. Is that what you did?"

She sat behind the wheel letting the motor idle. Her answer when it came was another question, off at another tangent: "Do you know my husband, Mr. Archer?"

The question took me by surprise. "Your husband?"

"Henry Fellows. Colonel Henry Fellows."

"I don't know him."

She fed gas to the motor, and the heavy car moved on the crackling gravel. "I really don't know him myself very well. We were married only recently." She added after a moment's pause: "As a matter of fact, we're on our honeymoon."

"Why don't you go home and get acquainted with him? No time like the present."

"He wasn't at the Inn when I left. I came out looking for him. Are you sure you don't know him, Mr. Archer?"

"I know several thousand people, several dozen colonels. I don't know a Henry Fellows."

"Then it couldn't have been Henry who struck you and knocked you unconscious?"

I felt out of touch with reality, wherever it was. The big car rolling across the star-blanched desert might have been a space-ship just landed on the moon. "Where did you get that idea?"

"I just wondered."

"Did you see him?"

"No, I didn't." She sounded uncomfortable. "It was a silly idea. I shouldn't have put it into words."

"What does he look like?"

She answered reluctantly, then warmed to her work: "He's a large man, in his forties—a great tall powerful creature. I need a big man to set me off, you know. Henry's quite distinguished looking with his nice brown wavy hair, and the gray at his temples." A sharper note entered her voice: "He's very attractive to women."

I tried to dredge up an image of the man who had knocked me out, but nothing came. I had had no time to turn and look at him. Perhaps I had seen his shadow on the veranda floor. I couldn't even be sure of that.

"I'm pretty sure it wasn't Henry," I said. "You don't have any reason to think it was?"

"No. I shouldn't have said it."

"How do you spell the last name?"

She spelled it out for me. "I'm Marjorie Fellows. But if he thinks he can carry on like this, even before our honeymoon is over—I shan't be Marjorie Fellows for long!" Her mind was helplessly hung up between love for Henry and resentment of him. New tears glittered like rhinestones on her lashes.

I felt sorry for the big soft woman, driving her car along unpeopled streets in early-morning darkness—a poor sort of way to pass a honeymoon. She seemed out of place on the California desert.

"Where did you meet Colonel Fellows?"

"In Reno." But she had remembered her pride, and it stiffened her voice: "I don't care to discuss it. Please forget what I said."

At the next corner, she jerked the steering-wheel viciously, cutting the wheels so the tires ground in the stones. There was a little settlement of lights ahead, which became a scattering of buildings behind an adobe wall. A score of cars were parked with their noses to the wall, a single taxi at the end of the line. A blue neon sign, OASIS INN, hung over the entrance of the largest building, which fronted on the road.

She turned her car into an empty space between two others, switched off the engine and headlights. We got out together.

As we walked down the line of cars towards the entrance, a man emerged from the shadows under the stucco portico. He strode towards us, literally shouting: "Marjorie! Where have you been?"

She stood still, frightened stiff, unable to answer him. He stepped up close to her, tall and wide and angry. "Where have you been?"

I said: "Fortunately for me, your wife decided to go for a midnight drive. I was lost in the desert, my car broke down, and she gave me a lift to civilization." This was civilization. And I was back on the little-boy-lost routine again.

"What made you do that, Marjorie?" One of his hands closed over one of her arms. The flesh bulged out on either side of it, and she winced.

I thought of hitting him. He was big enough to make it worth while, a powerful-looking heavyweight with a nose like a battering ram. It would give me a good deal of satisfaction, but on the other hand it wouldn't help Marjorie. Henry would have the rest of their life together to take it out on her, and he looked like the man to do just that.

"Why shouldn't I go for a ride by myself?" She jerked her arm free. "What do you care? You go away and neglect me all the time."

"Now, darling, that's not fair. You had me worried sick when you didn't come home."

"Were you really worried, Henry?"

"You know I was. I can't have my sweet girl wandering around in the desert at all hours of the night." His pale eyes glared in my direction, as if I had kidnapped his bride.

Marjorie was doing fine, it seemed. I thanked her and said good night. She fluttered a hand at me, then tucked it possessively under the big man's arm.

Chapter 11

IT WAS nearly eight by my watch, and delivery trucks were honking their matins, when I got back to town. I was feeling accident-prone, and I drove within the speed limit. The twisted scrap of mind the night had left me was concentrated on Keith Dalling. He had escorted me gracefully into a very queer setup, and gracefully run out. I owed him an opportunity to explain. His yellow Buick was in the parking lot behind the Casa Loma. I eased my car in beside it and got out. The Buick was locked and empty.

An outside wooden staircase led up from the parking lot to a series of long porches across the rear wall of the building. Dalling's back door, if he had one, would be on the second floor at the far right end. A milkman ran down the stairs, a metal basket full of empty bottles clanking in each hand. "Morning," he cried. "Up early, eh?" He disappeared down the alley.

I climbed the stairs to the second floor and followed the veranda to the end. Dalling's apartment had a back door, with a black 8 stenciled on it. The door was an inch ajar, and it opened wider when I knocked. An alarm clock chirped on the other side of the wall, uneager feet shuffled across a floor. Neither my knocking nor the neighbor's alarm clock wakened Dalling.

I pushed the door wide open and entered his kitchen. It was a bachelor's kitchen done by an expressionist scene-designer, probably a Russian. The sink was brimming with dirty water in which a half-submerged pagoda of dirty dishes stood precariously. There were more dirty dishes and a bottle half full of sour milk on the folding table attached to the wall in the breakfast corner. What I could see of the linoleum floor was glazed with grime. But most of it was covered with empty whisky bottles in staggered rows, a sad little monument to Dalling's thirst. Many of the bottles were pints and some were half-pints, which meant that Dalling had sometimes had no more than a dollar between him and sobriety.

I picked my way across the floor to the open door of the living-room. Someone had smashed a bottle on the door frame. The jagged dried splash on the wall still smelled of bourbon,

58

and the floor was littered with brown shards of glass which crunched under my feet.

The living-room was dim behind closed Venetian blinds. I jerked the cord to let the morning in, and looked around me. A scarred prewar radio-phonograph stood by the window, with piles of records on the floor beside it. There was a shallow fireplace in the inside wall, containing a cold gas heater unnecessarily protected by a brass fire-screen. On the wall above the fireplace Van Gogh's much reproduced sunflowers burned in a bamboo frame. The mantel held some old copies of *Daily Variety* and *Hollywood Reporter*, and a few books: cheap reprints of Thorne Smith, Erskine Caldwell, the poems of Joseph Moncure March, and *The Lost Weekend*. There was one handsome book, a copy of *Sonnets from the Portuguese* bound in green tooled leather. Its flyleaf was inscribed: "If thou must love me, let it be for naught except for love's sake only.—Jane." Jane wrote a precise small hand.

The most conspicuous piece of furniture was a Murphy bed standing on its hind legs in a doorway across the room. I had to push it aside before I could get through the door. I did this with my elbow, instead of my fingerprint surfaces. I suppose I smelled the blood before I was conscious of it.

There was a great deal of blood in the little hallway on the other side of the door. It covered the floor from wall to wall, a dark pool filming over now and beginning to cake at the edges. Dalling lay in the middle of it, prone on his back and finished. His waxen profile caught the light that shone through the bathroom door. At first glance I couldn't make out the hole through which the blood had wasted. Leaning over, I saw the puncture in the far slope of his neck and the powder burns on his collar. He was dressed as I had seen him in Palm Springs, and he made a handsome corpse. Any mortician would have been proud of Dalling.

A sheaf of envelopes and folded papers lay on the unbreathing chest halfway out of the jacket's inside pocket. Hugging the door frame with one crooked elbow, I leaned further out over the red pool and got them. It wasn't legal, but on the other hand paper seldom took usable fingerprints.

I went back to the window with the papers, and read through them quickly. A Third Street auto agency intended to repossess the Buick if Dalling didn't pay overdue installments of one hundred and sixty-five dollars and fifty cents. A note on the letterhead of a talent agency, signed by one of its partners, stated that things were tough all over in show biz, if that was any comfort, but TV might make a few more jobs in the fall. An overdraft notice from a downtown bank hinted at a threat of legal proceedings. A Beverly Hills tailor was turning over his account to a collection agency.

I returned to the door of the hallway and took a second look for a gun. There was none in sight, and it wasn't likely that Dalling had fallen on it in his position. Somebody else had done him the final favor.

There was only one personal letter, written on an interoffice memo form from a Hollywood radio station. It was handwritten in neat small calligraphy, and signed Jane:

Dear Keith, It may be difficult for you to believe, under the circumstances, that I was glad to hear from you, but, even under the circumstances, I truly was. I shall always be glad to hear from you, whatever the reason. I don't think, however, that it would be good for either of us to try to renew our relationship, as you suggest. What's past is past, though I think of you often and bear you no ill feeling. I do hope, Keith, that you are taking better care of yourself now. I enclose my personal check for one hundred dollars, and trust it will tide you over your current embarrassment.

Yours sincerely,

Jane

Jane's full name was written above the station call-letters that were printed on the envelope. It was Jane Starr Hammond. The envelope had been postmarked early in March.

I found her name again in the small red leather address-book that was the last of the items from Dalling's breast pocket. There were a great many names in the book, nine out of ten of them female, and a great many telephone numbers. The only addresses and telephone numbers that interested me deeply were the ones on the last page: Mrs. Samuel Lawrence's and my own. I tore out that last page, and put the book and the bills and the letters back where I had got them.

Dalling had no more use for Malibu telephone numbers or hundred-dollar loans. He'd keep no more whisky vigils in the Murphy bed, with desperation and a dying bottle for bedmates. No one would ever send him another book of poems with love written small and neat on the flyleaf.

There were two men starting their cars in the parking lot, but they didn't pay any special attention to me. I got into my car and switched on the engine. The yellow Buick stood there waiting to be repossessed.

Chapter 12

I CALLED Jane Starr Hammond's number from a short-order restaurant on the boulevard. If I reached her before the body was discovered and the police visited her, I might learn something that I otherwise wouldn't. A maid with a Negro lilt in her voice answered the phone immediately. Miss Hammond had already left for the studio; she would be in her office there the rest of the morning. I went back to my seat at the counter and contemplated the ham and eggs I had ordered. The yolk of one of the eggs had leaked out onto the plate like a miniature pool of yellow blood. I had black coffee for breakfast.

Parking spaces in downtown Hollywood were as scarce as the cardinal virtues. I found a place on Cahuenga and walked back to the studio, which occupied the third and fourth floors of a stone-faced building on Sunset. When I asked for Miss Hammond's office, the blue-uniformed elevator attendant let me off on the third floor and pointed down the corridor. Her name was on the translucent glass pane of a door, with PRIVATE printed underneath. I knocked lightly and waited, undergoing a rare attack of embarrassment. It passed.

"Come in," a cool voice answered, "it isn't locked."

I stepped into a light and airy office and closed the door behind me. Its opposite wall was a giant studio window. A young woman sat with her back to the light, working at a bleached mahogany desk. She was as crisp and exact as the daffodils in the square white bowl at her elbow. She was shiny and trim in a navy blue faille suit and a flat blue sailor hat, too trim and shiny. She looked as if she was made of rustless alloys, synthetic rubber and dyes, powered by a chrome-plated engine clicking away inside her porcelain chest. She wore a fresh gardenia on her lapel.

She looked up from the typescript she was penciling, and caught me regarding the hat. "Pay no attention to the flying saucer." She showed her small even teeth in a practiced smile. "I have to interview a ladybird this morning. As a matter of fact, I thought you might be she."

"I'm usually compared to insects like the cockroach."

"I mean when you knocked. Don't you know what a ladybird is? A ladybird is a bird who thinks she's a lady. The hat helps me to dominate, you know? This particular ladybird has slain wild elephants with a wild elephant gun, so she'll take some dominating. Now tell me you're her husband." She smiled expertly again. If her nose had been a trifle less sharp, her eyes a few degrees warmer, she would have been a very pretty woman. I couldn't imagine her writing the inscription in the *Sonnets from the Portuguese*.

I said: "My name is Archer. You *are* Miss Hammond?"

"You surprise and distress me, Mr. Archer. My fair pan was on the cover of *Radio Mirror* last month." I wondered if she worked this hard selling herself all day every day.

"What can I do for you?" she said. "I only have a minute."

"I'm looking for a woman named Galley Lawrence. Mrs. Joseph Tarantine. Do you know her?"

A shadow crossed her face. Her hardening blue gaze reminded me that I hadn't shaved or changed my shirt for over twenty-four hours. "I think I've heard the name. Are you a detective?"

I admitted that I was.

"You should shave more often; it puts people off. What has this Mrs. Tarantine been up to?"

"I'm trying to find out. What did she used to be up to?"

"I really don't know Mrs. Tarantine. She lives in the same apartment building as a friend of mine. I've seen her once or twice, I think, that's all."

"Under what conditions?"

"Normal conditions. She dropped into my friend's apartment for a cocktail one afternoon when I was there. I didn't like her, if that's what you mean. Her appeal is to the opposite sex. Frank sexuality is her forte. If I wanted to be catty I'd call it blatant." Her forte was the cutting word.

"Do you know her husband?"

"He was there, too, I didn't like him either. He was sleek and crawling with charm, like a tomcat, you know? They made a well-suited couple. Keith—my friend implied that Tarantine was some sort of gangster, if that's the sort of thing you're looking for." She took a cigarette from a silver box on the desk and broke it clean in half between her carmine-tipped fingers. "What *are* you looking for, anyway?"

I didn't know myself. "Just information. Is this friend of yours Keith Dalling?"

"Yes. Have you talked to Keith—Mr. Dalling?" She managed to get the second cigarette between her lips.

I leaned across the desk and held my lighter to it. "I'd like to. He doesn't answer his phone."

She puffed hungrily on the cigarette. "What did she do? I've always considered her capable of anything. I named her Ignoble Savage."

"Her husband seems to have committed a theft."

"From whom?"

"I daren't say."

"And you want to question Keith?"

"Yes."

"He isn't involved in it, is he?" Now she was really worried. And that was just as well, if she loved Dalling or ever had.

"He may be. If he's mixed up with Mrs. Tarantine."

"Oh no." She'd come close to the edge of candor but I had pushed her too fast. She drew away from it, her personality almost visibly receding. "They're just the merest acquaintances, apartment-house neighbors."

"You said they were friends."

"I certainly did not, because they aren't." The clicking machine was back in place, everything under control. "I'm afraid we've run out of time, Mr. Archer. Good morning and good luck." She crushed out her cigarette in a silver ashtray, and the last smoke puffed from her nostrils like a tiny exhaust.

"Somethng I almost forgot," I said. "There's a radio producer, a friend of Dalling's, who does a crime show based on police work. He wouldn't work for this station?"

"You are checking up on Mr. Dalling, then. Is he in some kind of trouble?" Her voice was tense, though she had regained her composure.

"I hope not."

"Of course you wouldn't tell me if he was. You probably mean Joshua Severn. Mr. Dalling used to work for him. He doesn't work for the studio, he owns his own show, but he has an office down the hall. Sometimes he's even in it."

"Thank you, Miss Hammond."

"Don't mention it, Mr. Archer."

There was a telephone booth in the first-floor lobby of the building next door. The man behind the news counter wore the frosted glasses of the blind. I called police headquarters from the booth, and told the sergeant on duty that I was worried about a friend of mine. His name was Keith Dalling and he lived in the Casa Loma, Apartment 8. He didn't answer when I phoned or when I knocked on the door—

"And what is your name, sir?" he cut in sharply.

I deliberately misunderstood the question: "Keith Dalling. He lives at the Casa Loma."

"Just one minute, sir." His voice was soothing.

There was a buzzing silence on the line, terminated by a double click. It probably meant that the body had been found and they were tracing my call.

I hung up. I went back to the studio building and up in the elevator again to the third floor. I found the name Joshua Severn on a door at the rear of the building. It was standing slightly ajar; a continuous low murmur came from the other side. I knocked and was told to come in.

It was a working room, containing two desks piled with papers, a pair of metal filing-cabinets, a blackboard on one wall. At the moment the blackboard showed the odds on a half-dozen Derby candidates quoted from the winter book. A heavy middle-aged man switched off the dictating machine on the table beside him and straightened up in his chair.

"Mr. Severn?"

"That's what it says on the door." He said it cheerfully. He had a broad cheerful face surmounted by a brush of erect gray hair, like iron filings tempted by a magnet.

"My name is Archer."

"Wait a minute. Not Lew Archer?" He stood up and offered me a stubby hand. "I'm glad to meet you, Archer. Have a seat."

I said that I was glad to meet him, too, and sat in the chair he pushed up beside his desk. I added I hadn't been aware that my name was a byword in the upper echelons of the radio industry.

He grinned. Most of his features, nose and ears and chin, were a little larger than life-size and slightly squashed-looking, as if they'd outgrown their mold. "It's a darn funny thing, Archer. It happens to me all the time. The extra-sensory boys, the parapsychologists, have got me half convinced. I start thinking about somebody I haven't seen or heard of for maybe two years. Within twenty-four hours after I get the flash, I meet the guy on the street or he marches into my office, just like you." He glanced at the yachtsman's chronometer on his wrist. "It took you thirty-six."

"I'm always a little slow. I take it you were thinking about me around nine thirty Sunday night. Why?"

"A fellow I know called in from Palm Springs. He wanted the name of a good private detective, one who works alone. I gave him yours. I have a beach house in Santa Teresa, and Miranda Sampson was singing your praises last year. Okay?"

"Miranda's a nice girl," I said. "Who was the fellow that called you Sunday night?"

"Keith Dalling. Did he get in touch with you?"

I made a quick adjustment. "Yes, he did. I talked to him on the phone, but I haven't seen him yet."

"Funny, he sounded in a hurry. What sort of job does he want you for, anyway?"

"He asked me to keep it confidential. I have my doubts about it. That's why I'm here."

"Hell, there goes my extra-sensory perception. Dalling mentioned *me* to *you*, eh?" He took a long black Havana out of a box on the desk and bit its end off. "Have a cigar."

"Not in the morning, thanks. Yes, Dalling mentioned you. He said you told him a little story about a man called Dowser."

"The mobster?" Unconsciously he began to eat the unlit cigar. "Dowser's name never came up between us."

"You didn't give him any information about Dowser?"

"I don't know anything about Dowser. I've heard he was in the dope racket but they're saying that about them all these days. You were the only name I mentioned. What kind of a line has Keith been feeding you?"

"Grade B movie stuff," I said. "Is he a pathological liar?"

"Not when he's sober. You've got to watch him when he's drunk, and it's hard to tell when he is. He's a terrible alcoholic." Severn removed the cigar from his mouth and looked at the wet mashed end without seeing it. "I hope our Keith hasn't got himself mixed up with a crew of thugs. I warned him about the girl he was running with."

"Galley Tarantine?"

His eyebrows moved. "She comes into the picture, too, eh? Did Dalling tell you who her husband is? I don't know Tarantine, but he has a bad name with the police. I told Keith he better lay off her or he'd end up with a knife stuck under his ribs. Is he in trouble with Tarantine?"

"He may be. He didn't say very much. If you can fill me in on his background, it might help." I tried to sound as diffident as possible. Severn looked sharp.

Very sharp. The blue eyes under his heavy black brows were hard and bright as diamonds. "Are you working for Keith or against him? You're not very communicative yourself."

"I'm for him a hundred per cent." Which was true. I was a sucker for underdogs, and dead men were at the bottom of the heap.

"Good enough. I'll take Miranda's word for your honesty. I like the boy, you see, I've known him since he was a kid. He used to crew for me before the war when I had my Star boat, and we won the cup at Santa Monica one year. I didn't fire him until I was forced to; the sponsor was raising Cain."

"He worked for you?"

"He worked on a lot of shows, he's a good actor. Trouble was, he couldn't lay off the liquor and they canned him one by one and finally blacklisted him. I was the last one that kept him on; he played my detective-lieutenant for over two years. It got pretty rough. He fluffed so many lines I was scissoring the tape every bloody week. One day he passed out in the middle of a show and I had to go out on the streets for an actor. I cut him off, though it broke my heart to do it. It played hell with his life, I guess. He was going to get married, and he was building himself a house. I guess he lost the house. I know he lost the girl."

"Jane Hammond?"

"Yeah. I feel kind of sorry for Jane. She works here, you know. A lot of women have carried the torch for Keith—that's probably what ruined him—only Jane is different. He was the one big love in her life, but she was too successful for him. When I fired him, he ran out on her. I was afraid for a while she'd go crazy, though she keeps a stiff upper lip."

"When was this?"

"Around the first of the year. I fired him the day after Christmas." He made a sour face, champing savagely on the cigar.

"Nice timing, eh? Soon after that he started with Tarantine's wife. I see them in night spots now and then. As a matter of fact, I slip him a few lakhs of rupees when I can." He glanced at the dictating machiner in polite impatience. "Will that do? The things I know about Keith would take all day."

I rose and thanked him. He followed me to the door, massive and quick-moving: "I've let down the old back hair, Dalling's anyway. Do you care to tell me what it's all about?"

"He'll have to tell you himself."

He shrugged his heavy shoulders, easily, as if his weight of integrity was no burden. "Okay, Archer."

"Give my love to Miranda."

"I never see her. She moved to Hawaii. See you around."

I had to pass Jane Hammond's door to get to the elevator. The door was standing open. She was still behind her desk, sitting erect and trim with a telephone receiver in her left hand. Her right hand gripped her right breast, its carmine nails digging into the soft flesh. Her eyes were dark and deep in her head. They looked straight at me and failed to recognize me.

The police had found her name in the red leather address-book.

Chapter 13

I CROSSED to Pico Boulevard and drove to Mrs. Lawrence's house in Santa Monica. Tiredness was catching up with me. The glittering late-morning traffic hurt my eyes and feelings. I had a notion at the back of my mind that at worst Mrs. Lawrence could rent me a room to sleep in, out of reach of policemen's questions for a while. At best she might have heard from her daughter.

Mrs. Lawrence had done better, and worse, than that. The bronze Packard was parked at the curb in front of her house. The sight of it acted on me like benzedrine. I took the veranda steps in one stride, and leaned my weight on the doorbell. She came to the door immediately:

"Mr. Archer! I've been trying to get you by phone."

"Is Galley here?"

"She was. It's why I called you. Where have you been?"

"Too far. I'd like to come in, if I may."

"Excuse me. I've been so dreadfully upset I don't know if I'm coming or going." She looked distraught. Her gray hair, which had been so carefully done the previous morning, was unkempt, almost as if she'd been tearing at it with her hands. A single day had drawn deeper lines in her face.

Still she was very courteous as she stood back to let me enter and led me down the hall to her hoard of old furniture. "You look quite worn out, Mr. Archer. May I make you some tea?"

I said: "No, thanks. Where's Galley?"

"I don't know where she went. A man came to get her about ten o'clock, when I was just giving her her breakfast. I was frying the bacon, crisp, as she's always liked it, when this man came to the door. She went away with him, without a single word of explanation." She sat down in a platform rocker just inside the door of the room, her clenched hands resting stiffly on her knees.

"Could he have been her husband? Did you see him?"

"Her husband?" Her voice sounded weary and bewildered. She had encountered too much life in too short a time. "Surely she isn't married."

"She seems to be, to a man called Tarantine. Didn't she tell you?"

"We barely had a chance to talk. She came home late last night—I don't know how to thank you, Mr. Archer, for what you've done—"

"Galley mentioned me, then."

"Oh yes. She came straight home after you found her. It was very late, after dawn in fact, and she was too tired to want to talk very much. This morning I let her sleep in. It was so grand to have my girl back in her own bed. Now she's gone away again." She sat gazing at the fact, drearily blinking her eyes.

"This man," I nudged her attention. "Did you see the man she went with?"

"Certainly. I answered the door myself. I didn't like his looks at all. He was a very thin man, a walking skeleton. I thought when I looked at him he must have tuberculosis. Galley wouldn't marry a man like that." But her statement curled at the edges into a question.

"That isn't her husband. Did he threaten you, or her?"

"Heavens, no. He simply asked for Galley, very quietly. She came to the door and they talked together for a minute. I didn't hear what was said. Galley closed the door and stepped outside. Then she came back in and put on her coat and left."

"Without a word?"

"She said good-bye. She said she would be back soon. I tried to get her to eat her breakfast first, but she was in too great a hurry."

"Was she frightened?"

"I don't know. I've never seen my daughter show fear. She is a very courageous girl, Mr. Archer, she always has been. Her father and I tried to teach her to face the world with fortitude."

I was standing above her, resting part of my weight on the edge of the refectory table. I noticed that she was looking at me with growing disapproval.

"Is something the matter?"

"Please sit down in a *chair*, Mr. Archer. That table was one of the doctor's favorite pieces."

"Sorry." I sat down.

Her past-encumbered mind came back to the present again: "You've implied several times that Galley is in danger."

"I got the idea from you."

"Don't you believe she will come back soon, as she promised? Has something happened to my girl, Mr. Archer?" One of her fists was steadily pounding one of her bony knees.

"I don't know. All you can do is wait and see."

"Can't *you* do something? I'll give you anything I have. If only nothing dreadful happens to Galley."

"I'll do what I can. I'm in this case to stay."

"You're a good man." The fist stopped pounding.

"Hardly." She lived in a world where people did this or that because they were good or evil. In my world people acted because they had to. I gave her a little bulletin from my world: "Last night your daughter's husband knocked me out with a sandbag and left me lying. I make a point of paying back things like that."

"Goodness gracious! What kind of a man is Galley married to?"

"Not a good man." Perhaps our worlds were the same after all, depending on how you looked at them. The things you had to do in my world made you good or evil in hers. "You'll probably be hearing from the police some time today."

"The police? Is Galley in wrong with the police?" It was the final affront to Dr. Lawrence's memory and the furniture. Her hands rose to her head and lifted her hair in two gray tangled wings.

"Not necessarily. They'll want to ask some questions. Tell them the truth. Tell them I told you to tell them the truth." I moved to the door.

"Where are you going?"

"I think I know where Galley is. Did she go away in a car?"

"Yes, a big black car. There was a second man driving."

"I'll bring her back if I can."

"Wait a minute." She followed me down the dim hallway and detained me at the front door. "There's something I must tell you."

"About Galley? If it isn't you'd better save it."

Her roughened hand moved on my sleeve. "Yes, about Galley. I haven't been entirely candid, Mr. Archer. Now you tell me the police are coming here—"

"Nothing to worry about. They'll want to do some checking."

"A policeman was here Sunday night," she said. "He warned me not to divulge the fact to anyone, not even you."

"How did I come into the conversation? I entered this case on Monday."

"Lieutenant Dahl urged me to employ you. He's a detective in the Vice Squad, he said, a very lovely young man. He said my girl was living with a criminal whom he was shortly going to have to arrest. But he knew that Galley was an innocent good girl, and he didn't want to involve her if he could help it. So he gave me your name and telephone number. He said that you were honest and discreet, but even so I wasn't to tell you about his conversation with me." She bit her lip. "It's terribly wrong of me to violate his confidence like this."

"When did he come here?"

"Sunday night, after midnight. He got me up out of bed."

"What did he look like?"

"He was in civilian clothes—an extremely handsome young fellow."

"Tall, wavy reddish hair, purple eyes, movie-actor's profile, radio-actor's voice?"

"Do you know Lieutenant Dahl?"

"Very slightly," I said. "Our friendship never had a chance to come to its full flower."

Chapter 14

I WENT up the looping road in second and stopped at the green iron gate. The sentry was already out of the gatehouse with the shotgun. The sun burned on the oiled and polished barrels.

"How's the hunting?" I asked him.

He had a bulldog face whose only expression was a frozen ferocity intended to scare off trespassers. "You better beat it. This is private property."

"Dowser is expecting me. I'm Archer."

"You stay in your car and I'll check." He retired to the gatehouse, from which a telephone wire ran to the main building. When he came out he opened the gate for me. "You can park over here by the fence."

He moved up close to me as I got out of the car. I stood still and let his hands run down me. They paused at my empty holster. "Where's the gun?"

"I ditched it."

"Trouble?"

"Trouble."

Blaney met me at the front door, still wearing the wide black hat. "I didn't expect you back."

I took a long look at the mushroom-colored face, the ground glass eyes. They told me nothing. If Blaney had shot Dalling he'd done it without a second thought.

"I can't resist your charming hospitality," I said. "Where's the boss?"

"Eating lunch in the patio. You're to come on out, he says."

Dowser was sitting alone at a wrought-iron table by the swimming pool, a crabmeat salad with mayonnaise in front of him. His short hair was wet, and he was wrapped to the chin in a white terrycloth robe. With his bulging eyes and munching jaws he looked like an overgrown gopher masquerading as a man.

He went on eating for a while, to remind me of his importance in the world. He ate pieces of crabmeat and lettuce with his fingers, and then he licked his fingers. Blaney stood and watched him like an envious ghost. I looked around at the oval

73

pool still stirred and winking with the memory of Dowser's bathe, the spectrum of flowers that fringed the patio, all the fine things that Dowser had pushed and cheated and killed for. And I wondered what I could do to take them away from Dowser.

He pushed the demolished salad away and lit a cigarette. "You can go in, Blaney." The thin man vanished from my side.

"Did you get my special delivery?"

"Come again. Sit down if you want to."

I took a chair across the table from him. "I flushed the girl for you. Tarantine was too quick for me, or I'd have brought him in too."

"*You* flushed her! We had to find her ourselves. Some dame called in this morning that she was at her old lady's. That wasn't you on the phone, was it, doing a female impersonation?"

"I don't have the figure for it," I said, looking him up and down.

"So where do you come in?"

"I brought her from Palm Springs for you. You said it was worth a thousand."

"The way I understand it, she came by herself. I pay for value received."

"You've got her, haven't you? You wouldn't have her if I hadn't sent her home to mother. I talked her into it."

"That's not her story."

"What is her story?"

"She isn't talking much." He looked uncomfortable, and changed the subject: "Did you see Tarantine?"

"I didn't see him. He sapped me from behind. The girl tried to stop it, I think. There's a possibility she isn't in this with him. Whatever *this* is."

He laughed his unenjoyable laugh. "You'd like to know, huh?"

"When I get beaten over the head, I'm interested in the reason."

"I'll tell you the reason. Tarantine has something of mine, you maybe guessed it, huh? I'm going to get it back. The girl says she don't know nothing about it."

"What does it look like?"

"That doesn't matter. He won't be toting it around with him. When I get him, then I get *it* afterwards."

"Junk," I said under my breath. If he heard me he paid no attention.

"You working for me, Archer?"

"Not for love."

"I offered you five grand for Tarantine. I'll raise it five."

"You offered me one for Galley. You're full of offers." I was watching his face closely, to see how far I could go in that direction.

"Be reasonable," he said. "You brought her in, I'd of slipped you the cash just like an expressman at the door. You didn't bring her. Blaney had to go and get her himself. I can't afford to throw money away on good will. My expenses are a friggin' crime these days. I got a payroll that would break your heart and now the lawyers tell me I got to pay back income-tax to clear myself with the feds." His voice was throbbing with the injustice of it all. "Not to mention the politicians," he added. "The God-damn politicians bleed me white."

"Five hundred, then," I said. "We'll split the difference."

"Five hundred dollars for nothing?" But he was just haggling now, trying to convert a bargain to a steal.

"Last night it was a thousand. Only last night you didn't have the girl."

"The girl is no good to me. If she knows where Joe Tarantine is, she isn't telling."

"Let me talk to her?" Which was the point I had been aiming at from the beginning.

"She'll talk for me. It takes a little time." He stood up, tightening the sash around his flabby waist. There was something womanish about the gesture, though the muscles bulged like angry veins in his sleeves.

On his feet he looked smaller. His legs were proportionately shorter than his body. I stayed in my chair. Dowser would be more likely to do what I wanted him to do if he could look down at the top of my head. There were two-inch heels on the sandals that clasped his feet.

"A little time," I repeated. "Isn't that what Tarantine needs to get lost in Mexico? Or wherever he's gone."

"I can extradite him," he said with his canine grin. "All I need to know is where he is."

"And if she doesn't know?"

"She knows. She'll remember. A man don't leave behind a piece like her. Not Joey. He loves his flesh."

"Speaking of flesh, what have you been doing to the girl?"

"Nothing much." He shrugged his heavy shoulders. "Blaney pushed her around a little bit. I guess now I got my strength up I'll push her around a little bit myself." He punched himself in the abdomen, not very hard.

"I wish you'd let me talk to her," I said.

"Why all the eager interest, baby?"

"Tarantine sapped me."

"He didn't sap you in the moneybags, baby. That's where you get the real agony."

"No doubt. But here's my idea. The girl has a notion I might be on her side." If Galley had that notion, she was right. "If you muss my hair and shove me in alongside her, it should convince her. I suppose you've got her locked in some dungeon?"

"You want to stool for me, is that the pitch?"

"Call it that. When do I get my five hundred?"

He dug deep into the pocket of his robe, slipped a bill from the gold money-clip and tossed it on the table. "There's your money."

I rose and picked it up against my will, telling myself it was justified under the circumstances. Taking his money was the only way I knew to make Dowser trust me. I folded the bill and tucked it into my watch pocket, separate from my other money, promising myself that at the earliest opportunity I'd bet it on the horses.

"It might be a good idea," he said. "You have a talk with the girl before we rough her up too much. I kind of like her looks the way she is. Maybe you do too, huh?" The bulging eyes shone with a lewd cunning.

"She's a lovely piece," I said.

"Well, don't start getting any ideas. I'll put you in where she is, see, and all you do is talk to her. Along the lines we discussed. I got a mike in there, and a one-way window. I put the one-way window in for the politicians. They come to visit me sometimes, see. I take my own sex straight."

So does a coyote, I thought, and did not say.

Chapter 15

A FTER THE sunswept patio, the room was very dim behind three-quarters-drawn drapes. A thin partition of light fell through it from the uncovered strip of window, dividing it into two unequal sections. The section to my right held a dressing-table and a long chair upholstered in dark red satin. I saw myself in the mirror above the dressing-table. I looked disheveled enough without even trying. The heavy door slammed shut and a key turned in the lock.

In the section to my left there were more chairs, a wide bed with a red silk padded head, a portable cellarette beside the bed in lieu of a bedside table. Galley Tarantine crouched on the bed like a living piece of the dimness and the stillness. Only the amber discs of her eyes showed life. Then the point of her tongue made a slow circuit of her lips at the pace of a second hand:

"This is an unexpected pleasure. I didn't know I was going to have a cellmate. The right sex, too." There was some irony there. Her voice, low and intense, was well adapted to it.

"You're very observant." I went to the window and found that it was a casement, but bolted top and bottom on the outside.

"It isn't much use," she said. "Even if you smashed it, the place is too well guarded to get away from. Dowser plays with gunmen the way other spoiled little boys play with lead soldiers. He thinks he's Napoleon Bonaparte and he probably suffers from the same anatomical deficiency. I wouldn't know myself. I wouldn't let him touch me with a ten-foot pole." She spoke quietly but clearly, apparently taking pleasure in the sound of her own voice, though it had growling overtones. I hoped that Dowser was hearing all of this, and wondered where the mike was.

Perhaps in the cellarette. I turned from the window to look at it, and the light fell on my face. The woman sat up higher on her heels and let out a little gasp of recognition. "You're Archer! How did you get here?"

"It all goes back about thirty-seven years ago." She was too bright for a Lochinvar approach. "A few months before I was born, my mother was frightened by a tall dark stranger with a sandbag. It had a queer effect on my infant brain. Whenever anybody hits me with a sandbag, I fall down and get up angry."

"You touch me deeply," she said. "How did you know it was a sandbag?"

"I've been sandbagged before." I sat down on the foot of the bed and fingered the back of my head. The swelling there was as sore as a boil.

"I'm sorry. I tried to stop it, but Joe was too fast. He sneaked out the back of the house and around to the porch in his stocking feet. You're lucky he didn't shoot you." She shuffled towards me on her knees, her hips rotating with a clumsy kind of grace. "Let me look at it."

I bent my head. Her fingers moved cool and gentle on the swelling. "It doesn't look too bad. I don't think there's any concussion, not much anyway." Her fingers slid down the nape of my neck.

I looked up into the narrow face poised over me. The full red lips were parted and the black eyes dreamed downward heavily. Her hair was uncombed. She had sleepless hollows under her eyes, a dark bruise on her temple. She still was the fieriest thing I'd seen up close for years.

"Thanks, nurse."

"Don't mention it." The dark hawk face came down and kissed my mouth. For an instant her breast came hard against my shoulder, then she withdrew to the other end of the bed.

It made the blood run round in my veins too fast. But she was calm and cool, as if it were a thing she did for all her patients.

"What did Joe do after that?" I said.

"You haven't told me how you got here.—Have you a comb?"

I tossed her my pocket comb. Her hair crackled and ran smooth like black water through her hands. I looked around the room for Dowser's one-way window. There was a double band of black glass along the edges of the panel heater near the door.

"You wouldn't be one of Dowser's lead soldiers, would you?" She was still combing her hair, her bosom rising and falling with the movement of her arms.

"That bum? I wouldn't be here if I was. I told you your mother hired me."

"Ah yes, you're Mother's helper. Did you see her?"

"No more than an hour ago. Stop combing your hair, it disturbs me."

A white grin lit her face. "Poor mans, did I excite hims?"

"That was the idea, wasn't it?"

"Was it?" The tossed comb would have hit me in the face if I hadn't palmed it. "What did Mother say?"

"She said she'd give whatever she has if I could bring you back."

"Really?" For the first time she sounded and looked dead serious. "Did she mean it?"

"She meant it all right. I said I'd do what I can."

"So you came up here and got yourself locked up. It took you less than an hour. You move fast, Archer."

I assumed an angry tone which turned out to be half real: "If I had my gun, it wouldn't have happened. Your husband took my gun last night."

"He took mine, too," she said.

"Where did he go?"

"You'll never catch him now."

"You know where he is, then?"

"I can guess. He didn't tell me anything himself. He never did."

"Don't kid me."

"I wouldn't if I could," she said. "It's true. When I went to Las Vegas with him—we were married at Gretna Green—I thought he was a wrestling promoter. I knew he worked as a pinball machine collector before that, but that seemed fairly innocent. He didn't tell me different."

"How did you meet him?"

"In line of duty, I suppose you'd call it. I had a patient by the name of Speed who used to be Joe's boss. Joe came to see this Speed in the hospital. Joe is a good-looking man, and I guess I fell." She was leaning against the padded headboard with her knees turned sideways under her. On the other side of the red chenille desert that lay between us, her thighs rose under the blue skirt like the slopes of blue mountain foothills.

"This Speed," I said. "What was the matter with him?"

"You probably know, or you wouldn't ask." The reclining slopes of her body shifted, and my nerves recorded the seismic vibrations. "Mr. Speed had a bullet wound in the stomach."

"But that didn't give you any ideas about Mr. Speed's employee?"

"I hate to admit I must have been naïve. Mr. Speed said it was an accident. He shot himself cleaning a gun, at least that was his story."

"So you married Joe, who probably shot Speed himself." I made the suggestion at random, fishing for facts.

Her eyes widened, black and depthless beneath their amber surfaces. "Oh. Joe and Herman Speed were always good friends. When Joe took over, Mr. Speed gave him pointers about the business—"

"What business?"

"The pinball machines and the wrestling contracts and various other things."

"All Dowser's things?"

"I guess so. I didn't know Joe's business. He kept me up here in L.A., you see, and Joe and I weren't very good friends after the first week. Joe had a pleasant trick of slapping people. That's why I bought my gun. It cooled him off but I was still afraid of him, and he knew it. It didn't make for marital confidences."

"But you know what Dowser wants him for?"

"I have a rough idea. He absconded with something valuable of Dowser's. But Dowser won't catch him either." She looked at the watch on her slim brown wrist. "He's probably in Mexico by now. Over the hills and far away."

"You think he went to Mexico?"

"That's what it looks like to me. I'll never see him again," she added bitterly.

"Is that going to ruin your life?"

She sat up straight, her face set in angry planes. "Look what he did. Married me under false pretenses, took me for a ride, and now he's stood me up. Left me to take a beating from Dowser and his dirty rotten crew. The dirty rotten coward."

"Tell me where he went last night?"

"Why do you want to know?"

"I want to have the pleasure of hitting him over the head with a blackjack. If I bring him in, that will clear you with Dowser, won't it?"

"It will if you're man enough to do it. You weren't last night."

There was no answer to that. "Tell me about last night. I'd like to get it straight. I met your boy friend Dalling in a bar—I think he was expecting me—and he drove me out to Oasis—"

"Dalling is not my boy friend."

"All right, he likes you, though." I was careful about the tense. "He was worried about you."

"Keith is a terrible worrier. What next?"

"He parked down the road and stayed in his car. Joe slipped out of the house while I was talking to you at the door, and sapped me. Now it's your turn."

"To sap you?"

"To say what happened after that. Did he see Dalling's car?"

"Yes. He went after it, but Keith got away. Joe came back in a rage and told me to pack, we were leaving. We were off in fifteen minutes. You were still unconscious, and I think that saved your life. He made me drive him into Los Angeles though I didn't want to do it. I suspected he was after Keith for giving away his hideout. I could tell he blamed me for it, because Keith was my friend. *Not* my boy friend.

"He was so blind mad he went back to the Casa Loma, that's where we had our apartment. I told him Dowser's men would be watching it, but he shut me up. Keith's car was in the parking lot. Joe told me to stay down there and he went up the back way himself."

"What time was this?"

"Around three, I think."

"You got there in a hurry."

"Yes, I was hitting ninety and ninety-five. I kind of hoped we'd have a blowout and put an end to the business, but no such luck." She stroked the side of her face with one hand, her eyes unfocused. "Anyway, Joe came down in a couple of minutes and said Keith wasn't at home. He made me drive him to Pacific Point and let him out near the yacht basin. That was the last I saw of him. He didn't even say good-bye to me." She smiled narrowly. "It might have been smart of him to say good-bye."

"Why don't you tell Dowser about all this? He'll turn you loose."

"I'll tell you why: Dowser let his gorilla put his paws on me. I wouldn't tell him which direction was up."

I sat and looked at her, waiting for the key to turn in the lock. The more I looked at her proud body and head, the more I liked her, and the more I liked her, the more I felt like a heel.

I had to remind myself that a man was dead, that all was for the best in the best of all possible worlds, and that anything was fair in love and war and murder. I leaned sideways on one elbow, and sleep came over my head like a gunny sack. Just before I dozed off, I heard a car engine start with a roar somewhere outside the house.

Chapter 16

WHEN I awoke the strip of sunlight had moved to the foot of the bed. It drew a broad bright band diagonally across my body, like the sash of yellow satin that went with a South American decoration. I sat up, feeling my legs constricted, and saw that Galley had pulled the spread across me.

She stirred sleepily at her end of the bed. "You've been dead to the world for two hours. It isn't very flattering. Besides, you snore."

"Sorry. I missed my sleep last night."

"I didn't mind, really. You sounded like my father. My father was quite a guy. He died when I was eight."

"And you remember what his snoring sounded like?"

"I have an excellent memory." She stretched and yawned. "Do you suppose they'll ever let us out of here?"

"Your guess is as good as mine." I threw aside the spread and stood up. "Nice of you to tuck me in."

"Professional training. Which reminds me, now that Joe is gone, I suppose I'll have to get myself a job. He didn't leave me anything but my clothes."

I remembered the condition of the clothes in the Casa Loma apartment, and kept quiet on the subject. "You're giving him up pretty easily, aren't you?"

"He won't be back," she said flatly. "If he does come back, he won't survive. And even if he did, I wouldn't take him back. Not after what he said to me last night."

I looked my question.

"We won't go into it," she said.

She flung herself off the bed and walked to the other end of the room, soft-footed in her stockings. Her narrow high-heeled shoes stood together neatly on the floor. She leaned toward the dressing-table mirror, lifting her hair to examine the bruise on her temple.

"God damn it, I can't stand waiting. I think I'll smash something." She swung around fiercely.

"Go ahead."

There was a perfume atomizer on the table. She picked it up and hurled it at the door. The perfume splattered, and bits of glass rained down.

"You've made the place smell like a hothouse."

"I feel better, anyway. Why don't *you* break something?"

"It takes a skull to satisfy me. Is Joe long-headed or round-headed? Better put on your shoes or you'll cut your feet."

"Round-headed, I guess." Standing first on one leg and then on the other, she slipped the narrow shoes on. Her legs were beautiful.

"I like the round-headed ones especially. They're like cracking walnuts, one of the happiest memories of my childhood."

She stood and faced me with her hands on her hips. "You talk a good fight, Archer. Joe can be rough, you know that."

"Tell me more."

But there were hustling footsteps in the corridor. The key turned in the lock. It was Dowser himself, in beige slacks and a chocolate jacket.

He jerked his thumb at me. "Out. I want to talk to you."

"What about me?" the girl said.

"Calm down. You can go home as far as I'm concerned. Only don't try to skip out, I want you around." He turned to Blaney behind him. "Take her home."

Blaney looked disappointed. She called out "Good luck, Archer" as he marched her away.

I followed Dowser into the big room with the bar. The curly-headed Irishman was shooting practice shots on the snooker table. He straightened up as the boss came in, presenting arms with his cue.

"I got a job for you, Sullivan," Dowser said. "You're going to Ensenada and see Torres. I talked to him on the telephone, so he knows you're coming. You stick with Torres until Joe shows up."

"Is Joe in Ensenada?"

"There's a chance he'll turn up there. The *Aztec Queen* is gone, and it looks as if he took it. You can have the Lincoln, and make it fast, huh?"

Sullivan started out and paused, fingering his black bow-tie: "What do I do with Joe?"

"Give him my best regards. You take orders from Torres."

Dowser turned to me, the big executive with more responsibility on his shoulders than one man should rightly have to bear. But always a genial host: "Want a drink?"

"Not on an empty stomach."

"Something to eat?"

"Most jails provide board for the prisoners."

He gave me a hurt look, and beat on the floor with the butt of the abandoned cue. "You're not my prisoner, baby, you're my guest. You can leave whenever you want."

"How about now?"

"Don't be in such a hurry." He hammered the floor still harder, and raised his voice: "Where the hell is everybody around here? I pay them double wages so they leave me stranded in the middle of the day. Hey! Fenton!"

"You should have a bell to ring."

An old man answered the summons at a limping run. "I was lying down, Mr. Dowser. You want something?" His eyes were bleared with sleep.

"Get Archer here something to eat. A couple of ham sandwiches, and some buttermilk for me. Hurry."

The old man ran out of the room, his shirtsleeved elbows flapping, the long white hair on his head ruffled by his own wind.

"He's the butler," Dowser said with satisfaction. "He's English, he used to work for a producer in Bel-Air. I should of made him talk for you, you ought to hear him talk. I'll make him talk when he comes back, huh? Ten-dollar words!"

"I'm afraid I have to leave," I said.

"Stick around, baby. I might have plenty of use for a man like you. That was the straight dope you got from the girl. I went to the Point and checked it personally. The bastard lammed in his brother's boat all right."

"Did you have to keep me locked up until you checked?"

"Come on, boy, I was doing you a favor. Don't tell me you didn't make out?" He leaned over the green table and sank a long shot in one of the far pockets. "How about a game of snooker, huh? A dollar a point, and I'll spot you twenty. You'll make money off me."

I was getting restless. The friendlier Dowser grew, the less I liked him. On the other hand, I didn't want to offend him. An idea for taking care of Dowser was forming at the back of my head, where it hurt, and I wanted to be able to come back to his house. I said that he was probably a shark and that I hadn't played the game for years. But I took a cue from the rack at the end of the bar.

I hardly got a chance to use my cue. Dowser made a series of brilliant runs, and took me for thirty dollars in ten minutes.

"You know," he said reminiscently, chalking his cue, "I made my living at this game for three years when I was a kid. I was going to be another Willie Hoppe. Then I found out I could fight: there's quicker money in fighting. I come up the hard way." He touched his rosebud ear with chalk-greened fingers. "How about another?"

"No, thanks. I'll have to be shoving off."

But then the butler came back with the sandwiches. He was wearing a black coat now, and had brushed his hair. "Do you wish to eat at the bar, sir?"

"Yeah. Fenton, say a ten-dollar word for Archer here."

The old man answered him with a straight face: "Antidisestablishmentarianism. Will that do, sir? It was one of Mr. Gladstone's coinages, I believe."

"How about that?" Dowser said to me. "This Gladstone was one of those English big shots, a lord or something."

"He was Prime Minister, sir."

"Prime Minister, that's it. You can go now, Fenton."

Dowser insisted that I share the buttermilk, on the grounds that it was good for the digestion. We sat side by side at the bar and drank it from chilled metal mugs. He became vivacious over his. He could tell that I was an honest man, and he liked me for it. He wanted to do things for me. Before he finished, he had offered me a job at four hundred dollars a week, and showed me the money-clip twice. I told him I liked working for myself.

"You can't make twenty thousand a year working for yourself."

"I do all right. Besides, I have a future."

I had touched a sore spot. "What do you mean by that?" His eyes seemed to swell like leeches sucking blood from his face.

"You don't last so long in the rackets. If you're lucky, you last as long as a pitcher or a fighter—"

"I run a legitimate business," he said with intensity. "I used to handle bets, sure, but that's over and done. I hardly ever break a law any more."

"Not even the murder laws?" I was getting very impatient, and it made me indiscreet.

But the question appealed to his vanity in some way. "I never even been indicted," he said.

"How many men have you lost in the last five years?"

"How the hell should I know? I got a rapid turnover, sure, it's the nature of the business. I got to protect myself from competition, I got to protect my friends." He slid off his stool and began to pace the floor: "I'll tell you one thing, Archer, I'm going to live a long time. I come from a long-lived family. My grandfather's still living, believe it or not, he's over ninety years old. I keep myself in shape, by God, and I'm going to live to be a hundred. What do you think of that?" He punched himself in the stomach, easily.

I thought that Dowser was afraid to die, and I realized why he couldn't bear to be left alone. I didn't answer him.

"I'm going to live to be a hundred," he repeated, like a man talking in his sleep.

I heard the front door open and close. Blaney appeared in the hallway.

"Did you take her home?" Dowser asked him.

"I dropped her off at the corner. There was a patrol car in front of the house."

"Cops? What do cops want with her?"

"A man named Dalling was killed this morning," I said, looking from one to the other.

Apparently the name meant nothing to Dowser. "Who's he?"

"A friend of Galley's. The cops will be asking her a lot of questions."

"She better not answer too many." He sounded unworried. "What happened to the guy?"

"I wouldn't know. Good-bye."

"Gimme a rumble if you hear anything." And he gave me his private number.

Now that Blaney was back, Dowser lost interest in me. I walked to the door unescorted and let myself out. But I didn't entirely relax until I was back on the highway.

Chapter 17

I HAD questions I wanted to ask Galley Lawrence in private, but the police had got to her first. I always believed in giving the police an official priority, when they got there first. So I stayed on the highway and drove south through Santa Monica.

It was after four o'clock when I reached the Pacific Point Hospital. I passed up the information desk and went straight upstairs to Room 204. Mario Tarantine's bed was empty. The other bed in the room was occupied by a small boy reading a comic book.

I checked on the room number again, and went down the corridor to the nurse's station. A gimlet-eyed head nurse looked up from a chart: "Visiting hours are over. We can't run a hospital if visitors don't obey regulations."

"You're absolutely right," I said. "Did Mr. Tarantine go home?"

"Mr. who?"

"Tarantine, in 204. Where is he?"

Her sharp little angled face expressed stern disapproval. "Yes, he did go home. Against his doctor's orders and his own best interests, he put on his clothes last night and walked out of the hospital. I suppose you're a friend of his?"

"I know him."

"Well, you can tell him that if he has a relapse, on his own head be it. We can't run a hospital if patients won't co-operate." The waspish buzzing followed me down the corridor.

I drove across town to the end of Sanedres Street, and parked in front of Mrs. Tarantine's cottage. The late afternoon sun shining through the laurels in the front yard made gold filigree patterns on the worn lawn. I tapped on the glass door and a man's voice called: "Come in."

I turned the knob and stepped directly into a small dim living-room. The air in the room smelled of spices and scrubbed floors and rotting flowers. The plaster wall opposite the door was almost covered with a crude painting of a four-masted schooner in full sail. Above the warped mantelpiece a tarnished gold Christ writhed on a dark wood cross.

In front of the dead fireplace, Mario Tarantine was sitting with his legs up on a time-eaten mohair davenport, a white pillow behind his bandaged head. "You again," was all he said when he saw me.

"Me again. I tried the hospital first. Are you all right?"

"Now that I'm getting some decent food I'm all right. You know what they tried to feed me in that hospital? Chicken broth. Fruit salad. Cottage cheese." His swollen mouth spat out the words as if he could taste their flavor. "How can I get my strength back on cottage cheese? I just sent Mama down to the butcher shop for the biggest steak she can find." He smiled painfully, showing his broken front teeth. "What's the word?"

"About your brother? He's been getting around. Your boat is gone, but I suppose you know that."

"The *Aztec Queen*?" He leaned toward me, heavy-shouldered, the old davenport creaking under his weight. "Gone where?"

"To Mexico, perhaps. Wherever Joe's gone."

"For Christ's sake!" His dark eyes, peering distracted from the ruined face, glanced around the room. His gaze rested on the gilt Christ above the mantel, and dropped. He stood up and moved towards me. "How long has the boat been gone? How do you know Joe took it?"

"I talked to Galley. She dropped him near the yacht basin early this morning, four or five o'clock. Does Joe have a key to the boat?"

"The bastard has *my* keys. You got a car with you? I got to get down there."

"I'll drive you if you're feeling up to it."

"I'm feeling up to it. Wait, I'll get my shoes on." He shuffled out of the room in stocking feet, and stamped back wearing boots and a leather jacket. "Let's go."

He noticed that I was looking at the painted schooner on the wall. It wasn't a lithograph, as I'd thought at first glance, but a mural painted directly on the plaster, with a black frame painted around it. The colors were garish, made worse by an impossible sunset raying the stiff water, and the draftsmanship was wobbly. Still, the leaning ship looked as if it was moving, and that was something.

"How do you like the picture?" Mario said from the open door. "Joe did it when he was a kid. He wanted to be an artist. Too bad he had to grow up into an all-round heel."

I saw then that the painting had a signature, carefully painted in script: Joseph Tarantine, 1934. It had a title, too, probably copied from a calendar: *When My Ship Comes In.*

I drove downhill to the palm-lined boulevard that skirted the seashore, and along it to the dock. Mario directed me to a lot at the base of the breakwater, where I parked beside a weather-beaten Star boat perched on a trailer. A brisk offshore wind was blowing the sand, and tossing puffs of spray across the concrete breakwater. In its lee a hundred boats lay at their moorings, ranging from waterlogged skiffs to seventy-foot sailing yachts with masts like telephone poles.

Mario looked across the bright water of the basin and groaned out loud. "It's gone all right. He took my boat." He sounded ready to cry.

I followed him up the sand-drifted steps to a gray one-room building marked HARBORMASTER. Its door was locked. We could see through the window that the office was empty.

An old man in a dinghy with an outboard chugged up to the landing platform below. Mario hailed him. "Where's the Chief?"

The old man's answer was blown away by the wind. We went down the slanting gangway to the platform, which rose and dropped with the swells. "Where's Chief Schreiber?"

"He went out on the Coast Guard cutter," the old man said. "They got a radio call from a San Pedro tuna boat." He lifted the outboard motor clear of the stern and heaved it onto the dock. "There's a boat on the rocks at Sanctuary. They said it looks as if it's breaking up. What happened to your face, chum?"

"Never mind that." Mario's hand closed on the old man's arm. "Did you catch the name of the boat?"

The old man pulled away. "Don't get excited, friend. Just take it easy. The tuna boat didn't get close enough to read the name. You lose a boat?"

"You guessed it."

"It's a sport-fishing boat with aluminum outriggers."

Mario turned to me urgently: "Drive me out to Sanctuary, how about it?" The ugly bruises around his eyes were livid against his pallor.

"Don't you think you better take it easy?"

"When my boat's breaking up on the rocks? You don't want to drive me, I'll take my motorcycle."

"I'll drive you," I said. "How far is it?"

"Less than ten miles. Come on."

"Is it your boat?" The old man's question blew after us like a seagull's cry, and blew away unanswered.

We drove down the coast highway in silence. Mario sat glum beside me, glaring down at his skinned knuckles, which he rapped together fiercely time after time. With his bandage-helmeted head and damaged Latin features, he looked like a wounded gladiator. I hoped he wasn't going to pass out on my hands.

"Who beat you up, Mario?" I asked him after a while.

It was some time before he answered. When he did, his voice was thick with remembered anger. "There were three of them. Two of them held me while the other one sloughed me. Who they were is my own business. I'll take care of them personally, one at a time."

He dug into the pocket of his jacket and brought out a dully gleaming object. I took my eyes from the road to glance at it. It was a curved metal bar of aluminum, about five inches long, with four round fingerholes and a taped grip. Mario slipped it over his fingers and smacked his armed right hand in the open palm of his left. "I'll take care of them personally," he growled to himself.

"Put it away," I said. "It's a felony to carry knuckles like that. Where did you get it?"

"Took it away from a customer one time. I used to be a bartender in town." He kissed the cruel edge of the metal and dropped it back in his pocket. "I thought it might come in handy. I'm glad I kept it."

"You'll get yourself in worse trouble. Why did they beat you, Mario?"

"It was my lousy brother's fault," he said. "He skipped on Friday night and left me holding the bag. They thought I was in it with him. He didn't even warn me ahead of time. They came aboard the *Queen* in the middle of the night and dragged me out of my bunk. I couldn't handle three."

"Is that the night you and Joe got back from Ensenada?"

He looked at me suspiciously. "What about Ensenada? Joe and me went fishing off Catalina Thursday and Friday. We anchored off the island overnight."

"Catch anything?"

"Not a damn thing. What's this about Ensenada, anyway?"

"I heard that Dowser has a Mexican branch. Your loyalty to Dowser is very moving, especially after what he did to your face."

"I don't know any Dowser," he answered unconvincingly. "You wouldn't be Treasury, would you?"

"I would not. I told you I'm a private detective."

"What's your angle? You said you talked to Galley, you must of found her."

"Your brother slugged me last night. It bothers me, for some reason." But it was the dead man who lay heavy on my mind.

"I'll lend you my knucks when I finish with them," he said. "Turn down the next side road."

It was a rutted lane, meandering across a high meadow to the lip of a sea-cliff. Near the cliff's edge a grove of eucalyptus, with smooth pink trunks like naked flesh, huddled raggedly in the wind. There were weathered redwood tables for picnickers scattered among the trees. Mario ran down a path toward the edge of the cliff, and I followed him. I could see the moving water through the trees, as bright as mercury, and then the gray Coast Guard cutter a half-mile out from shore. It was headed north, back to Pacific Point.

The path ended in a sagging wooden barrier beyond which the cliff dropped sheer. A hundred feet below, which looked like a hundred yards, the running surges burst on its rocky base. Mario leaned on the barrier, looking down.

Where the surf boiled whitest on the jutting black basalt, the boat lay half-capsized. Wave after wave struck it and almost submerged it, pouring in foam-streaked sheets down its slanting deck. The boat rolled with their punches, and its smashed hull groaned on the rocks. The outriggers flopped loose like broken wings. It was a total loss.

Mario's body was swaying in sympathy with the boat. I didn't have to ask if it was his. He groaned when the surf went over it, and his face was wetter than the spray accounted for.

"I wonder what happened to Joe," I said.

"The bastard wrecked my boat. I hope he drowned."

A cormorant flew over the water from north to south like a sharp black soul hell-bent. Mario watched it out of sight.

Chapter 18

W E W E R E waiting at the yacht basin when the Coast Guard cutter docked. As the gray hull nudged the truck-tire buffers along the edge of the dock, two men jumped ashore. One was a tanned young Coast Guard lieutenant in working uniform, apparently the commander of the cutter. The other was a gray-bearded man in ancient suntans without insignia. He had the sea-scoured faded eyes, the air of quiet obstinacy and the occupational pot of an old Navy petty officer.

"The *Aztec Queen*'s on the rocks at Sanctuary," he said to Mario.

"I know it. We just got back from there."

"No chance to salvage it," the Coast Guard lieutenant said. "Even if we could get in close enough, it wouldn't be worth it now. It's breaking up."

"I know it."

"Let's get inside." The harbormaster hugged himself. "That's a cold wind."

We followed him to his office on the breakwater at the foot of the dock. I sat in on a conference in the barren cubicle, or stood in on it, because there were only three chairs. They had seen nobody aboard the wreck. The skipper of the tuna boat who had reported it in the first place had seen nobody, either. The question was: how did the *Aztec Queen* get out of the yacht basin and nine miles down the coast?

In official company, Mario wasn't outspoken. He said he had no idea. But he looked at me as if he expected me to do the talking.

"It's your boat, isn't it?" the harbormaster said.

"Sure it's my boat. I bought it secondhand from Rassi in January."

"Insured?" the lieutenant asked him.

He shook his head. "I couldn't afford the premiums."

"Tough tiddy. What were you using it for?"

"Fishing parties, off and on. Mostly off, in this season. *You* know that, Chief." He turned to Schreiber, who was leaning back in his chair against the wall. The coastal-waters chart behind his head showed a round grease spot where he had leaned before.

"Let's get back on the beam," he said heavily. "The boat didn't slip her moorings and steer herself onto the rocks. There must have been *some*body aboard her."

"*I* know that," Mario stirred uneasily in his chair. If talking had to be done, he wanted somebody else to do it for him.

"Well, it wasn't Captain Kidd. Didn't the engine have a lock on it?"

"Yeah. My brother had the keys, my brother Joe."

"Why didn't you say so? Now we're getting somewhere. Your boat was gone this morning when I come on duty. I thought you took it."

"I been laid up," Mario said. "I was in an accident."

"Yeah, I can see. Looks as if your brother got himself in a worse accident. Did you give him permission to take the boat?"

"He didn't need permission. He owned an interest in it."

"Well, it ain't worth much now," Schreiber said sententiously. "About two red cents. Are you sure it was your brother took her out?"

"How can I be sure? I was home in bed."

"Joe was here this morning," I said. "His wife drove him down before dawn."

"Did he say he was going out in the boat?" the lieutenant asked.

"He didn't say anything so far as I know."

"Where's his wife now?"

"She's staying in Santa Monica with her mother. Mrs. Samuel Lawrence."

Schreiber made a note of the name. "I guess we better get in touch with her. It looks as if her husband's lost at sea."

The lieutenant stood up and pulled his visored cap down over his forehead. "I'll call the sheriff's office. We'll have to make a search for him." He peered through the window across the yacht basin; red sunset streamers were unraveling on the horizon. "It's getting pretty late to do anything tonight. We can't get to the boat until low tide."

"Better try, though. There's an off chance he's still inside the cabin." Schreiber turned to Mario: "Your brother have heart attacks or anything like that?"

"Joe isn't aboard," Mario answered flatly.

"How do you know?"

"I got a feeling."

Schreiber rose, shrugging his thick shoulders. "You better go home, boy, and crawl back into the sack. I don't know how you feel, but you look God-awful."

We went back to my car and turned toward the city. It lay serene on its terraced slopes in the last of the sunset, a few lights winking on like early stars. The white African buildings lay in the red air like something seen through rose-colored glasses in memory. Everything was still except the sea, which drummed and groaned behind us to the slow blues-beat of time.

I was glad enough for once to get out of hearing of the sea. But I didn't get far. Mario wouldn't go home.

He stopped me at a waterfront bar and said he could use a drink. I parked the car and got out. I could use one, too. Below the sea-wall that lined the other side of the boulevard, the surf complained and pounded like a tired heart. The heavy closing door shut out the sound.

A fat old waiter came to the door, shook hands with Mario, lamented like a mother over his face. He seated us in a booth at the back of the room and lit a bottled red candle on our table. The bottle was thickly crusted with the meltings of other candles, like clotted blood. I thought of Dalling in his blood on the floor. He'd be on a mortuary slab by now, or under white light on an autopsy table, with a butterfly incision in his torso. Dalling seemed very distant and long ago.

The waiter finished dabbing at the table with the end of a soiled napkin. "Something to eat, gentlemen? Or you want drinks?"

I ordered a steak and a bottle of beer. Mario wanted a double whisky, straight.

"Aren't you going to eat? You'll knock yourself out."

"We got minestrone tonight, Mario," the waiter said. "It's pooty good for a change."

"I got to save my appetite," he explained. "Mama is waiting dinner for me."

"You want to phone your mama?"

"Naw, I don't want to talk to her."

The waiter padded away on flat feet.

"What am I going to tell her?" Mario asked no one in particular. "I lost the boat, that's bad enough, she never wanted me to buy the boat. I was a damn fool, I let Joe talk me into it. I put up all my cash, and now what have I got? Nothing. I'm on the rocks. And I could of bought an interest in this place, you know that? I tended bar here all last fall and I got on fine with the customers. I got on fine with George, the old guy. He's getting ready to retire and I could of been sitting pretty instead of on my uppers the way I am."

He was falling into the singsong of a man with a grievance, as if the whisky he ordered had hit him in the emotions before he drank it. George brought our drinks, silencing Mario. I looked around the room he might have bought a piece of. It had more decorations than a briefcase general: strings of colored bulbs above the bar, deer heads and stuffed swordfish, photographs of old baseball teams, paintings of cardboard mountains, German beer-mugs. On a platform over the kitchen door, an eagle with glaring glass eyes was attacking a stuffed mountain-lion. All the group needed to complete it was a stuffed taxidermist.

"The boat is bad enough," Mario repeated dismally. "What am I going to tell her about Joe? Joe's always been her favorite, she'll go nuts if she thinks he's drowned. She used to drive us crazy when we were kids, worrying about the old man when he was out. It was kind of a relief when the old man died in bed—"

"You said you had a feeling Joe isn't aboard. Where do you get that feeling?"

He drained his double shot-glass and rapped on the table for another. "Joe's awful smart. Joe would never get caught. He was shoplifting in the stores before he was out of grade school, and he never got caught. He was the bright young brother, see, he had that innocent look. I tried it once and they hauled me off to Juvenile and Mama said I was disgracing the family. Not Joe."

The waiter brought his whisky, and told me that my steak would soon be ready.

"Besides," Mario said, "the bastard can swim like a seal. He used to be a lifeguard on the beach. He's been a lot of things, most of them lousy. I got a pretty good inkling where Joe is. He isn't on the *Queen* and he isn't on the bottom of the sea. He skipped again and left me holding the bag."

"How could he skip at sea?"

"He abandoned the *Queen*, if you want my opinion. He had five hundred in it, I had fifteen. What did it matter to him, he makes big money. The bastard took her out and ditched her, so it would look as if he drowned himself. He probably made a rendezvous with the guy that has the cabin cruiser in Ensenada—" He cut himself off short, peered anxiously into my face.

"Torres?" I said as casually as I could.

His bruises served as a mask for whatever feelings he had. Deliberately, he emptied his second shot-glass, and sipped with fumbling lips at a glass of water. "I don't know anything about any Torres. I was making it up as I went along, trying to figure how he ditched the boat."

"Why would he go to all that trouble?"

"Take a look at my face and figure it out for yourself. They did this to me because I'm Joey's brother, that's all the reason they had. What would they do to him?" He answered his own question in pantomime, twisting his doubled fists in opposing directions, the way you behead a chicken.

The steak came, and I washed down what I could eat of it with the remnant of my beer. Mario had his third double. He was showing signs of wear, and I decided not to let him have any more. But it turned out that I didn't have to interfere.

Customers had been drifting in by ones and twos, most of them heading for the bar at the front, where they perched like roosting chickens in a row. I was trying to catch the waiter's eye, to signal for my check, when a man opened the front door. He stood with his hand on the knob, scanning the bar-flies, a big man with a ten-gallon hat who looked like a rancher in his Saturday suit. Then his glance caught the back of Mario's bandaged head, and he strode toward us.

Mario half-turned in his seat and saw him coming. "Dammit," he muttered. "It's the deputy sheriff."

The big man laid a hand on his shoulder. "I thought you might be in here. What's this about your brother? Move over, eh?"

Mario slid reluctantly into the corner. "Your guess is as good as mine. Joe doesn't tell me his plans."

The deputy sat down heavily beside him. Mario leaned away as if contact with the law might be contagious.

"You had some trouble with Joe, I hear."

"Trouble? What kind of trouble?"

"Take a look in a mirror, it might stir up your memory."

"I haven't seen Joe since last Friday night."

"Friday night, eh? Was that before or after you got your face ploughed under?"

Mario touched his cheekbone with an oil-grained finger. "Hell, that wasn't Joe."

"Who was it?"

"A friend of mine. It was a friendly fight."

"You got nice friends," the deputy said with sarcasm. A downward smile drew his sun-wrinkles deeper. "What about Joe?"

"I told you I didn't see him since Friday night. We got in from a fishing trip and he beat it back to L.A. He lives in L.A. with his wife."

"If he doesn't live in Davy Jones's locker with a mermaid. I heard he dropped out of sight last Friday, hasn't been back here since."

"He came back this morning," I said. "His wife drove him down."

"Yeah, I mean until this morning. I got in touch with the wife, she's on her way. She didn't see the other one, though."

"What other one?"

"That's what I'm trying to find out," he snapped, and turned his flat red face on Mario: "Were you down here this morning? Aboard your boat?"

"I was home in bed. The old lady knows I was home in bed." Mario looked bewildered, and his words were whisky-slurred.

"Yeah? I was talking to her on the telephone. She didn't wake up until seven. Your boat went out around four."

"How do you know that?"

"Trick Curley, he's a lobsterman, he just got in from the island. You know him?"

"Seen him around."

"He was up early this morning, and he saw the skiff go out to the *Aztec Queen*. The skiff is still there, by the way, tied to the moorings. There were two men in it when it passed Trick's boat."

"Joe?"

"He couldn't tell, it was dark. He hailed them but they didn't answer him. He heard them go aboard, and then the boat went out past the end of the breakwater." He turned on Mario suddenly, and rasped: "Why didn't you answer him?"

"Me? Answer who?"

"Trick, when he hailed you in the skiff."

"For Christ's sake!" The appalling face looked genuinely appalled. "I was home in bed. I didn't get up till nine. Mama gave me breakfast in bed, you ask her."

"I already did. That wouldn't stop you from sneaking out in the middle of the night and coming down here."

"Why would I do a crazy thing like that?" His upturned hands moved eloquently in the air.

"There was bad blood between you and Joe," the deputy said dramatically. "That's common knowledge. Last week in this very bar you threatened to kill him, in front of witnesses. You told him it would be a public service. If you killed him, it would be the only public service you ever did, Tarantine."

"I was drunk when I said that," Mario whined. "I don't know what happened to him, sheriff, honest to God. He took my boat and wrecked it and now you're blaming me. It isn't fair."

"Aw, shut your yap."

"Okay, arrest me!" Mario cried. "I'm a sick man, so go ahead and arrest me."

"Take it easy, Tarantine." The deputy rose ponderously, his wavering shadow climbing the opposite wall as high as the ceiling. "We haven't even got a *corpus delicti* yet. When we do we'll come and see you. Stick around."

"I'm not going any place."

He sat slack and miserable in the corner. The only life in his face came from the small jumping reflections of the candle in the black centers of his eyes. I waited until the deputy was out of sight, and steered him out to my car. Mario cursed steadily under his breath in a mixture of English, *bracero* Spanish, and Italian.

Chapter 19

WE DROVE down Sanedres Street on the way to Mario's house. From a distance I could see a small crowd gathering in front of the arena, clotting in groups of two and four and six. A string of naked bulbs above the entrance threw a one-sided light on their faces. There were many kinds of faces: the fat rubber faces of old sports wearing cigar butts in their lower middle, boys' Indian faces under ducktail haircuts, experienced and hopeful faces of old tarts, the faces of girls, bright-eyed and heavy-mouthed, gleaming with youth and interest in the kill. And the black slant face of Simmie, who was taking tickets at the door.

Mario clutched my right forearm with both hands and cried out: "Stop!"

I swerved and almost crashed into a parked car, then braked to a stop. "That wasn't very smart."

He was halfway out of the car, and didn't hear me. He crossed the road in a loose-kneed run. The faces turned toward him as he floundered into the crowd. He moved among them violently, like a killer dog in a flock of sheep. His hand came out of his pocket wearing metal. There was going to be trouble.

I could have driven away: he wasn't my baby. But a light jab to the head might easily kill him. I looked for a parking place, found none. Both sides of the road were lined with cars. I backed and turned up the alley beside the arena. The faces were regrouping. Most of the mouths were open. All of the eyes were turned toward the door where Mario and Simmie had disappeared.

I started to get out of my car. The exit door in the wall in front of my headlights burst open with sudden force, as if a rectangular piece of the wall had been kicked out. Simmie, in a yellow shirt, came out of the door head down and crossed the alley in three strides. Mario came after him, running clumsily with his striking arm upraised. Simmie had one knee hooked over the top of the fence when Mario overtook him. The glaring whites of his eyes rolled backward in terror. The metal fist came down across his face. The black boy fell in slow motion to the gravel.

I took hold of Mario from behind. His metal knuckles flailed my thigh and left it numb. I shifted my grip and held him more securely.

"Calm down, boy."

"I'll kill him," he cried out hoarsely between laboring breaths. "Let me go!" His shoulders heaved and almost took me off my feet.

"Take it easy, Mario. You'll kill yourself."

Simmie got onto his knees. The blood was running free from a cut on his brow. He rose to his feet, swaying against the fence. The blood splashed his shirt.

"Mr. Blaney will shoot you dead for this, Mr. Tarantine." He spat dark on the gravel.

Mario cried out loudly, making no words. His muscles jerked iron-hard and broke my grip. His striking arm swung up again. Simmie flung himself over the fence. I pinned Mario against it and wrenched his metal knuckles off. His knee tried for my groin, and I had to stamp the instep of his other foot. He sat down against the fence and held the foot in both hands.

The Negro woman I had seen the day before came around the corner of the building on the other side of the fence. She was the first of a line of Negro men and women who stood at the end of their row of hutches and watched us silently. One of the men had the black-taped stock of a sawed-off shotgun in his hands. Simmie moved to his side and turned:

"Come on over here and try it."

"Yeah," the man beside him said. "Come on over the fence, why don't you?"

The woman touched the bloody side of the boy's face, moaning. I looked around and saw that the faces were dense in the alley around my car. One of the fat rubber faces opened and called out:

"Attaboy, Tarantine. Go and get the black bastard. Let him have it." The face's owner stayed where he was, in the second line of spectators.

I pulled Mario to his feet and walked him toward the car.

"Did the dirty nigger hit him?" a woman said.

"He's drunk. He knocked himself out. You might as well break it up."

I got in first, pulled Mario after me, and backed slowly through the crowd.

"I got one of them," Mario said to himself. "Christ! did you see him bleed? I'll get the others."

"You'll get yourself a case of sudden death." But he paid no attention.

One of the bright-eyed girls followed the car to the sidewalk and hooked one arm over the door on Mario's side. "Wait!"

I stopped the car. She had short fair hair that clasped her head like a cap made out of gold leaf. Her young red-sweatered breasts leaned at the open window, urgently. "Where's Joey, Mario? I'm awful hard up."

"Beat it. Leave me alone." He tried to push her away.

"Please, Mario." Her red-shining mouth curved in some kind of anguish. "Fix me, will you?"

"I said beat it." He struck at her with the back of his open hand. She held on to it with both of hers.

"I heard you lost your boat. I can tell you something about it. Honest, Mario—"

"Liar." He jerked his hand free and turned the window up. "Let's get out of here, I'm feeling lousy."

I took him home. When he stepped out of the car, he staggered and fell to his knees on the edge of the curb.

I helped him to the door. "You better call the doctor and let him look at your head."

"To hell with the doctor." He said it without energy. "I just need a little rest, that's all."

His mother opened the door. "Mario, where you been, what you been doing?" Her voice was thin and piping with anxiety, as if a frightened small girl were sunk in the inflation of her flesh.

"Nothing," he said. "Nothing to worry, Mama. I went out for some fresh air, that's all."

Chapter 20

THERE WAS no sign of Simmie when I got back to the arena. The man in the box office who sold me my ticket tore it in half himself and told me to go on in. The crowd was gone, except for a few small boys waiting around the door for a chance to duck in free. They watched me with great dark eyes full of silent envy, as if Achilles was fighting Hector inside, or Jacob was wrestling with the angel.

Inside, a match was under way. A thousand or more people were watching the weekly battle between right and wrong. Right was represented by a pigeon-chested young Mediterranean type, covered back and front with a heavy coat of black hair. Wrong was an elderly Slav with a round bald spot like a tonsure and a bushy red beard by way of compensation. His belly was large and pendulous, shaped like a tear about to fall. The belly and the beard made him a villain.

I found my seat, three rows back from ringside, and watched the contest for a minute or two. Redbeard took a tuft of hair on the other's chest between the thumb and forefinger of his right hand and tugged at it delicately, like someone plucking lilies of the valley. Pigeon Chest howled with pain and terror, and cast a pleading look at the referee. The referee, a small round man in a sweatshirt, rebuked Redbeard severely for thus maltreating his colleague. Redbeard wiggled his beard disdainfully. The crowd roared with anger.

Redbeard waddled across the ring to the corner where Pigeon Chest was gamely enduring his anguish, and smote the young hero lightly on the shoulder with his forearm. Pigeon Chest sank to his knees, pitifully shaken by the blow. Wrong beat its breast with both fists and looked around with arrogance at the crowd.

"Kill him, Gino," a grandmotherly lady said beside me. "Get up and kill the dirty Russian coward." She looked as if she meant it, stark and staring. The rest of the crowd was making similar suggestions.

Warmed by their encouragement, Gino struggled manfully to his feet. Redbeard swung again, with the speed and violence of a feather falling, but this time Gino ducked the blow and hit back. The crowd went mad with delight. "Murder him, Gino." Wrong cowered and skulked away; all bullies were cowards. Wrong had a yellow streak down its back a yard wide, as the old lady said beside me. She could probably see the yellow streak through her bifocal glasses.

Since Right was triumphing, I could afford to take my eyes off the ring for a little while. The girl I was looking for was easy to find. Her bright hair gleamed from a ringside seat on the other side of the platform. She was sitting very close to a middle-aged man in a gabardine suit a little too light for the season and a Panama hat with a red-blue-yellow band. He had a convention badge on his lapel. She was practically sitting in his lap. With a kind of calculated excitement, her fingers moved up and down his arm, and played with his vest-buttons and tie. His face was red and loose, as if he'd been drinking. Hers was on her work.

Now Redbeard was on his hands and knees on the canvas beside the ropes. Gino was begging the referee to make him get up and fight. The referee grasped the evil Russian by the beard and raised him to his feet. Gino went into swift and murderous action. He threw himself into the air feet first and brushed the jutting red beard with the toe of one wrestling shoe. Redbeard, felled by the breeze or the idea of the kick, went down heavily on his back. Right landed neatly on the back of its neck and sprang to its feet in triumph like a tumbler. Wrong lay prostrate while the referee counted it out and declared Right the winner. The crowd cheered. Then Wrong opened its eyes and got up and disputed the decision, its red beard wagging energetically. "Oh, you dirty cheater," the old lady cried. "Throw him out!"

The gilt-haired girl and the man in the Panama hat got up and started to move toward the entrance. I waited until they were out of sight and followed them. The rest of the crowd, heartened by their moral victory, were laughing and chattering, buying peanuts and beer and coke from the white-capped boys in the aisles. Right and Wrong had left the ring together.

When I went out the man and the girl were standing by the box-office, and the ticket man inside was phoning a taxi for them. She was clinging to the man like lichen to a rock. What

I could see of her face looked sick and desperate. The fat gabardine arm was hugging her small waist.

By the time the taxi came, I was waiting in my car with the motor idling, a hundred feet short of the entrance. The taxi paused to pick them up and headed for downtown. It was easy to follow in the light evening traffic, six straight blocks to a stop sign, left on Main Street past Mexican movies and rumdum-haunted bars, down to the ocean boulevard again. Another leftward jog along the shore. The taxi paused and let them out.

Their destination was a small motel standing between a dog hospital and a dark and immobile merry-go-round. A sign over the entrance inscribed its name, THE COVE, in blue neon on the night. As I went by, the girl's face, drawn and hollowed by the glare, was intent on the open wallet in the man's hands. Her lean and sweatered body cast a jagged shadow beside the man's squat open-handed one.

I parked my car at the curb on the other side of the boulevard. Beyond a row of dwarf palms the sea was snoring and complaining like a drunk in a doorway. I spat in its direction and walked back to the motel. This was a long narrow building at right angles to the street, with a row of single rooms reached by a gallery on each side, and open carports below, most of them empty. A light went on toward the rear of the gallery on my side, and for an instant I saw the ill-assorted couple framed in the doorway. Then a T-shirted boy came out, closing the door solicitously behind him. He heel-and-toed along the gallery towards the open stairway at the front. I kept on walking.

When I heard the door of the front office close, I turned and sauntered back. There was a pickup truck in the driveway beside the dog hospital. I went and sat on its running board in the shadow, and watched the lighted window. In no time at all the light in the room went out.

I noticed then that the boy in the T-shirt shared my interest in it. He had mounted the steps without my seeing him, and was walking very lightly toward the closed door. When he reached it, he flattened himself against the wall, tense and still like a figure in a frieze. I sat and watched him. He looked as if he were waiting for a signal to move. I heard it when it came: the girl's voice calling softly behind the door. I couldn't make out the words; perhaps the call was wordless.

The boy unlocked the door and stepped inside and closed it. The curtained window lit up again. I decided to move in closer.

There was another set of stairs at the rear of the building, where the gallery widened into an open sun-porch. I stepped across a scrubby eugenia hedge and climbed the stairs; moved softly along the gallery to the lighted window, staying close to the wall where the boards were less likely to creak. I could hear the voices before I reached the window: the boy's voice speaking with quiet intensity: "How can she be your wife? You're registered from Oregon, and she lives here. I thought I recognized her, and now I know it." And the man's, strained and subdued by anxiety: "We just got married today, didn't we? Didn't we?"

The boy was scornful: "I bet she doesn't even know your name."

"I don't," the girl admitted. "What are you going to do?"

"You didn't have to tell him that!" Hysteria threatened the man, but it was still controlled by the fear of being heard. "You didn't have to bring me here in the first place. You said it was safe, that you had an understanding with the management."

"I guess I was wrong," the girl said wearily.

"I guess you were! Now look at the mess I'm in. How old are you anyway?"

"Fifteen, nearly sixteen."

"God." The word came out with a rush of air, as if he'd been rammed in the stomach by a piledriver. I leaned at the edge of the window trying to see him, but the window was covered completely with curtains of rough tan cloth.

"That makes it worse," the boy said virtuously. He sounded very virtuous for a night clerk in a waterfront motel. "Contributing to the delinquency of a minor. Statutory rape, even."

The man said without inflection: "I got a daughter at home as old as her. What am I going to do? I got a wife."

The virtuous youth said: "You're remembering a little late. I tell you what I have to do. I have to call the police."

"No! You don't have to call the *police*. She doesn't want you to call them, do you? Do you? I paid her money, she won't testify. Will you?"

"They'll make me," she said glumly. "They'll send me away. You, too."

"This isn't a call-house, mister," the boy said. "The manager says if this sort of thing comes up, I got to call the police. *I* didn't invite you here."

"*She* did! It's all her fault. I'm a stranger in town, son. I didn't realize the situation. I came down here from Portland for the ad convention. I didn't realize the situation."

"Now you do. We let this sort of thing go on, they take away our license. The manager hears about it, I lose my job. And I'm not your son."

"You don't have to get nasty." The older man's voice was querulous. "Maybe what you need is a punch in the nose."

"Try it on, you old goat. Only button yourself up first."

The girl's voice cut in shrilly: "Talk to him. You won't get anywhere like that. He'll tag you for assault along with the rest."

"I'm sorry," the older man said.

"You've got plenty to be sorry about."

The girl began to sob mechanically. "They'll send me away, and you too. Can't you do anything, mister?"

"Maybe I could talk to the manager? It isn't good business if you call the police—"

"He's out of town," the boy said. "Anyway, I can handle this myself."

After a pause, the man asked haltingly: "How much money do you make a week?"

"Forty a week. Why?"

"I'll pay you to forget this business. I haven't got much ready cash—"

"You've got some twenties in your wallet," the girl said. She had given over sobbing as suddenly as she'd started. "I saw them."

"You shut up," the boy said. "I couldn't take a bribe, mister. It would mean my job."

"I have about eighty-five in cash here. You can have it."

The boy laughed flatly. "For contributing and statutory rape? That would be cheap now, wouldn't it? Jobs are scarce around here."

"I have a hundred-dollar traveler's check." The man's voice was brightening. "I'll give you a hundred and fifty. I got to keep a little to pay my hotel."

"I'll take it," the boy said. "I don't like to do it, but I'll take it."

"Thank God."

"Come on down to the office, mister. You can use the fountain pen in the office."

"Gee, thanks, mister," the girl said softly. "You saved my life for sure."

"Get away from me, you dirty little tart." His voice was furious.

"Quiet," the boy said. "Quiet. Let's get out of here."

I moved back to the sun-porch, and watched them around the corner as they came out. The boy moved briskly ahead, swinging his arms. The older man slouched behind with his hat in his hand. His untied shoelaces dragged on the floor of the gallery.

Chapter 21

I TAPPED on the door.

"Who is it?" the girl whispered.

I tapped on the door again.

"Is that you, Ronnie?"

I answered yes. Her bare feet padded across the floor, and the door opened. "He was easy—" she started to say. Then her hand flew up to her mouth, and her eyes darkened at the sight of me. "Augh?"

She tried to shut the door in my face. I pushed through past her and leaned on the door, closing it behind me. She backed away, the fingers of both hands spread across her red-smeared mouth. She had nothing on but a skirt, and after a moment she remembered this. Her hands slid down to cover her breasts. They were young and small, easy to cover. The bones in her shoulders stood out, puny as a chicken's. A part of her left arm was pitted like ancient marble by hypo marks.

"Yours is a keen racket, sister. Can't you think of anything better to do with your body?"

She retreated further, as far as the unmade bed in the corner of the room. It was an ugly little room, walled and ceiled with sick green plaster that reminded me of public locker rooms, furnished with one bed, one chair, one peeling veneer dresser and a rug the moths had been at. It was a hutch for quick rabbit-matings, a cell where lonely men could beat themselves to sleep with a dark brown bottle. The girl looked too good for the room, though I knew she wasn't.

She picked her sweater off the floor and pulled it over her head. "What business of yours is it, what I do with my body?" Her red-eyed breast looked dully at me for an instant before she covered it. "You get out of here or I'll call the key-boy."

"Good. I want to talk to him."

Her eyes widened. "You're a policeman." There was something peculiar about her eyes.

"A private cop," I said. "Does that make you feel any better?"

"Get out of my room and leave me alone, then I'll feel better."

I moved toward her instead. Her face was pinched thin and white by an internal chill. The peculiar thing about her eyes was that they had no centers. I looked through them into darkness, cold darkness inside her. A tremor started in her hands, moved up her arms to her shoulders and down her body. She sat down on the edge of the bed and gripped her knees with both hands, bracing her limbs against each other to keep them from flying apart. A shadow crossed her face as dark and final as the shadow of death. She looked like a little old woman in a gold wig.

"How long has it been?" I said.

"Three days. I'm going crazy." Her teeth began to chatter. She closed them hard over her lower lip.

"The bad stuff, kid?"

"Uh-huh."

"I'm sorry for you."

"A lot of good that does me. I haven't slept for three nights."

"Since Tarantine went away."

She straightened up, having repressed the tremor. "Do you know where Joey is? Can you get me some? I've got the money to pay for it—"

"I'm not in the business, kid. What's your name, anyway?"

"Ruth. Do you know where he is? Do you work for him?"

"Not me. So far as Joey's concerned, you'll have to sweat it out."

"I can't. I'll die." And maybe she was right.

"How long have you been on the kick?"

"Since last fall. Ronnie started me."

"How often?"

"Once a week, about. Then twice a week. Every day the last couple of months."

"How much?"

"I don't know. They cut it. It was costing me fifty dollars a day."

"Is that why you started shaking down the tourists?"

"It's a living." She raised her heavy eyes. "How do you know so much about me?"

"I don't. But I know one thing. You should see a doctor."

"What's the use? They'll send me away to a Federal hospital, and then I'll die for certain."

"They'll taper you off."

"How do you know, have you had it?"

"No."

"Then you don't know what you're talking about. It turns you inside out. I was down on the beach last night and every time a wave slapped the sand it hit me like an earthquake, the end of the world. I lay back and looked straight up and there wasn't any sky. Nothing but yellow specks in my eyes, and the black. I felt the beach slanting down under me and I slid off in the black. It's funny, it felt as if I was falling into myself, I was hollow like a well and falling down me." She touched her stomach. "It's funny I'm still alive. It was like dying."

She lay back on the rumpled bed and looked at the ceiling with her arms under her head, her breasts pulled almost flat, her nose and mouth and chin carved stark by strain. Sweat was darkening her narrow golden temples. The sick-green ceiling was her only sky. "I guess I'll have to go through it again, though, before I really die."

"You're not going to die, Ruth." That was my statement. But I felt like a prosecutor cross-questioning a dead girl in the lower courts of hell. "What were you doing on the beach last night?"

"Nothing." Her answer was like a memory of an earlier, happier life: "We used to go down to the beach all the time before Dad went away. We had a dog then, a little golden cocker, and he used to chase the birds and we used to take our lunch down to the beach and have a picnic and light a fire and have a lot of fun. Dad always collected seashells for me: we made a real collection." She propped herself up on her elbows, wrinkling her blank young brow. "I wonder where my seashells are, I don't know what happened to them."

"What happened to your father?"

"I hardly ever see him any more. He went away when my mother left him: they ran a photographer's studio in town. He got a job as radio operator on a ship, and he's always way off somewhere, India or Japan. He sends my grandmother money for me, though." Her tone was defensive. "He writes me letters."

"You live with your grandmother, do you?"

She dropped back flat on the bed. "More or less. She's a waitress in a truck-stop down the line. She isn't home at night and she sleeps in the daytime. That was the trouble last night. The house began to breathe around me, in and out, and I got scared and I was all alone. I thought if I went down to the beach, maybe I'd feel better. It always used to make me feel good when I smelled the ocean. It didn't work. It was worse in the open. I told you about the stars, how they were like holes in my head, and falling into the black. When I woke up from that, I saw the man come out of the sea and I guess I blew my top. I thought he was a merman like the poem we had in English last year. I still don't know for sure if he was real."

"Tell me about the man. Where did you see him?"

"Mackerel Beach, where they have the barbecue pits: that's where we always used to have our picnics." She raised one hand and gestured vaguely southward. "It's about a mile down the boulevard. I was lying behind one of the wind-shelters on the sand, and I was awful cold." The recollection made her shiver a little. "The black was gone, though, and I wasn't falling. I thought the worst was over. There was a little light on the water, and I always feel better in daylight when I can see things. Then this man stood up in the surf and walked out of the water up on the beach. It scared me stiff. I had a crazy idea that he belonged to the sea and was coming to get me. It was still pretty dark, though, and I lay still and he didn't even see me. He walked into the bushes behind the barbecue pits. I think he had a car parked in the lane back there. I heard a motor starting after a while. He was real enough, I guess. Do you think he was real?"

"He was a real man, sure. Did he have a bandage on his head?"

"No, I don't think so. It wasn't Mario. Ronnie told me about Mario's boat getting wrecked, and I thought it might have something to do with Mario's boat—"

"Did you see the boat?"

"No. Maybe I heard it, I don't know. Half the time if a seagull screams it blasts my ears like a steam whistle and half the time I'm deaf, I can't hear a thing." Like most dope addicts she was hypochondriac, more interested in her symptoms than anything else and talented in describing them.

I said: "What did he look like?"

"There wasn't much light. I couldn't see his face. He was mother-naked, or else he was wearing a light-colored bathing suit. I think he had a bundle around his neck."

"Was it anybody you know?"

"I don't think so."

"Not Joe Tarantine?"

"It couldn't have been Joey. I wish it was. I'd have known Joey, mother-naked or not."

"He's your source of supply, I take it."

"I've got no source of supply," she said to the ceiling. "For three days now like three years. What would you do in my place, mister? Ronnie's got weed, but that just makes me sicker. What would you do?"

"Go to a doctor and taper off."

"I can't do that, I told you. I can't. You're from L.A., aren't you? You know where I can get it in L.A.? I made two hundred dollars the last three nights."

I thought of Dowser, who liked blondes. She'd be better sweating it out than going to Dowser, even if Dowser had the stuff to give her. "No, I don't know."

"Ronnie knows a man in San Francisco. Ronnie was a runner for Herman Speed, before old Speed got shot. Do you think I could get some if I went to Frisco? I've been waiting for Joey to come back. He doesn't come. Do you think he'll ever come?"

"Joey's either dead or out of the country now. He won't come back."

"I was afraid he wouldn't. To hell with waiting for Joey any more. I'm going to Frisco." She sat up suddenly and began to comb her hair.

"Who's the man there Ronnie told you about?"

"I don't know his name, they don't use names. He calls himself Mosquito. He pushed the stuff for Speed last year. Now he's doing it in Frisco." She leaned over to pull on her shoes.

"That's a big city."

"I know where to go, Ronnie told me." She covered her mouth with her hand in a schoolgirl's gesture. "I'm talking too much, aren't I? I always talk too much when people are nice to me. You've been awful nice to me, and I thought you were a policeman."

"I used to be," I said, "but I won't spoil your chance."

She was looking much better, now that she'd made up her mind to travel that night. There was some blood moving under her skin, some meaning in her eyes. But she still looked old enough to be her own mother.

Chapter 22

THE DOOR sprang open without warning, as doors were always opening in my life. The boy Ronnie came in. A big nineteen or twenty, he had the face of a juvenile lead instead of a juvenile delinquent, keen and dark with a black brush of hair, a heavy single eyebrow barring his brow. His arms below the T-shirt were tanned and heavy-looking. The right one held a tire-iron.

I saw this in the instant before he swung at my head. I ducked and moved in on him before he could swing again. The girl was silent behind me. My fingers found the wrist that held the tire-iron. I twisted it away with my other hand and tossed it clanking in a corner of the room. Then I pushed him away, looped an obvious left at his head, to bring up his guard, and put my weight behind a straight right to his center. It was a sucker punch, not on the side of the angels. A single futile blow for the damned.

He fell turning on his face, and writhed on the floor for air. The girl joined him there, kneeling across him with little cries of love. He'd started her on heroin, given her yellow fever and white death, so she was crazy about him.

His paralyzed diaphragm began to work again. He drew deep sighing breaths. I stood and watched him sit up, and thought I should have hit him harder.

The girl's white face slanted up towards me. "You big bully."

"You wait outside, Ruth. I want to talk to Ronnie."

"Who are you?" The boy's words came hard between gulps of air. "What goes on?"

"He says he's a private cop." Her arms were around his shoulders; one of her hands was gently stroking his flank.

He pushed her away and rose unsteadily. "What do you think you want?" His voice was higher than it had been, as if my blow had reversed his adolescence.

"Sit down." I glanced at the single chair standing under the ceiling light. "I want some information."

"Not from me you don't." But he sat down. A nerve was twitching in his cheek, so that he seemed to be winking at me gaily again and again.

"Close the door," I said to the girl. "Behind you."

"I'm staying. I'm not going to let you hurt him any more."

The boy's face screwed up in sudden fury. "Get out of here, God damn you. Sell yourself for dog meat, only get out." He was talking to the girl, taking out his humiliation on her.

She answered him soberly: "If you say so, Ronnie," and went out, dragging her feet.

"You were a runner for Speed," I said to the boy.

Fury took hold of his face again and pulled it sharp and ratty. His ears were unnaturally small and close to his head. "Ruth's been flapping at the mouth, eh? She's a real fun person, Ruth is. I'll have to talk to Ruth."

"You'll lay off her entirely. I've got some more punches that you haven't seen. No girl would look twice at your face again."

His light eyes flicked towards the tire-iron in the corner, and quickly away from it. He groped for a boyish and dutiful expression and presented it to me. "I can't stay here, mister, honest. I got to get out in the office."

"There won't be any more easy marks tonight."

He managed to show me crooked teeth in a crooked little smile. "I guess maybe I'm stupid, mister. I don't get you at all."

"A century and a half is a lot of money to earn for five minutes' fast talking."

The cheek twitched, and he winked again. He was the least charming boy I had ever talked to. "You'd never get him to testify," he said.

"Don't kid yourself. He'll wake up mad tomorrow morning. I can easily find him."

"The old goat was asking for it, wasn't he?"

"You're the one that's asking for it, boy. They don't like badger games in a tourist town."

"I get it. You want a split." He smiled and winked again.

"I wouldn't touch it. Information is what I want."

"What kind of information? I got no information."

"About Herman Speed. I want to know what happened to him, and why."

Without moving his body, he gave the impression of squirming. He ran his hand nervously over his dark brush of hair. "You a State agent, mister? Federal?"

"Relax. It's not you I want. Though I'll turn you in for extortion if I have to."

"If I don't talk, you mean?"

"I'm getting impatient."

"I don't know what you want me to say. I—"

"You worked for Speed. You don't any more. Why not?"

"Speed isn't in business any more."

"Who do you work for?"

"Myself. Tarantine doesn't like me."

"I can't understand that," I said. "You've got looks, brains, integrity, everything. What more could Tarantine ask?"

That nicked his vanity and he showed a little shame. Only a little. "I was a runner for Speed, so Tarantine doesn't like me."

"He worked for Speed himself."

"Yeah, but he double-crossed him. When the corporation moved in, he changed sides. He saw an independent like Speed couldn't hold out against them."

"So he shot Speed and took over the business for the corporation."

"Not exactly. Tarantine's too smart to do any shooting himself. Maybe he fingered Speed. I heard he did."

"How did it happen?"

"I wasn't there, I only know what I heard." He did some more of his motionless squirming. Under the single eyebrow his eyes looked very small and close together. Transparent pimples of sweat dotted his forehead. "I shouldn't be talking like this, mister. It could get me blasted. How do I know I can trust you?"

"You'll have to take the chance."

"You couldn't use me for witness, I only know what I heard."

"Tell me."

"I'll tell you the best I can, mister. Speed was driving up from Tijuana that night. He had some packages of white in his tires; his system was pockets vulcanized on the inside of the tubes. Tarantine was riding with him and I guess he tipped off the mob. They hijacked Speed on the highway this side of Delmar, blocked him off the road with an old truck or something. Speed objected so they shot him down, drove his car away and left him for dead. Tarantine brought him in, he was Speed's palsy-walsy.

That's what Speed thought. When Speed got out of the hospital, he left town. He almost died, I guess that scared him off. He couldn't stand a shooting war, he was a gentleman."

"I can see that. Where's the gentleman now?"

"I wouldn't know. He blew, that's all. He sold the Arena lease to Tarantine and blew."

"Describe the gentleman, Ronnie."

"Speed? He's a sharp dresser. Two-hundred-dollar suits and custom shirts and ties with his own monogram. A big stout guy, but sharp. He talks like a college graduate, the genuine class."

"Does he have a face?"

"Yeah, he's pretty good-looking for an older guy. He's still got most of his hair—light brown hair. A little fair mustache." He drew a finger across his upper lip. "Pretty good features, except for his nose. He has a bump on his nose where he had it broken."

"About how old?"

"Middle-aged, forty or so. About your age, maybe a little older. Speed hasn't got your looks, though, mister." He tried to look earnest and appealing.

He was the kind of puppy who would lick any hand that he was afraid to bite. It was depressing not to be able to hit him again because he was younger and softer and too easy. If I really hurt him, he'd pass it on to somebody weaker, like Ruth. There was really nothing to be done about Ronnie, at least that I could do. He would go on turning a dollar in one way or another until he ended up in Folsom or a mortuary or a house with a swimming pool on top of a hill. There were thousands like him in my ten-thousand-square-mile beat: boys who had lost their futures, their parents and themselves in the shallow jerry-built streets of the coastal cities; boys with hot-rod bowels, comic-book imaginations, daring that grew up too late for one war, too early for another.

He said: "What's the matter, mister? I told you the truth so far as I know the truth." His cheek twitched, and I realized that I had been gazing down sightlessly into his empty hazel eyes.

"Maybe you have at that. You didn't make it all up, you haven't the brains. What was Tarantine's system?"

"I wouldn't know about that." He ran his uneasy fingers through his short black hair again.

"Sorry, I forgot. You're a respectable citizen. You don't have truck with crooks like Tarantine."

"Him and his brother bought this boat," he said. "The boat that got wrecked today. How would I know what they used it for? They went on a couple of fishing trips, maybe they went to Mexico. That's where Speed got the stuff when he was here, from a guy in Mexico City that manufactured it out of opium." He leaned forward toward me, without leaving the security of the chair. "Mister, let me go out to the office now, I told you all I know. What do you say?"

"Don't be such an eager beaver, Ronnie. There's another friend of yours I want to hear about. Where do I get in touch with Mosquito, in case I ever have the urge?"

"Mosquito?"

"He's selling in San Francisco now, Ruth says. He used to sell for Speed here."

"I don't know any Mosquito," he said without conviction, "only the ones that bite me."

I clenched my fist and held it for him to look at, telling myself that I was a great hand at frightening boys.

The hazel eyes crossed slightly looking at it. "I'll tell you, mister, promise you won't use my name. They wouldn't appreciate me talking around. He wrote me I might get a job up there this summer—"

"I'm not making any promises, Ronnie. I'm getting impatient again."

"You want to know where to find him, is that it?"

"That will do."

"I contacted him through a musician plays the piano in a basement bar, a place called The Den. It's right off Union Square, it's easy enough to find."

"When was this?"

"About a month ago. I flew up for a week-end last month. I get a buzz out of Frisco. It suits my personality, not like this one-horse town—"

"Yeah. Did you see Mosquito to talk to?"

"Sure, he's a big shot now, but he's a good friend of mine. I knew him in high school." Ronnie expanded in the thought. He knew Mosquito when.

"What's his real name?"

"You won't tell him I told you, mister, will you? Gilbert Moreno."

"And the musician?"

"I don't know his name. You'll find him in The Den, he plays piano every night in The Den. He's a snowbird, you can't miss him."

"Does Mosquito know where Speed is?"

"He said Speed was up there Christmas trying to raise a stake. Then he went to Reno, I think he said Reno. Can I go now, mister?"

The pattern was starting to form on the map at the back of my mind. It was an abstract pattern, a high thin triangle drawn in red. Its base was the short straight line between Palm Springs and Pacific Point. Its apex was San Francisco. Another, shadowier triangle on the same base pointed its apex at Reno. But when I tried to merge the two into a single picture, the entire pattern blurred.

I said: "All right, get."

When we went out, the girl had disappeared. I felt relieved. She was a bigger responsibility than I wanted.

Chapter 23

THE LIGHTED clock on the tower of the county courthouse said that it was only five minutes after eleven. I didn't believe it. I had a post-midnight feeling. My tongue was already furred with the dregs of a long bad evening. A criminal catechism ran on like a screechy record in my head. What? Blood. Where? There. When? Then. Why? Who knows. Who? Him. They. She. It. Us. Especially us.

I parked in front of the wing of the courthouse that held the county jail. The windows on the second and third floors were barred with ornamental ironwork, to appeal to the æsthetic sense of the thieves and muggers and prostitutes behind them. Part of the first floor of this wing was occupied by the sheriff's office, whose windows showed the only lights in the building below the tower clock.

The tall black oak door stood open, and I walked in under white fluorescent light. Behind the counter that divided the anteroom in two, a fat young man was talking into a telephone. No, he said, the chief wasn't there. He couldn't give out his private number. Anyway, he was probably in bed. Is that right, he was very sorry to hear it. He'd bring it to the chief deputy's attention in the morning.

He set the receiver down and sighed with relief. "A nut," he said to me. "We hear from her every day or two. She thinks she can receive radio waves, and foreign agents are bombarding her nervous system with propaganda. Next time I'm going to tell her to get her tubes adjusted so she can receive television."

He left his desk and lumbered to the counter: "What can I do for you, sir?" He had the friendly manner of a corner grocer, dispensing justice instead of bread and potatoes.

"I don't suppose the chief *is* here?"

"Not since supper. Anything I can do?"

"One of the deputies is working on a disappearance case: Joe Tarantine."

"One of the deputies, hell. There's three or four working on it." He buried his eyes in a smile.

121

"Let me talk to one of them."

"They're pretty busy. You a reporter?"

I showed him my photostat. "The one I was talking to is a big man in a ten-gallon hat, or do they all wear ten-gallon hats?"

"Just Callahan. He's in there with Mrs. Tarantine just now." He jerked his thumb towards an inner door. "You want to wait?"

"Which Mrs. Tarantine, mother or wife?"

"The young one. If I was Tarantine, I wouldn't run out on a bundle of goodies like that one." A leer started in his eyes and moved across his face in sluggish ripples.

I swallowed my irritation. "Is that the official view, that Tarantine ran out? Maybe you've got some inside dope that he can walk on water, or maybe a Russian sub was waiting to pick him up."

"Maybe." He fanned his face with his hand. "You and the old lady should get together. She says the voices in her head talk with a Russian accent. Matter of fact, there ain't no official view, won't be until we complete our investigation."

"Did they get aboard the *Aztec Queen*?"

"Yeah, it's all broken up on the rocks. Nobody in the cabin. What's your interest, if I may ask, Mister—?"

"Archer. I have some information for Callahan."

"He should be out any minute. They been in there nearly an hour." Casting an envious glance at the inner door, he meandered back to his desk and inserted his hips between the arms of the swivel chair.

I had time to smoke a cigarette, almost my first of the day. I sat on a hard bench against the wall. The minute hand of the electric clock on the opposite wall inched round in little nervous jumps to eleven thirty. The deputy on duty was yawning over a news magazine.

The latch of the inner door clicked finally, and Callahan appeared in the doorway. His big hat was in his hand, exposing a sun-freckled pate to the inclement light. He stood back awkwardly to let Galley precede him, smiling down at her as if he owned her.

She looked as trim and vital as she had in the afternoon. She was wearing a dark brown suit and a dark hat, their suggestion of widow's weeds denied by a lime-green blouse under her jacket. Only the bluish crescents under her eyes gave me an idea of what she had been through.

I stood up and she paused, one knee forward and bent in an uncompleted step. "Why, Mr. Archer! I didn't expect to run into you tonight." She completed the step and gave me her gloved hand. Even through the leather, it felt cold.

"I thought I might run into you. If you don't mind waiting a minute, I want to see Callahan."

"Of course I'll wait."

She sat down on the bench. Callahan hung over her and thanked her profusely for her aid. Her smile was a little strained. The fat young man leaned across the counter, his fleshbound eyes regarding her hungrily.

The big man put on his hat as he turned to me. "What's the story, mac? Let's see, you were with Mario down on the water-front. You a friend of his?"

"A private detective, looking for Joe Tarantine. The name is Archer."

"For her?" He cocked his head towards Galley.

"Her mother." I walked him to the other end of the counter. "A girl I've been talking to saw something this morning that ought to interest you. She was lying behind a wind-shelter on Mackerel Beach at dawn, all by herself."

"All by herself?" Perplexity or amusement corrugated the skin around his eyes.

"She says all by herself. A man swam in to shore with a bundle around his neck, probably clothes because he had nothing on. She saw him cross the beach and then she heard a car start up in the grove of trees behind the barbecue pits."

"So that's what happened to Tarantine," he drawled.

"It wasn't Joe, according to her, and it wasn't Mario either. She knows both of them—"

"Who is this girl? Where is she?"

"I met her at the wrestling match. I tried to bring her in but she ran out on me."

"What does she look like?"

"Blonde and thin."

"Hell, half the girls in town are blondies nowadays. When did you say she saw this guy?"

"Shortly before dawn. It was still too dark to see him very clearly."

"She wouldn't be having delusions?" he muttered. "Any girl that was lying on the beach by herself at that time."

"I don't think so." But perhaps he had something. There were better witnesses than Ruth, a hundred and fifty million of them, roughly.

He turned to Galley, removing his hat again. Even his voice changed when he spoke to her, as if he had a separate personality for each sex: "Oh, Mrs. Tarantine. What time did you say you drove your husband down here?"

She rose and came toward us, walking with precision. "I don't know the time exactly. About four a.m., I think it was."

"Before dawn, though?"

"At least an hour before dawn. It wasn't fully daylight when I got back to Santa Monica."

"That's what I thought you told me."

"Is it important?"

He answered her with solemnity: "Everything is important in a murder case."

"You think he was murdered?" I said.

"Tarantine? No telling what happened to him. We'll start dragging operations in the morning."

"But you mentioned murder."

"Tarantine is wanted for murder," he said. "L.A. has an all-points out for him. Didn't you hear about the Dalling killing?"

I glanced at Galley. Her head moved in a barely perceptible negative. I said: "Oh, that."

"I'm horribly tired," she said. "I'm going to ask Mr. Archer to drive me home."

I said I'd be glad to.

Chapter 24

SHE TOOK my arm on the courthouse steps, her fingers gripping me hard but not unpleasantly. "I'm grateful you showed up, Archer. I've been answering policemen's questions for hours and hours, and I feel quite unreal, like a character in a movie. You're something solid to hold on to, aren't you?"

"Solid enough. I weigh a hundred and eighty-five."

"That's not what I mean, and you know it. All those official faces are like death masks. You have a human face, you're made of flesh and blood."

"Flesh and blood and all things nice," I said. "I used to be a policeman. And I think you're walking on eggs."

Her grip on my arm tightened. "Walking on eggs?"

"You heard me. I can't understand why the L.A. cops haven't locked you up as a material witness."

"Why should they put me in jail? I'm perfectly innocent."

"Maybe you are in deed. Not in the mind. You're much too smart to be taken in by Tarantine. You couldn't live with him for over two months without knowing what he was up to."

She dropped my arm, and hung back when I opened the door of the car for her.

"Get in, Mrs. Tarantine. You asked me to drive you home. Where's your own car, by the way?"

"I didn't trust myself to drive tonight. I had a terrible day, and now you're cross-questioning me." Her voice broke, whether artificially or naturally I couldn't tell.

"Get in. I want to hear the story you told the cops."

"You've got no right to speak to me like this. A woman can't be forced to accuse her husband." But she got in.

I said: "She can if she's accessory." And slammed the door to punctuate the sentence.

She stayed in the far corner of the seat while I started the engine. "I didn't even know that Joe was wanted for murder until Mr. Callahan told me. Actually there is no warrant for him. He's simply wanted for questioning. They found his fingerprints in Keith's apartment." Her voice was thin.

"You must have known." I turned left towards the main street. "As soon as they told you Dalling had been shot, you must have thought about Joe's visit to Dalling this morning. What did you give Homicide on that?"

"Nothing. I left it out entirely. I said I drove him straight to Pacific Point."

"And you don't know what I mean by walking on eggs?"

"I couldn't tell them," she whispered. "They'd use it to put him in the gas chamber, if they ever find him."

I stopped for a flashing red light, and crossed the main street in the direction of the highway. "This afternoon you were strongly anti-Tarantine. What transformed you into the loyal wife?"

"You can save your sarcasm, Archer." Her spirit was flickering up again. "Joe isn't a very nice person, but he's incapable of killing anyone. Besides, I'm married to him."

"I know it. It didn't make him incapable of peddling heroin."

"How did you find that out?"

"The hard way. The point is that I didn't find out from you."

"I only knew the last few weeks. I hated it. I'd have left him if I hadn't been afraid to. Does that make me a criminal?"

"Afraid of what, Galley? Joe wouldn't hurt a fly, the way you tell it."

"He didn't kill Keith," she cried. "I'm certain he didn't. He had no reason to."

"Come off it, you know he had. You won't admit it, because you're afraid of getting involved yourself. As if you weren't up to your neck already."

"What reason did he have?"

"You gave me one reason this afternoon: Joe was blind mad, you said, because Dalling brought me to the hideout in Oasis. You've changed your story, now that the thing's come real."

"Keith wasn't in his apartment. There was no shot. I would have heard the shot."

"Nobody else heard it, either, but there was one. You want more motives? Joe must have known that you and Dalling were having an affair. Everybody else did."

"You're a liar!"

"About what, the fact, or the public knowledge of it?"

"It isn't a fact. Keith was a friend, and that's all. What do you think I am?"

"A woman who hated her husband. Call the thing platonic if you want to. Joe isn't the kind to split hairs. You won't deny that Dalling was crazy about you."

"Certainly I deny it. I gave him no encouragement."

"He didn't need encouragement. He was a romantic kid. He would have died for you, and perhaps he did. He brought me into the case, you know."

"I thought you said my mother—"

"Keith persuaded her. He paid a visit to her Sunday night and talked her into hiring me."

"Did she tell you that?"

"She did. And it's the truth."

"She didn't know Keith."

"She met him Sunday."

"How can you be sure?"

"The whole thing was a setup, when I met him in Palm Springs. He wanted me to find him there. Keith was afraid to come to me openly on his own, on account of Joe and Dowser. He felt caught in the middle between them. Still, he had guts enough to take me out there. It must have been hard to do, for a tender personality like Keith. And it really meant something."

"Yes, it meant something." I thought she added under her breath: "Poor fool." She was quiet then.

We were on the open highway, headed north toward Long Beach. A strong wind was blowing across it, and I reduced my speed to keep the car from weaving. I caught occasional glimpses of the sea, whitecapped and desolate under a driving sky. The unsteady wind whined in the corners of the cut-banks and fell off in unexpected silences. In one of the silences, under the drive of the motor, I heard Galley crying to herself.

The lights of Long Beach angered the moving sky ahead of us. The wind rose and fell and rose, and the woman's crying continued through strata of peace and violence. She moved against me gently and leaned her head on my shoulder. I drove left-handed so as not to disturb her.

"Did you love him, Galley?"

"I don't know, he was sweet to me." She sighed in the corners of her grief; her breath tickled my neck. "It was too late when I met him. I was married to Joe, and Keith was going to marry another woman. I took him away from her, but it couldn't work out. He wasn't quite a man, except when he was loaded. Then he was worse than a man."

"He's finished now."

"Everything's finished," she said. "Everything's on its last legs. I wish I had had a blowout when I was driving Joe in from Oasis. There wouldn't be all these loose ends to gather up and live with, would there?"

"You didn't strike me as the kind of a girl who wants an easy out."

"There are no easy outs, I guess. I thought I was taking an easy out when I married Joe. I was sick of taking hospital orders, fighting off internes in the linen room, waiting for something good to happen to me. Joe looked like something good for a little while. He wasn't."

"How did you meet him?"

"I told you that, this afternoon. It seems like years ago, doesn't it?"

"Tell me again."

"There are things I'd rather talk about, but I will if you insist. I was on twenty-four hour duty with Mr. Speed for over two weeks. Joe came to see him nearly every day. He was running the Arena for him."

"Who shot Speed?"

"One of Dowser's men, Blaney I think. I didn't dare speak out this afternoon. They might have been listening."

"Did Speed tell you that?"

"No, he never admitted anything about the shooting. When the police questioned him in the hospital, he claimed he shot himself by accident. I suppose he was afraid they'd finish him off if he talked. It was Joe told me, after we were married. I promised him I'd never tell a soul, but I guess my promises to Joe are canceled now. He's gone away without caring what happens to me."

"Gone where? Surely he gave you a hint."

"I only know what I told you," she said. "I believe he took Mario's boat."

"The *Aztec Queen* didn't get very far."

"Joe might have been covering his tracks. He could have had another boat waiting at sea for him."

"His brother had the same idea."

"Mario? Mario would know, better than I. Joe has friends in Ensenada—"

"I wonder. He may have business connections, but they really belong to Dowser. If Joe's as sharp as he sounds, he'll be running in the opposite direction.—Did anybody meet him at the yacht basin?"

"I didn't see anyone, no. I heard what you told Mr. Callahan about the man on the beach. It might have been Joe, mightn't it, in spite of what the girl said?"

"It might. I think it was somebody else."

"Who?"

"I haven't any idea."

"What do you think happened to Joe?"

"God knows. He may be in Los Angeles or San Francisco. He may have flown to Cleveland or New York. He may be at the bottom of the sea."

"I almost hope he is."

"What was he carrying, Galley?"

"He didn't tell me, but I can guess that it was heroin. It's what he deals in."

"Does he take it himself?"

"Not Joe. I've seen some of his customers, and that's when I started to hate him. I didn't even like his money after that."

"He ran out with Dowser's shipment, is that it?"

"Evidently. I didn't dare to ask him."

"How much?"

"I couldn't even guess."

"Where did he keep it?"

"I don't know that, either." Her body turned inward to me, and she sighed. "Please stop talking like a policeman. I really can't stand it any longer."

The traffic was still fairly heavy in the Long Beach area, and I concentrated on my driving. On both sides of the road, the oilfield derricks marched like platoons of iron men across the suburban wilderness. I felt as if I were passing through dream country, trying to remember the dream that went along with the landscape and not being able to. Galley removed her hat and lay heavy and still against me until I stopped the car in front of her mother's house.

"Wake up," I said. "You're home."

Chapter 25

IT WAS nearly two o'clock when I reached my section of the city. I lived in a five-room bungalow on a middle-class residential street between Hollywood and Los Angeles. The house and the mortgage on it were mementos of my one and only marriage. Since the divorce I never went home till sleep was overdue. It was overdue now. The last few miles down the night-humming boulevard I drove by muscle memory, half-asleep. My consciousness didn't take over until I was in my driveway. I saw the garage door white in my headlights, a blank wall at the end of a journey from nowhere to nowhere.

Leaving the motor idling, I got out of the car to open the garage. Two men walking abreast emerged from the shadows on the porch beside me. I waited in the narrow passage between the house and the open door of the car. They were big young men, dressed in dark suits and hats. In the half-light reflected from the garage door, their wide shoulders and square faces looked almost identical. A pair of heavenly twins, I guessed, from the Los Angeles police. The thought of Dalling in his blood had followed me all day. Now Dalling was catching up.

"Archer?" one of them said. "Mr. Lew Archer?"

"You have me. Hearthstone of the Death Squad, I presume." I was running short of élan. "Accompanied by Deathstone of the Hearth Squad. Where's Squadstone of the Death Hearth?"

"I'm Sergeant Fern," said First Policeman. "This is Sergeant Tolliver."

"Pronounced Taliaferro, no doubt."

Second Policeman said: "It's pretty late to be making corny jokes, isn't it, Mr. Archer?"

"Bloody late. Can't this wait until morning?"

"Lieutenant Gary said to bring you in whenever you showed. He wants to talk to you now."

"About the Dalling killing?"

The plain-clothes sergeants looked at each other as if I had said something significant. The first one said: "Lieutenant Gary will be glad to explain."

"I suppose there's no way out of it." I switched off the head-lights and slammed the car door shut. "Let's go."

The patrol car was waiting around the corner. Lieutenant Gary was waiting in his Homicide Division cubicle.

It was a small square room dismally equipped with gray-painted steel furniture: a filing-cabinet, a desk with a squawk-box and In and Out baskets piled with reports, a water-cooler in a corner. A street map of the city nearly covered one wall. The single window opened on the windowless side of an adjacent building. A ceiling fixture filled the room with bright and ugly light.

Gary stood up behind his desk. He was a man in his forties with prematurely white hair. It stuck up all over his head in thistly spikes, as if his fingers had been busy at it. Gary had the shoulders of a football guard, but there was nothing beef-trust about his face. He had quarterback's eyes, alert and shifting, a thin inquiring nose, a mobile mouth.

"Lew Archer, eh?" he said, not unpleasantly. His shirt was open and his tie hung askew. He tugged at it half-heartedly and forgot it. "Okay, Fern, thanks."

The sergeant who had escorted me into the station closed the glass door behind him. Gary sat down at his desk and studied me. There was a green cloth board on the wall beside him, with several pictures of wanted men, full-face and profile, pinned to it. I had a fellow-feeling with the black-and-white smudged faces.

"You'll always remember me, Lieutenant."

"I do remember you. I've been checking your record, as a matter of fact. A pretty good record, as records go, in your job, in this town. I can't say you've ever co-operated very freely, but you've never tried to cheat us, and that's something. Also, I've talked to Colton on the D.A.'s staff about you. He's in your corner, one hundred percent."

"I served under him in Intelligence during the war. What are you working up to, lieutenant? You didn't haul me in at two in the morning to compliment me on my record."

"No. I mention the record because if it wasn't for that you'd be under arrest."

It took me a little while to swallow that. He watched me, his nervous mouth chewing on itself.

I decided to come up smiling. "As it is I'm paying you a social call. Charming occasion, isn't it?"

His eyes narrowed and brightened. They were like rifle slits in his walled face, with blue steel glinting behind them. "The warrant's drawn," he said softly. "If I decided to execute it, you wouldn't think it was funny."

"What's it for? Spitting on the sidewalk?"

I got no rise out of him. He answered me with a question: "What have you been doing with yourself all day?"

"Eating. Working. Drinking. Having laughs."

He answered his own question: "Looking for Joe Tarantine. Tell me why."

"I have a client."

"Name him."

"My memory for names is very lousy."

He shifted in his chair, his blue gaze circling the room as if he wanted out. "I have several questions to ask you, Archer. I hope this isn't going to be typical of your answers."

"You seem to know the answers."

"Hell, let's get down to cases. Soft-pedal the repartee."

"I'm afraid when you wave a warrant at me it brings out the comedian."

"Forget the warrant. It wasn't my idea." Against all the odds, he sounded like a fair man. "Sit down and tell me why in God's name you should start running errands for Dowser at this late date."

"What have you got against Dowser?" I sat in the one straight chair in front of the desk. "Dowser's a solid citizen. He's got a swimming pool and a private bar to prove it. He entertains politicians in his charming ranch-type home on an exclusive hilltop. He even supports a butler and a blonde."

"I don't get it, Archer." He sounded disappointed. "You're working for him?"

"Why not? He must be on good terms with the law or he wouldn't be running loose. I wonder how many cops he has on his payroll. I'm just an ex-cop with a living to hustle."

His eyes shut tight. For an instant the long gray face looked dead. "Don't tell me about Dowser's payoff. I know. I also know why you left the Long Beach force. You wouldn't take Sam Schneider's monthly cut, and he forced you out."

"Colton's been talking too much," I said. "If you know all about Dowser, go out and bring him in and put him in Alcatraz where he belongs. Don't take out your official frustrations on me."

"He isn't my department." Gary was masticating his lip again. "The boys knock off his peddlers two and three a month, but that's as far as it goes. Tarantine's one of his right-hand men, you know that?"

"He was. Not any more."

"Where is Tarantine now?"

"Nobody knows."

"We found his fingerprints in Dalling's apartment." He changed the subject suddenly: "What were you doing in Dalling's apartment this morning?"

I let it go by, trying not to show that he had startled me.

He went on: "A driver for Western Dairy gave us your description this afternoon. He also described your car. You or your twin went in the Casa Loma the back way some time around eight o'clock this morning." He sat back and waited for me to have a reaction.

I had a number of them. This meant that his questions about Dowser were by-play. He'd told me to forget the warrant, but he remembered it.

There was nothing in being cagey. "At eight o'clock Dalling had been dead for hours. The autopsist will tell you that, if he hasn't already."

"You admit you were there? You admit that Dalling was dead."

"I was there. He was dead."

"You didn't report it to us. We had to wait until the blood soaked through the floor and made a spot on the ceiling of the apartment underneath and somebody finally got around to noticing it. That wasn't smart of you, Archer, it wasn't co-operative, it wasn't even legal. It's the kind of thing that makes for license trouble." He leaned forward across the desk, his eyes jumping like blue Bunsen flames, and tossed me a change-of-pace: "Of course license trouble is the least of your worries."

"Go on."

"You rushed straight from the Casa Loma to interview a couple of witnesses, Severn and the Hammond woman. God knows what you thought you were trying to do. The kindest interpretation is that you suddenly remembered you were an aging boy-wonder and decided to cut us out entirely and run a murder investigation as a one-man show. Have you been seeing a lot of movies lately? Reading *The Rover Boys at Hollywood and Vine*?"

"Maybe I have. What's the unkindest interpretation?"

"It's possible you were covering up for yourself." He dropped it very casually. "We found the gun, you see. A member of my detail picked it out of a storm drain on the street behind the Casa Loma parking lot."

Gary opened the drawer in front of him and set a squat black .38 automatic on the desk. "Recognize it?"

I recognized it. It was my own gun.

"You should," he said. "It's registered to you. Our ballistics man just completed some firing tests with this gun a couple of hours ago. It's his opinion, based on examination with a comparison microscope, that this gun fired the slug that was dug out of Dalling's cortex. It severed the jugular vein and imbedded itself in the cortex. Dalling bled to death. How do you like that, Archer?"

"Not very much. Go on. You haven't warned me that anything I say may be used against me yet."

"I'll give it to you now. Have you got anything to say?"

"I'm very smart," I said, "and very devious. I saw Dalling for the first time last night and decided that he was too pretty to live, a fit subject for the perfect crime. So I committed it. I shot him with a gun that could easily be identified as mine and carefully deposited it in the nearest drain, where any cop would be sure to look for it. Four or five hours later I returned to the scene of the crime, as murderers must, in order to admire my handiwork. Also to let a milkman spot me for you. I wanted to make things difficult for myself—"

"You have." Gary was using his gentle voice once more. "This isn't very funny. It doesn't make me laugh."

"It isn't funny. It has some funny elements, though—"

He cut me off again: "You've acted like a damn fool, and you know it. I could probably get an indictment and possibly make it stick—"

"The hell you could. I was just going to tell you the funniest thing of all. I shot Dalling at a range of one hundred and twenty miles. Pretty good for a .38 automatic that normally can't hit a barn door at fifty paces."

"Failing a murder indictment," he went on imperturbably, "I could be very nasty about your failure to report discovery of the corpse. It happens I don't want to be nasty. Colton doesn't want me to be nasty, and I value his judgment. But you're going to force me to be nasty if you go on talking like a damn fool on top of acting like one." He chewed his upper lip. "Now what was that about an alibi?"

It struck me that vaudeville was dead. "At the time Dalling was shot, I was fifteen or twenty miles on the other side of Palm Springs, talking to a woman by the name of Marjorie Fellows. Why don't you get in touch with her? She's staying at the inn there."

"Perhaps I will. What time was that?"

"Around three in the morning."

"If you know that Dalling was shot at three, you know more than we do. Our doctor places it around four, give or take an hour." He spread his hands disarmingly, as if to underline the fact of his candor. "There's no way to determine how long he lived after he was shot, or exactly when he was shot. It's evident from the blood that he lived for some time, though he was almost certainly unconscious from the slug in his cortex. Anyway, you can see how that plays hell with any possible alibi. Unless you have better information?" There was irony in the question.

I said that I had.

"You want to make a statement?"

I said that I did.

"Good. It's about time." He flipped the switch on the squawk-box on the corner of his desk, and summoned a stenographer.

My obligation to Peter Colton was growing too big for comfort. Apparently the conversation up to this point had been off the record. That suited me, because my performance had been painful. I'd bungled like an amateur when I found Dalling's body; gambled and lost on the chance that Miss Hammond or Joshua Severn might tell me something important if I got to them before policemen did. Gary had driven that home, in spite of my efforts to talk around the point. Vaudeville was dead as Dalling, and the Rover Boys were as out of date as the seven sleepers of Ephesus.

Gary gave up his chair to the young male stenographer.

"Do you want it in detail?" I asked him.

"Absolutely."

I gave the thing in detail from the beginning. The beginning was Dalling's visit to Mrs. Lawrence, which brought me into the case. The night died gradually, bleeding away in words. The police stenographer filled page after page of his notebook with penciled hieroglyphics. Gary paced from wall to wall, still looking for a way out. Occasionally he paused to ask me a question. When I told him that Tarantine had taken my gun, he interrupted to ask:

"Will Mrs. Tarantine corroborate that?"

"She already has."

"Not to us." He took a paper-bound typescript from his desk and riffled through it. "There's nothing in her statement about your gun. Incidentally, you didn't report the theft."

"Call her up and ask her."

He left the room. The stenographer lit a cigarette. We sat and looked at each other until Gary came back:

"I sent a car for her. I talked to her on the phone and she doesn't seem to object. She a friend of yours?"

"She won't be after this. She has a queer old-fashioned idea that a woman should stick by her husband."

"He hasn't done much of a job of sticking by her. What do you make of Mrs. Tarantine, anyway?"

"I think she made the mistake of her life when she married Tarantine. She has a lot of stuff, though."

"Yeah," he said dryly. "Is she trying to cover for him, that's what I want to know."

"She has been, I think." And I recited what she had told me about the early-morning visit to Dalling's apartment.

That stopped him in his tracks. "There's a discrepancy there, all right." He consulted her statement again. "According to what she said this afternoon, she drove him straight over from Palm Springs to Long Beach by the canyon route. The question is, which time was she telling the truth?"

"She told me the truth," I said. "She didn't know then that Dalling was dead. When she found out that he was, she switched her story to protect her husband."

"When did you talk to her?"

"Early this afternoon—yesterday afternoon." It was four o'clock by my wristwatch.

"You knew that Dalling was dead."

"I didn't tell her."

"Why? Could she have killed him herself, or set him up for her husband?"

"I entertained the possibility, but she's crazy if she did. She was half in love with Dalling."

"What was the other half?"

"Mother feeling or something. She couldn't take him seriously; he was alcoholic, for one thing."

"Yeah. Did she communicate all this, or you dream it up?"

"You wouldn't be interested in my dreams."

"Okay. Let's have the rest of the statement, eh?" And he went back to filling the room with his pacing.

It was ten to five when I finished my statement. The stenographer left the room with orders to have it typed as quickly as possible.

"If you've been leveling," Gary said to me, "it looks very much like Tarantine. Why would he do it?"

"Ask Mrs. Tarantine."

"I'm going to. Now."

"I'd like to sit in if possible."

"Uh-uh. Good night."

She met me in the corridor, walking in step with Sergeant Tolliver.

"We're always meeting in police stations," I said.

"As good a place as any, I guess." She looked exhausted, but she had enough energy left to smile with.

Chapter 26

I WOKE up looking for the joker that would freeze the pile and win the hand for me. It wasn't under the pillow. It wasn't between the sheets. It wasn't on the floor beside the bed. I was climbing out of the bed to look underneath it when I realized that I had been dreaming.

It was exactly noon by my bedside alarm. A truck started up in the street outside with an impatient clash of gears, as if to remind me that the world was going on without me. I let it go. First I took a long hot shower and then a short cold one. The pressure of the water hurt the back of my head. I shaved and brushed my teeth for the first time in two days and felt unreasonably virtuous. My face looked the same as ever, as far as I could tell. It was wonderful how much a pair of eyes could see without being changed by what they saw. The human animal was almost too adaptable for its own good.

The kitchen was brimful of yellow sunlight that poured in through the window over the sink. I started a pot of coffee, fried some bacon, broke four eggs in the sizzling grease, toasted half a dozen slices of stale bread. After eating, I sat in the breakfast nook with a cigarette and a cup of black coffee, thinking of nothing. Silence and loneliness were nice for a change. The absence of dialogue was a positive pleasure that lasted through the second cup of coffee. But I noticed after a while that I was tapping one heel on the floor in staccato rhythm and beginning to bite my left thumbnail. A car passed in the street with the sound of a bus I was about to miss. The yellow sunlight was bleak on the linoleum. The third cup of coffee was too bitter to drink.

I went to the phone in the hall and dialed my answering service. A Mrs. Caroline Standish had phoned on Monday and again on Tuesday. No, she hadn't left her number; she said she would call again. A Mrs. Samuel Lawrence had phoned twice Tuesday morning. Tuesday afternoon a certain Lieutenant Gary had wanted to speak to me, very urgently. There had also been a call from Mr. Colton of the D.A.'s office. The only Wednesday call was long-distance from Palm Springs. A Mrs. Marjorie Fellows wanted me to call her back at the Oasis Inn.

"When did you get that last one?"

"About two hours ago. Mrs. Fellows called about ten thirty."

I thanked the cool female voice, depressed the bar, and dialed Long Distance. They got me Marjorie Fellows person-to-person.

"This is Archer. You wanted to talk to me."

"I do, very much. So many things have been happening, I don't know which way to turn." She sounded rather beaten and bewildered.

"Give me an example."

"What did you say?"

"Give me an example, of the things that have been happening."

"Oh, so many things. The police and—other things. I don't like to speak of them over the telephone. You know these switchboard operators." She said it with direct malice, to a hypothetical operator listening on the line. "Could you possibly come out and talk to me here?"

"It might be more convenient if you came to town."

"I can't. I have no car. Besides, I'm quite disorganized. I've been so depending on you. I don't know anyone at all in southern California." A whine ran through the flat midwestern voice, in and out in a pattern of self-pity. "You *are* a private detective, as Lieutenant Gary said?"

"I am. What happened to your car?"

"Henry—is using it."

"You can fly in from Palm Springs in half an hour."

"No, I couldn't possibly fly. Don't you understand, I'm terribly upset. I need your help, Mr. Archer."

"Professionally speaking?"

"Yes, professionally speaking. Won't you come out and have lunch with me at the Inn?"

I said I would, if she was willing to wait for a late lunch. I put on a tie and jacket, and loaded a revolver.

By-passing Palm Springs, I reached Oasis shortly after two thirty. Its grid of roads lay on the flat desert, a blueprint for a boom hopefully waiting for the boom to happen. An escarpment of black stone overshadowed the unbuilt town, its steep sides creased and folded like a stiff black tarpaulin thrown carelessly on the horizon. Beyond it the desert stretched into rainbow distances. The bright new copper penny of the sun spun in its heat against a flat painted sky.

The stucco buildings of the Oasis Inn were dazzling white in the daytime. It was a pueblo hotel with the main building fronting the road and about twenty detached cottages scattered behind it. The watered lawn around them looked artificial and out of place, like a green broadloom carpet spread on the arid earth. I parked against the adobe wall beside the portico, and entered the lobby. Its air-conditioning chilled the sweat on my forehead. The big room was lined and furnished with light wood and leather, draped and upholstered with desert-colored cloth in Indian patterns. Whoever did it had both money and taste, an unusual combination anywhere.

The man behind the desk was expecting me. He called me by name and turned me over to a Filipino in a white-drill steward's jacket. I followed his thin impassive back down a concrete walk between spaced rows of cottages. Several half-naked bodies, male and female, were broiling in the sun or reclining on long chairs in the shadowed porches: castaways from Hollywood and Chicago and New York. More castaways were grouped around the pool that shimmered at the rear of the compound. *Dolce far niente* with a dollar sign.

My Filipino guide led me onto the porch of one of the smaller cottages and knocked discreetly on the screen door. When Marjorie Fellows appeared he said "Mr. Archer" and vanished.

She looked larger than life in a sleeveless linen dress that emphasized the width of her shoulders and hips. "I'm so glad you could come, I really am." She held the door for me and extended her hand at arm's length. It was large and cold and moist, and it held on for some time.

I murmured appropriate greetings as I disengaged myself. She led me into her sitting-room and seated me in an armchair.

"I took the liberty of ordering for you," she said. "They close the kitchens at three. I'm having shirred eggs with those cute little pork sausages they have. I ordered the same for you. Shirred eggs Bercy?"

I said that shirred eggs Bercy sounded delectable.

"Perhaps you'd like something to drink. You've had a long hot drive and all on my account. I *owe* you a nice cool drink." She was hovering around my chair. She wasn't built to hover, but she was hovering.

I said that I could do with a bottle of beer.

She went to the phone in a little skipping run that jolted the foundations of the building; turned with her hand on the receiver: "They have some very nice imported Loewenbrau, at least Henry likes it. Dark or light?"

"Dark will be fine." While she placed the order, I looked around the room for traces of Henry. There were no traces of Henry.

When she returned to her hovering, I asked her: "Where's your husband?"

Her face arranged itself in a meditative pout. Her large arms hung awkwardly at her sides. I felt a sudden sympathy for her, with a little insight mixed in. Her type had been invented to make men comfortable. Without a man to be nice to, she didn't know what to do with herself at all. And she was without a man.

I wished I could recall my brusque question and wrap it up in a prettier parcel for her.

She understood the look on my face and answered it along with the question: "I'm glad you brought it up, honestly. It's what I want to talk to you about, but I hated to broach the subject. I'm an awful dreamer, Mr. Archer. I live in a world of my own unless somebody snaps me out of it like you just did."

She flung herself on a bright-patterned sofa, which sagged and creaked under her weight. Curiously enough, her legs were good. She arranged them in such a way that I couldn't fail to notice the slimness of her ankles.

"The dirty bastard picked up and left me," she said in a deep harsh voice. Her eyes were round with anger, or surprise at her own language. "Good heavens," she said in her normal voice, "I never swear, honestly."

"Swear some more. It will probably do you good."

"Oh no, I couldn't." She had flushed to the ears. But she said: "I call him a dirty bastard because I believe he is one."

"You'd better go back and take it from the beginning."

"I hate to. I hate to talk about it, or even think about it. I've acted like a great fool. I let him take advantage of me all along the line."

"Where did you get on?"

"Get on?"

"How did you happen to meet him?"

"Oh," she said. "He was staying at the guest-ranch near Reno when I was waiting for my divorce. Everything was so romantic, and Henry could ride so well, and his conversation was so interesting. I sort of fell in love with him on the rebound."

"Rebound?"

"From George, I mean. I was married to George for sixteen years and I guess I got bored with him, or we got bored with each other. It would have been seventeen years this coming June the 10th. We never went anywhere or did anything together any more. All George wanted to do was go out to the country club when he got finished at the office and try to break eighty. I always wanted to come out west but George never took me further than Minneapolis. The only reason we went to Minneapolis was because the business has a branch in Minneapolis. George is the secretary-treasurer of the Simplex Ball Bearing Company." Pride and resentment and nostalgia warred in her expression. Nostalgia won. "I was a fool to leave him, a great fool, and now I'm having to take my medicine. I walked out on George, now Henry walks out on me. My second marriage lasted sixteen *days*." The contrast was too much for her. It brought tears to her eyes, still puffed and red from previous tears.

"Henry walked out on you?"

"Yes." The syllable lengthened shakily into a sob. "He left this morning, with the car and the money and—everything."

"After a quarrel?"

"We didn't even quarrel," as if Henry had denied her her rightful due. "The police called from Los Angeles early this morning, and Henry answered the telephone, and afterwards he heard me talking to them over the phone. He started packing right away, before I put down the receiver, even. I begged him to tell me what was the matter. He wouldn't say a word, except that he had to go away on business. He checked out and drove away without even eating breakfast."

"In your car?"

"I paid for it, only it's registered in his name. Henry wanted it that way, and he was so masterful, and besides we bought it for our honeymoon. It was really my idea to put it in his name, it made me feel more married." She hugged her large fine bosom, but there was cold comfort in that.

"You also mentioned money, Mrs. Fellows?"

"Yes." A nervous hurt plucked at her eyebrows, drawing them closer together. "Please don't call me Mrs. Fellows, I hate it. Call me Marjorie, or Mrs. Barron."

"George's name?"

"Yes." She managed a weak smile, with tears still standing in her eyes. "George made me a very generous settlement, and I've thrown a lot of it away already. Great fool that I am."

"How much did Henry get into you for?"

"Thirty thousand dollars." The sound of the numbers seemed to appall her. Unconsciously, she reached for the alligator purse that was lying on the couch beside her, and pressed it to her girdled abdomen. "He said he had a wonderful chance to make a good investment for both of us: this apartment building in Hollywood. He showed me the apartment building, too. Now I guess it's gone with the wind."

There was a gentle tapping on the door behind me. She opened it, and an elderly waiter wheeled in our lunch on a cart. While he set the table, Marjorie left the room. She came back in time to tip him heavily, smiling with a washed and reconstructed face. At least Henry hadn't taken her for all she had, financially or otherwise.

She ate her lunch with appetite, and asked me how I liked mine. I said that the German beer was very good, and that the quality of the shirred eggs Bercy was not strained. I waited until we had lighted cigarettes, and asked her:

"What did you say to the police on the telephone this morning? Apparently that's what frightened Henry off."

"Do you think so? This Lieutenant Gary wanted to come and talk to me but I explained that I was on my honeymoon and he said he would get in touch with me again and arrange to have me make a deposition, or something of the sort. Then he asked me a lot of questions about Mr. Dalling's house: what I was doing there and if I found you unconscious, and of course I said I did—and what time it was. Finally he told me that Mr. Dalling was dead, isn't that dreadful?"

"Dreadful. Did Lieutenant Gary ask you what you were doing at the house when you found me?"

"Yes."

"What did you tell him?"

"The same as I told you." She dropped her eyes demurely, and tapped the ash from the end of her cigarette. "That I was just driving by, and saw you lying there on the porch."

"I think it's time you told somebody the truth about that."

She flared up feebly, like a moist firecracker. "How could I tell him the truth? Henry was standing right beside me at the phone, listening to everything I said. I didn't dare to say a word about my suspicions of him—"

"You'd been having suspicions, then."

"I was suspicious of Henry from the very beginning, if I'd admitted it to myself. Only he made me *feel* so good, I couldn't face up to the facts. I knew he hadn't much money, and he knew I had. I knew I was foolish to marry again so quickly before I checked his background. But I wanted so hard to believe that he loved me for myself, I deliberately blinded myself and rushed right in. I'd never have given him the thirty thousand if I hadn't wanted to blind myself. I'm stupid, but I'm not that stupid, Mr. Archer."

"I doubt that you're stupid at all," I said. "You're too darn emotional, is all. You probably made a mistake divorcing George, but a lot of women make the same mistake. Or else they make the mistake of not divorcing George."

"You're an awful cynic, aren't you? But what you say is perfectly true. I *am* too emotional. I'm a great emotional fool, and you've put your finger on my central weakness. It was my foolish emotions that made me give him the money. I trusted him because I wanted to so badly. I had to trust him to make the whole thing stay real for a little longer. I guess it was slipping already."

"When was this?"

"Last Thursday, the day after we came here. We were in Santa Barbara at the Biltmore before that. Our week there was a perfect idyll. They have a lovely big pool, and Henry actually taught me how to swim. Henry's a splendid athlete, and that's one of the things that appealed to me so much. I love to see a man be able to *do* things. He told me when he was younger, before he got his wound, that he was a boxing champion in the army." She noticed that she was softening towards Henry, and caught herself up short, the harsh disgusted note breaking out in her voice again: "I suppose that was a lie, like everything else."

"His wound?" I prompted her.

"His war wound. He was a colonel in the war, until he was invalided out because of his wound. He was living on his disability pension."

"Did he ever show you a government check?"

"No, but I know he wasn't lying about that. I saw the wound."

"Where was he wounded?"

"In Germany. He fought under General Patton."

"Not geographically. Physiologically."

"Oh." She blushed. "He had a dreadful scar on his abdomen. It still wasn't completely healed, after all these years."

"Too bad."

"That week in Santa Barbara he told me the whole story of his life. But even then I began to have my suspicions. There was this waiter at the Biltmore who knew him. The waiter called him by some other name: apparently he remembered Henry from when he worked at another hotel somewhere. Henry was quite put out. He explained to me that it was a nickname, but I knew waiters don't address hotel guests by their nicknames, and I wondered about it afterwards."

"What was the name?"

"It's queer, I don't remember. It'll probably come back, though. Anyway, that was when I started to have my real suspicions of him. Then when we came out here he was always going away, on business he said, and he wouldn't tell me where he went. On Sunday night we had a quarrel about it. He wanted to go out by himself and I wouldn't give him the keys to the car, so he had to take a taxi. When the taxi-driver got back to his stand, I tipped him to tell me where he had taken Henry, and he said it was this Mr. Dalling's house. I waited up for him, but he wouldn't tell me what he was doing there. The same thing happened Monday night. He went out and I waited and waited, and finally I drove out to the house to look for him."

"And found me instead."

"And found you instead." She smiled.

"But you didn't tell any of this to Lieutenant Gary."

"Not a smidgen. I couldn't, with Henry right there."

"Are you going to, when you give your evidence?"

"Do you think I should?"

"Definitely."

"I don't know." She pushed her chair back from the table, marched up and down the length of the Indian-patterned rug, her plump hips teetering at the top of her long straight legs. "I don't know whether I will or whether I won't. He might have really gone on a business trip, and be coming back tomorrow like he said. Henry's a strange silent sort of man."

"He said that, did he, that he's coming back tomorrow?"

"Something like that. Do you think I should believe him? It would be terrible if this was all a mistake, and I had called the police in, and he really did come back." She stood facing the door, with a funny look of expectant remorse, as if Henry was there to upbraid her for having disloyal thoughts. "What shall I do, Mr. Archer? It's taken me a long time to get around to it, but that's really what I wanted to talk to you about."

"What do you want to do, get Henry back?"

"No, I don't think so, even if he would come. I don't trust him any more, I'm afraid of him. It isn't only his deception of me. I might be able to forgive that if he came back and proved that he loves me by turning over a new leaf. But I can't help feeling that he's mixed up in this terrible murder, that that's why he rushed away so unexpectedly. You see, I don't know who he is or what he is." She sat down on the edge of the couch, suddenly and weakly, as if her legs had given way.

"I have a good idea who and what he is. Did the waiter in Santa Barbara call him Speed?"

Her head jerked up: "Speed! That was it. I knew it would come back to me. How did you guess? Do you know him?"

"By reputation," I said. "His reputation is bad. He didn't get his abdominal wound in the war. He got it in a gang fight last fall."

"I knew it," she cried, and shook her head from side to side so the bright dyed hair swung forward and brushed her cheeks. "I want to go back to Toledo, where people are nice. I always wanted to live in California but now that I've seen it, it's a hellish place. I've fallen among thieves, that's what I've done. Thieves and murderers and confidence men. I want to go back to George."

"It sounds like a very good plan."

"I can't though, he'd never forgive me. I'd be a laughingstock for the rest of my days. What could I tell him about the thirty thousand? It's nearer forty when you count the car and all the money I've spent." She kneaded her alligator bag with both clenched hands.

"There's a possibility you can get it back. You have no notion where Henry went, I don't suppose."

"He didn't tell me *anything*. He just went away. Now I know I'll never see him again. But if I ever do, I'll scratch his eyes out." Her eyes glared from the ambush of her hair. I didn't know whether to laugh at her or weep with her.

I looked out the window onto the lawn, where spray from a sprinkling system danced in the sun. "No letters? No telephone calls? No telegrams? No visitors?"

There was a long pause while I watched the dancing water.

"He had a person-to-person call from San Francisco yesterday. I answered the phone myself, then he made me go into the bedroom and close the door. Does that mean anything?"

"It may." I stood up. "I'll try it anyway. You got no hint of who was calling, no names given?"

"No."

"But you're positive it was a San Francisco call."

"Oh, yes. The operator said so." She had pushed back her hair from her face and was looking less upset. There was an ice-chip hardness in her eyes I hadn't noticed before.

"I ought to tell you, Mrs. Fellows—"

"Mrs. Barron," she said stubbornly. "I was never really married to him."

"Mrs. Barron, then. You might get better results if you took your story to the police."

"I can't. It would be in all the papers. I could never go home at all then. Don't you see?"

"If I recover your money, or any part of it, I'll take a percentage, fifteen percent. That would be forty-five hundred out of thirty thousand."

"All right."

"Otherwise I'll charge you for my expenses and nothing else. I usually work for a daily fee, but this case is different."

"Why is it so different?"

"I have my own reasons for wanting to talk to Henry. And if I find him, I'll do what I think best. I'm making you no promises."

Chapter 27

IT WAS midnight when I parked my car under Union Square. A wet wind blew across the almost deserted square, blowing fogged breath from the sea on the dark pavements. Flashing neons on all four sides repudiated the night. I turned down a slanting street past a few late couples strolling and lingering on the sidewalk.

The Den's orange sign was one of a dozen bar signs in its block. I went down a dirty flight of stairs and looked into the place through a swinging glass door at the bottom. It was a large square room with rounded corners and a ceiling so low you could feel the weight of the city over it. A curved bar arched out from the left-hand wall, making space for a bartender and his array of bottles. The other walls were lined with booths and tables. In the cleared space in the middle of the room, a tired-looking man in a worn tuxedo was beating the life out of an exhausted grand piano. All the furniture, including the piano, was enameled a garish orange. A sequence of orange-haired nudes romped and languished along the walls under a glaze of grime. I went in.

There were several customers at the bar: a couple well-dressed and young and looking out of place, and a pair of lone-wolfing sailors. A few others, all of them men, were propped like dummies at the tables, waiting for something wonderful to happen, a new life to begin, in more delightful places, under different names. Five or six revelers, all of them women, and hard cases by their looks, were standing around the piano in a choryban-tic circle, moving various members in approximate time to the music. One of them, a streaked blonde in a green dress with a drooping hemline, raised what passed for her voice in a banshee sort of singing. The whole thing had the general effect of a wake.

The pianist could have passed for a corpse in any mortuary if he had only stayed still, instead of tossing his fingers in bunches at the suffering keyboard. His batting average in hitting the notes was about .333, which would have been good enough for a Coast League ball-player. He was white and loaded to the gills, it was hard to tell with what. I sat down at a table near the piano and watched him until he turned his face in my direction. He had the sad bad centerless eyes I expected, wormholes in a withered apple with a dark rotten core.

I ordered a beer from a sulky waitress in an orange apron. When I left her the change from a dollar, she hoisted a long-suffering smile from the depths of her despair and offered it to me: "Zizi's as high as a kite. They ought to make him shut up when he's so wild, instead of encouraging him."

"I'd like to buy him a drink."

"He doesn't drink." She corrected herself: "With the customers, I mean."

"Tell him I want to talk to him when he stops. If he can stop."

She gave me the twice-over then, and I tried to look as degenerate as hell. Maybe it came easier than I thought. I wanted to drink the beer, but I let it stand on the table, going flat, while Zizi battered his way through half a dozen requests. *Moonlight and Roses,* the girls wanted. *Stardust* and *Blue Moon* and other pieces that brought other times and places into the midnight basement at the bottom of the city. One of the sailors made up his mind and left the bar. Without preliminary, he attached himself to the blonde in the green dress and steered her out, lean-hipped and swaggering. The bartender's face watched them over the bar like a dead white moon. *Happy Days Are Here Again,* and *Stormy Weather.* One of the women tried to sing it and burst loosely into tears. The others comforted her. The pianist struck a plangent discord and gave up. A lone drunk sitting against the wall behind me was talking in a monotone to his absent mother, explaining very reasonably, in great detail, why he was a no-good son-of-a-gun and a disgrace to the family.

A stranger voice, husky and loose, wandering between the masculine and feminine registers, rustled like damp dead leaves in the corners of the room. It was Zizi announcing a break: "Excuse me folks my stint is done but I'll be back when the clock strikes one to bring you more hot music and fun." He pushed the mike away and rose unsteadily.

The waitress elbowed through the group of women around him and whispered in his ear, gesturing in my direction. He crossed to my table, a tall middle-aged man who had once been handsome, fixed by that fact in the mannerisms of a boy.

Leaning with one hand spread on the table in an attitude of precarious grace, he inclined towards me. His jaw dropped lackadaisically, showing discolored teeth.

"You wanted to speak with me, boy friend? I am Zizi. You like my music?"

"I'm tone deaf."

"You are fortunate." He smiled sickly, revealing pale gums above the discolored teeth.

"It isn't music that's on my mind."

"Yes?" He leaned closer, his long frail body half-collapsed against the edge of the table.

I lowered my voice, and plucked at the sleeve of his greening tux in what I hoped was an appealing gesture. "I need a fix real bad," I said. "I'm going off my stick."

His thin weeded eyebrows rose towards his thinning hair-line. "Why do you come to me?"

"I've been getting it from Ronnie in Pacific Point. He said you knew Mosquito."

He straightened slowly, swaying like a willow, and peered into my eyes. I let them glaze: "For God's sake, Zizi, give me a break."

"I don't know you," he said.

"Here's my card, then." I put a twenty on the table by his hand. "I got to have it. Where can I find Mosquito?"

The hand crawled over the bill. I noticed that its nails were broken and bleeding. "Okay, boy friend. He lives in the Grand-view Hotel. It's just around the corner, a block above Market. Ask the night clerk for him." The hand closed over the bill and dove into his pocket. "Remember I haven't the faintest notion why you want to see him. Tee hee."

"Thank you," I said emotionally.

"Sweet dreams, boy friend."

The Grandview Hotel was an old four-story building of dirty brick squeezed between taller buildings. An electric sign over the entrance advertised SINGLE WITH BATH, $1.50. The brass fittings on the front door looked as if they went back to the earth-quake. I pulled it open and entered the lobby, a deep narrow room poorly lit by a couple of ancient wall-fixtures on each side. Two women and three men were playing draw poker at a table under one of the lights. The women were bulldog-faced, and wore coats trimmed with the fur of extinct animals. Two of the men were fat and old, bald probably under their hats. The third was young and hatless. They were using kitchen matches instead of chips.

I moved toward the lighted desk at the rear, and the hatless youth got up and followed me. "You want a room?" Apparently he was the curator. He suited the role. Bloodless and narrow, his face was set in a permanent sneer.

"I want to see Mosquito."

"Does he know you?"

"Not yet."

"Somebody send you?"

"Zizi."

"Wait a minute." He leaned across the desk and lifted a house-phone from a niche at one end, plugging it in to the old-fashioned switchboard above it. He spoke softly into the mouth-piece and glanced at me, with the receiver to his ear. He hung up and unplugged the connection: "He says you can go up."

"What room?"

He sneered at my ignorance of his mysteries. "307. Take the elevator if you want." His feet were soundless on the decayed rubber matting as he padded back to the poker game.

I piloted the ramshackle elevator cage to the third floor, and stepped out into an airless corridor. The brown numbered doors stood like upended coffins on each side, bathed in the static red flames of fire-exit bulbs that dotted the ceiling at intervals. 307 was halfway down the corridor to the left. Its door was open a crack, throwing a yellow ribbon of light across the threadbare carpeting of the hallway and up the opposite wall.

Then the light was half obscured by someone watching me from the other side of the door. I raised my hand to knock. The door swung inward sharply before I touched it. A young man stood in the doorway with his back to the light. He was middle-sized, but the great black bush of hair on top of his head made him seem almost tall. "Zizi's little friend, eh? Come on in." His voice was adenoidal.

One of his hands was on his hip, the other on the door-knob. I had to brush against him to enter the room. He wasn't heavy-looking but his flesh was soft and tremulous like a woman's. His movements seemed invertebrate as he closed the door and turned. He was wearing a soft green shirt, six-pleated high-rise trousers of dark green gabardine, a brilliant green and yellow tie held by a large gold clasp.

His other hand moved to his other hip. He cocked his head on one side, his face small and pointed under the top-heavy hair. "Carrying iron, old man?"

"I use it in my business." I patted my heavy jacket pocket.

"And what's your business, old man?"

"Whatever I can knock off. Do I need references?"

"Long as you don't try to knock off daddy." He smiled at the ridiculousness of the idea. His teeth were small and fine like a child's first set. "Where you from?"

"Pacific Point."

"I never see you in the Point."

"I work the whole coast," I said impatiently. "You want to know my history, send me a questionnaire."

"Hard up for it?"

"I wouldn't be here if I wasn't."

"All right, take it easy, I like to know who I'm dealing with, that's natural, isn't it? You want to use my needle or you snuff it?"

"The needle," I said.

He crossed the room to a chest of drawers in the corner, and opened the top drawer. Mosquito wasted no money on front. The room stood as he had found it: bare discolored walls, broken-backed iron bed, cracked green blind over the single window, the rug on the floor marked with a threadbare path from the bed to the door of the bathroom. He could move at a minute's notice into any one of ten thousand similar rooms in the city.

He set an alcohol lamp on top of the chest of drawers and lit it with a silver cigarette-lighter. A new-looking needle gleamed in his other hand. "You want the forty, or the sixty-five main-liner?" he asked me over his shoulder.

"Sixty-five. Your prices are high."

"Yeah, aren't they? I like to see the money first, old man."

I showed him money.

"Bring it over here."

He was melting some yellowish-white powder in a spoon. I counted sixty-five dollars down beside the hissing lamp.

Water began to run behind the bathroom door. Somebody coughed. "Who's in there?" I asked him.

"Only a friend of mine, don't get your wind up. Better take off your coat, or do you take it in the thigh?"

"I want to see who's in there. I'm loaded. I can't take chances."

"It's only a girl, old man." His voice was soothing. "There ain't the teensiest danger. Take off your coat and lie down like a good boy now."

He dipped the needle in the spoon and charged it, turning to me. I slapped it out of his hand.

Mosquito's face turned purplish red. The loose flesh under his tiny chin shook like a turkey's wattles. His hand was in and out of the open drawer before I could hold him, and the blade of a spring-knife jumped up under my nose. "You dirty filthy beast, don't you dare touch me." He backed against the wall and crouched with the knife advanced, its double-edged blade pointing at the ceiling. "I'll cut you if you lay a finger on me."

I brought the revolver out of my jacket pocket. "Put it away, Mosquito."

His small black eyes watched me uncertainly, looked down at the knife and crossed slightly, focused on its point. I swung the gun on him, cutting the wrist of his knife hand with the muzzle. The knife dropped to the floor. I stepped on it and moved in closer to Mosquito. He tried to scratch my face. Since it was necessary to hit him, I hit him: a short right hook under the ear. He slid down the wall like a rag doll.

I crunched the hypodermic needle into the carpet with my heel, stooped for the knife, which I closed and dropped into my pocket. Mosquito was out, quick adenoidal breathing his only sign of life, his eyeballs under the heavy lids as blank-white as a statue's. His head was jammed against the wall, and I lifted him away from it so he wouldn't choke. His narrow black suède shoes pointed to opposite corners of the ceiling.

The bathroom door clicked behind me. I straightened up quickly and turned. The door creaked inward slowly, opening on darkness. It was the girl Ruth who emerged from the darkness, moving like a sleepwalker. She had on pajamas that were much too big for her, yellow nylon piped with red. Thin soft hanging folds obscured her lines and enhanced the dreaminess of her walk. Her eyes were dark craters in her smooth blanched face.

"Hello hello hello," she said. "Hello hello." She noticed the gun in my hand, without fear or curiosity: "Don't shoot, cowboy, I give up." Her hands jerked upward in a token gesture of surrender, then hung limp from her wrists again. "I absolutely give up." She stood swaying.

I put the gun away and took her by the elbow. Her face didn't change. I identified its look of frozen expectancy. I had seen it on the face of a man who had just been struck by a bullet, mortally.

"Unhand me villain," she said without rancor; pulled away from me and crossed to the end of the bed where she sat down. She didn't notice Mosquito until then, though he was lying practically at her feet. She nudged his leg with a red-tipped toe: "What happened to the nasty little man?"

"He fell and hurt himself. Too bad."

"Too bad," she echoed. "Too bad he isn't dead. He's still breathing. Look, he bit me." She pulled the pajama collar to one side to show me the red tooth-marks on her shoulder. "He couldn't hurt me, though. I was a thousand miles away. Ten thousand miles away. A hundred thousand miles away." She was chanting.

I cut in: "Where were you, Ruth?"

"On my island, the island I go to. My little white island in the deep dark blue ocean."

"All alone?"

"All alone." She smiled. "I shut the door and lock it with a key and bar the door and fasten the chains and sit in my chair and no one can touch me. No one. I sit and listen to the water on the beach and never open the door until my father comes. Then we go down to the water and look for shells. We find the prettiest shells, pink and red and purple, great big ones. I keep them in my house, in a special room. Nobody knows where it is, I'm the only one that knows." Her voice trailed off. She drew her knees up to her chin and sat with her eyes closed, rocking gently back and forth on a remote inward surge.

The breathing of the man on the floor had changed for the better, easing and slowing down. His eyes were closed now. I went to the bathroom for a glass of water: Ruth's clothes were scattered on the bathroom floor: and poured the water over Mosquito's face. The little eyes snapped open. He gasped and spluttered.

"Upsadaisy," I said, and dragged him to a sitting position against the wall. His head hung sideways but he was conscious, his eyes pointed with malice. "You won't get away with this, old man," he whispered.

I disregarded him, turned to the girl on the bed: "Have you seen Speed?"

"Speed?" she repeated from a great distance. Her face was closed and smooth as a shell listening to its own murmurings.

Mosquito struggled up onto his knees: "Don't tell him anything, he's a heister." Which told me that Mosquito had something to tell.

I bunched his tie and shirt-collar in both hands and lifted him against the wall. He hung limp, afraid to resist.

"You tell me where Speed is, then."

He twisted his wet head back against the plaster, his eyes watching me from their corners. "Never heard of him." His voice was thin, almost a rodent squeak. "Take your dirty hands—off me." His face was purpling again, and the breath piped in his throat.

"There's no way out of this one." I loosened the pressure of my fingers slightly. "I want Speed."

He tried to spit in my face. The bubbly white saliva ran down his chin. I tightened the pressure, carefully. He invited death, like a soft and loathsome insect.

He struggled feebly, gasping. "Turn me loose."

I released him. He dropped onto his hands and knees, coughing and shaking his head from side to side.

"Where is Speed?" I said.

"I don't know." He crouched like a dog at my feet.

"Listen to me, Mosquito. I don't like you. I don't like your business. Just give me a slight excuse, and I'll give you the beating of your life. Then I'll call the feds to cart you away. You won't be back for a long time if I do."

He looked up at me through a rat's-nest of hair. "You're talking big for a hood."

"No. It's what I'm going to do if you don't take me to Speed."
I showed him my Special Deputy's badge to clinch it.

"I guess you win," he said to the threadbare carpet. Slowly he got to his feet.

I held my gun on him while he combed his hair and put on a green tweed coat. He blew out the alcohol lamp, replacing it in the drawer.

The girl was still balanced on the end of her spine, rocking blindly. I gave her a shove as I passed her. She tumbled sideways onto the bed and lay as she had fallen, with her knees up to her chin, waiting to be born into the world or out of it.

Mosquito locked the door. I took his key away before he could pocket it. He backed against the door, the malice on his face canceled by fear into a kind of stupidity. The red corridor light shone down on him like a dirty little sun, scaled to the world in his head. His outstretched hand was questioning.

"You won't speak to the night clerk, you won't even look at him. Is it far to Speed?"

"He's at Half Moon Bay, in a cabin. Don't take me there. He'll kill me."

"Worry about him," I said, "unless you're lying to me."

Behind one or another of the numbered doors, a woman cried out sorrowfully. A man laughed. Down the corridor, in the elevator, across the lobby, up the steep street to the empty square, I stuck to Mosquito like a brother. He walked as if every step he took had to be willed in advance.

Chapter 28

There were clouds in the hills along the skyline route, obscuring the winding road and spraying my windshield with fine droplets of water. I used my yellow foglights and kept the wipers metronoming, but it was a long slow drive. Between the San Francisco limits and the bay, we passed no lighted houses and few cars. The city with all its lights had sunk behind us as if it had never existed.

The man beside me was quiet. Occasionally he uttered a little moan. Once he said: "He'll kill me. Speed will kill me."

"Small loss if he did," I said to cheer him up.

"He'll kill you too!" he cried. "I hope he does kill you."

"Naturally. Is he alone?"

"Far as I know he is."

"You'll go up to the door. You'll do the talking."

"I can't. I'm sick. You hurt me."

"Buck up. I hate a whiner."

He was quiet again, though he still moaned occasionally to himself. We crept on under the smothering gray sky, through the gray cloud-drowned hills. The sun and the other stars had burned out long ago, and Mosquito and I were journeying for our sins through a purgatory of gray space.

Eventually the road dipped below the cloudline. Below it to the right, a flat gray arm of the sea meandered among the hills like a slow river. The opposite bank was black with trees. I followed the shore for miles, losing it and coming back to it again as the road determined. In a narrow valley close by the forsaken shore, the road branched left and right.

I stopped the car. "Which way?"

"I don't know."

"Sure you do, Mosquito. Bear this in mind: you'll take your chance with Speed, or have the certainty of a Federal pen. Now which is it going to be? Which way?"

"To the right," he answered drearily. "It's only about a mile from here."

We crossed a long low bridge and followed a gravel road up the opposite bank of the bay. After a while we passed a dirt road that straggled downward towards the landlocked water. "That's it," he said.

I braked and backed, turning into the rutted lane. "How far down is it?"

"Just around the curve."

I cut my lights, stopped short of the curve and set my emergency brake. "Get out and walk ahead of me. If you give him warning, I'll drop you."

"Speed will kill me," he said slowly and distinctly, as if he was stating a theory I had failed to understand. In the dim light from the dashboard, I could see the water shining in his eyes. I took my flashlight out of the glove compartment, and tested it on his face. It looked sick.

"Get out." I leaned across him to open the door, and crowded out behind him. I closed the windows and locked both doors.

"I'm afraid," he said, "afraid of the dark. I never been out here at night."

"You'll never go back if you keep this up. Now walk ahead of me."

He was clinging to the door handle. I pushed him upright with the revolver muzzle, and prodded him into the road. He lurched ahead of me.

Below the curve the lane broadened into a small clearing. A cabin of rough-hewn logs sat in the clearing, one square lit window facing us. A man's shadow moved there, growing until it covered the whole window. Then the light died behind it. There was a long dark car parked beside the cabin.

"Call him," I said to the man at the end of my gun. The flashlight was in my left hand.

His first attempt was a dry gasp.

"Keep moving and call him. Tell him who you are. Tell him that I'm a friend."

"Mr. Speed," he cried thinly. "It's Mosquito."

We were halfway across the clearing. "Louder," I said in his ear, and jabbed him in the kidneys with the muzzle.

"Mr. Speed." His voice cracked.

I pushed him on ahead of me. The door opened inward as Mosquito set his feet on the plank stoop.

"Who is it?" a man's voice said from the deep inside shadow.

"Mosquito."

"What do you want? Who's with you?"

"A friend."

"What friend?" The hidden voice rose in pitch.

I'd got as far as I could with that approach. Even with tear gas, tommyguns and a police cordon, there is no way to take a desperate man without risking your life. I had an advantage over Speed, of course. I knew that he was still convalescing from Blaney's bullet, and was probably gun-shy.

I stepped around Mosquito. "The name is Archer. A Mrs. Henry Fellows"—I pronounced the name carefully—"hired me to look for you."

Before I finished speaking, I pressed my flashlight button. The white beam fanned the doorway. Speed crouched there, a massive figure with a black gun in his hand. We faced each other for a long tense instant. Either of us could have shot the other. I was so sharply aware of him, I felt his gun wound burning a hole in my own belly.

The starch went out of him suddenly. Without seeming to move, he shifted from the offensive to the defensive. "What do you want?" His pale bright eyes looked down at his gun, as if it was the gun that had somehow failed him.

"You might as well drop it," I said. "I have you covered."

He flung it down in a gesture of self-disgust. It skittered across the rough planks toward me. Instinctively, Mosquito moved to retrieve it. I set my foot on the gun and elbowed him back.

"Go away, Mosquito," I said, watching Speed. "I don't want to see you again."

"Where should I go?" He sounded both hurt and unbelieving.

"Anywhere but San Francisco. Start walking."

"All by myself? Out here?"

"Start walking."

He stepped off the porch into gray gloom. I didn't waste a backward glance on him. "We'll go into the house," I said to Speed. "You better hold your hands on top of your head."

"You're exceedingly masterful." He was recovering his style, or whatever it was that kept him upright and made him interesting to women. On the shooting level he was a bum, as useless as a cat in a dogfight. But he had his own feline dignity, even with his hands up.

I picked up his gun, a light automatic with the safety still on, and juggled it into my pocket, holding the flash under my arm. "About face, colonel. No false moves, unless you want a hole in the back to match the one in the front."

He turned in the doorway. I stayed close behind him as he crossed the room and relit the oil lamp. The flame steadied and brightened, casting a widening circle of light across the bare floor and up into the rafters. The room contained a built-in bunk, a cheap pine table, two kitchen chairs and a canvas deck-chair placed by the stone fireplace. A pair of new leather suitcases stood unopened at the end of the bunk. There was no fire in the fireplace, and the room was cold.

"Sit down." I waved my gun at the deck-chair.

"You're very kind." He sprawled in the chair with his long legs spraddled in front of him. "Is it necessary for me to retain the hands-on-head position? It makes me feel ridiculous."

"You can relax." I sat down facing him in one of the kitchen chairs.

"Thank you." He lowered his hands and clasped them in his lap, but he didn't relax. His entire body was taut. The attempt he made to smile was miserable, and he abandoned it. He raised one hand to shield his worried mouth. The hand stayed there of its own accord, brushing back and forth across his thin brown eyebrow of mustache. Its fingernails were bitten down to the quick. "I know you, don't I?" he said.

"We've seen each other. This is a comedown after the Oasis Inn."

"It is, rather. Are you a detective?"

I nodded.

"I'm surprised at Marjorie." But he showed no emotion of any kind. His face was unfocused, sagging wearily on its bones. Deep lines dragged from his nose to the corners of his mouth. His fingers began to explore them. "I didn't think she would go to such lengths."

"You hurt her feelings," I said. "It's never a good idea to hurt a woman's feelings. If you have to rob them, you should try to do it without hurting their feelings."

"Rob is a pretty strong word to use. She gave me the money to invest for her. She'll get it back, I promise you."

"And your word is as good as your bond, eh? How good is your bond?"

"One week," he said. "Give me one week. I'll pay it back with interest gladly."

"How about now?"

"That's impossible. I don't have the money now. It's already invested."

"In real estate?"

"In real estate, yes." The pale eyes flickered. The exploring hand climbed up to them and masked them for a moment.

"Don't rack your brain for a story, Speed. I know where the money went."

He peered at me, still hiding behind his fingers. "I suppose Mosquito told you?"

"Mosquito told me nothing."

"She tapped my phone at the Inn, then. The sweet sow." The hand slid down his face to his throat, where it pinched the loose skin between thumb and forefinger. "Oh, the sweet sow." But he couldn't work up any anger. The things that had been done to him looked worse and more important than the things he could do in return. He was sick of himself. "Well, what do you want with me? I guarantee she'll have her money back in a week."

"You can't see over the edge of the next five minutes, and you're talking about a week. In a week you may be dead."

A half-smile deepened the lines on one side of his face. "I may at that. And you may too. I certainly wish it for you."

"Who did you pay the money to?"

"Joe Tarantine. I wouldn't try to get it back from him if I were you."

"Where is he?"

He lifted his broad shoulders, and dropped them. "I don't know, and I haven't any desire to. Joe isn't one of my bosom pals, exactly."

"When did you see him last?"

"Two nights ago," he said, after some reflection.

"When you bought the heroin from him?"

"You seem to know my business better than I do." He leaned toward me, drawing his legs back. I moved the revolver to remind him of it.

"Put the gun away, please. What did you say your name was?"

"Archer." I kept the gun where it was, supported on my knee.

"How much is Marjorie paying you, Archer?"

"Enough."

"Whatever it is, I could pay you much better. If you'll give me a little leeway. A little time."

"I don't think so."

"I have two kilos of pure heroin. Do you know how much that's worth on the present market?"

"I haven't been following the quotations. Fill me in."

"A clean hundred thousand, if I have the time to make the necessary contacts. A hundred thousand, over and above my debt to the sweet sow." For the first time, he was showing a little animation. "I'm not even suggesting you double-cross her. All I ask is time. Four days should do it."

"While I sit holding a gun on you?"

"You can put it away."

"I think you're trying to con me the way you conned Marjorie. For all I know, you have the money on you."

He compressed the flesh around his eyes, trying to force them into an expression of earnest sincerity. Surrounded by puckered skin, they stayed pale and cold and shallow. "You're quite mistaken, old man." I'd wondered where Mosquito got the phrase. "You can take a look at my wallet if you like." His hand moved toward the inner pocket of his jacket.

"Keep your hands in sight. What about your suitcases?"

"Go right ahead and search them. They're not locked." Which probably meant there was nothing important in the suitcases.

He turned his head to look at the expensive luggage, and revealed a different face. Full-face, he looked enough like a gentleman to pass for one in southern California: his face was oval and soft, almost gentle around the mouth, with light hair waving back from a wide sunburned forehead. In profile, his saddle nose and lantern jaw gave him the look of an aging roughneck; the slack skin twisted into diagonal folds under his chin.

He had fooled me in a way: I hadn't been able to reach in behind the near-gentlemanly front. My acceptance of the front had even built it up for Speed a little. He was more at ease than he had been, in spite of the gun on my knee.

I spoke to the ravaged old man behind the front: "You're on your last legs, Speed. I guess you know that."

His head turned back to me, losing ten years. He said nothing, but there was a kind of questioning assent in the eyes.

"You can't buy me," I said. "The way things stand, you can't angle out of this rap. You've made your big try for a comeback, and it's failed."

"What is this leading up to? Or do you simply enjoy hearing yourself make speeches?"

"I have to take you back with me. There's the matter of Marjorie's money, for one thing—"

"She'll never get it if you take me back, not a red cent of it."

"Then she'll have the satisfaction of jailing you. She's in the mood to push it to the limit. Not to mention what the police will do. They'll have a lot of questions to ask you about this and that, particularly Dalling's murder."

"Dalling's murder?" His face thinned and turned sallow. "Who is Dalling?" But he knew who Dalling was, and knew I knew he knew.

"If they ever let you out, Dowser and Blaney will be waiting for you." I piled it on. "Last time they had no special grudge against you. All they wanted was your territory. This time they'll cut you to pieces, and you know it. I wouldn't insure your life for a dime if you paid me a hundred-dollar premium."

"You're one of Dowser's troopers." He looked at my gun and couldn't look away. I raised it so he could see the round hole in the barrel, the peephole into darkness.

"How about it, Speed? Do you come south with me, or settle with me here?"

"Settle?" he said, still with his eyes on the gun.

"I'm going back with you or the heroin, one or the other."

"To Dowser?"

"You're a good guesser. If Danny gets his shipment back, he won't care so much about you."

He said, with an effort: "I'll split with you. We can clear a hundred thousand between us. Fifty thousand for you. I have a contact in the east, he's flying out tomorrow." The effort left him breathless.

"You can't buy me," I repeated. "Hand it over."

"If I do, what happens to me?"

"It's up to you. Climb into your car and drive as fast as you can as far as you can. Or walk due west until you hit the ocean and keep on walking."

He raised his eyes to mine. His face was old and sick. "I should have shot you when I had the chance."

"You should have, but you didn't. You're washed up, as I said."

"Yes," he said to himself. "I am washed up." His voice was almost cheerful, in a wry thin way. I got the impression that he had never really expected to succeed, and was taking a bitter satisfaction from his own foresight.

"You're wasting my time. Where is it?"

"I'll give you a straight answer to that if you'll give me a straight answer to this. Who tipped my hand to you? I don't expect to do anything about it. I'd simply like to know."

"Nobody did."

"Nobody?"

"I put together a couple of hunches and a lot of legwork, and worked it out for myself. You won't believe that, naturally."

"Oh, I believe it. Anyway, what difference does it make?" He shook his head fretfully, bored by the answer to his own question. "The lousy stuff is in a tobacco can in the kitchen cupboard."

I found it there.

Chapter 29

I HAD made up my mind about Ruth before I got back to the Grandview Hotel. I knew if I didn't go back for her I wouldn't be able to forget her. A teen-aged girl with heroin in her veins was the stuff bad dreams were made of.

The lobby was dark and deserted except where the night clerk sat behind his desk with a science-fiction magazine propped in front of him. He descended from inter-galactic space to give me a quick once-over. Neither of us spoke. I went up in the elevator and down the red-lit corridor again to 307.

The girl was sleeping as I had left her, on her side, her knees bent double and her long thighs clasped to her breast. She stirred and sighed when I closed the door and crossed the room to look at her. The short gold hair fallen across her face moved in and out with her breathing. I pushed it back and tucked it behind her ear. She raised her free arm as if to protect her head from attack, but she slept on. She was sunk deep in sleep, maybe beyond my reach.

I filled the bathroom glass with cold water again, straightened her out on the bed, and poured the water over her face. Her eyelids fluttered open, and she swore.

"Rise and shine, Ruth."

"Go away, you're rocking my dreamboat." She flipped over onto her stomach, and buried her wet face in the soaking pillow.

I flipped her back. "Hey, kid! You've got to get up."

"No. Please," she whined, her eyes tight shut again.

I refilled the glass and brought it back from the bathroom. "More water?"

"No!" She sat up, calling me names.

"Get dressed. You're coming with me. You don't want to stay with Mosquito, do you?"

Her head lolled on her neck, to one side and then the other. "No. He's nasty." She spoke with childish earnestness, casting an orphaned look around the barren walls. "Where is Mosquito?"

"He's on his way. You've got to get out of here."

"Yes." She repeated after me like a lesson she had learned: "I've got to get out of here."

I gathered up her clothes from the bathroom floor and tossed them to her: sweater and skirt, shoes and stockings. But she was still far gone, unequal to the task of putting them on. I had to strip off the pajamas and dress her. Her entire body was cold to the touch. It was like dressing a doll.

Her polo coat was hanging on the bathroom door. I wrapped it around her and pulled her to her feet. She couldn't stand alone, or didn't choose to. Ruth had flown back to her island, leaving her vacant body for me to deal with. In one way and another I got her to the elevator and propped her in a corner while I ran it down to the lobby. I pushed back the metal door and lifted her in my arms. She was light enough.

The night clerk looked up as I passed the desk. He didn't say a word. No doubt he had seen more remarkable couples step out of that elevator.

My car was parked at the yellow curb in front of the hotel. I unlocked the door and deposited her on the seat with her head propped in the corner against a baseball cushion. She stayed in that position for the next six hours, though she had a tendency to slide toward the floor. Every hour or so, I had to stop the car in order to lift her back into her corner. Most of the rest of the time I kept the speedometer needle between seventy-five and eighty. She slept like the dead while I drove from foggy night to dawn and through the long bright morning, heading south.

She woke up finally when I braked for the stoplight at the Santa Barbara wye. The light changed suddenly, taking me by surprise, and I had to burn rubber. Ruth was flung from her seat. I held her back from the windshield with my right arm. She opened her eyes then, and looked around and wondered where she was.

"Santa Barbara." The light changed back to green, and I shifted gears.

She stretched and sat up straight, staring at the combed green lemon groves and the blue mountains in the near distance. "Where are we going?" she asked me, her voice still thickened by sleep.

"To see a friend of mine."

"In San Francisco?"

"Not in San Francisco."

"That's good." She yawned and stretched some more. "I don't really want to go there after all. I had an awful dream about San Francisco. An awful little man with bushy hair took me up to his room and made me do terrible things. I don't exactly remember what they were, though. God, I feel lousy. Was I on a jag last night?"

"A kind of one. Go to sleep again if you want to. Or how about something to eat?"

"I don't know if I can scarf anything, but maybe I better try. God knows how long since I have."

We were approaching the freeway, and there was a truck-stop restaurant ahead. I pulled into the service station beside it and helped her out of the car. We were a sorry couple. She still moved like a sleepwalker, and her pallor was ghastly under the noon sun. I had three hundred and forty brand-new miles on my gauge, and I felt as if I had walked them. I needed food, sleep, shave, and shower. Most of all I needed a talk with or even a look at somebody who was happy, prosperous, and virtuous, or any one of the three.

A steak and a pint of coffee did a lot for me. The girl nibbled half-heartedly at a piece of toast that she dipped in the yolk of one of her eggs. Heroin was her food and drink and sleep. It was going to be her death if she stayed with the kick to the end. The idea bothered me.

I said that to her, in slightly different words, when we were back in the car: "I've known weed- and opium-smokers, coke-sniffers, hemp-chewers, laudanum drinkers, plain and fancy drunks. Guys and girls who lived on canned heat and rubbing alcohol. There are even people in the world who can't leave arsenic alone, and other people who would sell themselves into slavery for a long cool drink of ether. But your habit is the worst habit there is."

"A lecture," she said, with adolescent boredom. I might have been a high-school teacher objecting to bubble-gum. "What do you know about my habits, Mr. Drag?"

"Plenty."

"Who are you?"

"I'm a private detective. I told you that before, but you've forgotten it."

"Yeah, I suppose I did. Was I in San Francisco last night? I think I remember, I rode up there on a bus."

"You were there. I don't know how you got there."

"What happened to my shoulder? I noticed in the rest room, it looks like somebody bit me."

"You were bitten by a mosquito."

I turned from the road to look at her, and our eyes met for a moment. Hers were uncomprehending.

"That isn't funny," she said icily.

I was angry and amused at the same time. "Hell, I didn't bite you." But not angry enough to remind her unnecessarily of the night she had forgotten. Even to me, Mosquito seemed unreal, the figment of a red-lit dream.

I glanced at the girl's face, and saw that she was remembering: the shadow of the memory shaded her eyes. "It's true," she said, "what you said about the habit. It's terrible. I started out trying it for kicks, with Ronnie. The first few times he gave it to me free. Now it's the only thing that makes me feel good. In between, I feel awful. How do you think I feel now?"

"Half dead, the way you look."

"Completely dead, and I don't even care. I don't even care."

After a while she dropped off to sleep again. She slept through the heavy truck-traffic on 101 Alternate and the even heavier traffic on the boulevard. It took Main Street to wake her finally.

I found a parking place near the Hall of Justice. It was nearly two o'clock, a good time to catch Peter Colton in his office. She came along quietly enough, still walking as if the sidewalk were foam rubber, until she saw the building. Then she jerked to a stop:

"You're going to turn me in!"

"Don't be silly," I said, but I was lying. A couple of sidewalk loungers were drifting toward us, prepared to witness anything we cared to do. "Come along with me now, or I'll bite your other shoulder."

She glared at me, but she came, on stiff unwilling legs. Our short black shadows stumped up the steps together.

Colton was in his office, a big jut-nosed man in his fifties, full of quiet energy. When I opened the door, his head was bowed over papers on his desk, and he stayed in that position for a measurable time. His light brown hair, cut *en brosse*, gave him a bearish look that went with his disposition. I pushed the girl ahead of me into the room, and shut the door rather sharply. She moved sideways along the wall, away from me.

Colton looked up with calculated effect, his powerful nose pointed accusingly at me. "Well. The prodigal son. You look terrible."

"That comes of living on the husks that the swine did eat."

"A Biblical scholar yet, and I wasn't even certain you could read." Before I could answer, he aimed his face at the girl, who was trembling against the wall: "Who's this, the prodigal daughter?"

"This is Ruth," I said. "What's your last name, Ruth?"

She stammered: "I won't tell you."

Colton regarded her with cold blue interest. "What's the girl been taking?"

"Heroin."

"It's a lie," she said woodenly.

Colton shrugged his shoulders. "You're in the wrong department, aren't you? I'm busy. Why bring her to me?"

"Busy on the Dalling case?"

"You've got nerve, Lew, even to bring up the name. Lucky for you the Tarantine woman backed up your story about the gun. The Assistant D.A. wanted to clap you in one of the nice new cells till I talked him out of it. Stick around and waste my time and I'll talk him right back into it. And it won't be hard to do. We've had a lot of trouble with private operators the last couple of years."

"Yeah," I said. "Like when I took Dwight Troy for you."

"Don't brag, I know you're hot. Now why don't you take all that Fahrenheit and peddle it someplace else? You can't polish apples with us by bringing in a little old junkie. They're two for a nickel. I could round up fifty any time between here and Union Station." Colton was angry. He had kept me out of a cell, but he hadn't forgiven me for what I had done to the law.

The girl looked at me sideways, smiling slightly. It gave her pleasure to see me taking it. She sat down in a straight-backed chair against the wall and crossed her legs.

"Go ahead and ride me," I said. "It's the old Army play, when somebody's riding you."

"Nobody's riding me. I'll tell you frankly, though, this Hammond woman has been ugly to deal with. And all day yesterday she was after us to release the body to her. Why in God's name did you have to go and stir up Jane Starr Hammond?"

"It seemed like a promising lead at the time. I'm not infallible."

"Don't act as if you thought you were, then. Next time the wolves can have you." He rose and moved to the window, his back to the room.

"All right," I said. "I apologize. Now if your wounded feelings have had enough of a therapeutic workout, let's get back to business."

He growled something unintelligible.

"You haven't found Tarantine, have you?"

That brought him back from the window. "We have not." He added with heavy irony: "No doubt he gave you his forwarding address."

"I think I know where to look for him. In the sea."

"You're a little late. The Sheriff's Aero Squadron in Pacific Point has been working on that for two days. The Coast Guard's carrying on dragging operations."

"Any trace of his companion?"

"None. They're not even sure he had a companion. The only witness they have won't swear there were two in the skiff. It was just an impression he had."

"Ruth is a witness. She saw him swim ashore."

"I heard something about that." He turned on the girl: "Where have you been?"

"Around." She drew herself together, shrinking in his shadow.

"What about this man you saw?"

She told her story, haltingly.

He considered it. "Are you sure it wasn't a dream? You junkies have funny dreams, I hear."

"I'm no junkie." Her voice was strained thin by fright. "I saw the man come out of the water, just like I said."

"Was it Tarantine? Do you know Tarantine?"

"It wasn't Joe. The man on the beach was bigger than Joe. He had a smooth shape." She giggled unexpectedly.

Colton looked at me: "She know Tarantine?"

"He sold her heroin."

The giggle ceased. "It's a lie."

"Show her a picture of Dalling," I said. "It's what I brought her here for."

He leaned across his desk and took some blown-up photographs out of a drawer. I looked at them over his shoulder as he shuffled them. Dalling lying full-length in his blood, his face like plaster in the magnesium light. Dalling close up and full face. Dalling right profile, with the black leaking hole in the side of his neck. Dalling left profile, looking as handsome as ever, and very dead.

One at a time, he handed them to the girl. She gasped when she saw the first one. "I think it's him." And when she had looked at them all: "It's him all right. He was a neat-looking fellow. What happened to him?"

Colton scowled down at her. He hated questions that he couldn't answer. After a pause he said more or less to himself: "We've practically assumed that Tarantine killed Dalling. If it was the other way around, wouldn't that be a boff?" He gave no sign of laughing, though.

"If Dalling killed Tarantine, who killed Dalling?" I said.

He looked at me quizzically. "Maybe you shot him yourself, after all."

Though Colton didn't mean it seriously, the warmed-over accusation irritated me. "If you can take time off from making funny remarks, I want you to do something for me." I emphasized the "me."

"Well?"

"Call up the head of the Narcotics Bureau and ask him nicely to come over here."

The girl looked up at me sharply, her mouth working. I was threatening her food and drink and sleep, threatening to sink her island in the sea.

"For her?" Colton snorted. "Maybe you need a rest, Lew. I'll get a matron for her."

The girl had shrunk up small again, her thin shoulders curved forward like folded wings to nullify her chest. Matron was another word she feared. Her mouth worked miserably, but no words came. She gazed dully toward the open casement window as if she might be contemplating a running jump. I moved between her and the window. We were several floors from the street.

"Yeah, send for a matron. Ruth doesn't want to take a cure, but she needs it."

Colton lifted the receiver of his phone. The girl collapsed on herself, her head bent forward into her lap. The back of her neck was white and thin, feathered with a light soft fuzz of hair.

When Colton had given his order and hung up, I said: "Now call Narcotics."

"Why?"

"Because I've got a hundred thousand dollars' worth of heroin in my car. Maybe you want me to peddle that elsewhere along with my Fahrenheit, you lousy phrasemonger."

For the first time in my experience, Colton blushed. It wasn't a pretty sight.

Chapter 30

IT WAS late afternoon when I drove up the hill to Dowser's house for the third and last time. The guard at the gate had changed, but it was the same shotgun, its double muzzle watching me like a pair of binoculars. After the usual palaver and frisking, I was admitted to the sacred portals. My gun was locked in the glove compartment of the car, along with the can of heroin and Speed's automatic and Mosquito's knife.

Sullivan, the curly-headed Irishman, met me at the door. His face was sunburned fiery red.

"Have a nice time in Mexico?" I asked him.

"Rotten. I can't eat their rotten food." He looked at me sullenly, as if he could smell policeman on my clothes. "What do you want?"

"The boss. I phoned him, he knows I'm coming."

"He didn't say nothing to me." Sullivan was jealous.

"Maybe he doesn't trust you."

He gazed at me blankly, his slow brain taken by the plausibility of my suggestion.

"Let's get in to the boss," I said. "He's very eager to see me. I think he wants to offer me your job."

Dowser and his blonde were playing two-handed canasta in the patio. They were in the middle of a hand when I stepped out through the French doors, and Dowser was losing. The woman had half a dozen melds on the table; Dowser had nothing down. He was so intent on the cards in his hand that he didn't look up.

She did, though. "Why, hello, there," she said to me. She was looking very pleased with herself in a strapless white bathing suit that justified her pleasure.

"Hello."

Dowser grunted. With infinite reluctance, he disengaged a king of hearts from the fan of cards in his hand and tossed it onto the pile.

"Ha!" she cried. "I was holding out a pair." And she reached for the pile of discards.

Dowser was quicker. He snatched up the king of hearts and tucked it back in his hand: "I didn't mean to give you a king. I thought it was a jack."

"The hell you thought it was a jack," she said. "Give me back my king." She grabbed for his hand across the table, and missed.

"Settle down, Irene. I made a mistake. You wouldn't want to take advantage of me because my eyes are bothering me, would you now?"

"Take advantage of him, he says!" She slapped her cards on the table, faces up, and rose from her chair. "Why should I try to play cards with a damn cheat? It should happen to you what happened to Rothstein."

He crouched forward, heavy arms on the table: "Take that back."

The righteous indignation drained out of her suddenly. "I didn't mean it the way it sounded, Danny. I was only talking, that's all."

"You talk too friggin' much. You get your mouth washed out with something stronger than soap."

"I'm sorry," she said meekly. "You want to finish the game?"

"Nah!" He stood up, wide and pudgy in his bathrobe. "Why should I play you for it when I can take it any time I want? Beat it, Irene."

"If you say so." She transported her physical equipment through the French doors and out of sight.

Dowser threw down his cards and turned to me. "Psychiatry! That's what you got to use on them. Psychiatry! Sullivan, you can beat it too."

Sullivan departed with a backward unwanted glance. I sat down across the table from Dowser and looked him over. He took a few strutting paces on the patio tiles, his arms folded across his chest. With his swollen body wrapped in a white beach robe, he reminded me a little of a Roman emperor sawed off and hammered down. It was strange that men like Dowser could gain the power they had. No doubt they got the power because they wanted it so badly, and were willing to take any responsibility, run any risk, for the sake of seizing power and holding on. They would bribe public officials, kill off rivals, peddle women and drugs; and they were somehow tolerated because they did these things for money and success, not for the things themselves.

I looked at the bold eyes bulging in the greased face and felt no compunction at all for what I was going to do to him.

"Well, baby?" When he smiled, his thick lower lip protruded. "You said you got something for me?" He sat down.

"I couldn't be very definite over the phone. It might be tapped."

"Uh-uh. Not any more. But that's showing good sense."

"Speaking of your phone, I've been intending to ask you: you said a woman called you on Tuesday morning, and told you that Galley Tarantine was home at her mother's."

"That's right. I talked to her myself, but she wouldn't say who she was."

"And you haven't any idea?"

"No."

"How would she know your number?"

"You've got me. She may have been a friend of Irene's, or one of the women the boys have on the string." He moved restlessly, brushing his rosebud ear with the tips of his fingers. "You said you had something for me, baby. You didn't say you wanted to come up and ask me a slew of questions."

"That was the only question.—You offered me ten grand for Tarantine."

"I did. You're not going to try and tell me you got him stashed someplace." He gathered up the cards and began to shuffle them absently. In spite of the swollen displaced bones in the knuckles, his touch was delicate.

"Not Tarantine," I said. "But it wasn't really Tarantine you wanted."

"Is that so? Maybe you can tell me what I really wanted."

"Maybe I can. Joe was carrying a tobacco can. It didn't have much tobacco in it, though."

His gaze was sticky on my face. "If I thought you heisted it from Joe," he said, "you know what I'd do to you, baby?" He picked up one card and tore it neatly in half.

"I know it, and I didn't. Joe sold it to a third party."

"Who?"

"I couldn't say."

"Where is it now?"

"I have it. Joe got thirty thousand for it. I'm not so greedy."

"How much?"

"Make a bid. You offered ten for Joe. He's in the deep freeze somewhere, out of my reach. But the heroin is worth more."

"Fifteen," he said. "I've already paid for it once."

"I'll take it. Now."

"Don't rush me. Fifteen grand is a lot of green. I got to be sure you're giving me the McCoy. Where's the stuff?"

"The money first," I said.

He half-lowered the thick eyelids over his bulging eyeballs, and the sharp pink point of his tongue did several laps around his mouth. "Whatever you say, baby. Wait here for a minute. And I mean in this chair."

I sat there for ten minutes, keenly aware that my skin was in one piece and might not be for long. I dealt myself a few poker hands, and got nothing worth betting on. When Dowser returned, he had changed to soft flannels. Blaney and Sullivan were with him, one at either elbow. The three made a curious picture as they advanced across the patio, like a fat powerful shark attended by a pair of oversize scavenger fish. Dowser had money in his hand, but it gave off a fishy smell. I saw when he came up to me that the money consisted of thousand-dollar bills.

He tossed them on the table: "Fifteen, count 'em."

Blaney and Sullivan watched me count the money as if it were edible and they were starving. I put it in my wallet.

"Not so fast," Dowser said. "I want a look at the stuff, that's natural."

"You can roll in the stuff. It's in the glove compartment of my car. Shall I go and get it?"

"I'll do that." He held out his hand for my keys.

I sat some more, with Blaney and Sullivan looking down at me. To indicate my general carefreeness, I laid out a hand of solitaire on the tabletop. When I tried to play it, though, the numbers on the cards didn't make sense. Blaney and Sullivan were perfectly silent. I could hear the tiny lapping of the swimming pool, then Dowser's footsteps coming back through the house. The wallet in my hip pocket felt heavy as lead.

Dowser was smiling his canine smile. Gold-capped molars gleamed in the corners of his mouth. Blaney and Sullivan stepped apart so that he could come between and ahead of them.

"It's the McCoy," he said. "Now tell us where you got it. That's included."

"I don't think so."

"Think again." His voice had softened, and he was still smiling. His lower lip stuck out far enough to stand on. "You got about ten seconds."

"Then what?"

He clicked his teeth with a sound like a pistol hammer. "Then we start over again. Only this time you got nothing to sell me. Just information is all. You were up in Frisco last night. There's a tag from the Union Square parking lot on your windshield. Who did you meet in Frisco?"

"I'm the detective, Danny. You're stealing my stuff."

"I'll tell you who it was," he said. "Gilbert the Mosquito, am I right?"

"Gilbert the who?"

"Brighten up. You're dumb, but not that dumb. Mosquito worked for me till he set up for himself. He was peddling in Frisco."

"Was?" I said.

"I said *was*. They found him on the road near Half Moon Bay this morning. Killed. A hit-run ran him down."

"It couldn't have happened to a nicer fellow."

"And what do you know, I find his knife in your car." He brought the spring-knife out of his jacket pocket. "Recognize it? It's got his initials on the handle." He handed it to Blaney, who nodded his head.

"I took it away from him when he tried to knife me."

Dowser grinned. "Sure, it was self-defense. You laid him out in the road and ran over him in self-defense. Don't get me wrong, he got what was coming to him, and you did me a favor when you did it. But I'm in business, baby, you got to realize that."

"Selling old knives?" I said.

"Maybe you're not so dumb. You catch on pretty fast." He dropped his voice to a whisper. "Pass the lettuce, huh?"

Blaney and Sullivan showed their guns. I stood up, raising my hands. This was the moment I had been living over and over for the past half-hour. Now that it was happening, it seemed hackneyed.

"You dirty double-crossers," I said from the script I had written in my head.

"Come on now, don't be like that. You sold me something valuable of mine, I sell you something valuable of yours. It's just that I'm smarter than you are." He said it with deep sincerity. "I'll mail you the knife some time, if you're sweet about things. Make trouble, though, and I'll deliver it in person." He dropped it back in his pocket, and reached around me. My wallet was lighter when he replaced it on my hip.

"Double-crossing dip." I counterfeited anger, but I was inwardly relieved. If Dowser hadn't dreamed up something to pin on me, he might have thought it necessary to kill me. It was the chance I had to face from the beginning.

Dowser's pleasure was more obvious than mine. His face was shining with it. "Where would Mosquito get thirty grand? The sprout was strictly small-time for my money. Or maybe that was just part of the spiel. Maybe he used the knife on Joe, huh, and didn't need thirty grand?"

"That would be nice," I said.

"You still around?" He pantomimed surprise, and his gunmen smiled dutifully over their guns. "You can go now. Remember, you go quiet and stay sweet. I'm holding on to the knife for you."

Blaney and Sullivan escorted me to the car. In order to keep their minds occupied, I swore continuously without repeating myself. The guns were missing from the glove compartment. The guard at the gate held his shotgun on me until I was out of sight. Dowser was careful.

A quarter mile south of the private road, two black sedans, unmarked, were parked on the left side of the highway. Peter Colton was beside the driver of the lead car. The other eleven men were strangers to me.

I U-turned illegally under the eyes of twelve policemen, local and Federal, and stopped by the lead car.

"He has the can," I told Colton, "probably in his safe. Do you want me to go in with you?"

"Dangerous and unnecessary," he snapped. "By the way, they found Tarantine's body. He was drowned all right."

I wanted to ask him questions, but the black cars started to roll. Two cars coming from the other direction joined them at the entrance to the private road. All four turned up toward the hilltop where Dowser lived, not forever.

Chapter 31

THE PACIFIC POINT morgue was in the rear of a mortuary two blocks from the courthouse. I avoided the front entrance—white pseudo-Colonial columns lit by a pink neon sign—and went up the driveway at the side. It curved around the back, past the closed doors of the garage, and led me to the rear door. Callahan was smoking a cigarette just outside the door, his big hat brushing the edge of the brown canvas canopy. A pungent odor drifted through the open door and disinfected the twilight.

He showed me the palm of his hand in salutation. "Well, we found your man. He's not much good to anybody, in his condition."

"Drowned?"

"Sure looks like it. Doc McCutcheon's coming over to do an autopsy on him soon as he can. Right now he's delivering a baby. So we don't lose any population after all." A smile cracked his weathered face as dry heat cracks the earth. "Want to take a look at the corpus?"

"I might as well. Where did you find him?"

"On the beach, down south of Sanctuary. There's a southerly current along here, about a mile an hour. The wind blew the boat in fast, but Tarantine was floating low in the water and the current drifted him further south before the tide brought him in. That's how I figure it." His butt pinwheeled into the gathering darkness, and he turned toward the door.

I followed him into a low deep room walled with bare concrete blocks. Five or six wheeled tables with old-fashioned marble tops stood against the walls. All but one were empty. Callahan switched on a green-shaded lamp that hung above the occupied table. A pair of men's feet, one of them shoeless, protruded from under the white cotton cover. Callahan pulled the cover off with a sweeping showman's gesture.

Joe Tarantine had been roughly used by the sea. It was hard to believe that the battered, swollen face had once been handsome, as people said. There was white sand in the curled black hair and white sand on the eyeballs. I peered into the gaping mouth. It was packed with wet brown sand.

"No foam," I said to Callahan. "Are you sure he drowned?"

"You can't go by that. And those marks on his face and head are probably posthumous. The stiffs all get 'em when the surf rolls 'em in on the rocks."

"You have a lot of them?"

"One or two a month along here. Drownings, suicides. This is a plain ordinary drowning in my book."

"In spite of what the girl said, about the man swimming ashore?"

"I wouldn't worry about that if I was you. Even if the girl was telling the truth, which I doubt—some of these biddies will say anything to get their picture in the paper—even if she was, it was probably one of these midnight bathers or something. We have a lot of nuts in this town."

I leaned closer to the dead man to examine his clothing. He had on worn blue levis and a work-shirt, still dark with sea-stain and smelling of the sea. There was sand in the pockets and nothing else.

I glanced at Callahan. "You're certain this is Tarantine?"

"Him or his brother. I knew the guy."

"Did he usually wear dungarees? I understood he was a flashy dresser."

"Nobody wears good clothes on a boat."

"I suppose not. Speaking of his brother, where is his brother?"

"Mario should be on his way now. Him and the old lady were out all afternoon; we finally got in touch with them. They're coming in for a formal identification."

"What about Mrs. Tarantine? The wife?"

"She's coming, too. We notified her soon as we found the body. Seems to be taking her time about it, doesn't she?"

"I'll stick around, if you don't mind."

"It's all right with me," he said, "if you like the scenery. It suits me better outside." Raising his arm in an exaggerated movement, he squeezed his veined nose between thumb and forefinger.

The dead man lay under the light, battered and befouled and awesome. Callahan turned the switch and we went outside.

Leaning against the wall with a cigarette, I told him about Dalling's early morning swim and Dalling's early morning death. I didn't expect the information to do him any good. I was talking against the stillness that circled outward from the dead man as sound waves spread from their source. The late green twilight faded from the sky as I talked, and darkness rolled in a slow surge over the rooftops. All I could see of Callahan was his dark hulk like a buttress against the wall, and the orange eye of the cigarette glowing periodically under his hatbrim.

A pair of bright headlights swept into the driveway and froze in the massive stillness.

"Bet that's the patrol car," he said, and moved to the corner of the building.

Over his shoulder, I saw Mario step out of the sheriff's car. He came into the glare of the headlights, towing his mother like a captive balloon. I stepped back into the shadow to let them pass, and followed them to the door.

Callahan switched on the lamp above the dead man's face. Mario stood looking down, his mother leaning heavily on his shoulder. The bruise marks on his face were turning yellowish and greenish. Other men had been as rough on him as the sea had been on his brother. He might have been thinking that, from the look in his eyes. They were mocking and grim.

"That's Joe," he said finally. "Was there any doubt about it?"

"We like to have a relative, just to make it legal." Callahan had removed his hat and assumed an expression of solemnity.

Mrs. Tarantine had been silent, her broad face almost impassive. She cried out now, as if the fact had sunk through layers of flesh to her quick: "Yes! It is my son, my Giuseppe. Dead in his sins. Yes!" Her great dark eyes were focused for distance. She saw the dead man lying far down in hell.

Mario glanced at Callahan in embarrassment, and jerked at his mother's arm. "Be quiet, Mama."

"Look at him!" she cried out scornfully. "Too smart to go to Mass. For many years no confession. Now look at my boy, my Giuseppe. Look at him, Mario."

"I already did," he said between his teeth. He pulled at her roughly. "Come away now."

She laid one arm across the dead man's waist to anchor herself. "I will stay here, with Giuseppe. Poor baby." She spoke in Italian to the dead man, and he answered her with silence.

"You can't do that, Mrs. Tarantine." Callahan rocked in pain from one foot to the other. "The doctor's going to perform an autopsy, you wouldn't want to see it. You don't object, do you?"

"Naw, she don't object. Come on, Mama, you get yourself all dirty."

She allowed herself to be drawn towards the door. Mario paused in front of me: "What do you want?"

"I'll drive you home if you like."

"We're riding with the chief deputy. He wants to ask me some questions, he says."

The mother looked at me as if I was a shadow on the wall. There was a stillness in her to match the stillness of the dead.

"Answer a couple for me."

"Why should I?"

I moved up close to him: "You want me to tell you in Mexican?"

His attempt to smile when he got it was grotesque. He shot a nervous glance at Callahan, who was crossing the room toward us. "Okay, Mr. Archer. Shoot."

"When did you see your brother last?"

"Friday night, like I told you."

"Are those the clothes he was wearing?"

"Friday night, you mean? Yeah, those are the same clothes. I wouldn't be sure it was him if it wasn't for the clothes."

Callahan spoke up behind him: "There's no question of identification. You recognize your son, don't you, Mrs. Tarantine?"

"Yes," she said in a deep voice. "I know him. I ought to know him, the boy I nursed from a little baby." Her hands moved on her black silk expanse of bosom.

"That's fine—I mean, thank you very much. We appreciate you coming down here and all." With a disapproving glance at me, Callahan ushered them out.

He turned to me when they were out of earshot: "What's eating you? *I* knew the guy, knew him well enough not to grieve over him. His mother and his brother certainly knew him."

"Just an idea I had. I like to be sure."

"Trouble with you private dicks," he grumbled, "you're always looking for an angle, trying to find a twist in a perfectly straight case."

Chapter 32

A N INNER door opened, and a plump coatless man in a striped shirt appeared in the opening. "Telephone for you," he said to Callahan. "It's your office calling." He had an undertaker's soft omniscient smile.

"Thanks," Callahan said as he passed him in the doorway.

The man in the striped shirt moved like a wingless moth toward the lighted table. His bright black boots hissed on the concrete floor.

"Well," he said to the dead man, "you aren't as pretty as you might be, are you? When doctor's through with you, you won't be pretty in the least. However, we'll fix you up, I give you my word." His voice dripped in the stillness like syrup made from highly refined sugar.

I stepped outside and closed the door and lit a cigarette. It was half burned down when Callahan reappeared. He was bright-eyed, and his cheeks had a rosy shine.

"What have you been doing, drinking embalming fluid?"

"Teletype from Los Angeles. Keep it to yourself, and I'll let you in on it." I couldn't have prevented him from telling me. "They raided the Dowser mob—Treasury agents and D.A.'s men. Caught them with enough heroin to give the whole city a jag."

"Any casualties?" I was thinking of Colton.

"Not a one. They came in quiet as lambs. And get this: Tarantine worked for the corporation, he fronted for Dowser down at the Arena right here in town. You were looking for an angle, weren't you? There it is."

"Fascinating," I said.

A car came up the driveway, turned the corner of the building and parked beyond the canopy. A slope-shouldered man with a medical bag climbed out.

"Sorry I'm so late," he said to Callahan. "It was a slow delivery, and then I snatched some supper."

"The customer's still waiting." He turned to me. "This is Dr. McCutcheon. Mr. Archer."

"How long will it take?" I asked the doctor.

"For what?"

"To determine cause of death."

"An hour or two. Depends on the indications." He glanced inquiringly at Callahan: "I understood he was drowned."

"Yah, we thought so. Could be a gang murder, though," Callahan added knowingly. "He ran with the Dowser gang."

"Take a good look for anything else that might have caused his death," I said. "If you don't mind my shoving an oar in."

He shook his tousled gray head impatiently. "Such as?"

"I wouldn't know. Blunt instrument, hypo, even a bullet wound."

"I always make a thorough examination," McCutcheon stated. That ended the conversation.

I left my car parked in front of the mortuary and walked the two blocks to the main street. I was hungry in spite of the odors that seemed to have soaked into my clothes, of fish and kelp and disinfected death. In spite of the questions asking themselves like a quiz program tuned in to my back fillings, with personal comments on the side.

Callahan had recommended a place called George's Café. It turned out to be a restaurant-bar, lower-middle-class and middle-aged. A bar ran down one side, with a white-capped short-order cook at a gas grill that crowded the front window. There were booths along the other side, and a row of tables covered with red-checked tablecloths down the center. Three or four ceiling fans turned languidly, mixing the smoky air into a uniform blue-gray blur. Everything in the place, including the customers phalanxed at the bar, had the air of having been there for a long time.

As soon as I sat down in one of the empty booths, I felt that way myself. The place had a cozy subterranean quality, like a time capsule buried deep beyond the reach of change and violence. The fairly white-coated waiters, old and young, had a quick slack economy of movement surviving from a dead regretted decade. The potato chips that came with my sizzling steak tasted exactly the same as the chips I ate out of greasy newspaper wrappings when I was in grade school in Oakland in 1920. The scenic photographs that decorated the walls—Route of the Union Pacific—reminded me of a stereopticon I had found in my mother's great-aunt's attic. The rush and whirl of bar conversation sounded like history.

I was finishing my second bottle of beer when I caught sight of Galley through the foam-etched side of the glass. She was standing just inside the door, poised on high heels. She had on a black coat, a black hat, black gloves. For an instant she looked unreal, a ghost from the present. Then she saw me and moved toward me, and it was everything else that seemed unreal. Her vitality blew her along like a strong wind. Yet her face was haggard, as if her vitality was something separate from her, feeding on her body.

"Archer!" The ghastly face smiled at me, and the smile came off. "I'm so glad I found you."

I pulled a chair out for her. "How did you?"

"The deputy sheriff said you were here. Callahan?"

"You've seen the body, then."

"Yes. I saw—him." Her eyes were as dark as a night without stars. "The doctor was cutting him up."

"They shouldn't have let you in."

"Oh, I wanted to. I had to know. But it's queer to see a man in pieces after you've lived with him. Even if I am a nurse."

"Have a drink."

"I will. Thanks. Straight whisky." She was breathing quickly and shallowly, like a dog on a warm day.

I let her down the drink before I asked her: "What did the doctor say?"

"He thinks it's drowning."

"He does, eh?"

"Don't you?"

"I'm just a floating question-mark, waiting for an answer to hook onto me. Have another drink."

"I guess I will. They got Dowser, did you hear? Mr. Callahan told me."

"That's fine." I didn't feel like bragging about my part in it. Dowser had friends, and the friends had guns. "Tell me, Galley."

"Yes?" There were stars in her eyes again, and no whisky in her shot-glass.

"I'd like a better picture of that week-end you spent with Joe in the desert."

"It was a lost one, believe me. Joe was wild. It was like being shut up in four rooms with a sick mountain-lion. I was pretty wild myself. He wouldn't tell me what it was all about, and it drove me crazy."

"Facts, please. A few objective facts."

"Those are facts."

"Not the kind that help much. I want details. What was he wearing, for example?"

"Joe was in his underwear most of the time. Is that important? It was hot out there, in spite of the air-conditioning—"

"Didn't he have any clothes with him?"

"Of course."

"Where are they now?"

"I wouldn't know. He had them in a club-bag when I drove him down here."

"What was he wearing?"

"Blue work-clothes."

"The same as he has on now?"

"He hadn't anything on when I saw him. I suppose they're the same. Why?"

"His brother said he was wearing those clothes Friday night. Was he?"

Her curved brows knitted in concentration. "Yes. He didn't change when he got home Friday night."

"And he wore them, when he wasn't in his underwear, right through to Tuesday morning. It doesn't fit in with what I've heard about Joe."

"I know. He wasn't himself. He was in a sort of frenzy. I had dinner waiting for him when he got home—he phoned that he was coming—but he wouldn't even stop to eat it. I barely had time to pack anything, he was in such a hurry. We rushed out to Oasis, and then we sat and looked at each other for three days."

"No explanations?"

"He said he was getting out, that we were waiting for money. I thought he had broken with the gang, as I'd been urging him to. I knew he was afraid, and I thought they were hunting him. If I hadn't believed that, I wouldn't have gone with him, or stayed. Then when he did go, he went by himself."

"You wouldn't want to have gone along, not where he's gone."

"Maybe I would at that." She raised the empty shot-glass in her fist and stared down into its thick bottom like a crystal-gazer rapt in tragic visions.

The waiter, a fat old Greek who moved on casters, appeared beside our booth. "Another drink?"

Galley came out of her trance. "I think I should eat something. I don't know whether I can."

"A steak like the gentleman's?" The waiter molded an imaginary steak with his hands. She nodded absently.

"A beer for me." When he had gone: "Another detail, Galley." Her head came up. "You didn't say a word about Herman Speed."

"Speed?" Her fine white teeth closed over her lower lip. "I told you I nursed him."

"That's the point. You must have recognized him."

"I don't know what you mean. When should I have recognized him?"

"Sunday night, when he came to your house in Oasis. You must have known he bought the heroin from Joe."

"I don't believe it."

"Didn't you see him?"

"I wasn't there Sunday night. I haven't seen Mr. Speed since he got out of the hospital. I heard he left the country."

"You heard wrong. Where were you?"

"Sunday? About eight o'clock, Joe told me to get out, not to come back for a couple of hours. He let me take the car. How do you know Speed was there?"

"It's beside the point. He was there, and he did buy the heroin—"

"This heroin you've been talking about, did Joe steal it from Dowser?" Her face was intent on mine.

"Apparently."

"And sold it to Speed?"

"For thirty thousand dollars."

"Thirty thousand dollars," she repeated slowly. "Where is it now?"

"It could be in Joe's club-bag at the bottom of the sea, or making a fat roll in somebody's pocket."

"Whose?"

"Possibly Speed's." It seemed in retrospect that he'd handed over the heroin to me much too easily. "He might have known Joe's plans, and been waiting for him on the boat Tuesday morning. He had a motive, in addition to the money. Your sainted husband fingered him for the mob last fall."

Her eyes dilated. "I thought they were friends."

"Speed thought so, too. Perhaps he found out different, and decided to do something about it. I say perhaps. There's another possibility I like better."

"Yes," she said softly. "Keith Dalling."

"You're a quick girl."

"Not really." Her smile was one-sided. "I've been thinking about him for days, trying to understand why he acted as he did, and why he was killed. He was spying on us in Oasis, you know. I thought he was carrying a torch for me. I didn't suspect it was money he was after, though God knows he needed it."

"You saw him Sunday night, I believe."

"Yes. Did he tell you? He was waiting up the road when I left the house. He pretended to be worried about me. We went to a little place in Palm Springs, and he drank too much and tried to persuade me to run away with him."

"Did he know what Joe was carrying?"

"If he did, he didn't tell me. Frankly, I thought he was naïve, quite a bit of a fool. A nice fool, even."

"So did I. But it's pretty clear that he was on the boat, Tuesday morning. He was seen swimming ashore."

"No!" She leaned forward across the red-checked tablecloth. "That would seem to make it definite, wouldn't it?"

"Except for a couple of things that bother me. One is the fact that he was shot himself within an hour or two."

"With your gun."

"With my gun. It would be a nice irony if Dowser's men shot him because they thought he was Joe's partner. But how would they get hold of my gun? You said Joe took it. Are you sure of that?"

"I saw him. He put it in the club-bag along with his own."

"There is a way it could have happened," I said. "If Dalling took my gun when he took the money and brought it ashore with him, then Dowser's men took it away from him in his apartment. It's an old gang trick, shooting a man with his own iron."

"Is it? I wouldn't know." Her head was sagging again, under the weight of too much information at once.

"It would be a nice irony," I said, "but a little too neat for real life. And it doesn't begin to cover the second thing that bothers me. Why did Dalling go to the trouble of talking your mother into hiring me? It doesn't make sense. Unless he was really schizo?"

"No. I think I know the answer to that one. One possible answer, anyway."

"If you can figure it out, I'll give you a job."

"I could use one. The point is that Keith was deathly afraid of Joe. He wanted you to come out there and make trouble, the worse the better. If both of you got killed, that would be perfect. I'd be there in his house, unencumbered, complete with dowry. He wouldn't even have to carry me across the threshold. Does it make sense? He'd be afraid to hire you personally for a job like that—too many things to go wrong."

The waiter set a steak in front of her, and poured beer for me.

"The job is yours," I said. "The steak is an advance on your first week's salary."

She paid no attention to the food, or to me. "It didn't work out the way Keith wanted it to. Joe survived, and so did you. What did happen was, Joe thought that the gang was closing in, and he had to run for it. Maybe that's all Keith counted on. Anyway, he was there at the dock, or on the boat, when Joe got there. And he did his own dirty work after all."

"Very fine," I said. "But how did he know where Joe was heading? You didn't tell him?"

"I didn't know. He might have followed us down here."

"He might have. Or he might have had an accomplice."

"Who?" Her eyes burned black.

"We'll discuss that later. Eat your steak now, before it gets cold. I'll be back shortly." I slid out of my seat.

"Where are you going?"

"I want to catch the doctor before he leaves. Guard my beer, will you?"

"With my life."

Chapter 33

M<small>CCUTCHEON</small>, assisted by the man in the striped shirt, was sewing up an incision that ran from the base of the dead man's throat to his lower abdomen. The doctor was wearing rubber gloves, a white coverall, and a hat that gave him an oddly casual appearance. A dead cigar projected from his mouth.

It didn't turn in my direction till the sewing job was finished. Then McCutcheon straightened, using his forearm to push the hat back on his head. "Rotten sort of task," he said. "I shouldn't kick, I guess. He's fresher than some."

"Exactly how fresh, can you tell?"

"It's a hard question, with bodies found in water. Rate of deterioration depends on water temperature and other factors. We happen to know that this laddie's been in the water between fifty and sixty hours. If I didn't know that, I'd say he'd been in longer. Decomposition's rather far advanced for this time of year." He started to reach for a pocket under the coverall, then remembered his gloved hands: "Light my cigar for me, will you?"

I gave him a light. "What about cause of death?"

He dragged deep, regarding me through a cloud of blue smoke. "It isn't definite yet. I need some work from the pathology lab before I stick my neck out." He pointed a thumb at a row of jars the undertaker was labeling on the adjacent table. "Stomach contents, blood, lung tissue, neck structures. You a reporter?"

"Detective. Private, more or less. I've been working on this case from the beginning. And I simply want to know if he was drowned."

"It's not impossible," he said around the cigar. "Some of the indications are consistent with drowning. The lungs are waterlogged, for one thing. The right side of the heart is dilated. Trouble is, those conditions are equally consistent with asphyxia. There are chemical tests we can use on the blood to determine which it is, but I won't have a report on them before tomorrow."

"In your opinion, though, he was drowned or smothered?"

"I don't have an opinion until the facts are in."

"No signs of violence?"

"None that I can ascertain. I'll tell you this: if he was drowned, it was an unusual drowning; he must have died as soon as he hit the water."

The mortician glanced up brightly from his jars. "I've seen it happen, doctor. Sometimes they die *before* they strike the water. Shock. Their poor hearts just stop ticking." He coughed delicately.

McCutcheon ignored him. "If you don't mind, I'd like to get out of here."

"Sorry. But would you call it murder?"

"That depends on a lot of things. Frankly, there's something a little peculiar about the tissues. If it weren't a patent impossibility, I'd say he might have frozen to death. Anyway, I'm making a couple of microscopic sections. So there you have three alternatives. See what you can make of them." He turned back to the table where Tarantine lay.

I drove to the sheriff's office and found Callahan. He was huddled over a typewriter that looked too small for his hands, filling out an official form of some kind. He looked pleased when I walked in, providing him with an excuse to leave off typing.

"How was George's?"

"Fine. I left Mrs. Tarantine there."

"Did her brother-in-law find you all right?"

"Mario? I didn't see him."

"He left here a few minutes ago. He wanted to invite her for overnight—you wouldn't think a dame with her class would want to stay with them guineas, though. Hell, I wanted to hold him in a cell but the Chief says no. We need the Italian vote in the election. Matter of fact, the Chief is one himself, shut my big mouth."

"If the vote depends on Mario, you'll probably lose it. I've just been talking to McCutcheon."

"What did he say?"

"A lot of things. Which boil down to three possibilities: drowning, suffocation, freezing."

"Freezing?"

"That's what he said. He also said that it was impossible, but I don't know. Maybe you can tell me if Mario's boat had a freezer."

"I doubt it. The big commercial boats have. You don't see them on a sport boat that size. There's an ice plant down near the dock, though. Maybe we better take a look at it."

"Later. Right now I want to see Mario."

I was frustrated. When we reached George's Café, the booth I had occupied was empty.

The old Greek waiter hustled across the room. "I'm sorry, sir, I poured out your beer after the lady left. I thought—"

"When did she leave?"

"Five minutes, ten minutes, hard to tell. When her friend came in—"

"The man with the bandaged head?"

"That's him. He sat down with her for a minute, then they got up and left." He twisted his head towards Callahan. "Is something the matter, sheriff?"

"Huh. Did he threaten her? Show any kind of a weapon?"

"Oh, no, nothing like that." The old man's face had turned a dull white, like bread dough. "I see any trouble, I call you on the telephone, you know that. They just walked out like anybody else."

"No argument?"

"Maybe they argued a little. How can I tell? I was busy."

I drew Callahan to one side.

"Did she have her car?"

He nodded. "They're probably in it, eh?"

"It looks to me like a general alarm, with road-blocks. The quicker the better."

But the alarm and the road-blocks were too late. I waited in the sheriff's office for an hour, and nobody was brought in. By ten o'clock I was ready to try a long shot in the dark.

Chapter 34

FOR TWO hours I drove down the white rushing tunnel carved by my headlights in the solid night. At the end of the run the unbuilt town lay dark around me, its corners desolate under the sparse street-lights. When I stepped out of my car the night shot up like a tree and branched wide into blossoming masses of stars. Under their far cold lights I felt weak and little. If a fruit fly lived for one day instead of two, it hardly seemed to matter. Except to another fruit fly.

There was light behind the Venetian blinds of the house that Dalling built, the kind of warm and homey light a lonely man might envy as he passed the house. The same light that murderers worked in when they killed their wives or husbands or lovers or best friends. The house was as quiet as a burial vault.

The light was in the living-room. I mounted the low veranda and looked in between the slats of the blind. Galley lay prone on the tan rug, one arm supporting her head, the other outstretched. The visible side of her face was smeared darkly with something that looked like blood. Her visible eye was closed. There was a heavy automatic gun in her outstretched hand. The too-late feeling that had driven me across the desert went to my knees and loosened them.

The front door was standing open and I went in, letting the screen door close itself behind me. From the hall I heard her breathing and sighing in slow alternation. She sounded like a runner who has run a fast race and fallen and broken his heart.

I was halfway across the room toward the prostrate girl when she became aware of me. She rose on her knees and elbows, her breasts sharp-pointed at the floor, the blunt gun in her right hand pointed at me. Behind the tangled black hair that hung down over her face, her eyes gleamed like an animal's. I froze.

She straightened gradually, rocking back on her heels and rising to her feet; stood swaying a little with her legs apart, both hands holding the gun up. She tossed her hair back. Her eyes were wide and fixed.

"What happened to you?"

She answered me in a small tired voice: "I don't know. I must have passed out for a while."

"Give me the gun." I took a step toward her. Another step would put me within kicking distance, but my feet stuck to the floor.

"Stand back. Back to where you were." Her voice had changed. It cracked like an animal trainer's whip. And her hands were steady as stone.

The soles of my feet came unstuck and slid away from her. Her eyes were blank and ominous, like the gun's round eye.

"Where's Mario?"

She shrugged impatiently. "How should I know?"

"You left the café together."

Her mouth twisted. "God, I despise you, Archer! You're a dirty little sees-all hears-all tells-all monkey, aren't you? What difference does it make to you what people do?"

"I like to pretend I'm God. But I don't really fool myself. It takes a murderer to believe it about himself. Personally, I'm just another fruit fly. If I don't care what happens to fruit flies, what is there to care about? And if I don't care, who will? It makes no difference to the stars." My talk was postponing the gun's roaring period, but I couldn't talk it out of her hands and out the window.

"You're talking nonsense, chattering like a monkey." Her foot felt for the armchair behind her, and she sat down carefully, cradling the gun on her knee. "If you must talk, we'll talk seriously. You sit down, too."

I squatted uncomfortably on a leatherette hassock by the fireplace. Yellow light fell like an ugly truth from the bulbs in the ceiling fixture. Galley was bleeding from a wide cut on one cheekbone.

I said: "There's blood on your face."

"It doesn't matter."

"Blood on your hands, too."

"Not yours. Not yet." She smiled her bitter smile. "I want to explain to you why I killed Keith Dalling. Then we'll decide what to do."

"You have the gun."

"I know. I'm going to keep it. I didn't have the gun when I shot Keith. I had to fight him for it."

"I see. Self-defense. Neat. Only, can you get away with it?"

"I'm telling you the truth," she said.

"It's the first time if you are."

"Yes, the first time." She spoke rapidly and low. "When I drove Joe to the Point Tuesday morning, I saw Keith's car at the docks. He knew Joe would turn up there: I told him myself. I didn't realize what Keith was planning. I went back to Los Angeles, to Keith's apartment, and waited for him there. When he came home I asked him what he had done, and he confessed to me. He'd fought with Joe on the boat and pushed him into the ocean. He thought the way was clear now for us to marry. I couldn't conceal what I thought of him, I didn't try. He was a murderer, and I told him so. Then he pulled a gun on me, the gun he'd taken from Joe, your gun, as you guessed he did. I pretended to be convinced—I had to save my life—and I made up to him and got the gun away from him. I shot him. I had to. Then I panicked and ran out and threw the gun in the drain, and when the police questioned me I lied about everything. I was afraid. I knew that Joe was dead, and it made no difference to him if I blamed Keith's death on him. I know now I made a mistake. I should have called the police when it happened, and told them the truth."

Her breast rose and fell irregularly. Like any pretty woman with mussed hair, blood on her face, she had a waiflike appeal, which the steady gun destroyed. I thought of Speed, and saw how easy it was to wilt in a gun's shadow. Though I had faced them before, single and multiple, each time was a fresh new experience. And a single gun in the hands of a woman like Galley was the most dangerous weapon. Only the female sex was human in her eyes, and she was its only really important member.

"What truth?" I said. "You've changed your story so often I doubt if you know what really happened."

"Don't you believe me?" Her face seemed to narrow and lengthen. I had never seen her look ugly before. An ugly woman with a gun is a terrible thing.

"I believe you partly. No doubt you shot Dalling. The circumstances sound a bit artificial."

The blood from her cut cheek wriggled like a black worm at the corner of her mouth. "The police will believe me, if you're not there to deny it. I can turn Gary round my little finger." It was a forlorn boast.

"You're losing your looks," I said. "Murders take it out of a woman. You pay so much for them that they're never the bargain they seem to be." I had heard a noise from the back of the house, and was talking to cover it. It sounded like a drunk man floundering in the dark.

She glanced at the gun in her hands and back to my face, imagining the flight of the bullet. I saw her knuckles tense around the butt.

And I leaned forward a little without rising, shifting my weight to the balls of my feet, still talking: "If you shoot me, I'll get to you before I die, I promise. You'll have no looks left, even if you survive. Even if you survive, the police will finish the job. You're vulnerable as hell." The back door creaked. "Vulnerable as hell," I repeated loudly. "Two murders, or three, already, and more coming up. You can't kill everybody. We're too many for one crazy girl with a gun."

The floundering footsteps moved on the kitchen floor. She heard them. Her eyes shifted from me to the door on her right, came back to me before I could stir. She stepped sideways out of the chair, retreating with her back to the window, so that her gun commanded my side of the room and the kitchen doorway.

Mario came into the doorway and leaned there for an instant with one raised hand gripping the frame. His chin had been smashed by something heavier than a fist. Blood coursed down his neck into the black hair that curled over his open shirt-collar. There was death in his face. I wasn't sure he could see until he advanced on Galley. His smashed mouth blew a bubble in which the room hung upside down, tiny and blood-colored.

She yelped once like a dog and fired point-blank. The slug spun Mario on his heels and flung him bodily against the wall. He pushed himself away from the wall with his hands and turned to face her. She fired again, the black gun jumping like a toad. Still her white hands held it firm, and her white devoted face was watching us both.

Mario doubled forward and sank to his knees. The indestructible man crawled toward the woman, leaking blood like black oil on the rug. Her third shot drilled the bandaged top of his head, and finished Mario. Still she was not content. Standing over him, she pumped three bullets into his back as fast as she could fire.

I counted them, and when the gun was empty I took it away from her. She didn't resist.

Chapter 35

WHEN I set the telephone down, she was sitting in the chair I had pushed her into, her closed eyelids tremorless as carved ivory, her passionate mouth closed and still. From where I stood on the other side of the room, she seemed tiny and strange like a figurine, or an actress sitting on a distant stage. Mario lay face down between us.

A shudder ran through her body and her eyes came open. "I'm glad I didn't kill you, Archer. I didn't want to kill you, honestly." Her voice had the inhuman quality of an echo.

"That was nice of you." I stepped over the prone body and sat down facing her. "You didn't want to kill Mario, either. Like Dalling, you killed him in self-defense." I sounded strange to myself. The fear of death had made a cold lump in my throat which I was still trying to swallow.

"You're a witness to that. He attacked me with a deadly weapon." She glanced at the metal knuckles on the dead man's fist, and touched her cheek. "He struck me with it."

"When?"

"In the garage a few minutes ago."

"How did you get there?"

"He came into George's Café and forced me to leave with him. I had no gun. He'd got the idea that I knew where his brother had left the money. I knew there was a gun out here, in the garage where Joe had hidden it. I told Mario the money was here, and he made me drive him out." Her voice was clear and steady, though the words came out with difficulty. "He was almost crazy, threatening to kill me, with that awful thing on his hand. I got hold of Joe's gun and shot him with it, once. I thought he was dead. I managed to get into the house before I fainted." She sighed. With the emotional versatility of a good actress, she was slipping back into the brave-little-woman role that had taken me in before, and wouldn't again.

"You might get by with a self-defense plea if you'd only killed one man. Two in a week is too many. Three is mass murder."

"Three?"

"Dalling and Mario and Joe."

200

"I didn't kill Joe. How could I? I can't even swim."

"You're a good liar, Galley. You have the art of mixing fact with your fantasy, and it's kept you going for a week. But you've run out of lies now."

"I didn't kill him," she repeated. Her body was stiff in the chair, her hands clenched tight on the arms. "Why should I kill my own husband?"

"Spare me the little-wife routine. It worked for a while, I admit. You had me and the cops convinced that you were shielding Joe. Now it turns my stomach. You had plenty of reasons to kill him, including thirty thousand dollars. It must have looked like a lot of money after years of nurse's work on nurse's pay. You probably married Joe with the sole intention of killing him as soon as he was loaded."

"What kind of a woman do you think I am?" Her face had lost its impassivity and was groping for an expression that might move me.

I touched the dead man with the toe of my shoe. "I just saw you pump six .45 slugs into a man who was dying on his feet. Does that answer your question?"

"I had to. I was terrified."

"Yeah. You have the delicate sensitivity of a frightened rattlesnake, and you react like one. You killed Mario because he figured out that you murdered his brother. Joe probably warned him about you."

"You'd have a hard time proving that." Her eyes were like black charred holes in her white mask.

"I don't have to. Wait until the police lab men have a look at the deep-freeze unit in your kitchen."

"How—?" Her mouth closed tight, an instant too late. She had confirmed my guess.

"Go on. How did I know that you kept Joe in cold storage for three days?"

"I'm not talking."

"I didn't know it until now. Not for certain. It clears up a lot of things."

"You're talking nonsense again. Do I have to listen to you?"

"Until the sheriff's car gets here from Palm Springs, yes. There's a lot of truth to be told, after all the lies, and if you won't tell it I will. It might give you a little insight into yourself."

"What do you think you are, a psychoanalyst?"

"Thank God I'm not yours. I wouldn't want to have to explain what made you do what you did. Unless you were in love with Herman Speed?"

She laughed. "That old stallion? Don't be a silly boy. He was my patient."

"You used him then. You got the lowdown on Joe's dope-smuggling from him. I take it he was glad enough to spoil the game for the man who fingered him and stole his business. Perhaps Speed was using you, at that. After talking to both of you, I imagine it was his idea in the first place. He was the brains—"

"Speed?" I had touched a nerve. So it had been her idea.

"Anyway, you went to San Francisco with him when he got out of the hospital. You sent your mother a Christmas card from there, and that was your first mistake—mixing sentiment with business. After you'd worked out the plan, you let your mother sweat out the next two months without hearing from you, because you intended to use her. You came back to Pacific Point and married Joe: no doubt he'd asked you before and was waiting for your answer. Speed went to Reno to try and raise the necessary money. Unfortunately he succeeded. Which brings us down to last Friday night—"

"You," she said, "not us. You lost me long ago. You're all by yourself."

"Maybe some of the details are wrong or missing: they'll be straightened out in court. I don't know, for example, what you put in Joe's food or drink Friday night when he came home from his last boat-trip. Chloral hydrate, or something that leaves no trace? You know more about things like that than I do."

"I thought you were omniscient."

"Hardly. I don't know whether Dalling pushed in on your project, or was invited. Or was it a combination of both? In any case, you needed the use of this house of his, and you needed help. Speed was busy holding up his end of a phony honeymoon. Dalling was the best you could get in the clutch. When Joe went to sleep, Dalling helped you carry him out through his apartment and down the back way to the car. At this end, you hoisted him into the freezer and let him smother. So far it had been simple. Joe was dead, and you had the heroin. Speed had the money and the contacts. But your biggest problem still faced you. You knew if Dowser caught on to you, you wouldn't live to enjoy your money. Perhaps you heard what his gorillas did to Mario Friday night, just on the off chance that he knew something about it. You had to clear yourself with Dowser. That's where I came in, and that's where you made your big mistake."

"Anything with you in it is a mistake. I only hope you repeat this fable in public, to the police. I'll put you out of business." But she couldn't muster enough conviction to support the words. They sounded desperately thin.

"I'll be in business when you're in Tehachapi, or in the gas chamber. You thought you could call me in to take a fall, then turn me off like a tap, or kiss me off with a little casual sex. It was a tricky idea, a little too tricky to work. You and your radio actor persuaded your mother to hire me to look for you: you probably wrote the script. Then you arranged for me to find you and be convinced that Joe was alive and kicking. Dalling sneaked up on the porch behind me and sandbagged me. You even faked a warning that came too late, to demonstrate good faith. You removed my gun and filed it for future reference. I don't know whether you were already planning to kill your partner. You must have seen that he was going to pieces. But you kept him alive as long as possible, because you still needed his help.

"Joe went back into the trunk of your car. In his condition, he must have made an awkward piece of luggage. You and Keith drove separately to Pacific Point. He got the body aboard the *Aztec Queen*, took it to sea, dumped it into the water, and swam ashore to your headlights. You took him back to the dock, where his car was, and the two of you drove to Los Angeles. That took care of the body, and more important, it took care of Dowser. It would be obvious, if and when the body was found, that Joe had drowned in a getaway attempt.

"That left just one fly in your ointment, your partner. He was useful for physical work that you couldn't do, like rowing dead bodies around harbors and starting boat-engines, but he was a moral weakling. You knew he couldn't stand the pressure that was coming. Besides, he'd be wanting his share of the cash. So you went up to his apartment with him and paid him off with a bullet. A bullet from my gun. Hid my gun where the cops would be sure to find it. Went home to bed and, if I know your type, slept like a baby."

"Did I?"

"Why not? You'd killed two men and kept yourself in the clear. I have an idea that you like killing men. The real payoff for you wasn't the thirty thousand. It was smothering Joe, and shooting Keith and Mario. The money was just a respectable excuse, like the fifty dollars to a call-girl who happens to be a nymphomaniac. You see, Galley, you're a murderer. You're different from ordinary people, you like different things. Ordinary people don't throw slugs into a dead man's back for the hell of it. They don't arrange their lives so they have to spend a week-end with a corpse. Did it give you a thrill, cooking your meals in the same room with him?"

I had finally got to her. She leaned out of the chair towards me and spoke between bared teeth: "You're a dirty liar! I couldn't eat. I hated it. I had to get out of the house. By Sunday night I was going crazy with it—Joe crouched in there with frost on him—" A dry sob racked her. She covered her face with her hands.

Somewhere in the distance a siren whined.

"That's right," I said. "Sunday night Speed came to babysit for you. Later, when I talked to him, he covered for you. It will convict him along with you."

She mastered her sobbing, and spoke behind her hands: "I should have saved a bullet for you."

"I served your purpose, didn't I? I couldn't have done it better if you had briefed me. Of course you set it up for me rather nicely, phoning Dowser Tuesday morning to let him know you were available. You must have trusted me pretty far at that. I know three or four private operators who wouldn't have followed you up to Dowser's house. Ironic, isn't it? I thought I was rescuing a maiden from a tower. Fall guys usually do, I guess. And the women who use them often make the mistake you did. They forget that even fall guys have minds of their own, until they fall for keeps." I looked down at Mario, and her gaze followed mine. Her fingers were still spread across her face, as if she needed them to hold it together.

The siren rose nearer and higher, building a thin arch of sound across the desert.

"It's sort of sad about you," I said. "All that energy and ingenuity wasted, because you had to tie it in with murder. Now before the police get here, do you want to tell me where the money is? I need it for a client, and if I get it I'll give you the best break I can."

"Go to hell." Her eyes burned furiously between her fingers. "They won't be able to hold me, you know that? They can't prove anything, not a thing. I'm innocent, do you hear me?"

I heard her.

The siren whooped like a wolf in the street. Headlights swept the window.

Chapter 36

A FTER GALLEY was taken away, a deputy named Runceyvall and I spent an hour or so going over the house. Mario had left a trail of blood across the kitchen floor and out the back door to the attached garage. We followed it and found the place where the gun had been cached, behind a loose board in the wall between the garage and the house. It contained a box of .45 cartridges, but no money. We found only one other thing of any significance: a couple of black hairs stuck to the interior wall of the deep-freeze. I told Runceyvall to seal it shut, and explained why. Runceyvall thought the whole thing was delightful.

Shortly after two I checked in at the Oasis Inn for the rest of the night. The clerk informed me that Mrs. Fellows was still registered. I asked to be called at eight.

I was. When I had showered and looked at my beard in the bathroom mirror and put on the same dirty clothes, I strolled across the lawn to Marjorie's bungalow. It was a dazzling morning. The grass looked as fresh as paint. Beyond a palm-leaf fence at the rear of the enclosure, a red tractor was pulling a cultivator up and down through a grove of date-palms that stood squat against the sky. High above them in ultramarine space, too high to be identified, a single bird circled on still wings. I thought it was an eagle or a hawk, and I thought of Galley.

Marjorie was breakfasting alfresco under a striped orange beach umbrella. She had on a Japanese kimono that harmonized with the umbrella, if nothing else. At the table with her a gray-headed man in shorts was munching diligently on a piece of toast.

She glanced up brightly when I approached, her round face glowing with sunburn and *Gemütlichkeit*: "Why, Mr. Archer, what a nice surprise! We were just talking about you, and wondering where you were."

"I slept here last night. Checked in late, and thought I wouldn't disturb you."

"Now wasn't that thoughtful," she said to the gray-headed man. "George, this is Mr. Archer. My husband, Mr. Archer—my ex, I guess I should say." Surprisingly, the large kimonoed body produced a girlish titter.

George stood up and gave me a brisk hand-shake. "Glad to know you, Archer. I've heard a lot about you." He had a thin flat chest, a sedentary stomach, a kind bewildered face.

"I've heard a lot about you. From Marjorie."

"You have?" He bestowed a loving look on the top of her head. "I feel darn silly in these shorts. She made me wear 'em. Oh well, as long as there's nobody here from Toledo—" He gazed short-sightedly around him, seeking spies.

"You look handsome in them, George. Pull in your stomach now. I love you in them." She turned to me with a queenly graciousness: "Please sit down, Mr. Archer. Have you had your breakfast? Let me order you some. George, bring Mr. Archer a chair from the porch and order more ham and eggs." George marched away with his stomach held tautly in, his head held high.

"I didn't expect to find him here."

"Neither did I. Isn't it wonderful? He saw my name in the papers and flew right down from Toledo on the first plane, just like a movie hero. I almost fainted yesterday when he walked in. To think that he really cares! Of course it was somewhat embarrassing last night. He had to sleep in a separate bungalow because we're not legally married yet."

"Yet? Don't you mean 'any more'?"

"Yet." She blushed rosier. "We're flying to San Francisco at noon to pick up the car there, and then we'll drive over to Reno and be married. They don't make you wait in Reno and George says he won't wait a single minute longer than necessary."

"Congratulations, but won't there be legal difficulties? You can have your marriage to Speed annulled, of course, since he married you under a false name. Only that will take time, even in Nevada."

"Haven't you heard?" Her face, blank and unsmiling now, showed the strain she was under. "The San Francisco police recovered my Cadillac last night. He left it in the middle of the Golden Gate Bridge."

"No."

"Yes, he's dead. Several persons saw him jump."

It hit me hard, though Speed meant nothing to me. Now there were four men violently dead, five if I counted Mosquito. Galley and I between us had swept the board clean.

"You didn't find him, did you?" she was saying. "You didn't reach him?"

"I beg your pardon?"

"I mean, you had nothing to do with his suicide? If I thought he did it because I hunted him down—it would be dreadful, wouldn't it? I couldn't face it." She shut her eyes and looked like a well-fed baby blown up huge.

There was only one possible answer: "I didn't find him."

She breathed out. "I'm so relieved, so glad. I don't give a hang for the money, now that I've got George back. I suppose it was swept out to sea with his body. George says we can probably deduct it from our income tax anyway."

George stepped off the porch with a deck-chair. "Is somebody using my name in vain?" he called out cheerfully.

She smiled in response: "I was just telling Mr. Archer how wonderful it is to have you back, darling. It's like waking up from a nightmare. Did you order the food?"

"Coming right up."

"I'm afraid I can't stay," I said.

They were nice people, hospitable and rich. I couldn't stand their company for some reason, or eat their food. My mind was still fixed on death, caught deep in its shadow. If I stayed I'd have to tell them things that they wouldn't like. Things that would spoil their fun, if anything could spoil their fun.

"Must you go? I'm so sorry." She was already reaching for her bag. "Anyway, you must let me pay you for your time and trouble."

"Fine. A hundred dollars will do it."

"I'm sorry it turned out the way it did. It's hardly fair to you." She rose and pressed the money into my hand.

"Marjorie's taken quite a shine to you, Archer. She's actually a very remarkable woman. I never realized before what a very remarkable woman Marjorie is."

"Go on with you." She pushed George playfully.

"You are. You know you are." He pushed her back.

"I'm the silliest fat old woman in the world." She tried to push him again but he clung to her hand.

"Good-bye. Good luck. Give my regards to Toledo."

I left them playing and laughing like happy children. Above the date-palms, half-hidden in space, the unknown bird described its dark circles.

The case ended where it began, among the furniture in Mrs. Lawrence's sitting room. It was noon by then. The dim little room was pleasant after the heat of the desert. Mrs. Lawrence herself was pleasant enough, though she looked haggard. The police had come and gone.

We sat together like strangers mourning at the funeral of a common friend. She was wearing a rusty black dress. Even her stockings were black. Her drawn and sallow cheeks were spottily coated with white powder. She offered me tea which I refused because I had just eaten. Her speech and movements were slower but she hadn't changed. Nothing would change her. She sat like a monument with her fists clenched on her knees:

"My daughter is perfectly innocent, of course. As I told Lieutenant Gary this morning, she wouldn't hurt a hair of anyone's head. When she was a child, I couldn't even force her to swat a fly, not if her life depended on it." Her eyes were sunk deep in her head, under brows like stony caverns. "You believe her innocent." It was a statement.

"I hope she is."

"Of course. She's never been well-liked. Girls who are pretty *and* clever are never well-liked. After her father died and our money went, she withdrew more and more into herself. She lived a dream-life all through high school and that didn't help to make her popular. It earned her enemies, in fact. More than once they tried to get her into trouble. Even in the hospital it happened. There were unfounded accusations from various people who resented Galley's having had a distinguished father—"

"What sort of accusations?"

"I wouldn't taint my tongue with them, or offend your ears, Mr. Archer. I know that Galley is inherently good, and that's enough. She always has been good, and she is now. I learned many years ago to close my ears to the base lying chatter of the world." Her mouth was like iron.

"I'm afraid your conviction isn't enough. Your daughter is in a cell with a great deal of firm evidence against her."

"Evidence! A wild fabrication the police made up to conceal their own incompetence. They shan't use my daughter for a scapegoat."

"Your daughter murdered her husband," I said. It was the hardest speech I ever uttered. "The only question is, what are you going to do about it? Do you have any money?"

"A little. About two hundred dollars. You are quite mistaken about Galley's guilt, however. I realize that things look black for my girl. But as her mother I know that she is absolutely incapable of murder."

"We won't argue. Two hundred dollars isn't enough. Even with twenty thousand, and the best defenders in southern California, she wouldn't get off with less than second-degree murder. She's going to spend years in prison anyway. Whether she spends the rest of her life there depends on just one thing: her defense in Superior Court."

"I can raise some money on this house, I believe."

"It's mortgaged, isn't it?"

"Yes, but I do have an equity—"

"I have some money here." I took Dowser's folded bill from my watch pocket and scaled it into her lap. "It's money I have no use for."

Her mouth opened and shut. "Why?"

"She needs a break. I'm going to have to testify against her."

"You are kind. You can't afford this." Tears came into her eyes like water wrung from stone. "You must believe that Galatea is innocent, to do this."

"No. I was police-trained and the harness left its marks on me. I know she's guilty, and I can't pretend I don't. But I feel responsible in a way. For you, if not for her."

She understood me. The tears made tracks on her cheeks. "If only you'd believe she's innocent. If only someone would believe me."

"She'll need twelve and she won't get them. Did you see the papers this morning?"

"Yes. I saw them." She leaned forward, crumpling the bill in her lap. "Mr. Archer."

"Is there something I can do?"

"No, nothing more. You are being so good, I really feel I can trust you. I must tell you—" She rose abruptly and went to the sewing machine beside the window. Raising the lid, she reached far inside and brought out an oblong packet wrapped in brown paper. "Galley gave me this to keep for her, Tuesday morning. She made me promise not to tell anyone, but things are different now, aren't they? It may be evidence in her favor. I haven't opened it."

I broke the tape that sealed one end, and saw the hundred-dollar bills. It was Galley's thirty thousand. Speed's thirty thousand. Marjorie's thirty thousand. Thirty thousand dollars that had lain hidden in an old lady's sewing machine while men were dying for it.

I handed it back to her. "It's evidence, all right: the money she killed her husband for."

"That's impossible."

"Impossible things are happening all the time."

She looked down at the money in her hand. "Galley really killed him?" she whispered. "What shall I do with this?"

"Burn it."

"When we need the money so badly?"

"Either burn it, or take it to a lawyer and let him contact the police. You may be able to make a deal of some kind. It's worth trying."

"No," she said. "I will not. My girl is innocent, and Providence is watching over her. I know that now. God has provided for her in her hour of greatest need."

I stood up and moved to the door. "Do as you like. If the police discover the source of the money, it will wreck your daughter's defense."

She followed me down the hallway: "They shan't know a thing about it. And you won't tell them, Mr. Archer. You believe that my daughter is innocent, even though you won't admit it."

I knew that Galley Lawrence was guilty as hell.

The colored fanlight over the door washed her mother in sorrowful purple. She opened the door, and noon glared in on her face. The tear-tracks resembled the marks of sparse rain on a dusty road.

"You won't tell them?" Her voice was broken.

"No."

I looked back from the sidewalk. She was standing on the steps, using the brown paper package to shield her eyes from the cruel light. Her other hand rose in farewell, and dropped to her side.

THE BARBAROUS COAST

For Stanley Tenny

The people and institutions named in this book are imaginary.
Any coincidence with the names or characteristics of actual people or
institutions is unintentional and without meaning.

Chapter 1

THE CHANNEL CLUB lay on a shelf of rock overlooking the sea, toward the southern end of the beach called Malibu. Above its long brown buildings, terraced gardens climbed like a richly carpeted stairway to the highway. The grounds were surrounded by a high wire fence topped with three barbed strands and masked with oleanders.

I stopped in front of the gate and sounded my horn. A man wearing a blue uniform and an official-looking peaked cap came out of the stone gatehouse. His hair was black and bushy below the cap, sprinkled with gray like iron filings. In spite of his frayed ears and hammered-in nose, his head had the combination of softness and strength you see in old Indian faces. His skin was dark.

"I seen you coming," he said amiably. "You didden have to honk, it hurts the ears."

"Sorry."

"It's all right." He shuffled forward, his belly overhanging the belt that supported his holster, and leaned a confidential arm on the car door. "What's your business, mister?"

"Mr. Bassett called me. He didn't state his business. The name is Archer."

"Yah, sure, he is expecting you. You can drive right on down. He's in his office."

He turned to the reinforced wire gate, jangling his key-ring. A man came out of the oleanders and ran past my car. He was a big young man in a blue suit, hatless, with flying pink hair. He ran almost noiselessly on his toes toward the opening gate.

The guard moved quickly for a man of his age. He whirled and got an arm around the young man's middle. The young man struggled in his grip, forcing the guard back against the gatepost. He said something guttural and inarticulate. His shoulder jerked, and he knocked the guard's cap off.

The guard leaned against the gatepost and fumbled for his gun. His eyes were small and dirty like the eyes of a potato. Blood began to drip from the end of his nose and spotted his

219

blue shirt where it curved out over his belly. His revolver came up in his hand. I got out of my car.

The young man stood where he was, his head turned sideways, halfway through the gate. His profile was like something chopped out of raw planking, with a glaring blue eye set in its corner. He said:

"I'm going to see Bassett. You can't stop me."

"A slug in the guts will stop you," the guard said in a reasonable way. "You move, I shoot. This is private property."

"Tell Bassett I want to see him."

"I already told him. He don't want to see you." The guard shuffled forward, his left shoulder leading, the gun riding steady in his right hand. "Now pick up my hat and hand it to me and git."

The young man stood still for a while. Then he stooped and picked up the cap and brushed at it ineffectually before he handed it back.

"I'm sorry. I didn't mean to hit you. I've nothing against you."

"I got something against you, boy." The guard snatched the cap out of his hands. "Now beat it before I knock your block off."

I touched the young man's shoulder, which was broad and packed with muscle. "You better do what he says."

He turned to me, running his hand along the side of his jaw. His jaw was heavy and pugnacious. In spite of this, his light eyebrows and uncertain mouth made his face seem formless. He sneered at me very youngly:

"Are you another one of Bassett's muscle boys?"

"I don't know Bassett."

"I heard you ask for him."

"I do know this. Run around calling people names and pushing in where you're not wanted, and you'll end up with a flat profile. Or worse."

He closed his right fist and looked from it to my face. I shifted my weight a little, ready to block and counter.

"Is that supposed to be a threat?" he said.

"It's a friendly warning. I don't know what's eating you. My advice is go away and forget it—"

"Not without seeing Bassett."

"And, for God's sake, keep your hands off old men."

"I apologized for that." But he flushed guiltily.

The guard came up behind him and poked him with the revolver. "Apology not accepted. I used to could handle two like you with one arm tied behind me. Now are you going to git or do I have to show you?"

"I'll go," the young man said over his shoulder. "Only, you can't keep me off the public highway. And sooner or later he has to come out."

"What's your beef with Bassett?" I said.

"I don't care to discuss it with a stranger. I'll discuss it with him." He looked at me for a long moment, biting his lower lip. "Would *you* tell him I've got to see him? That it's very important to me?"

"I guess I can tell him that. Who do I say the message is from?"

"George Wall. I'm from Toronto." He paused. "It's about my wife. Tell him I won't leave until he sees me."

"That's what you think," the guard said. "March now, take a walk."

George Wall retreated up the road, moving slowly to show his independence. He dragged his long morning shadow around a curve and out of sight. The guard put his gun away and wiped his bloody nose with the back of his hand. Then he licked his hand, as though he couldn't afford to waste the protein.

"The guy's a cycle-path what they call them," he said. "Mr. Bassett don't know him, even."

"Is he what Bassett wants to see me about?"

"Maybe, I dunno." His arms and shoulders moved in a sinuous shrug.

"How long has he been hanging around?"

"Ever since I come onto the gate. For all I know, he spent the night in the bushes. I ought to have him picked up, but Mr. Bassett says no. Mr. Bassett is too softhearted for his own good. Handle him yourself, he says, we don't want trouble with law."

"You handled him."

"You bet you. Time was, I could take on two like him, like I said." He flexed the muscle in his right arm and palpated it admiringly. He gave me a gentle smile. "I was a fighter one time—pretty good fighter. Tony Torres? You ever hear my name? The Fresno Gamecock?"

"I've heard it. You went six with Armstrong."

"Yes." He nodded solemnly. "I was an old man already, thirty-five, thirty-six. My legs was gone. He cut my legs off from under me or I could of lasted ten. I felt fine, only my legs. You know that? You saw the fight?"

"I heard it on the radio. I was a kid in school, I couldn't make the price."

"What do you know?" he said with dreamy pleasure. "You heard it on the radio."

Chapter 2

ILEFT my car on the asphalt parking-lot in front of the main building. A Christmas tree painted brilliant red hung upside-down over the entrance. It was a flat-roofed structure of field-stone and wood. Its Neutraesque low lines and simplicity of design kept me from seeing how big it was until I was inside. Through the inner glass door of the vestibule I could see the fifty-yard swimming-pool contained in its U-shaped wings. The ocean end opened on bright blue space.

The door was locked. The only human being in sight was a black boy bisected by narrow white trunks. He was sweeping the floor of the pool with a long-handled underwater vacuum. I tapped on the door with a coin.

After a while he heard me and came trotting. His dark, intelligent eyes surveying me through the glass seemed to divide the world into two groups: the rich, and the not so rich. I qualified for the second group, it seemed. He said when he opened the door:

"If you're selling, mister, the timing could be better. This is the off-season, anyway, and Mr. Bassett's in a rotten mood. He just got through chopping *me* out. It isn't my fault they threw the tropical fish in the swimming-pool."

"Who did?"

"The people last night. The chlorine water killed them, poor little beggars, so I got to suck them out."

"The people?"

"The tropical fish. They scooped 'em out of the aquarium and chunked 'em in the pool. People go out on a party and get drunk, they forget all the ordinary decencies of life. So Mr. Bassett takes it out on me."

"Don't hold it against him. My clients are always in a rotten mood when they call me in."

"You an undertaker or something?"

"Something."

"I just wondered." A white smile lit his face. "I got an aunt in the undertaking business. I can't see it myself. Too creepy. But she enjoys it."

"Good. Is Bassett the owner here?"

"Naw, just the manager. The way he talks, you'd think he owns it, but it belongs to the members."

I followed his wedge-shaped lifeguard's back along the gallery, through shifting green lights reflected from the pool. He knocked on a gray door with a MANAGER sign. A high voice answered the knock. It creaked along my spine like chalk on a damp blackboard:

"Who is it, please?"

"Archer," I said to the lifeguard.

"Mr. Archer to see you, sir."

"Very well. One moment."

The lifeguard winked at me and trotted away, his feet slapping the tiles. The lock snicked, and the door was opened slightly. A face appeared in the crack, just below the level of my own. Its eyes were pale and set too wide apart; they bulged a little like the eyes of a fish. The thin, spinsterly mouth emitted a sigh:

"I *am* glad to see you. Do come in."

He relocked the door behind me and waved me to a chair in front of his desk. The gesture was exaggerated by nerves. He sat down at the desk, opened a pigskin pouch, and began to stuff a big-pot briar with dark flakes of English tobacco. This and his Harris tweed jacket, his Oxford slacks, his thick-soled brown brogues, his Eastern-seaboard accent, were all of a piece. In spite of the neat dye job on his brown hair, and the unnatural youth which high color lent his face, I placed his age close to sixty.

I looked around the office. It was windowless, lit by hidden fluorescence and ventilated by an air-conditioning system. The furniture was dark and heavy. The walls were hung with photographs of yachts under full sail, divers in the air, tennis-players congratulating each other with forced smiles on their faces. There were several books on the desk, held upright between elephant bookends made of polished black stone.

Bassett applied a jet lighter to his pipe and laid down a blue smoke screen, through which he said:

"I understand, Mr. Archer, that you're a qualified bodyguard."

"I suppose I'm qualified. I don't often take on that kind of work."

"But I understood— Why not?"

"It means living at close quarters with some of the damnedest jerks. They usually want a bodyguard because they can't get anybody to talk to them. Or else they have delusions."

He smiled crookedly. "I can hardly take that as a compliment. Or perhaps I wasn't intended to?"

"You're in the market for a bodyguard?"

"I hardly know." He added carefully: "Until the situation shapes up more clearly, I really can't say what I need. Or why."

"Who gave you my name?"

"One of our members mentioned you to me some time ago. Joshua Severn, the television producer. You'll be interested to know that he considers you quite a fireball."

"Uh-huh." The trouble with flattery was that people expected to be paid for it in kind. "Why do you need a detective, Mr. Bassett?"

"I'll tell you. A certain young chap has threatened my—threatened my safety. You should have heard him on the telephone."

"You've talked to him?"

"Just for a minute, last night. I was in the midst of a party—our annual post-Christmas party—and he called from Los Angeles. He said he was going to come over here and assault me unless I gave him certain information. It jarred me frightfully."

"What kind of information?"

"Information which I simply don't possess. I believe he's outside now, lying in wait for me. The party didn't break up until very late and I spent the night here, what remained of it. This morning the gateman telephoned down that he had a young man there who wished to see me. I told him to keep the fellow out. Shortly after that, when I'd gathered my wits together, I telephoned you."

"And what do you want me to do, exactly?"

"Get rid of him. You must have ways and means. I don't want any violence, of course, unless it should prove to be absolutely necessary." His eyes gleamed palely between new strata of smoke. "It may be necessary. Do you have a gun?"

"In my car. It's not for hire."

"Of course not. You misinterpret my meaning, old boy. Perhaps I didn't express myself quite clearly. I yield to no man in my abhorrence of violence. I merely meant that you might have use for a pistol as an—ah—instrument of persuasion. Couldn't you simply escort him to the station, or the airfield, and put him aboard a plane?"

"No." I stood up.

He followed me to the door and took hold of my arm. I disliked the coziness, and shook him off.

"Look here, Archer, I'm not a wealthy man, but I do have some savings. I'm willing to pay you three hundred dollars to dispose of this fellow for me."

"Dispose of him?"

"Without violence, of course."

"Sorry, no sale."

"Five hundred dollars."

"It can't be done. What you want me to do is merely kidnapping under California law."

"Good *Lord*, I didn't mean *that*." He was genuinely shocked.

"Think about it. For a man in your position, you're pretty dim about law. Let the police take care of him, why don't you? You say he threatened you."

"Yes. As a matter of fact, he mentioned horse-whipping. But you can't go to the police with that sort of thing."

"Sure you can."

"Not I. It's so ridiculously old-fashioned. I'd be the laughingstock of the entire Southland. You don't seem to grasp the personal aspects, old boy. I'm manager and secretary of a very, very exclusive club. The finest people on the coast confide their children, their young daughters, to my trust. I have to be clear of any breath of scandal—Calpurnia, you know."

"Where does the scandal come in?"

Calpurnia took his pipe out of his mouth and blew a wobbly smoke-ring. "I'd hoped to avoid going into it. I certainly didn't expect to be cross-questioned on the subject. However. Something has to be done, before the situation deteriorates irreparably."

His choice of words annoyed me, and I let the annoyance show. He gave me an appealing look, which fell with a thud between us:

"Can I trust you, *really* trust you?"

"So long as it's legal."

"Oh, heavens, it's legal. I am in a bit of a jam, though, through no fault of my own. It's not what I've done, but what people might think I've done. You see, there's a woman involved."

"George Wall's wife?"

His face came apart at the seams. He tried to put it together again around the fixed point of the pipe, which he jammed into his mouth. But he couldn't control the grimace tugging like hooks at the end of his lips.

"You know her? Does everybody know?"

"Everybody soon will if George Wall keeps hanging around. I ran into him on my way in—"

"Good God, he is on the grounds, then."

Bassett crossed the room in awkward flight. He opened a drawer of his desk and took out a medium-caliber automatic.

"Put that thing away," I said. "If you're worried about your reputation, gunfire can really blow it to hell. Wall was outside the gate, trying to get in. He didn't make it. He did give me a message for you: he won't leave until you see him. Over."

"Damn it, man, why didn't you say so? Here we've been wasting time."

"You have."

"All *right*. We won't quarrel. We've got to get him away from here before any members come."

He glanced at the chronometer strapped to his right wrist, and accidentally pointed the automatic at me.

"Put the gun down, Bassett. You're too upset to be handling a gun."

He laid it on the embossed blotter in front of him and gave me a shamefaced smile. "Sorry. I am a bit nervy. I'm not accustomed to these alarums and excursions."

"What's all the excitement about?"

"Young Wall seems to have some melodramatic notion that I stole his wife from him."

"Did you?"

"Don't be absurd. The girl is young enough to be my daughter." His eyes were wet with embarrassment. "My relations with her have always been perfectly proper."

"You do know her, then?"

"Of course. I've known her for years—much longer than George Wall has. She's been using the pool for diving practice ever since she was in her teens. She's not far out of her teens now, as a matter of fact. She can't be more than twenty-one or two."

"Who is she?"

"Hester Campbell, the diver. You may have heard of her. She came close to winning the national championship a couple of years ago. Then she dropped out of sight. Her family moved away from here and she gave up amateur competition. I had no idea that she was married, until she turned up here again."

"When was this?"

"Five or six months ago. *Six* months ago, in June. She seemed to have had quite a bad time of it. She'd toured with an aquacade for a while, lost her job and been stranded in Toronto. Met this young Canadian sportswriter and married him in desperation. Apparently the marriage didn't work out. She left him after less than a year together, and came back here. She was on her uppers, and rather beaten, spiritually. Naturally I did what I could for her. I persuaded the board to let her use the pool for diving instruction, on a commission basis. She did rather well at that while the summer season lasted. And when she lost her pupils, I'm frank to say I helped her out financially for a bit." He spread his hands limply. "If that's a crime, then I'm a criminal."

"If that's all there is to it, I don't see what you're afraid of."

"You don't understand—you don't understand the position I'm in, the enmities and intrigues I have to contend with here. There's a faction among the membership who would like to see me discharged. If George Wall made it appear that I was using my place to procure young women—"

"How could he do that?"

"I mean if he brought court action, as he threatened to. An unprincipled lawyer could make some kind of case against me. The girl told me that she planned a divorce, and I suppose I wasn't thoroughly discreet. I was seen in her company more than once. As a matter of fact, I cooked several dinners for her." His color rose slightly. "Cooking is one of my hobby-horses. I realize now it wasn't wise to invite her into my home."

"He can't do anything with that. This isn't the Victorian age."

"It is in certain circles. You just don't grasp how precarious my position is. I'm afraid the accusation would be enough."

"Aren't you exaggerating?"

"I hope I am. I don't feel it."

"My advice to you is, level with Wall. Tell him the facts."

"I tried to, on the telephone last night. He refused to listen. The man's insane with jealousy. You'd think I had his wife hidden somewhere."

"You haven't, though?"

"Of course not. I haven't seen her since the early part of September. She left here suddenly without a good-by or a thank-you. She didn't even leave a forwarding address."

"Run off with a man?"

"It's more than likely," he said.

"Tell Wall that. In person."

"Oh, no. I couldn't possibly. The man's a raving maniac, he'd assault me."

Bassett ran tense fingers through his hair. It was soaked at the temples, and little rivulets ran down in front of his ears. He took the folded handkerchief out of his jacket pocket and wiped his face with it. I began to feel a little sorry for him. Physical cowardice hurts like nothing else.

"I can handle him," I said. "Call the gate. If he's still up there, I'll go and bring him down."

"Here?"

"Unless you can think of a better place."

After a nervous moment, he said: "I suppose I have to see him. I can't leave him rampaging around in public. There are several members due for their morning dip at any moment."

His voice took on a religious coloring whenever he mentioned the members. They might have belonged to a higher race, supermen or avenging angels. And Bassett himself had a slipping toehold on the edge of the earthly paradise. Reluctantly, he picked up the intramural phone:

"Tony? Mr. Bassett. Is that young maniac still rampaging around? . . . Are you certain? Absolutely certain? . . . Well, fine. Let me know if he shows up again." He replaced the receiver.

"Gone?"

"It seems so." He inhaled deeply through his open mouth. "Torres says he took off on foot some time ago. I'd appreciate it, though, if you stayed around for a bit, just in case."

"All right. This trip is costing you twenty-five dollars, anyway."

He took the hint and paid me in cash from a drawer. Then he got an electric razor and a mirror out of another drawer. I sat and watched him shave his face and neck. He clipped the hairs in his nostrils with a tiny pair of scissors, and plucked a few hairs out of his eyebrows. It was the sort of occasion that made me hate the job of guarding bodies.

I looked over the books on the desk. There were a Dun and Bradstreet, a Southern California Blue Book, a motion-picture almanac for the previous year, and a thick volume bound in worn green cloth and entitled, surprisingly, *The Bassett Family.* I opened this to the title page, which stated that the book was an account of the genealogy and achievements of the descendants of William Bassett, who landed in Massachusetts in 1634; down to the outbreak of the World War in 1914. By Clarence Bassett.

"I don't suppose you'd be interested," Bassett said, "but it's quite an interesting story to a member of the family. My father wrote that book: he occupied his declining years with it. We really did have a native aristocracy in New England, you know—governors, professors, divines, men of affairs."

"I've heard rumors to that effect."

"Sorry, I don't mean to bore you," he said in a lighter tone, almost self-mocking. "Curiously enough, I'm the last of my branch of the family who bears the name of Bassett. It's the one sole reason I have for regretting my not having married. But then I've never been the philoprogenitive type."

Leaning forward toward the mirror, he began to squeeze a blackhead out of one of the twin grooves that ran from the base of his nose. I got up and roamed along the walls, examining the photographs. I was stopped by one of three divers, a man and two girls, taking off in unison from the high tower. Their bodies hung clear of the tower against a light summer sky, arched in identical swan dives, caught at the height of their parabolas before gravity took hold and snatched them back to earth.

"That's Hester on the left," Bassett said behind me.

Her body was like an arrow. Her bright hair was combed back by the wind from the oval blur of her face. The girl on the right was a dark brunette, equally striking in her full-breasted way. The man in the middle was dark, too, with curly black hair and muscles that looked hammered out of bronze.

"It's one of my favorite photographs," Bassett said. "It was taken a couple of years ago, when Hester was in training for the nationals."

"Taken here?"

"Yes. We let her use our tower for practicing, as I said."

"Who are her friends in the picture?"

"The boy used to be our lifeguard. The girl was a young friend of Hester's. She worked in the snack bar here, but Hester was grooming her for competitive diving."

"Is she still around?"

"I'm afraid not." His face lengthened. "Gabrielle was killed."

"In a diving accident?"

"Hardly. She was shot."

"Murdered?"

He nodded solemnly.

"Who did it to her?"

"The crime was never solved. I doubt that it ever will be now. It happened nearly two years ago, in March of last year."

"What did you say her name was?"

"Gabrielle. Gabrielle Torres."

"Any relation to Tony?"

"She was his daughter."

Chapter 3

THERE WAS a heavy knock on the door. Bassett shied like a frightened horse.

"Who is it?"

The knock was repeated. I went to the door. Bassett neighed at me:

"Don't open it."

I turned the key in the lock and opened the door a few inches against my foot and shoulder. George Wall was outside. His face was greenish-gray in the reflected light. The torn white meat of his leg showed through a rip in his trousers. He breathed hard into my face:

"Is he in here?"

"How did you get in?"

"I came over the fence. Is Bassett in here?"

I looked at Bassett. He was crouched behind the desk, with only his white eyes showing, and his black gun. "Don't let him come in. Don't let him touch me."

"He's not going to touch you. Put that down."

"I will not. I'll defend myself if I have to."

I turned my back on his trigger-happy terror. "You heard him, Wall. He has a gun."

"I don't care what he has. I've got to talk to him. Is Hester here?"

"You're on the wrong track. He hasn't seen her for months."

"Naturally he says that."

"I'm saying it, too. She worked here during the summer, and left some time in September."

His puzzled blue look deepened. His tongue moved like a slow red snail across his upper lip. "Why wouldn't he see me before, if she's not with him?"

"You mentioned horsewhipping, remember? It wasn't exactly the approach diplomatic."

"I don't have time for diplomacy. I have to fly home tomorrow."

"Good."

His shoulder leaned into the opening. I felt his weight on the door. Bassett's voice rose an octave:

"Keep him away from me!"

Bassett was close behind me. I turned with my back against the door and wrenched the gun out of his hand and put it in my pocket. He was too angry and scared to say a word. I turned back to Wall, who was still pressing in but not with all his force. He looked confused. I spread one hand on his chest and pushed him upright and held him. His weight was stubborn and inert, like a stone statue's.

A short, broad-shouldered man came down the steps from the vestibule. He walked toward us fussily, almost goose-stepping, glancing out over the pool and at the sea beyond it as if they were his personal possessions. The wind ruffled his crest of silver hair. Self-importance and fat swelled under his beautifully tailored blue flannel jacket. He was paying no attention to the woman trailing along a few paces behind him.

"Good Lord," Bassett said in my ear, "it's Mr. and Mrs. Graff. We can't have a disturbance in front of Mr. Graff. Let Wall come in. Quickly, man!"

I let him in. Bassett was at the door, bowing and smiling, when the silver-haired man came up. He paused and chopped the air with his nose. His face was brown and burnished-looking.

"Bassett? You've got the extra help lined up for tonight? Orchestra? Food?"

"Yes, Mr. Graff."

"About drinks. We'll use the regular bar bourbon, not my private stock. They're all barbarians, anyway—none of them knows the difference."

"Yes, Mr. Graff. Enjoy your swim."

"I always enjoy my swim."

The woman came up behind him, moving a little dazedly, as though the sunlight distressed her. Her black hair was pulled back severely from a broad, flat brow, to which her Greek nose was joined without indentation. Her face was pale and dead, except for the dark searchlights of her eyes, which seemed to contain all her energy and feeling. She was dressed in black jersey, without ornament, like a widow.

Bassett bade her good-morning. She answered with sudden

animation that it was a lovely day for December. Her husband strode away toward the *cabañas*. She followed like a detached shadow. Bassett sighed with relief.

"Is he the Graff in Helio-Graff?" I said.

"Yes."

He edged past Wall to his desk, rested a haunch on one corner, and fumbled with his pipe and tobacco pouch. His hands were shaking. Wall hadn't moved from the door. His face was red in patches, and I didn't like the glacial stare of his eyes. I kept my bulk between the two men, watching them in turn like a tennis referee.

Wall said throatily: "You can't lie out of it, you must know where she is. You paid for her dancing lessons."

"Dancing lessons? I?" Bassett's surprise sounded real.

"At the Anton School of Ballet. I spoke to Anton yesterday afternoon. He told me she took some dancing lessons from him, and paid for them with your check."

"So that's what she did with the money I lent her."

Wall's lip curled to one side. "You've got an answer for everything, haven't you? Why would you lend her money?"

"I like her."

"I bet you do. Where is she now?"

"Frankly, I don't know. She left here in September. I haven't set eyes on Miss Campbell since."

"The name is Mrs. Wall, Mrs. George Wall. She's my wife."

"I'm beginning to suspect that, old boy. But she used her maiden name when she was with us. She was planning to divorce you, I understood."

"Who talked her into that?"

Bassett gave him a long-suffering look. "If you want the truth, I tried to talk her out of it. I advised her to go back to Canada, to you. But she had other plans."

"What other plans?"

"She wanted a career," Bassett said with a trace of irony. "She was brought up in the Southland here, you know, and she had the movie fever in her blood. And of course her diving gave her a taste for the limelight. I honestly did my best to talk her out of it. But I'm afraid I made no impression on her. She was determined to find an outlet for her talent—I suppose that explains the dancing lessons."

"Does she have talent?" I said.

Wall answered: "She thinks she has."

"Come now," Bassett said with a weary smile. "Let's give the lady her due. She's a lovely child, and she could develop—"

"So you paid for her dancing lessons."

"I lent her money. I don't know how she spent it. She took off from here very suddenly, as I was telling Archer. One day she was living quietly in Malibu, working at her diving, making good contacts here. And the next day she'd dropped out of sight."

"What sort of contacts?" I said.

"A good many of our members are in the industry."

"Could she have gone off with one of them?"

Bassett frowned at the idea. "Certainly not to my knowledge. You understand, I made no attempt to trace her. If she chose to leave, I had no right to interfere."

"I have a right." Wall's voice was low and choked. "I think you're lying about it. You know where she is, and you're trying to put me off."

His lower lip and jaw stuck out, changing the shape of his face into something unformed and ugly. His shoulders leaned outward from the door. I watched his fists clench, white around the knuckles.

"Act your age," I said.

"I've got to find out where she is, what happened to her."

"Wait a minute, George." Bassett pointed his pipe like a token gun, a wisp of smoke at the stem.

"Don't call me George. My friends call me George."

"I'm not your enemy, old boy."

"And don't call me old boy."

"*Young boy*, then, if you wish. I was going to say, I'm sorry this ever came up between us. Truly sorry. I've done you no harm, believe me, and I wish you well."

"Why don't you help me, then? Tell me the truth: is Hester alive?"

Bassett looked at him in dismay.

I said: "What makes you think she isn't?"

"Because she was afraid. She was afraid of being killed."

"When was this?"

"The night before last. Christmas night. She phoned long-distance to the flat in Toronto. She was terribly upset, crying into the telephone."

"What about?"

"Someone had threatened to kill her, she didn't say who. She wanted to get out of California. She asked me if I was willing to take her back. I was, and I told her so. But before we could make any arrangements, the call was cut off. Suddenly she wasn't there, there was nobody there on the end of the line."

"Where was she calling from?"

"Anton's Ballet School on Sunset Boulevard. She had the charges reversed, so I was able to trace the call. I flew out here as soon as I could get away, and saw Anton yesterday. He didn't know about the telephone call, or he said he didn't. He'd been throwing some kind of a party for his students that night, and things were pretty confused."

"Your wife is still taking lessons from him?"

"I don't know. I believe so."

"He should have her address, then."

"He says not. The only address she gave him was the Channel Club here." He threw a suspicious look in Bassett's direction. "Are you certain she doesn't live here?"

"Don't be ridiculous. She never did. I invite you to check on that. She rented a cottage in Malibu—I'll look up the address for you. The landlady lives next door, I believe, and you can talk to her. She's Mrs. Sarah Lamb—an old friend and employee of mine. Just mention my name to her."

"So she can lie for you?" Wall said.

Bassett rose and moved toward him, tentatively. "Won't you listen to reason, old boy? I befriended your wife. It's rather hard, don't you think, that I should have to suffer for my good deeds. I can't spend the whole day arguing with you. I've an important party to prepare for tonight."

"That's no concern of mine."

"No, and your affairs are no concern of mine. But I do have a suggestion. Mr. Archer is a private detective. I'm willing to pay him, out of my own pocket, to help you find your wife. On condition that you stop badgering me. Now, is that a fair proposal or isn't it?"

"You're a detective?" Wall said.

I nodded.

He looked at me doubtfully. "If I could be sure this isn't a put-up job— Are you a friend of Bassett's?"

"Never saw him until this morning. Incidentally, I haven't been consulted about this deal."

"It's right down your alley, isn't it?" Bassett said smoothly. "What's your objection?"

I had none, except that there was trouble in the air and it was the end of a rough year and I was a little tired. I looked at George Wall's pink, rebellious head. He was a natural-born troublemaker, dangerous to himself and probably to other people. Perhaps if I tagged along with him, I could head off the trouble he was looking for. I was a dreamer.

"How about it, Wall?"

"I'd like to have your help," he answered slowly. "I'd rather pay you myself, though."

"Absolutely not!" Bassett said. "You must let me do something—I'm interested in Hester's welfare, too."

"So I gather." Wall's voice was surly.

I said: "We'll toss for it. Heads Bassett pays, tails Wall."

I flipped a quarter and slapped it down on the desk. Tails. I was George Wall's boy. Or he was mine.

Chapter 4

G RAFF WAS floating on his back in the pool when George Wall and I went outside. His brown belly swelled above its surface like the humpback of a Galápagos tortoise. Mrs. Graff, fully clothed, was sitting by herself in a sunny corner. Her black dress and black hair and black eyes seemed to annul the sunlight. Her face and body had the distinction that takes the place of beauty in people who have suffered long and hard.

She interested me, but I didn't interest her. She didn't even raise her eyes when we passed.

I led Wall out to my car. "You better duck down in the seat when we get up to the gate, Tony might take a pot shot at you."

"Not really?"

"He might. Some of these old fighters can get very upset very quickly, especially when you take a poke at them."

"I didn't mean to do that. It was a rotten thing to do."

"It wasn't smart. Twice this morning you nearly got yourself shot. Bassett was scared enough to do it, and Tony was mad enough. I don't know how it is in Canada, but you can't throw your weight around too much in these parts. A lot of harmless-looking souls have guns in their drawers."

His head sank lower. "I'm sorry."

He sounded more than ever like an adolescent who hadn't caught up with his growth. I liked him pretty well, in spite of that. He had the makings, if he lived long enough for them to jell.

"Don't apologize to me. The life you save may be your own."

"But I'm really sorry. The thought of Hester with that old sissy— I guess I lost my head."

"Find it again. And, for God's sake, forget about Bassett. He's hardly what you'd call a wolf."

"He gave her money. He admitted it."

"The point is, he did admit it. Probably somebody else is paying her bills now."

He said in a low, growling voice: "Whoever it is, I'll kill him."

"No, you won't."

He sat in stubborn silence as we drove up to the gate. The gate was open. From the door of the gatehouse, Tony waved to me and made a face at Wall.

"Wait," George said. "I want to apologize to him."

"No. You stay in the car."

I made a left turn onto the coast highway. It followed the contour of the brown bluffs, then gradually descended toward the sea. The beach cottages began, passing like an endless and dilapidated freight train.

"I know how terrible I look to you," George blurted. "I'm not usually like this. I don't go around flexing my muscles and threatening people."

"That's good."

"Really," he said. "It's just—well, I've had a bad year."

He told me about his bad year. It started at the Canadian National Exhibition, in August of the previous year. He was a sportswriter on the Toronto *Star*, and he was assigned to cover the aquacade. Hester was one of the featured tower divers. He'd never cared much about diving—football was his sport—but there was something special about Hester, a shine about her, a kind of phosphorescence. He went back to see her on his own time, and took her out after the show.

The third night, she came out of a two-and-a-half too soon, struck the water flat, and was pulled out unconscious. They took her away before he could get to her. She didn't appear for her act the following night. He found her eventually in a hotel on lower Yonge Street. Both her eyes were black and bloodshot. She said she was through with diving. She'd lost her nerve.

She cried on his shoulder for some time. He didn't know what to do to comfort her.

It was his first experience with a woman, except for a couple of times that didn't count, in Montreal, with some of his football buddies. He asked her to marry him in the course of the night. She accepted his proposal in the morning. They were married three days later.

Perhaps he hadn't been as frank with Hester as he should have been. She'd assumed, from the way he spent money, that he had plenty of it. Maybe he'd let on that he was a fairly important figure in Toronto newspaper circles. He wasn't. He was a cub, just one year out of college, at fifty-five dollars a week.

Hester had a hard time adjusting to life in a two-room flat on Spadina Avenue. One trouble was her eyes, which were a long time clearing. For weeks she wouldn't leave the flat. She gave up grooming her hair, making up, even washing her face. She refused to cook for him. She said she'd lost her looks, lost her career, lost everything that made her life worth living.

"I'll never forget last winter," George Wall said.

There was such intensity in his voice, I turned to look at him. He didn't meet my eyes. With a dreaming expression on his face, he was staring past me at the blue Pacific. Winter sunlight crumpled like foil on its surface.

"It was a cold winter," he said. "The snow creaked under your feet and the hair froze in your nostrils. The frost grew thick on the windows. The oil furnace in the basement kept going out. Hester got quite chummy with the custodian of the building, a woman named Mrs. Bean who lived in the next flat. She started going to church with Mrs. Bean—some freakish little church that carried on in an old house on Bloor. I'd get home from work and hear them in the bedroom talking about redemption and reincarnation, stuff like that.

"One night after Mrs. Bean left, Hester told me that she was being punished for her sins. That was why she missed her dive and got stuck in Toronto with me. She said she had to purify herself so her next incarnation would be on a higher level. For about a month after that, I slept on the chesterfield. Jesus, it was cold.

"On Christmas Eve she woke me up in the middle of the night and announced that she was purified. Christ had appeared in her sleep and forgiven all her sins. I didn't take her seriously at first—how could I? I tried to kid her out of it, laugh it off. So she told me what she meant, about her sins."

He didn't go on.

"What did she mean?" I said.

"I'd just as soon not say."

His voice was choked. I looked at him out of the corner of my eyes. Blood burned in his half-averted cheek and reddened his ear.

"Anyway," he continued, "we had a kind of reconciliation. Hester dropped the phony-religious kick. Instead, she developed a sudden craze for dancing. Dance all night and sleep all day. I couldn't stand the pace. I had to go to work and drum up the old enthusiasm for basketball and hockey and other childish pastimes. She got into the habit of going out by herself, down into the Village."

"I thought you said you were living in Toronto."

"Toronto has its own Village. It's very much like the original in New York—on a smaller scale, of course. Hester got in with a gang of ballet buffs. She went overboard for dancing lessons, with a teacher by the name of Padraic Dane. She had her hair clipped short, and her ears pierced for earrings. She took to wearing white silk shirts and matador pants around the flat. She was always doing entrechats or whatever you call 'em. She'd ask me for things in French—not that she knew French—and when I didn't catch on, she'd give me the silent treatment.

"She'd sit and stare at me without blinking for fifteen or twenty minutes at a time. You'd think I was a piece of furniture that she was trying to think of a better place for. Or maybe by that time I didn't exist at all for her. You know?"

I knew. I'd had a wife and lost her in those silences. I didn't tell George Wall, though. He went on talking, pouring out the words as though they'd been frozen in him for a long time and finally been thawed by the California sun. He probably would have spilled his soul that day to an iron post or a wooden Indian.

"I know now what she was doing," he said. "She was getting her confidence back, in a crazy, unreal way, pulling herself together to make a break with me. The crowd she was playing with, Paddy Dane and his gang of pixies, were encouraging her to do it. I should have seen it coming.

"They put on some kind of a dance play late in the spring, in a little theater that used to be a church. Hester played the boy lead. I went to see it, couldn't make head nor tail of it. It was something about a split personality falling in love with itself. I heard them afterwards filling her up with nonsense about herself. They told her she was wasting herself in Toronto, married to a slob like me. She owed it to herself to go to New York, or back to Hollywood.

"We had a battle when she finally came home that night. I laid it on the line for her: she had to give up those people and their ideas. I told her she was going to drop her dancing lessons and her acting and stay home and wear ordinary women's clothes and look after the flat and cook a few decent meals."

He laughed unpleasantly. It sounded like broken edges rubbing together inside him.

"I'm a great master of feminine psychology," he said. "In the morning after I left for work she went to the bank and drew out the money I'd saved towards a house and got on a plane for Chicago. I found that out by inquiring at the airport. She didn't even leave me a note—I guess she was punishing me for *my* sins. I didn't know where she'd gone. I looked up some of her rum friends in the Village, but they didn't know, either. She dropped them just as flat as she dropped me.

"I don't know how I got through the next six months. We hadn't been married long, and we hadn't been close to each other, the way married people should be. But I was in love with her, I still am. I used to walk the streets half the night and every time I saw a girl with blond hair I'd get an electric shock. Whenever the telephone rang, I'd *know* that it was Hester. And then one night it was.

"It was Christmas night, the night before last. I was sitting in the flat by myself, trying not to think about her. I felt like a nervous breakdown getting ready to happen. Wherever I looked, I kept seeing her face on the wall. And then the telephone rang, and it was Hester. I told you what she said, that she was afraid of being killed and wanted to get out of California. You can imagine how I felt when she was cut off. I thought of calling the Los Angeles police, but there wasn't much to go on. So I had the call traced, and caught the first plane I could get out of Toronto."

"Why didn't you do that six months ago?"

"I didn't know where she was—she never wrote me."

"You must have had some idea."

"Yes, I thought she'd probably come back here. But I didn't have the heart to track her down. I wasn't making much sense there for a while. I pretty well convinced myself she was better off without me." He added after a silence: "Maybe she is, at that."

"All you can do is ask her. But first we have to find her."

Chapter 5

WE ENTERED a dead-end street between the highway and the beach. The tires shuddered on the pitted asphalt. The cottages that lined the street were rundown and disreputable-looking, but the cars that stood in front of them were nearly all late models. When I turned off my engine, the only sound I could hear was the rumble and gasp of the sea below the cottages. Above them a few gulls circled, tattletale gray.

The one that Hester had lived in was a board-and-batten box which had an unused look, like a discarded container. Its walls had been scoured bare and grained by blowing sands. The cottage beside it was larger and better kept, but it was losing its paint, too.

"This is practically a slum," George said. "I thought that Malibu was a famous resort."

"Part of it is. This is the other part."

We climbed the steps to Mrs. Lamb's back porch, and I knocked on the rusty screen door. A heavy-bodied old woman in a wrapper opened the inside door. She had a pleasantly ugly bulldog face and a hennaed head, brash orange in the sun. An anti-wrinkle patch between her eyebrows gave her an air of calm eccentricity.

"Mrs. Lamb?"

She nodded. She held a cup of coffee in her hand, and she was chewing.

"I understand you rent the cottage next door."

She swallowed whatever was in her mouth. I watched its passage down her withered throat. "I may as well tell you right off, I don't rent stag. Now if you're married, that's another matter." She paused expectantly and took a second swallow, leaving a red half-moon on the rim of the cup.

"I'm not married."

That was as far as I got.

"Too bad," she said. Her nasal Kansas voice hummed on like a wire in a rushing wind: "I'm all for marriage myself, went out with four men in my lifetime and married two of them. The first one lasted thirty-three years, I guess I made him happy. He didn't bother *me* with his Copenhagen snuff and his dirt around the house. It takes more than that to bother *me*. So when he died I married again, and that one wasn't so bad. Could have been better, could have been worse. It was kind of a relief, though, when *he* died. He didn't do a lick of work in seven years. Luckily I had the strength to support him."

Her sharp eyes, ringed with concentric wrinkles, flicked from me to George Wall and back again. "You're both nice-appearing young men, you ought to be able to find a girl willing to take a chance with you." She smiled fiercely, swirled her remaining coffee around in the cup, and drank it down.

"I had a wife," George Wall said heavily. "I'm looking for her now."

"You don't say. Why didn't you say so?"

"I've been trying to."

"Don't get mad. I like a little sociability, don't you? What's her name?"

"Hester."

Her eyes flattened. "Hester Campbell?"

"Hester Campbell Wall."

"Well, I'll be darned, I didn't know she was married. What happened, did she run away?"

He nodded solemnly. "Last June."

"What do you know? She's got less sense than I thought she had, running away from a nice young fellow like you." She inspected his face intently through the screen, clucking in decrescendo. " 'Course I never did give her credit for too much sense. She was always full of razzmatazz, ever since she was a kid."

"Have you known her long?" I said.

"You bet I have. Her and her sister and her mother both. She was a hoity-toity one, her mother, always putting on airs."

"Do you know where her mother is now?"

"Haven't seen her for years, or the sister either."

I looked at George Wall.

He shook his head. "I didn't even know she had a mother. She never talked about her family. I thought she was an orphan."

"She had one," the old woman said. "Her and her sister, Rina, they were both well supplied with a mother. Mrs. Campbell was bound to make something out of those girls if it killed them. I

don't know how she afforded all those lessons she gave them—
music lessons and dancing lessons and swimming lessons."

"No husband?"

"Not when I knew her. She was clerking in the liquor store
during the war, which is how we became acquainted, through
my second. Mrs. Campbell was always bragging about her girls,
but she didn't really have their welfare at heart. She was what
they call a movie-mother, I guess, trying to get her little girls
to support her."

"Does she still live here?"

"Not to my knowledge. She dropped out of sight years ago.
Which didn't break my heart."

"And you don't know where Hester is, either?"

"I haven't laid eyes on the girl since September. She moved
out, and that was that. We have some turnover in Malibu, I can
tell you."

"Where did she move to?" George said.

"That's what I'd like to know." Her gaze shifted to me: "Are
you a relative, too?"

"No, I'm a private detective."

She showed no surprise. "All right, I'll talk to you, then.
Come inside and have a cup of coffee. Your friend can wait
outside."

Wall didn't argue; he merely looked disgruntled. Mrs. Lamb
unhooked her screen door, and I followed her into the tiny
white kitchen. The red plaid of the tablecloth was repeated in
the curtains over the sink. Coffee was bubbling on an electric
plate.

Mrs. Lamb poured some of it for me in a cup which didn't
match hers, and then some more for herself. She sat at the table,
motioned to me to sit opposite.

"I couldn't exist without coffee. I developed the habit when I
ran the snack bar. Twenty-five cups a day, silly old woman." But
she sounded very tolerant of herself. "I do believe if I cut myself
I'd bleed coffee. Mr. Finney—he's my adviser at the Spiritualist
Church—says I should switch to tea, but I say no. Mr. Finney,
I told him, the day I have to give up my favorite vice, I'd just
as soon lay down and fold my hands around a lily and pass on
into another life."

"Good for you," I said. "You were going to tell me something about Hester."

"Yes, I was. I hated to say it right out in front of the husband. I had to evict her."

"What for?"

"Carrying on," she said vaguely. "The girl's a fool about men. Doesn't he know that?"

"It seems to be at the back of his mind. Any particular men?"

"One particular man."

"Not Clarence Bassett?"

"Mr. Bassett? Heavens, no. I've known Mr. Bassett going on ten years—I ran the snack bar at the club until my legs give out—and you can take my word for it, he ain't the carrying-on *type*. Mr. Bassett was more like a father to her. I guess he did his best to keep her out of trouble, but his best wasn't good enough. Mine, either."

"What kind of trouble did she get into?"

"Man trouble, like I said. Nothing that you could put your finger on, maybe, but I could see she was heading for disaster. One of the men she brought here to her house was a regular gangster type. I *told* Hester if she was going to have bums like him visiting her, spending the night, she'd have to find another house to do it in. I felt I had a right to speak out, knowing her from childhood and all. But she took it the wrong way, said she would look after her affairs and I could look after mine. I told her what she did on my property *was* my affair. She said, all right, if that's the way you feel about it she'd get out, said I was an interfering old bag. Which maybe I am, at that, but I don't take talk like that from any flibberty-gibbet who plays around with gunmen."

She paused for breath. An ancient refrigerator throbbed emotionally in the corner of the kitchen. I took a sip of my coffee and looked out the window which overlooked the street. George Wall was sitting in the front seat of my car with a rejected expression on his face. I turned back to Mrs. Lamb:

"Who was he, do you know?"

"I never did learn his name. Hester wouldn't tell me his name. When I took the matter up with her, she said he was her boyfriend's manager."

"Her boyfriend?"

"The Torres boy. Lance Torres, he calls himself. He was a fairly decent boy at one time, least he put up a nice front when he had his lifeguard job."

"Was he a lifeguard at the club?"

"Used to be, for a couple of summers. His Uncle Tony got him the job. But lifeguard was too slow for Lance, he had to be a big shot. I heard he was a boxer for a while and then he got into some trouble, I think they put him in jail for it last year."

"What kind of trouble?"

"I don't know, there's too many good people in the world to make it worth my while to keep track of bums. You could of knocked me over with a brick when Lance turned up here with his gunman friend, sucking around Hester. I thought he had more self-respect."

"How do you know he was a gunman?"

"I saw him shooting, that's how. I woke up one morning and heard this popping noise down on the beach. It sounded like gunfire. It was. This fellow was out there shooting at beer bottles with a nasty black gun he had. That was the day I said to myself, either she stops messing around with bums or good-by Hester."

"Who was he?"

"I never did learn his name. That nasty snub-nosed gun and the way he handled it was all I needed to know about him. Hester said he was Lance's manager."

"What did he look like?"

"Looked like death to me. Those glassy brown eyes he had, and kind of a flattened-out face, fishbelly color. But I talked right up to him, told him he ought to be ashamed of himself shooting up bottles where people could cut themselves. He didn't even look at me, just stuck another clip in his gun and went on shooting at the bottles. He'd probably just as soon been shooting at me, least that was how he acted."

Remembered anger heightened her color. "I don't like being brushed off like that—it ain't *human*. And I'm touchy about shooting, specially since a friend of mine was shot last year. Right on this very beach, a few miles south of where you're sitting."

"You don't mean Gabrielle Torres?"

"I should say I do. You heard about Gabrielle, eh?"

"A little. So she was a friend of yours."

"Sure, she was. Some people would have a prejudice, her being part Mex, but I say if a person is good enough to work with you, a person is good enough to be your friend." Her monolithic bosom rose and fell under the flowered-cotton wrapper.

"Nobody knows who shot her, I hear."

"Somebody knows. The one that did it."

"Do you have any ideas, Mrs. Lamb?"

Her face was as still as stone for a long moment. She shook her head finally.

"Her cousin Lance, maybe, or his manager?"

"I wouldn't put it past them. But what reason could they have?"

"You've thought about it, then."

"How could I help it, with them going in and out of the cottage next door, shooting off guns on the beach? I told Hester the day she left, she should learn a lesson from what happened to her friend."

"But she went off with them anyway?"

"I guess she did. I didn't see her leave. I don't know where she went, or who with. That day I made a point of going to visit my married daughter in San Berdoo."

Chapter 6

IRELAYED as little as possible of this to George Wall, who showed signs of developing into a nuisance. On the way to Los Angeles, I turned into the drive of the Channel Club. He gave a wild look around, as though I was taking him into an ambush.

"Why are we coming back here?"

"I want to talk to the guard. He may be able to give me a lead to your wife. If not, I'll try Anton."

"I don't see the point of that. I talked to Anton yesterday, I told you all he said."

"I may be able to squeeze out some more. I know Anton, did a piece of work for him once."

"You think he was holding out on me?"

"Could be. He hates to give anything away, including information. Now you sit here and see that nobody swipes the hubcaps. I want to get Tony talking, and you have bad associations for him."

"What's the use of my being here at all?" he said sulkily. "I might as well go back to the hotel and get some sleep."

"That's an idea, too."

I left him in the car out of sight of the gate, and walked down the curving drive between thick rows of oleanders. Tony heard me coming. He shuffled out of the gatehouse, gold gleaming in the crannies of his smile.

"What happened to your loco friend? You lose him?"

"No such luck. You have a nephew, Tony."

"Got a lot of nephews." He spread his arms. "Five-six nephews."

"The one that calls himself Lance."

He grunted. Nothing changed in his face, except that he wasn't smiling any more. "What about him?"

"Can you tell me his legal name?"

"Manuel," he said. "Manuel Purificación Torres. The name my brother give him wasn't good enough for him. He had to go and change it."

"Where is he living now, do you know?"

"No, sir, I don't know. I don't have nothing to do with that one no more. He was close to me like a son one time. No more." He wagged his head from side to side, slowly. The motion shook a question loose: "Is Manuel in trouble again?"

"I couldn't say for sure. Who's his manager, Tony?"

"He don't got no manager. They don't let him fight no more. I was his manager couple years ago, trained him and managed him both. Brought him along slow and easy, gave him a left and taught him the combinations. Kept him living clean, right in my own house: up at six in the morning, skip-the-rope, light and heavy bag, run five miles on the beach. Legs like iron, beautiful. So he had to ruinate it."

"How?"

"Same old story," Tony said. "I seen it too many times. He wins a couple-three fights, two four-rounders and a six-rounder in San Diego. Right away he's a bigshot, he *thinks* he's a bigshot. Uncle Tony, poor old Uncle Tony, he's too dumb in the head to tell him his business. Uncle Tony don't know from nothing, says lay off muscadoodle, lay off dames and reefers, sell your noisy, stinky motycycle before you break your neck, you got a future. Only he wants it now. The whole world, right now.

"Then something come up between us. He done something I don't like, I don't like it at all. I says, you been wanting out from me, now you can get out. We didden have no contract, nothing between us any more, I guess. He clumb on his motycycle and tooted away, back to Los Angeles. There he was, a Main Street bum, and he wasn't twenty-one years old yet.

"My sister Desideria blamed me, I should go after him on my hands and knees." Tony shook his head. "No, I says, Desideria, I been around a long time. So have you, only you're a woman and don't see things. A boy gets ants in his pants, you can't hire no exterminator for that. Let him do it the hard way, we can't live his life.

"So one of these crooks he wants to be like—this crook sees Manny working out in the gym. He asks him for a contract and Manny gives it to him. He wins some fights and throws some, makes some dirty money, spends it on dirty things. They caught him with some caps in his car last year, and put him in jail. When he gets out, he's suspended, no more fights—back where he started in the starvation army."

Tony spat dry. "Long ago, I tried to tell him, my father, his grandfather, was *bracero*. Manny's father and me, we was born in a chickenhouse in Fresno, nowhere, from nothing. We got two strikes on us already, I says, we got to keep our nose clean. But would he listen to me? No, he got to stick his neck under the chopper."

"How much time did he serve?"

"I guess he was in all last year. I dunno for sure. I got troubles of my own then."

His shoulders moved as if they felt the entire weight of the sky. I wanted to ask him about his daughter's death, but the grief in his face tied my tongue. The scars around his eyes, sharp and deep in the sun, had been left there by crueller things than fists. I asked a different question:

"Do you know the name of the man that held his contract?"

"Stern, his last name is."

"Carl Stern?"

"Yeah." Squinting at my face, he saw the effect of the name on me. "You know him?"

"I've seen him in nightclubs, and heard some stories about him. If ten per cent of them are true, he's a dangerous character. Is your nephew still with him, Tony?"

"I dunno. I bet you he is in trouble. I think you know it, only you won't tell me."

"What makes you think that?"

"Because I seen him last week. He was all dressed up like a movie star and driving one of those sporty cars." He made a low sweeping motion with his hands. "Where would he get the money? He don't work, and he can't fight no more."

"Why didn't you ask him?"

"Don't make me laugh, ask him. He wooden say hello to his Uncle Tony. He is too busy riding around with blondes in speedy cars."

"He was with a blonde girl?"

"Sure."

"Anybody you know?"

"Sure. She used to work here last summer. Hester Campbell, her name is. I thought she had more brains, to run around with my nephew Manny."

"How long has she been running with him?"

"I wooden know. I got no crystal ball."

"Where did you see them?"

"Venice Speedway."

"Wasn't the Campbell girl a friend of your daughter's?"

His face set hard and dark. "Maybe. What is this all about, mister? First you ask for my nephew, now it's my daughter."

"I just heard about your daughter this morning. She was a friend of the Campbell girl, and I'm interested in the Campbell girl."

"I'm not, and I don't know nothing. It's no use asking me. What do I know?" His mood had swung heavily downward. He made an idiot face. "I'm a punchy bum. My brains don't think straight. My daughter is dead. My nephew is a crooked *pachuco*. People come and punch me in the nose."

Chapter 7

A NTON'S WINDOWS overlooked the boulevard from the second floor of a stucco building in West Hollywood. The building was fairly new, but it had been painted and scraped and repainted in blotches of color, pink and white and blue, to make it look like something from the left bank of the Seine. You entered it through a court which contained several small arty shops and had a terrazzo fountain in the center. A concrete nymph stood with her feet in its shallow water, covering her pudenda with one hand and beckoning with the other.

I climbed the outside stairs to the second-floor balcony. Through an open door, I saw a half-dozen girls in leotards stretching their ligaments on barres along the wall. A woman with flat breasts and massive haunches called out orders in a drill-sergeant's voice:

"Grand battement, s'il vous plaît. Non, non, grand *battement."*

I walked on to the end of the balcony, trailed by the salt-sweet odor of young sweat. Anton was in his office, short and wide behind the desk in a gabardine suit the color of lemon ice cream. His face was sunlamp brown. He rose very lightly, to demonstrate his agelessness. The hand he extended had rings on two of the fingers, a seal ring and a diamond to go with the diamond in his foulard tie. His grip was like a bull lobster's.

"Mr. Archer."

Anton had been in Hollywood longer than I had, but he still pronounced my name "Meester Arshair." The accent was probably part of his business front. I liked him in spite of it.

"I'm surprised you remember my name."

"I think of you with gratitude," he said. "Frequently."

"What wife are you on now?"

"Please, you are very vulgar." He raised his hands in a fastidious gesture, and while he was at it, examined his manicure. "Number five. We are very happy. You are not needed."

"Yet."

"But you didn't come to discuss my marital problems. Why do you come?"

"Missing girl."

"Hester Campbell again?"

"Uh-huh."

"Are you employed by that big *naïf* of a husband?"

"You're psychic."

"He is a fool. Any man of his age and weight who runs after a woman in this city is a fool. Why doesn't he stand still, and they'll come swarming?"

"He's only interested in the one. Now what about her?"

"What about her?" he repeated, offering his hands palms up to show how clean they were. "She has had some ballet lessons from me, three or four months of lessons. The young ladies come and go. I am not responsible for their private lives."

"What do you know about her private life?"

"Nothing. I wish to know nothing. My friend Paddy Dane in Toronto did me no favor when he sent her here. There is a young lady very much on the make. I could see trouble in her."

"If you could see all that, why turn her husband loose on Clarence Bassett?"

His shoulders rose. "*I* turned him loose on Bassett? I merely answered his questions."

"You made him believe that she was living with Bassett. Bassett hasn't seen her for nearly four months."

"What would I know about that?"

"Don't kid me, Anton. Did you know Bassett before this?"

"*Pas trop.* He would not remember, probably."

He moved to the window and cranked the louvers wider. The sound of traffic rose from the Boulevard. Under it, his voice was sibilant:

"But I do not forget. Five years ago, I applied for membership in the Channel Club. They refused me, with no reason given. I heard through my sponsor that Bassett never presented my name to the membership committee. He wanted no dancing-masters in his club."

"So you thought you'd make trouble for him."

"Perhaps." He looked at me over his shoulder, his eye bright and empty as a bird's. "Did I succeed?"

"I stopped it before it happened. But you could have triggered a murder."

"Nonsense." He turned and came toward me, stepping with

feline softness on the carpet. "The husband is a nothing, a hysterical boy. There is no danger in him."

"I wonder. He's big and strong, and crazy about his wife."

"Is he rich?"

"Hardly."

"Then tell him to forget her. I have seen many like her, in love with themselves. They think they aspire to an art, acting or dancing or music. But all they really aspire to is money and clothes. A man comes along who can give them these things, and there is the end of aspiration." His hands went through the motions of liberating a bird and throwing it a good-by kiss.

"Did one come along for Hester?"

"Possibly. She seemed remarkably prosperous at my Christmas party. She had a new mink stole. I complimented her on it, and she informed me that she was under personal contract to a movie producer."

"Which one?"

"She did not say, and it does not matter. She was lying. It was a little fantasy for my benefit."

"How do you know?"

"I know women."

I was ready to believe him. The wall behind his desk was papered with inscribed photographs of young women.

"Besides," he said, "no producer in his right mind would give that girl a contract. There is something lacking in her—essential talent, feeling. She became cynical so young, and she makes no attempt to hide it."

"How did she act the other night?"

"I did not observe her for very long. I had over a hundred guests."

"She made a telephone call from here. Did you know?"

"Not until yesterday. The husband told me she was frightened of something. Perhaps she drank too much. There was nothing at my party to frighten anyone—a lot of nice young people amusing themselves."

"Who was she with?"

"A boy, a good-looking boy." He snapped his fingers. "She introduced him to me, but I forget his name."

"Lance Torres?"

His eyelids crinkled. "Possibly. He was quite dark, Spanish-looking. A very well-built boy—one of those new young types with the *apache* air. Perhaps Miss Seeley can identify him for you. I saw them talking together." He pushed his right cuff back and looked at his wristwatch. "Miss Seeley is out for coffee, but she should be back very soon."

"While we're waiting, you could give me Hester's address. Her real address."

"Why should I make things easy for you?" Anton said with his edged smile. "I don't like the fellow you are working for. He is too aggressive. Also, I am old and he is young. Also, my father was a streetcar conductor in Montreal. Why should I help an Anglo from Toronto?"

"So you won't let him find his wife?"

"Oh, you can have the address. I simply wished to express my emotions on the subject. She lives at the Windsor Hotel in Santa Monica."

"You know it by heart, eh?"

"I happen to remember. I had a request for her address from another detective last week."

"Police detective?"

"Private. He claimed to be a lawyer with money for her, a bequest, but his story was very clumsy and I am not stupid." He glanced at his wristwatch again. "If you'll excuse me, now, I have to dress for a class. You can wait here for Miss Seeley if you wish."

Before I could ask him any more questions, he went out through an inner door and closed it behind him. I sat down at his desk and looked up the Windsor Hotel in the telephone directory. The desk clerk told me that Miss Hester Campbell didn't stay there any more. She'd moved out two weeks ago, leaving no forwarding address.

I was masticating this fact when Miss Seeley came in. I remembered her from the period when Anton divorced his third wife, with my assistance. She was a little older, a little thinner. Her tailored pinstriped suit emphasized the boniness of her figure. But she still wore hopeful white ruffles at her wrists and throat.

"Why, Mr. Archer." The implications of my presence struck her. "We're not having wife trouble again?"

"Wife trouble, yes, but nothing to do with the boss. He says you may be able to give me some information."

"My telephone number, by any chance?" Her smile was warm and easygoing behind her lipstick mask.

"That I could do with, too."

"You flatter me. Go right ahead. I can stand a smattering of flattering for a change. You don't meet many eligible males in this business."

We exchanged some further pleasantries, and I asked her if she remembered seeing Hester at the party. She remembered.

"And her escort?"

She nodded. "Dreamy. A real cute thing. That is, if you like the Latin type. I don't go for the Latin type myself, but we got along just fine. Until he showed his true colors."

"You talked to him?"

"For a while. He was kind of shy with all the people, so I took him under my wing. He told me about his career and all. He's an actor. Helio-Graff Studios have him under long-term contract."

"What's his name?"

"Lance Leonard. It's kind of a cute name, don't you think? He told me he chose it himself."

"He didn't tell you his real name?"

"No."

"And he's under contract to Helio-Graff?"

"That's what he said. He's certainly got the looks for it. *And* the artistic temperament."

"You mean he made a pass at you?"

"Oh, no. Not that I'd permit it. He's stuck on Hester anyway, I could see that. They were at the bar after, drinking out of the same glass, just as close as close." Her voice was wistful. She added by way of consolation to herself: "But then he showed his true colors."

"How did he do that?"

"It was awful," she said with relish. "Hester came in here to put in a telephone call. I let her have the key. It must have been to another man, because he followed her in and made a scene. These Latins are so emotional."

"You were here?"

"I heard him yelling at her. I had things to do in my own office, and I couldn't *help* overhearing. He called her some awful names: b-i-t-c-h and other words I won't repeat." She tried to blush, and failed.

"Did he threaten her in any way?"

"You bet he did. He said she wouldn't last a week unless she played along with the operation. She was in it deeper than anybody, and she wasn't going to ruin his big chance." Miss Seeley was a fairly decent woman, but she couldn't quite restrain the glee fluttering at the corners of her mouth.

"Did he say what the operation was?"

"Not that I heard."

"Or threaten to kill her?"

"He didn't say that *he* was going to do anything to her. What he said—" She looked up at the ceiling and tapped her chin. "He said if she didn't stay in line, he'd get this friend of his after her. Somebody called Carl."

"Carl Stern?"

"Maybe. He didn't mention the last name. He just kept saying that Carl would fix her wagon."

"What happened after that?"

"Nothing. They came out and left together. She looked pretty subdued, I mean it."

Chapter 8

THERE WAS an outdoor telephone booth in the court, and I immured myself with the local directories. Lance Leonard wasn't in them. Neither was Lance Torres, or Hester Campbell, or Carl Stern. I made a telephone call to Peter Colton, who had recently retired as senior investigator in the D.A.'s office.

Carl Stern, he told me, had also retired recently. That is, he'd moved to Vegas and gone legit, if you could call Vegas legit. Stern had invested his money in a big new hotel-and-casino which was under construction. Personally Colton hoped he'd lose his dirty gold-plated shirt.

"Where did the gold come from, Peter?"

"Various sources. He was a Syndicate boy. When Siegel broke with the Syndicate and died of it, Stern was one of the heirs. He made his heavy money out of the wire service. When the Crime Commission broke that up, he financed a narcotics ring for a while."

"So you put him away, no doubt."

"You know the situation as well as I do, Lew." Colton sounded angry and apologetic at the same time. "Our operation is essentially a prosecuting agency. We work with what the cops bring in to us. Carl Stern was using cops for bodyguards. The politicians that hire and fire the cops went on fishing trips with him to Acapulco."

"Is that how he wangled himself a gambling license in Nevada?"

"He didn't get a license in Nevada. With his reputation, they couldn't give him one. He had to get himself a front."

"Do you know who his front man would be?"

"Simon Graff," Colton said. "You must have heard of him. They're going to call their place Simon Graff's Casbah."

That stopped me for a minute. "I thought Helio-Graff was making money."

"Maybe Graff saw his chance to make some more money. I'd tell you what I think of that, but it wouldn't be good for my blood pressure." He went ahead and told me anyway, in a voice that was choked with passion: "They've got no decency, they've got no sense of public responsibility—these goddam lousy big Hollywood names that go to Vegas and decoy for thieves and pander for mobsters and front for murderers."

"Is Stern a murderer?"

"Ten times over," Colton said. "You want his record in detail?"

"Not just now. Thanks, Peter. Take it easy."

I knew a man at Helio-Graff, a writer named Sammy Swift. The studio switchboard put me on to his secretary, and she called Sammy to the phone.

"Lew? How's the Sherlock kick?"

"It keeps me in beer and skittles. By the way, what are skittles? You're a writer, you're supposed to know these things."

"I let the research department know them for me. Division of labor. Will you cut it short now, boy? Any other time. I'm fighting script, and the mimeographers are hounding me." His voice was hurried, in time with a rapid metronome clicking inside his head.

"What's the big project?"

"I'm flying to Italy with a production unit next week. Graff's doing a personal on the Carthage story."

"The Carthage story?"

"*Salammbô*, the Flaubert historical. Where you been?"

"In geography class. Carthage is in Africa."

"It was, not any more. The Man is building it in Italy."

"I hear he's doing some building in Vegas, too."

"The Casbah, you mean? Yeah."

"Isn't it kind of unusual for a big independent producer to put his money in a slot-machine shop?"

"Everything the Man does is unusual. And moderate your language, Lew."

"You bugged?"

"Don't be silly," he said uncertainly. "Now, what's your problem? If you think you're broke, I'm broker, ask my broker."

"No problem. I want to get in touch with a new actor you have. Lance Leonard?"

"Yeah, I've seen him around. Why?"

I improvised. "A friend of mine, newspaperman from the east, wants an interview."

"About the Carthage story?"

"Why, is Leonard in it?"

"Minor role, his first. Don't you read the columns?"

"Not when I can help it. I'm illiterate."

"So are the columns. So's Leonard, but don't let your friend print that. The kid should do all right as a North African barbarian. He's got prettier muscles than Brando, used to be a fighter."

"How did he get into pictures?"

"The Man discovered him personally."

"And where does he board his pretty muscles?"

"Coldwater Canyon, I think. My secretary can get you the address. Don't let on you got it from me, though. The kid is afraid of the press. But he can use the publicity." Sammy caught his breath. He liked to talk. He liked anything that interrupted his work. "I hope this isn't one of your fast ones, Lew."

"You know better than that. I lost my fast one years ago. I'm down to my slider."

"So are we all, boy. With bursitis yet. See you."

I got the address in Coldwater Canyon, and went out to the street. The sun shimmered on the car roof. George Wall was slumped in the front seat with his head thrown back. His face was flushed and wet. His eyes were closed. The interior was oven-hot.

The starting engine woke him. He sat up, rubbing his eyes. "Where are we going?"

"Not we. I'll drop you off at your hotel. Which one?"

"But I don't want to be dropped off." He took hold of my right arm. "You found out where she is, haven't you? You don't want me to see her."

I didn't answer. He tugged at my arm, causing the car to swerve. "That's the idea, isn't it?"

I pushed him away, into the far corner of the seat. "For God's sake, George, relax. Take a sedative when you get back to the hotel. Now, where is it?"

"I'm not going back to the hotel. You can't force me."

"All right, all right. If you promise to stay in the car. I have a lead that may pan out and it may not. It won't for sure, if you come barging in."

"I won't. I promise." After a while he said: "You don't understand how I feel. I dreamed of Hester just now when I was asleep. I tried to talk to her. She wouldn't answer, and then I saw she was dead. I touched her. She was as cold as snow—"

"Tell it to your head-shrinker," I said unpleasantly. His self-pity was getting on my nerves.

He withdrew into hurt silence, which lasted all the way to the Canyon. Lance Leonard lived near the summit, in a raw new redwood house suspended on cantilevers over a steep drop. I parked above the house and looked around. Leonard had no close neighbors, though several other houses dotted the further slopes. The hills fell away from the ridge in folds like heavy drapery trailing in the horizontal sea.

I nailed George in place with one of my masterful looks, and went down the slanting asphalt drive to the house. The trees in the front yard, lemons and avocados, were recently planted: I could see the yellow burlap around their roots. The open garage contained a dusty gray Jaguar two-door and a light racing motorcycle. I pressed the button beside the front door, and heard chimes in the house softly dividing the silence.

A young man opened the door. He was combing his hair with a sequined comb. His hair was black, curly on top and straight at the sides. The height of the doorstep brought his head level with mine. His face was darkly handsome, if you overlooked the spoiled mouth and slightly muddy eyes. He had on blue nylon pajamas, and his brown feet were bare. He was the central diver in Bassett's photograph.

"Mr. Torres?"

"Leonard," he corrected me. Having arranged the curls low on his forehead to his satisfaction, he dropped the comb in his pajama pocket. He smiled with conscious charm. "Got a new name to go with my new career. What's the mission, cap?"

"I'd like to see Mrs. Wall."

"Never heard of her. You got the wrong address."

"Her maiden name was Campbell. Hester Campbell."

He stiffened. "Hester? She ain't married—isn't married."

"She's married. Didn't she tell you?"

He glanced over his shoulder into the house, and back at me. His movements were lizard-quick. He took hold of the knob and started to shut the door. "Never heard of her. Sorry."

"Who does the comb belong to? Or do you merely adore bright things?"

He paused in indecision, long enough for me to get my foot in the door. I could see past him through the house to the sliding glass wall at the rear of the living-space, and through it the outside terrace which overhung the canyon. A girl was lying on a metal chaise in the sun. Her back was brown and long, with a breathtaking narrow waist from which the white hip arched up. Her hair was like ruffled silver feathers.

Leonard stepped outside, forcing me back onto the flagstone walk, and shut the front door behind him. "Drag 'em back into their sockets, cousin. No free shows today. And get this, I don't know any Hester what's-her-name."

"You did a minute ago."

"Maybe I heard the name once. I hear a lot of names. What's yours, for instance?"

"Archer."

"What's your business?"

"I'm a detective."

His mouth went ugly, and his eyes blank. He'd come up fast out of a place where cops were hated and feared: the hatred was still in him like a chronic disease. "What you want with me, cop?"

"Not you. Hester."

"Is she in a jam?"

"She probably is if she's shacked up with you."

"Naw, naw. She gave me the brush-off, frankly." He brushed his nylon flanks illustratively. "I haven't seen the chick for a long time."

"Have you tried looking on your terrace?"

His hands paused and tightened on his hips. He leaned forward from the waist, his mouth working like a red bivalve: "You keep calling me a liar. I got a public position to keep up, so I stand here and take it like a little gentleman. But you better get off my property or I'll clobber you, cop or no cop."

"That would go good in the columns. The whole set-up would."

"What set-up? What do you mean?"

"You tell me."

He squinted anxiously up toward the road where my car was parked. George's face hung at the window like an ominous pink moon.

"Who's your sidekick?"

"Her husband."

Leonard's eyes blurred with thought. "What is this, a shake-down? Let's see your buzzer."

"No buzzer. I'm a private detective."

"Dig him," he said to an imaginary confidant on his left.

At the same time, his right shoulder dropped. The hooked arm swinging from it drove a fist into my middle below the rib-cage. It came too fast to block. I sat down on the flagstones and discovered that I couldn't get up right away. My head was cool and clear, like an aquarium, but the bright ideas and noble intentions that swam around in it had no useful connection with my legs.

Leonard stood with his fists ready, waiting for me to get up. His hair had fallen forward over his eyes, blue-black and shining like steel shavings. His bare feet danced a little on the stone. I reached for them and clutched air. Leonard smiled down at me, dancing:

"Come on, get up. I can use a workout."

"You'll get it, sucker-puncher," I said between difficult breaths.

"Not from you, old man."

The door opened behind him, and featherhead looked out. She wore dark harlequin glasses whose sequined rims matched the comb. Oil glistened on her face. A terrycloth towel held under her armpits clung to the bulbs and narrows of her body.

"What's the trouble, hon?"

"No trouble. Get inside."

"Who is this character? Did you hit him?"

"What do you think?"

"I think you're crazy, taking the chances you take."

"*Me* take chances? Who shot off her mouth on the telephone? You *brought* the bastard here."

"All right, so I wanted out. So I changed my mind."

"Shut it off." He threatened her with a movement of his shoulders. "I said inside."

Running footsteps clattered on the driveway. George Wall called out: "Hester! I'm here!"

What I could see of her face didn't change expression. Leonard spread a hand on her terrycloth breast and pushed her in and shut the door on her. He turned as George charged in on him, met him with a stiff left to the face. George stopped dead.

Leonard waited, his face smooth and intent like a man's listening to music.

I got my legs under me and stood up and watched them fight. George had been wanting a fight: he had the advantage of height and weight and reach: I didn't interfere. It was like watching a man get caught in a machine. Leonard stepped inside of a looping swing, rested his chin on the big man's chest, and hammered his stomach. His elbows worked like pistons in oiled grooves close to his body. When he stepped back, George doubled over. He went to his knees and got up again, very pale.

The instant his hands left the flagstone, Leonard brought up his right hand into George's face, his back uncoiling behind it. George walked backward onto the tender new lawn. He looked at the sky in a disappointed way, as if it had dropped something on him. Then he shook his head and started back toward Leonard. He tripped on a garden hose and almost fell.

I stepped between them, facing Leonard. "He's had it. Knock it off, eh?"

George shouldered me aside. I grabbed his arms.

"Let me at the little runt," he said through bloody lips.

"You don't want to get hurt, boy."

"Worry about him."

He was stronger than I was. He broke loose and spun me away. Threw another wild one which split the back of his suit coat and accomplished nothing else. Leonard inclined his head two or three inches from the vertical and watched the fist go by. George staggered off balance. Leonard hit him between the eyes with his right hand, hit him again with his left as he went down. George's head made a dull noise on the flagstone. He lay still.

Leonard polished the knuckles of his right fist with his left hand, as though it were a bronze object of art.

"You shouldn't use it on amateurs."

He answered reasonably: "I don't unless I have to. Only sometimes I get damn browned off, big slobs thinkin' they can push me around. I been pushed around plenty, I don't have to take it no more." He balanced himself on one foot and touched George's outflung arm with the tip of his big toe. "Maybe you better take him to a doctor."

"Maybe I better."

"I hit him pretty hard."

He showed me the knuckles of his right hand. They were swelling and turning blue. Otherwise, the fight had done him good. He was cheerful and relaxed, and he pranced a little when he moved, like a stallion. Featherhead was watching him from the window. She had on a linen dress now. She saw me looking at her, and moved back out of sight.

Leonard turned on the hose and ran cold water over George's head. George opened his eyes and tried to sit up. Leonard turned off the hose.

"He'll be all right. They don't come out of it that fast when they're bad hurt. Anyway, I hit him in self-defense, you're a witness to that. If there's any beef about it, you can take it up with Leroy Frost at Helio."

"Leroy Frost is your fixer, eh?"

He gave me a faintly anxious smile. "You know Leroy?"

"A little."

"Maybe we won't bother him about it, eh? Leroy, he's got a lot of troubles. How much you make in a day?"

"Fifty when I'm working."

"Okay, how's about I slip you fifty and you take care of the carcass?" He turned on all his neon charm. "Incidently, I should apologize. I kind of lost my head there for a minute, I shouldn't ought to of took the sucker punch on you. You can pay me back some time."

"Maybe I will, at that."

"Sure you will, and I'll let you. How's the breadbasket, cap?"

"Feels like a broken tennis racquet."

"But no hard feelings, eh?"

"No hard feelings."

"Swell, swell."

He offered me his hand. I set myself on my heels and hit him in the jaw. It wasn't the smartest thing in the world to do. My legs were middle-aging, and still wobbly. If I missed the nerve, he could run circles around me and cut me to ribbons with his left alone. But the connection was good.

I left him lying. The front door was unlocked, and I went in. The girl wasn't in the living-room or on the terrace. Her terrycloth towel was crumpled on the bedroom floor. A sun-hat woven of plaited straw lay on the floor beside it. The leather band inside the hat was stamped with the legend: "Handmade in Mexico for the Taos Shop."

A motor coughed and roared behind the wall. I found the side door which opened from the utility room into the garage. She was at the wheel of the Jaguar, looking at me with her mouth wide open. She locked the door on her side before I got hold of the handle. Then it was torn from my fist.

The Jaguar screeched in the turnaround, laying down black spoor, and leaped up the driveway to the road. I let it go. I couldn't leave George with Leonard.

They were sitting up in front of the house, exchanging dim looks of hatred across the flagstone walk. George was bleeding from the mouth. The flesh around one of his eyes was changing color. Leonard was unmarked, but I saw when he got to his feet that there was a change in him.

He had a hangdog air, a little furtive, as if I'd jarred him back into his past. He kept running his fingers over his nose and mouth.

"Don't worry," I said, "you're still gorgeous."

"Funny boy. You think it's funny? I kill you, it wasn't for this." He displayed his swollen right hand.

"You offered me a sucker punch, remember. Now we're even. Where did she go?"

"*You* can go to hell."

"What's her address?"

"Go to hell."

"You might as well give me her address. I got her license number. I can trace her."

"Go right ahead." He gave me a superior look, which probably meant that the Jaguar was his.

"What did she change her mind about? Why did she want out?"

"I can't read minds. I dunno nothin' about her. I service plenty of women, see? They ask me for it, I give 'em a bang sometimes. Does that mean I'm responsible?"

I reached for him. He backed away, his face sallow and pinched. "Keep your hands off of me. And drag your butt off of my property. I'm warning you, I got a loaded shotgun in the house."

He went as far as the door, and turned to watch us. George was on his hands and knees now. I got one of his arms draped over my shoulders and heaved him up to his feet. He walked like a man trying to balance himself on a spring mattress.

When I turned for a last look at the house, Leonard was on the doorstep, combing his hair.

Chapter 9

I DROVE down the long grade to Beverly Hills, slowly, because I was feeling accident-prone. There were days when you could put your finger on the point of stress and everything fell into rational patterns around you. And there were the other days.

George bothered me. He sat hunched over with his head in his hands, groaning from time to time. He had a fine instinct, even better than mine, for pushing his face in at the wrong door and getting it bloodied. He needed a keeper: I seemed to be elected.

I took him to my own doctor, a G.P. named Wolfson who had his office on Santa Monica Boulevard. Wolfson laid him out on a padded metal table in a cubicle, went over his face and skull with thick, deft fingers, flashed a small light in his eyes, and performed other rituals.

"How did it happen?"

"He fell down and hit his head on a flagstone walk."

"Who pushed him? You?"

"A mutual friend. We won't go into that. Is he all right?"

"Might be a slight concussion. You ever hurt your head before?"

"Playing football, I have," George said.

"Hurt it bad?"

"I suppose so. I've blacked out a couple of times."

"I don't like it," Wolfson said to me. "You ought to take him to the hospital. He should spend a couple of days in bed, at least."

"No!" George sat up, forcing the doctor backward. His eyes rolled heavily in their swollen sockets. "A couple of days is all I've got. I have to see her."

Wolfson raised his eyebrows. "See who?"

"His wife. She left him."

"So what? It happens every day. It happened to you. He's still got to go to bed."

George swung his legs off the table and stood up shakily. His face was the color of newly poured cement. "I refuse to go to the hospital."

269

"You're making a serious decision," Wolfson said coldly. He was a fat doctor who loved only medicine and music.

"I can put him to bed at my house. Will that do?"

Wolfson looked at me dubiously. "Could you keep him down?"

"I think so."

"Very well," George stated solemnly, "I accept the compromise."

Wolfson shrugged. "If that's the best we can do. I'll give him a shot to relax him, and I'll want to see him later."

"You know where I live," I said.

In a two-bedroom stucco cottage on a fifty-foot lot off Olympic. For a while the second bedroom hadn't been used. Then for a while it had been. When it was vacated finally, I sold the bed to a secondhand-furniture dealer and converted the room into a study. Which for some reason I hated to use.

I put George in my bed. My cleaning woman had been there that morning, and the sheets were fresh. Hanging his torn clothes on a chair, I asked myself what I thought I was doing and why. I looked across the hall at the door of the bedless bedroom where nobody slept any more. An onion taste of grief rose at the back of my throat. It seemed very important to me that George should get together with his wife and take her away from Los Angeles. And live happily ever after.

His head rolled on the pillow. He was part way out by now, under the influence of paraldehyde and Leonard's sedative fists:

"Listen to me, Archer. You're a good friend to me."

"Am I?"

"The only friend I have within two thousand miles. You've got to find her for me."

"I did find her. What good did it do?"

"I know, I shouldn't have come tearing down to the house like that. I frightened her. I always do the wrong thing. Christ, I wouldn't hurt a hair of her head. You've got to tell her that for me. Promise you will."

"All right. Now go to sleep."

But there was something else he had to say: "At least she's alive, isn't she?"

"If she's a corpse, she's a lively one."

"Who are these people she's mixed up with? Who was the little twerp in the pajamas?"

"Boy named Torres. He used to be a boxer, if that's any comfort to you."

"Is he the one who threatened her?"

"Apparently."

George raised himself on his elbows. "I've heard that name Torres. Hester used to have a friend named Gabrielle Torres."

"She told you about Gabrielle, did she?"

"Yes. She told me that night she—confessed her sins to me." His gaze moved dully around the room and settled in a corner, fixed on something invisible. His dry lips moved, trying to name the thing he saw:

"Her friend was shot and killed, in the spring of last year. Hester left California right after."

"Why would she do that?"

"I don't know. She seemed to blame herself for the other girl's death. And she was afraid of being called as a witness, if the case ever came to trial."

"It never did."

He was silent, his eyes on the thing in the empty corner.

"What else did she tell you, George?"

"About the men she'd slept with, from the time that she was hardly in her teens."

"That Hester had slept with?"

"Yes. It bothered me more than the other, even. I don't know what that makes me."

Human, I thought.

George closed his eyes. I turned the venetian blinds down and went into the other room to telephone. The call was to CHP headquarters, where a friend of mine named Mercero worked as a dispatcher. Fortunately he was on the daytime shift. No, he wasn't busy but he could be any minute, accidents always came in pairs and triples to foul him up. He'd try to give me a quick report on the Jaguar's license number.

I sat beside the telephone and lit a cigarette and tried to have a brilliant intuition, like all the detectives in books and some in real life. The only one that occurred to me was that the Jaguar belonged to Lance Leonard and would simply lead me around in a circle.

Cigarette smoke rumbling in my stomach reminded me that I was hungry. I went out to the kitchen and made myself a ham-and-cheese sandwich on rye and opened a bottle of beer. My cleaning woman had left a note on the kitchen table:

> Dear Mr. Archer, Arrived nine left twelve noon, I need the money for today will drive by and pick it up this aft, please leave $3.75 in mailbox if your out. Yours truly, Beatrice M. Jackson.
>
> P.S.—There is mouse dirt in the cooler, you buy a trap Ill set it out, mouse dirt is not sanitary.
>
> Yours truly, Beatrice M. Jackson.

I sealed four dollars in an envelope, wrote her name across the face, and took it out to the front porch. A pair of house wrens chitchatting under the eaves made several snide references to me. The mailbox was full of mail: four early bills, two requests for money from charitable organizations, a multigraphed letter from my Congressman which stated that he was alert to the threat, a brochure describing a book on the Secrets of Connubial Bliss marked down to $2.98 and sold only to doctors, clergymen, social-service workers, and other interested parties; and a New Year's card from a girl who had passed out on me at a pre-Christmas party. This was signed "Mona" and carried a lyric message:

> True friendship is a happy thing
> Which makes both men and angels sing.
> As the year begins, and another ends,
> Resolved: that we shall still be friends.

I sat down at the hall table with my beer and tried to draft an answer. It was hard. Mona passed out at parties because she had lost a husband in Korea and a small son at Children's Hospital. I began to remember that I had no son, either. A man got lonely in the stucco wilderness, pushing forty with no chick, no child. Mona was pretty enough, and bright enough, and all she wanted was another child. What was I waiting for? A well-heeled virgin with her name in the Blue Book?

I decided to call Mona. The telephone rang under my hand. "Mercero?" I said.

But it was Bassett's voice, breathy in my ear: "I tried to get you earlier."

"I've been here for the last half-hour."

"Does that mean you've found her, or given up?"

"Found her and lost her again." I explained how, to the accompaniment of oh's and ah's and tut-tut's from the other end of the line. "This hasn't been one of my days so far. My biggest mistake was taking Wall along."

"I hope he's not badly hurt?" There was a vein of malice in Bassett's solicitude.

"He's a hardhead, he'll survive."

"Why do you suppose she ran away from him this time?"

"Simple panic, maybe. Maybe not. There seems to be more to this than a lost-wife case. Gabrielle Torres keeps cropping up."

"It's odd you should mention her. I've been thinking about her off and on all morning—ever since you commented on her picture."

"So have I. There are three of them in the picture: Gabrielle and Hester and Lance. Gabrielle was murdered, the murderer hasn't been caught. The other two were very close to her. Lance was her cousin. Hester was her best friend."

"You're not suggesting that Lance, or Hester—?" His voice was hushed, but buzzing with implications.

"I'm only speculating. I don't think Hester killed her friend. I do think she knows something about the murder that nobody else knows."

"Did she say so?"

"Not to me. To her husband. It's all pretty vague. Except that nearly two years later she turns up in Coldwater Canyon. She's suddenly prosperous, and so is her little friend with the big fists."

"It does give one to think, doesn't it?" He tittered nervously. "What do *you* have in mind?"

"Blackmail is most obvious, and I never rule out the obvious. Lance spread the word that he's under contract at Helio-Graff, and it seems to be legit. The question is, how did he latch on to a contract with a big independent? He's a good-looking boy, but it takes more than that these days. You knew him when he was a lifeguard at the Club?"

"Naturally. Frankly, I wouldn't have hired him if his uncle hadn't been extremely persistent. We generally use college boys in the summer."

"Did he have acting ambitions?"

"Not to my knowledge. He was training to be a pugilist." Bassett's voice was contemptuous.

"He's an actor now. It could be he's an untutored genius—stranger things have happened—but I doubt it. On top of that, Hester claims to have a contract, too."

"With Helio-Graff?"

"I don't know. I intend to find out."

"You'll probably find it's with Helio-Graff." His voice had become sharper and more definite. "I've hesitated to tell you this, though it's what I called you about. In my position, one acquires the habit of silence. However, I was talking to a certain person this morning, and Hester's name came up. So did the name of Simon Graff. They were seen together in rather compromising circumstances."

"Where?"

"In a hotel in Santa Monica—the Windsor, I believe."

"It fits. She used to live there. When was this?"

"A few weeks ago. My informant saw them coming out of a room on one of the upper floors. At least, Mr. Graff came out. Hester only came as far as the door."

"Who is your informant?"

"I couldn't possibly tell you that, old man. It was one of our members."

"So is Simon Graff."

"Don't think I'm not aware of it. Mr. Graff is the most powerful single member of the Club."

"Aren't you sticking your neck out, telling me this?"

"Yes. I am. I hope my confidence in you—in your discretion—hasn't been misplaced."

"Relax. I'm a clam. But what about your switchboard?"

"I'm on the switchboard myself," he said.

"Is Graff still out there?"

"No. He left hours ago."

"Where can I find him?"

"I have no idea. He's having a party here tonight, but you mustn't approach him. You're not on any account to approach him."

"All right." But I made a mental reservation. "This secret informant of yours—it wouldn't be Mrs. Graff?"

"Of course not." His voice was fading. Either he was lying, or the decision to tell me about the Windsor Hotel episode had drained his energy. "You mustn't even consider such a thought."

"All right," I said, considering it.

I called the Highway Patrol number and got Mercero:

"Sorry, Lew, no can do. Three accidents since you called, and I've been hopping." He hung up on me.

It didn't matter. A pattern was forming in the case, like a motif in discordant, angry music. I had the slimmest of leads, a sun-hat from a shop in Santa Monica. I also had the queer tumescent feeling you get when something is going to break.

I looked in on George before I left the house. He was snoring. I shouldn't have left him.

Chapter 10

THE TAOS SHOP was a little tourist trap on the Coast Highway. It sold Navajo blankets and thunderbird necklaces and baskets and hats and pottery in an atmosphere of disordered artiness. A mouse blonde in a brown Indian blouse clicked her wampum at me languidly and asked me what I desired, a gift for my wife perhaps? I told her I was looking for another man's wife. She had romantic plum-colored eyes, and it seemed like the right approach. She said:

"How fascinating. Are you a detective?"

I said I was.

"How fascinating."

But when I told her about the hat, she shook her head regretfully. "I'm sorry. I'm sure it's one of ours, all right—we import them ourselves from Mexico. But we sell so many of them, I couldn't possibly—" She waved a willowy arm toward a tray piled with hats at the far end of the counter. "Perhaps if you described her?"

I described her. She shook her head dolefully. "I never could tell one Hollywood blonde from another."

"Neither could I."

"Ninety-nine and forty-four one-hundredths of them are blonde out of a bottle, anyway. I could be a blonde if I wanted to, just with a rinse now and then. Only I've got too much personal pride." She leaned toward me, and her wampum swung invitingly over the counter. "I'm sorry I can't help you."

"Thanks for trying. It was an off-chance anyway." I started out, and turned. "Her name is Hester Wall, by the way. That doesn't ring a bell?"

"Hester? I know of a Hester, but her last name isn't Wall. Her mother used to work here."

"What is her last name?"

"Campbell."

"She's the one. Campbell's her maiden name."

"Now, isn't that fascinating?" She smiled in dimpled glee, and her large eyes glowed. "The most exciting things happen to *people*, don't you think? I suppose you're looking for her about her inheritance?"

"Inheritance?"

"Yes. It's why Mrs. Campbell quit her job, on account of her daughter's inheritance. Don't tell me she's come into another fortune!"

"Who did she inherit the first one from?"

"Her husband, her late husband." She paused, and her soft mouth quivered. "It's sort of sad, when you realize, nobody inherits anything unless somebody else dies."

"That's true. And you say her husband died?"

"Yes. She married a wealthy husband in Canada, and he died."

"Is that what Hester told you?"

"No. Mrs. Campbell told me. I don't know Hester myself." Her face went blank suddenly. "I certainly hope it's not a false alarm. We were all so thrilled when Mrs. Campbell got the news. She's a dear, really, such a cute little duck for her age, and she used to have money, you know. Nobody begrudges her good fortune."

"When did she find out about it?"

"A couple of weeks ago. She only quit the beginning of this week. She's moving in with her daughter."

"Then she can tell me where her daughter is. If you'll tell me where *she* lives."

"I have her address someplace."

"Doesn't she have a phone?"

"No, she uses a neighbor's phone. Teeny Campbell's had hard sledding these last few years." She paused, and gave me a liquid look. "I'm not going to give you her address if it means trouble for her. Why are you looking for Hester?"

"One of her Canadian relatives wants to get in touch with her."

"One of her husband's relatives?"

"Yes."

"Cross your heart and hope to die."

"Cross my heart," I said. It felt like the kind of lie that would bring me bad luck. It was. "And hope to die."

Mrs. Campbell lived on a poor street of stucco and frame cottages half hidden by large, ancient oak trees. In their sun-flecked shadows, pre-school children played their killing games: Bang bang, you're dead; I'm not dead; you are so dead. A garbage truck on its rounds started a chorus of dogs barking in resentment at the theft of their masters' garbage.

Mrs. Campbell's cottage stood behind a flaked stucco wall in which a rusty gate stood permanently open. There was a new cardboard FOR SALE sign wired to the gate. In the courtyard, red geraniums had thrust up through a couple of stunted lime trees and converted them into red-flowering bushes which seemed to be burning in the sun. The thorned and brighter fire of a bougainvillæa vine surged up the front porch and the roof.

I stepped in under its cool shade and knocked on the screen door, which was tufted with cotton to ward off flies. A tiny barred window was set in the inner door. Its shutter snapped open, and an eye looked out at me. It was a blue eye, a little faded, surrounded with curled lashes and equipped with a voice like the sparrows' in the oak trees:

"Good morning, are you from Mr. Gregory?"

I mumbled something indistinguishable which might have been, yes, I was.

"Goodie, I've been expecting you." She unlocked the door and opened it wide. "Come in, Mr.—?"

"Archer," I said.

"I'm absotively delighted to see you, Mr. Archer."

She was a small, straight-bodied woman in a blue cotton dress too short and frilly for her age. This would be about fifty, though everything about her conspired to deny it. For an instant in the dim little box of a hallway, her bird voice and quick graces created the illusion that she was an adolescent blonde.

In the sunlit living-room, the illusion died. The dry cracks of experience showed around her eyes and mouth, and she couldn't smile them away. Her ash-blond boyish bob was fading into gray, and her neck was withering. I kind of liked her, though. She saw that. She wasn't stupid.

She ankled around the small living-room, lifting clean ashtrays and setting them down again. "Do have a chair, or would you prefer to stand up and look around? How nice of you to be interested in my little nest. Please notice the sea view, which is one of the little luxuries I have. Isn't it lovely?"

She posed her trim, small body, extended her arm toward the window and held it stiff and still, slightly bent up at the elbow, fingers apart. There was a view of the sea: a meager blue ribbon, tangled among the oak-tree branches.

"Very nice." But I was wondering what ghostly audience or dead daddy she was playing to. And how long she would go on taking me for a prospective buyer.

The room was crammed with dark old furniture made for a larger room, and for larger people: a carved refectory table flanked by high-backed Spanish chairs, an overstuffed red plush divan, thick red drapes on either side of the window. These made a cheerless contrast with the plaster walls and ceiling, which were dark green and mottled with stains from old leaks in the roof.

She caught me looking at the waterstains. "It won't happen again, I can guarantee you that. I had the roof repaired last fall, and, as a matter of fact, I've been saving up to redecorate this room. When all of a sudden my big move came up. I've had the most wondrous good luck, you know, or I should say my daughter has." She paused in a dramatic listening attitude, as if she were receiving a brief message in code on her back fillings. "But let me tell you over coffee. Poor man, you look quite peaked. I know what house-hunting is."

Her generosity disturbed me. I hated to accept anything from her under false pretenses. But before I could frame an answer she'd danced away through a swinging door to the kitchen. She came back with a breakfast tray on which a silver coffee set shone proudly, laid it on the table, and hovered over it. It was a pleasure to watch her pour. I complimented the coffeepot.

"Thank you very mooch, kind sir. It was one of my wedding presents, I've kept it all these years. I've held on to a lot of things, and now I'm glad I did, now that I'm moving back into the big house." She touched her lips with her fingertips and chuckled musically. "But of course you can't know what I'm talking about, unless Mr. Gregory told you."

"Mr. Gregory?"

"Mr. Gregory the realtor." She perched on the divan beside me, confidentially. "It's why I'm willing to sell without a cent of profit, as long as I get my equity out of this place. I'm moving out the first of the week, to go and live with my daughter. You see, my daughter is flying to Italy for a month or so, and she wants me to be in the big house, to look after it while she's gone. Which I'll be very happy to do, I can tell you."

"You're moving into a larger house?"

"Yes indeedy I am. I'm moving back into my own house, the one my girls were born in. You might not think it to look around you, unless you have an eye for good furniture, but I used to live in a grand big house in Beverly Hills." She nodded her head vigorously, as though I'd contradicted her. "I lost it— we lost it way back before the war when my husband left us. But now that clever daughter of mine has bought it back! And she's asked me to live with her!" She hugged her thin chest. "How she must love her little mother! Eh? Eh?"

"She certainly must," I said. "It sounds as if she's come into some money."

"Yes." She plucked at my sleeve. "I *told* her it would happen, if she kept faith and worked hard and made herself agreeable to people. I told the girls the very day we moved out that some-day we'd move back. And, sure enough, it's happened, Hester's come in to all this uranium money."

"She found uranium?"

"Mr. Wallingford did. He was a Canadian mining tycoon. Hester married an older man, just as I did in my time. Unfortunately the poor man died before they'd been married a year. I never met him."

"What was his name?"

"George Wallingford," she said. "Hester draws a substantial monthly income from the estate. And then she's got her movie money, too. Everything seems to have broken for her at once."

I watched her closely, but could see no sign that she was lying consciously.

"What does she do in the movies?"

"Many things," she said with a wavy flip of her hand. "She dances and swims and dives—she was a professional diver—and of course she acts. Her *father* was an actor, back in the good old days. You've heard of Raymond Campbell?"

I nodded. The name belonged to a swashbuckling silent-movie star who had tried to make the transition to the talkies and been tripped by advancing years and a tenor voice. I could remember a time in the early twenties when Campbell's serials filled the Long Beach movie houses on Saturday afternoons. Me they had filled with inspiration: his Inspector Fate of Limehouse series had helped to make me a cop, for good or ill. And when the cops went sour, the memory of Inspector Fate had helped to pull me out of the Long Beach force.

She said: "You do remember Raymond, don't you? Did you know him personally?"

"Just on the screen. It's been a long time. What ever happened to him?"

"He died," she said, "he died of a broken heart, way back in the depression. He hadn't had a picture for years, his friends turned against him, he was terribly in debt. And so he died." Her eyes became glazed with tears, but she smiled bravely through them like one of Raymond Campbell's leading ladies. "I carried on the faith, however. I was an actress myself, before I subordinated my life to Raymond's, and I brought up my girls to follow in his footsteps, just as he would have wished. One of them, at least, has made the most of it."

"What does your other daughter do?"

"Rina? She's a psychiatric nurse, can you imagine? It's always been a wonder to me that two girls so close in age and looks could differ so in temperament. Rina actually doesn't *have* any temperament. With all the artistic training I gave her, she grew up just as cold and hard and practical as they come. Why, I'd drop dead with shock if Rina ever offered me a home. No!" she cried melodramatically. "Rina would rather spend her time with crazy people. Why would a pretty girl do a thing like that?"

"Maybe she wants to help them."

Mrs. Campbell looked blank. "She could have found a more feminine way. Hester brings real joy to others without demeaning herself."

A funny look must have crossed my face. She regarded me shrewdly, then snapped her eyelids wide and turned on her brights. "But I mustn't bore you with my family affairs. You came to look at the house. It's got just the three rooms, but it's *most* convenient, especially the kitchen."

"Don't bother with that, Mrs. Campbell. I've been imposing on your hospitality."

"Why, no you haven't. Not at all."

"I have, though. I'm a detective."

"A detective?" Her tiny fingers clawed at my arm and took hold. She said in a new voice, a full octave lower than her bird tones: "Has something happened to Hester?"

"Not that I know of. I'm simply looking for her."

"Is she in trouble?"

"She may be."

"I knew it. I've been so afraid that something would go wrong. Things never work out for us. Something goes wrong, always." She touched her face with her fingertips: it was like crumpled paper. "I'm in a damned hole," she said hoarsely. "I gave up my job on the strength of this, and I owe half the people in town. If Hester falls down on me now, I don't know what I'll do." She dropped her hands, and raised her chin. "Well, let's have the bad news. Is it all a bunch of lies?"

"Is what a bunch of lies?"

"What I've been telling you, what she told me. About the movie contract and the trip to Italy and the rich husband who died. I had my doubts about it, you know—I'm not that much of a fool."

"Part of it may be true. Part of it isn't. Her husband isn't dead. He isn't old, and he isn't rich, and he wants her back. Which is where I come in."

"Is that all there is to it? No." Her eyes regarded me with hard suspicion. The shock had precipitated a second personality in her, and I wondered how much of the hardness belonged to her, and how much to hysteria. "You're holding out on me. You admitted she's in trouble."

"I said she may be. What makes you so sure?"

"You're a hard man to get information out of." She stood up in front of me, planting her fists on her insignificant hips and leaning forward like a bantam fighter. "Now don't try to give me the runaround, though God knows I'm used to it after thirty years in this town. Is she or isn't she in trouble?"

"I can't answer that, Mrs. Campbell. So far as I know, there's nothing against her. All I want to do is talk to her."

"On what subject?"

"The subject of going back to her husband."

"Why doesn't he talk to her himself?"

"He intends to. At the moment he's a little under the weather. And we've had a lot of trouble locating her."

"Who is he?"

"A young newspaperman from Toronto. Name's George Wall."

"George Wall," she said. "George Wallingford."

"Yes," I said, "it figures."

"What sort of a man is this George Wall?"

"I think he's a good one, or he will be when he grows up."

"Is he in love with her?"

"Very much. Maybe too much."

"And what you want from me is her address?"

"If you know it."

"I ought to know it. I lived there for nearly ten years. 14 Manor Crest Drive, Beverly Hills. But if that's all you wanted, why didn't you say so? You let me beat my gums and make a fool of myself. Why do that to me?"

"I'm sorry. It wasn't very nice. But this may be more than a runaway-wife case. You suggested yourself that Hester's in trouble."

"Trouble is what the word detective means to me."

"Has she been in trouble before?"

"We won't go into that."

"Have you been seeing much of her this winter?"

"Very little. I spent one weekend with her—the weekend before last."

"In the Beverly Hills house?"

"Yes. She'd just moved in, and she wanted my advice about redecorating some of the rooms. The people who had it before Hester didn't keep it up—not like the days when we had our Japanese couple." Her blue gaze strained across the decades, and returned to the present. "Anyway, we had a good time together, Hester and I. A wonderful weekend all by our lonesomes, chatting and tending to her clothes and pretending it was old times. And it ended up with Hester inviting me to move in the first of the year."

"That was nice of her."

"Wasn't it? I was so surprised and pleased. We hadn't been close at all for several years. I'd hardly seen her, as a matter of fact. And then, out of the blue, she asked me to come and live with her."

"Why do you think she did?"

The question seemed to appeal to her realistic side. She sat on the edge of her chair, in thinking position, her fingertips to her temple. "It's hard to say. Certainly not on account of my beautiful blue eyes. Of course, she's going to be away and she needs someone to stay in the house and look after it. I think she's been lonely, too."

"And frightened?"

"She didn't act frightened. Maybe she was. She wouldn't tell me if she was. My girls don't tell me anything." She inserted the knuckle of her right thumb between her teeth, and wrinkled her face like a baby monkey. "Will I still be able to move the first of the year? Do you think I will?"

"I wouldn't count on it."

"But the house must belong to her. She wouldn't spend all that money on redecorating. Mr. Archer—is that your name? Archer?—where is all the money coming from?"

"I have no idea," I said, though I had several.

Chapter 11

MANOR CREST DRIVE was one of those quiet palm-lined avenues which had been laid out just before the twenties went into their final convulsions. The houses weren't huge and fantastic like some of the rococo palaces in the surrounding hills, but they had pretensions. Some were baronial pseudo-Tudor with faked half-timbered façades. Others were imitation Mizener Spanish, thick-walled and narrow-windowed like stucco fortresses built to resist imaginary Moors. The street was good, but a little disappointed-looking, as though maybe the Moors had already been and gone.

Number 14 was one of the two-story Spanish fortresses. It sat well back from the street behind a Monterey cypress hedge. Water from a sprinkling system danced in the air above the hedge, rainbowed for an instant as I passed. A dusty gray Jaguar was parked in the driveway.

I left my car in front of one of the neighboring houses, walked back, and strolled down the driveway to the Jaguar. According to the white slip on the steering-post, it was registered to Lance Leonard.

I turned and surveyed the front of the house. Tiny gusts from the sprinkler wet my face. It was the only sign of life around. The black oak door was closed, the windows heavily draped. The pink tile roof pressed down on the house like a lid.

I mounted the stoop and pressed the bellpush and heard the electric buzzer sound deep inside the building. I thought I heard footsteps approaching the ironbound door. Then I thought I heard breathing. I knocked on the door and waited. The breathing on the other side of the door, if it was breathing, went away or ceased.

I knocked a few more times and waited some more, in vain. Walking back toward the driveway, I caught a movement from the corner of my eye. The drape in the end window twitched at the edge. When I looked directly at it, it had fallen back in place. I reached across a spiky pyracantha and tapped on the window, just for kicks. Kicks were all I got.

I returned to my car, U-turned at the next intersection, drove back past the pink-roofed house, and parked where I could watch its front in my rear-view mirror. The street was very quiet. Along both sides of it, the fronds of the palms hung in the air like static green explosions caught by a camera. In the middle distance, the tower of the Beverly Hills City Hall stood flat white against the flat blue sky. Nothing happened to mark the passage of time, except that the hands of my wristwatch bracketed two o'clock and moved on past.

About two ten, a car rolled into sight from the direction of the City Hall. It was an old black Lincoln, long and heavy as a hearse, with gray curtains over the rear windows completing the resemblance. A man in a black felt hat was at the wheel. He was doing about fifty in a twenty-five-mile zone. As he entered the block I was in, he started to slow down.

I reached for a yesterday's newspaper in the back seat and propped it up on the wheel to hide my face. Its headlines read like ancient history. The Lincoln seemed to take a long time to pass me. Then it did. Small-eyed, saddle-nosed, rubber-mouthed, its driver's face was unforgettable. Unforgettably ugly.

He turned into the driveway of Number 14, entering my rear-view mirror, and parked beside the Jaguar and got out. He moved quickly and softly, without swinging his arms. In a long charcoal-gray raglan topcoat, his slope-shouldered body looked like a torpedo sliding on its base.

The door opened before he knocked. I couldn't see who opened it. The door closed for a while, two or three long minutes, and then opened again.

Lance Leonard came out of the house. In a queer little hustling run, like a puppet jerked by wires, he descended the steps and crossed the lawn to the Jaguar, not noticing the sprinkler, though it wet his white silk open-necked shirt and spotted his light-beige slacks.

The Jaguar backed roaring into the street. As it raced past on squealing tires I caught a glimpse of Lance Leonard's face. His face was a blank, dead yellow. The nose and chin were drawn sharp. The eyes blazed black. They didn't see me.

The Jaguar plunged away into silence. I got out the .38 Special which I kept in the dash compartment and crossed the street. The Lincoln was registered to a Theodore Marfeld who lived at a Coast Highway address in South Malibu. Its black leather interior was shabby and smelled of cat. The back seat and floor were covered with sheets of heavy wrapping paper. The dashboard clock had stopped at eleven twenty.

I went to the door of the house and lifted my fist to knock and saw that the door was standing slightly ajar. I pushed it wider, stepped into a dim hall with a round Moorish ceiling. Ahead to my left a flight of red tile steps rose cumbrously through the ceiling. To the right, an inner door threw a bent fan of brightness across the floor and up the blank plaster side of the staircase.

A hatted shadow moved into the brightness and blotted most of it out. The head and shoulder of Saddlenose leaned from the doorway.

"Mr. Marfeld?" I said.

"Yeah. Who the hell are you? You got no right barging into a private residence. Get the hell out."

"I'd like to speak to Miss Campbell."

"What about? Who sent you?" he said mouthily.

"Her mother sent me, as a matter of fact. I'm a friend of the family. Are you a friend of the family?"

"Yeah. A friend of the family."

Marfeld raised his right hand to his face. His left hand was out of sight behind the door frame. I was holding the gun in my pocket with my finger on the trigger. Marfeld seemed puzzled. He took hold of the entire lower part of his face and pulled it sideways. There was a red smear on the ball of his thumb. It left a red thumbprint on the side of his indented nose.

"Cut yourself?"

He turned his hand around and looked at his thumb and closed his fist over it. "Yeah, I cut myself."

"I'm an expert at First Aid. If you're in pain, I have some monoacetic acid ester of salicylic acid in the car. I also have some five-per-cent tincture of iodine to offset the risk of blood-poisoning or other serious infection."

His right hand pushed the words away from his face. Neurosis cheeped surprisingly in his voice. "Shut up, God damn you, I can't stand doubletalk." He got himself under control and returned to his lower-register personality. "You heard me tell you to get out of here. What are you waiting for?"

"That's no way for a friend of the family to talk to another friend of the family."

He leaned round-shouldered out of the doorway, a metal rod glittering in his left hand. It was a brass poker. He shifted it to his right hand and lunged toward me, so close I could smell his breath. His breath was sour with trouble. "God-damn doublemouth."

I could have shot him through my pocket. Maybe I should have. The trouble was, I didn't know him well enough to shoot him. And I trusted the speed of my reflexes, forgetting Leonard's knockdown punch and the residue of languor in my legs.

Marfeld raised the poker. A dark drop flew from its hooked point and spattered the plaster wall like a splash of wet red paint. My eye stayed on it a millisecond too long. The poker seared and chilled the side of my head. It was a glancing blow, or I would have gone all the way out. As it was, the floor upended and rapped my knees and elbows and my forehead. The gun went skittering through a hole in the broken light.

I crawled up the steep floor toward it. Marfeld stamped at my fingers. I got my hands on one of his feet, my shoulder against his knee, and threw him over backward. He went down hard and lay whooping for breath.

I groped for the gun among jagged shards of light. The bright room beyond the doorway flashed on my angled vision with a hallucination's vividness. It was white and black and red. The blonde girl in the linen dress lay on a white rug in front of a raised black fireplace. Her face was turned away. An inkblot of red darkness spread around it.

Then there were footsteps behind me, and as I turned, the front end of the Sunset Limited hit the side of my head and knocked me off the rails into deep red darkness.

I came to, conscious of motion and a rumbling noise in my stomach which gradually detached itself from me and became the sound of a car engine. I was sitting propped up in the middle of the front seat. Shoulders were jammed against me on both sides. I opened my eyes and recognized the dashboard clock which had stopped at eleven twenty.

"People are dying to get in there," Marfeld said across me from the right.

My eyeballs moved grittily in their sockets. Marfeld had my gun on his knee. The driver, on my left, said:

"Brother, you kill me. You pull the same old gag out of the file every time you pass the place."

We were passing Forest Lawn. Its Elysian fields were distorted by moving curves, heat waves in the air or behind my eyes. I felt a craving nostalgia for peace. I thought how nice it would be to lie down in the beautiful cemetery and listen to organ music. Then I noticed the driver's hands on the wheel. They were large, dirty hands, with large, dirty fingernails, and they made me mad.

I reached for the gun on Marfeld's knee. Marfeld pulled it away like somebody taking candy from a baby. My reactions were so feeble and dull it scared me. He rapped my knuckles with the gun muzzle.

"How about that? The sleeper awakes."

My wooden tongue clacked around in my desiccated mouth and produced some words: "You jokers know the penalty for kidnapping?"

"Kidnapping?" The driver had a twisted little face which sprouted queerly out of a massive body. He gave me a corkscrew look. "I didn't hear of any kidnapping lately. You must of been dreaming."

"Yeah," Marfeld said. "Don't try to kid me, peeper. I was on the county cops for fifteen years. I know the law and what you can do and what you can't do. You can't go bulling into a private house with a deadly weapon. You was way out of line and I had a right to stop you. Christ, I could of killed you, they wouldn't even booked me."

"Count your blessings," the driver said. "You peepers, some of you, act like you think you can get away with murder."

"Somebody does."

Marfeld turned violently in the seat and pushed the gun muzzle into the side of my stomach. "What's that? Say that again. I didn't catch it."

My wits were still widely scattered around Los Angeles County. I had just enough of them with me to entertain a couple of ideas. They couldn't be sure, unless I told them, that I had seen the girl in the bright room. If she was dead and they knew I knew, I'd be well along on my way to a closed-coffin funeral.

"What was that about murder?"

Marfeld leaned hard on the gun. I tensed my stomach muscles against its pressure. The taste of the little seeds they put in rye bread rose in my throat. I concentrated on holding it down.

Marfeld got tired of prodding me after a while, and sat back with the gun on his knee. "Okay. You can do your talking to Mr. Frost."

He made it sound as if nothing worse could ever happen to me.

Chapter 12

L EROY FROST was not only head of Helio-Graff's private police force. He had other duties, both important and obscure. In certain areas, he could fix a drunk-driving or narcotics rap. He knew how to bring pressure to settle a divorce suit or a statutory-rape charge out of court. Barbiturate suicides changed, in his supple hands, to accidental overdoses. Having served for a time as deputy security chief of a Washington agency, he advised the editorial department on the purchase of scripts and the casting department on hiring and firing. I knew him slightly, about as well as I wanted to.

The studio occupied a country block surrounded by a high white concrete wall on the far side of San Fernando. Twisty-face parked the Lincoln in the semicircular drive. The white-columned colonial façade of the administration building grinned emptily into the sun. Marfeld got out and put my gun in his coat pocket and pointed the pocket at me.

"March."

I marched. Inside in the vestibule a blue-uniformed guard sat in a glass cage. A second uniformed guard came out of the white oak woodwork. He led us up a curved ramp, along a windowless corridor with a cork floor and a glass roof, past rows of bigger-than-life-size photographs: the heads that Graff and, before him, Heliopoulos had blown up huge on the movie screens of the world.

The guard unlocked a door with a polished brass sign: SECURITY. The room beyond was large and barely furnished with filing cabinets and typewriter desks, one of which was occupied by a man in earphones typing away like mad. We passed into an anteroom, with a single desk, unoccupied, and Marfeld disappeared through a further door which had Leroy Frost's name on it.

The guard stayed with me, his right hand near the gun on his hip. His face was heavy and blank and content to be heavy and blank. Its lower half stuck out like the butt end of a ham, in which his mouth was a small, meaningless slit. He stood with his chest pushed out and his stomach held in, wearing his unofficial uniform as though it was very important to him.

I sat on a straight chair against the wall and didn't try to make conversation. The dingy little room had the atmosphere of an unsuccessful dentist's waiting-room. Marfeld came out of Frost's office looking as if the dentist had told him he'd have to have all his teeth pulled. The uniform that walked like a man waved me in.

I'd never seen Leroy Frost's office. It was impressively large, at least the size of a non-producing director's on long-term contract. The furniture was heavy but heterogeneous, probably inherited from various other rooms at various times: leather chairs and a camel-backed English settee and a bulging rosewood Empire desk which was big enough for table tennis.

Frost sat behind the desk, holding a telephone receiver to his head. "Right now," he said into it. "I want you to contact her right now."

He laid the receiver in its cradle and looked up, but not at me. I had to be made to realize how unimportant I was. He leaned back in his swivel chair, unbuttoned his waistcoat, buttoned it up again. It had mother-of-pearl buttons. There were crossed cavalry sabers on the wall behind him, and the signed photographs of several politicians.

In spite of all this backing, and the word on the outer door, Frost looked insecure. The authority that thick brown eyebrows lent his face was false. Under them, his eyes were glum and yellowish. He had lost weight, and the skin below his eyes and jaw was loose and quilted like a half-sloughed snakeskin. His youthful crewcut only emphasized the fact that he was sick and prematurely aging.

"All right, Lashman," he said to the guard. "You can wait outside. Lew Archer and me, we're buddy-buddy from way back."

His tone was ironic, but he also meant that I had eaten lunch at Musso's with him once and made the mistake of letting him pick up the tab because he had been on an expense account and I hadn't. He didn't invite me to sit down. I sat down anyway, on the arm of one of the leather chairs.

"I don't like this, Frost."

"*You* don't like it. How do you think I feel? Here I thought we were buddy-buddy like I said, I thought there was a basis of mutual live-and-let-live there. My God, Lew, people got to be able to have faith and confidence in each other, or the whole fabric comes to pieces."

"You mean the dirty linen you're washing in public?"

"Now what kind of talk is that? I want you to take me seriously, Lew, it offends my sense of fitness when you don't. Not that *I* matter personally. I'm just another joe working my way through life—a little cog in a big machine." He lowered his eyes in humility. "A *very* big machine. Do you know what our investment is, in plant and contracts and unreleased film and all?"

He paused rhetorically. Through the window to my right, I could see hangarlike sound stages and a series of open sets: Brownstone Front, Midwestern Town, South Sea Village, and the Western Street where dozens of celluloid heroes had taken the death walk. The studio seemed to be shut down, and the sets were deserted, dream scenes abandoned by the minds that had dreamed them.

"Close to fifteen million," Frost said in the tone of a priest revealing a mystery. "A huge investment. And you know what its safety depends on?"

"Sun spots?"

"It isn't sun spots," he said gently. "The subject isn't funny, fifteen million dollars isn't funny. I'll tell you what it depends on. You know it, but I'll tell you anyway." His fingers formed a Gothic arch a few inches in front of his nose. "Number one is glamour, and number two is goodwill. The two things are interdependent and interrelated. Some people think the public will swallow anything since the war—any stinking crud—but I know different. I'm a student of the problem. They swallow just so much, and then we lose them. Especially these days, when the industry's under attack from all sides. We got to keep our glamour dry for the public. We got to hold on to our strategic goodwill. It's psychological warfare, Lew, and I'm on the firing line."

"So you send your troopers out to push citizens around. You want a testimonial from me?"

"You're not just any old ordinary citizen, Lew. You get around so fast and you make so many mistakes. You go bucketing up to Lance Leonard's house and invade his privacy and throw your weight around. I was on the phone to Lance just now. It wasn't smart what you did, and it wasn't ethical, and nobody's going to forget it."

"It wasn't smart," I admitted.

"But it was brilliant compared with the rest of it. Merciful God, Lew, I thought you had some feeling for situations. When we get to the payoff—you trying to force your way into the house of a lady who shall be nameless—" He spread his arms wide and dropped them, unable to span the extent of my infamy.

"What goes on in that house?" I said.

He munched the inside corner of his mouth, watching my face. "If you were smart, as smart as I used to think, you wouldn't ask that question. You'd let it lie. But you're so interested in facts, I'll tell you the one big fact. The less you know, the better for you. The more you know, the worse for you. You got a reputation for discretion. Use it."

"I thought I was."

"Uh-uh, you're not that stupid, kiddo. Nobody is. Your neck's out a mile, and you know it. You follow the thought, or do I have to spell it out in words of one syllable?"

"Spell it out."

He got up from behind the desk. His sick yellow glance avoided mine as he moved around me. He leaned on the back of my chair. His allusive little whisper was scented with some spicy odor from his hair or mouth:

"A nice fellow like you that percolates around where he isn't wanted—he could stop percolating period."

I stood up facing him. "I was waiting for that one, Frost. I wondered when we were getting down to threats."

"Call me Leroy. Hell, I wouldn't threaten you." He repudiated the thought with movements of his shoulders and hands. "I'm not a man of violence, you know that. Mr. Graff doesn't like violence, and I don't like it. That is, when I can prevent it. The trouble with a high-powered operation like this one, sometimes it runs over people by accident when they keep getting in the way. It's our business to make friends, see, and we got friends all over, Vegas, Chicago, all over. Some of them are kind of rough, and they might get an idea in their little pointed heads—you know how it is."

"No. I'm very slow on the uptake. Tell me more."

He smiled with his mouth; his eyes were dull yellow flint. "The point is, I like you, Lew. I get a kick out of knowing that you're in town, in good health and all. I wouldn't want your name to be bandied about on the long-distance telephone."

"It's happened before. I'm still walking around, and feeling pretty good."

"Let's keep it that way. I owe it to you to be frank, as one old friend to another. There's a certain gun that would blast you in a minute if he knew what you been up to. For his own reasons he'd do it, in his own good time. And it could be he knows now. That's a friendly warning."

"I've heard friendlier. Does he have a name?"

"You'd know it, but we won't go into that." Frost leaned forward across the back of the chair, his fingers digging deep into the leather. "Get wise to yourself, Lew. You trying to get yourself killed and drag us down with you, or what?"

"What's all the melodrama about? I was looking for a woman. I found her."

"You found her? You mean you saw her—you talked to her?"

"I didn't get to talk to her. Your goon stopped me at the door."

"So you didn't actually see her?"

"No," I lied.

"You know who she is?"

"I know her name. Hester Campbell."

"Who hired you to find her? Who's behind this?"

"I have a client."

"Come on now, don't go fifth-amendment on me. Who hired you, Lew?"

I didn't answer.

"Isobel Graff? Did she sick you onto the girl?"

"You're way off in left field."

"I used to play left field. Let me tell you something, just in case it's her. She's nothing but trouble—schizzy from way back. I could tell you things about Isobel you wouldn't believe."

"Try me."

"Is she the one?"

"I don't know the lady."

"Scout's honor?"

"Eagle Scout's honor."

"Then where's the trouble coming from? I got to know, Lew. It's my job to know. I got to protect the Man and the organization."

"What do you have to protect them against?" I said experimentally. "A murder rap?"

The experiment got results. Fear crossed Leroy Frost's face like a shadow chased by shadows. He said very mildly and reasonably: "Nobody said a word about murder, Lew. Why bring up imaginary trouble? We got enough real ones. The trouble I'm featuring just this minute is a Hollywood peeper name of Archer who is half smart and half stupid and who has been getting too big for his goddam breeches." While he spoke, his fear was changing to malice. "You going to answer my question, Lew? I asked you who's your principal and why."

"Sorry."

"You'll be sorrier."

He came around the chair and looked me up and down and across like a tailor measuring me for a suit of clothes. Then he turned his back on me, and flipped the switch on his intercom.

"Lashman! Come in here."

I looked at the door. Nothing happened. Frost spoke into the intercom again, on a rising note:

"Lashman! Marfeld!"

No answer. Frost looked at me, his yellow eyes dilating.

"I wouldn't slug a sick old man," I said.

He said something in a guttural voice which I didn't catch. Outside the window, like his echo vastly amplified, men began to shout. I caught some words:

"He's comin' your way." And further off: "I see him."

A pink-haired man in a dark suit ran under the window, chasing his frenzied shadow across the naked ground. It was George Wall. He was running poorly, floundering from side to side and almost falling. Close behind him, like a second bulkier shadow struggling to make contact with his heels, Marfeld ran. He had a gun in his hand.

Frost said: "What goes on?"

He cranked open the casement window and shouted the same question. Neither man heard him. They ran on in the dust, up Western Street, through the fake tranquillity of Midwestern

Town. George's legs were pumping weakly, and Marfeld was closing up the distance between them. Ahead of George, in South Sea Village, Lashman jumped into sight around the corner of a palm-thatched hut.

George saw him and tried to swerve. His legs gave under him. He got up, swaying in indecision as Lashman and Marfeld converged on him. Marfeld's shoulder took him in the side, and he went down again. Lashman dragged him up to his feet, and Marfeld's dark bulk blotted out his face.

Frost was leaning on the window sill, watching the distant figures. Marfeld's shoulder, leaning over George, moved in a jerky rhythm from side to side. I pushed Frost out of the way—he was light as straw—and went out through the window and across the lot.

Marfeld and Lashman were fascinated and oblivious. Marfeld was pistol-whipping George while Lashman held him up. Blood streaked his blind face and spotted his charcoal-gray suit. I noticed the irrelevant fact that the suit belonged to me: I'd last seen it hanging in my bedroom closet. I moved on them in ice-cold anger, got one hand on Marfeld's collar and the other on the slippery barrel of the gun. I heaved. The man and the gun came apart. The man went down backward. The gun stayed in my hand. It belonged to me, anyway. I reversed it and held it on Lashman:

"Turn him loose. Let him down easy."

The little, cruel mouth in his big jaw opened and closed. The fever left his eyes. He laid George out on the white imported sand. The boy was out, with the whites of his eyes glaring.

I took the revolver off Lashman's hip, stepped back and included Marfeld in the double line of fire. "What are you cookies up to, or you just do this for fun?"

Marfeld got to his feet, but he remained silent. Lashman answered the guns in my hands politely:

"The guy's a crackpot. He bust into Mr. Graff's office, threatened to kill him."

"Why would he do that?"

"It was something about his wife."

"Button it down," Marfeld growled. "You talk too much, Lashman."

There were muffled footsteps in the dust behind me. I circled

Marfeld and Lashman, and backed against the bamboo wall of a hut. Frost and the guard from the vestibule were crossing the lot toward us. This guard had a carbine on his arm. He stopped, and raised it into firing position.

"Drop it," I said. "Tell him to drop it, Frost."

"Drop it," he said to the guard.

The carbine thudded on the ground and sent up a little dust cloud. The situation was mine. I didn't want it.

"What goes on?" Frost said in a querulous tone. "Who is he?"

"Hester Campbell's husband. Kick him around some more if you really want bad publicity."

"Jesus Christ!"

"You better get him a doctor."

Nobody moved. Frost slid his hand up under his waistcoat and fingered his rib-cage to see if his heart had stopped. He said faintly:

"You brought him here?"

"You know better than that."

"The guy tried to kill Mr. Graff," Lashman said virtuously. "He was chasing Mr. Graff around the office."

"Is Graff all right?"

"Yeah, sure. I heard the guy yelling and run him out of there before he did any damage."

Frost turned to the guard who had dropped the carbine: "How did he get in?"

The man looked confused, then sullen. He broke his lips apart with difficulty:

"He had a press card. Said he had an appointment with Mr. Graff."

"You didn't clear it with me."

"You were busy, you said not to disturb—"

"Don't tell me what I said. Get out of here. You're finished here. Who hired you?"

"You did, Mr. Frost."

"I ought to be shot for that. Now get out of my sight." His voice was very mild. "Tell anybody about this, anybody at all, and you might as well leave town, it'll save you hospital bills."

The man's face had turned a grainy white, the color of rice pudding. He opened and closed his mouth several times without speaking, turned on his heel, and trudged toward the gate.

Frost looked down at the bloody man in the sand. He whined with pity, all of it for himself:

"What am I going to do with him?"

"Move your butt and get him an ambulance."

Frost turned his measuring look on me. Over it, he tried on a Santa Claus smile that didn't fit. A fluttering tic in one eyelid gave him the air of having a secret understanding with me:

"I talked a little rough back there in the office. Forget it, Lew. I like you. As a matter of fact, I like you very much."

"Get him an ambulance," I said, "or you'll be needing one for yourself."

"Sure, in a minute." He rolled his eyes toward the sky like a producer having an inspiration. "I been thinking for some time, long before this came up, we can use you in the organization, Lew. How would you like to go to Italy, all expenses paid? No real work, you'll have men under you. It'll be a free vacation."

I looked at his sick, intelligent face and the cruel, stupid faces of the two men beside him. They went with the unreal buildings which stood around like the cruel, sick pretense of a city.

"I wouldn't let you pay my way to Pismo Beach. Now turn around and walk, Frost. You too, Marfeld, Lashman. Stay close together. We're going to a telephone and call the Receiving Hospital. We've wasted enough time."

I had very little hope of getting out of there and taking George out with me. I merely had to try. What hope I had died a sudden death. Two men appeared ahead of us in Midwestern Town, running stooped over behind a clean white picket fence. One was the guard Frost had fired. Both of them had Thompson guns at the ready.

They saw me and ducked behind a deep front porch with an old-fashioned glider on it. Frost and his goons stopped walking. I said to Frost's back:

"You're going to have to handle this with care. You'll be the first one drilled. Tell them to come out into the middle of the street and put their tommyguns down."

Frost turned to face me, shaking his head. Out of the tail of my left eye, I saw a third man running and crouching toward me, hugging the walls of the South Sea huts. He had a riot gun. I felt like a major strike which was being broken. Frost made a mock-lugubrious face which fitted all his wrinkles.

"You'd never get out alive." He raised his voice. "Drop 'em, Lew. I'll count to three."

The man in the tail of my left eye was on his elbows and knees, crawling. He lay still and aimed as Frost began to count. I dropped the guns on the count of two. Marfeld and Lashman turned at the sound.

Frost nodded. "Now you're being smart."

Marfeld scooped up the guns. Lashman took a step forward. He had a black leather sap in his right hand. The man with the riot gun was on his feet now, trotting. The commandos behind the front porch came out from behind it, cautiously at first and then more quickly. The one Frost had fired had a silly, sickly grin on his face. He was ashamed of what he was doing, but couldn't stop doing it.

Away off on the other side of the lot, Simon Graff stood in a doorway and watched Lashman swing his sap.

Chapter 13

TIME BEGAN to tick again, in fits and starts. Pain glowed in my mind like lightning in a cloud, expanding and contracting with my heartbeat. I lay on my back on a hard surface. Somewhere above me, Lance Leonard said through flutter and wow:

"This is a neat layout Carlie's got himself here. I been out here plenty of times. He gives me the run of the place. I get the use of it any time he's away. It's swell for dames."

"Be quiet." It was Frost.

"I was just explaining." Leonard's voice was aggrieved. "I know this place like I know the back of my hand. Anything you want, any kind of booze or wine, I can get it for you."

"I don't drink."

"Neither do I. You on drugs?"

"Yah, I'm on drugs," Frost said bitterly. "Now shut it off. I'm trying to think."

Leonard subsided. I lay in the unblessed silence for a while. Sunlight was hot on my skin and red through my eyelids. When I raised my eyelids slightly, scalpels of light probed the inside of my head.

"His eyelids just fluttered," Leonard said.

"Better take a look at him."

Boots scraped concrete. I felt a toe in my side. Leonard squatted and pulled open one of my eyelids. I had turned up my eyes.

"He's still out."

"Throw some water on him. There's a hose on the other side of the pool."

I waited, and felt its stream gush into my face, hot from the sun, then lukewarm. I let a little of the water run into my dry mouth.

"Still out," Leonard said glumly. "What if he don't wake up? What do we do then?"

"That's your friend Stern's problem. He will, though. He's a hardhead, bone all the way through. I almost wish he wouldn't."

"Carlie ought to been here long ago. You think his plane crashed?"

"Yah, I think his plane crashed. Which makes you a goddam orphan." There was a rattlesnake buzz in Frost's voice.

"You're stringing me, ain't you? Aren't you?" Leonard was dismayed.

Frost failed to answer him. There was another silence. I kept my eyes shut, and sent a couple of messages down the red-lit avenues behind them. The first one took a long time getting there, but when it arrived it flexed the fingers of my right hand. I willed my toes to wiggle, and they wiggled. It was very encouraging.

A telephone rang behind a wall.

"I bet that's Carlie now," Leonard said brightly.

"Don't answer it. We'll sit here and guess who it is."

"You don't have to get sarcastic. Flake can answer it. He's in there watching television."

The telephone hadn't rung again. A sliding wall hissed in its grooves and bumped. Twistyface's voice said:

"It's Stern. He's in Victorville, wants to be picked up."

"Is he still on the line?" Leonard asked.

"Yeah, he wants to talk to you."

"Go and talk to him," Frost said. "Put him out of his misery."

Footsteps receded. I opened my eyes, looked up into glaring blue sky in which the declining sun hung like an inverted hot-plate. I raised my pulsating head, a little at a time. A winking oval pool was surrounded on three sides by a blue Fiberglas fence, on the fourth side by the glass wall of an adobe-colored desert house. Between me and the pool, Frost sat lax in a long aluminum chair under a blue patio umbrella. He was half-turned away from me, listening to a murmur of words from the house. An automatic hung from his limp right hand.

I sat up slowly, leaning my weight on my arms. My vision had a tendency to blur. I focused on Frost's neck. It looked like a scrawny plucked rooster's, easy to wring. I gathered my legs under me. They were hard to control, and one shoe scraped the concrete.

Frost heard the little sound it made. His eyes swiveled toward me. His gun came up. I crawled toward him anyway, dripping reddish water. He scrambled out of the long chair and backed toward the house.

"Flake! Come out here."

Twistyface appeared in the opening of the wall. I wasn't thinking well, and my movements were sluggish. I got up, made a staggering lunge for Frost, and fell short, onto my knees. He aimed a kick at my head, which I was too slow to avoid. The sky broke up in lights. Something else hit me, and the sky turned black.

I swung in black space, supported by some kind of sky hook above the bright scene. I could look down and see everything very clearly. Frost and Leonard and Twistyface stood over a prostrate man, palavering in doubletalk. At least, it sounded like doubletalk to me. I was occupied with deep thoughts of my own. They flashed on my mind like brilliant lantern slides: Hollywood started as a meaningless dream, invented for money. But its colors ran, out through the holes in people's heads, spread across the landscape and solidified. North and south along the coast, east across the desert, across the continent. Now we were stuck with the dream without a meaning. It had become the nightmare that we lived in. Deep thoughts.

I realized with some embarrassment that the body on the deck belonged to me. I climbed air down to it and crawled back in, a rat who lived in a scarecrow. It was familiar, even cozy, except for the leaks. But something had happened to me. I was hallucinating a little bit, and self-pity opened up in front of me like a blue, inviting pool where a man could drown. I dove in. I swam to the other side, though. There were barracuda in the pool, hungry for my manhood. I climbed out.

Came to my senses and saw I hadn't moved. Frost and Leonard had gone away. Twistyface sat in the aluminum chair and watched me sit up. He was naked to the waist. Black fur made tufted patterns on his torso. He had breasts like a female gorilla. The inevitable gun was in his paw.

"That's better," he said. "I don't know about you, but ole Flake feels like going in and watching some TV. It's hotter than the hinges out here."

It was like walking on stilts, but I made it inside, across a large, low room, into a smaller room. This was paneled in dark wood and dominated by the great blind eye of a television set. Flake pointed with his gun at the leather armchair beside it.

"You sit there. Get me a Western movie."

"What if I can't?"

"There's always a Western movie at this time of day."

He was right. I sat for what seemed a long time and listened to the clop-clop and bang-bang. Flake sat close up in front of the screen, fascinated by simple virtue conquering simple evil with fists and guns and rustic philosophy. The old plot repeated itself like a moron's recurrent wish-fulfillment dream. The pitchman in the intervals worked hard to build up new little mechanical wishes. Colonel Risko says buy Bloaties, they're yum-yum delicious, yum-yum nutritious. Get your super-secret badge of membership. You'll ell-oh-vee-ee Bloaties.

I flexed my arms and legs from time to time and tried to generate willpower. There was a brass lamp on top of the television set. It had a thick base, and looked heavy enough to be used as a weapon. If I could find the will to use it, and if Flake would forget his gun for two consecutive seconds.

The movie ended in a chaste embrace which brought tears to Flake's eyes. Or else his eyes were watering from eyestrain. The gun sagged between his spread knees. I rose and got hold of the lamp. It wasn't as heavy as it looked. I hit him on the head with it anyway.

Flake merely looked surprised. He fired in reflex. The pitchman on the television screen exploded in the middle of a deathless sentence. In a hail of glass I kicked at the gun in Flake's hand. It hopped through the air, struck the wall, and went off again. Flake lowered his little dented head and charged me.

I sidestepped. His wild fist cracked a panel in the wall. Before he recovered his balance, I got a half-nelson on him and then a full nelson.

He was a hard man to bend. I bent him, and rapped his head on the edge of the television box. He lunged sideways, dragging me across the room. I retained my hold, clenched hands at the back of his neck. I rapped his head on the steel corner of an air-conditioning unit set in the window. He went soft, and I dropped him.

I got down on my knees and found the gun and had a hard time getting up again. I was weak and trembling. Flake was worse off, snoring through a broken nose.

I found my way to the kitchen and had a drink of water and went outside. It was already evening. There were no cars in the carport, just a flat-tired English bicycle and a motor scooter that wouldn't start. Not for me it wouldn't. I thought of waiting there for Frost and Leonard and Stern, but all I could think of to do with them was shoot them. I was sick and tired of violence. One more piece of violence and they could reserve my room at Camarillo, in one of the back wards. Or such was my opinion at the time.

I started down the dusty private road. It descended a low rise toward the bed of a dry stream in the middle of a wide, flat valley. There were mountain ranges on two sides of the valley, high in the south and medium high in the west. On the slopes of the southern range, drifts of snow gleamed impossibly white between the deep-blue forests. The western range was jagged black against a sky where the last light was breaking up into all its colors.

I walked toward the western range. Pasadena was on the other side of it. On my side of it, in the middle of the valley, tiny cars raced along a straight road. One of them turned toward me, its headlights swinging up and down on the bumps. I lay down in the sage beside the road.

It was Leonard's Jaguar, and he was driving it. I caught a glimpse of the face in the seat beside him: a pale, flat oval like a dish on which flat eyes were painted, a pointed chin resting on a spotted bow tie. I'd seen that old-young face before, in the papers after Siegel died, on television during the Kefauver hearings, once or twice at nightclub tables flanked by bodyguards. Carl Stern.

I stayed off the road, cutting at an angle across the high desert toward the highway. The air was turning chilly. In the darkness rising from the earth and spreading across the sky, the evening star hung alone. I was a bit lightheaded, and from time to time I thought that the star was something I had lost, a woman or an ideal or a dream.

Self-pity stalked me, snuffing at my spoor. He was invisible, but I could smell him, a catty smell. Once or twice he fawned on the backs of my legs, and once I kicked at him. The joshua trees waved their arms at me and tittered.

Chapter 14

THE FOURTH car I thumbed stopped for me. It was a cut-down jalopy with a pair of skis strapped to the top, driven by a college boy on his way back to Westwood. I told him I'd turned my car over on a back road. He was young enough to accept my story without too many questions, and decent enough to let me go to sleep in the back seat.

He took me to the ambulance entrance of St. John's Hospital. A resident surgeon put some stitches in my scalp, gave me quiet hell, and told me to go to bed for a couple of days. I took a taxi home. Traffic was sparse and rapid on the boulevard. I sat back in the seat and watched the lights go by, flashing like thrown knives. There were nights when I hated the city.

My house looked shabby and small. I turned on all the lights. George Wall's dark suit lay like a crumpled man on the bedroom floor. To hell with him, I thought, and repeated the thought aloud. I took a bath and turned off all the lights and went to bed.

It didn't do any good. A nightmare world sprang up around the room, a world of changing faces which wouldn't hold still. Hester's face was there, refracted through George Wall's mind. It changed and died and came alive and died again smiling, staring with loveless eyes out of the red darkness. I thrashed around for a while and gave up. Got up and dressed and went out to my garage.

It hit me then, and not until then, that I was minus a car. If the Beverly Hills cops hadn't hauled it away, my car was parked on Manor Crest Drive, across the street from Hester's house. I called another taxi and asked to be let off on a corner half a block from the house. My car was where I had left it, with a parking ticket under the windshield-wiper.

I crossed the street for a closer look at the house. There was no car in the drive, no light behind the windows. I climbed the front steps and leaned on the bellpush. Inside, the electric bell chirred like a cricket on an abandoned hearth. The nobody-home sound, the empty-house girl-gone one-note blues.

I tried the door. It was locked. I glanced up and down the street. Lights shone at the intersections and from the quiet houses. The people were all inside. They had given up night walks back in the cold war.

Call me trouble looking for a place to happen. I went around to the side of the house, through a creaking wooden gate into a walled patio. The flagstone paving was uneven under my feet. Crab grass grew rank in the spaces between the stones. I made my way among wrought-iron tables and disemboweled chaises to a pair of French doors set into the wall.

My flashlight beam fell through dirty glass into a lanai full of obscene shadows. They were cast by rubber plants and cacti growing in earthenware pots. I reversed the light and used its butt to punch out one of the panes, drew back a reluctant bolt, and forced the door open.

The house was mostly front, like the buildings on Graff's sets. Its rear had been given over to ghosts and spiders. Spiders had rigged the lanai's bamboo furniture and black oak rafters with loops and hammocks and wheels of dusty webbing. I felt like an archæologist breaking into a tomb.

The door at the end of the lanai was unlocked. I passed through a storeroom full of once-expensive junk: high, unsittable Spanish chairs, a grand piano with grinning yellow keys, brownish oil paintings framed in gilt: through another door, into the central hallway of the house. I crossed to the door of the living-room.

White walls and a half-beamed ceiling rose in front of me, supported by the upward beam from my light. I lowered it to the floor, which was covered with ivory carpeting. White and black sectional furniture, low-slung and cubistic, was grouped in angular patterns around the room. The fireplace was faced with black tile and flanked by a square white leather hassock. On the other side of the fireplace, a faint dark patch showed in the carpet.

I got down on my knees and examined it. It was a wet spot the size of a large dinner plate, of no particular color. Through the odor of detergent, and under the other odors in the room, perfume and cigarette smoke and sweet mixed drinks, I could smell blood. The odor of blood was persistent, no matter how you scrubbed.

Still on my knees, I turned my attention to the raised fireplace. It was equipped with a set of brass fire tools in a rack:

brush, shovel, a pair of leather bellows with brass handles. The set was new, and looked as if it had never been used or even touched. Except that the poker was missing.

Beyond the fireplace there was a doorless arch which probably opened into the dining-room. Most of the houses of this style and period had similar floor plans, and I had been in a lot of them. I moved to the arch, intending to go over the rest of the downstairs, then the upstairs.

A motor droned in the street. Light washed the draped front windows and swept past. I went to the end window and looked out through the narrow space between the drape and the window frame. The old black Lincoln was standing in the driveway. Marfeld was at the wheel, his face grotesquely shadowed by the reflection of the headlights. He switched them off and climbed out.

Leroy Frost got out on the far side. I knew him by his hurrying feeble walk. The two men passed within three or four feet of me, headed for the front door. Frost was carrying a glinting metal rod which he used as a walking-stick.

I went through the archway into the next room. In its center a polished table reflected the wan light filtered through lace-curtained double windows. A tall buffet stood against the wall inside the arch, a chair in the corner behind it. I sat down in the deep shadow, with my flashlight in one hand and my gun in the other.

I heard a key turn in the front door, then Leroy Frost's voice, jerking with strain:

"I'll take the key. What happened to the other key?"

"Lance give it to the pig."

"That was a sloppy way to handle it."

"It was your idea, chief. You told me not to talk to her myself."

"All right, as long as she got it." Frost mumbled something indistinguishable. I heard him shuffling in the entrance to the living-room. Suddenly he exploded: "Where is the goddam light? You been in and out of this house, you expect me to grope around in the dark all night?"

The lights went on in the living-room. Footsteps crossed it. Frost said:

"You didn't do a very good job on the rug."

"I did the best I could in the time. Nobody's gonna go over it with a fine-tooth comb, anyway."

"You hope. You better bring that hassock over here, cover it up until it dries. We don't want her to see it."

Marfeld grunted with effort. I heard the hassock being dragged across the carpet.

"Fine," Frost said. "Now wipe my prints off the poker and put it where it belongs."

There was the sound of metal coming in contact with metal.

"You sure you got it clean, chief?"

"Don't be a birdbrain, it isn't the same poker. I found a match for it in the prop warehouse."

"I be damned, you think of everything." Marfeld's voice was moist with admiration. "Where did you ditch the other one?"

"Where nobody's going to find it. Not even you."

"Me? What would I want with it?"

"Skip it."

"Hell, don't you *trust* me, chief?"

"I trust nobody. I barely trust myself. Now let's get out of here."

"What about the pig? Don't we wait for her?"

"No, she won't be here for a while. And the less she sees of us, the better. Lance told her what she's supposed to do, and we don't want her asking us questions."

"I guess you're right."

"I don't need you to tell me I'm right. I know more about heading off blackmail than any other two men in this town. Bear it in mind in case you develop any ideas."

"I don't get it, chief. What kind of ideas you mean?" Marfeld's voice was full of injured innocence.

"Ideas of retiring, maybe, with a nice fat pension."

"No, sir. Not me, Mr. Frost."

"I guess you know better, at that. You try to put the bite on me or any friend of mine—it's the quickest way to get a hole in the head to go with the hole in the head you already got."

"I know that, Mr. Frost. Christ amighty, I'm *loyal*. Didn't I prove it to you?"

"Maybe. Are you sure you saw what you said you saw?"

"When was that, chief?"

"This afternoon. Here."

"Christ, yes." Marfeld's plodding mind caught the implication and was stung by it. "Christ, Mr. Frost, I wouldn't lie to you."

"You would if you did it yourself. That would be quite a trick, to do a murder and con the organization into covering for you."

"Aw now, chief, you wouldn't accuse me. Why would I kill anybody?"

"For kicks. You'd do it for kicks, any time you thought you could get away with it. Or to make yourself into a hero, if you had a few more brains."

Marfeld whined adenoidally: "Make myself into a hero?"

"Yah, Marfeld to the rescue, saving the company's cookies for it again. It's kind of a coincidence that you been in on both killings, Johnny-on-the-spot. Or don't you think so?"

"That's crazy, chief, honest to God." Marfeld's voice throbbed with sincerity. It ran down, and began on a new note: "I been loyal all my life, first to the sheriff and then to you. I never asked for anything for myself."

"Except a cash bonus now and then, eh?" Frost laughed. Now that Marfeld was jittery, too, Frost was willing to forgive him. His laughter rustled like a Santa Ana searching among dry leaves. "Okay, you'll get your bonus, if I can get it past the comptroller."

"Thank you, chief. I mean it very sincerely."

"Sure you do."

The light went out. The front door closed behind them. I waited until the Lincoln was out of hearing, and went upstairs. The front bedroom was the only room in use. It had quilted pink walls and a silk-canopied bed, like something out of a girl's adolescent dream. The contents of the dressing-table and closet told me that the girl had been spending a lot of money on clothes and cosmetics, and hadn't taken any of it with her.

Chapter 15

I LEFT the house the way I had entered, and drove up into the Canyon. A few sparse stars peered between the streamers of cloud drifting along the ridge. Houselights on the slopes islanded the darkness through which the road ran white under my headlight beam. Rounding a high curve, I could see the glow of the beach cities far below to my left, phosphorescence washed up on the shore.

Lance Leonard's house was dark. I parked on the gravel shoulder a hundred yards short of the entrance to his driveway. Its steep grade was slippery with fog. The front door was locked, and nobody answered my knock.

I tried the garage door. It opened easily when I lifted the handle. The Jaguar had returned to the fold, and the motorcycle was standing in its place. I moved between them to the side entrance. This door wasn't locked.

The concentric ovals of light from my flash slid ahead of me across the floor of the utility room, the checkerboard linoleum in the kitchen, the polished oak in the living-room, up along the glass walls on which the gray night pressed heavily, around and over the fieldstone-faced fireplace, where a smoking log was disintegrating into talc-like ash and dull-red flakes of fire. The mantel held a rack of pipes and a tobacco jar, an Atmos clock which showed that it was three minutes to eleven, a silver-framed glamour shot of Lance Leonard smiling with all his tomcat charm.

Lance himself was just inside the front door. He wore a plaid evening jacket and midnight-blue trousers and dull-blue dancing-pumps, but he wasn't going anywhere. He lay on his back with his toes pointing at opposite corners of the ceiling. One asphalt eye looked into the light, unblinking. The other had been broken by a bullet.

I put on gloves and got down on my knees and saw the second bullet wound in the left temple. It was bloodless. The hair around it was singed, the skin peppered with powder marks. I covered the floor on my hands and knees. Pushing aside one of the stiff legs, I found a used copper shellcase, medium caliber.

Apparently it had rebounded from the wall or from the murderer's clothes and rolled across the floor where Leonard fell on it.

It took me a long time to find the second shell. I opened the front door, finally, and saw it glinting in the crack between the lintel and the concrete stoop. I squatted in the doorway with my back to the dead man and tried to reconstruct his murder. It looked simple enough. Someone had knocked on the door, waited with a gun for Lance to open it, shot him in the eye, shot him again after he fell to make certain, and gone away, closing the door behind him. The door had a self-locking mechanism.

I left the shells where they were, and shook down the rest of the house. The living-room was almost as impersonal as a hotel room. Even the pipes on the mantel had been bought by the set, and only one of them had ever been smoked. The tobacco in the jar was bone dry. There was nothing but tobacco in the jar, nothing but wood in the woodbox. The portable bar in one corner was well stocked with bottles, most of which were unopened.

I went into the bedroom. The blond oak chests of drawers were stuffed with loot from the Miracle Mile haberdasheries: stacks of shirts custom-made out of English broadcloth and wool gabardine and Madras, hand-painted ties, Argyle socks, silk scarves, a rainbow of cashmere sweaters. A handkerchief drawer contained gold cufflinks and monogrammed tie-bars; a gold identification bracelet engraved with the name Lance Leonard; a tarnished medal awarded to Manuel Torres (it said on the back) for the Intermediate Track and Field Championships, Serena Junior High School, 1945; five expensive wrist-watches and a stopwatch. The boy had been running against time.

I looked into the closet. A wooden shoe-rack held a dozen pairs of shoes to go with the dozen suits and jackets hanging above them. A double-barreled shotgun stood in a corner beside a two-foot pile of comic books and crime magazines. I leafed through some of the top ones: Fear, Lust, Horror, Murder, Passion.

On the shelves at the head of the bed there were some other books of a different kind. A morocco-bound catechism inscribed in a woman's hand: "Manuel Purificación Torres, 1943." An old life of Jack Dempsey, read to pieces, whose flyleaf bore the legend: "Manny 'Terrible' Torres, 1734 West Nopal Street, Los Angeles, California, The United States, The Western Hemisfear, the World, The Universe." A manual of spoken English whose first few pages were heavily underscored in pencil. The name on the flyleaf of this one was Lance Leonard.

The fourth and final book was a stamped-leather album of clippings. The newspaper picture on the first page showed a boyish Lance leaning wide-shouldered and wasp-waisted into the camera. The caption stated that Manny Torres was being trained by his Uncle Tony, veteran club-fighter, and experts conceded him an excellent chance of capturing the lightweight division of the Golden Gloves. There was no follow-up to this. The second entry was a short account of Lance Torres' professional debut; he had knocked out another welterweight in two minutes of the second round. And so on for twenty fights, through six-rounders up to twelve. None of the clippings mentioned his arrest and suspension.

I replaced the album on the shelf and went back to the dead man. His breast pocket contained an alligator billfold thick with money, a matching address book filled with girls' names and telephone numbers scattered from National City to Ojai. Two of the names were Hester Campbell and Rina Campbell. I wrote down their Los Angeles telephone numbers.

There was a gold cigarette case full of reefers in the side pocket of his dinner jacket. In the same pocket, I found an engraved invitation in an envelope addressed to Lance Leonard, Esq., at the Coldwater Canyon address. Mr. and Mrs. Simon Graff requested his presence at a Roman Saturnalia to be held at the Channel Club tonight.

I put everything back and stood up to leave, turned at the door for a final look at the boy. He lay exhausted by his incredible leap from nowhere into the sun. His face was old-ivory in the flashlight beam. I switched it off and let the darkness take him.

"Lance Manuel Purificación Torres Leonard," I said out loud by way of epitaph.

Outside, a wisp of cloud dampened my face like cold and meager tears. I climbed on heavy legs to my car. Before I started the motor, I heard another motor whining up the grade from the direction of Ventura Boulevard. Headlights climbed the hanging cloud. I left my own lights off.

The headlights swerved around the final curve, projected by a dark sedan with a massive chrome cowcatcher. Without hesitating, they entered Leonard's driveway and lit up the front of his house. A man got out of the driver's seat and waded through the flowing light to the front door. He wore a dark raincoat belted tight at the waist, and he stepped lightly, with precision. All I could see of his head was the short, dark crewcut that surmounted it.

Having knocked and got no answer, he pulled out a flashing keyring and opened the door. The lights came on in the house. A minute later, half muffled by its redwood walls, a man's voice rose in a scream which sounded like a crow cawing. The lights went out again. The cawing continued for some time in the dark interior of the house.

There was an interval of silence before the door was opened. The man stepped out into the glare of his own headlights. He was Carl Stern. In spite of the crewcut and the neat bow tie, his face resembled an old woman's who had been bereaved.

He turned his sedan rather erratically and passed my car without appearing to notice it. I had to start and turn my car, but I caught him before he reached the foot of the hill. He went through boulevard stops as if he had a motorcycle escort. So did I. I had him.

Then we were on Manor Crest Drive, and I was completing the circuit of the roller-coaster. There was a difference, though. Hester's house was lighted upstairs and down. On the second floor, a woman's shadow moved across a blind. She moved like a young woman, with an eager rhythm.

Stern left his sedan in the driveway with the motor running, knocked and was admitted, came out again before I'd decided what to do. He got in and drove away. I didn't follow him. It was beginning to look as though Hester was home again.

Chapter 16

I WENT in by the broken lanai door and through to the front. Feet were busy on the floor over my head. I heard quick, clacking heels and a girl's tuneless humming. I climbed the stairs, leaning part of my weight on the banister. At the end of the upstairs hallway, light spilled from the doorway of the front bedroom. I moved along the wall to a point from which I could see into the room.

The girl was standing by the canopied bed with her back to me. She was very simply dressed in a tweed skirt and a short-sleeved white blouse. Her bright hair was brushed slick around the curve of her skull. A white leather suitcase with a blue silk lining lay open on the bed. She was folding some kind of black dress into it, tenderly.

She straightened and went to the far side of the room, her hips swinging from a flexible small waist. She opened the mirrored door of a closet and entered its lighted interior. When she came out, with more clothes in her arms, I was in the room.

Her body went stiff. The bright-colored dresses fell to the floor. She stepped backward against the mirrored door, which closed with a snap.

"Hello, Hester. I thought you were dead."

Her teeth showed, and she pressed her knuckles against them. She said behind the knuckles: "Who are you?"

"The name is Archer. Don't you remember me from this morning?"

"Are you the detective—the one that Lance had a fight with?"

I nodded.

"What do you want with me?"

"A little talk."

"You get out of here." She glanced at the ivory telephone on the bedside table, and said uncertainly: "I'll call the police."

"I doubt that very much."

She took her hand away from her mouth and laid it against her side below the swell of her breast, as though she felt a pain there. Anger and anxiety wrenched at her face, but she was one of those girls who couldn't look ugly. There was a sculptured

315

beauty built into her bones, and she held herself with a sense that her beauty would look after her.

"I warn you," she said, "some friends of mine are coming here, any minute now."

"Fine. I'd like to meet them."

"You think so?"

"I think so."

"Stick around if you like, then," she said. "Do you mind if I go on with my packing?"

"Go right ahead, Hester. You are Hester Campbell, aren't you?"

She didn't answer me or look at me. She picked up the fallen dresses, carried the rustling sheaf to the bed, and began to pack.

"Where are you going at this time of night?" I said.

"It's no concern of yours."

"Cops might be interested."

"Might they? Go and tell them, why don't you? Do anything you like."

"That's kind of reckless talk for a girl on the lam."

"I'm not on the lam, as you put it, and you don't frighten me."

"You're just going away for a weekend in the country."

"Why not?"

"I heard you tell Lance this morning that you wanted out."

She didn't react to the name as I'd half suspected she would. Her deft hands went on folding the last of the dresses. I liked her courage, and distrusted it. There could be a gun in the suitcase. But when she finally turned she was empty-handed.

"Wanted out of what?" I said.

"I don't know what you're talking about, and I couldn't care less." But she cared.

"These friends of yours who are coming here—is Lance Leonard one of them?"

"Yes, and you better get out before he does come."

"You're sure he's coming?"

"You'll see."

"It ought to be something to see. Who's going to carry the basket?"

"The basket?" she said in a high little voice.

"Lance isn't getting around much any more. They have to carry him in a basket."

Her hand went to her side again. The pain had risen higher. Her body moved angrily, hips and shoulders, trying to pass through the narrow space between the bed and me. I blocked her way.

"When did you see him last?"

"Tonight."

"What time tonight?"

"I don't know. Several hours ago. Does it matter?"

"It matters to you. How was he when you left him?"

"He was fine. Why, has something happened to him?"

"You tell me, Hester. You leave a trail of destruction like Sherman marching through Georgia."

"What happened? Is he hurt?"

"Badly hurt."

"Where is he?"

"At home. He'll soon be in the morgue."

"He's dying?"

"He's dead. Didn't Carl Stern tell you?"

She shook her head. It was more of a convulsion than a denial. "Lance couldn't be dead. You're crazy."

"Sometimes I think I'm the only one who isn't."

She sat down on the edge of the bed. A row of tiny droplets stood along her peaked hairline. She brushed at them with her hand, and her right breast rose with the movement of her arm. She looked up at me, her eyes sleepy with shock. She was a very good actress, if she was acting.

I didn't think she was. "Your good friend is dead," I said. "Somebody shot him."

"You're lying."

"Maybe I should have brought along the body. Shall I tell you where he took the slugs? One in the temple, one in the eye. Or do you know all this? I don't want to bore you to death."

Her forehead crinkled. Her mouth stretched in the tragic rectangle.

"You're horrible. You're making all this up, trying to make me tell you things. You said the same thing about—about me—that I was dead." Tears started in her eyes. "You'd say anything to make me talk."

"What kind of things could you tell me if you did?"

"I don't have to answer your questions, any of them."

"Give it a little thought, and you might want to. It looks as though they're using you for a patsy."

She gave me a bewildered look.

"You're kind of naïve, aren't you, in view of the company you keep? Nice company. They're setting you up for a murder rap. They saw a chance to kill two birds with one stone, to knock off Lance and fix you at the same time."

I was playing by ear, but it was a familiar tune to me, and she was listening hard. She said in a hushed voice:

"Who would do such a thing?"

"Whoever talked you into taking a trip."

"Nobody talked me into it. I wanted to."

"Whose idea was it? Leroy Frost's?"

Her gaze flickered and dimmed.

"What did Frost tell you to do? Where did he tell you to go?"

"It wasn't Mr. Frost. It was Lance who contacted me. So what you say can't be true. He wouldn't plan his own murder."

"Not if he knew what the plan was. Obviously he didn't. They conned him into it the same way they conned you."

"Nobody conned me," she said stubbornly. "Why would anybody try to con me?"

"Come off it, Hester, you're no ingenue. You know better than I do what you've been doing."

"I haven't done anything wrong."

"People have different standards, don't they? Some of us think that blackmail is the dirtiest game in the world."

"Blackmail?"

"Look around you, and stop pretending. Don't tell me Graff's been giving you things because he likes the way you do your hair. I've seen a lot of blackmail in this town, it's got so I can smell it on people. And you're in it up to your neck."

She fingered her neck. Her resistance to suggestion was wearing thin. She looked around at the pink walls and slowly turned their color. It was an authentic girlish blush, the first I had seen for some time, and it made me doubtful. She said:

"You're inventing all this."

"I have to. You won't tell me anything. I go by what I see and hear. A girl leaves her husband, takes up with a washed-up fighter who runs with mobsters. In no time at all, you're in the chips. Lance has a movie contract, you have your nice big house in Beverly Hills. And Simon Graff turns out to be your fairy godfather. Why?"

She didn't answer. She looked down at her hands twisting in her lap.

"What have you been selling him?" I said. "And what has Gabrielle Torres got to do with it?"

The color had drained out of her face, leaving it wan, blue-shadowed around the eyes. Her gaze turned inward on an image in her mind. The image seemed to appall her.

"I think you know who killed her," I said. "If you do, you'd better tell me. It's time to break these things out into the open, before more people are killed. Because you'll be next, Hester."

Her lips flew open like a dummy's controlled by a ventriloquist: "I'm not—" Her will took over, biting the sentence off.

She shook her head fiercely, dislodging tears from her eyes. She covered her streaked face with her hands and flung herself sideways on the bed. Fear ran through her, silent and rigorous as an electric current, shaking her entire body. Something that felt like pity rose from the center of mine. The trouble with pity was that it always changed to something else—repulsion or desire. She lay still now, one hip arching up in a desolate slope.

"Are you going to tell me about Gabrielle?"

"I don't know anything to tell you." Her voice was small and muffled.

"Do you know who shot Lance?"

"No. Leave me alone."

"What did Carl Stern say to you?"

"Nothing. We had a date. He wanted to postpone it, that's all."

"What kind of a date?"

"It's none of your business."

"Is he going to take you for a ride?"

"Perhaps." She seemed to miss the implication.

"A one-way ride?"

This time she caught it, and sat up almost screaming: "Get away from me, you sadist. I know your kind. I've seen police detectives, and the way they torment helpless people. If you're a man at all, you'll get out of here."

Her torso was twisted sideways, her breasts sharp under the white blouse. Her red lips curled, and her eyes sparked blue. She was an extraordinarily good-looking girl, but there was more to her than that. She sounded like a straight one.

I caught myself doubting my premises, doubting that she could be any kind of hustler. Besides, there was just enough truth in her accusation, enough cruelty in my will to justice, enough desire in my pity, to make the room uncomfortable for me. I said good-night and left it.

The problem was to love people, try to serve them, without wanting anything from them. I was a long way from solving that one.

Chapter 17

THERE WAS no guard on duty when I got to the Channel Club. The gate was open, though, and the party was still going on. Music and light spilled from one wing of the building. Several dozen cars stood in the parking-lot. I left mine between a black Porsche and a lavender Cadillac convertible with wine-colored leather upholstery and gold trim; and went in under the inverted red Christmas tree. It seemed to be symbolic of something, but I couldn't figure out what.

I knocked on Bassett's office door and got no answer. The pool was a slab of green brilliance, lit from below by underwater floodlights and spotlit from above. People were gathered at the far end under the aluminum-painted diving tower. I went down a shallow flight of steps and along the tiled edge toward the people.

Most of them were Hollywood fillies, sleek and self-conscious in strapless evening gowns or bathing suits not intended for the water. Among the men, I recognized Simon Graff and Sammy Swift and the Negro lifeguard I had talked to in the morning. Their faces were turned up toward a girl who stood absolutely still on the ten-meter platform.

She ran and took off into the light-crossed air. Her body bowed and turned in a smooth flip-and-a-half, changed from a bird to a fish as it entered the water. The spectators applauded. One of them, an agile youth in a dinner jacket and his middle forties, took a flashbulb picture as she came dripping up the ladder. She shook the water out of her short black hair contemptuously, and retired to a corner to dry herself. I followed her.

"Nice dive."

"You think so?" She turned up her taut brown face and I saw that she wasn't a girl and hadn't been for years. "I wouldn't give myself a score of three. My timing was way off. I can do it with a twist when I'm in shape. But thank you anyway."

She toweled one long brown leg, and then the other, with a kind of impersonal affection, like somebody grooming a racehorse.

"You dive competitively?"

"I did at one time. Why?"

"I was just wondering what makes a woman do it. That tower's high."

"A person has to be good at something, and I'm not pretty." Her smile was thin and agonized. "Dr. Frey—he's a psychiatrist friend of mine—says the tower is a phallic symbol. Anyway, you know what the swimmers say—a diver is a swimmer with her brains knocked out."

"I thought a diver was a swimmer with guts."

"That's what the *divers* say. Do you know many divers?"

"No, but I'd like to. Would Hester Campbell be a friend of yours?"

Her face became inert. "I know Hester," she said cautiously. "I wouldn't call her a friend."

"Why not?"

"It's a long story, and I'm cold." She turned brusquely and trotted away toward the dressing-room. Her hips didn't bounce.

"Quiet, everyone," a loud voice said. "You are about to witness the wonder of the century, brought to you at fabulous expense."

It came from a gray-haired man on the five-meter platform of the tower. His legs were scrawny, his chest pendulous, his belly a brown leather ball distending his shorts. I looked again and saw it was Simon Graff.

"Ladies and gentlemen." Graff shaded his eyes with a hand and looked around facetiously. "Are there any ladies present? Any gentlemen?"

The women tittered. The men guffawed. Sammy Swift, who was standing near me, looked more than ever like a ghost who had seen a goblin.

"Watch it, boys and girls," Graff shouted in a high, unnatural voice. "The Great Graffissimo, in his unique and death-defying leap."

He took a flat-footed little run and launched himself with his arms at his sides in what boys used to call a dead-soldier dive. His people waited until he came to the surface and then began to applaud, clapping and whistling.

Sammy Swift noticed my silence and moved toward me. He didn't recognize me until I called him by name. I could have set fire to his breath.

"Lew Archer, by damn. What are you doing in this *galère?*"

"Slumming."

"Yah, I bet. Speaking of slumming, did you get to see Lance Leonard?"

"No. My friend got sick and we gave up on the interview."

"Too bad, the boy's had quite a career. He'd make a story."

"Fill me in."

"Uh-uh." He wagged his head. "You tell your friend to take it up with Publicity. There's an official version and an unofficial version, I hear."

"What do you hear in detail?"

"I didn't know you did leg work for newspapers, Lew. What's the pitch, you trying to get something on Leonard?"

His fogged eyes had cleared and narrowed. He wasn't as drunk as I'd thought, and the subject was touchy. I backed away from it:

"Just trying to give a friend a lift."

"You looking for Leonard now? I haven't seen him here tonight."

Graff raised his voice again:

"*Achtung*, everyone. Time for lifesaving practice." His eyes were empty and his mouth was slack. He stepped toward the twittering line of girls and pointed at one who was wearing a silver gown. His forefinger dented her shoulder. "You! What is your name?"

"Martha Matthews." She smiled in an agony of delight. The lightning was striking her.

"You're a cute little girl, Martha."

"Thank you." She towered over him. "Thank you very much, Mr. Graff."

"Would you like me to save your life, Martha?"

"I'd simply adore it."

"Go ahead, then. Jump in."

"But what about my dress?"

"You can take it off, Martha."

Her smile became slightly dazed. "I can?"

"I just said so."

She pulled the dress off over her head and handed it to one of the other girls. Graff pushed her backward into the pool. The agile photographer took a shot of the action. Graff went in after her and towed her to the ladder, his veined hand clutching her flesh. She smiled and smiled. The lifeguard watched them with no expression at all on his black face.

I felt like slugging somebody. There wasn't anybody big enough around. I walked away, and Sammy Swift tagged along. At the shallow end of the pool, we leaned against a raised planter lush with begonia, and lit cigarettes. Sammy's face was thin and pale in the half-light.

"You know Simon Graff pretty well," I stated.

His light eyes flickered. "You got to know him well to feel the way I do about him. I been making a worm's-eye study of the Man for just about five years. What I don't know about him isn't worth knowing. What I do know about him isn't worth knowing, either. It's interesting, though. You know why he pulls this lifesaving stunt, for instance? He does it every party, just like clockwork, but I bet I'm the only one around who's got it figured out. I bet Sime doesn't even know, himself."

"Tell me."

Sammy assumed an air of wisdom. He said in the jargon of the parlor analyst:

"Sime's got a compulsion neurosis, he has to do it. He's fixated on this girl that got herself killed last year."

"What girl would that be?" I said, trying to keep the excitement out of my voice.

"The girl they found on the beach with the bullets in her. It happened just below here." He gestured toward the ocean, which lay invisible beyond the margin of the light. "Sime was stuck on her."

"Interesting if true."

"Hell, you can take my word for it. I was with Sime that morning when he got the news. He's got a ticker in his office— he always wants to be the first to know—and when he saw her name on the tape he turned as white as a sheet, to coin a simile. Shut himself up in his private bathroom and didn't come out for an hour. When he finally did come out, he passed it off as a hangover. Hangover is the word. He hasn't been the same since the girl died. What was her name?" He tried to snap his fingers, unsuccessfully. "Gabrielle something."

"I seem to remember something about the case. Wasn't she a little young for him?"

"Hell, he's at the age when they really go for the young ones. Not that Sime's so old. It's only the last year his hair turned gray, and it was the girl's death that did it to him."

"You're sure about this?"

"Sure, I'm sure. I saw them together a couple of times that spring, and I got X-ray eyes, boy, it's one thing being a writer does for you."

"Where did you see them?"

"Around, and once in Vegas. They were lying beside the pool of one of the big hotels, smoking the same cigarette." He looked down at the glowing butt of his own cigarette, and threw it spinning into the water. "Maybe I shouldn't be telling tales out of school, but you won't quote me, and it's all in the past, anyway. Except that he keeps going through these crazy lifesaving motions. He's re-enacting her death, see, trying to save her from it. Only please note that he does it in a heated pool."

"This is your own idea, no doubt."

"Yeah, but it makes sense," he said with some fanaticism. "I been watching him for years, like you watch the flies on the wall, and I *know* him. I can read him like a book."

"Who wrote the book? Freud?"

Sammy didn't seem to hear me. His gaze had roved to the far end of the pool, where Graff was posing for more pictures with some of the girls. I wondered why picture people never got tired of having their pictures taken. Sammy said:

"Call me Œdipus if you want to. I really hate that bastard."

"What did he do to you?"

"It's what he does to Flaubert. I'm writing the Carthage script, version number six, and Sime Graff keeps breathing down my neck." His voice changed; he mimicked Graff's accent: "Matho's our juvenile lead, we can't let him die on us. We got to keep him alive for the girl, that's basic. I got it. I got it. She nurses him back to health after he gets chopped up, how about that? We lose nothing by the gimmick, and we gain heart, the quality of heart. Salammbô rehabilitates him, see? The boy was kind of a revolutionary type before, but he is saved from himself by the influence of a good woman. He cleans up on the barbarians for her. The girl watches from the fifty-yard line. They clinch. They marry." Sammy resumed his own voice: "You ever read *Salammbô*?"

"A long time ago, in translation. I don't remember the story."

"Then you wouldn't see what I'm talking about. *Salammbô* is a tragedy, its theme is dissolution. So Sime Graff tells me to tack a happy ending onto it. And I write it that way. Jesus," he said in a tone of surprise, "this is the way I've written it. What makes me do it to myself and Flaubert? I used to worship Flaubert."

"Money?" I said.

"Yeah. Money. Money." He repeated the word several times, with varying inflections. He seemed to be finding new shades of meaning in it, subtle drunken personal meanings which brought the tears into his voice. But he was too chancy and brittle to hold the emotion. He slapped himself across the eyes, and giggled. "Well, no use crying over spilled blood. How about a drink, Lew? How about a drink of Danziger Goldwasser, in fact?"

"In a minute. Do you know a girl called Hester Campbell?"

"I've seen her around."

"Lately?"

"No, not lately."

"What's her relation to Graff, do you know?"

"No, I wouldn't know," he answered sharply. The subject disturbed him, and he took refuge in clowning: "Nobody tells me anything, I'm just an intellectual errand boy around here. An ineffectual intellectual errand boy. Song." He began to sing in a muffled tenor to an improvised tune: "He's so reprehensible yet so indispensable he makes things comprehensible he's my joy. That intellectual—ineffectual—but oh so sexual—intellectual errand boy. Whom nothing can alloy. . . . Dig that elegant whom."

"I dug it."

"It's the hallmark of genius, boy. Did I ever tell you I was a genius? I had an I.Q. of 183 when I was in high school in Galena, Illinois." His forehead crinkled. "What ever happened to me? Wha' happen? I used to like people, by damn, I used to have talent. I didn't know what it was worth. I came out here for the kicks, going along with the gag—seven fifty a week for playing word games. Then it turns out that it isn't a gag. It's for keeps, it's your life, the only one you've got. And Sime Graff has got you by the short hairs and you're not inner-directed any more. You're not yourself."

"Who are you, Sam?"

"That's my problem." He laughed, and almost choked. "I had a vision of myself last week, I could see it as plain as a picture. Dirty word, picture, but let it pass. I was a rabbit running across a desert. Rear view." He laughed and coughed again. "A goddam white-tailed bunny rabbit going lickety-split across the great American desert."

"Who was chasing you?"

"I don't know," he said with a lopsided grin. "I was afraid to look."

Chapter 18

GRAFF CAME strutting toward us along the poolside, trailed by his twittering harem and their eunuchs. I wasn't ready to talk to him, and turned my back until he'd passed. Sammy was yawning with hostility.

"I really need a drink," he said. "My eyes are focusing. How's about joining me in the bar?"

"Later, maybe."

"See you. Don't quote me on anything."

I promised that I wouldn't, and Sammy went away toward the lights and the music. At the moment the pool was deserted except for the Negro lifeguard, who was moving around under the diving tower. He trotted in my direction with a double armful of soiled towels, took them into a lighted room at the end of the row of *cabañas*.

I went over and tapped on the open door. The lifeguard turned from a canvas bin where he had dumped the towels. He had on gray sweat-clothes with CHANNEL CLUB stenciled across the chest.

"Can I get you something, sir?"

"No, thanks. How are the tropical fish?"

He gave me a quick grin of recognition. "No tropical-fish trouble tonight. People trouble is all. There's always people trouble. Why they want to go swimming on a night like this! I guess it's the drinking they do. The way they pour it down is a revelation."

"Speaking of pouring it down, your boss is pretty good at it."

"Mr. Bassett? Yeah, he's been drinking like a fish lately, ever since his mother died. A tropical fish. Mr. Bassett was very devoted to his mother." The black face was smooth and bland, but the eyes were sardonic. "He told me she was the only woman he ever loved."

"Good for him. Do you know where Bassett is now?"

"Circulating." He stirred the air with his finger. "He circulates around at all the parties. You want me to find him for you?"

"Not just now, thanks. You know Tony Torres?"

"Know him well. We worked together for years."

"And his daughter?"

"Some," he said guardedly. "She worked here, too."

"Would Tony still be around? He isn't on the gate."

"No, he goes off at night, party or no party. His fill-in didn't show up tonight. Maybe Mr. Bassett forgot to call him."

"Where does Tony live, do you know?"

"I ought to. He lives under your feet, practically. He's got a place next to the boiler room, he moved in there last year. He used to get so cold at night, he told me."

"Show me, will you?"

He didn't move, except to look at his wristwatch. "It's half past one. You wouldn't want to wake him up in the middle of the night."

"Yes," I said. "I would."

He shrugged and took me along a corridor filled with a soapy shower-room odor, down a flight of concrete steps into hot-house air, through a drying-room where bathing suits hung like sloughed snakeskins on wooden racks, between the two great boilers which heated the pool and the buildings. Behind them, a room-within-a-room had been built out of two-by-fours and plywood.

"Tony lives here because he wants to," the lifeguard said rather defensively. "He won't live in his house on the beach any more, he rents it out. I wish you wouldn't wake him up. Tony's an old man, he needs his rest."

But Tony was already awake. His bare feet slithered on the floor. Light came on, blazing through all the cracks in the ply-wood walls and framing the door. Tony opened it and blinked at us, a big-bellied little old man in long underwear with a reli-gious locket hanging around his neck.

"Sorry to get you out of bed. I'd like to talk to you."

"What about? What's the trouble?" He scratched at his tousled, graying hair.

"No trouble." Just two murders in his family, one of which I wasn't supposed to know about. "May I come in?"

"Sure thing. Matter 'fact, I been thinking I'd like to talk to you."

He pushed the door wide and stepped back with a gesture that was almost courtly. "You comin' in, Joe?"

"I got to get back upstairs," the lifeguard said.

I thanked him and went in. The room was hot and small, lit by a naked bulb on an extension cord. I'd never seen a monk's cell, but the room could probably have served as one. A blistered oak-veneer bureau, an iron cot, a kitchen chair, a doorless cardboard wardrobe containing a blue serge suit, a horsehide windbreaker, and a clean uniform. Faded blue flannelette sheets covered the cot, and an old brass-fitted suitcase protruded from underneath it. Two pictures shared the wall above the head of the bed. One was a hand-tinted studio photograph of a pretty dark-eyed girl in a white dress that looked like a high-school graduation dress. The other was a Virgin in four colors, holding a blazing heart in her extended hand.

Tony indicated the kitchen chair for me, and sat on the bed himself. Scratching his head again, he looked down at the floor, his eyes impassive as anthracite. The big knuckles of his right hand were jammed and swollen.

"Yeah, I been thinkin'," he repeated. "All day and half of the night. You're a detective, Mr. Bassett says."

"A private one."

"Yeah, private. That's for me. These county cops, who can trust 'em? They run around in their fancy automobiles and arrest people for no-taillight or throw-a-beer-can-in-the-highway-ditch. Something real bad happens, they ain't there."

"They're usually there, Tony."

"Maybe. I seen some funny things in my time. Like what happened last year, right in my own family." His head turned slowly to the left, under intangible but irresistible pressure, until he was looking at the girl in the white dress. "I guess you heard about Gabrielle, my daughter."

"Yes. I heard."

"Shot on the beach, I found her. March twenty-first, last year. She was gone all night supposed to be with a girl friend. I found her in the morning, eighteen years old, my only daughter."

"I'm sorry."

His black glance probed my face, gauging the depth of my sympathy. His wide mouth was wrenched by the pain of truth-telling: "I ain't no bleeding heart. It was my fault, I seen it coming. How could I bring her up myself? A girl without a mother? A pretty young girl?" His gaze rotated in a quarter-circle again, and returned to me. "What could I tell her what to do?"

"What happened to your wife, Tony?"

"My wife?" The question surprised him. He had to think for a minute. "She run out on me, many years now. Run away with a man, last I heard she's in Seattle, she's always crazy for men. My Gabrielle took after her, I think. I went to Catholic Welfare, ask them what I should do, my girl is running out of control like a loco mare in heat—I didden say that to the Father, not them words.

"The Father says, put her in a convent school, but it was too much money. Too much money to save my daughter's life. All right, I saved the money, I got the money in the bank, nobody to spend it for." He turned and said to the Virgin: "I am a dirty old fool."

"You can't live their life for them, Tony."

"No. What I could do, I coulda kept her locked up with good people looking after her. I coulda kept Manuel out of my house."

"Did he have something to do with her death?"

"Manuel is in jail when it happens. But he was the one started her running wild. I didden catch on for a long time, he taught her to lie to me. It was high-school basketball, or swimming team, or spend-the-night-with-a-friend. Alla time she was riding around on the back of motycycles from Oxnard, learning to be a dirty—" His mouth clamped down on an unspoken word.

After a pause, he went on more calmly: "That girl I seen with Manuel on the Venice Speedway in the low-top car. Hester Campbell. She's the one Gabrielle's supposed to spend the night with, the night that she got killed. Then you come here this morning asking about Manuel. It started me thinking, about who done it to her. Manuel and the blondie girl, why do they get together, can you tell me?"

"Later on I may be able to. Tell me, Tony, is thinking all you've been doing?"

"Huh?"

"Did you leave the Club today or tonight? Did you see your nephew Manuel?"

"No. No to both questions."

"How many guns do you have?"

"Just the one."

"What caliber?"

"Forty-five Colt revolver." His mind was one-track and too preoccupied to catch the inference. "Here."

He reached behind the mashed pillow and handed me his revolver. Its chambers were full, and it showed no signs of having been fired recently. In any case, the shells I had found beside his nephew's body were medium-caliber, probably thirty-two's.

I hefted the Colt. "Nice gun."

"Yeah. It belongs to the Club. I got a permit to carry it."

I gave it back to him. He pointed it at the floor, sighting along the barrel. He spoke in a very old voice, dry, sexless, dreadful:

"If I ever know who killed her, this is what he gets. I don't wait for crooked cops to do my business." He leaned forward and tapped my arm with the barrel, very lightly: "You're a detective, mister, find me who killed my girl, you can have all I got. Money in the bank, over a thousand dollars, I *save* my money these days. Piece of rented property onna beach, mortgage all paid off."

"Keep it that way. And put the gun away, Tony."

"I was a gunner's mate in the World War Number One. I know how to handle guns."

"Prove it. Too many people would get a boot out of it if I got myself drilled in a shooting accident."

He slipped the revolver under the pillow and stood up. "It's too late, huh? Nearly two years, a long time. You are not interested in wild-duck cases, you got other business."

"I'm very much interested. In fact, this is why I wanted to talk to you."

"It's what you call a coincidence, eh?" He was proud of the word.

"I don't believe much in coincidences. If you trace them back far enough, they usually have a meaning. I'm pretty sure this one has."

"You mean," he said slowly, "Gabrielle and Manuel and Manuel's blondie?"

"And you, and other things. They all fit in together."

"Other things?"

"We won't go into them now. What did the cops tell you last March?"

"No evidence, they said. They poked around here a few days and closed down the case. They said some robber, but I dunno. What robber shoots a girl for seventy-five cents?"

"Was she raped?"

Something like dust gathered on the surface of his anthracite eyes. The muscles stood out in his face like walnuts of various sizes in a leather bag, altering its shape. I caught a glimpse of the gamecock passion that had held him up for six rounds against Armstrong in the old age of his legs.

"No rape," he said with difficulty. "Doctor at the autopsy says a man was with her some time in the night. I don't wanna talk about it. Here."

He stooped and dragged the suitcase out from under the bed, flung it open, rummaged under a tangle of shirts. Stood up breathing audibly with a dog-eared magazine in his hand.

"Here," he said violently. "Read it."

It was a lurid-covered true-crime book which fell open to an article near the middle entitled "The Murder of the Violated Virgin." This was an account of the murder of Gabrielle Torres, illustrated with photographs of her and her father, one of which was a smudgy reproduction of the photograph on the wall. Tony was shown in conversation with a sheriff's plainclothesman identified in the caption as Deputy Theodore Marfeld. Marfeld had aged since March of the previous year. The account began:

It was a balmy Spring night at Malibu Beach, gay playground of the movie capital. But the warm tropical wind that whipped the waves shoreward seemed somehow threatening to Tony Torres, onetime lightweight boxer and now watchman at the exclusive Channel Club. He was not easily upset after many years in the squared circle, but tonight Tony was desperately worried about his gay young teen-aged daughter, Gabrielle.

What could be keeping her? Tony asked himself again and again. She had promised to be in by midnight at the latest. Now it was three o'clock in the morning, now it was four o'clock, and still no Gabrielle. Tony's inexpensive alarm clock ticked remorselessly on. The waves that thundered on the beach below his modest seaside cottage seemed to echo in his ears like the very voice of doom itself. . . .

I lost patience with the clichés and the excess verbiage, which indicated that the writer had nothing much to say. He hadn't. The rest of the story, which I scanned in a hurry, leered a great deal under a veil of pseudo-poetic prose, on the strength of a few facts:

Gabrielle had a bad reputation. There had been men in her life, unnamed. Her body had been found to contain male seed and two bullets. The first bullet had inflicted a superficial wound in her thigh. This had bled considerably. The implication was that several minutes at least had elapsed between the firing of the first bullet and the firing of the second. The second had entered her back, found its way through the ribs, and stopped her heart.

Both slugs were twenty-two long, and had been fired from the same long-barreled revolver, location unknown. That is what the police ballistics experts said. Theodore Marfeld said—the quotation ended the article: "Our daughters must be protected. I am going to solve this hideous crime if it takes me the rest of my life. At the moment I have no definite clues."

I looked up at Tony. "Nice fellow, Marfeld."

"Yah." He heard the irony. "You know him, huh?"

"I know him."

I stood up. Tony took the magazine from my hand, tossed it into the suitcase, kicked the suitcase under the bed. He reached for the string that controlled the light, and jerked the grief-stricken room downward into darkness.

Chapter 19

I WENT upstairs and along the gallery to Bassett's office. He still wasn't in it. I went in search of a drink. Under the half-retracted roof of a great inner court, dancers were sliding around on the waxed tiles to the music of a decimated orchestra. JEREMY CRANE AND HIS JOY BOYS was the legend on the drum. Their sad musicians' eyes looked down their noses at the merrymaking squares. They were playing lilting melancholy Gershwin: "Someone to Watch Over Me."

My diving friend whose hips didn't bounce was dancing with the perennial-bachelor type who loved taking pictures. Her diamonds glittered on his willowy right shoulder. He didn't like it when I cut in, but he departed gracefully.

She had on a tiger-striped gown with a slashed neckline and a flaring skirt which didn't become her. Her dancing was rather tigerish. She plunged around as if she was used to leading. Our dance was politely intense, like an amateur wrestling match, with no breath wasted on words. I said when it ended:

"Lew Archer is my name. May I talk to you?"

"Why not?"

We sat at one of several marble-topped tables separated by a glass windscreen from the pool. I said:

"Let me get you a drink."

"Thank you, I don't drink. You're not a member, and you're not one of Sime Graff's regulars. Let me guess." She fingered her pointed chin, and her diamonds flashed. "Reporter?"

"Guess again."

"Policeman?"

"You're very acute, or am I very obvious?"

She studied me from between narrowed eyelids, and smiled narrowly. "No, I wouldn't say you're obvious. It's just you asked me something about Hester Campbell before. And it kind of made me wonder if you were a policeman."

"I don't follow your line of reasoning."

"Don't you? Then how does it happen that you're interested in her?"

"I'm afraid I can't tell you that. My lips are sealed."

"Mine aren't," she said. "Tell me, what is she wanted for? Theft?"

"I didn't say she was wanted."

"Then she ought to be. She's a thief, you know." Her smile had a biting edge. "She stole from me. I left my wallet in the dressing-room in my *cabaña* one day last summer. It was early in the morning, no one was around except the staff, so I didn't bother locking up the place. I did a few dives and showered, and when I went to dress, my wallet was gone."

"How do you know she took it?"

"There's no doubt whatever that she did. I saw her slinking down the shower-room corridor just before I found it missing. She had something wrapped in a towel in her hand, and a guilty smirk on her face. She didn't fool me for a minute. I went to her afterwards and asked her point-blank if she had it. Of course she denied it, but I could see the deceitful look in her eyes."

"A deceitful look is hardly evidence."

"Oh, it wasn't only that. Other members have suffered losses, too, and they always coincided with Miss Campbell's being around. I know I sound prejudiced, but I'm not, really. I'd done my best to help the girl, you see. I considered her almost a protégée at one time. So it rather hurt when I caught her stealing from me. There was over a hundred dollars in the wallet, and my driver's license and keys, which had to be replaced."

"You say you caught her."

"Morally speaking, I did. Of course she wouldn't admit a thing. She'd cached the wallet somewhere in the meantime."

"Did you report the theft?" My voice was sharper than I intended.

She drummed on the tabletop with blunt fingertips. "I must say, I hardly expected to be cross-questioned like this. I'm voluntarily giving you information, and I'm doing so completely without malice. You don't understand, I *liked* Hester. She had bad breaks when she was a kid, and I felt sorry for her."

"So you didn't report it."

"No, I didn't, not to the authorities. I did take it up with Mr. Bassett, which did no good at all. She had him thoroughly hoodwinked. He simply couldn't believe that she'd do wrong—until it happened to him."

"What happened to him?"

"Hester stole from him, too," she said with a certain complacency. "That is, I can't swear that she did, but I'm morally certain of it. Miss Hamblin, his secretary, is a friend of mine, and I hear things. Mr. Bassett was dreadfully upset the day she left." She leaned toward me across the table: I could see the barred rib-cage between her breasts. "And Miss Hamblin said he changed the combination of his safe that very day."

"All this is pretty tenuous. Did he report a theft?"

"Of course he didn't. He never said a word to anybody. He was too ashamed of being taken in by her."

"And you've never said a word to anybody, either?"

"Until now."

"Why bring it all out now?"

She was silent, except for her drumming fingers. The lower part of her face set in a dull, thick expression. She had turned her head away from the source of light, and I couldn't see her eyes. "You asked me."

"I didn't ask you anything specific."

"You talk as if you were a friend of hers. Are you?"

"Are *you*?"

She covered her mouth with her hand, so that her whole face was hidden, and mumbled behind it: "I thought she was my friend. I could have forgiven her the wallet, even. But I saw her last week in Myrin's. I walked right up to her, prepared to let bygones be bygones, and she snubbed me. She pretended not to know me." Her voice became deep and harsh, and the hand in front of her mouth became a fist. "So I thought, if she's suddenly loaded, able to buy clothes at Myrin's, the least she can do is repay me my hundred dollars."

"You need the money, do you?"

Her fist repelled the suggestion, fiercely, as if I'd accused her of having a moral weakness or a physical disease. "Of course I don't need the money. It's the principle of the thing." After a thinking pause she said: "You don't like me the least little bit, do you?"

I hadn't expected the question, and I didn't have an answer ready. She had the peculiar combination of force and meanness you often find in rich, unmarried women. "You're loaded,"

I said, "and I'm not, and I keep remembering the difference. Does it matter?"

"Yes, it matters. You don't understand." Her eyes emerged from shadow, and her meager breast leaned hard against the table edge. "It isn't the money, so much. Only I thought Hester *liked* me. I thought she was a true friend. I used to coach her diving, I let her use Father's pool. I even gave a party for her once—a birthday party."

"How old was she?"

"It was her eighteenth birthday. She was the prettiest girl in the world then, and the nicest. I can't understand—what happened to all her niceness?"

"It's happening to a lot of people."

"Is that a crack at me?"

"At me," I said. "At all of us. Maybe it's atomic fallout or something."

Needing a drink more than ever, I thanked her and excused myself and found my way to the drinking-room. A curved mahogany bar took up one end of it. The other walls were decorated with Hollywood-Fauvist murals. The large room contained several dozen assorted couples hurling late-night insults at each other and orders at the Filipino bartenders. There were actresses with that numb and varnished look, and would-be actresses with that waiting look; junior-executive types hacking diligently at each other with their profiles; their wives watching each other through smiles; and others.

I sat at the bar between strangers, wheedled a whisky-and-water out of one of the white-coated Filipinos, and listened to the people. These were movie people, but a great deal of their talk was about television. They talked about communications media and the black list and the hook and payment for second showings and who had money for pilot films and what their agents said. Under their noise, they gave out a feeling of suspense. Some of them seemed to be listening hard for the rustle of a dropping option. Some of their eyes were knowing previews of that gray, shaking hangover dawn when all the mortgage payments came due at once and the options fell like snow.

The man on my immediate right looked like an old actor and sounded like a director. Maybe he was an actor turned director.

He was explaining something to a frog-voiced whisky blonde: "It means it's happening to you, you see. You're the one in love with the girl, or the boy, as the case may be. It's not the girl on the screen he's making a play for, it's you."

"Empathy-schwempathy," she croaked pleasantly. "Why not just call it sex?"

"It isn't sex. It includes sex."

"Then I'm for it. Anything that includes sex, I'm for it. That's my personal philosophy of life."

"And a fine philosophy it is," another man said. "Sex and television are the opium of the people."

"I thought marijuana was the opium of the people."

"Marijuana is the *marijuana* of the people."

There was a girl on my left. I caught a glimpse of her profile, young and pretty and smooth as glass. She was talking earnestly to the man beside her, an aging clown I'd seen in twenty movies.

"You said you'd catch me if I fell," she said.

"I was feeling stronger then."

"You said you'd marry me if it ever happened."

"You got more sense than to take me seriously. I'm two years behind on alimony now."

"You're very romantic, aren't you?"

"That's putting it mildly, sweetheart. I got some sense of responsibility, though. I'll do what I can for you, give you a telephone number. And you can tell him to send the bill to me."

"I don't want your dirty telephone number. I don't want your dirty money."

"Be reasonable. Think of it like it was a tumor or something— that is, if it really exists. Another drink?"

"Make mine prussic acid," she said dully.

"On the rocks?"

I left half my drink standing. It was air I needed. At one of the marble-topped tables in the court, under the saw-toothed shadow of a banana tree, Simon Graff was sitting with his wife. His gray hair was still dark and slick from the shower. He wore a dinner jacket with a pink shirt and a red cummerbund. She wore a blue mink coat over a black gown figured with gold which was out of style. His face was brown and pointed, talking at her. I couldn't see her face. She was looking out through the windscreen at the pool.

I had a contact mike in my car, and I went out to the parking-lot to get it. There were fewer cars than there had been, and one additional one: Carl Stern's sedan. It had Drive-Yourself registration. I didn't take time to go over it.

Graff was still talking when I got back to the poolside. The pool was abandoned now, but wavelets still washed the sides, shining in the underwater light. Hidden from Graff by the banana tree, I moved a rope chair up against the windscreen and pressed the mike to the plate glass. The trick had worked before, and it worked again. He was saying:

"Oh, yes, certainly, everything is my fault, I am your personal *bête noire*, and I apologize deeply."

"Please, Simon."

"Simon who? There is no Simon here. I am Mephisto Bête Noire, the famous hell husband. No!" His voice rose sharply on the word. "Think a minute, Isobel, if you have any mind left to think with. Think of what I have done for you, what I have endured and continue to endure. Think where you would be if it weren't for my support."

"This is support?"

"We won't argue. I know what you want. I know your purpose in attacking me." His voice was smooth as butter salted with tears. "You have suffered, and you want me to suffer. I refuse to suffer. You cannot make me suffer."

"God damn you," she said in a rustling whisper.

"God damn me, eh? How many drinks have you had?"

"Five or ten or twelve. Does it signify?"

"You know you cannot drink, that alcohol is death for you. Must I call Dr. Frey and have you locked up again?"

"No!" She was frightened. "I'm not drunk."

"Of course not. You are sobriety personified. You are the girl ideal of the Women's Christian Temperance Union, *mens sana in corpore sano*. But let me tell you one thing, Mrs. Sobriety. You are not going to ruin my party, no matter what. If you cannot or will not act as hostess, you will take yourself off, Toko will drive you."

"Get *her* to be your hostess, why don't you?"

"Who? Who are you talking about?"

"Hester Campbell," she said. "Don't tell me you're not seeing her."

"For business purposes. I have seen her for business purposes. If you have hired detectives, you will regret it."

"I don't need detectives, I have my sources. Did you give her the house for business purposes? Did you buy her those clothes for business purposes?"

"What do you know about that house? Have you been in that house?"

"It's none of your business."

"Yes." The word hissed like steam escaping from an overloaded pressure system. "I make it my business. Were you in that house today?"

"Maybe."

"Answer me, crazy woman."

"You can't talk to me like that." She began to call him names in a low, husky voice. It sounded like something tearing inside of her, permitting the birth of a more violent personality.

She rose suddenly, and I saw her walking across the patio in a straight line, moving among the dancers as though they were phantoms, figments of her mind. Her hip bumped the door frame as she went into the bar.

She came right out again, by another door. I caught a glimpse of her face in the light from the pool. It was white and frightened-looking. Perhaps the people frightened her. She skirted the shallow end of the pool, clicking along on high heels, and entered a *cabaña* on the far side.

I strolled toward the other end of the pool. The diving tower rose gleaming against a bank of fog that hid the sea. The ocean end was surrounded by a heavy wire fence. From a locked gate in the fence, a flight of concrete steps led down to the beach. High tides had gnawed and crumbled the lower steps.

I leaned on the gatepost and lit a cigarette. I had to cup the match against the stream of cold air which flowed upward from the water. This and the heavy shifting sky overhead created the illusion that I was on the bow of a slow ship, and the ship was headed into foggy darkness.

Chapter 20

SOMEWHERE BEHIND me, a woman's voice rose sharp. A man's voice answered it and drowned it out. I turned and looked around the bright, deserted pool. The two were standing close together at the wavering margin of the light, so close they might have been a single dark and featureless body. They were at the far end of the gallery, maybe forty yards away from me, but their voices came quite clearly across the water.

"No!" she repeated. "You're crazy. I did not."

I crossed to the gallery and walked toward them, keeping in its shadow.

"I'm not the one who is crazy," the man was saying. "We know who's crazy, sweetheart."

"Leave me alone. Don't touch me."

I knew the woman's voice. It belonged to Isobel Graff. I couldn't place the man's. He was saying:

"You bitch. You dirty bitch. Why did you do it? What did he do to you?"

"I didn't. Leave me alone, you filth." She called him other names which reflected on his ancestry and her vocabulary.

He answered her in a low, blurred voice I didn't catch. There were Lower East Side marbles in his mouth. I was close enough to recognize him now. Carl Stern.

He let out a feline sound, a mewling growl, and slapped her face, twice, very hard. She reached for his face with hooked fingers. He caught her by the wrists. Her mink coat slid from her shoulders and lay on the concrete like a large blue animal without a head. I started to run on my toes.

Stern flung her away from him. She thudded against the door of a *cabaña* and sat down in front of it. He stood over her, dapper and broad in his dark raincoat. The greenish light from the pool lent his head a cruel bronze patina.

"Why did you kill him?"

She opened her mouth and closed it and opened it, but no sound came. Her upturned face was like a cratered moon. He leaned over her in silent fury, so intent on her that he didn't know I was there until I hit him.

I hit him with my shoulder, pinned his arms, palmed his flanks for a gun. He was clean, in that respect. He bucked and snorted like a horse, trying to shake me off. He was almost as strong as a horse. His muscles cracked in my grip. He kicked at my shins and stamped my toes and tried to bite my arm.

I released him and, when he turned, chopped at the side of his jaw with my right fist. I didn't like men who bit. He spun and went down with his back to me. His hand dove up under his trouser-leg. He rose and turned in a single movement. His eyes were black nailheads on which his face hung haggard. A white line surrounded his mouth and marked the edges of his black nostrils, which glared at me like secondary eyes. Protruding from the fist he held at the center of his body was the four-inch blade of the knife he carried on his leg.

"Put it away, Stern."

"I'll carve your guts." His voice was high and rasping, like the sound of metal being machined.

I didn't wait for him to move. I threw a sneak right hand which crashed into his face and rocked him hard. His jaw turned to meet the left hook that completed the combination and finished Stern. He swayed on his feet for a few seconds, then collapsed on himself. The knife clattered and flashed on the concrete. I picked it up and closed it.

Footsteps came trotting along the gallery. It was Clarence Bassett, breathing rapidly under his boiled shirt. "What on earth?"

"Cat fight. Nothing serious."

He helped Mrs. Graff to her feet. She leaned on the wall and straightened her twisted stockings. He picked up her coat, brushing it carefully with his hands, as though the mink and the woman were equally important.

Carl Stern got up groggily. He gave me a dull-eyed look of hatred. "Who are you?"

"The name is Archer."

"You're the eye, uh?"

"I'm the eye who doesn't think that women should be hit."

"Chivalrous, eh? You're going to hate yourself for this, Archer."

"I don't think so."

"I think so. I got a lot of friends. I got connections. You're through in L.A., you know that? All finished."

"Put it in writing, will you? I've been wanting to get out of the smog."

"Speaking of connections," Bassett said quietly to Stern, "you're not a member of this club."

"I'm a guest of a member. And you're going to get crucified, too."

"Oh, my, yes. What fun. Whose guest would you happen to be?"

"Simon Graff's. I want to see him. Where is he?"

"We won't bother Mr. Graff just now. And may I make a suggestion? It's getting latish, more for some than for others. Don't you think you'd better leave?"

"I don't take orders from servants."

"Don't you indeed?" Bassett's smile was a toothy mask which left his eyes sad. He turned to me.

I said: "You want to be hit again, Stern? It would be a pleasure."

Stern glared at me for a long moment, red lights dancing on his shallow eyes. The lights went out. He said:

"All right. I'll leave. Give me back my knife."

"If you promise to cut your throat with it."

He tried to go into another fury, but lacked the energy. He looked sick. I tossed him the closed knife. He caught it and put it in the pocket of his coat, turned and walked away toward the entrance. He stumbled several times. Bassett marched behind him, at a distance, like a watchful policeman.

Mrs. Graff was fumbling with a key at the door of the *cabaña*. Her hands were shaking, out of control. I turned the key for her and switched on the light. It was indirect, and shone from four sides on a bellying brown fishnet ceiling. The room was done in primitive Pacific style, with split-bamboo screens at the windows, grass matting on the floor, rattan armchairs and chaise longues. Even the bar in one corner was rattan. Beside it, at the rear of the room, two louvered doors opened into the dressing-rooms. The walls were hung with tapa cloths and Douanier Rousseau reproductions, bamboo-framed.

The only discordant note was a Matisse travel poster lithographed in brilliant colors and advertising Nice. Mrs. Graff paused in front of it, and said to no one in particular:

"We have a villa near Nice. Father gave it to us as a wedding present. Simon was all for it in those days. All for me, and all for one." She laughed, for no good reason. "He won't even take me to Europe with him any more. He says I always make trouble for him when we go away together, any more. It isn't true, I'm as quiet as a quilt. He flies away on his trans-polar flights and leaves me here to rot in the heat and cold."

She clasped her head with both hands, tightly, for a long moment. Her hair stuck up between her fingers like black, untidy feathers. The silent pain she was fighting to control was louder than a scream.

"Are you all right, Mrs. Graff?"

I touched her blue mink back. She sidestepped away from my touch, whirled the coat off, and flung it on a studio bed. Her back and shoulders were dazzling, and her breast overflowed the front of her strapless dress like whipped cream. She held her body with a kind of awkward pride mixed with shame, like a young girl suddenly conscious of her flesh.

"Do you like my dress? It isn't new. I haven't been to a party for years and years and years. Simon doesn't take me any more."

"Nasty old Simon," I said. "Are you all right, Mrs. Graff?"

She answered me with a bright actress's smile which didn't go with the stiffness of the upper part of her face, the despair in her eyes:

"I'm wonderful. Wonderful."

She did a brief dance-step to prove it, snapping her fingers at the end of rigid arms. Bruises were coming out on her white forearms, the size and color of Concord grapes. Her dancing was mechanical. She stumbled and lost a gold slipper. Instead of putting it on again, she kicked off the other slipper. She sat on one of the bar stools, wriggling her stockinged feet, clasping and rubbing them together. They looked like blind, flesh-colored animals making furtive love under the hem of her skirt:

"Incidentally," she said, "and accidentally, I haven't thanked you. I thank you."

"What for?"

"For saving me from a fate worse than life. That wretched little drug-peddler might have killed me. He's terribly strong, isn't he?" She added resentfully: "They're not supposed to be strong."

"Who aren't? Drug-peddlers?"

"Pansies. All pansies are supposed to be weak. Like all bullies are cowards, and all Greeks run restaurants. That isn't a good example, though. My father was a Greek, at least he was a Cypriot, and, by God, he ran a restaurant in Newark, New Jersey. Great oaks from little acorns grow. Miracles of modern science. From a greasy spoon in Newark to wealth and decadence in one easy generation. It's the new accelerated pace, with automation."

She looked around the alien room. "He might as well have stayed in Cyprus, for God's sake. What good did it do me? I ended up in a therapy room making pottery and weaving rugs like a God-damn cottage industry. Except that *I* pay them. I always do the paying."

Her contact seemed to be better, which encouraged me to say: "Do you always do the talking, too?"

"Am I talking too much?" She gave me her brilliant, disorganized smile again, as if her mouth could hardly contain her teeth. "Am I making any sense, for God's sake?"

"From time to time you are, for God's sake."

Her smile became slightly less intense and more real. "I'm sorry, I get on a talking jag sometimes and the words come out wrong and they don't mean what I want them to. Like in James Joyce, only to me it just *hap*pens. Did you know his daughter was schizzy?" She didn't wait for an answer. "So sometimes I'm a wit and sometimes I'm a nitwit, so they tell me." She extended her bruise-mottled arm: "Sit down and have a drink and tell me who *you* are."

I sat on the stool beside her. "I'm nobody in particular. My name is Archer."

"Archer," she repeated thoughtfully, but she wasn't interested in me. Memory flared and smoked inside of her like a fire in changing winds: "I'm nobody in particular, either. I used to think I was. My father was Peter Heliopoulos, at least that's what he called himself, his real name was longer than that and much more complicated. And I was much more complicated, too. I was the crown princess, my father *called* me Princess. So now—" her voice jangled harshly off-key—"so now a cheap

Hollywood drug-peddler can push me around and get away with it. In my father's day they would have flayed him alive. So what does my husband do? He goes into business with him. They're palsy-walsies, cerebral palsy-walsies."

"Do you mean Carl Stern, Mrs. Graff?"

"Who else?"

"What kind of business are they in?"

"Whatever people do in Las Vegas, gambling and helling around. I never go there myself, never go anywhere."

"How do you know he's a drug-peddler?"

"I bought drugs from him myself when I ran out of doctors —yellow jackets and demerol and the little kind with the red stripe. I'm off drugs now, however. Back on liquor again. It's one thing Dr. Frey did for me." Her eyes focused on my face, and she said impatiently: "You haven't made yourself a drink. Go ahead and make yourself a drink, and make one for me, too."

"Do you think that's a good idea, Isobel?"

"*Don't* talk to me as though I were a child. I'm not drunk. I can hold my liquor." The bright smile gashed her face. "The only trouble with me is that I am somewhat crazy. But not at the moment. I was upset there for a moment, but you're very soothing and smoothing, aren't you? Kind of kind of kind." She was mimicking herself.

"Any more," I said.

"Any more. But you won't make fun of me, will you? I get so mad sometimes—angry-mad, I mean—when people mock my dignity. I may be going into a wind-up, I don't know, but I haven't taken off yet. On my trans-polar flight," she added wryly, "into the wild black yonder."

"Good for you."

She nodded in self-congratulation. "That was one of the wit ones, wasn't it? It isn't really true, though. When it happens, it isn't like flying or any sort of arrival or departure. The *feel* of things changes, that's all, and I can't tell the difference between me and other things. Like when Father died and I saw him in the coffin and had my first breakdown. I thought *I* was in the coffin. I felt dead, my flesh was cold. There was embalming fluid in my veins, and I could smell myself. At the same time I was lying dead in the coffin and sitting in the pew in the Orthodox

Church, mourning for my own death. And when they buried him, the earth—I could hear the earth dropping on the coffin and then it smothered me and I was the earth."

She took hold of my hand and held it, trembling. "Don't let me talk so much. It does me harm. I almost *went*, just then."

"Where did you go?" I said.

"Into my dressing-room." She dropped my hand and gestured toward one of the louvered doors. "For a second I was in there, watching us through the door and listening to myself. *Please* pour me a drink. It does me good, honestly. Scotch on the rocks."

I moved around behind the bar and got ice cubes out of the small beige refrigerator and opened a bottle of Johnnie Walker and made a couple of drinks, medium strength. I felt more comfortable on the wrong side of the bar. The woman disturbed me basically, the way you can be disturbed by starvation in a child, or a wounded bird, or a distempered cat running in yellow circles. She seemed to be teetering on the verge of a psychotic episode. Also, she seemed to know it. I was afraid to say anything that might push her over the edge.

She raised her glass. The steady tremor in her hand made the brown liquor slosh around among the ice cubes. As if to demonstrate her self-control, she barely sipped at it. I sipped at mine, leaned on my elbow across the formica counter in the attitude of a bartender with a willing ear.

"What was the trouble, Isobel?"

"Trouble? You mean with Carl Stern?"

"Yes. He got pretty rough."

"He hurt me," she said, without self-pity. A taste of whisky had changed her mood, as a touch of acid will change the color of blue litmus paper. "Interesting medical facts. I bruise very easily." She exhibited her arms. "I bet my entire body is covered with bruises."

"Why would Stern do it to you?"

"People like him are sadists, at least a lot of them are."

"You know a lot of them?"

"I've known my share. I attract them, apparently, I don't know why. Or maybe I do know why. Women like me, we don't expect too much. *I* don't expect *any*thing."

"Lance Leonard one of them?"

"How should I know? I guess so. I hardly knew—I hardly knew the little mackerel."

"He used to be a lifeguard here."

"I don't mess with lifeguards," she said harshly. "What is this? I thought we were going to be friends, I thought we were going to have fun. I never have any *fun*."

"Any more."

She didn't think it was funny. "They lock me up and punish me, it isn't fair," she said. "I did one terrible thing in my life, and now they blame me for everything that happens. Stern's a filthy liar. I never touched his lover-boy, I didn't even know that he was dead. Why would I shoot him? I have enough on my conscious—on my conscience."

"Such as?"

She peered at my face. Hers was as stiff as a board. "Such as, you're trying to pump me, aren't you, such as? Trying to dig things out of me?"

"Yes, I am. What terrible thing did you do?"

Something peculiar happened to her face. One of her eyes became narrow and sly, one became hard and wide. On the sly side, her upper lip lifted and her white teeth gleamed under it. She said: "I'm a naughty, naughty, naughty girl. I watched them doing it. I stood behind the door and watched them doing it. Miracles of modern science. And I was in the room and behind the door."

"What did you do?"

"I killed my mother."

"How?"

"By wishing," she said slyly. "I wished my mother to death. Does that take care of your questions, Mr. Questionnaire? Are you a psychiatrist? Did Simon hire you?"

"The answer is no and no."

"I killed my father, too. I broke his heart. Shall I tell you my other crimes? It's quite a decalogue. Envy and malice and pride and lust and rage. I'd sit at home and plan his death, by hanging, burning, shooting, drowning, poison. I'd sit at home and imagine him with them, all the young girls with their bodies and waving white legs. I sat at home and tried to have men friends. It never seemed to work out. They were exhausted by the heat and cold or else I frightened them. One of them told me I frightened him, the lousy little nance. They'd drink up my liquor and never come back." She sipped from her glass. "Go ahead," she said. "Drink up your liquor."

"Drink up yours, Isobel. I'll take you home. Where do you live?"

"Quite near here, on the beach. But I'm not going home. You won't make me go home, will you? I haven't been to a party for so long. Why don't we go and dance? I am very ugly to look at, but I am a good dancer."

"You are very beautiful, but I am a lousy dancer."

"I'm ugly," she said. "You mustn't mock me. I know how ugly I am. I was born ugly through and through, and nobody ever loved me."

The door opened behind her, swinging wide. Simon Graff appeared in the opening. His face was stony.

"Isobel! What kind of *Walpurgisnacht* is this? What are you doing in here?"

Her reaction was slow, almost measured. She turned and rose from the stool. Her body was tense and insolent. The drink was shaking in her hand.

"What am I doing? I'm telling my secrets. I'm telling all my dirty little secrets to my dear friend."

"You fool. Come home with me."

He took several steps toward her. She threw her glass at his head. It missed him and dented the wall beside the door. Some of the liquid spattered his face.

"Crazy woman," he said. "You come home now with me. I will call Dr. Frey."

"I don't have to go with you. You're not my father." She turned to me, the look of lopsided cunning still on her face. "Do I have to go with him?"

"I don't know. Is he your legal guardian?"

Graff answered: "Yes, I am. You will keep out of this." He said to her: "There is nothing but grief for you, for all of us, if you try to break loose from me. You would be really lost." There was a new quality in his voice, a largeness and a darkness and an emptiness.

"I'm lost now. How lost can a woman get?"

"You will find out, Isobel. Unless you come with me and do as I say."

"Svengali," I said. "Very old-hat."

"Keep out of this, I warn you." I felt his glance like an icicle parting my hair. "This woman is my wife."

"Lucky her."

"Who are you?"

I told him.

"What are you doing in this club, at this party?"

"Watching the animals."

"I expect a specific answer."

"Try using a different tone, and you might get one." I came around the end of the bar and stood beside Isobel Graff. "You've been spoiled by all those yes-men in your life. I happen to be a no-man."

He looked at me in genuine shock. Maybe he hadn't been contradicted for years. Then he remembered to be angry, and turned on his wife:

"Did he come here with you?"

"No." She sounded intimidated. "I thought he was one of your guests."

"What is he doing in this *cabaña?*"

"I offered him a drink. He helped me. A man hit me." Her voice was monotonous, threaded by a whine of complaint.

"What man hit you?"

"Your friend Carl Stern," I said. "He slapped her around and pushed her down. Bassett and I threw him out."

"You threw him out?" Graff's alarm turned to anger, which he directed against his wife again: "You permitted this, Isobel?"

She hung her head and assumed an awkward, ugly posture, standing on one leg like a schoolgirl.

"Didn't you hear me, Graff? Or don't you object to thugs pushing your wife around?"

"I will look after my wife in my own way. She is mentally disturbed, sometimes she requires to be firmly handled. You are not needed. Get out."

"I'll finish my drink first, thank you." I added conversationally: "What did you do with George Wall?"

"George Wall? I know no George Wall."

"Your strong-arm boys do—Frost and Marfeld and Lashman." The names piqued his interest. "Who is this George Wall?"

"Hester's husband."

"I am not acquainted with any Hester."

His wife gave him a swift, dark look, but said nothing. I fixed him with my steeliest glance and tried to stare him down. It didn't work. His eyes were like holes in a wall; you looked through them into a great, dim, empty place.

"You're a liar, Graff."

His face turned purple and white. He went to the door and called Bassett in a loud, trembling voice. When Bassett appeared, Graff said: "I want this man thrown out. I don't permit party-crashers—"

"Mr. Archer is not exactly a party-crasher," Bassett said coolly.

"Is he a friend of yours?"

"I think of him as a friend, yes. A friend of brief standing, shall we say. Mr. Archer is a detective, a private detective I hired for personal reasons."

"What reasons?"

"A crackpot threatened me last night. I hired Mr. Archer to investigate the matter."

"Instruct him, then, to leave my friends alone. Carl Stern is an associate of mine. I want him treated with respect."

Bassett's eyes gleamed wetly, but he stood up to Graff. "I am manager of this club. As long as I am, I'll set the standards for the behavior of the guests. No matter whose friends they are."

Isobel Graff laughed tinnily. She had sat down on her coat, and was plucking at the fur.

Graff clenched his fists at his sides and began to shake. "Get out of here, both of you."

"Come along, Archer. We'll give Mr. Graff a chance to recover his manners."

Bassett was white and scared, but he carried it off. I didn't know he had it in him.

Chapter 21

W E WENT along the gallery to his office. His walk was a stiff-backed, high-shouldered march step. His movements seemed to be controlled by a system of outside pressures that fitted him like a corset.

He brought glasses out of his portable bar and poured me a stiff slug of whisky, a stiffer one for himself. The bottle was a different bottle from the one I had seen in the morning, and it was nearly empty. Yet the long day's drinking, like a passage of years, had improved Bassett in some ways. He'd lost his jaunty self-consciousness, and he wasn't pretending to be younger than he was. The sharp skull pressed like a death mask behind the thin flesh of his face.

"That was quite a performance," I said. "I thought you were a little afraid of Graff."

"I am, when I'm totally sober. He's on the board of trustees, and you might say he controls my job. But there are limits to what a man can put up with. It's rather wonderful not to feel frightened, for a change."

"I hope I didn't get you into trouble."

"Don't worry about me. I'm old enough to look after myself." He waved me into a chair and sat behind his desk with the half-glass of neat whisky in his hand. He drank from it and regarded me over the rim. "What brings you here, old man? Has something happened?"

"Plenty has happened. I saw Hester tonight."

He looked at me as though I'd said that I had seen a ghost. "You saw her? Where?"

"In her house in Beverly Hills. We had some conversation, which got us nowhere—"

"Tonight?"

"Around midnight, yes."

"Then she's alive!"

"Unless she was wired for sound. Did you think she was dead?"

It took him a while to answer. His eyes were wet and glassy. Behind them, something obscure happened to him. I guessed

353

he was immensely relieved. "I was mortally afraid that she was dead. I've been afraid all day that George Wall was going to kill her."

"That's nonsense. Wall has disappeared himself. He may be in a bad way. Graff's people may have killed him."

Bassett wasn't interested in Wall. He came around the desk and laid a tense hand on my shoulder. "You're not lying to me? You're certain that Hester's all right?"

"She was all right, physically, a couple of hours ago. I don't know what to make of her. She looks and talks like a nice girl, but she's involved with the crummiest crew in the Southwest. Carl Stern, for instance. What do you make of her, Bassett?"

"I don't know what to make of her. I never have."

He leaned on the desk, pressed his hand to his forehead, and stroked his long horse face. His eyelids lifted slowly. I could see the dull pain peering out from under them.

"You're fond of her, aren't you?"

"Very fond of her. I wonder if you can understand my feeling for the girl. It's what you might call an avuncular feeling. There's nothing—nothing fleshly about it at all. I've known Hester since she was an infant, her and her sister, too. Her father was one of our members, one of my dearest friends."

"You've been here a long time."

"Twenty-five years as manager. I was a charter member of the Club. There were twenty-five of us originally. Each of us put up forty thousand dollars."

"You put up forty thousand?"

"I did. Mother and I were fairly well fixed at one time, until the crash of '29 wiped us out. When that happened, my friends in the Club offered me the post of manager. This is the first and only job I've ever had."

"What happened to Campbell?"

"He drank himself to death. As I am doing, on a somewhat retarded schedule." Grinning sardonically, he reached for his glass and drained it. "His wife was a silly woman, completely impractical. Lived up Topanga Canyon after Raymond's death. I did what I could for the fatherless babes."

"You didn't tell me all this yesterday morning."

"No. I was brought up not to boast of my philanthropies."

His speech was very formal, and slightly blurred. The whisky was getting to him. He looked from me to the bottle, his eyes swiveling heavily. I shook my head. He poured another quadruple shot for himself, and sipped at it. If he drank enough of it down, there would be no more pain behind his eyelids. Or the pain would take strange forms. That was the trouble with alcohol as a sedative. It floated you off reality for a while, but it brought you back by a route that meandered through the ash-dumps of hell.

I threw out a question, a random harpoon before he floated all the way down to Lethe: "Did Hester doublecross you?"

He looked startled, but he handled his alcohol-saturated words with care: "What in heaven's name are you talking about?"

"It was suggested to me that Hester stole something from you when she left here."

"Stole from me? Nonsense."

"She didn't rob your safe?"

"Good Lord, no. Hester wouldn't do a thing like that. Not that I have anything worth stealing. We handle no cash at the club, you know, all our business is done by chit—"

"I'm not interested in that. All I want is your word that Hester didn't rob your safe in September."

"Of course she didn't. I can't imagine where you got such a notion. People have such poisonous tongues." He leaned toward me, swaying slightly. "Who was it?"

"It doesn't matter."

"I say it does matter. You should check your sources, old man. It's character-assassination. What kind of a girl do you think Hester is?"

"It's what I'm trying to find out. You knew her as well as anyone, and you say she isn't capable of theft."

"Certainly not from me."

"From anyone?"

"I don't know what she's capable of."

"Is she capable of blackmail?"

"You ask the weirdest questions—weirder and weirder."

"Earlier in the day, you didn't think blackmail was so far-fetched. You might as well be frank with me. Is Simon Graff being blackmailed?"

He wagged his head solemnly. "What could Mr. Graff be blackmailed for?"

I glanced at the photograph of the three divers. "Gabrielle Torres. I've heard that there was a connection between her and Graff."

"What kind of connection?"

"Don't pretend to be stupid, Clarence. You're not. You knew the girl—she worked for you. If there was a thing between her and Graff, you'd probably know it."

"If there was," he said stolidly, "it never came to my knowledge." He meditated for a while, swaying on his feet. "Good Lord, man, you're not suggesting he *killed* her?"

"He could have. But Mrs. Graff was the one I had in mind."

Bassett gave me a stunned and murky look. "What a perfectly dreadful notion."

"That's what you'd say if you were covering for them."

"But thish ish utterly—" He grimaced and started over: "This is utterly absurd and ridiculous—"

"Why? Isobel is crazy enough to kill. She had a motive."

"She isn't crazy. She was—she did have serious emotional problems at one time."

"Ever been committed?"

"Not committed, I don't believe. She's been in a private sanitorium from time to time. Dr. Frey's in Santa Monica."

"When was she in last?"

"Last year."

"What part of last year?"

"All of it. So you shee—" He waved his hand in front of his face, as if a buzzing fly had invaded his mouth. "You see, it's quite impossible. Isobel was incarcerated at the time the girl was shot. Absolutely imposible."

"Do you know this for a fact?"

"Shertainly I do. I visited her regularly."

"Isobel is another old friend of yours?"

"Shertainly is. Very dear old friend."

"Old enough and dear enough to lie for?"

"Don't be silly. Ishobel wouldn't harm a living creashur."

His eyes were clouding up, as well as his voice, but the glass in his hand was steady. He raised it to his mouth and drained it, then sat down rather abruptly on the edge of his desk. He swayed gently from side to side, gripping the empty glass in both hands as though it was his only firm support.

"Very dear old friend," he repeated sentimentally. "Poor Ishbel, hers is a tragic story. Her mother died young, her father gave her everything but love. She needed sympathy, someone to talk to. I tried to be that shomeone."

"You did?"

He gave me a shrewd, sad look. The jolt of whisky had partly and temporarily sobered him, but he had reached the point of diminishing returns. His face was the color of boiled meat, and his thin hair hung lank at the temples. He detached one hand from its glass anchor and pushed his hair back.

"I know it sounds unlikely. Remember, this was twenty years ago. I wasn't always an old man. At any rate, Isobel liked older men. She was devoted to her father, but he couldn't give her the understanding she needed. She'd just flunked out of college, for the third or fourth time. She was terribly withdrawn. She used to spend her days here, alone on the beach. Gradually she discovered that she could talk to me. We talked all one summer and into the fall. She wouldn't go back to school. She wouldn't leave me. She was in love with me."

"You're kidding."

I was deliberately needling him, and he reacted with alcoholic emotionalism. Angry color seeped into his capillaries, stippling his gray cheeks with red:

"It's true, she loved me. I'd had emotional problems of my own, and I was the only one who understood her. And she respected me! I am a Harvard man, did you know that? I spent three years in France in the first war. I was a stretcher-bearer."

That would make him about sixty, I thought. And twenty years ago he would have been forty to Isobel's twenty, say.

"How did you feel about her?" I said. "Avuncular?"

"I loved her. She and my mother were the only two women I ever loved. And I'd have married her, too, if her father hadn't stood in the way. Peter Heliopoulos disapproved of me."

"So he married her off to Simon Graff."

"To Simon Graff, yah." He shuddered with the passion of a weak and timid man who seldom lets his feelings show. "To a climber and a pusher and a whoremonger and a cheat. I knew Simon Graff when he was an immigrant nobody, a nothing in this town. Assistant director on quickie Westerns with one decent suit to his name. I liked him, he pretended to like me. I lent him money, I got him a guest membership in the Club, I introduced him to people. I introduced him to Heliopoulos, by heaven. Within two years he was producing for Helio, and married to Isobel. Everything he has, everything he's done, has come out of that marriage. And he hasn't the common decency to treat her decently!"

He stood up and made a wide swashbuckling gesture which carried him sideways all the way to the wall. Dropping the glass, he spread the fingers of both hands against the wall to steady himself. The wall leaned toward him, anyway. His forehead struck the plaster. He jackknifed at the hips and sat down with a thud on the carpeted floor.

He looked up at me, chuckling foolishly. One of his boiled blue eyes was straight, and one had turned outward. It gave him the appearance of mild, ridiculous lunacy.

"There's a seavy hea running," he said.

"We'll hatten down the batches."

I took him by the arms and set him on his feet and walked him to his chair. He collapsed in it, hands and jaw hanging down. His divided glance came together on the bottle. He reached for it. Five or six ounces of whisky swished around in the bottom. I was afraid that another drink might knock him out, or maybe even kill him. I lifted the bottle out of his hands, corked it, and put it away. The key of the portable bar was in the lock. I turned it and put it in my pocket.

"By what warrant do you sequester the grog?" Working his mouth elaborately around the words, Bassett looked like a camel chewing. "This is illegal—false seizure. I demand a writ of habeas corpus."

He leaned forward and reached for my glass. I snatched it away. "You've had enough, Clarence."

"Make those decisions myself. Man of decision. Man of distinction. Bottle-a-day man, by God. Drink you under table."

"I don't doubt it. Getting back to Simon Graff, you don't like him much?"

"Hate him," he said. "Lez be frank. He stole away only woman I ever loved. 'Cept Mother. Stole my maître dee, too.

Best maître dee in Southland, Stefan. They offered him double shallery, spirited him away to Las Vegas."

"Who did?"

"Graff and Stern. Wanted him for their slo-called club."

"Speaking of Graff and Stern, why would Graff be fronting for a mobster?"

"Sixty-four-dollar question, *I* don't know the ansher. Wouldn't tell *you* if did know. *You* don't like me."

"Buck up, Clarence. I like you fine."

"Liar. Cruel and inhuman." Two tears detached themselves from the corners of his eyes and crawled down his grooved cheeks like little silver slugs. "Won't give me a drink. Trying make me talk, withholding my grog. 'Snot fair, 'snot humane."

"Sorry. No more grog tonight. You don't want to kill yourself."

"Why not? All alone in the world. Nobody loves me." He wept suddenly and copiously, so that his whole face was wet. Transparent liquid streamed from his nose and mouth. Great sobs shook him like waves breaking in his body.

It wasn't a pretty sight. I started out.

"Don't leave me," he said between sobs. "Don't leave me alone."

He came around the desk, buckled at the knees as if he'd struck an invisible wire, and lay full-length on the carpet, blind and deaf and dumb. I turned his head sideways so that he wouldn't smother and went outside.

Chapter 22

THE AIR was turning chilly. Laughter and other party sounds still overflowed the bar, but the music in the court had ceased. A car toiled up the drive to the highway, and then another. The party was breaking up.

There was light in the lifeguard's room at the end of the row of *cabañas*. I looked in. The young Negro was sitting inside, reading a book. He closed it when he saw me, and stood up. The name of the book was *Elements of Sociology*.

"You're a late reader."

"Better late than never."

"What do you do with Bassett when he passes out?"

"Is he passed out again?"

"On the floor of his office. Does he have a bed around?"

"Yeah, in the back room." He made a resigned face. "Guess I better put him in it, eh?"

"Need any help?"

"No, thanks, I can handle him myself, I had plenty of practice." He smiled at me, less automatically than before. "You a friend of Mr. Bassett's?"

"Not exactly."

"He give you some kind of a job?"

"You could say that."

"Working around the Club here?"

"Partly."

He was too polite to ask what my duties were. "Tell you what, I'll pour Mr. Bassett in bed, you stick around, I'll make you a cup of coffee."

"I could use a cup of coffee. The name is Lew Archer, by the way."

"Joseph Tobias." His grip was the kind that bends horseshoes. "Kind of an unusual name, isn't it? You can wait here, if you like."

He trotted away. The storeroom was jammed with folded beach umbrellas, piled deckchairs, deflated plastic floats and beach balls. I set up one of the deckchairs for myself and stretched out on it. Tiredness hit me like pentothal. Almost immediately, I went to sleep.

When I woke up, Tobias was standing beside me. He had opened a black iron switchbox on the wall. He pulled a series of switches, and the glimmering night beyond the open door turned charcoal gray. He turned and saw that I was awake.

"Didn't like to wake you up. You look tired."

"Don't you ever get tired?"

"Nope. For some reason I never do. Only time in my life I got tired was in Korea. There I got bone-tired, pushing a jeep through that deep mud they have. You want your coffee now?"

"Lead me to it."

He led me to a brightly lighted white-walled room with SNACK BAR over the door. Behind the counter, water was bubbling in a glass coffee-maker. An electric clock on the wall was taking spasmodic little bites of time. It was a quarter to four.

I sat on one of the padded stools at the counter. Tobias vaulted over the counter and landed facing me with a deadpan expression.

"Cuchulain the Hound of Ulster," he said surprisingly. "When Cuchulain was weary and exhausted from fighting battles, he'd go down by the riverside and exercise. That was his way of resting. I turned the fire on under the grill in case we wanted eggs. I could use a couple of eggs or three, personally."

"Me, too."

"Three?"

"Three."

"How's about some tomato juice to start out with? It clarifies the palate."

"Fine."

He opened a large can and poured two glasses of tomato juice. I picked up my glass and looked at it. The juice was thick and dark red in the fluorescent light. I put the glass down again.

"Something the matter with the juice?"

"It looks all right to me," I said unconvincingly.

He was appalled by this flaw in his hospitality. "What is it— dirt in the juice?" He leaned across the counter, his forehead wrinkled with solicitude. "I just opened the can, so if there's something in it, it must be the cannery. Some of these big corporations think that they can get away with murder, especially now that we have a businessmen's administration. I'll open another can."

"Don't bother."

I drank the red stuff down. It tasted like tomato juice.

"Was it all right?"

"It was very good."

"I was afraid there for a minute that there was something the matter with it."

"Nothing the matter with it. The matter was with me."

He took six eggs out of the refrigerator and broke them onto the grill. They sputtered cozily, turning white at the edges. Tobias said over his shoulder:

"It doesn't alter what I said about the big corporations. Mass production and mass marketing do make for some social benefits, but sheer size tends to militate against the human element. We've reached the point where we should count the human cost. How do you like your eggs?"

"Over easy."

"Over easy it is." He flipped the six eggs with a spatula, and inserted bread in the four-hole toaster. "You want to butter your own toast, or you want me to butter it for you? I have a butter brush. Personally, I prefer that, myself."

"You butter it for me."

"Will do. Now how do you like your coffee?"

"At this time in the morning, black. This is a very fine service you have here."

"We endeavor to please. I used to be snack-bar bus-boy before I switched over to lifeguard. Lifeguard doesn't pay any better, but it gives me more time to study."

"You're a student, are you?"

"Yes, I am." He dished up our eggs and poured our coffee. "I bet you're surprised at the facility with which I express myself."

"You took the words right out of my mouth."

He beamed with pleasure, and took a bite of toast. When he had chewed and swallowed it, he said: "I don't generally let the language flow around here. People, the richer they get, the more they dislike to hear a Negro express himself in well-chosen words. I guess they feel there's no point in being rich unless you can feel superior to somebody. I study English on the college level, but if I talked that way I'd lose my job. People are very sensitive."

"You go to U.C.L.A.?"

"Junior College. I'm working up to U.C.L.A. Heck," he said, "I'm only twenty-five, I've got plenty of time. 'Course I'd be way ahead of where I am now if I'd of caught on sooner. It took a hitch in the Army to jolt me out of my unthinking complacency." He rolled the phrase lovingly on his tongue. "I woke up one night on a cold hill on the way back from the Yalu. And suddenly it hit me—wham!—I didn't know what it was all about."

"The war?"

"Everything. War and peace. Values in life." He inserted a forkful of egg into his mouth and munched at me earnestly. "I realized I didn't know who *I* was. I wore this kind of mask, you know, over my face and over my mind, this kind of blackface mask, and it got so I didn't know who I was. I decided I had to find out who I was and be a man. If I could make it. Does that sound like a foolish thing for a person like me to decide?"

"It sounds sensible to me."

"I thought so at the time. I still do. Another coffee?"

"Not for me, thanks. You have another."

"No, I'm a one-cup man, too. I share your addiction for moderation." He smiled at the sound of the words.

"What do you plan to do in the long run?"

"Teach school. Teach and coach."

"It's a good life."

"You bet it is. I'm looking forward to it." He paused, taking time out to look forward to it. "I love to tell people important things. Especially kids. I love to communicate values, ideas. What do you do, Mr. Archer?"

"I'm a private detective."

Tobias looked a little disappointed in me. "Isn't that kind of a dull life? I mean, it doesn't bring you into contact with ideas very much. Not," he added quickly, for fear he had hurt my feelings, "not that I place *ideas* above other values. Emotions. Action. Honorable action."

"It's a rough life," I said. "You see people at their worst. How's Bassett, by the way?"

"Dead to the world. I put him to bed. He sleeps it off without any trouble, and *I* don't mind putting him to bed. He treats me pretty well."

"How long have you worked here?"

"Over three years. I started out in the snack bar here, and shifted over to lifeguard summer before last."

"You knew Gabrielle here, then."

He answered perfunctorily: "I knew her. I told you that."

"At the time that she was murdered?"

His face closed up entirely. The brightness left his eyes like something quick and timid retreating into its hole. "I don't know what you're getting at."

"Nothing to do with you. Don't run out on me, Joseph, just because I ask you a couple of questions."

"I'm not running out." But his voice was dull and singsong. "I already answered all the questions there are."

"What do you mean?"

"You know what I mean, if you're a detective. When Gabrielle—when Miss Torres was killed, I was the very first one that they arrested. They took me down to the sheriff's station and questioned me in relays, all day and half the night."

He hung his head under the weight of the memory. I hated to see him lose his fine *élan*.

"Why did they pick on you?"

"For no good reason." He raised his hand and turned it before his eyes. It was burnished black in the fluorescent light.

"Didn't they question anybody else?"

"Sure, when I proved to them I was at home all night. They picked up some winos and sex deviates that live around Malibu and up the canyons, and some hoboes passing through. And they asked Miss Campbell some questions."

"Hester Campbell?"

"Yes. She was the one that Gabrielle was supposed to be spending the evening with."

"How do you know?"

"Tony said so."

"Where did she really spend the evening?"

"How would I know that?"

"I thought you might have some idea."

"You thought wrong, then." His gaze, which had been avoiding mine, returned slowly to my face. "Are you reopening that murder case? Is that what Mr. Bassett hired you to do?"

"Not exactly. I started out investigating something else, but it keeps leading me back to Gabrielle. How well did you know her, Joseph?"

He answered carefully: "We worked together. Weekends, she took orders for sandwiches and drinks around the pool and in the *cabañas*. She was too young to serve the drinks herself, so I did that. Miss Torres was a very nice young lady to work with. I hated to see the thing that happened to her."

"You saw what happened to her?"

"I don't mean that. I didn't see what happened to her when it happened. But I was right here in this room when Tony came up from the beach. Somebody shot her, I guess you know that, shot her and left her lying just below the Club. Tony lived down the shore a piece from here. He expected Gabrielle home by midnight. When she didn't come home, he phoned the Campbells' house. They said they hadn't seen her, so he went out looking for her. He found her in the morning with bulletholes in her, the waves splashing up around her. She was supposed to be helping Mrs. Lamb that day, and Tony came up here first thing to tell Mrs. Lamb about it."

Tobias licked his dry lips. His eyes looked through me at the past. "He stood right there in front of the counter. For a long time he couldn't say a word. He couldn't open his mouth to tell Mrs. Lamb that Gabrielle was dead. She could see that he needed comfort, though. She walked around the end of the counter and put her arms around him and held him for a while like he was a child. Then he told her. Mrs. Lamb sent me to call the police."

"You called them yourself?"

"I was going to. But Mr. Bassett was in his office. He called them. I went down to the end of the pool and peeked down through the fence. She was lying there in the sand, looking up at the sky. Tony had pulled her up out of the surf. I could see sand in her eyes, I wanted to go down and wipe the sand out of her eyes, but I was afraid to go down there."

"Why?"

"She had no clothes on. She looked so *white*. I was afraid they'd come and catch me down there and get a crazy idea about me. They went ahead and got their ideas anyway. They arrested me right that very morning. I was half expecting it."

"You were?"

"People have to blame somebody. They've been blaming us for three hundred years now. I guess I had it coming. I shouldn't have let myself get—friendly with her. And then, to make it worse, I had this earring belonging to her in my pocket."

"What earring was that?"

"A little round earring she had, made of mother-of-pearl. It was shaped like a lifesaving belt, with a hole in the middle, and U.S.S. Malibu printed on it. The heck of it was, she was still— the other earring that matched it was still on her ear."

"How did you happen to have the earring?"

"I just picked it up," he said, "and I was going to give it back to her. I found it alongside the pool," he added after a moment.

"That morning?"

"Yes. Before I knew she was dead. That Marfeld and the other cops made a big deal about it. I guess they thought they had it made, until I proved out my alibi." He made a sound which was half snort and half groan. "As if I'd lay a hand on Gabrielle to hurt her."

"Were you in love with her, Joseph?"

"I didn't say that."

"It's true, though, isn't it?"

He rested his elbow on the counter and his chin on his hand, as though to steady his thinking. "I could have been," he admitted, "if I'd had a chance with her. Only there was no mileage in it. She was only half Spanish-American, and she never really saw me as a human being."

"That could be a motive for murder."

I watched his face. It lengthened, but it showed no other sign of emotion. The planes of his cheeks, his broad lips, had the look of a carved and polished mask balanced on his palm.

"You didn't kill her yourself, Joseph?"

He winced, but not with surprise, as though I'd pressed on the scar of an old wound. He shook his head sadly. "I wouldn't hurt a hair on her head, and you know it."

"All right. Let it pass."

"I won't let it pass. You can take it back or get out of here."

"All right. I take it back."

"You shouldn't have said it in the first place. She was my friend. I thought you were my friend."

"I'm sorry, Joseph. I have to ask these questions."

"Why do you have to? Who makes you? You should be careful what you say about who did what around here. Do you know what Tony Torres would do if he thought I killed his girl?"

"Kill you."

"That's right. He threatened to kill me when the police turned me loose. It was all I could do to talk him out of it. He gets these fixed ideas in his head, and they stick there like a bur. And he's got a lot of violence in him yet."

"So do we all."

"I know it, Mr. Archer. I know it in myself. Tony's got more than most. He killed a man with his fists once, when he was young."

"In the ring?"

"Not in the ring, and it wasn't an accident. It was over a woman, and he meant to do it. He asked me down to his room one night and got drunk on muscatel and told me all about it."

"When was this?"

"A couple of months ago. I guess it was really eating him up. Gabrielle's mother was the woman, you see. He killed the man that she was running with, and she left him. The other man had a knife, so the judge in Fresno called it self-defense, but Tony blamed himself. He connected it up with Gabrielle, said that what happened to her was God's punishment on him. Tony's very superstitious."

"You know his nephew Lance?"

"I know him." Joseph's tone defined his attitude. It was negative. "He used to have the job I have a few years back, when I started in the snack bar. I hear he's a big wheel now, it's hard to believe. He was so bone lazy he couldn't even hold a lifeguard job without his uncle filling in for him. Tony used to do his clean-up work while Lance practiced fancy diving."

"How does Tony feel about him now?"

Joseph scratched his tight hair. "He finally caught on to him. I'd say he almost hates him."

"Enough to kill him?"

"What's all this talk about killing, Mr. Archer? Did somebody get killed?"

"I'll tell you, if you can keep a secret."

"I can keep a secret."

"See that you do. Your friend Lance was shot last night."

He didn't lift his eyes from the counter. "He was no friend of mine. He was nothing in my life."

"He was in Tony's."

He shook his head slowly from side to side. "I shouldn't have told you what I did about Tony. He did something once when he was young and crazy. He wouldn't do a thing like that again. He wouldn't hurt a flea, unless it was biting him."

"You can't have it both ways at once, Joseph. You said he hated Lance."

"I said almost."

"Why did he hate him?"

"He had good reason."

"Tell me."

"Not if you're going to turn it against Tony. That Lance isn't fit to tie his shoelaces for him."

"You think yourself that Tony may have shot him."

"I'm not saying what I think, I don't think anything."

"You said he had good reason. What was the reason?"

"Gabrielle," he said to the floor. "Lance was the first one she went with, back when she was just a kid in high school. She told me that. He started her drinking, he taught her all the ways of doing it. If Tony shot that *pachuco*, he did a good service to the world."

"Maybe, but not to himself. You say Gabrielle told you all these things?"

He nodded, and his black, despondent shadow nodded with him.

"Were you intimate with her?"

"I never was, not if you mean what I think you mean. She treated me like I had no human feelings. She used to torture me with these things she told me—the things he taught her to do." His voice was choked. "I guess she didn't know she was torturing me. She just didn't know I had feelings."

"You've got too many feelings."

"Yes, I have. They break me up inside sometimes. Like when she told me what he wanted her to do. He wanted her to go to L.A. with him and live in a hotel, and he would get her dates with men. I blew my top on that one, and went to Tony with it. That was when he broke off with Lance, got him fired from here and kicked him out of the house."

"Did Gabrielle go with him?"

"No, she didn't. I thought with him out of the way, maybe she'd straighten out. But it turned out to be too late for her. She was already gone."

"What happened to her after that?"

"Listen, Mr. Archer," he said in a tight voice. "You could get me in trouble. Spying on the members is no part of my job."

"What's a job?"

"It isn't the job. I could get another job. I mean really bad trouble."

"Sorry. I didn't mean to frighten you. I thought you wanted to be serviceable."

Chapter 23

H E LOOKED up at the light. His face was smooth. No moral strain showed. But I could feel the cracking tension in him.

"Gabrielle is dead," he said to the unblinking light. "What service can I do her by talking about her?"

"There are other girls, and it could happen to them."

His silence stretched out. Finally he said:

"I'm not as much of a coward as you think. I tried to tell the policemen, when they were asking me questions about the earring. But they weren't interested in hearing about it."

"Hearing about what?"

"If I've got to say it, I'll say it. Gabrielle used to go in one of the *cabañas* practically every day and stay there for an hour or more."

"All by herself?"

"You know I don't mean that."

"Who was with her, Joseph?"

I was almost certain what his answer would be.

"Mr. Graff used to be with her."

"You're sure of that?"

"I'm sure. You don't understand about Gabrielle. She was young and silly, proud that a man like Mr. Graff would take an interest in her. Besides, she wanted me to cover for her by taking orders in the other *cabañas* when she was—otherwise occupied. She wasn't ashamed for me to know," he added bitterly. "She was just ashamed for Mrs. Lamb to know."

"Did they ever meet here at night?" I said. "Graff and Gabrielle?"

"Maybe they did. I don't know. I never worked at night in those days."

"She was in the Club the night she was killed," I said. "We know that."

"How do we know that? Tony found her on the beach."

"The earring you found. Where was it you found it?"

"On the gallery in front of the *cabañas*. But she could have dropped it there any time."

"Not if she was still wearing the other one. Do you know for a fact that she was, or is this just what they told you?"

"I know it for a fact. I saw it myself. When they were asking me questions, they took me down to where she was. They opened up the drawer and made me look at her. I saw the little white earring on her ear."

Tears started in his eyes, the color of blue-black ink. Memory had given him a sudden stab. I said:

"Then she must have been in the Club shortly before she was killed. When a girl loses one earring, she doesn't go on wearing the other one. Which means that Gabrielle didn't have time to notice the loss. It's possible that she lost it at the precise time that she was being killed. I want you to show me where you found it, Joseph."

Outside, first light was washing the eastern slopes of the sky. The sparse stars were melting in it like grains of snow on stone. Under the dawn wind, the pool was gray and restless like a coffined piece of the sea.

Tobias led me along the gallery, about half the length of the pool. We passed the closed doors of half-a-dozen *cabañas*, including Graff's. I noticed that the spring had gone out of his walk. His sneakered feet slapped the concrete disconsolately. He stopped and turned to me:

"It was right about here, caught in this little grid." A circular wire grating masking a drain was set into a shallow depression in the concrete. "Somebody'd hosed down the gallery and washed it into the drain. I just happened to see it shine."

"How do you know somebody hosed the gallery?"

"It was still wet in patches."

"Who did it, do you know?"

"Could have been anybody, anybody that worked around the pool. Or any of the members. You never can tell what the members are going to do."

"Who worked around the pool at that time?"

"Me and Gabrielle, mostly, and Tony and the lifeguard. . . . No, there wasn't any lifeguard just then—not until I took over in the summer. Miss Campbell was filling in as lifeguard."

"Was she there that morning?"

"I guess she was. Yes, I remember she was. What are you trying to get at, Mr. Archer?"

"Who killed Gabrielle, and why and where and how."

He leaned against the wall, his shoulders high. His eyes and mouth gleamed in his black basalt face. "For God's sake, Mr. Archer, you're not pointing the finger at me again?"

"No. I'd like your opinion. I think that Gabrielle was killed in the Club, maybe right on this spot. The murderer dragged her down to the beach, or else she crawled there under her own power. She left a trail of blood, which had to be washed away. And she dropped an earring, which didn't get washed away."

"A little earring isn't much to go on."

"No," I said. "It isn't."

"You think Miss Campbell did all this?"

"It's what I want your opinion about. Did she have any reason, any motive?"

"Could be she had." He licked his lips. "She made a play for Mr. Graff herself, only he didn't go for her."

"Gabrielle told you this?"

"She told me Miss Campbell was jealous of her. She didn't have to tell me. I can see things for myself."

"What did you see?"

"The dirty looks between them, all that spring. They were still friends in a way, you know how girls can be, but they didn't like each other the way they used to. Then, right after it happened, right after the inquest, Miss Campbell took off for parts unknown."

"But she came back."

"More than a year later she came back, after it all died down. She was still very interested in the case, though. She asked me a lot of questions this last summer. She gave me a story that her and her sister Rina were going to write it up for a magazine, but I don't think that was their interest."

"What kind of questions did they ask?"

"I don't know," he said wearily. "Some of the ones you asked me, I guess. You've asked me about a million of them now."

"Did you tell her about the earring?"

"Maybe I did. I don't remember. Does it matter?" He pushed himself away from the wall, shuffled across the gallery, and looked up at the whitening sky. "I got to go home and get some sleep, Mr. Archer. I go back on duty at nine o'clock."

"I thought you never got tired."

"I get depressed. You stirred up a lot of things I want to forget. In fact, you've been giving me kind of a hard time."

"I'm sorry. I'm tired, too. It'll be worth it, though, if we can solve this murder."

"Will it? Say you do, then what will happen?" His face was grim in the gray light, and his voice drew on old reserves of bitterness. "The same thing will happen that happened before. The cops will take over your case and seal it off and nothing will happen, nobody get arrested."

"Is that what happened before?"

"I'm telling you it did. When Marfeld saw he couldn't railroad me, he suddenly lost interest in the case. Well, I lost interest, too."

"I can go higher than Marfeld if I have to."

"What if you do? It's too late for Gabrielle, too late for me. It was always too late for me."

He turned on his heel and walked away. I said after him:

"Can I drop you someplace?"

"I have my own car."

Chapter 24

I SHOULD have handled it better. I walked to the end of the pool, the last man at the party, feeling that early-morning ebb of heart when the blood runs sluggish and cold. The fog had begun to blow out to sea. It foamed and poured in a slow cataract toward the obscure west. Black-marble patches of ocean showed through here and there.

I must have seen it and known what it was before I was conscious of it. It was a piece of black driftwood with a twist of root at one end, floating low in the water near the shore. It rode in slowly and discontinuously, pushed by a series of breaking waves. Its branches were very flexible for a log. A wave lodged it on the wet brown sand. It was a man in a dark, belted raincoat, lying face-down.

The gate in the fence was padlocked. I picked up a DO NOT RUN sign with a heavy concrete base and swung it at the padlock. The gate burst open. I went down the concrete steps and turned Carl Stern over onto his back. His forehead was deeply ridged where it had struck or been struck by a hard object. The wound in his throat gaped like a toothless mouth shouting silently.

I went to my car, remembering from my bottom-scratching days that there was a southward current along this shore, about a mile an hour. Just under three miles north of the Channel Club, a paved view-point for sightseers blistered out from the highway to the fenced edge of a bluff which overhung the sea. Stern's rented sedan was parked with its heavy chrome front against the cable fence. Blood spotted the windshield and dashboard and the front seat. Blood stained the blade of the knife which lay on the floor-mat. It looked like Stern's own knife.

I didn't mess with any of it. I wanted no part of Stern's death. I drove home on automatic pilot and went to bed. I dreamed about a man who lived by himself in a landscape of crumbling stones. He spent a great deal of his time, without much success, trying to reconstruct in his mind the monuments and the buildings of which the scattered stones were the only vestiges. He vaguely remembered some kind of oral tradition to the effect that a city had stood there once. And a still vaguer tradition: or perhaps it was a dream inside of the dream: that the people who had built the city, or their descendants, were coming back eventually to rebuild it. He wanted to be around when the work was done.

Chapter 25

M Y ANSWERING service woke me at seven thirty. "Rise and shine, Mr. Archer!"

"Do I have to shine? I'm feeling kind of dim. I got to bed about an hour ago."

"I haven't been to bed yet. And, after all, you could have canceled your standing order."

"I hereby cancel it, forever." I was in one of those drained and chancy moods when everything seems either laughable or weepworthy, depending on the position you hold your head in. "Now hang the hell up and let me get back to sleep. This is cruel and unusual punishment."

"My, but we're in splendid spirits this morning!" Her secretarial instinct took over: "Wait now, don't hang up. Couple of long-distance calls for you, both from Las Vegas. First at one forty, young lady, seemed very anxious to talk to you, but wouldn't leave her name. She said she'd call back, but she never did. Got that? Second at three fifteen, Dr. Anthony Reeves, intern at the Memorial Hospital, said he was calling on behalf of a patient named George Wall, picked up at the airport with head injuries."

"The Vegas airport?"

"Yes. Does that mean anything to you?"

It meant a surge of relief, followed by the realization that I was going to have to drag myself out to International Airport and crawl aboard a plane. "Make me a reservation, will you, Vera?"

"First plane to Vegas?"

"Right."

"One other call, yesterday afternoon. Man named Mercero from the CHP, said the Jag was registered to Lance Leonard. Is that the actor that got himself shot last night?"

"It's in the morning papers, eh?"

"Probably. I heard it on the radio."

"What else did you hear?"

"That was all. It was just a flash bulletin."

"No," I said. "It isn't the same one. What did you say the name was again?"

"I forget." She was a jewel among women.

Shortly before ten o'clock I was talking to Dr. Anthony Reeves in his room in the Southern Nevada Hospital. He'd had the night duty on Emergency, and had given George Wall a preliminary examination when George was brought in by the sheriff's men. They had found him wandering around McCarran Airfield in a confused condition. He had a fractured cheekbone, probably a brain concussion, and perhaps a fractured skull. George had to have absolute quiet for at least a week, and would probably be laid up for a month. He couldn't see anyone.

It was no use arguing with young Dr. Reeves. Butter wouldn't melt in his mouth. I went in search of a susceptible nurse, and eventually found a plump little redhead in an L.A. General cap who was impressed by an old Special Deputy badge I carried. On the strength of it, she led me to a semi-private room with a NO VISITORS sign on the door. George was the only occupant, and he was sleeping. I promised not to wake him.

The window shades were tightly drawn, and there was no light on in the room. It was so dim that I could barely make out George's white-bandaged head against the pillow. I sat in an armchair between his bed and the empty one, and listened to the susurrus of his breathing. It was slow and steady. After a while I almost went to sleep myself.

I was startled out of it by a cry of pain. I thought at first it was George, but it was a man on the other side of the wall. He cried loudly again.

George stirred and groaned and sat up, raising both hands to his half-mummified face. He swayed and threatened to fall out of bed. I held him by the shoulders.

"Take it easy, boy."

"Let me go. Who are you?"

"Archer," I said. "The indigent's Florence Nightingale."

"What happened to me? Why can't I see?"

"You've pulled the bandages down over your eyes. Also, it's dark in here."

"Where is here? Jail? Am I in jail?"

"You're in the hospital. Don't you remember asking Dr. Reeves to phone me long-distance?"

"I'm afraid I don't remember. What time is it?"

"It's Saturday morning, getting along towards noon."

The information hit him hard. He lay back quietly for a while, then said in a puzzled tone:

"I seem to have lost a day."

"Relax. You wouldn't want it back."

"Did I do something wrong?"

"I don't know what you did. You ask too many questions, George."

"You're just letting me down easy, aren't you?" Embarrassment thickened in his throat like phlegm. "I suppose I made a complete ass of myself."

"Most of us do from time to time. But hold the thought."

He groped for the light-switch at the head of the bed, found the cord, and pulled it. Fingering the bandages on his face, he peered at me through narrow slits in them. Below the bandages, his puffed lips were dry and cracking. He said with a kind of awe in his voice:

"That little pug in the pajamas—did he do this to me?"

"Part of it. When did you see him last, George?"

"You ought to know, you were with me. What do you mean, part of it?"

"He had some help."

"Whose help?"

"Don't you remember?"

"I remember something." He sounded childishly uncertain. Physical and moral shock had cut his ego down small. "It must have been just a nightmare. It was like a jumble of old movies running through my head. Only I was in it. A man with a gun was after me. The scene kept changing—it couldn't have been real."

"It was real. You got into a hassle with the company guards at Simon Graff's studio. Does the name Simon Graff mean anything to you?"

"Yes, it does. I was in bed in some wretched little house in Los Angeles, and someone talking on the telephone said that name. I got up and called a taxicab and asked the driver to take me to see Simon Graff."

"It was me on the telephone, George. In my house."

"Have I ever been in your house?"

"Yesterday." His memory seemed to be functioning very conveniently. I didn't doubt his sincerity, but I was irritated. "You also lifted a wretched little old charcoal-gray suit of mine which cost me one-two-five."

"Did I? I'm sorry."

"You'll be sorrier when you get the bill. But skip it. How did you get from the Graff studio to Vegas? And what have you been doing between then and now?"

The mind behind his blood-suffused eyes groped dully in limbo. "I think I came on a plane. Does that make any sense?"

"As much as anything does. Public or private plane?"

After a long pause, he said: "It must have been private. There were just the two of us, me and another fellow. I think it was the same one who chased me with the gun. He told me that Hester was in danger and needed my help. I blacked out, or something. Then I was walking down a street with a lot of signs flashing in my eyes. I went into this hotel where she was supposed to be, but she had gone, and the desk clerk wouldn't tell me where."

"Which hotel?"

"I'm not sure. The sign was in the shape of a wineglass. Or a martini glass. The Dry Martini? Does that sound possible?"

"There is one in town. When were you there?"

"Some time in the course of the night. I'd lost all track of time. I must have spent the rest of the night looking for her. I saw a number of girls who resembled her, but they always turned out to be someone different. I kept blacking out and coming to in another place. It was awful, with those lights in my eyes and the people milling about. They thought I was drunk. Even the policeman thought I was drunk."

"Forget it, George. It's over now."

"I won't forget it. Hester is in danger. Isn't that so?"

"She may be, I don't know. Forget about her, too, why don't you? Fall in love with the nurse or something. With your win-and-loss record, you ought to marry a nurse anyway. And, incidentally, you better lie down or the nurse will be reaming both of us."

Instead of lying down, he sat up straighter, his shoulders arching under the hospital shirt. Between the bandages, his red eyes were fixed on my face. "Something has happened to Hester. You're trying to keep me from knowing."

"Don't be crazy, kid. Relax. You've sparked enough trouble."

He said: "If you won't help me, I'm getting up and walking out of here now. Somebody has to do something."

"You wouldn't get far."

For answer, he threw off the covers, swung his legs over the edge of the high bed, reached for the floor with his bare feet, and stood up tottering. Then he fell forward onto his knees, his head swinging loose, slack as a killed buck. I hoisted him back onto the bed. He lay inert, breathing rapidly and lightly.

I pressed the nurse's signal, and passed her on my way out.

Chapter 26

THE DRY MARTINI was a small hotel on the edge of the older downtown gambling district. Two old ladies were playing Canasta for money in the boxlike knotty-pine lobby. The desk clerk was a fat man in a rayon jacket. His red face was set in the permanently jovial expression which people expect of fat men.

"What can I do for you, sir?"

"I have an appointment with Miss Campbell."

"I'm very much afraid Miss Campbell hasn't come in yet."

"What time did she go out?"

He clasped his hands across his belly and twiddled his thumbs. "Let's see, I came on at midnight, she checked in about an hour after that, stayed long enough to change her dress, and away she went again. Couldn't've been much later than one."

"You notice things."

"A sexburger like her I notice." The tip of his tongue protruded between his teeth, which were a good grade of plastic.

"Was anybody with her, going or coming?"

"Nope. She came and went by herself. You're a friend of hers, eh?"

"Yeah."

"Know her husband? Big guy with light-reddish hair?"

"I know him."

"What goes with him? He came in here in the middle of the night looking like the wrath of God. Big welts on his face, blood in his hair, yackety-yacking like a psycho. He had some idea in his head that his wife was in trouble and I was mixed up in it. Claimed I knew where she was. I had a hell of a time getting rid of him."

I looked at my watch. "She could be in trouble, at that. She's been gone eleven hours."

"Think nothing of it. They stay on the town for twenty-four, thirty-six hours at a time, some of them. Maybe she hit a winning streak and's riding it out. Or maybe she had a date. Somebody must've clobbered the husband. He *is* her husband, isn't he?"

"He is, and several people clobbered him. He has a way of leading with his chin. Right now he's in the hospital, and I'm trying to find her for him."

"Private dick?"

I nodded. "Do you have any idea where she went?"

"I can find out, maybe, if it's important." He looked me over, estimating the value of my clothes and the contents of my wallet. "It's going to cost me something."

"How much?"

"Twenty." It was a question.

"Hey, I'm not buying you outright."

"All right, ten," he said quickly. "It's better than getting poked in the eye with a carrot."

He took the bill and waddled into a back room, where I heard him talking on the telephone to somebody named Rudy. He came back looking pleased with himself:

"I called her a taxi last night, was just talking to the dispatcher. He's sending over the driver that took the call."

"How much is he going to cost me?"

"That's between you and him."

I waited inside the glass front door, watching the noon traffic. It came from every state in the Union, but most of the license plates belonged to Southern California. This carney town was actually Los Angeles's most farflung suburb.

A shabby yellow cab detached itself from the westbound stream and pulled up at the curb. The driver got out and started across the sidewalk. He wasn't old, but he had a drooping face and posture like a hound that had been fed too long on scraps. I stepped outside.

"You the gentleman interested in the blondie?"

"I'm the one."

"We're not supposed to give out information about our fares. Unless it's official—"

"A sawbuck official enough?"

He stood at attention and parodied a salute. "What was it you wanted to know, bud?"

"You picked her up what time?"

"One fifteen. I checked it on my sheet."

"And dropped her where?"

He gave me a yellow-toothed grin and pushed his peaked cap back. It hung almost vertically on the peaked rear of his skull. "Don't rush me, bud. Let's see the color of your money first."

I paid him.

"I set her out on the street," he said. "I didn't like to do it that time of night, but I guess she knew what she was doing."

"Where was this?"

"It's out past the Strip a piece. I can show you if you want. It's a two-dollar fare."

He opened the back door of his cab, and I got in. According to his identification card, his name was Charles Meyer. He told me about his troubles as we drove out past the Disney-Modern fronts where Hollywood and Times Square names decoyed for anonymous millionaires. Charles Meyer had many troubles. Drink had been his downfall. Women had wrecked his life. Gambling had ruined him. He told me in his singsong insistent whine:

"Three months I been hacking in this goddam burg trying to get together a stake to buy some clothes and a crate, get out of here. Last week I thought I had it made, two hundred and thirty bucks and all my debts paid off. So I went into the drugstore to get my insulin and they give me my change in silver, two dollars and a four-bits piece, and just for kicks I fed them in the machines and that was going to be that." He clucked. "There went two thirty. It took me a little over three hours to drop it. I'm a fast worker."

"You could buy a bus ticket."

"No, sir. I'm sticking here until I get a car, a postwar like the one I lost, and a suit of decent clothes. I'm not dragging my tail back to Dago looking like a bum."

We passed several buildings under construction, identified by signs as additional club-hotels with fancy names. One of them was Simon Graff's Casbah. Their girders rose on the edge of the desert like armatures for people to build their glad bad dreams on.

The Strip degenerated into a long line of motels clinging to the fringes of glamour. Charles Meyer U-turned and stopped in front of one of them, the Fiesta Motor Court. He draped his hound face over the seat back:

"This is where I set her off."

"Did anybody meet her?"

"Not that I saw. She was all by herself on the street when I pulled away."

"But there was traffic?"

"Sure, there's always some traffic."

"Did she seem to be looking for anybody?"

"How could I tell? She wasn't making much sense, she was in a kind of a tizzy."

"What kind of a tizzy?"

"You know. Upset. Hysterical-like. I didn't like to leave her alone like that, but she says beat it. I beat it."

"What was she wearing?"

"Red dress, dark cloth coat, no hat. One thing, she had on real high heels. I thought at the time, she wouldn't walk far with them on."

"Which way did she walk?"

"No way, she just stood there on the curb, long as I could see her. You want to go back to the Martini now?"

"Stick around for a few minutes."

"Okay, but I keep my meter running."

The proprietor of the Fiesta Motor Court was sitting at an umbrella table in the small patio beside his office. He was smoking a waterpipe and fanning himself with a frayed palm-leaf fan. He looked like a happy Macedonian or a disappointed Armenian. In the background several dark-eyed girls who could have been his daughters were pushing linen carts in and out of the tiny cottages.

No, he hadn't seen the young lady in the red dress. He hadn't seen anything after eleven thirty, got his NO VACANCY up at eleven twenty-five and went straight to bed. As I moved away he barked commands at one of the dark-eyed girls, as if to teach me by example how to keep my females out of trouble.

The Colonial Inn, next door, had a neat little office presided over by a neat little man with a clipped mustache and a north-by-northeast accent with asthmatic overtones. No, he certainly had not noticed the young lady in question, having better things to do with his time. He also had better things to do than answer questions about other people's wives.

Moving toward town and the unlit neon silo of the Flamingo, I tried the Bar-X Tourist Ranch and the Welcome Traveller and the Oasis. I got three different answers, all negative. Charles Meyer trailed me in his taxi, with many grins and nods.

The Rancho Eldorado was a double row of pastel chicken coops festooned with neon tubing. There was no one in the office. I rang until I got an answer, because it was close to the street and on a corner. A woman opened the door and looked at me down her nose, which was long and pitted with ancient acne craters. Her eyes were black and small, and her hair was up in pincurls. She was so homely that I felt sorry for her. It was practically an insult to offer her a description of a beautiful blonde in a red dress.

"Yes," she said. "I saw her." Her black eyes glinted with malice. "She stood on the corner for ten or twelve minutes last night. I don't set myself up as a judge of other people, but it made me mad to see her out there flaunting herself, deliberately trying to get herself picked up. I can tell when a girl's trying to get herself picked up. But it didn't work!" Her voice twanged triumphantly. "Men aren't as easily taken in as they used to be, and nobody stopped for her."

"What did she do to you?"

"Nothing, I just didn't like the way she flaunted herself under the light on my corner. That sort of thing is bad for business. This is a family motel. So I finally stepped outside and told her to move along. I was perfectly nice about it. I simply told her in a quiet way to peddle her papers elsewhere." Her mouth closed, lengthening in a horizontal line with right angles at the corners. "She's a friend of yours, I suppose?"

"No. I'm a detective."

Her face brightened. "I see. Well, I saw her go into the Dewdrop Inn, that's the second place down from here. It's about time somebody cleaned out that den of iniquity. Are you after her for some *crime?*"

"Third-degree pulchritude."

She chewed on this like a camel, then shut the door in my face. The Dewdrop Inn was a rundown stucco ell with sagging shutters and doors that needed paint. Its office door was opened by a woman who was holding a soiled bathrobe tight around her waist. She had frizzled red hair. Her skin had been seared by blowtorch suns, except where her careless breast gleamed white in the V of her robe. She caught and returned my dipping glance, letting the V and the door both open wider.

"I'm looking for a woman."

"What a lucky coincidence. I'm looking for a man. It's just it's just a leetle early for me. I'm still a teensy bit drunky from last night."

Yawning, she cocked one fist and stretched the other arm straight up over her head. Her breath was a blend of gin and fermenting womanhood. Her bare feet were dirty white.

"Come on in, I won't bite you."

I stepped up into the office. She held herself in the doorway so that I brushed against her from shoulder to knee. She wasn't really interested, just keeping in practice. The room was dirty and disordered, with a couple of lipsticky glasses on the registration desk, confession magazines scattered on the floor.

"Big night last night?" I said.

"Oh, sure. Big night. Drink cocktails until four and wake up at six and you can't get back to sleep. This divorce kick—well, it isn't all it's cracked up to be."

I braced myself for another life-story. Something about my face, maybe a gullible look, invited them. But she spared me:

"Okay, Joe, we won't beat around the bush. You want the girlie in the red dress."

"You catch on very quick."

"Yeah. Well, she isn't here. I don't know where she is. You a mobster or what?"

"That's a funny question."

"Yeah, sure, uproarious. You got a hand gun in your armpit, and you're not Davy Crockett."

"You shatter my illusions."

She gave me a hard and murky look. Her eyes resembled mineral specimens, malachite or copper sulphate, which had been gathering dust on somebody's back shelf. "Come on, now, what's it all about? The kid said there was mobsters after her. You're no mobster, are you?"

"I'm a private dick. Her husband hired me to find her." I realized suddenly that I was back where I'd started, twenty-eight hours later and in another state. It felt more like twenty-eight days.

The woman was saying: "You find her for him, what's he plan to do with her? Beat her up?"

"Look after her. She needs it."

"That could be. Was it all malarkey about the mobsters? I mean, was she stringing me?"

"I don't think so. Did she mention any names?"

She nodded. "One. Carl Stern."

"You know that name?"

"Yeah. The *Sun* dug into his record and spread it on the front page last fall when he put in for a gambling license. *He* wouldn't be her husband?"

"Her husband's a nice boy from Toronto. George Wall. Some of Stern's friends put him in the hospital. I want to get to his wife before they do it to her."

"No kidding?"

"I mean it."

"What did she do to Stern?"

"It's a question I want to ask her. Where is she now?"

She gave me the mineral look again. "Let's see your license. Not that a license means much. The guy that got me my divorce was a licensed private detective, and he was a prime stinker if I ever saw one."

"I'm not," I said with the necessary smile, and showed her my photostat.

She looked up sharply. "Your name is Archer?"

"Yes."

"Is this a funny coincidence or what? She tried to phone you last night, person to person. Knocked on the door along towards two o'clock, looking pretty white and shaky, and asked to use my phone. I asked her what the trouble was. She broke down and told me that there were mobsters after her, or there soon would be. She wanted to call the airport, catch a plane out right away quick. I put in a call for her, but I couldn't get her on a flight till morning. So then she tried to call you."

"What for?"

"She didn't tell me. If you're a friend of hers, why didn't you say so? *Are* you a friend of Rina Campbell's?"

"Who?" I said.

"Rina Campbell. The girl we're talking about."

I made a not very smooth recovery. "I think I am. Is she still here?"

"I gave her a nembutal and put her to bed myself. I haven't heard a peep out of her. She's probably still sleeping, poor dearie."

"I want to see her."

"Yeah, you made that clear. Only, this is a free country, and if she don't want to see you there's no way you can make her."

"I'm not planning to push her around."

"You better not, brother. Try anything with the kid, and I'll shoot you personally."

"You like her, do you?"

"Why not? She's a real good girl, as good as they come. I don't care what she's done."

"You're doing all right yourself."

"Am I? That I doubt. I had it once, when I was Rina's age. I tried to save a little of it for an emergency. If you can't pass on a little loving-kindness in this world, you might as well be a gopher in a hole."

"What did you say your name was?"

"I didn't say. My name is Carol, Mrs. Carol Busch." She offered me a red, unlovely hand. "Remember, if she changed her mind about wanting to see you, you amscray."

She opened an inner door, and shut it firmly behind her. I went outside where I could watch the exits. Charles Meyer was waiting in his cab.

"Hiyah. Any luck?"

"No luck. I'm quitting. How much do I owe you?"

He leaned sideways to look at the meter. "Three seventy-five. Don't you want a ride downtown? I'll let you have it for half-price."

"I'll walk. I need the exercise."

His look was sad and canine. He knew that I was lying, and he knew the reason: I didn't trust him. Mrs. Carol Busch called me from the doorway of the unit adjoining the office. "Okay, she's up, she wants to talk to you."

Chapter 27

M RS. BUSCH stayed outside and let me go in alone. The room was dim and cool. Blackout blinds and heavy drapes kept the sunlight out. A shaded bedside lamp was the only source of light. The girl sat on the foot of the unmade Hollywood bed with her face turned away from the lamp.

I saw the reason for this when she forgot her pose and looked up at me. Nembutal or tears had swollen her eyelids. Her bright hair was carelessly groomed. She wore her red wool dress as if it were burlap. Overnight, she seemed to have lost her assurance that her beauty would look after her. Her voice was small and high:

"Hello."

"Hello, Rina."

"You know who I am," she said dully.

"I do now. I should have guessed it was a sister act. Where is your sister, Rina?"

"Hester's in trouble. She had to leave the country."

"You're sure about that?"

"I'm not sure about anything since I found out Lance is dead."

"How did you find out? You didn't believe me when I told you last night."

"I have to believe you now. I picked up a Los Angeles paper at the hotel, and there was a headline about him—about his murder." Her eyelids lifted heavily. Her dark-blue eyes had changed subtly in thirteen hours: they saw more and liked it less. "Did my sister—did Hester kill him?"

"She may have, but I doubt it. Which way did they say she went—Mexico or Canada or Hawaii?"

"They didn't say. Carl Stern said it would be better if I didn't know."

"What are you supposed to be doing here? Giving her an alibi?"

"I guess so. That was the idea." She looked up again. "Please don't stand over me. I'm willing to tell you what I know, but please don't cross-question me. I've had a terrible night."

Her fingers dabbed at her forehead and came away wet. There was a box of Kleenex on the bedside table. I handed her a leaf of it, which she used to wipe her forehead and blow her nose. She said surprisingly, in a voice as thin as a flute:

"Are you a good man?"

"I like to think so," but her candor stopped me. "No," I said, "I'm not. I keep trying, when I remember to, but it keeps getting tougher every year. Like trying to chin yourself with one hand. You can practice off and on all your life, and never make it."

She tried to smile. The gentle corners of her mouth wouldn't lift. "You talk like a decent man. Why did you come to my sister's house last night? How did you get in?"

"I broke in."

"Why? Have you got something against her?"

"Nothing personal. Her husband asked me to find her. I've been trying to."

"She has no husband. I mean, Hester's husband is dead."

"She told you he was dead, eh?"

"Isn't it true?"

"She doesn't tell the truth when a lie will do."

"I know." She added in an unsentimental tone: "But Hester is my sister and I love her. I've always done what I could for her, I always will."

"And that's why you're here."

"That's why I'm here. Lance and Carl Stern told me that I could save Hester a lot of grief, maybe a penitentiary term. All I had to do was fly here under her name, and register in a hotel, then disappear. I was supposed to take a taxi out to the edge of the desert, past the airport, and Carl Stern was supposed to pick me up. I didn't meet him, though. I came back here instead. I lost my nerve."

"Is that why you tried to phone me?"

"Yes. I got to thinking, when I saw the piece about Lance in the paper. You'd told me the truth about that, perhaps you'd told me the truth about everything. And I remembered something you said last night—the very first thing you said when you saw me in Hester's room. You said—" her voice was careful, like a child's repeating a lesson by rote—"you thought I was Hester, and you said you thought I was dead—that *she* was dead."

"I said that, yes."

"Is it true?"

I hesitated. She got to her feet, swaying a little. Her hand pressed hard on my arm:

"Is Hester dead? Don't be afraid to tell me if she is. I can take it."

"Sorry, I don't know the answer."

"What do you think?"

"I think she is. I think she was killed in the Beverly Hills house yesterday afternoon. And the alibi they're trying to set up isn't for Hester. It's for whoever killed her."

"I'm sorry. I don't follow."

"Say she was killed yesterday. You assumed her identity, flew here, registered, disappeared. They wouldn't be asking questions about her in L.A."

"*I* would."

"If you got back alive."

It took her a second to grasp the idea, another to apply it to her present situation. She blinked, and the shock wave hit her. Her eyes were like cracked blue Easter eggs.

"What do you think I should do?"

"Fade. Disappear, until I get this thing settled. But first I want your story. You haven't explained why you let them use you for a patsy. Or how much you knew about your sister's activities. Did she tell you what she was doing?"

"She didn't intend to, but I guessed. I'm willing to talk, Mr. Archer. In a way, I'm as guilty as Hester. I feel responsible for the whole thing."

She paused, and looked around the yellow plaster walls. She seemed to be dismayed by the ugliness of the room. Her gaze stopped at the door behind me, and hardened. The door sprang open as I turned. Harsh sunlight slapped me across the eyes, and glinted on three guns. Frost held one of them. Lashman and Marfeld flanked him. Behind them Mrs. Busch crawled in the gravel. In the street Charles Meyer's shabby yellow taxi rolled away toward town. He didn't look back.

I saw all this while I reached for my left armpit. I didn't complete the motion. The day and the night and the day again had dulled me, and I wasn't reacting well, but I knew that a gun in my hand was all they needed. I stood with my right hand frozen on my chest.

Frost smiled like a death's-head against the aching blue sky. He had on a multicolored shot-silk shirt, a Panama hat with a matching colored band, and the kind of white flannels worn by tennis pros. The gun in his hand was a German machine pistol. He pressed its muzzle into my solar plexus and took my gun.

"Hands on your head. This is a real lovely surprise."

I put my hands on my head. "I like it, too."

"Now turn around."

Mrs. Busch had got to her feet. She cried out: "Dirty bullying bastards!" and flung herself on the back of the nearest gunman. This happened to be Marfeld. He pivoted and slapped her face with the barrel of his gun. She fell turning and lay still on her face, her hair splashing out like fire. I said:

"I'm going to kill you, Marfeld."

He turned to me, his eyes joyous, if Marfeld could feel joy. "You and who else, boysie? You won't be doing any pitching. You're the catcher, see?"

He slapped the side of my head with the gun. The sky swayed like a blue balloon on a string.

Frost spoke sharply to Marfeld. "Lay off. And, for God's sakes, lay off the woman." He spoke to me more gently: "Keep your hands on your head and turn around."

I did these things, tickled by worms of blood crawling through my hair and down the side of my face. Rina was sitting on the bed against the wall. Her legs were drawn up under her, and she was shivering.

"You disappoint me, doll," Frost said. "You do too, Lew."

"I disappoint myself."

"Yeah, after all the trouble I went to, giving you good advice, and our years of friendly relationship."

"You move me deeply. I haven't been so deeply moved since I heard a hyena howl."

Frost pushed the gun muzzle hard into my right kidney. Marfeld moved around me, swinging his shoulders busily. "That's no way to talk to Mr. Frost."

He swung the edge of his hand toward my throat. I pulled in my chin to protect my larynx and caught the blow on the mouth. I made a noise that sounded like *gar* and reached for him. Lashman locked my right arm and hung his weight on it. Marfeld's right shoulder dropped. At the end of his hooked right arm, his fist swung into my belly. It doubled me over. I straightened, gulping down bitter regurgitated coffee.

"That's enough of that," Frost said. "Hold a gun on him, Lash."

Frost moved past me to the bed. He walked slackly with his shoulders drooping. His voice was dry and tired:

"You ready to go now, baby?"

"Where is my sister?"

"You know she had to leave the country. You want to do what's right for her, don't you?" He leaned toward her in a parody of wheedling charm.

She hissed at him, grinning with all her teeth: "I wouldn't cross the street with you. You smell! I want my sister."

"You're coming if you have to be carried. So, on your horse."

"No. Let me out of here. You killed my sister."

She scrambled off the bed and ran for the door. Marfeld caught her around the waist and wrestled with her, grinning, his belly pressed to her hip. She slashed his cheek with her nails. He caught her by the hand and bent her fingers backward, struck savagely at her head with the flat of his hand. She stood submissive against the ghastly wall.

The gun at my back had lost contact, leaving a cold vacuum. I whirled. Lashman had been watching the girl being hurt with a voyeur's hot, dreamy eyes. I forced his gun down before he fired. I got the gun away from him and swung it at the left front corner of his skull. He crumpled in the doorway.

Marfeld was on my back. He was heavy and strong, with an innate sense of leverage. His arm looped around my neck and tightened. I swung him against the door frame. He almost pulled my head off, but he fell on top of Lashman, his face upturned. With the butt of the gun, I struck him between the eyes.

I turned toward Frost in the instant that he fired, and flung myself sideways. His slugs whanged into the wall wide of my head. I shot him in the right arm. His gun clanked on the floor. I got my free hand on it and stood up and backed to the wall and surveyed the room.

The air-conditioner thumped and whirred like a wounded bird in the wall behind my head. The girl leaned white-faced and still on the opposite wall. Frost sat on the floor between us, holding his right arm with his left hand. Blood laced his fingers. He looked from them to me. The fear of death which never left his eyes had taken over the rest of his face. In the doorway, Marfeld lay with his head on Lashman's chest. His veined eyeballs were turned up and in toward the deep blue dent in his forehead. Except for his hoarse breathing and the noise of the air-conditioner, the room was very tranquil.

Mrs. Busch appeared in the doorway, weaving slightly. One of her eyes was swollen and black, and her smiling mouth was bloody. She held a .45 automatic in both hands. Frost looked into its roving eye and tried to crawl under the bed. It was too low to receive him. He lay beside it, whimpering:

"Please. I'm a sick man. Don't shoot."

The redheaded woman laughed. "Look at him crawl. Listen to him whine."

"Don't kill him," I said. "Strange as it may seem, I have a use for him."

Chapter 28

RINA DROVE Frost's Cadillac. I rode in the back seat with Frost. She had made a pressure bandage and a sling for his arm out of several Dewdrop Inn bath towels. He sat and nursed his arm, refusing to talk, except to give directions.

Beyond the airport, we turned right toward mountains which lay naked and wrinkled under the sun. The road climbed toward the sun, and as it climbed it dwindled, changing to gravel. We came over the first low hump and overlooked a white-floored valley where nothing grew.

Near the crest of the inner slope, a concrete building with a rounded roof was set into the side of the hill. Squat and windowless, it resembled a military strongpoint. It was actually a disused ammunition dump.

Frost said: "She's in there."

Rina looked over her shoulder. Her nervous foot on the power brakes jolted the car to a stop. We slipped out under the brilliant sky. A jet track crossed it like a long white scar. I told Rina to stay in the car.

"You can put your gun away," Frost said. "There's nobody in there but her."

I made him climb ahead of me, up the slope to the single door of the building. Sheathed with rusting steel, the door swung half open. A broken padlock hung from its hasp. I pulled the door wide, holding my gun on Frost. A puff of warm air came from the interior. It smelled like an oven where meat had been scorched.

Frost hung back. I forced him to enter ahead of me. We stood on a narrow platform, peering down into dimness. The concrete floor of the dump was about six feet below the level of the entrance. Framed in light, our shadows fell across it. I pushed Frost out of the rectangle of light, and saw what lay on the floor: a wizened thing like a mummy, blackened and consumed by fire instead of by time.

"You did this to her?"

Frost said without conviction: "Hell, no, it was her

husband. You should be talking to him. He followed her here from L.A., did you know that? Knocked her off and set fire to the body."

"You'll have to do better than that, Frost. I've been talking to the husband. You flew him here in Stern's plane to frame him for the killing. You probably brought the body on the same flight. The frame didn't take, though, and it's not going to. None of your dirty little plans is working out."

He was silent for a period of time which was divided into shorter periods by the tic twitching at his eyelid. "It wasn't my idea, it was Stern's. And the gasoline was his idea. He said to put her to the torch, so that when they found the body they couldn't establish when she died. The girl was dead already, see, all we did was cremate her."

He looked down at the body. It was the image of the thing he feared, and it imposed silence on him. He reached out suddenly with his good arm, clawed at my shoulder and caught hold. "Can't we get out of here, Lew? I'm a sick man, I can't stand it in here."

I shook him off. "When you've told me who killed the girl."

There was another breathing silence. "Isobel Graff killed her," he said finally.

"How do you know?"

"Marfeld saw her. Marfeld saw her come tearing out of the house with the fantods. He went in, and there was Hester in the living-room. She had her head beaten in with a poker. The poker was lying across her. We couldn't leave her there. The cops would trace the Graff connection in no time—"

"What was Hester's connection with Graff?"

"Isobel thought they were shacked up, let's leave it at that. Anyway, it was up to me to do something with the body. I wanted to chuck it in the ocean, but Graff said no—he has a house on the ocean at Malibu. Then Lance Leonard got this other idea."

"How did Leonard get into the act?"

"He was a friend of Hester's. She borrowed his car, he came by to pick it up. Leonard had a key to her house, and he walked in on Marfeld and the body. He had his own reasons for wanting to cover it up, so he suggested getting her sister to help. The two sisters are look-alikes, almost like twins, and Leonard knew both of them. He talked the sister into flying here."

"What was going to happen to her?"

"That was Carl Stern's problem. But it looks as though Stern ran out on the whole deal. I don't see how he can afford to do that."

"You're kind of out of touch," I said. "You used to be an operator. When did you start letting goons and gunsills do your thinking for you?"

Frost grimaced and hung his head. "I'm not myself. I been full of demerol for the last three months."

"You're on a demerol kick?"

"I'm a dying man, Lew. My insides are being eaten away. I'm in terrible pain right at this moment. I shouldn't be walking around."

"You won't be walking around. You'll be sitting in a cell."

"You're a hard man, Lew."

"You keep calling me Lew. Don't do it. I ought to leave you here to find your own way back."

"You wouldn't do that to me?" He caught at me again, chattering. "Listen to me, Lew—Mr. Archer. About that Italy deal. I can get you five hundred a week for twenty-six weeks. No duties, nothing to do. A free holiday—"

"Save it. I wouldn't touch a nickel of yours with rubber gloves on."

"But you wouldn't leave me here?"

"Why not? You left her."

"You don't understand. I only did what I had to. We were caught. The girl fixed it herself so that we were caught. She had something on the Man and his wife, evidence against them, and she turned it over to Carl Stern. He forced the deal on us, in a way. I would have handled it differently."

"So everything you did was Stern's fault."

"I don't say that, but he was calling the signals. We had to co-operate with him. We've had to now for months. Stern even forced the Man to lend his name to his big new operation."

"What evidence does Stern hold against the Graffs?"

"Would I be likely to tell you?"

"You're going to tell me. Now. I'm getting sick of you, Frost."

He backed away from me against the doorpost. The light fell on one side of his face and made his profile look as pale and thin as paper. As if corruption had eaten him away till he was only a surface laid on darkness.

"A gun," he said. "A target pistol belonging to Mr. Graff. Isobel used it to kill a girl with, a couple of years ago."

"Where does Stern keep the gun?"

"In a safe-deposit box. I found out that much, but I couldn't get to it. He was carrying it with him last night, though, in the car. He showed it to me." His dull eyes brightened yellowly. "You know, Lew, I'm authorized to pay a hundred grand for that little gun. You're a strong, smart boy. Can you get it away from Stern?"

"Somebody already has. Stern got his throat cut in the course of the night. Or maybe you know that, Frost."

"No. I didn't know it. If it's true, it changes things."

"Not for you."

We went outside. Below, the valley floor shimmered in its own white heat. The jet trail which slashed the sky was blurring out. In this anti-human place, the Cadillac on the road looked as irrelevant as a space-ship stalled on the mountains of the moon. Rina stood at the foot of the slope, her face upturned and blank. It was heavy news I carried down to her.

Chapter 29

M UCH LATER, on the sunset plane, we were able to talk about it. Leroy Frost, denying and protesting and calling for lawyers and doctors, had been deposited with Marfeld and Lashman in the security ward of the hospital. The remains of Hester Campbell were in the basement of the same building, awaiting autopsy. I told the sheriff and the district attorney enough to have Frost and his men held for possible extradition on suspicion of murder. I didn't expect it to stick. The final moves in the case would have to be made in California.

The DC-6 left the runway and climbed the blue ramp of air. There were only a dozen other passengers, and Rina and I had the front end of the plane to ourselves. When the NO SMOKING sign went out, she crossed her legs and lit a cigarette. Without looking at me directly, she said in a brittle voice:

"I suppose I owe you my life, as they say in books. I don't know what I can do to repay you. No doubt I should offer to go to bed with you. Would you like that?"

"Don't," I said. "You've had a rough time and made a mistake, and I've been involved in it. But you don't have to take it out on me."

"I didn't mean to be snide," she said, a little snidely. "I was making a serious offer of my body. Having nothing better to offer."

"Rina, come off it."

"I'm not attractive enough, is that what you mean?"

"You're talking nonsense. I don't blame you. You've had a bad scare."

She sulked for a while, looking down at the Chinese Wall of mountains we were crossing. Finally she said in a chastened tone:

"You're perfectly right. I was scared, really scared, for the first time in my life. It does funny things to a girl. It made me feel—well, almost like a whore—as though I wasn't worth anything to myself."

"That's the way the jerks want you to feel. If everybody felt like a zombie, we'd all be on the same level. And the jerks could get away with the things jerks want to get away with. They're not, though. Jerkiness isn't as respectable as it used to be, not even in L.A. Which is why they had to build Vegas."

She didn't smile. "Is it such a terrible place?"

"It depends on who you pick for your playmates. You picked the worst ones you could find."

"I didn't pick them, and they're not my playmates. They never were. I despise them. I warned Hester years ago that Lance was poison for her. And I told Carl Stern what I thought of him to his face."

"When was this? Last night?"

"Several weeks ago. I went out on a double date with Lance and Hester. Perhaps it was a foolish thing to do, but I wanted to find out what was going on. Hester brought Carl Stern for me, can you imagine? He's supposed to be a millionaire, and Hester always believed that money was the important thing. She couldn't see, even at that late date, why I wouldn't play up to Stern.

"Not that it would have done me any good," she added wryly. "He was no more interested in me than I was in him. He spent the evening in various nightclubs playing footsie with Lance under the table. Hester didn't notice, or maybe she didn't care. She could be very dense about certain things. I cared, though, for her sake. Finally I told them off and walked out on the three of them."

"What did you say to them?"

"Just the plain, unvarnished truth. That Carl Stern was a pederast and probably much worse, and Hester was crazy to fool around with him and his pretty-boy."

"Did you mention blackmail?"

"Yes. I told them I suspected it."

"That was a dangerous thing to do. It gave Stern a reason to want you dead. I'm pretty sure he meant to kill you last night. Lucky for you he died first."

"Really? I can't believe—" But she believed it. Her dry throat refused to function. She sat swallowing. "Just because I—because I suspected something?"

"Suspected him of blackmail, and called him a fag. Killing always came easy to Stern. I went over his rap sheet this afternoon—the Nevada authorities have a full file on him. No wonder he couldn't get a gambling license in his own name. Back in the thirties he was one of Anastasia's boys, suspected of implication in over thirty killings."

"Why wasn't he arrested?"

"He was, but they couldn't convict him. Don't ask me why. Ask the politicians that ran the cops in New York and Jersey and Cleveland and the other places. Ask the people that voted for the politicians. Stern ended up in Vegas, but he belonged to the whole country. He worked for Lepke, for Game Boy Miller in Cleveland, for Lefty Clark in Detroit, for the Trans America gang in L.A. He finished his apprenticeship under Siegel, and after Siegel got it he went into business for himself."

"What sort of business?"

"Wire service for bookies, narcotics, prostitution, anything with a fast and dirty buck in it. He was a millionaire, all right, several times over. He sank a million in the Casbah alone."

"I don't understand why he would go in for blackmail. He didn't need the money."

"He was Syndicate-trained, and blackmail's been one of their main sources of power ever since Mafia days. No, it wasn't money he needed. It was status. Simon Graff's name gave him his chance to go legit, to really build himself into the countryside."

"And I helped him." The bones had come out in her face so that it was almost ugly. "I made it possible. I could bite my tongue out."

"Before you do, I wish you'd explain what you mean."

She drew in her breath sharply. "Well, in the first place, I'm a psychiatric nurse."

She fell silent. It was hard for her to get started.

"So your mother told me," I said.

She gave me a sidelong glance. "When did you run into Mother?"

"Yesterday."

"What did you think of her?"

"I liked her."

"Really?"

"I like women in general, and I'm not hypercritical."

"I am," Rina said. "I've always been suspicious of Mother and her little airs and graces and her big ideas. And it was mutual.

Hester was her favorite, her little pal. Or she was Hester's little pal. She spoiled my sister rotten, at the same time made terrible demands on her: all she wanted was for Hester to be great.

"I sat on the sidelines for fifteen years and watched the two girls play emotional ping-pong. Or pong-ping. I was the not-so-innocent bystander, the third one that made the crowd, the one that wasn't simpatico." It sounded like a speech she'd rehearsed to herself many times. There was bitterness in her voice, tempered with resignation. "I broke it up as soon as Mother would let me, as soon as I finished high school. I went into nurse's training in Santa Barbara, and took my P.G. work at Camarillo."

Talking about her profession, or talking out her feelings about her family, had given her back some of her self-assurance. She held her shoulders straighter, and her breasts were bold.

"Mother thought I was crazy. We had a knockdown-dragout quarrel the first year, and I haven't seen much of Mother since. It just happens I like doing things for sick people, especially working with disturbed people. Need to be needed, I guess. My main interest now is occupational therapy. It's mainly what I'm doing with Dr. Frey."

"This is the Dr. Frey who runs the sanitarium in Santa Monica?"

She nodded. "I've worked there for over two years."

"So you know Isobel Graff."

"Do I ever. She was admitted to the san not long after I started there. She'd been in before, more than once. The doctor said she was worse than usual. She's schizophrenic, you know, has been for twenty years, and when it's acute she develops paranoid delusions. The doctor said they used to be directed against her father when he was alive. This time they were directed against Mr. Graff. She believed that he was plotting against her, and she was going to get him first.

"Dr. Frey thought Mr. Graff should have her locked up for his own protection. Every now and then a paranoid delusion erupts into action. I've seen it happen. Dr. Frey gave her a series of metrazol treatments, and she gradually came out of the acute phase and quieted down. But she was still quite remote when this thing happened. I still wouldn't turn my back on her. But Dr. Frey said she wasn't dangerous, and he knew her better than I did and, after all, he was the doctor.

"In the middle of March, he gave her the run of the grounds. I shouldn't second guess a doctor, but that's where he made his mistake. She wasn't ready for freedom. The first little thing that happened set her off."

"What did happen?"

"I don't know exactly. Perhaps someone made a thoughtless remark, or simply looked at her in the wrong tone of voice. Paranoid people are like that, almost like radio receivers. They pick a tiny signal out of the air and build it up with their own power until they can't hear anything else. Whatever happened, Isobel took off, and she was gone all night.

"When she came back, she was *really* in a bad way. With that terrible glazed look on her face, like a fish with a hook in its mouth. She was right back where she started in January—worse."

"What night was she gone?"

"March 21, the first day of spring. I'm not likely to forget the date. A girl I used to know in Malibu, a girl named Gabrielle Torres, was killed that same night. I didn't connect the two events at the time."

"But you do now?"

She inclined her head somberly. "Hester made the connection for me. You see, she knew something I hadn't known, that Simon Graff and Gabrielle were—lovers."

"When did this come out?"

"One day last summer when we had lunch together. Hester was practically on her uppers then, I used to buy her lunch whenever I could. We were gossiping about this and that, and she brought up the case. It seemed to be on her mind: she was back at the Channel Club at the time, giving diving lessons. She told me about the love affair; apparently Gabrielle had confided in her. Without thinking what I was doing, I told her Isobel Graff had escaped that night. Hester reacted like a Geiger counter, and started asking me questions. I thought her only interest was in tracking down the person who killed her friend. I let down my back hair and told her all I knew, about Isobel and her runout and her mental condition when she came back.

"I had the early-morning duty that day, and I was the one who looked after her until Dr. Frey got there. Isobel dragged herself in some time around dawn. She was in bad shape, and not just mentally. She was physically exhausted. I think now she must have walked and run and crawled along the shore all the way from Malibu. The surf must have caught her, too, because her clothes were wet and matted with sand. I gave her a hot bath first thing."

"Did she tell you where she'd been?"

"No, she didn't say a thing. Actually, she didn't speak for days. Dr. Frey was worried for a while that she might be going into catatonia. Even when she did come out of it and started to talk again, she never mentioned that night—at least, not in words. I saw her in the crafts room, though, later in the spring. I saw some of the objects she made out of clay. I shouldn't have been shocked after what I've seen in mental wards, but I was shocked by some of those objects." She closed her eyes as if to shut out the sight of them, and went on in a hushed voice:

"She used to make these girl dolls and pinch their heads off and destroy them part by part, like some sort of jungle witch. And horrible little men dolls with huge—organs. Animals with human faces, coupling. Guns and—parts of the human body, all mixed up."

"Not nice," I said, "but it wouldn't necessarily mean anything, would it? Did she ever discuss these things with you?"

"Not with me, no. Dr. Frey doesn't encourage the nurses to practice psychiatry."

She turned in the seat and her knee nudged mine, withdrawing quickly. Her dark-blue gaze came up to my face. It was strange that a girl who had seen so much should have such innocent eyes.

"Will you be seeing Dr. Frey?" she said.

"Probably I will."

"Please don't tell him about me, will you?"

"There's no reason why I should."

"It's a terrible breach of ethics, you know, for a nurse to talk about her patients. I've worried myself sick these last few months since I spilled out everything to Hester. I was such a fool. I believed that she was sincere for once in her life, that all she wanted was the truth about Gabrielle's death. I should never have trusted her with dangerous information. It's obvious what she wanted it for. She wanted to use it to blackmail Mrs. Graff."

"How long have you known that, Rina?"

Her voice, or her candor, failed her for a time. I waited for her to go on. Her eyes were almost black with thought. She said:

"It's hard to say. You can know a thing and not know it. When you love a person, it takes so long to face the facts about them. I've really suspected the whole thing practically from the beginning. Ever since Hester left the Club and started living without any visible income. It came to a head on that horrible double date I told you about. Carl Stern got tight and started to boast about his new place in Vegas, and how he had Simon Graff under his thumb. And Hester sat there drinking it in, with stars in her eyes. I got a queer idea that she wanted me there to see how well she was doing. What a success she'd made of her life, after all. That was when I blew my top."

"What was their reaction?"

"I didn't wait for any reaction. I walked out of the place—we were in the Bar of Dixie—and went home in a taxi by myself. I never saw Hester again. I didn't see any of them again, until yesterday when Lance called me."

"To ask you to fly to Vegas under her name?"

She nodded.

"Why did you agree to do it?"

"You know why. I was supposed to be giving her an alibi."

"It doesn't explain why you wanted to."

"Do I have to explain? I simply wanted to." She added after a time: "I felt I owed it to Hester. In a way I'm as guilty as she is. This awful business would never have started if it hadn't been for me. I'd got her into it, I felt it was up to me to get her out. But Hester was dead already, wasn't she?"

A fit of shivering took hold of her, shaking her so that her teeth knocked together. I put my arm around her until the spasm passed. "Don't blame yourself too much."

"I have to. Don't you see, if Isobel Graff killed Hester, I'm to blame?"

"I don't see it. People are responsible for what they do themselves. Anyway, there's some doubt in my mind that Isobel killed your sister. I'm not even certain that she shot Gabrielle Torres. I won't be until I get hold of firm evidence: a confession, or an eyewitness, or the gun she used."

"You're just saying that."

"No, I'm not just saying it. I jumped to certain conclusions too early in this case."

She didn't ask me what I meant, and that was just as well. I still had no final answers.

"Listen to me, Rina. You're a girl with a lot of conscience, and you've taken some hard blows. You have a tendency to blame yourself for things. You were probably brought up to blame yourself for everything."

She sat stiff in the circle of my arm. "It's true. Hester was younger and always getting into trouble, and Mother blamed me. Only, how did you know that? You have a great deal of insight."

"Too bad it mostly takes the form of hindsight. Anyway, there's one thing I'm sure of. You're not responsible for what happened to Hester, and you didn't do anything very wrong."

"Do you really believe that?" She sounded astonished.

"Naturally I believe it."

She was a good girl, as Mrs. Busch had said. She was also a very tired girl, and a sad and nervous girl. We sat in uneasy silence for a while. The hum of the engines had changed. The plane had passed the zenith of its flight and begun the long descent toward Los Angeles and the red sun. Before the plane touched earth, Rina had cried a little on my shoulder. Then she slept a little.

Chapter 30

MY CAR was in the parking-lot at International Airport. Rina asked me to drop her off at her mother's house in Santa Monica. I did so, without going in myself, and drove up Wilshire and out San Vicente to Dr. Frey's sanitarium. It occupied walled grounds which had once belonged to a large private estate in the open country between Sawtelle and Brentwood. A male attendant in a business suit opened the automatic gate and told me that Dr. Frey was probably at dinner.

The central building was a white Edwardian mansion, with more recent additions, which stood on a terraced hillside. Dr. Frey lived in a guesthouse to one side of it. People who looked like anybody else were promenading on the terraces. Like anybody else, except that there was a wall around their lives. From Dr. Frey's veranda, I could see over the wall, as far as the ocean. Fog and darkness were gathering on its convex surface. Below the horizon the lost sun smoldered like a great plane that had crashed and burned.

I talked to a costumed maid, to a gray-haired housekeeper, finally to Dr. Frey himself. He was a stoop-shouldered old man in dinner clothes, with a highball glass in his hand. Intelligence and doubt had deeply lined his face. The lines deepened when I told him that I suspected Isobel Graff of murder. He set his glass on the mantelpiece and stood in front of it, rather belligerently, as though I had threatened the center of his house.

"Am I to understand that you are a policeman?"

"A private detective. Later I'll be taking this to the police. I came to you first."

"I hardly feel favored," he said. "You can't seriously expect me to discuss such a matter, such an accusation, with a stranger. I know nothing about you."

"You know quite a bit about Isobel Graff."

He spread his long gray hands. "I know that I am a doctor and that she is my patient. What do you expect me to say?"

"You could tell me there's nothing in it."

"Very well, I do so. There is nothing in it. Now if you'll excuse me, I have guests for dinner."

"Is Mrs. Graff here now?"

He countered with a question of his own: "May I ask, what is your purpose in making these inquiries?"

"Four people have been killed, three of them in the last two days."

He showed no surprise. "These people were friends of yours?"

"Hardly. Members of the human race, though."

He said with the bitter irony of age: "So you are an altruist, are you? A Hollywood culture-hero in a sports coat? You propose to cleanse the Augean stables single-handed?"

"I'm not that ambitious. And I'm not your problem, doctor. Isobel Graff is. If she killed four people, or one, she ought to be put away where she can't kill any more. Don't you agree?"

He didn't answer me for a minute. Then he said: "I signed voluntary commitment papers for her this morning."

"Does that mean she's on her way to the state hospital?"

"It should, but I'm afraid it doesn't." It was the third time in three minutes that he'd been afraid. "Before the papers could be—ah—implemented, Mrs. Graff escaped. She was very determined, much more so than we bargained for. I confess error. I should have had her placed in maximum security. As it was, she broke a reinforced window with a chair and made good her escape in the back of a laundry truck."

"When was this?"

"This morning, shortly before the lunch hour. She hasn't been found as yet."

"How hard is she being looked for?"

"You'll have to ask her husband. His private police are searching. He forbade—" Dr. Frey compressed his lips and reached for his drink. When he had sipped it: "I'm afraid I can't submit to further interrogation. If you were an official—" He shrugged, and the ice tinkled in his glass.

"You want me to call the police in?"

"If you have evidence."

"I'm asking you for evidence. Did Mrs. Graff kill Gabrielle Torres?"

"I have no way of knowing."

"What about the others?"

"I can't say."

"You've seen her and talked to her?"

"Of course. Many times. Most recently this morning."

"Was her mental condition consistent with homicide?"

He smiled wearily. "This is not a courtroom, sir. Next you'll be framing a hypothetical question. Which I would refuse to answer."

"The question isn't hypothetical. Did she shoot Gabrielle Torres on the night of March 21 last year?"

"It may not be hypothetical, but the question is certainly academic. Mrs. Graff is mentally ill now, and she was ill on March 21 of last year. She couldn't possibly be convicted of murder, or any other crime. So you are wasting both our times, don't you think?"

"It's only time, and I seem to be getting somewhere. You've practically admitted that she did that shooting."

"Have I? I don't think so. You are a very pertinacious young man, and you are making a nuisance of yourself."

"I'm used to that."

"I am not." He moved to the door and opened it. Male laughter came from the other side of the house. "Now if you will transport your rather shopworn charm to another location, it will save me the trouble of having you thrown out."

"One more question, doctor. Why did she pick that day in March to run away? Did she have a visitor that day, or the day before?"

"Visitor?" I had succeeded in surprising him. "I know nothing of any visitors."

"I understand Clarence Bassett visited her regularly here."

He looked at me, eyes veiled like an old bird's. "Do you have a paid spy among my employees?"

"It's simpler than that. I've talked to Bassett. As a matter of fact, he brought me into this case."

"Why didn't you say so? I know Bassett very well." He closed the door and took a step toward me. "He hired you to investigate these deaths?"

"It started out as a missing-girl case and turned into a murder case before I found her. The girl's name was Hester Campbell."

"Why, I know Hester Campbell. I've known her for years at the Club. I gave her sister a job." He paused, and the slight excitement ran through him and drained away. The only trace it left was a tremor in the hand that held his glass. He sipped from the glass to conceal its clinking. "Is Hester Campbell one of the victims?"

"She was beaten to death with a poker yesterday afternoon."

"And you have reason to believe that Mrs. Graff killed her?"

"Isobel Graff is involved, I don't know how deeply. She was at the scene of the crime, apparently. Her husband seems to accept her guilt. But that's not conclusive. Isobel may have been framed. Another possibility is this, that she has been used as a cat's-paw in these killings. I mean that she committed them, physically, but was incited to do it by somebody else. Would she be open to that kind of suggestion?"

"The more I know of the human mind, the less I know." He tried to smile, and failed miserably. "I predicted that you would be asking hypothetical questions."

"I keep trying not to, doctor. You seem to attract them. And you haven't answered my question about Bassett's visits here."

"Why, there was nothing unusual in them. He visited Mrs. Graff every week, I believe, sometimes more frequently when she asked for him. They were very close—indeed, they'd been engaged to be married at one time, many years ago, before her present marriage. I sometimes think she should have married Clarence instead of the man she did marry. He has an almost feminine quality of understanding, which she was badly in need of. Neither of them is adequate to stand alone. Together, if marriage had been possible for them, they might have made a functioning unit." His tone was elegiac.

"What do you mean when you say that neither of them is adequate?"

"It should be obvious in the case of Mrs. Graff. She has been subject to schizophrenic episodes since her middle teens. She has remained, in a sense, a teen-aged girl inside of a middle-aged body—unable to cope with the demands of adult life." He added with a trace of bitterness: "She has received little help from Simon Graff."

"Do you know what caused her illness?"

"The etiology of this disease is still mysterious, but I think I know something of this particular case. She lost her mother young, and Peter Heliopoulos was not a wise father. He pushed her towards maturity, at the same time deprived her of true human contact. She became in a social sense his second wife before she even reached puberty. Great demands were made on her as his little hostess, as the spearhead of his social ambition. The very vulnerable spearhead. These demands were too great for one who was perhaps predisposed from birth to schizophrenia."

"What about Clarence Bassett? Is he mentally ill?"

"I have no reason to think so. He is the manager of my club, not my patient."

"You said he was inadequate."

"I meant in the social and sexual sense. Clarence is the perennial bachelor, the giver of other people's parties, the man who is content to dwell on the sidelines of life. His interest in women is limited to young girls, and to flawed women like Isobel who have failed to outlive their childhood. All this is typical, and part of his adjustment."

"His adjustment to what?"

"To his own nature. His weakness requires him to avoid the storm centers of life. Unfortunately, his adjustment was badly shaken, several years ago, by his mother's death. Since then he has been drinking heavily. I would hazard the guess that his alcoholism is essentially a suicidal gesture. He is literally drowning his sorrows. I suspect he would be glad to join his beloved mother in the grave."

"You don't regard him as potentially dangerous?"

The doctor answered after a thinking pause: "Perhaps he could be. The death-wish is powerfully ambivalent. It can be turned against the self or against others. Inadequate men have been known to try to complete themselves in violence. A Jack the Ripper, for instance, is probably a man with a strong female component who is trying to annul it in himself by destroying actual females."

The abstract words fluttered and swerved like bats in the twilit room. "Are you suggesting that Clarence Bassett could be a mass murderer?"

"By no means. I have been speaking most generally."

"Why go to all the trouble?"

He gave me a complex look. There was sympathy in it, and tragic knowledge, and weariness. He had worn himself out in the Augean stables, and despaired of human action.

"I am an old man," he said. "I lie awake in the night watches and speculate on human possibility. Are you familiar with the newer interpersonal theories of psychiatry? With the concept of *folie à deux?*"

I said I wasn't.

"Madness for two, it might be translated. A madness, a violence, may arise out of a relationship even though the parties to the relationship may be individually harmless. My nocturnal speculations have included Clarence Bassett and Isobel. Twenty years ago their relationship might have made a marriage. Such a relationship may also sour and deteriorate and make something infinitely worse. I am not saying that this is so. But it is a possibility worth considering, a possibility which arises when two persons have the same unconscious and forbidden desire. The same death-wish."

"Did Bassett visit Mrs. Graff before her escape in March last year?"

"I believe he did. I would have to check the records."

"Don't bother, I'll ask him personally. Tell me this, Dr. Frey: do you have anything more to go on than speculation?"

"Perhaps I have. If I had, I would not and could not tell you." He raised his hand before his face in a faltering gesture of defense. "You deluge me with questions, sir, and there is no end to them. I am an old man, as I said. This is, or was, my dinner hour."

He opened the door a second time. I thanked him and went out. He slammed the heavy front door behind me. The people on the twilit terraces turned pale, startled, purgatorial faces toward the source of the noise.

Chapter 31

IT WAS full night when I got to Malibu. A single car stood in the Channel Club parking-lot, a beat-up prewar Dodge with Tony's name on the steering-post. Inside the club, around the pool, there was nobody in sight. I knocked on the door of Clarence Bassett's office and got no answer.

I walked along the gallery and down the steps to the poolside. The water shivered under a slow, cold offshore wind. The place seemed very desolate. I was the last man at the party for sure.

I took advantage of this circumstance by breaking into Simon Graff's *cabaña*. The door had a Yale-type lock which was easy to jimmy. I stepped in and turned on the light, half expecting to find someone in the room. But it was empty, its furnishings undisturbed, its pictures bright and still on the walls, caught out of time.

Time was running through me, harsh on my nerve-ends, hot in my arteries, impalpable as breath in my mouth. I had the sleepless feeling you sometimes get in the final hours of a bad case, that you can see around corners, if you want to, and down into the darkness in human beings.

I opened the twin doors of the dressing-rooms. Each had a back door opening into a corridor which led to the showers. The one on the right contained a gray steel locker and an assortment of men's beach clothes: robes and swimming trunks, Bermuda shorts and sports shirts and tennis shoes. The one on the left, which must have been Mrs. Graff's, was completely bare except for a wooden bench and an empty locker.

I switched on the light in the ceiling, uncertain what I was looking for. It was something vague yet specific: a sure sense of what had happened on that spring night when Isobel Graff had been running loose and the first young girl had died. *For a second*, Isobel had said, *I was in there, watching us through the door, and listening to myself. Please pour me a drink.*

I closed the door of her dressing-room. The louvers were set high in it, fairly wide apart, and loose, so that the windowless cubicle could air itself. By getting up on my toes, I could look down between the crosspieces into the outer room. Isobel Graff would have had to stand on the bench.

I dragged the bench over to the door and stood on it. Six inches below my eye-level, in the edge of one of the louvers, there was a series of indentations which looked like toothmarks, around them a faint red lipstick crescent, dark with age. I examined the underside of the soft wooden strip and found similar markings. Pain jerked through my mind like a knotted string, pulling an image after it. It was pain for the woman who had stood on this bench in the dark, watching the outer room through the cracks between the louvers and biting down on the wood in agony.

I turned out the light and crossed the outer room and stood in front of Matisse's Blue Coast lithograph. I had a fierce nostalgia for that brilliant, orderly world which had never quite existed. A world where nobody lived or died, held in the eye of a never-sinking sun.

Behind me someone cleared his throat delicately. I turned and saw Tony in the doorway, squinting against the light. His hand was on his gun butt.

"Mr. Archer, you broke the door?"

"I broke it."

He shook his head at me in a monitory way, and stooped to look at the damage I had done. A bright scratch crossed the setting of the lock, and the edge of the wood was slightly dented. Tony's blunt brown forefinger traced the scratch and the dent.

"Mr. Graff won't like this, he is crazy about his *cabaña*, he furnished it all himself, not like the others."

"When did he do that?"

"Last year, before the start of the summer season. He brought in his own decorators and cleaned it out like a whistle and put in all new stuff." His gaze was serious, black, unwavering. He removed his peaked cap and scratched his gray-flecked head. "You the one that bust the lock on the fence gate, too?"

"I'm the one. I seem to be in a destructive mood today. Is it important?"

"Cops thought so. Captain Spero was asking me back and forth who bust the gate. They found another dead one on the beach, you know that, Mr. Archer?"

"Carl Stern."

"Yah, Carl Stern. He was my nephew's manager, one time. Captain Spero said it was one of these gang killings, but I dunno. What do you think?"

"I doubt it."

Tony squatted on his heels just inside the open door. It seemed to make him nervous to be inside the Graffs' *cabaña*. He scratched his head again, and ran thumb and finger down the grooves that bracketed his mouth. "Mr. Archer. What happened to my nephew Manuel?"

"He was shot and killed last night."

"I know that. Captain Spero told me he was dead, shot in the eye." Tony touched the lid of his left eye with his right fore-finger. His upturned face resembled a cracked clay death mask. "What else did Spero say?"

"I dunno. Said it was maybe another gang killing, but I dunno. He asked me, did Manuel have enemies? I told him, yah, he had one big enemy, name of Manuel Torres. What did I know about his life, his friends? He bust up from me long ago and went on his own road, straight down to hell in a low-top car." Through the stoic Indian mask, his eyes shone with black, living grief. "I dunno, I coulden tear that boy loose from my heart. He was like my own son to me, one time."

His bowed shoulders moved with his breathing. He said: "I'm gonna get out of this place, it's bad luck for me and my family. I still got friends in Fresno. I ought to stayed in Fresno, never left it. I made the same mistake that Manuel made, thought I could come and take what I wanted. They wooden let me take it. They leave me with nothing, no wife, no daughter, no Manuel."

He balled his fist and struck himself on the cheekbone and looked around the room in confused awe, as though it was the lair of gods which he had offended. The room reminded him of his duty to it:

"What you doing in here, Mr. Archer? You got no right in here."

"I'm looking for Mrs. Graff."

"Why didden you say so? You didden have to break the door down. Mrs. Graff was here a few minutes ago. She wanted Mr. Bassett, only he ain't here."

"Where is Mrs. Graff now?"

"She went down on the beach. I tried to stop her, she ain't in very good shape. She wooden come with me, though. You think I ought to telephone Mr. Graff?"

"If you can get in touch with him. Where's Bassett?"

"I dunno, he was packing his stuff before. He's going away on his vacation, maybe. He always goes to Mexico for a month in the off-season. Used to show me colored pictures—"

I left him talking to the empty room and went to the end of the pool. The gate in the fence was open. Twenty feet below it, the beach sloped away to the water, delimited by the wavering line of white foam. The sight of the ocean gave me a queasy feeling: it reminded me of Carl Stern doing the dead man's float.

Waves rose like apparitions at the surf-line, and fell like masonry. Beyond them a padded wall of fog was sliding shoreward. I went down the concrete steps, met by a snatch of sound which blew up to me between the thumpings of the surf. It was Isobel Graff talking to the ocean in a voice like a gull's screek. She dared it to come and get her. She sat hunched over her knees, just beyond its reach, and shook her fist at the muttering water.

"Dirty old cesspool, I'm not afraid of you."

Her profile was thrust forward, gleaming white with a gleaming dark eye in it. She heard me moving toward her and cowered away, one arm thrown over her face.

"Leave me alone. I won't go back. I'll die first."

"Where have you been all day?"

Her wet black eyes peered up from under her arm. "It's none of your business. Go away."

"I think I'll stay with you."

I sat beside her on the impacted sand, so close that our shoulders touched. She drew away from the contact, but made no other move. Her dark and unkempt bird's-head twisted toward me suddenly. She said in her own voice:

"Hello."

"Hello, Isobel. Where have you been all day?"

"On the beach, mostly. I felt like a nice long walk. A little girl gave me an ice-cream cone, she cried when I took it away from her, I am an old horror. But it was all I had to eat all day. I promised to send her a check, only I'm afraid to go home. That dirty old man might be there."

"What dirty old man?"

"The one that made a pass at me when I took the sleeping-pills. I saw him when I passed out. He had a rotten breath like Father's when he died. And he had worms that were his eyes." Her voice was singsong.

"Who had?"

"Old Father Deathmas with the long white dirty beard." Her mood was ugly and ambiguous. She wasn't too far gone to know what she was saying, just far enough gone to say it. "He made a pass at me, only I was too tired, and there I was in the morning back at the old stand with the same hot and cold running people. What am I going to do? I'm afraid of the water. I can't stand the thought of the violent ways, and sleeping-pills don't work. They simply pump you out and walk you up and down and feed you coffee and there you are back at the old stand."

"When did you try sleeping-pills?"

"Oh, a long time ago, when Father made me marry Simon. I was in love with another man."

"Clarence?"

"He was the only one I ever. Clare was so sweet to me."

The wall of fog had crossed the foam-line and was almost on top of us. The surf pounded behind it like a despondent visitor. I didn't know whether to laugh or cry. I looked down at her face, which slanted up close to mine: a pale ghost of a face with two dark eye-holes and a mouth-hole in it. She was tainted by disease and far from young, but in the foggy night she looked more like a child than a woman. A disordered child who had lost her way and met death on the detour.

Her head leaned on my shoulder. "I'm caught," she said. "I've been trying all day to get up the nerve to walk into the water. What am I going to do? I can't endure forever in a room."

"In the church you were brought up in, suicide is a sin."

"I've committed worse."

I waited. The fog was all around us now, an element composed of air and water and a fishy chill. It made a kind of limbo, out of this world, where anything could be said. Isobel Graff said:

"I committed the worst sin of all. They were together in the light and I was alone in the darkness. Then the light was like broken glass in my eyes, but I could see to shoot. I shot her in the groin and she died."

"This happened in your *cabaña?*"

She nodded faintly. I felt the movement rather than saw it. "I caught her there with Simon. She crawled out here and died on the beach. The waves came up and took her. I wish that they would take me."

"What happened to Simon that night?"

"Nothing. He ran away. To do it again another day and do it and do it and do it. He was terrified when I came out of the back room with the gun in my hand. He was the one I really intended to kill, but he scuttled out the door."

"Where did you get the gun?"

"It was Simon's target pistol. He kept it in his locker. He taught me to fire it himself, on this very beach." She stirred in the crook of my arm. "What do you think of me now?"

I didn't have to answer her. There was a moving voice in the fog above our heads. It was calling her name, Isobel.

"Who is it? Don't let them take me." She turned on her knees and clutched my hand. Hers was fish-cold.

Footsteps and light were descending the concrete steps. I got up and went to meet them. The beam of light wavered toward me. Graff's dim and nimbused figure was behind it. The long, thin nose of a target pistol protruded from his other hand. My gun was already in mine.

"You're covered, Graff. Drop it directly in front of you."

His pistol thudded softly in the sand. I stooped and picked it up. It was an early-model German Walther, .22 caliber, with a custom-made walnut grip too small to fit my hand. The gun was loaded. Distrusting its hair-trigger action, I set the safety and shoved it down under my belt.

"I'll take the light, too."

He handed me his flashlight. I turned its beam upward on his face and saw it naked for an instant. His mouth was soft and twisted, his eyes were frightened.

"I heard my wife. Where is she?"

I swung the flash-beam along the beach. Its cone of brilliance filled with swirling fog. Isobel Graff ran away from it. Black and huge on the gray air, her shadow ran ahead of her. She seemed to be driving off a fury which dwarfed her and tormented her and mimicked all her movements.

Graff called her name again and ran after her. I followed along behind and saw her fall and get up and fall again. Graff helped her to her feet. They walked back toward me, slowly and clumsily. She dragged her feet and hung her head, turning her face away from the light. Graff's arm around her waist propelled her forward.

I took the target pistol out of my belt and showed it to her. "Is this the gun you used to shoot Gabrielle Torres?"

She glanced at it and nodded mutely.

"No," Graff said. "Admit nothing, Isobel."

"She's already confessed," I said.

"My wife is mentally incompetent. Her confession is not valid evidence."

"The gun is. The sheriff's ballistics department will have the matching slugs. The gun and the slugs together will be unshakable evidence. Where did you get the gun, Graff?"

"Carl Walther made it for me, in Germany, many years ago."

"I'm talking about the last twenty-four hours. Where did you get it this time?"

He answered carefully: "I have had it in my possession continuously for over twenty years."

"The hell you have. Stern had it last night before he was killed. Did you kill him for it?"

"That is ridiculous."

"Did you have him killed?"

"I did not."

"Somebody knocked off Stern to get hold of this gun. You must know who it was, and you might as well tell me. Everything's going to come out now. Not even your kind of money can stop it."

"Is money what you want from me? You can have money." His voice dragged with contempt—for me, and perhaps for himself.

"I'm not for sale like Marfeld," I said. "Your boss thug tried to buy me. He's in the Vegas clink with a body to explain."

"I know that," Graff said. "But I am talking about a very great deal of money. A hundred thousand dollars in cash. Now. Tonight."

"Where would you get that much in cash tonight?"

"From Clarence Bassett. He has it in his office safe. I paid it to him this evening. It was the price he set on the pistol. Take it away from him, and you can have it."

Chapter 32

THERE WAS light in Bassett's office. I knocked so hard that I bruised my knuckles. He came to the door in shirt sleeves. His face was putty-colored, with blue hollows under the eyes. His eyes had a Lazarus look, and hardly seemed to recognize me.

"Archer? What's the trouble, man?"

"You're the trouble, Clarence."

"Oh, I *hope* not." He noticed the couple behind me, and did a big take. "You've found her, Mr. Graff. I'm so glad."

"Are you?" Graff said glumly. "Isobel has confessed everything to this man. I want my money back."

Bassett's face underwent a process of change. The end product of the process was a bright, nervous grin which resembled the rictus of a dead horse.

"Am I to understand this? I return the money, and we drop the whole matter? Nothing more will be said?"

"Plenty more will be said. Give him his money, Clarence."

He stood tense in the doorway, blocking my way. Visions of possible action flitted behind his pale-blue eyes and died. "It's not here."

"Open the safe and we'll see for ourselves."

"You have no warrant."

"I don't need one. You're willing to co-operate. Aren't you?"

He reached up and plucked at his neck above the open collar of his button-down shirt, stretching the loose skin and letting it pull itself back into place. "This has been a bit of a shock. As a matter of fact, I am willing to co-operate. I have nothing to hide."

He turned abruptly, crossed the room, and took down the photograph of the three divers. A cylindrical safe was set in the wall behind it. I covered him with the target pistol as he spun the bright chrome dials. The gun he had used on Leonard was probably at the bottom of the sea, but there could be another gun in the safe. All the safe contained was money, though— bundles of money done up in brown bank paper.

"Take it," Graff said. "It is yours."

"It would only make a bum out of me. Besides, I couldn't afford to pay the tax on it."

"You are joking. You must want money. You work for money, don't you?"

"I want it very badly," I said. "But I can't take this money. It wouldn't belong to me, I would belong to it. It would expect me to do things, and I would have to do them. Sit on the lid of this mess of yours, the way Marfeld did, until dry rot set in."

"It would be easy to cover up," Graff said.

He turned a basilisk eye on Clarence Bassett. Bassett flattened himself against the wall. The fear of death invaded his face and galvanized his body. He swatted the gun out of my hand, went down on his hands and knees, and got a grip on the butt. I snaked it away from him before he could consolidate his grip, lifted him by the collar, and set him in the chair at the end of his desk.

Isobel Graff had collapsed in the chair behind the desk. Her head was thrown back, and her undone hair poured like black oil over the back of the chair. Bassett avoided looking at her. He sat hunched far over to one side away from her, trembling and breathing hard.

"I've done nothing that I'm ashamed of. I shielded an old friend from the consequences of her actions. Her husband saw fit to reward me."

"That's the gentlest description of blackmail I ever heard. Not that blackmail covers what you've done. Are you going to tell me you knocked off Leonard and Stern to protect Isobel Graff?"

"I have no idea what you're talking about."

"When you tried to frame Isobel for the murder of Hester Campbell, was that part of your protection service?"

"I did nothing of the sort."

The woman echoed him: "Clare did nothing of the sort."

I turned to her. "You went to her house in Beverly Hills yesterday afternoon?"

She nodded.

"Why did you go there?"

"Clare told me she was Simon's latest chippie. He's the only one who tells me things, the only one who cares what happens to me. Clare said if I caught them together, I could force Simon to give me a divorce. Only she was already dead. I walked into the house, and she was already dead." She spoke resentfully, as though Hester Campbell had deliberately stood her up.

"How did you know where she lived?"

"Clare told me." She smiled at him in bright acknowledgement. "Yesterday morning when Simon was having his dip."

"All this is utter nonsense," Bassett said. "Mrs. Graff is imagining it. I didn't even *know* where she lived, you can bear witness to that."

"You wanted me to believe you didn't, but you knew, all right. You'd had her traced, and you'd been threatening her. You couldn't afford to let George Wall get to her while she was still alive. But you wanted him to get to her eventually. Which is where I came in. You needed someone to lead him to her and help pin the frame on him. Just in case it didn't take, you sent Mrs. Graff to the house to give you double insurance. The second frame was the one that worked—at least, it worked for Graff and his brilliant cohorts. They gave you a lot of free assistance in covering up that killing."

"I had nothing to do with it," Graff said behind me. "I'm not responsible for Frost's and Marfeld's stupidity. They acted without consulting me." He was standing by himself, just inside the door, as if to avoid any part in the proceedings.

"They were your agents," I told him, "and you're responsible for what they did. They're accessory after the fact of murder. You should be handcuffed to them."

Bassett was encouraged by our split. "You're simply fishing," he said. "I was fond of Hester Campbell, as you know. I had nothing against the girl. I had no reason to harm her."

"I don't doubt you were fond of her, in some peculiar way of your own. You were probably in love with her. She wasn't in love with you, though. She was out to take you if she could. She ran out on you in September, and took along your most valuable possession."

"I'm a poor man. I have no valuable possessions."

"I mean this gun." I held the Walther pistol out of his reach. "I don't know exactly how you got it the first time. I think I know how you got it the second time. It's been passed around quite a bit in the last four months, since Hester Campbell stole it from your safe. She turned it over to her friend Lance Leonard. He wasn't up to handling the shakedown himself, so he co-opted Stern, who had experience in these matters. Stern also had connections which put him beyond the reach of Graff's strong-arm boys. But not beyond your reach.

"I'll give you credit for one thing, Clarence. It took guts to tackle Stern, even if I did soften him up for you. More guts than Graff and his private army had."

"I didn't kill him," Bassett said. "You know I didn't kill him. You saw him leave."

"You followed him out, though, didn't you? And you didn't come back for a while. You had time to slug him in the parking-lot, bundle him into his car, and drive it up the bluff where you could slit his throat and push him into the sea. That was quite an effort for a man your age. You must have wanted this gun back very badly. Were you so hungry for a hundred grand?"

Bassett looked up past me at the open safe. "Money had nothing to do with it." It was his first real admission. "I didn't know he had that gun in his car until he tried to pull it on me. I hit him with a tire-iron and knocked him out. It was kill or be killed. I killed him in self-defense."

"You didn't cut his throat in self-defense."

"He was an evil man, a criminal, meddling in matters he didn't understand. I destroyed him as you would destroy a dangerous animal." He was proud of killing Stern. The pride shone in his face. It made him foolish. "A gangster and drug-peddler—is he more important than I? I'm a civilized man, I come from a good family."

"So you cut Stern's throat. You shot Lance Leonard's eye out. You beat in Hester Campbell's skull with a poker. There are better ways to prove you're civilized."

"They deserved it."

"You admit you killed them?"

"I admit nothing. You have no right to bullyrag me. You can't prove a thing against me."

"The police will be able to. They'll trace your movements, turn up witnesses to pin you down, find the gun you used on Leonard."

"Will they really?" He had enough style left to be sardonic.

"Sure they will. You'll show them where you ditched it. You've started to tattle on yourself already. You're no hard-faced pro, Clarence, and you shouldn't try to act like one. Last night when it was over and the three of them were dead, you had to knock yourself out with a bottle. You couldn't face the thought of what you had done. How long do you think you can hold out sitting in a cell without a bottle?"

"You hate me," Bassett said. "You hate me and despise me, don't you?"

"I don't think I'll answer that question. Answer one of mine. You're the only one who can. What sort of man would use a sick woman as his cat's-paw? What sort of man would cut a young girl like Gabrielle off from the light so he could collect a bounty on her death?"

Bassett made an abrupt squirming gesture of denial. The movement involved the entire upper half of his body, and resembled a convulsion. He said through rigid jaws:

"You've got it all wrong."

"Then straighten me out."

"What's the use? You would never understand."

"I understand more than you think. I understand that you spied on Graff when his wife was in the sanitarium. You saw him using his *cabaña* for meetings with Gabrielle. You undoubtedly knew about the gun in his locker. Everything you knew or learned, you passed on to Isobel Graff. Probably you helped her to run away from the sanitarium, and provided her with the necessary pass-keys. It all adds up to remote-control murder. That much I understand. I don't understand what you had against Gabrielle. Did you try for her yourself and lose her to Graff? Or was it just that she was young and you were getting old, and you couldn't stand to see her living in the world?"

He stammered: "I had nothing to do with her death." But he turned in his chair as if a powerful hand had him by the nape of the neck. He looked at Isobel Graff for the first time, quickly and guiltily.

She was sitting upright now, as still as a statue. A statue of a blind and schizophrenic Justice, stonily returning Bassett's look:

"You did so, Clarence."

"No, I mean I didn't plan it that way. I had no idea of black-mail. I didn't want to see her killed."

"Who did you want to see killed?"

"Simon," Isobel Graff said. "Simon was to be the one. But I spoiled everything, didn't I, Clare? It was my fault it all went wrong."

"Be quiet, Belle." It was the first time that Bassett had spoken to her directly. "Don't say anything more."

"You intended to shoot your husband, Mrs. Graff?"

"Yes. Clare and I were going to be married."

Graff let out a snort, half angry and half derisive. She turned on him:

"Don't you dare laugh at me. You locked me up and stole my property. You treated me like a chattel-beast." Her voice rose. "I'm *sorry* I didn't kill you."

"So you and your moth-eaten fortune-hunter could live happily ever after?"

"We could have been happy," she said. "Couldn't we, Clare? You love me, don't you, Clare? You've loved me all these years."

"All these years," he said. But his voice was empty of feeling, his eyes were dead. "Now if you love me, you'll be quiet, Belle." His tone, brusque and unfriendly, denied his words.

He had rebuffed her, and she had a deep, erratic intuition. Her mood swung violently. "I know you," she said in a hoarse monotone. "You want to blame me for everything. You want them to put me in the forever room and throw the key away. But you're to blame, too. You said I could never be convicted of any crime. You said if I killed Simon *in fragrante — in flagrante —* the most they could do was lock me up for a while. Didn't you say that, Clare? Didn't you?"

He wouldn't answer her or look at her. Hatred blurred his features like a tight rubber mask. She turned to me:

"So you see, it was Simon I meant to kill. His chippie was just an animal he used — a little fork-legged animal. I wouldn't kill a pretty little animal."

She paused, and said in queer surprise: "But I did kill her. I shot her and smashed the connections. It came to me in the dark behind the door. It came to me like a picture of sin that she was the source of the evil. And she was the one the dirty old man was making the passes at. So I smashed the connections. Clare was angry with me. He didn't see the wicked things she did."

"Wasn't he with you?"

"Afterwards he was. I was trying to wipe up the blood—she bled on my nice clean floor. I was trying to wipe up the blood when Clare came in. He must have been waiting outside, and seen the chippie crawling out the door. She crawled away like a little white dog and died. And Clare was angry with me. He bawled me out."

"How many times did you shoot her, Isobel?"

"Just once."

"In what part of the body?"

She hung her head in ghastly modesty. "I don't like to say, in public. I told you before."

"Gabrielle Torres was shot twice, first in the upper thigh, then in the back. The first wound wasn't fatal, it wasn't even serious. The second wound pierced her heart. It was the second shot that killed her."

"I only shot her once."

"Didn't you follow her down to the beach and shoot her again in the back?"

"No." She looked at Bassett. "Tell him, Clare. You know I couldn't have done that."

Bassett glared at her without speaking. His eyes bulged like tiny pale balloons inflated by a pressure inside his skull.

"How would he know, Mrs. Graff?"

"Because he took the gun. I dropped it on the *cabaña* floor. He picked it up and went out after her."

The pressure forced words from Bassett's mouth. "Don't listen to her. She's crazy—hallucinating. I wasn't within ten miles—"

"You were so, Clare," she said quietly.

At the same time, she leaned across the desk and struck him a savage blow on the mouth. He took it stoically. It was the woman who began to cry. She said through tears:

"You had the gun when you went out after her. Then you came back and told me she was dead, that I had killed her. But you would keep my secret because you loved me."

Bassett looked from her to me. A line of blood lengthened from one corner of his mouth like a red crack in his livid mask. The blind worm of his tongue came out and nuzzled at the blood.

"I could use a drink, old man. I'll talk, if you'll only let me have a drink first."

"In a minute. Did you shoot her, Clarence?"

"I had to." He had lowered his voice to a barely audible whisper, as though a recording angel had bugged the room.

Isobel Graff said: "Liar, pretending to be my friend! You let me live in hell."

"I kept you out of worse hell, Belle. She was on her way to her father's house. She would have blabbed out everything."

"So you did it all for me, you filthy liar! Young Lochinvar did it for Honeydew Heliopoulos, the girl of the golden west!" Her feelings had caught up with her. She wasn't crying now. Her voice was savage.

"For himself," I said. "He missed the jackpot when you failed to kill your husband. He saw his chance for a consolation prize if he could convince your husband that you murdered Gabrielle. It was a perfect set-up for a frame, so perfect that he even convinced you."

The convulsion of denial went through Bassett again, leaving his mouth wrenched to one side. "It wasn't that way at all. I never thought of money."

"What's that we found in your safe?"

"It was the only money I got, or asked for. I needed it to go away, I planned to go to Mexico and live. I never thought of blackmail until Hester stole the gun and betrayed me to those criminals. They forced me to kill them, don't you see, with their greed and their indiscretion. Sooner or later the case would be reopened and the whole truth would come out."

I looked to Graff for confirmation, but he had left the room. The empty doorway opened on darkness. I said to Bassett:

"Nobody forced you to kill Gabrielle. Why couldn't you let her go?"

"I simply couldn't," he said. "She was crawling home along the beach. I'd started the whole affair, I had to finish it. I could never bear to see an animal hurt, not even a little insect or a spider."

"So you're a mercy killer?"

"No, I can't seem to make you understand. There we were, just the two of us in the dark. The surf was pounding in, and she was moaning and dragging her body along in the sand.

Naked and bleeding, a girl I'd known for years, when she was an innocent child. The situation was so dreadfully horrible. Don't you see, I had to put an end to it somehow. I had to make her stop crawling."

"And you had to kill Hester Campbell yesterday?"

"She was another one. She pretended to be innocent and wormed her way into my good graces. She called me Uncle Clarence, she pretended to like me, when all she wanted was the gun in my safe. I gave her money, I treated her like a daughter, and she betrayed me. It's a tragic thing when the young girls grow up and become gross and deceitful and lascivious."

"So you see that they don't grow up, is that it?"

"They're better dead."

I looked down into his face. It wasn't an unusual face. It was quite ordinary, homely and aging, given a touch of caricature by the long teeth and bulging eyes. Not the kind of face that people think of as evil. Yet it was the face of evil, drawn by a vague and passionate yearning toward the deed of darkness it abhorred.

Bassett looked up at me as if I were a long way off, communicating with him by thought-transference. He looked down at his clasped hands. The hands pulled apart from each other, and stretched and curled on his narrow thighs. The hands seemed remote from him, too, cut off by some unreported disaster from his intentions and desires.

I picked up the telephone on the desk and called the county police. They had routines for handling this sort of thing. I wanted it out of my hands.

Bassett leaned forward as I laid the receiver down. "Look here, old fellow," he said civilly, "you promised me a drink. I could use a drink in the worst way."

I went to the portable bar at the other end of the desk and got a bottle out. But Bassett received a more powerful sedative. Tony Torres came in through the open door. He slouched and shuffled forward, carrying his heavy Colt revolver. His eyes were dusty black. The flame from his gun was pale and brief, but its roar was very loud. Bassett's head was jerked to one side. It remained in that position, resting on his shoulder.

Isobel Graff looked at him in dull surprise. She rose and hooked her fingers in the neck of her denim blouse. Tore the blouse apart and offered her breast to the gun. "Kill me. Kill me, too."

Tony shook his head solemnly. "Mr. Graff said Mr. Bassett was the one."

He thrust the revolver into its holster. Graff entered behind him, diffidently. Stepping softly like an undertaker, Graff crossed the room to the desk where Bassett sat. His hand reached out and touched the dead man's shoulder. The body toppled, letting out a sound as it struck the floor. It was a mewling sound, like the faint and distant cry of a child for its mother.

Graff jumped back in alarm, as if his electric touch had knocked the life out of Bassett. In a sense, it had.

"Why drag Tony into this?" I said.

"It seemed the best way. The results are the same in the long run. I was doing Bassett a favor."

"You weren't doing Tony one."

"Don't worry about me," Tony said. "Two years now, two years in March, this is all I been living for, to get the guy that done it to her. I don't care if I never get back to Fresno or not." He wiped his wet forehead with the back of his hand, and shook the sweat off his hand. He said politely: "Is it okay with you gentlemen I step outside? It's hot in here. I'll stick around."

"It's all right with me," I told him.

Graff watched him go out, and turned to me with renewed assurance: "I noticed that you didn't try to stop him. You had a gun, you could have prevented that shooting."

"Could I?"

"At least we can keep the worst of it out of the papers now."

"You mean the fact that you seduced a teen-aged girl and ran out on her in the clutch?"

He shushed me and looked around nervously, but Tony was out of hearing.

"I'm not thinking of myself only."

He glanced significantly toward his wife. She was sitting on the floor in the darkest corner of the room. Her knees were drawn up to her chin. Her eyes were shut, and she was as still and silent as Bassett was.

"It's a little late to be thinking about Isobel."

"No, you are wrong. She has great recuperative powers. I have seen her in worse condition than this. But you could not force her to face a public courtroom, you are not so inhuman."

"She won't have to. Psychiatric Court can be held in a private hospital room. You're the one who has to face the public rap."

"Why? Why should I have to suffer more? I have been victimized by an Iago. You don't know what I have endured in this marriage. I am a creative personality, I needed a little sweetness and gentleness in my life. I made love to a young woman, that is my only crime."

"You lit the match that set the whole thing off. Lighting a match can be a crime if it sets fire to a building."

"But I did nothing wrong, nothing out of the ordinary. A few tumbles in the hay, what do they amount to? You wouldn't ruin me for such a little thing? Is it fair to make me a public scapegoat, wreck my career? Is it just?"

His earnest eloquence lacked conviction. Graff had lived too long among actors. He was a citizen of the unreal city, a false front leaning on scantlings.

"Don't talk to me about justice, Graff. You've been covering up murder for nearly two years."

"I have suffered terribly for those two years. I have suffered enough, and paid enough. It has cost me tremendous sums."

"I wonder. You used your name to pay off Stern. You used your corporation to pay off Leonard and the Campbell girl. It's a nice trick if you can work it, letting Internal Revenue help you pay your blackmail."

My guess must have been accurate. Graff didn't try to argue with it. He looked down at the valuable gun in my hand. It was the single piece of physical evidence that would force his name into the case. He said urgently:

"Give me my gun."

"So you can put me down with it?"

Somewhere on the highway, above the rooftop, a siren whooped.

"Hurry up," he said. "The police are coming. Remove the shells and give me the gun. Take the money in the safe."

"Sorry, Graff, I have a use for the gun. It's Tony's justifiable-homicide plea."

He looked at me as if I was a fool. I don't know how I looked at Graff, but it made him drop his eyes and turn away. I closed the safe and spun the dials and rehung the photograph of the three young divers. Caught in unchanging flight, the two girls and the boy soared between the sea and the sky's bright desolation.

The siren's whoop was nearer and louder, like an animal on the roof. Before the sheriff's men walked in, I laid the Walther pistol on the floor near Bassett's outflung hand. Their ballistics experts would do the rest.

THE DOOMSTERS

Purissima is an imaginary city. The people who "live" in and around it are imaginary. No reference to actual people or places is intended.

For John and Dick, Hill-climbers

Chapter 1

I WAS dreaming about a hairless ape who lived in a cage by himself. His trouble was that people were always trying to get in. It kept the ape in a state of nervous tension. I came out of sleep sweating, aware that somebody was at the door. Not the front door, but the side door that opened into the garage. Crossing the cold kitchen linoleum in my bare feet, I saw first dawn at the window over the sink. Whoever it was on the other side of the door was tapping now, quietly and persistently. I turned on the outside light, unlocked the door, and opened it.

A very large young man in dungarees stepped awkwardly backward under the naked garage bulb. There was dirt in his stubble of light hair. His unblinking pale blue eyes looked up at the light in an oddly pathetic way.

"Turn it off, will you?"

"I like to be able to see."

"That's just it." He glanced through the open garage door, out to the quiet gray street. "I don't want to be seen."

"You could always go away again." Then I took another look at him, and regretted my surliness. There was a kind of oily yellowish glaze on his skin which was more than a trick of the light. He could be in a bad way.

He looked again at the hostile street. "May I come in? You're Mr. Archer, aren't you?"

"It's kind of early for visiting. I don't know your name."

"Carl Hallman. I know it's early. I've been up all night."

He swayed, and steadied himself against the doorpost. His hand was black with grime, and there were bleeding scratches on the back of it.

"Been in an accident, Hallman?"

"No." He hesitated, and spoke more slowly: "There was an accident. It didn't happen to me. Not the way you mean."

"Who did it happen to?"

"My father. My father was killed."

"Last night?"

"Six months ago. It's one of the things I want to ask you—speak to you about. Can't you give me a few moments?"

437

A pre-breakfast client was the last thing I needed that morning. But it was one of those times when you have to decide between your own convenience and the unknown quantity of another man's trouble. Besides, the other man and his way of talking didn't go with his ragbag clothes, his mud-stained work shoes. It made me curious.

"Come in then."

He didn't seem to hear me. His glazed eyes stayed on my face too long.

"Come in, Hallman. It's cold in these pajamas."

"Oh. Sorry." He stepped up into the kitchen, almost as broad as the door. "It's hellish of me to bother you like this."

"No bother if it's urgent."

I shut the door and plugged in the coffee-maker. Carl Hallman remained standing in the middle of the kitchen floor. I pulled out a chair for him. He smelled of country.

"Sit down and tell me about it."

"That's just it. I don't *know* anything. I don't even know if it is urgent."

"Well, what's all the excitement about?"

"I'm sorry. I don't make much sense, do I? I've been running half the night."

"Where from?"

"A certain place. It doesn't matter where." His face closed up in blankness, almost stuporous. He was remembering that certain place.

A thought I'd been suppressing forced its way through. Carl Hallman's clothes were the kind of clothes they give you to wear in prison. He had the awkward humility men acquire there. And there was a strangeness in him, stranger than fear, which might be one of guilt's chameleon forms. I changed my approach:

"Did somebody send you to me?"

"Yes. A friend gave me your name. You *are* a private detective?"

I nodded. "Your friend has a name?"

"I don't know if you'd remember him." Carl Hallman was embarrassed. He popped his dirty knuckles and looked at the floor. "I don't know if my friend would want me to use his name."

"He used mine."

"That's a little different, isn't it? You hold a—sort of a public job."

"So I'm a public servant, eh? Well, we won't play guessing games, Carl."

The water in the coffee-maker boiled. It reminded me how cold I was. I went to my bedroom for a bathrobe and slippers. Looked at the gun in my closet, decided against it. When I came back to the kitchen, Carl Hallman was sitting in the same position.

"What are you going to do?" he asked me dully.

"Have a cup of coffee. How about you?"

"No, thanks. I don't care for anything."

I poured him a cup, anyway, and he drank it greedily.

"Hungry?"

"You're very kind, but I couldn't possibly accept—"

"I'll fry a couple of eggs."

"No! I don't want you to." His voice was suddenly high, out of control. It came queerly out of his broad barrel chest, like the voice of a little boy calling from hiding. "You're angry with me."

I spoke to the little boy: "I don't burn so easy. I asked for a name, you wouldn't give it. You have your reasons. All right. What's the matter, Carl?"

"I don't know. When you brushed me off, just now, all I could think of was Father. He was always getting angry. That last night—"

I waited, but that was all. He made a noise in his throat which might have been a sob, or a growl of pain. Turned away from me and gazed at the coffee-maker on the breakfast bar. The grounds in its upper half were like black sand in a static hourglass that wouldn't let time pass. I fried six eggs in butter, and made some toast. Carl gobbled his. I gobbled mine, and poured the rest of the coffee.

"You're treating me very well," he said over his cup. "Better than I deserve."

"It's a little service we provide for clients. Feeling better?"

"Physically, yes. Mentally—" He caught himself on the down-beat, and held steady. "That's good coffee you make. The coffee on the ward was terrible, loaded with chicory."

"You've been in a hospital?"

"Yes. The State Hospital." He added, with some defiance: "I'm not ashamed of it." But he was watching closely for my reaction.

"What was the trouble?"

"The diagnosis was manic-depressive. I don't think I *am* manic-depressive. I know I was disturbed. But that's all past."

"They released you?"

He hung his head over his coffee cup and looked at me from underneath, on the slant.

"Are you on the run from the hospital?"

"Yes. I am." The words came hard to him. "But it's not the way you imagine. I was virtually cured, ready to be discharged, but my brother wouldn't let them. He wants to keep me locked up." His voice fell into a singsong rhythm: "As far as Jerry is concerned, I could stay there until I rotted."

The melody was familiar: incarcerated people always had to be blaming someone, preferably a close relative. I said:

"Do you know for a fact your brother was keeping you there?"

"I'm certain of it. He had me put away. He and Dr. Grantland made Mildred sign the commitment papers. Once I was there, he cut me off entirely. He wouldn't visit me. He made them censor my mail so I couldn't even write letters." The words had been rushing faster and faster, tumbling out of his mouth. He paused and gulped. His Adam's apple bobbed like a ball valve under the skin of his throat.

"You don't know what it's like being cut off like that, not knowing what goes on. Of course, Mildred came to see me, every chance she got, but she didn't know what it was all about, either. And we couldn't talk freely about family matters. They made her visit me on the ward, and they always kept a nurse there, within hearing. As if I couldn't be trusted with my own wife."

"Why, Carl? Were you violent?"

Suddenly and heavily, as if I'd rabbit-punched him, his head sank low between his shoulders. I looked him over, thinking that he could be formidable in a violent mood. His shoulders were overlaid with laminated muscle, and wide enough to yoke a pair of oxen. He was saying:

"I made a fool of myself the first few days—tore up a couple of mattresses, things like that. They put me in wet packs. But

I never hurt anyone. At least I don't remember, if I did." His voice had sunk almost out of hearing. He raised it, and lifted his head. "Anyway, I never stepped out of line after that, not once. I wasn't going to give them any excuse to keep me locked up. But they did. And they had no right to."

"So you came over the wall."

He looked at me in surprise, his pale eyes wide. "How did you know we came over the wall?"

I didn't bother explaining that it was only an expression, which seemed to have hit the literal truth. "More than one of you broke out, eh?"

He didn't answer. His eyes narrowed suspiciously, still watching my face.

"Where are the others, Carl?"

"There's only the one other," he said haltingly. "Who he is doesn't matter. You'll read about it in the papers, anyway."

"Not necessarily. They don't publicize these things unless the escapees are dangerous."

Chapter 2

I LET that last word hang in the silence, turning this way and that, a question and a threat and a request. Carl Hallman looked at the window over the sink, where morning shone unhampered. Sounds of sporadic traffic came from the street. He turned to look at the door he had come in by. His body was taut, and the cords in his neck stood out. His face was thoughtful.

He got up suddenly, in a brusque movement which sent his chair over backwards, crossed in two strides to the door. I said sharply:

"Pick up the chair."

He paused with his hand on the knob, tension vibrating through him. "Don't give me orders. I don't take orders from you."

"It's a suggestion, boy."

"I'm not a boy."

"To me you are. I'm forty. How old are you?"

"It's none of your—" He paused, in conflict with himself. "I'm twenty-four."

"Act your age, then. Pick up the chair and sit down and we'll talk this over. You don't want to go on running."

"I don't intend to. I never wanted to. It's just—I have to get home and clean up the mess. Then I don't care what happens to me."

"You should. You're young. You have a wife, and a future."

"Mildred deserves someone better than me—than I. My future is in the past."

But he turned from the door, from the bright and fearful morning on the other side of it, and picked up the chair and sat in it. I sat on the kitchen table, looking down at him. His tension had wrung sweat out of his body. It stood in droplets on his face, and darkened the front of his shirt. He said very youngly:

"You think I'm crazy, don't you?"

"What I think doesn't matter, I'm not your head-shrinker. But if you are, you need the hospital. If you're not, this is a hell of a way to prove you're not. You should go back and get yourself checked out."

"Go back? You must be cr—" He caught himself.

I laughed in his face, partly because I thought he was funny and partly because I thought he needed it. "I must be crazy? Go ahead and say it. I'm not proud. I've got a friend in psychiatry who says they should build mental hospitals with hinged corners. Every now and then they should turn them inside out, so the people on the outside are in, and the people on the inside are out. I think he's got something."

"You're making fun of me."

"What if I am? It's a free country."

"Yes, it is a free country. And you can't make me go back there."

"I think you should. This way, you're headed for more trouble."

"I can't go back. They'd never let me out, now."

"They will when you're ready. If you turn yourself in voluntarily, it shouldn't go against you very hard. When did you break out?"

"Last night—early last evening, after supper. We didn't exactly break out. We piled the benches against the wall of the courtyard. I hoisted the other fellow up to the top and he helped me up after him, with a knotted sheet. We got away without being seen, I think. Tom—the other fellow—had a car waiting. They gave me a ride part of the way. I walked the rest."

"Do you have a special doctor you can see, if you go back?"

"Doctor!" It was a dirty word in his vocabulary. "I've seen too many doctors. They're all a bunch of shysters, and Dr. Grantland is the worst of them. He shouldn't even be allowed to practice."

"Okay, we'll take away his license."

He looked up, startled. He was easy to startle. Then anger rose in him. "You don't take me seriously. I came to you for help in a serious matter, and all I get is cheap wisecracks. It makes me mad."

"All right. It's a free country."

"God damn you."

I let that pass. He sat with his head down for several minutes, holding himself still. Finally he said: "My father was Senator Hallman of Purissima. Does the name mean anything to you?"

"I read in the papers that he died last spring."

He nodded jerkily. "They locked me up the next day, and wouldn't even let me go to his funeral. I know I blew my top, but they had no right to do that. They did it because they didn't want me snooping."

"Who are 'they'?"

"Jerry and Zinnie. Zinnie is my sister-in-law. She's always hated me, and Jerry's under her thumb. They want to keep me shut up for the rest of their lives, so that they can have the property to themselves."

"How do you know that?"

"I've had a lot of time to think. I've been putting things together for six months. When I got the word on Dr. Grantland— Well, it's obvious they paid him to have me committed. They may even have paid him to kill Father."

"I thought your father's death was accidental."

"It was, according to Dr. Grantland." Carl's eyes were hot and sly, and I didn't like the look of them. "It's possible it really was an accident. But I happen to know that Dr. Grantland has a bad record. I just found that out last week."

It was hard to tell if he was fantasying. Like any other private detective, I'd had to do with my share of mental cases, but I was no expert. Sometimes even the experts had a hard time distinguishing between justified suspicion and paranoid symptoms. I tried to stay neutral:

"How did you get the word on Dr. Grantland?"

"I promised never to divulge that fact. There's a—there are other people involved."

"Have you talked to anybody else about these suspicions of yours?"

"I talked to Mildred, last time she visited me. Last Sunday. I couldn't say very much, with those hospital eavesdroppers around. I don't *know* very much. It's why I had to *do* something." He was getting tense again.

"Take it easy, Carl. Do you mind if I talk to your wife?"

"What about?"

"Things in general. Your family. You."

"I don't object if she doesn't."

"Where does she live?"

"On the ranch, outside Purissima— No, she doesn't live there now. After I went to the hospital, Mildred couldn't go on sharing the house with Jerry and Zinnie. So she moved back into Purissima, with her mother. They live at 220 Grant—but I'll show you, I'll come along."

"I don't think so."

"But I must. There are so many things to be cleared up. I can't wait any longer."

"You're going to have to wait, if you want my help. I'll make you a proposition, Carl. Let me take you back to the hospital. It's more or less on the way to Purissima. Then I'll talk to your wife, see what she thinks about these suspicions of yours—"

"She doesn't take me seriously, either."

"Well, I do. Up to a point. I'll circulate and find out what I can. If there's any real indication that your brother's trying to cheat you, or that Dr. Grantland pitched any low curves, I'll do something about it. Incidentally, I charge fifty a day and expenses."

"I have no money now. I'll have plenty when I get what's coming to me."

"Is it a deal then? You go back to the hospital, let me do the legwork?"

He gave me a reluctant yes. It was clear that he didn't like the plan, but he was too tired and confused to argue about it.

Chapter 3

THE MORNING turned hot and bright. The brown September hills on the horizon looked like broken adobe walls you could almost reach out and touch. My car went miles before the hills changed position.

As we drove through the valley, Carl Hallman talked to me about his family. His father had come west before the first war, with enough inherited money to buy a small orange grove outside of Purissima. The old man was a frugal Pennsylvania German, and by the time of his death he'd expanded his holdings to several thousand acres. The main single addition to the original grove had come from his wife, Alicia, who was the descendant of an old land-grant family.

I asked Carl if his mother was still alive.

"No. Mother died, a long time ago."

He didn't want to talk about his mother. Perhaps he had loved her too much, or not enough. He went on talking about his father instead, with a kind of rebellious passion, as though he was still living in his father's shadow. Jeremiah Hallman had been a power in the county, to some extent in the state: founding head of the water association, secretary of the growers' co-operative, head of his party's county central committee, state senator for a decade, and local political boss to the end of his life.

A successful man who had failed to transmit the genes of success to his two sons.

Carl's older brother Jerry was a non-practicing lawyer. For a few months after he graduated from law school, Jerry had had his shingle out in Purissima. He'd lost several cases, made several enemies and no friends, and retired to the family ranch. There he consoled himself with a greenhouseful of cymbidium orchids and dreams of eventual greatness in some unnamed field of activity. Prematurely old in his middle thirties, Jerry was dominated by his wife, Zinnie, a blonde divorcée of uncertain origin who had married him five years ago.

Carl was bitter on the subject of his brother and sister-in-law, and almost equally bitter about himself. He believed that he'd failed his father all the way down the line. When Jerry petered out, the Senator planned to turn over the ranch to Carl, and sent Carl to Davis to study agriculture. Not being interested in agriculture, Carl flunked out. His real interest was philosophy, he said.

Carl managed to talk his father into letting him go to Berkeley. There he met his present wife, a girl he'd known in high school, and shortly after his twenty-first birthday he married her, in spite of the family's objections. It was a dirty trick to play on Mildred. Mildred was another of the people he had failed. She thought that she was getting a whole man, but right at the start of their marriage, within a couple of months, he had his first big breakdown.

Carl spoke in bitter self-contempt. I took my eyes from the road and looked at him. He wouldn't meet my look:

"I didn't mean to tell you about my other—that other breakdown. Anyway, it doesn't prove I'm crazy. Mildred never thought I was, and she knows me better than anybody. It was the strain I was under—working all day and studying half the night. I wanted to be something great, someone even Father would respect—a medical missionary or something like that. I was trying to get together enough credits for admission to medical school, and studying theology at the same time, and— Well, it was too much for me. I cracked up, and had to be taken home. So there we were."

I glanced at him again. We'd passed through the last of the long string of suburbs, and were in the open country. To the right of the highway, the valley lay wide and peaceful under the bright sky, and the hills had stepped backwards into blueness. Carl was paying no attention to the external world. He had a queer air of being confined, almost as though he were trapped in the past, or in himself. He said:

"It was a rough two years, for all of us. Especially for Mildred. She did her best to put a good face on it, but it wasn't what she had planned to do with her life, keeping house for in-laws in a dead country hole. And I was no use to her. For months I was so depressed that I could hardly bear to get up and face the daylight. What there was of it. I know it can't be true, but the way I remember those months, it was cloudy and dark every day. So dark that I could hardly see to shave when I got up at noon.

"The other people in the house were like gray ghosts around me, even Mildred, and I was the grayest ghost of all. Even the house was rotting away. I used to wish for an earthquake, to knock it down and bury us all at once—Father and me and Mildred and Jerry and Zinnie. I thought a good deal about killing myself, but I didn't have the gumption.

"If I'd had any gumption, or any sense, I'd have gone for treatment then. Mildred wanted me to, but I was too ashamed to admit I needed it. Father wouldn't have stood for it, anyway. It would have disgraced the family. He thought psychiatry was a confidence game, that all I really needed was hard work. He kept telling me that I was pampering myself, just as Mother had, and that I'd come to the same bad end if I didn't get out in the open air and make a man of myself."

He snickered dolefully, and paused. I wanted to ask him how his mother had died. I hesitated to. The boy was digging pretty deep as it was, and I didn't want him to break through into something he couldn't handle. Since he'd told me of his earlier breakdown and the suicidal depression that followed it, my main idea was to get him back to the hospital in one mental piece. It was only a few miles more to the turnoff, and I could hardly wait.

"Eventually," Carl was saying, "I did go to work on the ranch. Father had been slowing down, with some sort of heart condition, and I took over some of his supervisory duties. I didn't mind the work itself, out in the groves with the pickers, and I suppose it did me some good at that. But in the long run it only led to more trouble.

"Father and I could never see eye to eye on anything. He was in orange-growing to make money, the more money the better. He never thought in terms of the human cost. I couldn't stand to see the way the orange-pickers were treated. Whole families, men and women and kids, herded into open trucks and hauled around like cattle. Paid by the box, hired by the day, then shunted on their way. A lot of them were wetbacks, without any legal rights. Which suited Father fine. It didn't suit me at all. I told Father what I thought of his lousy labor policy. I told him that this was a civilized country in the middle of the twentieth century and he had no right to push people around like peons, cut them off from employment if they asked for a living wage.

I told him he was a spoiled old man, and I wasn't going to sit idly by and let him oppress the Mexican people, and defraud the Japanese!"

"The Japanese?" I said.

Carl's speech had been coming in a faster rhythm, so fast that I could hardly follow it. There was an evangelical light in his eye. His face was flushed and hot.

"Yes. I'm ashamed to say it, but my father cheated some of his own best friends, Japanese people. When I was a kid, before the War, there used to be quite a few of them in our county. They had hundreds of acres of truck gardens between our ranch and town. They're nearly all gone now. They were driven out during the war, and never came back. Father bought up their land at a few cents on the dollar.

"I told him when I got my share of the ranch, I'd give those people their property back. I'd hire detectives to trace them and bring them back and give them what was theirs. I intended to do it, too. That's why I'm not going to let Jerry cheat me out of the property. It doesn't *belong* to us, you see. We've got to give it back. We've got to set things right, between us and the land, between us and other people.

"Father said that was nonsense, that he'd bought the land perfectly honestly. In fact, he thought that my ideas were crazy. They all did, even Mildred. We had a big scene about it that last night. It was terrible, with Jerry and Zinnie trying to turn him against me, and Mildred in the middle, trying to make peace. Poor Mildred, she was always in the middle. And I guess she was right, I *wasn't* making too much sense. If I had been, I'd have realized that Father was a sick man. Whether I was right or wrong—and of course I *was* right—Father couldn't stand that kind of a family ruction."

I turned off the highway to the right, onto a road which curved back through an underpass, across flat fields, past a giant hedge of eucalyptus trees. The trees looked ancient and sorrowful; the fields were empty.

Chapter 4

CARL SAT tense and quiet in the seat beside me. After a while he said:

"Did you know that words can kill, Mr. Archer? You can kill an old man by arguing with him. I did it to my father. At least," he added on a different note, "I've thought for the last six months that I was responsible. Father died in his bath that night. When Dr. Grantland examined him, he said he'd had a heart attack, brought on by overexcitement. I blamed myself for his death. Jerry and Zinnie blamed me, too. Is it any wonder I blew my top? I thought I was a parricide.

"But now I don't know," he said. "When I found out about Dr. Grantland, it started me thinking back all over again. Why should I go by the word of a man like that? He hasn't even the right to call himself a doctor. It's the strain of not knowing that I can't stand. You see, if Father died of a heart attack, then I'm responsible."

"Not necessarily. Old men die every day."

"Don't try to confuse me," he said peremptorily. "I can see the issue quite clearly. If Father died of a heart attack, I killed him with my words, and I'm a murderer. But if he died of something else, then someone else is the murderer. And Dr. Grantland is covering up for them."

I was pretty certain by now that I was listening to paranoid delusions. I handled them with kid gloves:

"That doesn't sound too likely, Carl. Why don't you give it a rest for now? Think about something else."

"I can't!" he cried. "You've got to help me get at the truth. You promised to help me."

"I will—" I started to say.

Carl grabbed my right elbow. The car veered onto the shoulder, churning gravel. I braked, wrestling the wheel and Carl's clutching hands. The car came to a stop at a tilt, one side in the shallow ditch. I shook him off.

"That was a smart thing to do."

He was careless or unaware of what had happened. "You've got to believe me," he said. "Somebody's got to believe me."

"You don't believe yourself. You've told me two stories already. How many others are there?"

"You're calling me a liar."

"No. But your thinking needs some shaking out. You're the only one who can do that. And the hospital is the place to do it in."

The buildings of the great hospital were visible ahead, in the gap between two hills. We noticed them at the same time. Carl said:

"No. I'm not going back there. You promised to help me, but you don't intend to. You're just like all the others. So I'll have to do it myself."

"Do what?"

"Find out the truth. Find out who killed my father, and bring him to justice."

I said as gently as possible: "You're talking a little wild, kid. Now you keep your half of the bargain, and I'll keep mine. You go back in and get well, I'll see what I can find out."

"You're only trying to humor me. You don't intend to do anything."

"Don't I?"

He was silent. By way of proving that I was on his side, I said:

"It will probably help if you'd tell me what you know about this Grantland. This morning you mentioned a record."

"Yes, and I wasn't lying. I got it from a good source—a man who knows him."

"Another patient?"

"He's a patient, yes. That doesn't prove anything. He's perfectly sane, there's nothing the matter with his mind."

"Is that what he says?"

"The doctors say it, too. He's in for narcotic addiction."

"That hardly recommends him as a witness."

"He was telling me the *truth*," Carl said. "He's known Dr. Grantland for years, and all about him. Grantland used to supply him with narcotics."

"Bad enough, if true. But it's still a long way to murder."

"I see." His tone was disconsolate. "You want me to think I did it. You give me no hope."

"Listen to me," I said.

But he was deep in himself, examining a secret horror. He

sobbed once in dry pain. Without any other warning, he turned on me. Dull sorrow filmed his eyes. His hooked hands swung together reaching for my throat. Immobilized behind the steering wheel, I reached for the doorhandle to gain some freedom of action. Carl was too quick for me. His large hands closed on my neck. I struck at his face with my right hand, but he was almost oblivious.

His close-up face was immense and bland, spotted with clear drops of sweat. He shook me. Daylight began to wane.

"Lay off," I said. "Damn fool." But the words were a rusty cawing.

I hit at him again, ineffectually, without leverage. One of his hands left my neck and came up hard against the point of my jaw. I went out.

I came to in the dry ditch, beside the tiremarks where my car had stood. As I got up the checkerboard fields fell into place around me, teetering slightly. I felt remarkably small, like a pin on a map.

Chapter 5

ITOOK off my jacket and slapped the dust out of it and started to walk toward the hospital. It lay, like a city state, in the middle of its own fields. It had no walls. Perhaps their place was taken by the hills which stood around it, jagged and naked, on three sides. Broad avenues divided the concrete buildings which gave no outward indication of their use. The people walking on the sidewalks looked not much different from people anywhere, except that there was no hurry, nowhere to hurry to. The sun-stopped place with its massive, inscrutable buildings had an unreal quality; perhaps it was only hurry that was missing.

A fat man in blue jeans appeared from behind a parked car and approached me confidentially. In a low genteel voice he asked me if I wanted to buy a leather case for my car keys. "It's very good hand-carved leather, sir, hand-crafted in the hospital." He displayed it.

"Sorry, I don't have any use for it. Where do I go to get some information, about a patient?"

"Depends what ward he's on."

"I don't know the ward."

"You'd better ask at Administration." He pointed toward a new-looking off-white building at the intersection of two streets. But he was unwilling to let me go. "Did you come by bus?"

"I walked."

"From Los Angeles?"

"Part of the way."

"No car, eh?"

"My car was stolen."

"That's too bad. I live in Los Angeles, you know. I have a Buick station wagon, pretty good car. My wife keeps it up on blocks in the garage. They say that keeps the tires from deteriorating."

"Good idea."

"Yes," he said. "I want that car to be in good condition."

Broad concrete steps led up to the entrance of the administration building. I put on my jacket over my wet shirt, and went in through the glass doors. The highly groomed brunette at the information desk gave me a bright professional smile. "Can I help you, sir?"

"I'd like to see the superintendent."

Her smile hardened a little. "His schedule is very full today. May I have your name, please?"

"Archer."

"And what do you wish to see him about, Mr. Archer?"

"A confidential matter."

"One of our patients?"

"Yes, as a matter of fact."

"Are you a relative?"

"No."

"Which patient are you interested in, and what exactly is your interest? Sir."

"I'd better save that for the superintendent."

"You might have to wait all morning to see him. He has a series of conferences. I couldn't promise even then that he could find time for you."

It was gently administered, but it was the brush-off. There was no way to get around her quiet watchdog poise, so I gave it a frontal push:

"One of your patients escaped last night. He's violent."

She was unruffled. "You wish to lodge a complaint?"

"Not necessarily. I need some advice."

"Perhaps I can help you to it, if you'll give me the patient's name. Otherwise, I have no way of knowing which doctor is responsible for him."

"Carl Hallman."

Her thin eyebrows twitched upward: she recognized the name. "If you'll sit down, sir, I'll try to get the information for you."

She picked up one of her telephones. I sat down and lit a cigarette. It was still early in the morning, and I was the only one in the waiting-room. Its colored furniture and shiny waxed tile floors were insistently cheerful. I cheered up slightly myself when a covey of bright young nurses came in, and went twittering down a corridor.

The woman behind the desk put down her telephone and crooked a finger at me. "Dr. Brockley will see you. He's in his office now. You'll find it in the building behind this one, in the main corridor."

The second building was enormous. Its central corridor looked long enough to stage a hundred-yard-dash in. I contemplated making one. Ever since the Army, big institutions depressed me: channels, red tape, protocol, buck-passing, hurry up and wait. Only now and then you met a man with enough gumption to keep the big machine from bogging down of its own weight.

The door with Dr. Brockley's name above it was standing open. He came around from behind his desk, a middle-sized, middle-aged man in a gray herringbone suit, and gave me a quick hard hand.

"Mr. Archer? I happened to come in early this morning, so I can give you fifteen minutes. Then I'm due on the ward."

He placed me in a straight chair against the wall, brought me an ashtray, sat at his desk with his back to the window. He was quick in movement, very still in repose. His bald scalp and watchful eyes made him resemble a lizard waiting for a fly to expose itself.

"I understand you have a complaint against Carl Hallman. Perhaps you should understand that the hospital is not responsible for his actions. We're interested, but not responsible. He left here without permission."

"I know that. He told me."

"You're a friend of Hallman's?"

"I don't know him at all. He came to my house early this morning to try and get my help."

"What sort of help did he want?"

"It's a pretty involved story, having to do with his family. I think a lot of it was pure delusion. The main thing seems to be, he feels responsible for his father's death. He wants to get rid of the feeling. So he came to me. I happen to be a private detective. A friend of his recommended me to him."

When I named my profession, or sub-profession, the temperature went down. The doctor said frostily:

"If you're looking for family information, I can't give it to you."

"I'm not. I thought the best thing I could do for Hallman was bring him back here. I talked him into it, and we almost made it. Then he got excited and started throwing his weight around. As a matter of fact—" I'd been holding it back, because I was ashamed of it—"he took me by surprise and stole my car."

"It doesn't sound like him."

"Maybe I shouldn't say he stole it. He was upset, and I don't think he knew what he was doing. But he took it, and I want it back."

"Are you sure he took it?"

Another bureaucrat, I thought, with a noose of red tape up his sleeve. Another one of those. I said:

"I confess, Doctor. I never had a car. It was all a dream. The car was a sex symbol, see, and when it disappeared, it meant I'm entering the change of life."

He answered without a flicker of expression, smile or frown: "I mean, are you sure it wasn't the other one who stole your car? Another patient was with him when he took off last night. Didn't they stick together?"

"I only saw the one. Who was the other?"

Dr. Brockley lifted a manila folder out of his in-basket and studied its contents, or pretended to. "Normally," he said after a while, "we don't discuss our patients with outsiders. On the other hand, I'd like—" He closed the folder and slapped it down. "Let me put it this way. What do you intend to do about this alleged car theft? You want to see Hallman punished, naturally."

"Do I?"

"Don't you?"

"No."

"Why not?"

"I think he belongs in the hospital."

"What makes you think so?"

"He's flying, and he could be dangerous. He's a powerful boy. I don't want to be an alarmist, but he tried to throttle me."

"Really? You're not exaggerating?"

I showed him the marks on my neck. Dr. Brockley forgot himself for a second, and let his humanity show through, like a light behind a door. "Damn it, I'm sorry." But it was his patient he was sorry for. "Carl was doing so well these last few months—no acting out at all. What happened to set him off, do you know?"

"It may have been the idea of coming back here—this happened just up the road. The situation was sort of complicated. I let him talk too much, about his family, and then I made the mistake of arguing with him."

"Do you remember what about?"

"A fellow patient of his. Carl said he was a narcotics addict. He claimed the man gave him some suspicious information about a doctor he knew, a Dr. Grantland."

"I've met him. He's the Hallman family doctor. Incidentally, Grantland was instrumental in having Carl committed. It's natural that Carl would have feelings against him."

"He made some accusations. I don't think I'll repeat them, at least to another doctor."

"As you please." Brockley had resumed his poker face. "You say the source of the accusation was another patient, a narcotics addict?"

"That's right. I told Carl he should consider the source. He thought I was calling *him* a liar."

"What was the addict's name?"

"He wouldn't tell me."

Brockley said thoughtfully: "The man who escaped with him last night was a heroin addict. He's just another patient, of course—we treat them all alike—but he's quite a different kettle of fish from Carl Hallman. In spite of his disturbance, Carl's essentially a naïve and idealistic young man. Potentially a valuable man." The doctor was talking more to himself than to me. "I'd hate to think he's under Tom Rica's influence."

"Did you say Tom Rica?"

But the doctor had reached for his phone: "Miss Parish. This is Dr. Brockley. Tom Rica's folder, please— No, bring it to my office."

"I used to know a Tom Rica," I said when he put down the phone. "Let's see, he was eighteen about ten years ago, when he left Compton High. That would make him twenty-eight or -nine now. How old is Carl Hallman's friend?"

"Twenty-eight or -nine," Brockley said drily. "He looks a good deal older. Heroin has that effect, and the things that heroin leads to."

"This Rica has a record, eh?"

"Yes, he has. I didn't think he belonged here, but the authorities thought he could be rehabilitated. Maybe he can, at that. Maybe he can. We've had a few heroin cures. But he won't get cured wandering around the countryside."

There was a tap at the door. A young woman carrying a folder came in and handed it to Brockley. She was tall and generously made, with a fine sweep of bosom and the shoulders to support it. Her black hair was drawn back severely in a chignon. She had on a rather severely tailored dress which seemed intended to play down her femininity, without too much success.

"Miss Parish, this is Mr. Archer," Brockley said. "Mr. Archer ran into Carl Hallman this morning."

Her dark eyes lit with concern. "Where did you see him?"

"He came to my house."

"Is he all right?"

"It's hard to say."

"There's been a little trouble," Brockley put in. "Nothing too serious. I'll fill you in later if you like. I'm a bit rushed right now."

She took it as a reproof. "I'm sorry, Doctor."

"Nothing to be sorry about. I know you're interested in the case."

He opened the folder and began to scan it. Miss Parish went out rather hastily, bumping one hip on the doorframe. She had the kind of hips that are meant for childbearing and associated activities. Brockley cleared his throat, and brought my attention back to him:

"Compton High School. Rica's your boy all right."

Chapter 6

I WASN'T surprised, just disappointed. Tom had played his part in the postwar rebellion that turned so many boys against authority. But he had been one of the salvageable ones, I thought. I'd helped to get him probation after his first major conviction—car theft, as usual—taught him a little boxing and shooting, tried to teach him some of the other things a man should know. Well, at least he remembered my name.

"What happened to Tom?" I said.

"Who can say? He was only in a short time, and we hadn't got to him yet. Frankly, we don't spend much time on personal work with addicts. It's mostly up to them. Some of them make it, some don't." He looked down into the folder on his desk. "Rica has a history of trouble. We'll have to notify the police of his escape."

"What about Carl Hallman?"

"I've been in touch with his family. They're contacting Ostervelt, the sheriff in Purissima—he knows Carl. I'd rather handle it unofficially, if it's all right with you. Keep this car trouble off the books until Carl has a chance to think twice about it."

"You think he'll come to his senses and bring it back?"

"It wouldn't surprise me. We could at least give him a chance."

"He's not dangerous, in your opinion?"

"Everybody's dangerous, given the wrong circumstances. I can't predict individual behavior. I know that Carl got rough with you. Still, I'd be willing to take a chance on him. His hospital record is good. And there are other considerations. You know what happens when a patient goes out of here, with or without leave, and gets into any kind of trouble. The newspapers play it up, and then there's public pressure on us to go back to the snake-pit days—lock the loonies up and forget about them." Brockley's voice was bitter. He passed his hand over his mouth, pulling it to one side. "Are you willing to wait a bit, Mr. Archer? I can get you transportation back to town."

"I'd like a few questions answered first."

"I'm overdue on the ward now." He glanced at the watch on his wrist, then shrugged. "All right. Shoot away."

"Was Carl being kept here by his brother Jerry, after he needed it?"

"No. It was a staff matter, essentially my decision."

"Did he tell you he blamed himself for his father's death?"

"Many times. I'd say that guilt feeling was central in his illness. He also attached it to his mother's death. Her suicide was a great shock to him."

"She killed herself?"

"Yes, some years ago. Carl thought she did it because he broke her heart. It's typical of psychotic patients to blame themselves for everything that happens. Guilt is our main commodity here." He smiled. "We give it away."

"Hallman has a lot on his mind."

"He's been getting rid of it, gradually. And shock therapy helped. Some of my patients tell me that shock treatment satisfies their need for punishment. Maybe it does. We don't know for certain how it works."

"How crazy is he, can you tell me that?"

"He was manic-depressive, manic phase, when he came in. He isn't now, unless he's starting to go into a windup. Which I doubt."

"Is he likely to?"

"It depends on what happens to him." Brockley stood up, and came around the desk. He added, in a casual voice, but glancing sharply down at me: "You needn't feel that it's any responsibility of yours."

"I get your message. Lay off."

"For a while, anyway. Leave your telephone number with Miss Parish down the hall. If your car turns up, I'll get in touch with you."

Brockley let me out, and walked rapidly away. A few steps down the hall, I found a door lettered with Miss Parish's name and her title, Psychiatric Social Worker. She opened it when I knocked.

"I've been hoping you'd come by, Mr. Archer, is it? Please sit down."

Miss Parish indicated a straight chair by her desk. Apart from the filing cabinets the chair and desk were about all the furniture the small office contained. It was barer than a nun's cell.

"Thanks, I won't take the time to sit down. The doctor asked me to leave my telephone number with you, in case our friend changes his mind and comes back."

I recited the number. She sat down at her desk and wrote it on a memo pad. Then she gave me a bright and piercing look which made me self-conscious. Tall women behind desks had always bothered me, anyway. It probably went back to the vice-principal of Wilson Junior High, who disapproved of the live bait I used to carry in the thermos bottle in my lunch pail, and other ingenious devices. Vice-Principal Trauma with Archer's Syndrome. The hospital atmosphere had me thinking that way.

"You're not a member of Mr. Hallman's immediate family, or a close friend." The statement lifted at the end into a question.

"I never saw him until today. I'm mainly interested in getting my car back."

"I don't understand. You mean he has your car?"

"He took it away from me." Since she seemed interested, I outlined the circumstances.

Her eyes darkened like thunderclouds. "I can't believe it."

"Brockley did."

"I'm sorry, I don't mean I doubt your word. It's simply— this eruption doesn't fit in with Carl's development. He's been making such wonderful strides with us—helping us look after the less competent ones— But of course you're not interested. You're naturally resentful about the loss of your car."

"Not so very. He's had a good deal of trouble. I can afford a little, if he had to pass it on."

She looked more friendly. "You sound as though you talked to him."

"He talked to me, quite a lot. I almost got him back here."

"Did he seem disturbed? Apart from the outburst of violence, I mean?"

"I've seen worse, but I'm no judge. He was pretty bitter about his family."

"Yes, I know. It was his father's death that set him off in the first place. The first few weeks he talked of nothing else. But the trouble had died down, at least I thought it had. Of course I'm not a psychiatrist. On the other hand, I've had a lot more to do with Carl than any of the psychiatrists." She added softly: "He's a sweet person, you know."

Under the circumstances, the sentiment seemed slightly sticky. I said: "He picked a funny way to show it."

Miss Parish had emotional equipment to match her splendid physical equipment. The thunderclouds came into her eyes again, with lightning. "He's not responsible!" she cried. "Can't you see that? You mustn't judge him."

"All right. I'll go along with that."

This seemed to calm her, though her brow stayed dark. "I can't imagine what happened to stir him up. Considering the distance he'd had to come back, he was the most promising patient on the ward. He was due for a P-card in a very few weeks. He'd probably have gone home in two or three months. Carl didn't have to run away, and he knew it."

"Remember he had another man with him. Tom Rica may have done some pretty good needling."

"Is Tom Rica with him now?"

"He wasn't when I saw Carl."

"That's good. I shouldn't say it about a patient, but Tom Rica is a poor risk. He's a heroin addict, and this isn't his first cure. Or his last, I'm afraid."

"I'm sorry to hear it. I knew him when he was a boy. He had his troubles even then, but he was a bright kid."

"It's queer that you should know Rica," she said with some suspicion. "Isn't that quite a coincidence?"

"No. Tom Rica sent Carl Hallman to me."

"They are together, then?"

"They left here together. Afterwards, they seem to have gone separate ways."

"Oh, I hope so. An addict looking for dope, and a vulnerable boy like Carl—they could make an explosive combination."

"Not a very likely combination," I said. "How did they happen to be buddies?"

"I wouldn't say they were buddies, exactly. They were committed from the same place, and Carl's been looking after Rica on the ward. We never have enough nurses and technicians to go around, so our better patients help to take care of the worse ones. Rica was in a bad way when he came in."

"How long ago was that?"

"A couple of weeks. He had severe withdrawal symptoms—
couldn't eat, couldn't sleep. Carl was a positive saint with him:
I watched them together. If I'd known how it was going to turn
out, I'd have—" She broke off, clamping her teeth down on her
lower lip.

"You like Carl," I said in a neutral tone.

The young woman colored, and answered rather sharply:
"You would, too, if you knew him when he's himself."

Maybe I would, I thought, but not the way Miss Parish
did. Carl Hallman was a handsome boy, and a handsome boy
in trouble was a double threat to women, a triple threat if he
needed mothering.

Not needing it, and none being offered, I left.

Chapter 7

THE ADDRESS which Carl had given me for his wife was near the highway in an older section of Purissima. The highway traffic thrummed invisibly like a damaged artery under the noon silence in the street. Most of the houses were frame cottages or stucco boxes built in the style of thirty years ago. A few were older, three-story mansions surviving from an era of elegance into an era of necessity.

220 was one of these. Its long closed face seemed abashed by the present. Its white wooden walls needed paint. The grass in the front yard had grown and withered, untouched by the human hand.

I asked the cab-driver to wait and knocked on the front door, which was surmounted by a fanlight of ruby-colored glass. I had to knock several times before I got an answer. Then the door was unlocked and opened, reluctantly and partially.

The woman who showed herself in the aperture had unlikely purplish red hair cut in bangs on her forehead and recently permanented. Blue eyes burned like gas-flames in her rather inert face. Her mouth was crudely outlined in fresh lipstick, which I guessed she had just dabbed on as a concession to the outside world. The only other concession was a pink nylon robe from which her breasts threatened to overflow. I placed her age in the late forties. She couldn't be Mrs. Carl Hallman. At least I hoped she couldn't.

"Is Mrs. Hallman home?"

"No, she isn't here. I'm Mrs. Gley, her mother." She smiled meaninglessly. There was lipstick on her teeth, too, gleaming like new blood. "Is it something?"

"I'd like very much to see her."

"Is it about—him?"

"Mr. Hallman, you mean?"

She nodded.

"Well, I would like to talk to him."

"Talk to him! It needs more than talk to him. You might as well talk to a stone wall—beat your head bloody against it trying to change his ways." Though she seemed angry and afraid, she

464

spoke in a low monotone. Her voice was borne on a heavy breath in which Sen-Sen struggled for dominance. You inhaled it as much as heard it.

"Is Mr. Hallman here?"

"No, thank God for small mercies. He hasn't been here. But I've been expecting him ever since she got that call from the hospital." Her gaze, which had swiveled past me to the street, returned to my face. "Is that your taxi?"

"Yes."

"Well, that's a relief. Are you from the hospital?"

"I just came from there."

I'd intended some misrepresentation, which she made me regret immediately:

"Why don't you keep them locked up better? You can't let crazy-men run around loose. If you knew what my girl has suffered from that man—it's a terrible thing." She took the short easy step from motherly concern to self-concern: "Sometimes I think I'm the one who suffered most. The things I hoped and planned for that girl, and then she had to bring *that* one into the family. I begged and pleaded with her to stay home today. But no, she has to go to work, you'd think the office couldn't go on without her. She leaves me here by myself, to cope."

She spread out her hands and pressed them into her bosom, the white flesh rising like dough between her fingers.

"It isn't fair. The world is cruel. You work and hope and plan, then everything goes to pieces. I didn't deserve it." A few easy tears ran down her cheeks. She found a ball of Kleenex in her sleeve and wiped her eyes. They shone, undimmed by her grief, with a remarkable intensity. I wondered what fuel fed them.

"I'm sorry, Mrs. Gley. I'm new on this case. My name is Archer. May I come in and talk to you?"

"Come in if you like. I don't know what *I* can tell you. Mildred ought to be home over the noon-hour, she promised she would."

She moved along the dim hallway, a middle-aged woman going to seed, but not entirely gone. There was something about the way she carried herself: old beauty and grace controlling her flesh, like an unforgotten discipline. She turned at a curtained archway behind which voices murmured.

"Please go in and sit down. I was just changing for lunch. I'll put something on."

She started up a flight of stairs which rose from the rear of the hallway. I went in through the curtains, and found myself in a twilit sitting-room with a lighted television screen. At first the people on the screen were unreal shadows. After I sat and watched them for a few minutes, they became realer than the room. The screen became a window into a brightly lighted place where life was being lived, where a beautiful actress couldn't decide between career and children and had to settle for both. The actual windows of the sitting-room were heavily blinded.

In the shifting light from the screen, I noticed an empty glass on the coffeetable beside me. It smelled of gin. Just to keep my hand in, I made a search for the bottle. It was stuffed behind the cushion of my chair, a half-empty Gordon's bottle, its contents transparent as tears. Feeling a little embarrassed, I returned it to its hiding place. The woman on the screen had had her baby, and held it up to her husband for his approval.

The front door opened and closed. Quick heels clicked down the hallway, and paused at the archway. I started to get up. A woman's voice said:

"Who—Carl? Is that you, Carl?"

Her voice was high. She looked very pale and dark-eyed in the light from the screen, almost like a projection from it. She fumbled behind the curtains for a lightswitch. A dim ceiling light came on over my head.

"Oh. Excuse me. I thought you were someone else."

She was young and small, with a fine small head, its modeling emphasized by a short boyish haircut. She had on a dark business suit which her body filled the way grapes fill their skins. She held a shiny black plastic bag, like a shield, in front of it.

"Mrs. Hallman?"

"Yes." Her look said: who are you, and what are you doing here?

I told her my name. "Your mother asked me to sit down for a minute."

"Where is Mother?" She tried to speak in an ordinary tone, but she looked at me suspiciously, as if I had Mother's body hidden in a closet.

"Upstairs."

"Are you a policeman?"

"No."

"I just wondered. She phoned me at the office about half an hour ago and said she was going to ask for police protection. I couldn't get away immediately."

She stopped abruptly, and looked around the room. Its furnishings would have been antiques if they'd ever possessed distinction. The carpet was threadbare, the wallpaper faded and stained brown in patches. The mohair sofa that matched the chair I'd sat in was ripped and spilling its guts. The mahogany veneer was peeling off the coffeetable which held the empty glass. It was no wonder Mrs. Gley preferred darkness and gin and television to the light of morning.

The girl went past me in a birdlike rush, snatched up the glass, and sniffed at it. "I thought so."

On the screen behind her a male announcer, not so very male, was telling women how to be odorless and beloved. The girl turned with the glass in her hand. For a second I thought she'd throw it at the screen. Instead she stooped and switched the television off. Its light faded slowly like a dream.

"Did Mother pour you a drink?"

"Not yet."

"Has anyone else been here?"

"Not that I know of. But your mother may have the right idea. I mean, about police protection."

She looked at me in silence for a minute. Her eyes were the same color as her mother's, and had the same intensity, almost tangible on my face. Her gaze dropped to the glass in her hand. Setting it down, she said under cover of the movement: "You know about Carl? Did Mother tell you?"

"I talked to Dr. Brockley at the hospital this morning. I had a run-in with your husband earlier. As a matter of fact he took my car." I told her about that.

She listened with her head bowed, biting one knuckle like a doleful child. But there was nothing childish about the look she gave me. It held a startled awareness, as if she'd had to grow up in a hurry, painfully. I had a feeling that she was the one who had suffered most in the family trouble. There was resignation in her posture, and in the undertones of her voice:

"I'm sorry. He never did anything like that before."

"I'm sorry, too."

"Why did you come here?"

I had several motives, some more obscure than others. I picked the easiest: "I want my car back. If I can handle it myself, without reporting it as a theft—"

"But you said yourself that we should call the police."

"For protection, yes. Your mother's frightened."

"Mother's very easily frightened. I'm not. Anyway, there's no basis for it. Carl's never hurt anyone, let alone Mother and me. He talks a lot sometimes—that's all it amounts to. I'm not afraid of him." She gave me a shrewd and very female glance. "Are you?"

Under the circumstances, I had to say I wasn't. I couldn't be sure, though. Perhaps that was my reason for coming there— the obscurest motive that underlay the others.

"I've always been able to handle Carl," she said. "I'd never have let them take him to the hospital, if I could have kept him here and looked after him myself. But somebody had to go to work." She frowned. "What can be keeping Mother? Excuse me for a minute."

She left the room and started up the stairs. The ringing of a telephone brought her down into the hallway again. From somewhere upstairs her mother called:

"Is that you, Mildred? The phone's ringing."

"Yes. I'll get it." I heard her lift the receiver. "This is Mildred. Zinnie? What do you want? . . . Are you sure? . . . No, I can't. I can't possibly. . . . I don't believe it. . . ." Then, on a rising note: "All *right*. I'll come."

The receiver dropped in its cradle. I went to the door and looked into the hallway. Mildred was leaning against the wall beside the telephone table. Her face was wan, her eyes shock-bright. Her gaze shifted to me, but it was so inward I don't think it took me in.

"Trouble?"

She nodded mutely and drew in a shuddering breath. It came out as a sigh:

"Carl's at the ranch now. One of the hands saw him. Jerry isn't there, and Zinnie's terrified."

"Where's Jerry?"

"I don't know. In town, probably. He follows the stock market every day until two, at least he used to."

"What's she so scared about?"

"Carl has a gun with him." Her voice was low and wretched.

"You're sure?"

"The man who saw him said so."

"Is he likely to use it?"

"No. I don't think so. It's the others I'm worried about—what they might do to Carl if there's any shooting."

"What others?"

"Jerry, and the sheriff and his deputies. They've always taken orders from the Hallmans. I've got to go and find Carl—talk to him, before Jerry gets back to the ranch."

But she was having a hard time getting under way. She stood stiff against the wall, hands knotted at the ends of their straight arms, immobilized by tension. When I touched her elbow, she shied:

"Yes?"

"I have a taxi waiting. I'll take you out there."

"No. Taxis cost money. We'll go in my car." She scooped up her bag and pressed it under her arm.

"Go where?" her mother cried from the top of the stairs. "Where are you going? You're not going to leave me alone."

Mrs. Gley came down in a rush. She had on a kind of tea gown whose draperies flew out behind her, like the tail of a blowzy comet. Her body swayed softly and heavily against the newel post at the foot of the stairs. "You can't leave me alone," she repeated.

"I'm sorry, Mother. I have to go to the ranch. Carl's out there now, so there's nothing for you to worry about."

"Nothing to worry about, that's a good one. I've got my life to worry about, that's all. And your place is with your mother at this time."

"You're talking nonsense."

"Am I? When all I ask is a little love and sympathy from my own daughter?"

"You've had all I've got."

The younger woman turned and started for the door. Her mother followed her, a clumsy ghost trailing yellowing draperies and the powerful odor of Sen-Sen. Either her earlier drinks were catching up with her, or she had another bottle upstairs. She made her final plea, or threat:

"I'm drinking, Mildred."

"I know, Mother."

Mildred opened the door and went out.

"Don't you care?" her mother screamed after her.

Mrs. Gley turned to me as I passed her in the doorway. The light from the window over the door lent her face a rosy youthfulness. She looked like a naughty girl who was trying to decide whether or not to have a tantrum. I didn't wait to find out if she did.

Chapter 8

MILDRED HALLMAN'S car was an old black Buick convertible. It was parked behind my cab, wide of the curb. I paid off the cab-driver and got in. Mildred was sitting on the righthand side of the front seat.

"You drive, will you?" She said as we started: "Between Carl and Mother, I'm completely squeezed out. They both need a keeper, and in the end it always turns out to be me. No, don't think I'm feeling sorry for myself, because I'm not. It's nice to be needed."

She spoke with a kind of wilted gallantry. I looked at her. She'd leaned her head against the cracked leather seat, and closed her eyes. Without their light and depth in her face, she looked about thirteen. I caught myself up short, recognizing a feeling I'd had before. It started out as paternal sympathy but rapidly degenerated, if I let it. And Mildred had a husband.

"You're fond of your husband," I said.

She answered dreamily: "I'm crazy about him. I had a crush on him in high school, the first and only crush I ever had. Carl was a big wheel in those days. He barely knew I existed. I kept hoping, though." She paused, and added softly: "I'm still hoping."

I stopped for a red light, and turned right onto the highway which paralleled the waterfront. Gas fumes mixed with the odors of fish and underwater oil wells. To my left, beyond a row of motels and seafood restaurants, the sea lay low and flat and solid like blue tiling, swept clean and polished. Some white triangular sails stood upright on it.

We passed a small-boat harbor, gleaming white on blue, and a long pier draped with fishermen. Everything was as pretty as a postcard. The trouble with you, I said to myself: you're always turning over the postcards and reading the messages on the underside. Written in invisible ink, in blood, in tears, with a black border around them, with postage due, unsigned, or signed with a thumbprint.

Turning right again at the foot of the main street, we passed through an area of third-rate hotels, bars, pool halls. Stunned by sun and sherry, unemployed field hands and rumdums paraded like zombies on the noon pavements. A Mexican movie house marked the upper limits of the lower depths. Above it were stores and banks and office buildings, sidewalks bright with tourists, or natives who dressed like tourists.

The residential belt had widened since I'd been in Purissima last, and it was still spreading. New streets and housing tracts were climbing the coastal ridge and pushing up the canyons. The main street became a country blacktop which wound up over the ridge. On its far side a valley opened, broad and floored with rich irrigation green. A dozen miles across it, the green made inlets between the foothills and lapped at the bases of the mountains.

The girl beside me stirred. "You can see the house from here. It's off the road to the right, in the middle of the valley."

I made out a sprawling tile-roofed building floating low like a heavy red raft in the ridged green. As we went downhill, the house sank out of sight.

"I used to live in that house," Mildred said. "I promised myself I'd never go back to it. A building can soak up emotions, you know, so that after a while it has the same emotions as the people who live in it. They're in the cracks in the walls, the smokestains on the ceiling, the smells in the kitchen."

I suspected that she was dramatizing a little: there was some of her mother in her after all: but I kept still, hoping she'd go on talking.

"Greed and hate and snobbery," she said. "Everyone who lived in that house became greedy and hateful and snobbish. Except Carl. It's no wonder he couldn't take it. He's so completely different from the others." She turned toward me, the leather creaking under her. "I know what you're thinking—that Carl is crazy, or he was, and I'm twisting the facts around to suit myself. I'm not, though. Carl is good. It's often the very best people who crack up. And when he cracked, it was family pressure that did it to him."

"I gathered that, from what he said to me."

"Did he tell you about Jerry—constantly taunting him, trying to make him mad, then running to his father with tales of the trouble Carl made?"

"Why did he do that?"

"Greed," she said. "The well-known Hallman greed. Jerry wanted control of the ranch. Carl was due to inherit half of it. Jerry did everything he could to ruin Carl with his father, and Zinnie did, too. They were the ones who were really responsible for that last big quarrel, before the Senator died. Did Carl tell you about that?"

"Not very much."

"Well, Jerry and Zinnie started it. They got Carl talking about the Japanese, how much the family owed them for their land—I admit that Carl was hipped on the subject, but Jerry encouraged him to go on and on until he was really raving. I tried to stop it, but nobody listened to me. When Carl was completely wound up, Jerry went to the Senator and asked him to reason with Carl. You can imagine how much reasoning they did, when they got together. We could hear them shouting all over the house.

"The Senator had a heart attack that night. It's a terrible thing to say about a man, but Jerry was responsible for his father's death. He may even have planned it that way: he knew his father wasn't to be excited. I heard Dr. Grantland warn the family myself, more than once."

"What about Dr. Grantland?"

"In what way do you mean?"

"Carl thinks he's crooked," I hesitated, then decided she could hold it: "In fact, he made some pretty broad accusations."

"I think I've heard them. But go on."

"Conspiracy was one of them. Carl thought Grantland and his brother conspired to have him committed. But the doctor at the hospital says there's nothing to it."

"No," she said. "Carl needed hospital treatment. I signed the necessary papers. That was all aboveboard. Only, Jerry made me and Carl sign other papers at the same time, making him Carl's legal guardian. I didn't know what it meant. I thought it was just a part of the commitment. But it means that as long as Carl is ill, Jerry controls every penny of the estate."

Her voice had risen. She brought it under control and said more quietly: "I don't care about myself. I'd never go back there anyway. But Carl needs the money. He could get better treatment—the best psychiatrists in the country. It's the last thing Jerry wants, to see his brother cured. That would end the guardianship, you see."

"Does Carl know all this?"

"No, at least he's never heard it from me. He's mad enough at Jerry as it is."

"Your brother-in-law sounds charming."

"Yes indeed he is." Her voice was thin. "If it was just a question of saving Jerry, I wouldn't move a step in his direction. Not a step. But you know what will happen to Carl if he gets into any kind of trouble. He's already got more guilt than he can bear. It could set him back years, or make him permanent— No! I won't think about it. Nothing is going to happen."

She twisted in the seat away from me, as though I represented the things she feared. The road had become a green trench running through miles of orange trees. The individual rows of trees, slanting diagonally from the road, whirled and jumped backward in staccato movement. Mildred peered down the long empty vistas between them, looking for a man with straw-colored hair.

A large wooden sign, painted black on white, appeared at the roadside ahead: Hallman Citrus Ranch. I braked for the turn, made it on whining tires, and almost ran down a big old man in a sheriff's blouse. He moved away nimbly, then came heavily back to the side of the car. Under a wide-brimmed white hat, his face was flushed. Veins squirmed like broken purple worms under the skin of his nose. His eyes held the confident vacancy that comes from the exercise of other people's power.

"Watch where you're going, bud. Not that you're going anywhere, on this road. What do you think I'm here for, to get myself a tan?"

Mildred leaned across me, her breast live against my arm:

"Sheriff! Have you seen Carl?"

The old man leaned to peer in. His sun-wrinkles deepened and his mouth widened in a smile which left his eyes as vacant as before. "Why hello, Mrs. Hallman, I didn't see you at first. I must be going blind in my old age."

"Have you seen Carl?" she repeated.

He made a production out of answering her, marching around to her side of the car, carrying his belly in front of him like a gift. "Not personally, I haven't. We know he's on the ranch, though. Sam Yogan saw him to talk to, not much more than an hour ago."

"Was he rational?"

"Sam didn't say. Anyway, what would a Jap gardener know about it?"

"A gun was mentioned," I said.

The sheriff's mouth drooped at the corners. "Yeah, he's carrying a gun. I don't know where in hell he got hold of it."

"How heavy a gun?"

"Sam said not so heavy. But any gun is too big when a man is off his rocker."

Mildred let out a small cry.

"Don't worry, Mrs. Hallman. We got the place staked out. We'll pick him up." Tipping his hat back, he pushed his face in at her window. "You better get rid of your boyfriend before we do pick him up. Carl won't like it if you got a boyfriend, driving his car and all."

She looked from him to me, her mouth a thin line. "This is Sheriff Ostervelt, Mr. Archer. I'm sorry I forgot my manners. Sheriff Ostervelt never had any to remember."

Ostervelt smirked. "Take a joke, eh?"

"Not from you," she said without looking at him.

"Still mad, eh? Give it time. Give it time."

He laid a thick hand on her shoulder. She took it in both of hers and flung it away from her. I started to get out of the car.

"Don't," she said. "He only wants trouble."

"Trouble? Not me," Ostervelt said. "I try to make a little joke. You don't think it's funny. Is that trouble, between friends?"

I said: "Mrs. Hallman's expected at the house. I said I'd drive her there. Much as I'd love to go on talking to you all afternoon."

"I'll take her to the house." Ostervelt gestured toward the black Mercury Special parked on the shoulder, and patted his holster. "The husband's lurking around in the groves, and I don't have the men to comb them for him. She might need protection."

"Protection is my business."

"What the hell does that mean?"

"I'm a private detective."

"What do you know? You got a license, maybe?"

"Yes. It's good statewide. Now do we go, or do we stay here and have some more repartee?"

"Sure," he said, "I'm stupid—just a stupid fool, and my jokes ain't funny. Only I got an official responsibility. So you better let me see that license you say you got."

Moving very slowly, the sheriff came around to my side of the car again. I slapped my photostat into his hand. He read it aloud, in an elocutionary voice, pausing to check the physical description against my appearance.

"Six-foot-two, one-ninety," he repeated. "A hunk of man. Love those beautiful blue eyes. Or are they gray, Mrs. Hallman? You'd know."

"Leave me alone." Her voice was barely audible.

"Sure. But I better drive you up to the house in person. Hollywood here has those beautiful powder-blue eyes, but it don't say here"—he flicked my photostat with his forefinger—"what his score is on a moving target."

I picked the black-and-white card out of his hand, released the emergency brake, stepped on the gas. It wasn't politic. But enough was enough.

Chapter 9

THE PRIVATE road ran ruler-straight through the geometric maze of the orange trees. Midway between the highway and the house, it widened in front of several barnlike packing-sheds. The fruit on the trees was unripe, and the red-painted sheds were empty and deserted-looking. In a clearing behind them, a row of tumble-down hutches, equally empty, provided shelter of a sort for migrant pickers.

Nearly a mile further on, the main house stood back from the road, half-shadowed by overarching oaks. Its brown adobe walls looked as indigenous as the oaks. The red Ford station wagon and the sheriff's patrol car on the curving gravel drive-way seemed out of place, or rather out of time. The thing that struck me most as I parked in the driveway was a child's swing suspended by new rope from a branch of one of the trees. No one had mentioned a child.

When I switched off the Buick's engine, the silence was almost absolute. The house and its grounds were tranquil. Shadows lay soft as peace in the deep veranda. It was hard to believe the other side of the postcard.

The silence was broken by a screen door's percussion. A blonde woman wearing black satin slacks and a white shirt came out on the front veranda. She folded her arms over her breasts and stood as still as a cat, watching us come up the walk.

"Zinnie," Mildred said under her breath. She raised her voice: "Zinnie? Is everything all right?"

"Oh fine. Just lovely. I'm still waiting for Jerry to come home. You didn't see him in town, did you?"

"I never see Jerry. You know that."

Mildred halted at the foot of the steps. There was a barrier of hostility, like a charged fence, between the two women. Zinnie, who was at least ten years older, held her body in a compact defensive posture against the pressure of Mildred's eyes. Then she dropped her arms in a rather dramatic gesture which may have been meant for me.

"I hardly ever see him myself."

She laughed nervously. Her laugh was harsh and unpleasant, like her voice. It was easy for me to overlook the unpleasantness. She was a beautiful woman, and her green eyes were interested in me. The waist above her snug hips was the kind you can span with your two hands, and would probably like to.

"Who's your friend?" she purred.

Mildred introduced me.

"A private detective yet," Zinnie said. "The place is crawling with policemen already. But come on in. That sun is misery."

She held the door for us. Her other hand went to her face where the sun had parched the skin, then to her sleek hair. Her right breast rose elastically under the white silk shirt. A nice machine, I thought: pseudo-Hollywood, probably empty, certainly expensive, and not new; but a nice machine. She caught my look and didn't seem to mind. She switch-hipped along the hallway, to a large, cool living-room.

"I've been waiting for an excuse to have a drink. Mildred, you'll have ginger ale, I know. How's your mother, by the way?"

"Mother is fine. Thank you." Mildred's formality broke down suddenly. "Zinnie? Where is Carl now?"

Zinnie lifted her shoulders. "I wish I knew. He hasn't been heard from since Sam Yogan saw him. Ostervelt has several deputies out looking for him. The trouble is, Carl knows the ranch better than any of them."

"You said they promised not to shoot."

"Don't worry about that. They'll take him without any fireworks. That's where you come in, if and when he shows up."

"Yes." Mildred stood like a stranger in the middle of the floor. "Is there anything I can do now?"

"Not a thing. Relax. I need a drink if you don't. What about you, Mr. Archer?"

"Gibson, if it's available."

"That's handy, I'm a Gibson girl myself." She smiled brilliantly, too brilliantly for the circumstances. Zinnie seemed to be a trier, though, whatever else she was.

Her living-room bore the earmarks of a trier with a restless urge to be up to the minute in everything. Its bright new furniture was sectional, scattered around in cubes and oblongs and arcs. It sorted oddly with the dark oak floor and the heavily beamed ceiling. The adobe walls were hung with modern reproductions in limed oak frames. A row of book-club books occupied the mantel above the ancient stone fireplace. A free-form marble coffeetable held *Harper's Bazaar* and *Vogue* and a beautiful old silver handbell. It was a room in which an uneasy present struggled to overcome the persistent past.

Zinnie picked up the bell and shook it. Mildred jumped at the sound. She was sitting very tense on the edge of a sectional sofa. I sat down beside her, but she paid no attention to my presence. She turned to look out the window, toward the groves.

A tiny girl came into the room, pausing near the door at the sight of strangers. With light blond hair and delicate porcelain features, she was obviously Zinnie's daughter. The child was fussily dressed in a pale blue frock with a sash, and a matching blue ribbon in her hair. Her hand crept toward her mouth. The tiny fingernails were painted red.

"I was ringing for Juan, dear," Zinnie said.

"I want to ring for him, Mummy. Let me ring for Juan."

Though the child wasn't much more than three, she spoke very clearly and purely. She darted forward, reaching for the handbell. Zinnie let her ring it. Above its din, a white-jacketed Filipino said from the doorway:

"Missus?"

"A shaker of Gibsons, Juan. Oh, and ginger ale for Mildred."

"I want a Gibson, too," the little girl said.

"All right, darling." Zinnie turned to the houseboy: "A special cocktail for Martha."

He smiled comprehendingly, and disappeared.

"Say hello to your Aunt Mildred, Martha."

"Hello, Aunt Mildred."

"Hello, Martha. How are you?"

"I'm fine. How is Uncle Carl?"

"Uncle Carl is ill," Mildred said in a monotone.

"Isn't Uncle Carl coming? Mummy said he was coming. She said so on the telephone."

"No," her mother cut in. "You didn't understand what I said, dear. I was talking about somebody else. Uncle Carl is far away. He's living far away."

"Who is coming, Mummy?"

"Lots of people are coming. Daddy will be here soon. And Dr. Grantland. And Aunt Mildred is here."

The child looked up at her, her eyes clear and untroubled. She said: "I don't want Daddy to come. I don't like Daddy. I want Dr. Grantland to come. He will come and take us to a nice place."

"Not *us,* dear. You and Mrs. Hutchinson. Dr. Grantland will take you for a ride in his car, and you'll spend the day with Mrs. Hutchinson. Maybe all night, too. Won't that be fun?"

"Yes," the child answered gravely. "That will be fun."

"Now go and ask Mrs. Hutchinson to give you your lunch."

"I ate my lunch. I ate it all up. You said I could have a special cocktail."

"In the kitchen, dear. Juan will give you your cocktail in the kitchen."

"I don't want to go in the kitchen. I want to stay here, with people."

"No, you can't." Zinnie was getting edgy. "Now be a nice girl and do what you're told, or I'll tell Daddy about you. He won't like it."

"I don't care. I want to stay here and talk to the people."

"Some other time, Martha." She rose and hustled the little girl out of the room. A long wail ended with the closing of a door.

"She's a beautiful child."

Mildred turned to me. "Which one of them do you mean? Yes, Martha is pretty. And she's bright. But the way Zinnie is handling her—she treats her as if she were a doll."

Mildred was going to say more, but Zinnie returned, closely followed by the houseboy with the drinks. I drank mine in a hurry, and ate the onion by way of lunch.

"Have another, Mr. Archer." One drink had converted Zinnie's tension into vivacity, of a sort. "We've got the rest of the shaker to knock back between us. Unless we can persuade Mildred to climb down off her high wagon."

"You know where I stand on the subject." Mildred gripped her glass of ginger ale defensively. "I see you've had the room redone."

I said: "One's enough for me, thanks. What I'd like to do, if you don't object, is talk to the man who saw your brother-in-law. Sam something?"

"Sam Yogan. Of course, talk to Sam if you like."

"Is he around now?"

"I think so. Come on, I'll help you find him. Coming, Mildred?"

"I'd better stay here," Mildred said. "If Carl comes to the house, I want to be here to meet him."

"Aren't you afraid of him?"

"No, I'm not afraid of him. I love my husband. No doubt it's hard for you to understand that."

The hostility between the two women kept showing its sharp edges. Zinnie said:

"Well, I'm afraid of him. Why do you think I'm sending Martha to town? And I've got half a mind to go myself."

"With Dr. Grantland?"

Zinnie didn't answer. She rose abruptly, with a glance at me. I followed her through a dining-room furnished in massive old mahogany, into a sunlit kitchen gleaming with formica and chrome and tile. The houseboy turned from the sink, where he was washing dishes:

"Yes, Missus?"

"Is Sam around?"

"Before, he was talking to policeman."

"I know that. Where is he now?"

"Bunkhouse, greenhouse, I dunno." The houseboy shrugged. "I pay no attention to Sam Yogan."

"I know that, too."

Zinnie moved impatiently through a utility room to the back door. As soon as we stepped outside, a young man in a western hat raised his head from behind a pile of oak logs. He came around the woodpile, replacing his gun in its holster, swaggering slightly in his deputy's suntans.

"I'd stay inside if I was you, Mrs. Hallman. That way we can look after you better." He looked inquiringly at me.

"Mr. Archer is a private detective."

A peevish look crossed the young deputy's face, as though my presence threatened to spoil the game. I hoped it would. There were too many guns around.

"Any sign of Carl Hallman?" I asked him.

"You check in with the sheriff?"

"I checked in." Ostensibly to Zinnie, I said: "Didn't you say there wouldn't be any shooting? That the sheriff's men would take your brother-in-law without hurting him?"

"Yes. Sheriff Ostervelt promised to do his best."

"We can't guarantee nothing," the young deputy said. Even as he spoke, he was scanning the tree-shaded recesses of the back yard, and the dense green of the trees that stretched beyond. "We got a dangerous man to deal with. He bust out of a security ward last night, stole a car for his getaway, probably stole the gun he's carrying."

"How do you know he stole a car?"

"We found it, stashed in a tractor turnaround between here and the main road. Right near where the old Jap ran into him."

"Green Ford convertible?"

"Yeah. You seen it?"

"It's my car."

"No kidding? How'd he happen to steal your car?"

"He didn't exactly steal it. I'm laying no charges. Take it easy with him if you see him."

The deputy's face hardened obtusely. "I got my orders."

"What are they?"

"Fire if fired upon. And that's leaning way over backwards. You don't play footsie with a homicidal psycho, Mister."

He had a point: I'd tried to, and got my lumps. But you didn't shoot him, either.

"He isn't considered homicidal."

I glanced at Zinnie for confirmation. She didn't speak, or look in my direction. Her pretty head was cocked sideways in a strained listening attitude. The deputy said:

"You should talk to the sheriff about that."

"He didn't threaten Yogan, did he?"

"Maybe not. The Jap and him are old pals. Or maybe he did, and the Jap ain't telling us. We do know he's carrying a gun, and he knows how to use it."

"I'd like to talk to Yogan."

"If you think it'll do you any good. Last I saw of him he was in the bunkhouse."

He pointed between the oaks to an old adobe which stood on the edge of the groves. Behind us, the sound of an approaching car floated over the housetop.

"Excuse me, Mr. Carmichael," Zinnie said. "That must be my husband."

Walking quickly, she disappeared around the side of the house. Carmichael pulled his gun and trotted after her. I followed along, around the attached greenhouse which flanked the side of the house.

A silver-gray Jaguar stopped behind the Buick convertible in the driveway. Running across the lawn toward the sports car, under the towering sky, Zinnie looked like a little puppet, black and white and gold, jerked across green baize. The big man who got out of the car slowed her with a gesture of his hand. She looked back at me and the deputy, stumbling a little on her heels, and assumed an awkward noncommittal pose.

Chapter 10

THE DRIVER of the Jaguar had dressed himself to match it. He had on gray flannels, gray suede shoes, a gray silk shirt, a gray tie with a metallic sheen. In striking contrast, his face had the polished brown finish of hand-rubbed wood. Even at a distance, I could see he used it as an actor might. He was conscious of planes and angles, and the way his white teeth flashed when he smiled. He turned his full smile on Zinnie.

I said to the deputy: "That wouldn't be Jerry Hallman."

"Naw. It's some doctor from town."

"Grantland?"

"I guess that's his name." He squinted at me sideways. "What kind of detective work do you do? Divorce?"

"I have."

"Which one in the family hired you, anyway?"

I didn't want to go into that, so I gave him a wise look and drifted away. Dr. Grantland and Zinnie were climbing the front steps. As she passed him in the doorway, Zinnie looked up into his face. She inclined her body so that her breast touched his arm. He put the same arm around her shoulders, turned her away from him, and propelled her into the house.

Without going out of my way to make a lot of noise, I mounted the veranda and approached the screen door. A carefully modulated male voice was saying:

"You're acting like a wild woman. You don't have to be so conspicuous."

"I want to be. I want everyone to know."

"Including Jerry?"

"Especially him." Zinnie added illogically: "Anyway, he isn't here."

"He soon will be. I passed him on the way out. You should have seen the look he gave me."

"He hates anybody to pass him."

"No, there was more to it than that. Are you sure you haven't told him about us?"

"I wouldn't tell him the time of day."

"What's this about wanting everybody to know then?"

"I didn't mean anything. Except that I love you."

"Be quiet. Don't even say it. You could throw everything away, just when I've got it practically made."

"Tell me."

"I'll tell you afterwards. Or perhaps I won't tell you at all. It's working out, and that's all you need to know. Anyway, it will work out, if you can act like a sensible human being."

"Just tell me what to do, and I'll do it."

"Then remember who you are, and who I am. I'm thinking about Martha. You should be, too."

"Yes. I forget her sometimes, when I'm with you. Thank you for reminding me, Charlie."

"Not Charlie. Doctor. Call me doctor."

"Yes, Doctor." She made the word sound erotic. "Kiss me once, Doctor. It's been a long time."

Having won his point, he became bland. "If you insist, Mrs. Hallman."

She moaned. I walked to the end of the veranda, feeling a little let down because Zinnie's vivacity hadn't been for me. I lit a consolatory cigarette.

At the side of the house, childish laughter bubbled. I leaned on the railing and looked around the corner. Mildred and her niece were playing a game of catch with a tennisball. At least it was catch for Mildred, when Martha threw the ball anywhere near her. Mildred rolled the ball to the child, who scampered after it like a small utility infielder in fairy blue. For the first time since I'd met her, Mildred looked relaxed.

A gray-haired woman in a flowered dress was watching them from a chaise longue in the shade. She called out:

"Martha! You mustn't get overtired. And keep your dress clean."

Mildred turned on the older woman: "Let her get dirty if she likes."

But the spell of the game was broken. Smiling a perverse little smile, the child picked up the ball and threw it over the picket fence that surrounded the lawn. It bounced out of sight among the orange trees.

The woman on the chaise longue raised her voice again:

"Now look what you've done, you naughty girl—you've gone and lost the ball."

"Naughty girl," the child repeated shrilly, and began to chant: "Martha's a naughty girl, Martha's a naughty girl."

"You're not, you're a nice girl," Mildred said. "The ball isn't lost. I'll find it."

She started for the gate in the picket fence. I opened my mouth to warn her not to go into the trees. But something was going on in the driveway behind me. Car wheels crunched in the ground, and slid to a stop. I turned and saw that it was a new lavender Cadillac with gold trim.

The man who got out of the driver's seat was wearing fuzzy tweeds. His hair and eyes had the same coloring as Carl, but he was older, fatter, shorter. Instead of hospital pallor, his face was full of angry blood.

Zinnie came out on the veranda to meet him. Unfortunately her lipstick was smeared. Her eyes looked feverish.

"Jerry, thank God you're here!" The dramatic note sounded wrong, and she lowered her voice: "I've been worried sick. Where on earth have you been all day?"

He stumped up the steps and faced her, not quite as tall as she was on her heels. "I haven't been gone all day. I drove down to see Brockley at the hospital. Somebody had to give him the bawling-out he had coming to him. I told him what I thought of the loose way they run that place."

"Was that wise, dear?"

"It was some satisfaction, anyway. These bloody doctors! They take the public's money and—" He jerked a thumb toward Grantland's car: "Speaking of doctors, what's he doing here? Is somebody sick?"

"I thought you knew, about Carl. Didn't Ostie stop you at the road?"

"I saw his car there, he wasn't in it. What about Carl?"

"He's on the ranch, carrying a gun." Zinnie saw the shock on her husband's face, and repeated: "I thought you knew. I thought that's why you were staying away, because you're afraid of Carl."

"I'm not afraid of him," he said, on a rising note.

"You were, the day he left here. And you should be, after the things he said to you." She added, with unconscious cruelty, perhaps not entirely unconscious: "I believe he wants to kill you, Jerry."

His hands clutched his stomach, as though she'd struck him a physical blow there. They doubled into fists.

"You'd like that, wouldn't you? You and Charlie Grantland?"

The screen door rattled. Grantland came out on cue. He said with false joviality: "I *thought* I heard someone taking my name in vain. How are you, Mr. Hallman?"

Jerry Hallman ignored him. He said to his wife: "I asked you a simple question. What's he doing here?"

"I'll give you a simple answer. I had no man around I could trust to take Martha into town. So I called Dr. Grantland to chauffeur her. Martha is used to him."

Grantland had come up beside her. She turned and gave him a little smile, her smudged mouth doubling its meaning. Of the three, she and Grantland formed the paired unit. Her husband was the one who stood alone. As if he couldn't bear that loneliness, he turned on his heel, walked stiffly down the veranda steps, and disappeared through the front door of the greenhouse.

Grantland took a gray handkerchief out of his breast pocket and wiped Zinnie's mouth. The center of her body swayed toward him.

"Don't," he said urgently. "He knows already. You must have told him."

"I asked him for a divorce—you know that—and he's not a complete fool. Anyway, what does it matter?" She had the false assurance, or abandon, of a woman who has made a sexual commitment and swung her whole life from it like a trapeze. "Maybe Carl will kill him."

"Be quiet, Zin! Don't even think it—!"

His voice broke off. Her gaze had moved across me as he spoke, and telegraphed my presence to him. He turned on his toes like a dancer. The blood seeped out from underneath his tan. He might have been a beady-eyed old man with jaundice. Then he pulled himself together and smiled—a downward-turning smile but a confident one. It was unsettling to see a man's face change so rapidly and radically.

I threw away the butt of my cigarette, which seemed to have lasted for a long time, and smiled back at him. Felt from inside, like a rubber Halloween mask, my smile was a stiff grimace. Jerry Hallman relieved my embarrassment, if that is what I was feeling. He came hustling out of the greenhouse with a pair of shears in his hand, a dull blotched look on his face.

Zinnie saw him, and backed against the wall. "Charlie! Look out!"

Grantland turned to face Jerry as he came up the steps, a dumpy middle-aging man who couldn't stand loneliness. His eyes had a very solitary expression. The shears projected outward from the grip of his two hands, gleaming in the sun, like a double dagger.

"Yah, Charlie!" he said. "Look out! You think you can get away with my wife and my daughter both. You're taking nothing of mine."

"I had no such intention." Grantland stuttered over the words. "Mrs. Hallman telephoned—"

"Don't 'Mrs. Hallman' me. You don't call her that in town. Do you?" Standing at the top of the steps with his legs planted wide apart, Jerry Hallman opened and closed the shears. "Get out of here, you lousy cod. If you want to go on being a man, get off my property and stay off my property. That includes my wife."

Grantland had put on his old-man face. He backed away from the threatening edges and looked for support to Zinnie. Greenfaced in the shadow, she stood still as a bas-relief against the wall. Her mouth worked, and managed to say:

"Stop it, Jerry. You're not making sense."

Jerry Hallman was at that trembling balance point in human rage where he might have alarmed himself into doing murder. It was time for someone to stop it. Shouldering Grantland out of my way, I walked up to Hallman and told him to put the shears down.

"Who do you think you're talking to?" he sputtered.

"You're Mr. Jerry Hallman, aren't you? I heard you were a smart man, Mr. Hallman."

He looked at me stubbornly. The whites of his eyes were yellowish from some internal complaint, bad digestion or bad conscience. Something deep in his head looked out through his eyes at me, gradually coming forward into light. Fear and shame, perhaps. His eyes seemed to be puzzled by dry pain. He turned and went down the steps and into the greenhouse, slamming the door behind him. Nobody followed him.

Chapter 11

Voices rose on the far side of the house, as if another door had opened there. Female and excited, they sounded like chickens after a hawk has swooped. I ran down the steps and around the end of the veranda. Mildred came across the lawn toward me, holding the little girl's hand. Mrs. Hutchinson trailed behind them, her head turned at an angle toward the groves, her face as gray as her hair. The gate in the picket fence was open, but there was no one else in sight.

The child's voice rose high and penetrating. "Why did Uncle Carl run away?"

Mildred turned and bent over her. "It doesn't matter why. He likes to run."

"Is he mad at you, Aunt Mildred?"

"Not really, darling. He's just playing a game."

Mildred looked up and saw me. She shook her head curtly: I wasn't to say anything to frighten the child. Zinnie swept past me and lifted Martha in her arms. The deputy Carmichael was close behind her, unhitching his gun.

"What happened, Mrs. Hallman? Did you see him?"

She nodded, but waited to speak till Zinnie had carried the little girl out of hearing. Mildred's forehead was bright with sweat, and she was breathing rapidly. I noticed that she had the ball in her hand.

The gray-haired woman elbowed her way into the group. "I saw him, sneaking under the trees. Martha saw him, too."

Mildred turned on her. "He wasn't sneaking, Mrs. Hutchinson. He picked up the ball and brought it to me. He came right up to me." She displayed the ball, as if it was important evidence of her husband's gentleness.

Mrs. Hutchinson said: "I was never so terrified in my born days. I couldn't even open my mouth to let out a scream."

The deputy was getting impatient. "Hold it, ladies. I want a straight story, and fast. Did he threaten you, Mrs. Hallman—attack you in any way?"

"No."

"Did he say anything?"

489

"I did most of the talking. I tried to persuade Carl to come in and give himself up. When he wouldn't, I put my arms around him, to try and hold him. He was too strong for me. He broke away, and I ran after him. He wouldn't come back."

"Did he show his gun?"

"No." She looked down at Carmichael's gun. "Please, don't use your gun if you see my husband. I don't believe he's armed."

"Maybe not," Carmichael said noncommittally. "Where did all this happen?"

"I'll show you."

She turned and started toward the open gate, moving with a kind of dogged gallantry. It wasn't quite enough to hold her up. Suddenly she went to her knees and crumpled sideways on the lawn, a small dark-suited figure with spilled brown hair. The ball rolled out of her hand. Carmichael knelt beside her, shouting as if mere loudness could make her answer:

"Which way did he go?"

Mrs. Hutchinson waved her arm toward the groves. "Right through there, in the direction of town."

The young deputy got up and ran through the gateway in the picket fence. I ran after him, with some idea of trying to head off violence. The ground under the trees was adobe, soft and moist with cultivation. I never had gone well on a heavy track. The deputy was out of sight. After a while he was out of hearing, too. I slowed down and stopped, cursing my obsolescent legs.

It was purely a personal matter between me and my legs, because running couldn't accomplish anything, anyway. When I thought about it, I realized that a man who knew the country could hide for days on the great ranch. It would take hundreds of searchers to beat him out of the groves and canyons and creekbeds.

I went back the way I had come, following my own footmarks. Five of my walking steps, if I stretched my legs, equaled three of my running steps. I crossed other people's tracks, but had no way to identify them. Tracking wasn't my forte, except on asphalt.

After a long morning crowded with people under pressure, it was pleasant to be walking by myself in the green shade. Over my head, between the tops of the trees, a trickle of blue sky meandered. I let myself believe that there was no need to hurry, that trouble had been averted for the present. Carl had done no harm to anybody, after all.

Back-tracking on the morning, I walked slower and slower. Brockley would probably say that it was unconscious drag, that I didn't want to get back to the house. There seemed to be some truth in Mildred's idea that a house could make people hate each other. A house, or the money it stood for, or the cannibalistic family hungers it symbolized.

I'd run further than I'd realized, perhaps a third of a mile. Eventually the house loomed up through the trees. The yard was empty. Everything was remarkably still. One of the french doors was standing open. I went in. The dining-room had a curious atmosphere, unlived in and unlivable, like one of those three-walled rooms laid out in a museum behind silk rope: Provincial California Spanish, Pre-Atomic Era. The living-room, with its magazines and dirty glasses and Hollywood-Cubist furniture, had the same deserted quality.

I crossed the hallway and opened the door of a study lined with books and filing cabinets. The venetian blinds were drawn. The room had a musty smell. A dark oil portrait of a bald old man hung on one wall. His eyes peered through the dimness at me, out of a lean rapacious face. Senator Hallman, I presumed. I closed the study door on him.

I went through the house from front to back, and finally found two human beings in the kitchen. Mrs. Hutchinson was sitting at the kitchen table, with Martha on her knee. The elderly woman started at my voice. Her face had sharpened in the quarter-hour since I'd seen her. Her eyes were bleak and accusing.

"What happened next?" Martha said.

"Well, the little girl went to the nice old lady's house, and they had tea-cakes." Mrs. Hutchinson's eyes stayed on me, daring me to speak. "Tea-cakes and chocolate ice cream, and the old lady read the little girl a story."

"What was the little girl's name?"

"Martha, just like yours."

"She couldn't eat chocolate ice cream, 'cause of her algery."

"They had vanilla. We'll have vanilla, too, with strawberry jam on top."

"Is Mummy coming?"

"Not right away. She'll be coming later."

"Is Daddy coming? I don't want Daddy to come."

"Daddy won't—" Mrs. Hutchinson's voice broke off. "That's the end of the story, dear."

"I want another story."

"We don't have time." She set the child down. "Now run into the living-room and play."

"I want to go into the greenhouse." Martha ran to an inner door, and rattled the knob.

"No! Stay here! Come back here!"

Frightened by the woman's tone, Martha returned, dragging her feet.

"What's the matter?" I said, though I thought I knew. "Where is everybody?"

Mrs. Hutchinson gestured toward the door that Martha had tried to open. I heard a murmur of voices beyond it, like bees behind a wall. Mrs. Hutchinson rose heavily and beckoned me to her. Conscious of the child's unwavering gaze, I leaned close to the woman's mouth. She said:

"Mr. Hallman was ess aitch oh tee. He's dee ee ay dee."

"Don't spell! You mustn't spell!"

In a miniature fury, the child flung herself between us and struck the old woman on the hip. Mrs. Hutchinson drew her close. The child stood still with her face in the flowered lap, her tiny white arms embracing the twin pillars of the woman's legs.

I left them and went through the inner door. An unlit passageway lined with shelves ended in a flight of steps. I stumbled down them to a second door, which I opened.

The edge of the door struck softly against a pair of hind quarters. These happened to belong to Sheriff Ostervelt. He let out a little snort of angry surprise, and turned on me, his hand on his gun.

"Where do you think you're going?"

"Coming in."

"You're not invited. This is an official investigation."

I looked past him into the greenhouse. In the central aisle, between rows of massed cymbidiums, Mildred and Zinnie and Grantland were grouped around a body which lay face up. The face had been covered by a gray silk handkerchief, but I knew

whose body it was. Jerry's fuzzy tweeds, his rotundity, his help-
lessness, gave him the air of a defunct teddy bear.

Zinnie stood above him, incongruously robed in ruffled
white nylon. Without makeup, her face was almost as colorless
as the robe. Mildred stood near her, looking down at the dirt
floor. A little apart, Dr. Grantland leaned on one of the planters,
controlled and watchful.

Zinnie's face worked stiffly: "Let him come in if he wants to,
Ostie. We can probably use all the help we can get."

Ostervelt did as she said. He was almost meek about it.
Which reminded me of the simple fact that Zinnie had just
fallen heir to the Hallman ranch and whatever power went with
it. Grantland didn't seem to need reminding. He leaned close
to whisper in her ear, with something proprietary in the angle
of his head.

She silenced him with a sidewise warning glance, and edged
away from him. Acting on impulse—at least it looked like
impulse from where I stood—Zinnie put her arm around Mildred and hugged her. Mildred made as if to pull away, then
leaned on Zinnie and closed her eyes. Through the white-
painted glass roof, daylight fell harsh and depthless on their
faces, sistered by shock.

Ostervelt missed these things, which happened in a moment.
He was fiddling with the lid of a steel box that stood on a workbench behind the door. Getting it open, he lifted out a piece of
shingle to which a small gun was tied with twine.

"Okay, so you want to be a help. Take a look at this."

It was a small, short-barreled revolver, of about .25 caliber,
probably of European make. The butt was sheathed in mother-
of-pearl, and ornamented with silver filigree work. A woman's
gun, not new: the silver was tarnished. I'd never seen it, or a gun
like it, and I said so.

"Mrs. Hallman, Mrs. *Carl* Hallman, said you had some
trouble with her husband this morning. He stole your car, is
that right?"

"Yes, he took it."

"Under what circumstances?"

"I was driving him back to the hospital. He came to my house
early this morning, with some idea I might be able to help him.

I figured the best thing I could do for him was talk him into going back in. It didn't quite work."

"What happened?"

"He took me by surprise—overpowered me."

"What do you know?" Ostervelt smirked. "Did he pull this little gun on you?"

"No. He had no gun that I saw. I take it this is the gun that killed Hallman."

"You take it correct, mister. This is also the gun the brother had, according to Yogan's description of it. The doctor found it right beside the body. Two shells fired, two holes in the man's back. The doctor said he died instantly, that right, Doctor?"

"Within a few seconds, I'd say." Grantland was cool and professional. "There was no external bleeding. My guess is that one of the bullets pierced his heart. Of course it will take an autopsy to establish the exact cause of death."

"Did you discover the body, Doctor?"

"I did, as a matter of fact."

"I'm interested in matters of fact. What brought you out to the greenhouse?"

"The shots, of course."

"You heard them?"

"Very clearly. I was taking Martha's clothes out to the car."

Zinnie said wearily: "We all heard them. I thought at first that Jerry—" She broke off.

"Jerry what?" Ostervelt said.

"Nothing. Ostie? Do we have to go through this again—all this palaver? I'm very anxious to get Martha out of the house. God knows what this is doing to her. And wouldn't you accomplish more if you went out after Carl?"

"I got every free man in the department looking for him now. I can't leave until the deputy coroner gets here."

"Does that mean we have to wait?"

"Not right here, if it's getting you down. I think you ought to stick around the house, though."

"I've told you all I can," Grantland said. "And I have patients waiting. In addition to which, Mrs. Hallman has asked me to drive her daughter and her housekeeper into Purissima."

"All right. Go ahead, Doctor. Thanks for your help."

Grantland went out the back door. The two women came down the funereal aisle between the rows of flowers, bronze and green and blood-red. They walked with their arms around each other, and passed through the door that led toward the kitchen. Before the door closed, one of them broke into a storm of weeping.

The noise of grief is impersonal, and I couldn't be sure which one of them it was. But I thought it must have been Mildred. Her loss was the worst. It had been going on for a long time, and was continuing.

Chapter 12

THE BACK door of the greenhouse opened, and two men came in. One was the eager young deputy who excelled at cross-country running. Carmichael's blouse was dark with sweat, and he was still breathing deeply. The other man was a Japanese of indeterminate age. When he saw the dead man on the floor, he stood still, with his head bowed, and took off his soiled cloth hat. His sparse gray hair stood erect on his scalp, like magnetized iron filings.

The deputy squatted and lifted the gray handkerchief over the dead man's face. His held breath came out.

"Take a good long look, Carmichael," the sheriff said. "You were supposed to be guarding this house and the people in it."

Carmichael stood up, his mouth tight. "I did my best."

"Then I'd hate to see your worst. Where in Christ's name did you go?"

"I went after Carl Hallman, lost him in the groves. He must of circled around and come back here. I ran into Sam Yogan back of the bunkhouse, and he told me he heard some shots."

"You heard the shots?"

The Japanese bobbed his head. "Yessir. Two shots." He had a mouthy old-country accent, and some trouble with his esses.

"Where were you when you heard them?"

"In the bunkhouse."

"Can you see the greenhouse from there?"

"Back door, you can."

"He must of left by the back door, Grantland was at the front, and the women came in the side here. You see him, going or coming?"

"Mr. Carl?"

"You know I mean him. Did you see him?"

"No sir. Nobody."

"Did you look?"

"Yessir. I looked out the door of the bunkhouse."

"But you didn't come and look in the greenhouse."

"No sir."

"Why?" The sheriff's anger, flaring and veering like fire in the wind, was turned on Yogan now. "Your boss was lying shot in here, and you didn't move a muscle."

"I looked out the door."

"But you didn't move a muscle to help him, or apprehend the killer."

"He was probably scared," Carmichael said. With the heat removed from him, he was relaxing into camaraderie.

Yogan gave the deputy a look of calm disdain. He extended his hands in front of his body, parallel and close together, as though he was measuring off the limits of his knowledge:

"I hear two guns—two shots. What does it mean? I see guns all morning. Shooting quail, maybe?"

"All right," the sheriff said heavily. "Let's get back to this morning. You told me Mr. Carl was a very good friend of yours, and that was the reason you weren't scared of him. Is that correct, Sam?"

"I guess so. Yessir."

"How good a friend, Sam? Would you let him shoot his brother and get away? Is that how good a friend?"

Yogan showed his front teeth in a smile which could have meant anything. His flat black eyes were opaque.

"Answer me, Sam."

Yogan said without altering his smile: "Very good friend."

"And Mr. Jerry? Was he a good friend?"

"Very good friend."

"Come off it, Sam. You don't like any of us, do you?"

Yogan grinned implacably, like a yellow skull.

Ostervelt raised his voice:

"Wipe the smile off, tombstone-teeth. You're not fooling anybody. You don't like me, and you don't like the Hallman family. Why the hell you came back here, I'll never know."

"I like the country," Sam Yogan said.

"Oh sure, you like the country. Did you think you could con the Senator into giving you your farm back?"

The old man didn't answer. He looked a little ashamed, not for himself. I gathered that he had been one of the Japanese farmers bought out by the Senator and relocated during the war. I gathered further that he made Ostervelt nervous, as though his presence was an accusation. An accusation which had to be reversed:

"You didn't shoot Mr. Jerry Hallman yourself, by any chance?"

Yogan's smile brightened into scorn.

Ostervelt moved to the workbench and picked up the shingle with the pearl-handled gun attached to it. "Come here, Sam."

Yogan stayed immobile.

"Come here, I said. I won't hurt you. I ought to kick those big white teeth down your dirty yellow throat, but I'm not gonna. Come here."

"You heard the sheriff," Carmichael said, and gave the small man a push.

Yogan came one step forward, and stood still. By sheer patience, his slight figure had become the central object in the room. Having nothing better to do, I went and stood beside him. He smelled faintly of fish and earth. After a while the sheriff came to him.

"Is this the gun, Sam?"

Yogan drew in his breath in a little hiss of surprise. He took the shingle and examined the gun minutely, from several angles.

"You don't have to eat it." Ostervelt snatched it away. "Is this the gun Mr. Carl had?"

"Yessir. I think so."

"Did he pull it on you? Threaten you with it?"

"No sir."

"Then how'd you happen to see it?"

"Mr. Carl showed it to me."

"He just walked up to you and showed you the gun?"

"Yessir."

"Did he say anything?"

"Yessir. He said, hello Sam, how are you, nice to see you. Very polite. Also, where is my brother? I said he went to town."

"Anything about the gun, I mean."

"Said did I recognize it. I said, yes."

"You recognized it?"

"Yessir. It was Mrs. Hallman's gun."

"Which Mrs. Hallman?"

"Old lady Mrs. Hallman, Senator's wife."

"This gun belonged to her?"

"Yessir. She used to bring it out to the back garden, shoot at the blackbirds. I said she wanted a better one, a shotgun. No, she said, she didn't want to hit them. Let them live."

"That must of been a long time ago."

"Yessir, ten-twelve years. When I came back here on the ranch, put in her garden for her."

"What happened to the gun?"

"I dunno."

"Did Carl tell you how *he* got it?"

"No sir. I didn't ask."

"You're a close-mouthed s.o.b., Sam. You know what that means?"

"Yessir."

"Why didn't you tell me all this this morning?"

"You didn't ask me."

The sheriff looked up at the glass roof, as if to ask for comfort and help in his deep tribulations. The only apparent result was the arrival of a moon-faced young man wearing shiny rimless spectacles and a shiny blue suit. I needed no intuition to tab him as the deputy coroner. He carried a black medical bag, and the wary good humor of men whose calling is death.

Surveying the situation from the doorway, he raised his hand to the sheriff and made a beeline for the body. A sheriff's captain with a tripod camera followed close on his heels. The sheriff joined them, issuing a steady flux of orders.

Sam Yogan bowed slightly to me, his forehead corrugated, his eyes bland. He picked up a watering can, filled it at a tin sink in the corner, and moved with it among the cymbidiums. Disregarding the flashbulbs, he was remote as a gardener bent in ritual over flowers in a print.

Chapter 13

I WALKED around to the front of the house and rapped on the screen door. Zinnie answered. She had changed to a black dress without ornament of any kind. Framed in the doorway, she looked like a posed portrait of a young widow, carefully painted in two dimensions. The third dimension was in her eyes, which had green fire in their depths.

"Are you still here?"

"I seem to be."

"Come in if you like."

I followed her into the living-room, noticing how corseted her movements had become. The room had altered, too, though there was no change in its physical arrangement. The murder in the greenhouse had killed something in the house. The bright furnishings looked cheap and out of place in the old room, as if somebody had tried to set up modern housekeeping in an ancestral cave.

"Sit down if you like."

"Am I wearing out my welcome?"

"Everybody is," she said, a little obscurely. "I don't even feel at home here myself. Come to think of it, maybe I never did. Well, it's a little late to go into that now."

"Or a little early. No doubt you'll be selling."

"Jerry was planning to sell out himself. The papers are practically all drawn up."

"That makes it convenient."

Facing me in front of the dead hearth, she looked into my eyes for a long minute. Being a two-way experience, it wasn't unpleasant at all. The pain she'd just been through, or something else, had wiped out a certain crudity in her good looks and left them pretty dazzling. I hoped it wasn't the thought of a lot of new money shining in her head.

"You don't like me," she said.

"I hardly know you."

"Don't worry, you never will."

"There goes another bubble, iridescent but ephemeral."

"I don't think I like you, either. That's quite a spiel you have, for a cheap private detective. Where do you come from, Los Angeles?"

"Yep. How do you know I'm cheap?"

"Mildred couldn't afford you if you weren't."

"Unlike you, eh? I could raise my prices."

"I bet you could. And I was wondering when we were going to get around to that. It didn't take long, did it?"

"Get around to what?"

"What everybody wants. Money. The *other* thing that everybody wants." She turned, handling her body contemptuously and provocatively, identifying the first thing. "You might as well sit down and we'll talk about it."

"It will be a pleasure."

I sat on the end of a white *bouclé* oblong, and she perched tightly on the other end, with her beautiful legs crossed in front of her. "What I ought to do is tell Ostie to throw you the hell out of here."

"For any particular reason? Or just on general principles?"

"For attempted blackmail. Isn't blackmail the idea?"

"It never crossed my mind. Until now."

"Don't kid me. I know your type. Maybe you like to wrap it up in different words. I pay you a retainer to protect my interests or something like that. It's still blackmail, no matter how you wrap it."

"Or baloney, no matter how you slice it. But go on. It's a long time since anybody offered me some free money. Or is this only a daydream?"

She sneered, not very sophisticatedly. "How dare you try to be funny, with my husband not yet cold in his grave?"

"He isn't in it yet. And you can do better than that, Zinnie. Try another take."

"Have you no respect for a woman's emotions—no respect for anything?"

"Show me some real ones. You have them."

"What do you know about it?"

"I'd have to be blind and deaf not to. You go around shooting them off like fireworks."

She was silent. Her face was unnaturally calm, except for

the deep dimension of the eyes. "You mean that scene on the front porch, no doubt. It didn't mean a thing. Not a thing." She sounded like a child repeating a lesson. "I was frightened and upset, and Dr. Grantland is an old friend of the family. Naturally I turned to him in trouble. You'd think even Jerry would understand that. But he's always been irrationally jealous. I can't even look at a man."

She sneaked a look at me to see if I believed her. Our eyes met. "You can now."

"I tell you I'm not in the least interested in Dr. Grantland. Or anybody else."

"You're young to retire."

Her eyes narrowed rather prettily, like a cat's. Like a cat, she was kind of smart, but too self-centered to be really smart. "You're terribly cynical, aren't you? I hate cynical men."

"Let's stop playing games, Zinnie. You're crazy about Grantland. He's crazy about you. I hope."

"What do you mean, you hope?" she said, laying my last doubt to rest.

"I hope Charlie is crazy about you."

"He is. I mean, he would be, if I let him. What makes you think he isn't?"

"What makes you think it?"

She put her hands over her ears and made a monkey face. Even then, she couldn't look ugly. She had such good bones, her skeleton would have been an ornament in any closet.

"All this talky-talk," she said. "I get mixed up. Could we come down to cases? That business on the porch, I know it looks bad. I don't know how much you heard?"

I put on my omniscient expression. She was still coming to me, pressed by a fear that made her indiscreet.

"Whatever you heard, it doesn't mean I'm glad that Jerry is dead. I'm sorry he's dead." She sounded surprised. "I felt *sorry* for the poor guy when he was lying there. It wasn't his fault he didn't have it—that we couldn't make it together— Anyway, I had nothing to do with his death, and neither did Charlie."

"Who said you did?"

"Some people would say it, if they knew about that silly fuss on the porch. Mildred might."

"Where is Mildred now, by the way?"

"Lying down. I talked her into taking some rest before she goes back to town. She's emotionally exhausted."

"That was nice of you."

"Oh, I'm not a total all-round bitch. And I don't blame her for what her husband did."

"*If* he did." With nothing much to go on, I threw that in to test her reaction.

She took it personally, almost as an insult. "Is there any doubt he did it?"

"There always is, until it's proved in court."

"But he hated Jerry. He had the gun. He came here to kill Jerry, and we know he was here."

"We know he was here, all right. Maybe he still is. The rest is your version. I'd kind of like to hear his, before we find him guilty and execute him on the spot."

"Who said anything about executing him? They don't execute crazy people."

"They do, though. More than half the people who go to the gas-chamber in this state are mentally disturbed—medically insane, if not legally."

"But they'd never convict Carl. Look what happened last time."

"What did happen last time?"

She put the back of her hand to her mouth and looked at me over it.

"You mean the Senator's death, don't you?" I was frankly fishing, fishing in the deep green of her eyes.

She couldn't resist the dramatic thing. "I mean the Senator's murder. Carl murdered him. Everybody knows it, and they didn't do a thing to him except send him away."

"The way I heard it, it was an accident."

"You heard it wrong then. Carl pushed him down in the bathtub and held him until he drowned."

"How do you know?"

"He confessed the very next day."

"To you?"

"To Sheriff Ostervelt."

"Ostervelt told you this?"

"Jerry told me. He talked the sheriff out of laying charges. He wanted to protect the family name."

"Is that all he was trying to protect?"

"I don't know what you mean by that. Why did Mildred bring you out here, anyway?"

"For the ride. My main idea was to get my car back."

"When you get it, will you be satisfied?"

"I doubt it. I've never been yet."

"You mean you're going to poke around and twist the facts and try to prove that Carl didn't do—what he did do?"

"I'm interested in facts, as I told Dr. Grantland."

"What's he got to do with it?"

"I'd like an answer to that. Maybe you can tell me."

"I know he didn't shoot Jerry. The idea is ridiculous."

"Perhaps. It was your idea. But let's kick it around a little. If Yogan's telling the truth, Carl had the pearl-handled gun, or one like it. We don't know for certain that it killed your husband. We won't until we get ballistic evidence."

"But Charlie found it in the greenhouse, right beside the—poor Jerry."

"Charlie could have planted it. Or he could have fired it himself. That would make it easy for him to find."

"You're making this up."

But she was frightened. She didn't seem to know for sure that it hadn't happened that way.

"Did Ostervelt show you the gun?"

"I saw it."

"Did you ever see it before?"

"No." Her answer was emphatic and quick.

"Did you know it belonged to your mother-in-law?"

"No." But Zinnie asked no questions, showed no surprise, and took my word for it.

"Did you know she had a gun?"

"No. Yes. I guess I did. But I never saw it."

"I heard your mother-in-law committed suicide. Is that right?"

"Yes. Poor Alicia walked into the ocean, about three years ago."

"Why would she commit suicide?"

"Alicia had had a lot of illness."

"Mental?"

"I suppose you'd call it that. The menopause hit her very hard. She never came back, entirely. She was practically a hermit the last few years. She lived in the east wing by herself, with Mrs. Hutchinson to look after her. These things seem to run in the family."

"Something does. Do you know what happened to her gun?"

"Evidently Carl got hold of it, some way. Maybe she gave it to him before she died."

"And he's been carrying it all these years?"

"He could have hid it right here on the ranch. Why ask me? I don't know anything about it."

"Or who fired it in the greenhouse?"

"You know what I think about that. What I *know*."

"I believe you said you heard the shots."

"Yes. I heard them."

"Where were you, at the time?"

"In my bathroom. I'd just finished taking a shower." With never-say-die eroticism, she tried to set up a diversion: "If you want proof of that, examine me. I'm clean."

"Some other time. Stay clean till then. Is that the same bathroom your father-in-law was murdered in?"

"No. He had his own bathroom, opening off his bedroom. I wish you wouldn't use that word murder. I didn't mean to tell you that. I said it in confidence."

"I didn't realize that. Would you mind showing me that bathroom? I'd like to see how it was done."

"I don't know how it was done."

"You did a minute ago."

Zinnie took time out to think. Thinking seemed to come hard to her. "I only know what people tell me," she said.

"Who told you that Carl pushed his father down in the bathtub?"

"Charlie did, and he ought to know. He was the old man's doctor."

"Did he examine him after death?"

"Yes, he did."

"Then he must have known that the Senator didn't die of a heart attack."

"I told you that. Carl killed him."

"And Grantland knew it?"

"Of course."

"You realize what you've just said, Mrs. Hallman? Your good friends Sheriff Ostervelt and Dr. Grantland conspired to cover up a murder."

"No!" She flung the thought away from her with both hands. "I didn't mean it that way."

"How did you mean it?"

"I don't really know anything about it. I was lying."

"But now you're telling the truth."

"You've got me all twisted up. Forget what I said, eh?"

"How can I?"

"What are you looking for? Money? You want a new car?"

"I'm sort of attached to the old one. We'll get along better if you stop assuming I can be bought. It's been tried by experts."

She rose and stood over me, looking down in mingled fear and hatred. Making a great convulsive effort, she swallowed both. In the same effort, she changed her approach, and practically changed her personality. Her shoulders and breasts slumped, her belly arched forward, one of her hips tilted up. Even her eyes took on a melting-iceberg look.

"We *could* get along, quite nicely."

"Could we?"

"You wouldn't want to make trouble for little old me. Why don't you make us a shakerful of Gibsons instead? We'll talk it over?"

"Charlie wouldn't like it. And your husband's not yet cold in his grave, remember?"

There was a greenhouse smell in the room, the smell of flowers and earth and trapped heat. I got up facing her. She placed her hands on my shoulders and let her body come forward until it rested lightly against me. It moved in small intricate ways.

"Come on. What's the matter? Are you scared? I'm not. And I'm very good at it, even if I am out of practice."

In a way, I was scared. She was a hard blonde beauty fighting the world with two weapons, money and sex. Both of them had turned in her hands and scarred her. The scars were invisible, but I could sense the dead tissue. I wanted no part of her.

She exploded against me hissing like an angry cat, fled across the room to one of the deep windows. Her clenched hand jerked spasmodically at the curtains, like somebody signaling a train to stop.

Footsteps whispered on the floor behind me. It was Mildred, small and waiflike in her stocking feet.

"What on earth's the matter?"

Zinnie glared at her across the room. Except for her thin red lips and narrow green eyes, her face was carved from chalk. In one of those instinctive female shifts that are always at least partly real, Zinnie released her fury on her sister-in-law:

"So there you are—spying on me again. I'm sick of your spying, talking behind my back, throwing mud at Charlie Grantland, just because you wanted him yourself—"

"That's nonsense," Mildred said in a low voice. "I've never spied on you. As for Dr. Grantland, I barely know him."

"No, but you'd like to, wouldn't you? Only you know that you can't have him. So you'd like to see him destroyed, wouldn't you? You hired this man to ruin him."

"I did no such thing. You're upset, Zinnie. *You* should lie down and have a rest."

"I should, eh? So you can carry on your machinations without any interference?"

Zinnie crossed the room in an unsteady rush. I stayed between her and Mildred.

"Mildred didn't hire me," I said. "I have no instructions from her. You're away off the beam, Mrs. Hallman."

"You lie!" She screamed across me at Mildred: "You dirty little sneak, you can get out of my house. Keep your maniac husband away from here or by God I'll have him shot down. Take your bully-boy along with you. Go on, get out, both of you."

"I'll be glad to."

Mildred turned to the door in weary resignation, and I went out after her. I hadn't expected the armistice to last.

Chapter 14

I WAITED for Mildred on the front veranda. There were several more cars in the driveway. One of them was my Ford convertible, gray with dust but looking none the worse for wear. It was parked behind a black panel truck with county markings.

A deputy I hadn't seen before was in the front seat of another county car, monitoring a turned-up radio. The rest of the sheriff's men were still in the greenhouse. Their shadows moved on its translucent walls.

"Attention all units," the huge voice of the radio said. "Be on the lookout for following subject wanted as suspect in murder which occurred at Hallman ranch in Buena Vista Valley approximately one hour ago: Carl Hallman, white, male, twenty-four, six-foot-three, two hundred pounds, blond hair, blue eyes, pale complexion, wearing blue cotton workshirt and trousers. Suspect may be armed and is considered dangerous. When last seen he was traveling across country on foot."

Mildred came out, freshly groomed and looking fairly brisk in spite of her wilted-violet eyes. Her head moved in a small gesture of relief as the screen door slammed behind her.

"Where do you plan to go?" I asked her.

"Home. It's too late to think of going back to work. I have to see to Mother, anyway."

"Your husband may turn up there. Have you thought of that possibility?"

"Naturally. I hope he does."

"If he does, will you let me know?"

She gave me a clear cold look. "That depends."

"I know what you mean. Maybe I better make it plain that I'm in your husband's corner. I'd like to get to him before the sheriff does. Ostervelt seems to have his mind made up about this case. I haven't. I think there should be further investigation."

"You want me to pay you, is that it?"

"Forget about that for now. Let's say I like the old-fashioned idea of presumption of innocence."

She took a step toward me, her eyes brightening. Her hand rested lightly on my arm. "You don't believe he shot Jerry, either."

508

"I don't want to build up your hopes with nothing much to go on. I'm keeping an open mind until we have more information. You heard the shots that killed Jerry?"

"Yes."

"Where were you at the time? And where were the others?"

"I don't know about the others. I was with Martha on the other side of the house. The child seemed to sense what had happened, and I had a hard time calming her. I didn't notice what other people were doing."

"Was Ostervelt anywhere around the house?"

"I didn't see him if he was."

"Was Carl?"

"The last I saw of Carl was in the grove there."

"Which way did he go when he left you?"

"Toward town, at least in that general direction."

"What was his attitude when you talked to him?"

"He was upset. I begged him to turn himself in, but he seemed frightened."

"Emotionally disturbed?"

"It's hard to say. I've seen him much worse."

"Did he show any signs of being dangerous?"

"Certainly not to me. He never has. He was a little rough when I tried to hold him, that's all."

"Has he often been violent?"

"No. I didn't say he was violent. He simply didn't want to be held. He pushed me away from him."

"Did he say why?"

"He said something about following his own road. I didn't have time to ask him what he meant."

"Do you have any idea what he meant?"

"No." But her eyes were wide and dark with possibility. "I'm certain, though, he didn't mean anything like shooting his brother."

"There's another question that needs answering," I said. "I hate to throw it at you now."

She squared her slender shoulders. "Go ahead. I'll answer it if I can."

"I've been told your husband killed his father. Deliberately drowned him in the bathtub. Have you heard that?"

"Yes. I've heard that."

"From Carl?"

"Not from him, no."

"Do you believe it?"

She took a long time to answer. "I don't know. It was just after Carl was hospitalized—the same day. When a tragedy cuts across your life like that, you don't know what to believe. The world actually seemed to fly apart. I could recognize the pieces, but all the patterns were unfamiliar, the meanings were different. They still are. It's an awful thing for a human being to admit, but I don't know *what* I believe. I'm waiting. I've been waiting for six months to find out where I stand in the world, what sort of a life I can count on."

"You haven't really answered my question."

"I would if I could. I've been trying to explain why I can't. The circumstances were so queer, and awful." The thought of them, whatever they were, pinched her face like cold.

"Who told you about this alleged confession?"

"Sheriff Ostervelt did. I thought at the time he was lying, for reasons of his own. Perhaps I was rationalizing, simply because I couldn't face the truth—I don't know."

Before she trailed off into further self-doubts, I said: "What reasons would he have for lying to you?"

"I can tell you one. It isn't very modest to say it, but he's been interested in me for quite a long time. He was always hanging around the ranch, theoretically to see the Senator, but looking for excuses to talk to me. I knew what he wanted; he was about as subtle as an old boar. The day we took Carl to the hospital, Ostervelt made it very clear, and very ugly." She shut her eyes for a second. A faint dew had gathered on her eyelids, and at her temples. "So ugly that I'm afraid I can't talk about it."

"I get the general idea."

But she went on, in a chilly trance of memory which seemed to negate the place and time: "He was to drive Carl to the hospital that morning, and naturally I wanted to go along. I wanted to be with Carl until the last possible minute before the doors closed on him. You don't know how a woman feels when her husband's being taken away like that, perhaps forever. I was afraid it was forever. Carl didn't say a word on the way. For days before he'd been talking constantly, about everything under the sun—the plans he had for the ranch, our life together, philosophy, social justice, and the brotherhood of man. Suddenly it was all over. Everything was over. He sat in the car, between me and the sheriff, as still as a dead man.

"He didn't even kiss me good-by at the admissions door. I'll never forget what he did do. There was a little tree growing beside the steps. Carl picked one of the leaves and folded it in his hand and carried it into the hospital with him.

"I didn't go in. I couldn't bear to, that day, though I've been there often enough since. I waited outside in the sheriff's car. I remember thinking that this was the end of the line, that nothing worse could ever happen to me. I was wrong.

"On the way back, Ostervelt began to act as if he owned me. I didn't give him any encouragement; I never had. In fact, I told him what I thought of him.

"It was then he got really nasty. He told me I'd better be careful what I said. That Carl had confessed the murder of his father, and he was the only one who knew. He'd keep it quiet if I'd be nice to him. Otherwise there'd be a trial, he said. Even if Carl wasn't convicted we'd be given the kind of publicity that people can't live through." Her voice sank despairingly. "The kind of publicity we're going to have to live through now."

Mildred turned and looked out across the green country as if it were a wasteland. She said, with her face averted:

"I didn't give in to him. But I was afraid to reject him as flatly as he deserved. I put him off with some sort of a vague promise, that we might get together sometime in the future. I haven't kept the promise, needless to say, and I never will." She said it calmly enough, but her shoulders were trembling. I could see the rim of one of her ears, between silky strands of hair. It was red with shame or anger. "The horrible old man hasn't forgiven me for that. I've lived in fear for the last six months, that he'd take action against Carl—drag him back to stand trial."

"He didn't, though," I said, "which means that the confession was probably a phony. Tell me one thing, could it have happened the way Ostervelt claimed? I mean, did your husband have the opportunity?"

"I'm afraid the answer is yes. He was roaming around the house most of the night, after the quarrel with his father. I couldn't keep him in bed."

"Did you ask him about it afterwards?"

"At the hospital? No, I didn't. They warned me not to bring up disturbing subjects. And I was glad enough to let sleeping dogs lie. If it was true, I felt better not knowing than knowing. There's a limit to what a person can bear to know."

She shuddered, in the chill of memory.

The front door of the greenhouse was flung open suddenly. Carmichael backed out, bent over the handles of a covered stretcher. Under the cover, the dead man huddled lumpily. The other end of the stretcher was supported by the deputy coroner. They moved awkwardly along the flagstone path toward the black panel truck. Against the sweep of the valley and the mountains standing like monuments in the sunlight, the two upright men and the prostrate man seemed equally small and transitory. The living men hoisted the dead man into the back of the truck and slammed the double doors. Mildred jumped at the noise.

"I'm terribly edgy, I'd better get out of here. I shouldn't have gone into—all that. You're the only person I've ever told."

"It's safe with me."

"Thank you. For everything, I mean. You're the only one who's given me a ray of hope."

She raised her hand in good-by and went down the steps into sunlight which gilded her head. Ostervelt's senescent passion for her was easy to understand. It wasn't just that she was young and pretty, and round in the right places. She had something more provocative than sex: the intense grave innocence of a serious child, and a loneliness that made her seem vulnerable.

I watched the old Buick out of sight and caught myself on the edge of a sudden hot dream. Mildred's husband might not live forever. His chances of surviving the day were not much better than even. If her husband failed to survive, Mildred would need a man to look after her.

I gave myself a mental kick in the teeth. That kind of thinking put me on Ostervelt's level. Which for some reason made me angrier at Ostervelt.

Chapter 15

THE DEPUTY coroner had lit a cigar and was leaning against the side of the panel truck, smoking it. I strolled over and took a look at my car. Nothing seemed to be missing. Even the key was in the ignition. The additional mileage added up, so far as I could estimate, to the distance from the hospital to Purissima to the ranch.

"Nice day," the deputy coroner said.

"Nice enough."

"Too bad Mr. Hallman isn't alive to enjoy it. He was in pretty good shape, too, judging from a superficial examination. I'll be interested in what his organs have to say."

"You're not suggesting he died of natural causes."

"Oh, no. It's merely a little game I play with myself to keep the interest up." He grinned, and the sunlight glinted on his spectacles in cold mirth. "Not every doctor gets a chance to know his patients inside and out."

"You're the coroner, aren't you?"

"Deputy coroner. Ostervelt's the coroner—he wears two hats. Actually I do, too. I'm pathologist at the Purissima Hospital. Name's Lawson."

"Archer." We shook hands.

"You from one of the L.A. papers? I just got finished talking to the local man."

"I'm a private investigator, employed by a member of the family. I was wondering about your findings."

"Haven't got any yet. I know there're two bullets in him because they went in and didn't come out. I'll get 'em when I do the autopsy."

"When will that be?"

"Tonight. Ostervelt wants it quick. I ought to have it wrapped up by midnight, sooner maybe."

"What happens to the slugs after you remove them?"

"I turn 'em over to the sheriff's ballistics man."

"Is he any good?"

"Oh, yeah, Durkin's a pretty fair technician. If it gets too tough, we send the work up to the L.A. Police Lab, or to

Sacramento. But this isn't a case where the physical evidence counts for much. We pretty well know who did it. Once they catch him, he shouldn't be hard to get a story out of. Ostervelt may not bother doing anything with the slugs. He's a pretty easy-going guy. You get that way after twenty-five or thirty years in office."

"Worked for him long?"

"Four-five years. Five." He added, a little defensively: "Purissima's a nice place to live. The wife won't leave it. Who can blame her?"

"Not me. I wouldn't mind settling here myself."

"Talk to Ostervelt, why don't you? He's understaffed—always looking for men. You have any police experience?"

"A few years back. I got tired of living on a cop's salary. Among other things."

"There are always ways of padding it out."

Not knowing how he meant me to take that, I looked into his face. He was sizing me up, too. I said:

"That was one of the other things I got tired of. But you wouldn't think there'd be much of that in this county."

"More than you think, brother, more than you think. We won't go into that, though." He took a bite out of the tip of his cigar and spat it into the gravel. "You say you're working for the Hallman family?"

I nodded.

"Ever been in Purissima before?"

"Over the years, I have."

He looked at me with curiosity. "Are you one of the detectives the Senator brought in when his wife drowned?"

"No."

"I just wondered. I spent several hours with one of them—a smart old bulldog named Scott. You wouldn't happen to know him? He's from L.A. Glenn Scott?"

"I know Scott. He's one of the old masters in the field. Or he was until he retired."

"My impression exactly. He knew more about pathology than most medical students. I never had a more interesting conversation."

"What about?"

"Causes of death," he said brightly. "Drowning and asphyxiation and so on. Fortunately I'd done a thorough post-mortem. I was able to establish that she died by drowning; she had sand and fragments of kelp in her bronchial tubes, and the indicated saline solution in her lungs."

"There wasn't any doubt of it, was there?"

"Not after I got through. Scott was completely satisfied. Of course I couldn't entirely rule out the possibility of murder, but there were no positive indications. It's almost certain that the contusions were inflicted after death."

"Contusions?" I prompted softly.

"Yeah, the contusions on the back and head. You often get them in drownings along this coast, with the rocks and the heavy surf. I've seen some cadavers that were absolutely macerated, poor things. At least they got Mrs. Hallman before that happened to her. But she was bad enough. They ought to print a few of my pictures in the papers. There wouldn't be so many suicides walking into the water. Not so many women, anyway, and most of them *are* women."

"Is that what Mrs. Hallman did, walk into the water?"

"Probably. Or else she jumped from the pier. Of course there's always an outside chance that she fell, and that's how she got the contusions. The Coroner's Jury called it an accident, but that was mainly to spare the family's feelings. Elderly women don't normally go down to the ocean at night and accidentally fall in."

"They don't normally commit suicide, either."

"True enough, only Mrs. Hallman wasn't what you'd call exactly normal. Scott talked to her doctor after it happened and he said she'd been having emotional trouble. It's not fashionable these days to talk about hereditary insanity, but you can't help noticing certain family tie-ups. This one in the Hallman family, for instance. It isn't pure chance when a woman subject to depression has a son with a manic-depressive psychosis."

"Mother had blue genes, eh?"

"Ouch."

"Who was her doctor?"

"G.P. in town named Grantland."

"I know him slightly," I said. "He was out here today. He seems like a good man."

"Uh-huh." In the light of the medical code that inhibits doctors from criticizing each other, his grunt was eloquent.

"You don't think so?"

"Hell, it's not for me to second-guess another doctor. I'm not one of these medical hotshots with the big income and the bedside manner. I'm purely and simply a lab man. I did think at the time he should have referred Mrs. Hallman to a psychiatrist. Might have saved her life. After all, he knew she was suicidal."

"How do you know that?"

"He told Scott. Until he did, Scott thought it could be murder, in spite of the physical evidence. But when he found out she'd tried to shoot herself—well, it all fitted into a pattern."

"When did she try to shoot herself?"

"A week or two before she drowned, I think." Lawson stiffened perceptibly, as if he realized that he'd been talking very freely. "Understand me, I'm not accusing Grantland of negligence or anything like that. A doctor has to use his own judgment. Personally I'd be helpless if I had to handle one of these—"

He noticed that I wasn't listening, and peered into my face with professional solicitude. "What's the trouble, fellow? You got a cramp?"

"No trouble." At least no trouble I wanted to put into words. It was the Hallman family that really had trouble: father and mother dead under dubious circumstances, one son shot, the second being hunted. And at each high point of trouble, Grantland cropped up. I said:

"Do you know what happened to the gun?"

"What gun?"

"The one she tried to shoot herself with."

"I'm afraid I don't know. Maybe Grantland would."

"Maybe he would."

Lawson tapped the lengthening ash from his cigar. It splattered silently on the gravel between us. He drew on the cigar, its glowing end pale salmon in the sun, and blew out a cloud of smoke. The smoke ascended lazily, almost straight up in the still air, and drifted over my head toward the house.

"Or Ostervelt," he said. "I wonder what's keeping Ostervelt. I suppose he's trying to make an impression on Slovekin."

"Slovekin?"

"The police reporter from the Purissima paper. He's talking to Ostervelt in the greenhouse. Ostervelt loves to talk."

Ostervelt wasn't the only one, I thought. In fifteen or twenty minutes, a third of a cigar length, Lawson had given me more information than I knew what to do with.

"Speaking of causes of death," I said, "did you do the autopsy on Senator Hallman?"

"There wasn't any," he said.

"You mean no autopsy was ordered?"

"That's right, there was no question about cause of death. The old man had a heart history. He'd been under a doctor's care practically from day to day."

"Grantland again?"

"Yes. It was his opinion the Senator died of heart failure, and I saw no reason to question it. Neither did Ostervelt."

"Then there was no indication of drowning?"

"Drowning?" He looked at me sharply. "You're thinking about his wife, aren't you?"

His surprise seemed real, and I had no reason to doubt his honesty. He wore the glazed suit and frayed shirt of a man who lived on his salary.

"I must have got my signals switched," I said.

"It's understandable. He did die in the bathtub. But not of drowning."

"Did you examine the body?"

"It wasn't necessary."

"Who said it wasn't necessary?"

"The family, the family doctor, Sheriff Ostervelt, everybody concerned. I'm saying it now," he added with some spirit.

"What happened to the body?"

"The family had it cremated." He thought about this for a moment, behind his glasses. "Listen, if you're thinking that there was foul play involved, you're absolutely wrong. He died of heart failure, in a locked bathroom. They had to break in to get to him." Then, perhaps to put his own doubts to rest: "I'll show you where it happened, if you like."

"I would like."

Lawson pressed out his cigar against the sole of his shoe, and dropped the smelly butt in his side pocket. He led me through the house to a large rear bedroom. With blinds drawn, dust covers on the bed and the other furniture, the room had a ghostly air.

We went into the adjoining bathroom. It contained a six-foot tub supported on cast-iron feet. Lawson switched on the lofty ceiling fixture above it.

"The poor old man was lying in here," he said. "They had to force the window to get to him." He indicated the single window high above the basin.

"Who had to force the window?"

"The family. His two sons, I believe. The body was in the bathtub most of the night."

I examined the door. It was thick and made of oak. The lock was the old-fashioned kind that has to be turned with a key. The key was in the keyhole.

I turned it back and forth several times, then pulled it out and looked at it. The heavy, tarnished key told me nothing in particular. Either Lawson was misinformed, or the Senator had died alone. Or I had a locked-room mystery to go with the other mysteries in the house.

I tried a skeleton key on the door, and after a little jiggling around, it worked. I turned to Lawson. "Was the key in the lock when they found him?"

"I couldn't say, really. I wasn't here. Maybe Ostervelt could tell you."

Chapter 16

WE RAN into Ostervelt in the front hallway, ran into him almost literally as he came out of the living-room. He pushed between us, his belly projecting like a football concealed in his clothes. His jowls became convulsive:

"What goes on?"

"Mr. Archer wanted to see the Senator's bathroom," Lawson said. "You remember the morning they found him, Chief. Was the key in the lock?"

"What lock, for Christ sake?"

"The lock on the bathroom door."

"I don't know." Ostervelt's head jerked as he hammered out the words: "I'll tell you what I do know, Lawson. You don't talk official business to strangers. How many times do we have to go into that?"

Lawson removed his glasses and wiped them with the inside of his tie. Without them, his face looked unformed and vulnerable. But he had guts and some professional poise:

"Mr. Archer isn't a stranger, exactly. He's employed by the Hallman family."

"To do what? Pick your brains, if you have any?"

"You can't talk to me like that."

"What do you think you're going to do about it? Resign?"

Lawson turned on his heel, stiffly, and walked out. Ostervelt called after him:

"Go ahead and resign. I accept your resignation."

Feeling some compunction, since I had been picking Lawson's brains, I said to Ostervelt:

"Lay off him. What's the beef?"

"The beef is you. Mrs. Hallman said you asked her for money, made a pass at her."

"Did she rip her dress open at the neck? They usually rip their dresses open at the neck."

"It's no joke. I could put you in jail."

"What are you waiting for? The suit for false arrest will make my fortune."

519

"Don't get flip with me." Under his anger, Ostervelt seemed to be badly shaken. His little eyes were dirty with dismay. He took out his gun to make himself feel better.

"Put it away," I said. "It takes more than a Colt revolver to change a Keystone cop into an officer."

Ostervelt raised the Colt and laid it raking and burning across the side of my head. The ceiling slanted, then rose away from me as I went down. As I got up, a thin young man in a brown corduroy jacket appeared in the doorway. Ostervelt started to raise the gun for another blow. The thin young man took hold of his arm and almost ascended with it.

Ostervelt said: "I'll cut him to pieces. Get away from me, Slovekin."

Slovekin held onto his arm. I held onto my impulse to hit an old man. Slovekin said:

"Wait a minute, Sheriff. Who is this man, anyway?"

"A crooked private dick from Hollywood."

"Are you arresting him?"

"You're damn right I'm arresting him."

"What for? Is he connected with this case?"

Ostervelt shook him off. "That's between him and I. You stay out of it, Slovekin."

"How can I, when I'm assigned to it? I'm just doing my job, the same as you are, Sheriff." The black eyes in Slovekin's sharp young face glittered with irony. "I can't do my job if you give me no information. I have to fall back on reporting what I see. I see a public official beating a man with a gun, naturally I'm interested."

"Don't try to blackmail me, you little twerp."

Slovekin stayed cool and smiling. "You want me to deliver that message to Mr. Spaulding? Mr. Spaulding's always looking for a good local topic for an editorial. This could be just what he needs."

"Screw Spaulding. You know what you can do with that rag you work for, too."

"That's pretty language from the top law-enforcement official in the county. An elected official, at that. I suppose you don't mind if I quote you." Slovekin produced a notebook from a side pocket.

Ostervelt's face tried various colors and settled for a kind of mottled purple. He put his gun away. "Okay, Slovekin. What else do you want to know?" His voice was a rough whisper.

"Is this man a suspect? I thought Carl Hallman was the only one."

"He is, and we'll have him in twenty-four hours. Dead or alive. You can quote me on that."

I said to Slovekin: "You're a newspaperman, are you?"

"I try to be." He looked at me quizzically, as if he wondered what I was trying to be.

"I'd like to talk to you about this murder. The sheriff's got Hallman convicted already, but there are certain discrepancies—"

"The hell there are!" Ostervelt said.

Slovekin whipped out a pencil and opened his notebook. "Clue me in."

"Not now. I need more time to pin them down."

"He's bluffing," Ostervelt said. "He's just trying to make me look bad. He's one of these jokers, tries to make a hero out of himself."

Disregarding him, I said to Slovekin: "Where can I get in touch with you, tomorrow, say?"

"You're not going to be here tomorrow," Ostervelt put in. "I want you out of this county in one hour, or else."

Slovekin said mildly: "I thought you were arresting him."

Ostervelt was getting frantic. He began to yammer: "Don't get too cocky, Mr. Slovekin. Bigger men than you thought they could cross me, and lost their jobs."

"Oh, come off it, Sheriff. Do you go to movies much?" Slovekin unwrapped a piece of gum, put it in his mouth, and began to chew it. He said to me: "You can reach me through the paper any time—Purissima *Record*."

"You think so, eh?" Ostervelt said. "After today you won't be working there."

"Phone 6328," Slovekin said. "If I'm not there, talk to Spaulding. He's the editor."

"I can go higher than Spaulding, if I have to."

"Take it to the Supreme Court, Sheriff." Slovekin's chewing face had an expression of pained superiority which made him look like an intellectual camel. "I'd certainly like to get what you have now. Spaulding's holding the city edition for this story."

"I'd like to give it to you, but it hasn't jelled."

"You see?" Ostervelt said. "He's got nothing to back it up. He's only trying to make trouble. You're crazy if you take his word against mine. Christ, he may even be in cahoots with the psycho. He let Hallman use his car, remember."

"It's getting pretty noisy in here," I said to Slovekin, and moved toward the door.

He followed me outside to my car. "What you said about the evidence—you weren't kidding?"

"No. I think there's a good chance that Hallman's getting the dirty end of the stick."

"I hope you're right. I rather like the guy, or used to before he got sick."

"You know Carl, do you?"

"Ever since high school. I've known Ostervelt for quite a long time, too. But this is no time to go into Ostervelt." He leaned on the car window, smelling of Dentyne chewing gum. "Do you have another suspect in mind?"

"Several."

"Like that, eh?"

"Like that. Thanks for the assist."

"Don't mention it." His black gaze shifted to the side of my head. "Did you know you've got a torn ear? You should see a doctor."

"I intend to."

Chapter 17

Ⅰ DROVE into Purissima and checked in at a waterfront motel named the Hacienda. Not being on expense account and having forty-odd dollars in my wallet to tide me over until I qualified for the old-age pension, I picked the cheapest one I could find with telephones in the rooms. The room I paid eight dollars for in advance contained a bed and a chair and a limed-oak veneer chest of drawers, as well as a telephone. The window overlooked a parking lot.

The room surprised me into a sharp feeling of pain and loss. The pain wasn't for Carl Hallman, though his fugitive image continually crossed my mind. Perhaps the pain was for myself; the loss was of a self I had once imagined.

Peering out through the slats of the dusty blind, I felt like a criminal hiding out from the law. I didn't like the feeling, so I clowned it away. All I needed was a suitcase full of hot money and an ash-blonde moll whining for mink and diamonds. The closest thing to an ash-blonde moll I knew was Zinnie, and Zinnie appeared to be somebody else's moll.

I was kind of glad that Zinnie wasn't my moll. It was a small room, and the printed notice under the glass top of the chest of drawers said that the room rented for fourteen dollars double. Checkout time was twelve noon. Lighting an ash-blond cigarette, I calculated that I had about twenty-four hours to wrap up the case. I wasn't going to pay for another day out of my own pocket. That would be criminal.

Try listening to yourself sometime, alone in a transient room in a strange town. The worst is when you draw a blank, and the ash-blonde ghosts of the past carry on long twittering long-distance calls with your inner ear, and there's no way to hang up.

Before I made a long-distance call of my own, I went into the bathroom and examined my head in the mirror over the sink. It looked worse than it felt. One ear was cut, and half full of drying blood. There were abrasions on temple and cheek. One eye was slightly blackened, and made me appear more dissipated than I was. When I smiled at a thought that struck me, the effect was pretty grim.

The thought that struck me sent me back to the bedroom. I sat down on the edge of the bed and looked up Zinnie's doctor friend in the local directory. Grantland maintained an office on upper Main Street and a residence on Seaview Road. I made a note of the addresses and telephone numbers, and called his office number. The girl who answered gave me, after some persuasion, an emergency appointment for five-thirty, the end of office hours.

If I hurried, and if Glenn Scott was at home, I should have time to see him and get back for my appointment with Grantland. Glenn had retired to an avocado ranch in the Malibu hinterland. I'd driven up two or three times in the last two years to play chess with him. He always beat me at chess, but his whisky was good. Also, I happened to like him. He was one of the few survivors of the Hollywood rat race who knew how to enjoy a little money without hitting other people over the head with it.

I thought as I put through the call to his house that money happened to Glenn the way poverty happened to a lot of others. He'd worked hard all his life, of course, but he'd never knocked himself out for money. He used to say that he'd never tried to sell himself for fear that somebody might be tempted to buy him.

The maid who'd been with the Scotts for twenty years answered the telephone. Mr. Scott was outside watering his trees. Far as she knew, he'd be there all afternoon, and he'd be glad to see me, far as she knew.

I found him about a half-hour later, wielding a hose on the side of a sunburnt hill. The rocky barrenness of the hillside was accentuated by the rows of scrawny young avocado trees. Glenn's jeep was at the side of the road. Turning and parking behind it, I could look down on the gravel roof of his cantilevered redwood house, and further down on the long white curve of the beach rimming the sea. I felt a twinge of envy as I crossed the field toward him. It seemed to me that Glenn had everything worth having: a place in the sun, wife and family, enough money to live on.

Glenn gave me a smile that made me ashamed of my thoughts. His keen gray eyes were almost lost in his sun-wrinkles. His wide-brimmed straw hat and stained khaki coveralls completed his resemblance to a veteran farmhand. I said:

"Hi, farmer."

"You like my protective coloration, eh?" He turned off the water and began to coil the hose. "How you been, Lew? Still brawling, I see."

"I ran into a door. You're looking well."

"Yeah, the life suits me. When I get bored, Belle and I go in to the Strip for dinner and take a quick look around and beat it the hell back home."

"How is Belle?"

"Oh, she's fine. Right now she's in Santa Monica with the kids. Belle had her first grandson last week, with a little help from the daughter-in-law. Seven and a half pounds, built like a middleweight, they're going to call him Glenn. But you didn't make a special trip to ask me about my family."

"Somebody else's family. You had a case in Purissima about three years ago. Elderly woman committed suicide by drowning. Husband suspected murder, called you in to check."

"Uh-huh. I wouldn't call Mrs. Hallman elderly. She was probably in her early fifties. Hell, I'm older than that myself, and I'm not elderly."

"Okay, grandpa," I said with subtle flattery. "Are you willing to answer a couple of questions about the Hallman case?"

"Why?"

"It seems to be kind of reopening itself."

"You mean it was homicide?"

"I wouldn't go that far. Not yet. But the woman's son was murdered this afternoon."

"Which son? She had two."

"The older one. His younger brother escaped from a mental ward last night, and he's prime suspect. He was at the ranch shortly before the shooting—"

"Jesus," Glenn breathed. "The old man was right."

I waited, with no result, and finally said: "Right about what?"

"Let's skip that, Lew. I know he's dead now, but it's still a confidential case."

"I get no answers, eh?"

"You can ask the questions, I'll use my judgment about answering 'em. First, though, who are you representing in Purissima?"

"The younger son. Carl."

"The psycho?"

"Should I give my clients a Rorschach before I take them on?"

"I didn't mean that. He hire you to clear him?"

"No, it's my own idea."

"Hey, you're not off on one of your crusades."

"Hardly," I said with more hope than I felt. "If my hunch pans out, I'll get paid for my time. There's a million or two in the family."

"More like five million. I get it. You're on a contingency basis."

"Call it that. Do I get to ask you any questions?"

"Go ahead. Ask them." He leaned against a boulder and looked inscrutable.

"You've answered the main one already. That drowning could have been homicide."

"Yeah. I finally ruled it out at the time because there were no positive indications—nothing you could take to court, I mean. Also on account of the lady's background. She was unstable, been on barbiturates for years. Her doctor wouldn't admit she was hooked on them, but that was the picture I got. In addition to which, she'd attempted suicide before. Tried to shoot herself right in the doctor's office, a few days before she drowned."

"Who told you this?"

"The doctor told me himself, and he wasn't lying. She wanted a bigger prescription from him. When he wouldn't give it to her, she pulled a little pearl-handled revolver out of her purse and pointed it at her head. He knocked it up just in time, and the slug went into the ceiling. He showed me the hole it made."

"What happened to the gun?"

"Naturally he took it away from her. I think he told me he threw it into the sea."

"That's a funny way to handle it."

"Not so funny, under the circumstances. She begged him not to tell her husband about the attempt. The old man was always threatening to stash her away in a snake-pit. The doctor covered for her."

"You get any confirmation of this?"

"How could I? It was strictly between him and her." He added with a trace of irritation: "The guy didn't have to tell me anything. He was sticking his neck out, telling me what he did. Speaking of necks, mine is out a mile right now."

"Then you might as well stick it out some more. What do you think of the local law?"

"In Purissima? They have a good police force. Undermanned, like most, but one of the better small-city departments, I'd say."

"I was thinking more of the county department."

"Ostervelt, you mean? We got along. He co-operated fine." Glenn smiled briefly. "Naturally he co-operated. Senator Hall- man swung a lot of votes."

"Is Ostervelt honest?"

"I never saw any evidence that he wasn't. Maybe some graft crept in here and there. He isn't as young as he used to be, and I heard a rumor or two. Nothing big, you understand. Senator Hallman wouldn't stand for it. Why?"

"Just checking." Very tentatively, I said: "I don't suppose I could get a peek at your report on the case?"

"Not even if I had one. You know the law as well as I do."

"You didn't keep a copy?"

"I didn't make a written report. The old man wanted it word- of-mouth, and that was the way I gave it to him. I can tell you what I said in one word. Suicide." He paused. "But maybe I was wrong, Lew."

"Do you think you were wrong?"

"Maybe I was. If I did make a mistake, like La Guardia said, it was a beaut: they don't come often like that. I know I shouldn't admit it to an ex-competitor. On the other hand, you were never a very serious competitor. They went to you when they couldn't afford me." Scott was trying to carry it off lightly, but his face was heavy. "On the other hand, I wouldn't want you to climb way out on a limb, and get it sawed off from under you."

"So?"

"So take a piece of advice from an old pro who started in the rack—in the business, before you learned toilet control. You're wasting your time on this one."

"I don't think so. You gave me what I need."

"Then I better give you something you don't need, just so you won't get elated." Scott looked the opposite of elated. His voice dragged slower and slower. "Don't start to spend your piece of that five million until after you deposit the check. You know there's a little rule of law that says a murderer can't benefit from the estate of his victim."

"Are you trying to tell me Carl Hallman murdered his father?"

"I heard the old man died of natural causes. I didn't investigate his death. It looks as if somebody ought to."

"I intend to."

"Sure, but don't be surprised if you come up with an answer you don't like."

"Such as?"

"You said it a minute ago yourself."

"You've got some inside information?"

"Only what you told me, and what the old man told me when his lawyer sent for me. You know why he wanted me to make a confidential investigation of that drowning?"

"He didn't trust the local law."

"Maybe. The main reason was, he suspected his own son of knocking out the mother and throwing her in the water. And I'm beginning to think that's what actually happened."

I'd seen it coming from a long way off, but it hit me hard, with the weight of Glenn Scott's integrity behind it.

"Do you know what the Senator's suspicions were based on?"

"He didn't tell me much about that. I assumed he knew his own boy better than I did. I never even got to meet the boy. I talked to the rest of the family, though, and I gathered that he was very close to his mother. Too close for comfort, maybe."

"Close like Oedipus?"

"Could be. There was apronstring trouble, all right. The mother raised a hell of a stink when he went away to college. She was a clutcher, for sure, and not very stable, like I said. Could be he thought he had to kill her to get free. There've been cases like that. I'm only brainstorming, understand. You won't quote me."

"Not even to myself. Where was Carl when she died?"

"That's just the trouble, I don't know. He was going to school in Berkeley at the time, but he left there about a week before it happened. Dropped out of sight for maybe ten days, all told."

"What did he say he was doing?"

"I don't know. The Senator wouldn't even let me ask him. It wasn't a very satisfactory case to work on. As you'll discover."

"I already have."

Chapter 18

I PARKED on upper Main Street, in front of a flat-topped building made of pink stucco and glass brick. An imitation flagstone walk led through well-trimmed shrubbery to a door inset in one corner. A small bronze plate beside the door announced discreetly: J. Charles Grantland, M.D.

The waiting-room was empty, except for a lot of new-looking furniture. A fairly new-looking young woman popped up behind a bleached oak counter in the far corner beside an inner door. She had dark, thin good looks which needed a quick paint job.

"Mr. Archer?"

"Yes."

"I'm sorry, doctor's still busy. We're behind schedule today. Do you mind waiting a few minutes?"

I said I didn't mind. She took down my address.

"Were you in an accident, Mr. Archer?"

"You could call it that."

I sat in the chair nearest her, and took a folded newspaper out of my jacket pocket. I'd bought it on the street a few minutes earlier, from a Mexican newsboy crying murder. I spread it out on my knees, hoping that it might make a conversation piece.

The Hallman story had Eugene Slovekin's by-line under a banner heading: Brother Sought in Shooting. There was a three-column picture of the Hallman brothers in the middle of the page. The story began in a rather stilted atmospheric style which made me wonder if Slovekin had been embarrassed by the writing of it:

"In a tragedy which may parallel the ancient tragedy of Cain and Abel, violent death paid a furtive and shocking visit today to a well-known local family. Victim of the apparent slaying was Jeremiah Hallman, 34, prominent Buena Vista Valley rancher. His younger brother, Carl Hallman, 24, is being sought for questioning in the shooting. Mr. Hallman, son of the recently deceased Senator Hallman, was found dead at approximately one o'clock this afternoon by his family physician, Dr. Charles Grantland, in the conservatory of the Hallman estate.

"Mr. Hallman had been shot twice in the back, and apparently died within seconds of the shooting. A pearl-handled revolver, with two cartridges discharged, was found beside the body, lending a touch of fantastic mystery to the case. According to family servants the murder gun formerly belonged to the late Mrs. Alicia Hallman, mother of the victim.

"Sheriff Duane Ostervelt, who was on the scene within minutes of the shooting, stated that the murder weapon was known to be in the possession of Carl Hallman. Young Hallman was seen on the ranch immediately prior to the shooting. He escaped last night from the State Hospital, where he had been a patient for some months. According to members of the family, young Hallman has been a long-time victim of mental illness. An all-points search is being made for him, by the local sheriff's department and city and state police.

"Contacted by long-distance telephone, Dr. Brockley of the State Hospital staff said that young Hallman was suffering from manic-depressive psychosis when admitted to the hospital six months ago. According to Dr. Brockley, Hallman was not considered dangerous, and was thought to be 'well on the road to recovery.' Dr. Brockley expressed surprise and concern at the tragic outcome of Hallman's escape. He said that the local authorities were informed of the escape as soon as it occurred, and expressed the hope that the public would 'take a calm view of the situation. There is no violence in Hallman's hospital record,' Dr. Brockley said. 'He is a sick boy who needs medical care.'

"A similar view was expressed by Sheriff Ostervelt, who says that he is organizing a posse of a hundred or more local citizens to supplement the efforts of his department in the search. The public is asked to be on the lookout for Hallman. He is six feet three inches tall, of athletic build, blue-eyed, with light hair cut very short. When last seen he was wearing a blue work shirt and blue dungaree trousers. According to Sheriff Ostervelt, Hallman may be accompanied by Thomas Rica, alias Rickey, a fellow-escapee from . . ."

The story was continued on the second page. Before turning over, I took a close look at the picture of the two brothers. It was a stiffly posed portrait of the sort that photographers make to commemorate weddings. Both brothers wore boiled shirts and fixed smiles. Their resemblance was accentuated by this, and by the fact that Jerry hadn't grown fat when the picture was taken. The caption was simply: "The Hallman brothers (Carl on the right)."

The dark girl coughed insinuatingly. I looked up and saw her leaning far out over her counter, slightly cross-eyed with desire to break the silence.

"Terrible, isn't it? What makes it worse, I know him." She shivered, and hunched her thin shoulders up. "I talked to him just this morning."

"Who?"

"The murderer." She rolled the "r's" like an actress in melodrama.

"He telephoned here?"

"He *came* here, personally. He was standing right here in front of me." She pointed at the floor between us with a finger-nail from which the red polish was flaking. "I didn't know him from Adam, but *I* could tell there was something funny. He had that wild look they have in their eyes." Her own look was slightly wild, in a girlish way, and she'd forgotten her reception-ist's diction: "Jeeze, it bored right through me."

"It must have been a frightening experience."

"*You're* not kidding. 'Course I had no way of knowing he was going to shoot somebody, he only *looked* that way. 'Where's the doctor?' he said, just like that. I guess he thought he was Napoleon or something. Only he was dressed like any old bum. You'd never think he was a Senator's son. His brother used to come in here, and *he* was a real gentleman, always nicely dressed in the height of fashion—cashmere jackets and stuff. It's too bad about him. I feel sorry for his wife, too."

"You know her?"

"Oh yes, Mrs. Hallman, she comes in all the time for her sinuses." Her eyes took on the waiting birdlike expression of a woman naming another woman she happens not to like.

"Did you get rid of him all right?"

"The crazy-man? I tried to tell him doctor wasn't in, but he wouldn't take no for an answer. So I called out Dr. Grantland, *he* knows how to handle them, Dr. Grantland hasn't got a nerve in his body." The birdlike expression subtly changed to the look of adoration which very young receptionists reserve for their doctor-employers. "'Hello, old man, what brings you here?' the doctor says, like they were buddy-buddy from way back. He put his arm around him, calm as anything, and off they went into the back room. I guess he got rid of him out the back way, 'cause that was the last I saw of him. 'Least I hope that's the last. Anyway, doctor told me not to worry about it, that things like that come up in every office."

"Have you worked here long?"

"Just three months. This is my first real job. I filled in for other girls before, when they went on vacation, but I consider this the real start of my career. Dr. Grantland is wonderful to work for. Most of his patients are the nicest people you'd ever want to meet."

As though to illustrate this boast, a fat woman wearing a small flat hat and a mink neckpiece emerged through the inner door. She was followed by Grantland who looked professional in a white smock. She had the vaguely frightened eyes of a hypochondriac, and she clutched a prescription slip in her chubby hand. Grantland escorted her to the front door and opened it, bowing her out. She turned to him on the threshold:

"Thank you so much, doctor. I know I'll be able to sleep tonight."

Chapter 19

G RANTLAND CLOSED the door and saw me. The lingering smile on his face gave up the ghost entirely. Shoved by a gust of anger, he crossed the room toward me. His fists were clenched.

I rose to meet him. "Hello, doctor."

"What are you doing here?"

"I have an appointment with you."

"Oh no you haven't." He was torn between anger and the need to be charming to his receptionist. "Did you make an appointment for this—this gentleman?"

"Why not?" I said, since she was speechless. "Are you retiring from practice?"

"Don't try to tell me you're here as a patient."

"You're the only doctor I know in town."

"You didn't tell me you knew Dr. Grantland," the reception-ist said accusingly.

"I must have forgotten to."

"Very likely," Grantland said. "You can go now, Miss Cullen, unless you've made some more of these special appointments for me."

"He told me it was an emergency."

"I said you can go."

She went, with a backward look from the doorway. Grant-land's face was trying various attitudes: outrage, dignified sur-prise, bewildered innocence.

"What are you trying to pull on me?"

"Not a thing. Look, if you don't want to treat me, I can find another doctor."

He weighed the advantages and disadvantages of this, and decided against it. "I don't do much in the surgical line, but I guess I can fix you up. What happened to you, anyway—did you run into Hallman again?" Zinnie had briefed him well, apparently.

"No. Did you?"

He let that go by. We went through a consulting-room fur-nished in mahogany and blue leather. There were sailing prints

533

on the walls, and above the desk a medical diploma from a college in the middle west. Grantland switched on the lights in the next room and asked me to remove my coat. Washing his hands at the sink in the corner, he said over his shoulder:

"You can get up on the examination table if you like. I'm sorry my nurse has gone home—I didn't know I'd be wanting to use her."

I stretched out on the leatherette top of the metal table. Lying flat on the back wasn't a bad position for self-defense, if it came to that.

Grantland crossed the room briskly and leaned over me, turning on a surgical light that extended on retractable arms from the wall. "You get yourself gun-whipped?"

"Slightly. Not every doctor would recognize the marks."

"I interned at Hollywood Receiving. Did you report this to the police?"

"I didn't have to. Ostervelt did it to me."

"You're not a fugitive, for God's sake?"

"No, for God's sake."

"Were you resisting arrest?"

"The sheriff just lost his temper. He's a hot-headed old youth."

Grantland made no comment. He went to work cleaning my cuts with swabs dipped in alcohol. It hurt.

"I'm going to have to put some clamps in that ear. The other cut ought to heal itself. I'll simply put an adhesive bandage over it."

Grantland went on talking as he worked: "A regular surgeon could do a better job for you, especially a plastic surgeon. That's why I was a little surprised when you came to me. You're going to have a small scar, I'm afraid. But that's all right with me if it's all right with you." He pressed a series of clamps into my torn ear. "That ought to do it. You ought to have a doctor look at it in a day or two. Going to be in town long?"

"I don't know." I got up, and faced him across the table. "It could depend on you."

"Any doctor can do it," he said impatiently.

"You're the only one who can help me."

Grantland caught the implication, and glanced at his watch. "I'm late for an appointment now—"

"I'll make it as fast as I can. You saw a pearl-handled gun today. You didn't mention that you'd seen it before."

He was a very quick study. Without a second's hesitation, he said: "I like to be sure of my facts before I sound off. I'm a medical man, after all."

"What are your facts?"

"Ask your friend the sheriff. He knows them."

"Maybe. I'm asking you. You might as well tell a straight story. I've been in touch with Glenn Scott."

"Glenn who?" But he remembered. His gaze flickered sideways.

"The detective Senator Hallman hired to investigate the murder of his wife."

"Did you say murder?"

"It slipped out."

"You're mistaken. She committed suicide. If you talked to Scott, you know she was suicidal."

"Suicidal people can be murdered."

"No doubt, but what does that prove?" A womanish petulance tugged at his mouth, disrupting his false calm. "I'm sick and tired of being badgered about it, simply because she happened to be my patient. Why, I saved her life the week before she drowned. Did Scott bother to tell you that?"

"He told me what you told him. That she attempted suicide in this office."

"It was in my previous office. I moved last year."

"So you can't show me the bullethole in the ceiling."

"Good Lord, are you questioning that? I got that gun away from her at the risk of my own life."

"I don't question it. I wanted to hear it from you, though."

"Well, now you've heard it. I hope you're satisfied." He took off his smock and turned to hang it up.

"Why did she try to commit suicide in your office?"

He was very still for an instant, frozen in the act of placing the white garment on a hook. Between the shoulderblades and under the arms, his gray shirt was dark with sweat. It was the only indication that I was giving him a hard time. He said:

"She wanted something I wasn't prepared to give her. A massive dose of sleeping pills. When I refused, she pulled this little revolver out of her purse. It was touch and go whether she was going to shoot me or herself. Then she pointed it at her head. Fortunately I managed to reach her, and take the gun away." He turned with a bland and doleful look on his face.

"Was she on a barb kick?"

"You might call it that. I did my best to keep it under control."

"Why didn't you have her put in a safe place?"

"I miscalculated, I admit it. I don't pretend to be a psychiatrist. I didn't grasp the seriousness of her condition. We doctors make mistakes, you know, like everybody else."

He was watching me like a chess-player. But his sympathy gambit was a giveaway. Unless he had something important to cover up, he'd have ordered me out of his office long ago.

"What happened to the gun?" I said.

"I kept it. I intended to throw it away, but never got around to it."

"How did Carl Hallman get hold of it?"

"He lifted it out of my desk drawer." He added disarmingly: "I guess I was a damn fool to keep it there."

I'd been holding back my knowledge of Carl Hallman's visit to his office. It was disappointing to have the fact conceded. Grantland said with a faint sardonic smile:

"Didn't the sheriff tell you that Carl was here this morning? I telephoned him immediately. I also got in touch with the State Hospital."

"Why did he come here?"

Grantland turned his hands palms outward. "Who can say? He was obviously disturbed. He bawled me out for my part in having him committed, but his main animus was against his brother. Naturally I tried to talk him out of it."

"Naturally. Why didn't you hold on to him?"

"Don't think I didn't try to. I stepped into the dispensary for a minute to get him some thorazine. I thought it might calm him down. When I came back to the office, he was gone. He must have run out the back way here." Grantland indicated the back door of the examination room. "I heard a car start, but he was gone before I could catch him."

I walked over to the half-curtained window and looked out. Grantland's Jaguar was parked in the paved lot. Back of the lot, a dirt lane ran parallel with the street. I turned back to Grantland: "You say he took your gun?"

"Yes, but I didn't know it at the time. It wasn't exactly *my* gun, either. I'd practically forgotten it existed. I didn't even think of it till I found it in the greenhouse beside poor Jerry's body. Then I couldn't be sure it was the same one, I'm no expert on guns. So I waited until I got back here this afternoon, and had a chance to check the drawer of my desk. When I found it gone I got in touch with the sheriff's department right away— much as I hated to do it."

"Why did you hate to do it?"

"Because I'm fond of the boy. He used to be my patient. You'd hardly expect me to get a kick out of proving that he's a murderer."

"You've proved that, have you?"

"You're supposed to be a detective. Can you think of any other hypothesis?"

I could, but I kept it to myself. Grantland said:

"I can understand your feeling let down. Ostervelt told me you're representing poor Carl, but don't take it too hard, old man. They'll take his mental condition into account. I'll see to it personally that they do."

I wasn't as sad as I looked. Not that I was happy about the case. Every time I moved, I picked up another link in the evidence against my client. But this happened with such clockwork regularity that I was getting used to it and beginning to discount it. Besides, I was encouraged by the firm and lasting faith which I was developing in Dr. Grantland's lack of integrity.

Chapter 20

TWILIGHT WAS thickening in the street outside. The white-walled buildings, fluorescent with last light, had taken on the beauty and mystery of a city in Africa or someplace else I'd never been. I nosed my car out into a break in the traffic, turned right at the next intersection, and parked a hundred feet short of the entrance to Grantland's back lane. I hadn't been there five minutes when his Jaguar came bumping along the lane. It arced out into the street on whining tires.

Grantland didn't know my car. I followed him fairly closely, two blocks south, then west on a boulevard that slanted toward the sea. I almost lost him when he made a left turn onto the highway on the tail end of a green light. I followed through on the yellow as it turned red.

From there the Jaguar was easy to keep in sight. It headed south on the highway through the outskirts where marginal operators purveyed chicken-fried steaks and saltwater taffy, Mexican basketry and redwood mementoes. The neon-cluttered sub-suburbs dropped behind. The highway snaked up and along brown bluffs which rose at a steep angle above the beach. The sea lay at their foot, a more somber reflection of the sky, still tinged at its far edge with the sun's red death.

About two miles out of town, as many minutes, the Jaguar's brakelights blazed. It heeled and turned onto a black top shelf overlooking the sea. There was one other car in the turnout, a red Cadillac with its nose against the guardrail. Before the next curve swept me out of sight, I saw Grantland's car pull up beside the Cadillac.

There was traffic behind me. I found another turnout a quarter of a mile further on. By the time I'd made my turn and got back to the first turnout, the Jaguar was gone and the Cadillac was going.

I caught a glimpse of the driver's face as he turned onto the highway. It gave me the kind of shock you might get from seeing the ghost of someone you'd once known. I'd known him ten years before, when he was a high-school athlete, a big boy, nice looking, full of fermenting energy. The face behind the wheel of the Cadillac: yellow skin stretched over skull, smokily lit by black unfocused eyes: could have belonged to that boy's grandfather. I knew him, though. Tom Rica.

I turned once again and followed him south. He drove erratically, slowing on the straightaway and speeding up on the curves, using two of the four lanes. Once, at better than seventy, he left the road entirely, and veered onto the shoulder. The Cadillac skidded sideways in the gravel, headlights swinging out into gray emptiness. The bumper clipped the steel guardrail, and the Cadillac slewed wildly in the other direction. It regained the road and went on as if nothing had happened.

I stayed close behind, trying to think my way into Tom Rica's brain and along his damaged nerves and do his driving for him. I'd always felt an empathy for the boy. When he was eighteen and his unmaturing youth had begun to go rank, I'd tried to hold him straight, and even run some interference for him. An old cop had done it for me when I was a kid. I couldn't do it for Tom.

The memory of my failure was bitter and obscure, mixed with the ash-blonde memory of a woman I'd once been married to. I put both memories out of my mind.

Tom was steadying down to his driving. The big car held the road, and even stayed in one lane most of the time. The road straightened out, and began to climb. Just beyond the crest of the rise, a hundred feet or more above the invisible sea, a red neon sign flashed at the entrance to a private parking lot: Buenavista Inn.

The Cadillac turned in under the sign. I stopped before I got to it, and left my car on the shoulder of the road. The inn lay below, a pueblo affair with a dozen or more stucco cottages staggered along the shadowy terraces. About half of them had lights behind their blinds. There was a red neon Office sign above the door of the main building beside the parking lot.

Tom parked the Cadillac with several other cars, and left it with its lights burning. I kept the other cars between me and him. I didn't think he saw me, but he began to run toward the main building. He moved in a jerky knock-kneed fashion, like an old man trying to catch a bus which had already left.

The door under the red sign opened before he reached it. A big woman stepped out onto the platform of light projected from the doorway. Her hair was gold, her skin a darker gold. She wore a gold lamé gown with a slashed neckline. Even at a distance, she gave the impression of a shining hardness, as though she'd preserved her body from age by having it cast in metal. Her voice had a metallic carrying quality:

"Tommy! Where've you been?"

If he answered, I couldn't hear him. He stopped on his heels in front of her, feinted to the left, and tried to move past her on the right. The action was a sad parody of the broken-field running he'd once been pretty good at. Her flashing body blocked him in the doorway, and one of her round gold arms encircled his neck. He struggled weakly. She kissed him on the mouth, then looked out over his shoulder across the parking lot.

"You took my car, you naughty boy. And now you left the lights on. Get inside now, before somebody sees you."

She slapped him half-playfully, and released him. He scuttled into the lighted lobby. She marched across the parking lot, an unlikely figure of a woman with a broad serene brow, deep eyes, an ugly hungry tortured mouth, a faint pouch under her chin. She walked as if she owned the world, or had owned it once and lost it but remembered how it felt.

She switched off the lights of the car, removed the ignition key and pulled up her skirt to slip it into the top of her stocking. Her legs were heavy and shapely, with slender ankles. She slammed the door of the Cadillac and said out loud, in a tone of mingled anger and indulgence:

"Silly damn little fool."

She breathed and sighed, and noticed me in the middle of the sigh. Without changing the rhythm of her breathing, she smiled and nodded: "Hello there. What can I do for you?"

"You look as if you could do plenty."

"Kidder." But her smile widened, revealing bright gold inlays in its corners. "Nobody's interested in Maude any more. Except Maude. I'm very much interested in Maude."

"That's because you're Maude."

"You bet your sweet life I am. Who are you?"

I told her as I got out of my car, and added: "I'm looking for a friend."

"A new friend?"

"No, an old friend."

"One of my dolls?"

"Could be."

"Come on inside if you want to."

I followed her in. I'd hoped to find Tom Rica in the lobby, but he'd evidently gone through into the private part of the building.

The lobby was surprisingly well furnished with pastel leather chairs, potted palms. One end wall was covered with a photo-mural of Hollywood at night, which gave the effect of a picture window overlooking the city. The opposite wall was an actual window overlooking the sea.

Maude went around the curved teakwood counter across from the door. The inner door behind the counter was partly open. She closed it. She unlocked a drawer and took out a type-written sheet, much interlined.

"I mayn't have her listed any more. My turnover is terrific. The girls get married."

"Good for them."

"But not so good for me. I've had a recruiting problem ever since the war. You'd think I was running a matrimonial bureau or something. Well, if she isn't with me any more I can always get you another one. It's early. What did you say her name was?"

"I didn't say. And it's not a her."

She gave me a slightly disappointed look. "You're in the wrong pew. I run a clean place, strictly from heterosex."

"Who said I had sex on my mind?"

"I thought everybody had," she said with a kind of habitual wiggle.

"All the time?"

She glanced at me from the hard gray surface of her deep-set eyes. "What happened to you?"

"A lot of things. I'm trying to sell the movie rights to my life. Somebody down here hates me."

"I mean your face."

"Oh, that."

"What are you stalling for? My God, don't tell me you're a lamster, too. The woods are crawling with them."

"Could you put me up if I was?"

She took it as the fact, with the gullibility of cynicism: "How hot are you?"

"Not very."

"That car outside belong to you?"

"It's mostly the bank's."

"My God, you robbed a bank?"

"They're robbing me. Ten per cent interest on the money I borrowed to buy the crate."

She leaned forward across the counter, her ringed hands flat on its top, her eyes hard-bright as the cut stones in the rings:

"What kind of a joker are you? If you're thinking of knocking me over, I warn you I got protection, plenty of it."

"Don't get hinky."

"I'm not hinky. I get a little irritated, is all, when a beat-up punk walks into my place and won't tell me what he wants." She moved quickly to a small switchboard at the end of the counter, picked up a headphone, and said over her shoulder: "So get to the point, brother."

"Tom Rica is the friend I'm looking for."

A ripple of nerves went through her. Then she stood heavy and solid again. Her eyes didn't shift, but their bright stare became more intense.

"Who sent you here?"

"I came on my own."

"I doubt that. Whoever it was gave you the wrong information." She put down the phone and returned to the counter. "Come to think of it, there was a boy named Rica worked here a while back. What did you say the first name was?"

"Tom."

"What do you want with him?"

"A chance to talk, that's all."

"What about?"

"Old times."

She struck the countertop with the front of her fist. "Cut the doubletalk, eh? You're no friend of his."

"Better than some he has. I hate to see him poison his brains with heroin. He used to be a smart boy."

"He still is," she said defensively. "It isn't his fault he was sick." In a sudden gesture of self-contempt, self-doubt, she tugged at the pouch of flesh under her chin, and went on worrying it. "Who are you, anyway? Are you from the hospital?"

"I'm a private detective investigating a murder."

"That shooting in the country?" For the first time she seemed afraid. "You can't tie Tom in with it."

"What makes you think I'm trying to?"

"You said you wanted to see him, didn't you? But you're not seeing him. He had nothing to do with that killer."

"They escaped together last night."

"That proves nothing. I got rid of that Hallman character soon as we hit the main road. Him I wanted no part of. I see enough of them in line of business. And Tom hasn't seen him since, or gone anywhere. He's been here all day. With me."

"So you helped them get away from the hospital."

"What if I did?"

"You weren't doing Hallman a favor. Or Tom, either."

"I beg to differ. They were torturing him. They cut him off cold turkey. He had nothing to eat for over a week. You ought to've seen him when I picked him up."

"So you put him back on horse."

"I did not. He begged me to get him some caps, but I wouldn't do it. It's the only one thing I wouldn't do for Tom. I did buy him some bottles of cough medicine with the codeine in it. I couldn't just sit there and watch him suffer, could I?"

"You want him to be a hype for the rest of his life? And die of it?"

"Don't say that."

"What are you trying to do to him?"

"Look after him."

"You think you're qualified?"

"I love the boy," she said. "I did what I could for him. Does that make me so lousy?"

"Nobody said you're lousy."

"Nobody has to say it. I tried to make him happy. I didn't have what it takes."

Fingering her heavy breasts, she looked down at herself in sorrow.

Chapter 21

THE DOOR behind her opened. Tom Rica leaned in the opening, with one frail shoulder propped against the doorframe. His sharp tweed jacket hung loosely on him.

"What's the trouble, Maudie?" His voice was thin and dry, denatured. His eyes were puddles of tar.

Maude resumed her smiling mask before she turned to him. "No trouble. Go back in."

She put her hands on his shoulders. He smiled past her at me, detachedly, pathetically, as if there was a thick glass wall between us. She shook him: "Did you get a needle? Is that where you were?"

"Wouldn't you like to know," he said in dull coquetry, using his hollow face as if it was young and charming.

"Where did you get it? Where did you get the money?"

"Who needs money, honey?"

"Answer me." Her shoulders bowed across him. She shook him so that his teeth clicked. "I want to know who gave you the stuff and how much you got and where the rest of it is."

He collapsed against the doorframe. "Lay off me, bag."

"That isn't a bad idea," I said, coming around the counter.

She whirled as if I'd stuck a knife in her back. "You stay out of this, brother. I'm warning you. I've taken enough from you, when all I want is to do what's right for my boy."

"You own him, do you?"

She yelled in a brass tenor: "Get out of my place."

Tom moved between us, like a vaudeville third man. "Don't talk like that to my old buddy." He peered at me through the glass wall. His eyes and speech were more focused, as though the first shock of the drug was passing off. "You still a do-gooder, old buddy? Myself, I'm a do-badder. Every day in every way I'm doing badder and badder, as dear old mother used to say."

"You talk too much," Maude said, laying a heavy arm across his shoulders. "Come in and lie down now."

He turned on her in a sudden spurt of viciousness. "Leave me

544

be. I'm in good shape, having a nice reunion with my old buddy. You trying to break up my friendships?"

"I'm the only friend you got."

"Is that so? Let me tell you something. You'll have dirt in your eyes, and I'll be riding high, living the life of Riley. Who needs you?"

"You need me, Tom," she said, without assurance. "You were on your uppers when I took you in. If it wasn't for me you'd be in the pen. I got your charge reduced, and you know it, and it cost me plenty. So here you go right back on the same crazy kick. Don't you ever learn?"

"I learn, don't worry. All these years I been studying the angles, see, like an apprenticeship. I know the rackets like I know the back of my hand. I know where you stupid hustlers make your stupid mistakes. And I'm not making any. I got a racket of my own now, and it's as safe as houses." His mood had swung violently upward, in anger and elation.

"Houses with bars on the windows," the blonde woman said. "You stick your neck out again, and I can't cover for you."

"Nobody asked you to. I'm on my own now. Forget me."

He turned his back on her and went through the inner door. His body moved loosely and lightly, supported by invisible strings. I started to follow him. Maude turned her helpless anger on me:

"Stay out of there. You got no right in there."

I hesitated. She was a woman. I was in her house. With the toe of her shoe, Maude pressed a faintly worn spot in the carpet behind the counter:

"You better beat it out of here, I'm warning you."

"I think I'll stay for a while."

She folded her arms across her breasts and looked at me like a lioness. A short broad man in a plaid shirt opened the front door and came in quietly. His smile was wide and meaningless under a hammered-in nose. A leather blackjack, polished like a keepsake, swung from his hand.

"Dutch, take this one out," Maude said, standing away.

I went around the counter and took Dutch out instead. Perhaps bouncing drunks had spoiled him. Anyway, he was easy to hit. Between his wild swings, I hit him with a left to the head, a right cross to the jaw, a long left hook to the solar plexus which bent him over into my right coming up. He subsided. I picked up his blackjack and moved past Maude through the inner door. She didn't say a word.

I went through a living-room crowded with overstuffed furniture in a green-and-white jungle design from which eyes seemed to watch me, down a short hallway past a pink satin bedroom which reminded me of the inside of a coffin in disarray, to the open door of a bathroom. Tom's jacket lay across the lighted threshold like the headless torso of a man, flattened by the passage of some enormous engine.

Tom was sitting on the toilet seat with his left shirtsleeve rolled up and a hypodermic needle in his right hand. He was too busy looking for a vein to notice me. The veins he had already used and ruined writhed black up his arm from wrist to wasted biceps. Blue tattoo marks disguised the scars on his wrists.

I took the needle away from him. It was about a quarter full of clear liquid. Upturned in the bright bathroom light, his face set in hard wrinkles like a primitive mask used to conjure evil spirits, its eyeholes full of darkness.

"Give it back. I didn't get enough."

"Enough to kill yourself?"

"It keeps me alive. I almost died without it, there in the hospital. My brains were running out of my ears."

He made a sudden grab for the needle in my hand. I held it out of his reach.

"Go back to the hospital, Tom."

He swung his head slowly from side to side. "There's nothing for me there. Everything I want is on the outside."

"What do you want?"

"Kicks. Money and kicks. What else is there?"

"A hell of a lot."

"You've got it?" He sensed my hesitation, and looked up slyly. "Do-gooder ain't doing so good, eh? Don't go into the old look-to-the-future routine. It makes me puke. It always made me puke. So save it for the birds. *This* is my future, *now*."

"You like it?"

"If you give me back my needle. It's all I need from you."

"Why don't you kick it, Tom? Use your guts for that. You're too young to go down the drain."

"Save it for the boy scouts, den-father. You want to know why I'm a hype? Because I got bored with double-mouthed bastards like you. You spout the old uplift line, but I never seen a one of you that believed in it for himself. While you're telling other people how to live, you're double-timing your wife and running after gash, drinking like a goddam fish and chasing any dirty nickel you can see."

There was enough truth in what he said to tie my tongue for a minute. The obscure pain of memory came back. It centered in an image in my mind: the face of the woman I had lost. I blotted the image out, telling myself that that was years ago. The important things had happened long ago.

Tom spoke to the doubt that must have showed in my face:

"Give me back my needle. What's to lose?"

"Not a chance."

"Come on," he wheedled. "The stuff is weak. The first shot didn't even give me a lift."

"Then you don't have so far to fall."

He beat his sharp knees with his fists. "Give me my needle, you hot-and-cold-running false-faced mother-lover. You'd steal the pennies off a dead man's eyes and sell his body for soap."

"Is that how you feel? Dead?"

"The hell I am. I'll show you. I can get more."

He got up and tried to push past me. He was frail and light as a scarecrow. I forced him back onto the seat, holding the needle carefully out of his reach.

"Where did you get it in the first place, Tom?"

"Would I tell you?"

"Maybe you don't have to."

"Then why ask?"

"What's this fine new racket of yours that you were warbling about?"

"Wouldn't you like to know."

"Pushing reefers to school kids?"

"You think I'm interested in peanuts?"

"Buying and selling old clothes?"

His ego couldn't stand to be downgraded. The insult blew it up like a balloon. "You think I'm kidding? I got a piece of the biggest racket in the world. Before I'm through I'll be buying and selling peanut-eaters like you."

"By saving green stamps, no doubt."

"By putting on the squeeze, jerk, where the money is. You get something on somebody, see, and you sell it back a little piece at a time. It's like an annuity."

"Or a death-warrant."

He looked at me imperviously. Dead men never die.

"The good doctor could be very bad medicine."

He grinned. "I got an antidote."

"What have you got on him, Tom?"

"Do I look crazy enough to tell you?"

"You told Carl Hallman."

"Did I? Maybe he thinks I did. I told him any little thing that came into my little pointed head."

"What were you trying to do to him?"

"Just stir him up a little. I had to get out of that ward. I couldn't make it alone."

"Why did you send Hallman to me?"

"Get him off my hands. He was in my way."

"You must have had a better reason than that."

"Sure. I'm a do-gooder." His wise grin turned malign. "I thought you could use the business."

"Carl Hallman's got a murder rap on his hands, did you know that?"

"I know it."

"If I thought you talked him into it—"

"What would you do? Slap my wrist, do-gooder?"

He looked at me through the glass wall with lazy curiosity, and added casually: "Anyway, he didn't shoot his brother. He told me so himself."

"Has he been here?"

"Sure he was here. He wanted Maude to hide him out. She wouldn't touch him with gloves on."

"How long ago was this?"

"A couple of hours, maybe. He took off for town when Maude and Dutch gave him the rush."

"Did he say where he was going in town?"

"No."

"He didn't shoot his brother, you say?"

"That's right, he told me that."

"Did you believe him?"

"I had to believe him, because I did it myself." Tom looked at me dead-pan. "I flew over there by helicopter, see. In my new supersonic helicopter with the synchronized death-ray gun."

"Turn off the stardrive, Tom. Tell me what really happened."

"Maybe I will, if you give me back my needle."

His eyes held a curious mixture of plea and threat. They looked expectantly at the bright instrument in my fist. I was tempted to let him have it, on the chance that he knew something I could use. A few more caps in those black veins wouldn't make any difference. Except to me.

I was sick of the whole business. I threw the needle into the square pink bathtub. It smashed to pieces.

Tom looked at me incredulously, "What did you do that for?"

Sudden fury shook him, too strong for his nerves to carry. It broke through into grief. He flung himself face down on the pink tile floor, sobbing in a voice like fabric tearing.

In the intervals of the noise he made, I heard other noises behind me. Maude was coming through the jungle-colored living-room. A gun gleamed dully blue in her white hand. The man called Dutch was a pace behind her. His grin was broken-toothed. I could see why my knuckles were sore.

"What goes on?" Maude cried. "What did you do to him?"

"Took his needle away. See for yourself."

She didn't seem to hear me. "Come out of there. Leave him alone." She pushed the gun toward my face.

"Let me at him. I'll clobber the bastard," the man behind her lisped in punchy eagerness.

An Argyle sock hung heavy and pendulous from his hand. It reminded me of the blackjack in my pocket. I backed out of the doorway to gain elbowroom, and swung the leather club over and down at Maude's wrist.

She hissed with pain. The gun clanked at her feet. Dutch went down on his hands and knees after it. I hit him on the back of the head with the blackjack, not too hard, just hard enough to stretch him on his face again. The heavy sock fell from his numb hand, some of its sand spilling out.

Maude was scrambling in the doorway for the gun. I pushed her back and picked it up and put it in my pocket. It was a medium-caliber revolver and it made a very heavy pocket. I put the blackjack in my other pocket so that I wouldn't walk lopsided.

Maude leaned on the wall outside the door, holding her right wrist in her left hand. "You're going to be sorry for this."

"I've heard that before."

"Not from me you haven't, or you wouldn't be running around making trouble for people. Don't think it's going to last. I got the top law in this county in my pocket."

"Tell me more," I said. "You have a lovely singing voice. Maybe I can arrange a personal appearance, in front of the Grand Jury."

Her ugly mouth said yah at me. Her left hand came out stiff, its carmine talons pointed at my eyes. It was more of a threat than attempt, but it made me despair of our relationship.

I left her and found a back way out. There were soft lights and loud noises in the cottages on the terraces, music, female laughter, money, kicks.

Chapter 22

I DROVE back toward Purissima, keeping a not very hopeful lookout for Carl Hallman. Just outside the city limits, where the highway dipped down from the bluffs toward the sea, I saw a huddle of cars on the shoulder. Two of the cars had red pulsating lights. Other lights were moving on the beach.

I parked across the highway and got the flashlight out of my dash compartment. Before I closed it, I relieved my pockets of the gun and the blackjack and locked them up. I descended a flight of concrete steps which slanted down to the beach. Near their foot, the vestiges of a small fire glowed. Beside it, a blanket was spread on the sand, weighted down by a picnic basket.

Most of the lights were far up the beach by now, bobbing and swerving like big slow fireflies. Between me and the dim thumping line of the surf, a dozen or so people were milling aimlessly. A man detached himself from the shadowy group and trotted toward me, soft-footed in the sand.

"Hey! That's my stuff. It belongs to me."

I flashed my light across him. He was a very young man in a gray sweatshirt with a college letter on the front of it. He moved as though he had won the letter playing football.

"What's the excitement about?" I said.

"I'm not excited. I just don't like people messing around with my stuff."

"Nobody's messing around with your stuff. I mean the excitement up the beach."

"The cops are after a guy."

"What guy is that?"

"The maniac—the one that shot his brother."

"Did you see him?"

"I hope to tell you. I was the one that raised the alarm. He walked right up to Marie when she was sitting here. Lord knows what would have happened if I hadn't been within reach." The boy arched his shoulders and stuck out his chest.

"What did happen?"

"Well, I went up to the car to get some cigarettes, and this guy came out of the dark and asked Marie for a sandwich. It

551

wasn't just a sandwich that he wanted, she could tell. A sandwich was just the thin edge of the wedge. Marie let out a yell, and I came down the bank and threw a tackle at him. I could have held him, too, except that it was dark and I couldn't see what I was doing. He caught me a lucky blow in the face, and got away."

I turned my light on his face. His lower lip was swollen.

"Which way did he go?"

He pointed along the shore to the multicolored lights of the Purissima waterfront. "I would have run him down, only maybe he had confederates, so I couldn't leave Marie here by herself. We drove to the nearest gas station and I phoned in the alarm."

The onlookers on the beach had begun to straggle up the concrete steps. A highway patrolman approached us, the light from his flash stabbing at the pockmarked sand. The boy in the sweatshirt called out heartily:

"Anything else I can do?"

"Not right now there isn't. He got clean away, it looks like."

"Maybe he swam out to sea and went aboard a yacht and they'll put him ashore in Mexico. I heard the family is loaded."

"Maybe," the patrolman said drily. "You're sure you saw the man? Or have you been seeing too many movies?"

The boy retorted hotly: "You think I smacked myself in the mouth?"

"Sure it was the man we're looking for?"

"Of course. Big guy with light-colored hair in dungarees. Ask Marie. She had a real good look at him."

"Where is your girlfriend now?"

"Somebody took her home, she was pretty upset."

"I guess we better have her story. Show me where she lives, eh?"

"I'll be glad to."

While the young man was dousing the fire with sand and collecting his belongings, another car stopped on the roadside above us. It was an old black convertible which looked familiar. Mildred got out and started down the steps. She came so blindly and precipitously that I was afraid she'd fall and plunge headlong. I caught her at the foot of the steps with one arm around her waist.

"Let me go!"

I let her go. She recognized me then, and returned to her mind's single track: "Is Carl here? Have you seen him?"

"No—"

She turned to the patrolman: "Has my husband been here?"

"You Mrs. Hallman?"

"Yes. The radio said my husband was seen on Pelican Beach."

"He's been and gone, ma'am."

"Gone where?"

"That's what we'd like to know. Do you have any ideas on the subject?"

"No. I haven't."

"Has he got any close friends in Purissima—somebody he might go to?"

Mildred hesitated. The faces of curious onlookers strained out of the darkness toward her. The boy in the sweatshirt was breathing on the back of her neck. He spoke as if she were deaf or dead:

"This is the guy's *wife*."

The patrolman looked disgusted. "Break it up, eh? Move along there now." He turned back to Mildred: "Any ideas, ma'am?"

"I'm sorry—it's hard for me to think. Carl had lots of friends in high school. They all dropped away. He didn't see anyone the last year or so." Her voice trailed off. She seemed confused by the lights and the people.

I said, as stuffily as possible: "Mrs. Hallman came here to look for her husband. She doesn't have to answer questions."

The patrolman's light came up to my face. "Who are you?"

"A friend of the family. I'm going to take her home."

"All right. Take her home. She shouldn't be running around by herself, anyway."

With a hand under her elbow, I propelled Mildred up the steps and across the highway. Her face was an oval blur in the dark interior of my car, so pale that it seemed luminous.

"Where are you taking me?"

"Home, as I said. Is it far from here?"

"A couple of miles. I have my own car, thank you, and I'm perfectly fit to drive it. After all, I drove it here."

"Don't you think it's time you relaxed?"

"With Carl still being hunted? How can I? Anyway, I've been home all day. You said he might come to the house, but he never did."

Exhaustion or disappointment overcame her. She sat inertly, propped doll-like in the seat. Headlights went by in the road like brilliant forlorn hopes rushing out of darkness into darkness.

"He may be on his way there now," I said. "He's hungry, and he must be bone-tired. He's been on the run for a night and a day." And another night was beginning.

Her hand moved from her mouth to my arm. "How do you know he's hungry?"

"He asked a girl on the beach for a sandwich. Before that he went to a friend, looking for shelter. Friend may be the wrong word. Did Carl ever mention Tom Rica to you?"

"Rica? Isn't that the fellow who escaped with him? His name was in the paper."

"That's right. Do you know anything else about him?"

"Just from what Carl said."

"When was that?"

"The last time I saw him, in the hospital. He told me how this Rica man had suffered in the ward. Carl was trying to make it easier for him. He said that Rica was a heroin addict."

"Did he tell you anything more about him?"

"Not that I remember. Why?"

"Rica saw Carl, not more than a couple of hours ago. If Rica can be believed. He's staying with a woman named Maude, at a place called the Buenavista Inn, just a few miles down the highway. Carl went there looking for a place to hole up."

"I don't understand," Mildred said. "Why would Carl go to a woman like that for help?"

"You know Maude, do you?"

"Certainly not. But everybody in town knows what goes on at that so-called Inn." Mildred looked at me with a kind of terror. "Is Carl mixed up with those people?"

"It doesn't follow. A man on the run will take any out he can think of."

The words didn't sound the way I'd meant them to. Her head went down under the weight of the heavy image they made. She sighed again.

It was hard to listen to. I put my arm around her. She held herself stiff and silent against my shoulder.

"Relax. This isn't a pass."

I didn't think it was. Possibly Mildred knew better. She pulled herself away from me and got out of my car in a single flurry of movement.

Most of the cars across the highway had left as we sat talking. The road was empty except for a heavy truck highballing down the hill from the south. Mildred stood at the edge of the pavement, silhouetted by its approaching lights.

The situation went to pieces, and came together in the rigid formal clarity of a photographed explosion. Mildred was on the pavement, walking head down in the truck's bright path. It bore down on her as tall as a house, braying and squealing. I saw its driver's lantern-slide face high above the road, and Mildred in the road in front of the giant tires.

The truck stopped a few feet short of her. In the sudden vacuum of sound, I could hear the sea mumbling and spitting like a beast under the bank. The truck-driver leaned from his cab and yelled at Mildred in relief and indignation:

"Damn fool woman! Watch where you're going. You damn near got yourself killed."

Mildred paid no attention to him. She climbed into the Buick, waited until the truck was out of the way, and made a sweeping turn in front of me. I was bothered by the way she handled herself and the car. She moved and drove obliviously, like someone alone in black space.

Chapter 23

M Y QUASI-PATERNAL instinct followed her home; I went along for the ride. She made it safely, and left the black convertible at the curb. When I pulled in behind it, she stopped in the middle of the sidewalk:

"What are you trying to do?"

"Seeing Millie home."

Her response was flat. "Well, I'm home."

The old house leaned like a tombstone on the night. But there were lights inside, behind cracked blinds, and the sound of a broken soprano voice. I got out and followed Mildred up the walk:

"You almost got yourself run over."

"Did I?" She turned at the top of the veranda steps. "I don't need a keeper, thank you. In fact, all I want is to be let alone."

"The deep tangled wildwood," the lost and strident voice sang from the house. "And all the loved songs that my infancy knew."

"Is your mother all right, Mildred?"

"Mother's just dandy, thank you. She's been drinking all day." She looked up and down the dark street and said in a different voice: "Even the crummy people who live on this street look down their noses at us. I can't put up a front any more. I'd simply like to crawl into a hole and die."

"You need some rest."

"How can I get any rest? With all this trouble on my shoulders? And that?"

Cast by the light from one of the front windows, her shadow lay broken on the steps. She gestured toward the window. Behind it her mother had finished her song and was playing some closing bars on a badly tuned piano.

"Anyway," Mildred said, "I have to go to work tomorrow morning. I can't miss another half day."

"Who do you work for, Simon Legree?"

"I don't mean that. Mr. Haines is very nice. It's just, if I go off schedule, I'm afraid I'll never get back on."

She fumbled in her black plastic bag for her key. The door-knob turned before she touched it. The outside light came on over our heads. Mrs. Gley opened the door, smiling muzzily:

"Bring your friend in, dear. I've said it before and I'll say it again. Your mother's always pleased and proud to entertain your friends."

Mrs. Gley didn't seem to recognize me; I was part of the indiscriminate past blurred out by the long day's drinking. She was glad to see me anyway.

"Bring your friend in, Mildred. I'll pour him a drink. A young man likes to be entertained; that's something you've got to learn. You've wasted too much of your youth on that good-for-nothing husband—"

"Stop making a fool of yourself," Mildred said coldly.

"I am not making a fool of myself. I am expressing the feelings of my womanly heart. Isn't that so?" she appealed to me. "You'll come in and have a drink with me, won't you?"

"Be glad to."

"And I'll be glad to have you."

Mrs. Gley spread her arms out in a welcoming gesture, and toppled toward me. I caught her under the arms. She giggled against my shirt front. With Mildred's help, I walked her into the sitting-room. She was awkward to handle in her draperies, like a loosely shrouded corpse.

But she managed to sit upright on the sofa and say in gracious tones:

"Excuse me. I was overcome by dizziness for a moment. The shock of the night air, you know."

Like someone struck by a bullet, invisible and inaudible, she fell softly sideways. Very soon, she began to snore.

Mildred straightened out her mother's legs, smoothed her purplish red hair and put a cushion under her head. She took off her own cloth coat and covered the lower part of her mother's body. She did these things with neutral efficiency, without ten-derness and without anger, as though she'd done them many times before and expected to do them many times again.

In the same neutral way, like an older woman speaking to a younger, she said: "Poor mother, have sweet dreams. Or no dreams. I wish you no dreams at all."

"Can I help to get her upstairs?" I said.

"She can sleep here. She often has. This happens two or three times a week. We're used to it."

Mildred sat at her mother's feet and looked around the room as if to memorize its shabby contents. She stared at the empty eye of the television set. The empty eye stared back at her. She looked down at her mother's sleeping face. My feeling that their ages were reversed was stronger when she spoke again:

"Poor redhead. She used to be a genuine redhead, too. I give her money to have it dyed. But she prefers to dye it herself, and save the money for drinking. I can't really blame her. She's tired. She ran a boarding-house for fourteen years and then she got tired."

"Is your mother a widow?"

"I don't know." She raised her eyes to my face. "It hardly matters. My father took off when I was seven years old. He had a wonderful chance to buy a ranch in Nevada for very little down. Father was always getting those wonderful chances, but this was the one that was really going to pay off. He was supposed to come back for us in three weeks or a month, when everything was settled. He never did come back. I heard from him just once. He sent me a present for my eighth birthday, a ten-dollar gold piece from Reno. There was a little note along with it, that I wasn't to spend it. I was to keep it as a token of his love. I didn't spend it, either. Mother did."

If Mildred felt resentment, she didn't show it. She sat for a time, silent and still. Then she twitched her slender shoulders, as though to shake off the dead hand of the past:

"I don't know how I got off on the subject of Father. Anyway, it doesn't matter." She changed the subject abruptly: "This man Rica, at the Buenavista Inn, what kind of a person is he?"

"Pretty dilapidated. There's not much left but hunger. He's been on dope for years. As a witness he may be useless."

"As a witness?"

"He said that Carl told him he didn't shoot Jerry."

Faint color rose in her face, and her eyes brightened. "Why didn't you tell *me* that?"

"You didn't give me a chance to. You seemed to have a rendezvous with a truck."

Her color deepened. "I admit I had a bad reaction. You oughtn't to have put your arm around me."

"I meant it in a friendly way."

"I know. It just reminded me of something. We were talking about those people at the Inn."

"I thought you didn't know them."

"I don't know them. I don't want to know them." She hesitated. "But don't you think you should inform the police about what that man said?"

"I haven't made up my mind."

"Did you believe what he said?"

"With reservations. I never did think that Carl shot his brother. But my opinion isn't based on Rica's testimony. He's a dream-talker."

"What is it based on?"

"It's hard to say. I had a strange feeling about the events at the ranch today. They had an unreal quality. Does that fit in with anything you noticed?"

"I think so, but I couldn't pin it down. What do you mean, exactly?"

"If I could say exactly, I'd know what happened out there. I don't know what happened, not yet. Some of the things I saw with my own eyes seemed as if they'd been staged for my benefit. Your husband's movements don't make sense to me, and neither do some of the others. That includes the sheriff."

"It doesn't mean Carl is guilty."

"That's just my point. He did his best to try and prove that he was, but I'm not convinced. You're familiar with the situation, the people involved. And if Carl didn't shoot Jerry, somebody else did. Who had a motive?"

"Zinnie had, of course. Only the idea of Zinnie is impossible. Women like Zinnie don't shoot people."

"Sometimes they do if the people are their husbands, and if they have strong enough motives. Love and money are a strong combination."

"You know about her and Dr. Grantland? Yes, of course, you must. She's pretty obvious."

"How long has it been going on?"

"Not long, I'm sure of that. Whatever there is between them

started after I left the ranch. I heard rumors downtown. One of my best friends is a legal secretary. She told me two or three months ago that Zinnie wanted a divorce from Jerry. He wasn't willing to give it to her, though. He threatened to fight her for Martha, and apparently she dropped the whole idea. Zinnie would never do anything that would lose her Martha."

"Shooting Jerry wouldn't lose her Martha," I said, "unless she was caught."

"You're not suggesting that Zinnie did shoot him? I simply don't believe it."

I didn't believe it, either. I didn't disbelieve it. I held it in my mind and turned it around to see how it looked. It looked as ugly as sin.

"Where's Zinnie now, do you know?"

"I haven't seen her since I left the ranch."

"What about Martha?"

"I suppose she's with Mrs. Hutchinson. She spends a lot of her life with Mrs. Hutchinson." Mildred added in a lower tone: "If I had a little girl like Martha, I'd stay with her and look after her myself. Only I haven't."

Her eyes brightened with tears. I realized for the first time what her barren broken marriage meant to her.

The telephone rang like an alarm clock in the hall. Mildred went to answer it.

"This is Mildred Hallman speaking." Her voice went higher. "No! I don't want to see you. You have no right to harass me. . . . Of course he hasn't. I don't need anyone to protect me."

I heard her hang up, but she didn't come back to the sitting-room. Instead she went into the front of the house. I found her in a room off the hallway, standing in the dark by the window.

"What's the trouble?"

She didn't answer. I found the light switch by the door, and pressed it. A single bulb winked on in the old brass chandelier. Against the opposite wall, an ancient piano grinned at me with all its yellow keys. An empty gin bottle stood on top of it.

"Was that Sheriff Ostervelt on the telephone?"

"How did you know?"

"The way you react to him. The Ostervelt reaction."

"I hate him," she said. "I don't like her, either. Ever since

Carl's been in the hospital, she's been acting more and more as if she owns him."

"I seem to have lost the thread. Who are we talking about?"

"A woman called Rose Parish, a social worker at the State Hospital. She's with Sheriff Ostervelt, and they both want to come here. I don't want to see them. They're people-eaters."

"What does that mean?"

"They're people who live on other people's troubles. I hope I headed them off. I've had enough bites taken out of me."

"I think you're wrong about Miss Parish."

"You know her?"

"I met her this morning, at the hospital. She seemed very sympathetic to your husband's case."

"Then what's she doing with Sheriff Ostervelt?"

"Probably straightening him out, if I know Miss Parish."

"He can use some straightening out. If he comes here, I won't let him in."

"Are you afraid of him?"

"I suppose I am. No. I hate him too much to be afraid of him. He did a dreadful thing to me."

"You mean the day you took Carl to the hospital?"

Mildred nodded. Pale and heavy-eyed, she looked as if her youth had run out through the unstopped wound of that day.

"I'd better tell you what actually happened. He tried to make me his—his whore. He tried to take me to Buenavista Inn."

"That same day?"

"Yes, on the way back from the hospital. He'd already made three or four stops, and every time he came back to the car he was drunker and more obnoxious. Finally I asked him to let me off at the nearest bus station. We were in Buena Vista by then, just a little way from home, but I couldn't put up with him any longer.

"I was forced to, however. Instead of taking me to the bus station, he drove out the highway to the Inn, and parked above it. The owner was a friend of his, he said—a wonderful woman, very broad-minded. If I wanted to stay there with her, she'd give me a suite to myself, and it wouldn't cost me a cent. I could take a week's vacation, or a month's—as long as I liked—and he would come and keep me company at night.

"He said he'd had this in mind for a long time, ever since his wife passed away, before that. Now that Carl was out of the way, he and I could get together at last. You should have heard him, trying to be romantic. The great lover. Leaning across me with his bald head, sweating and breathing hard and smelling of liquor."

Anger clenched in my stomach like a fist. "Did he try to use force on you?"

"He tried to kiss me. I was able to handle him, though, when he saw how I felt about him. He didn't assault me, not physically, if that's what you're getting at. But he treated me as if I—as if a woman whose husband was sick was fair game for anybody."

"What about Carl's alleged confession? Did he try to use it to make you do what he wanted?"

"Yes, he did. Only please don't do anything about it. The situation is bad enough already."

"It could get worse for him. Abuse of office cuts two ways."

"You mustn't talk like that. It will only make things worse for Carl."

A car purred somewhere out of sight. Then its headlights entered the street.

"Turn off the light," Mildred whispered, "I have a feeling it's them."

I pressed the switch and crossed to the window where she stood. A black Mercury Special pulled in to the curb behind my convertible. Ostervelt and Miss Parish got out of the back seat. Mildred pulled down the blind and turned to me:

"Will you talk to them? I don't want to see them."

"I don't blame you for not wanting to see Ostervelt. You ought to talk to Miss Parish, though. She's definitely on our side."

"I'll talk to her if I have to. But she'll have to give me a chance to change my clothes."

Their footsteps were on the porch. As I went to answer the door, I heard Mildred running up the stairs behind me.

Chapter 24

MISS PARISH and the sheriff were standing in uncomfortable relation to each other. I guessed they'd had an argument. She looked official and rather imposing in a plain blue coat and hat. Ostervelt's face was shadowed by his wide hatbrim, but I got the impression that he was feeling subdued. If there had been an argument, he'd lost.

"What are you doing here?" He spoke without force, like an old actor who has lost faith in his part.

"I've been holding Mrs. Hallman's hand. Hello, Miss Parish."

"Hello." Her smile was warm. "How *is* Mrs. Hallman?"

"Yeah," Ostervelt said. "How is she? She sounded kind of upset on the telephone. Did something happen?"

"Mrs. Hallman doesn't want to see you unless it's necessary."

"Hell, I'm just interested in her personal safety." He looked sideways at Miss Parish and added for her benefit, in an injured-innocent tone: "What's Mildred got against me?"

I stepped outside and shut the door behind me. "Are you sure you want an answer?"

I couldn't keep the heat out of my voice. In reflex, Ostervelt put his hand on his gun-butt.

"Good heavens!" Miss Parish said with a forced little laugh. "Haven't we got enough trouble, gentlemen?"

"I want to know what he means by that. He's been needling me all day. I don't have to take that stuff from any keyhole cop." Ostervelt sounded almost querulous. "Not in my own county I don't."

"You ought to be ashamed of yourself, Mr. Archer." She stepped between us, turning her back on me and her full maternal charm on Ostervelt. "Why don't you wait for me in the car, Sheriff? I'll talk to Mrs. Hallman if she'll let me. It's obvious that her husband hasn't been here. That's all you wanted to know, isn't it?"

"Yeah, but—" He glared at me over her shoulder. "I didn't like that crack."

"You weren't intended to. Make something out of it."

The situation was boiling up again. Miss Parish poured cool words on it: "I didn't hear any crack. Both you men are under a strain. It's no excuse for acting like boys with a chip on your shoulder." She touched Ostervelt's shoulder, and let her hand linger there. "You will go and wait in the car, won't you? I'll only be a few minutes."

With a kind of caressing firmness, she turned Ostervelt around and gave him a gentle push toward the street. He took it, and he went. She gave me a bright, warm look.

"How did you get him eating out of your hand?"

"Oh, that's my little secret. Actually, something came up."

"What came up?"

She smiled. "I did. Dr. Brockley couldn't make it; he had an important meeting. So he sent me instead. I asked him to."

"To check up on Ostervelt?"

"I have no official right to do anything like that." The door of the Mercury slammed in the street. "We'd better go inside, don't you think? He'll know we're talking about him."

"Let him."

"You men. Sometimes I feel as though the whole world were a mental hospital. It's certainly a safe enough assumption to act on."

After the day I'd put in, I wasn't inclined to argue.

I opened the door and held it for her. She faced me in the lighted hallway.

"I didn't expect to find you here."

"I got involved."

"I understand you have your car back."

"Yes." But she wasn't interested in my car. "If you're asking the question I think you are, I'm working for your friend Carl. I don't believe he killed his brother, or anybody else."

"Really?" Her bosom rose under her coat. She unbuttoned the coat to give it the room it needed. "I just got finished telling Sheriff Ostervelt the same thing."

"Did he buy it?"

"I'm afraid not. The circumstances are very much against Carl, aren't they? I did manage to cool the old man off a bit."

"How did you manage that?"

"It's official business. Confidential."

"Having to do with Carl?"

"Indirectly. The man he escaped with, Tom Rica. I really can't give you any more information, Mr. Archer."

"Let me guess. If I'm right, I know it already. If I'm wrong, there's no harm done. Ostervelt got Rica off with a state-hospital commitment when under the law he should have been sent to the pen."

Miss Parish didn't say I was wrong. She didn't say anything.

I ushered her into the front room. Her dark awareness took it in at a glance, staying on the empty bottle on top of the piano. There was a family photograph beside it, in a tarnished silver frame, and a broken pink conch shell.

Miss Parish picked up the bottle and sniffed it and set it down with a rap. She looked suspiciously toward the door. Her bold profile and mannish hat reminded me of a female operative in a spy movie.

"Where's the little wife?" she whispered.

"Upstairs, changing her clothes."

"Is she a drinker?"

"Never touches the stuff. Her mother drinks for both of them."

"I see."

Miss Parish leaned forward to examine the photograph. I looked at it over her shoulder. A smiling man in shirtsleeves and wide suspenders stood under a palm tree with a strikingly pretty woman. The woman held a long-dressed child on her arm. The picture had been amateurishly tinted by hand. The tree was green, the woman's bobbed hair was red, the flowers in her dress were red. All the colors were fading.

"Is this the mother-in-law?"

"Apparently."

"Where is she now?"

"Dreamland. She passed out."

"Alcoholic?"

"Mrs. Gley is working at it."

"What about the father?"

"He dropped away long ago. He may be dead."

"I'm surprised," Miss Parish murmured. "I understood Carl came from quite a wealthy—quite a good background."

"Wealthy, anyway. His wife doesn't."

"So I gather." Miss Parish looked around the mortuary room where the past refused to live or die. "It helps to fill in the picture."

"What picture?" Her patronizing attitude irked me.

"My understanding of Carl and his problems. The type of family a sick man marries into can be very significant. A person who feels socially inadequate, as sick people do, will often lower himself in the social scale, deliberately declass himself."

"Don't jump to conclusions too fast. You should take a look at his own family."

"Carl's told me a great deal about them. You know, when a person breaks down, he doesn't do it all by himself. It's something that happens to whole families. The terrible thing is when one member cracks up, the rest so often make a scapegoat out of him. They think they can solve their own problems by rejecting the sick one—locking him up and forgetting him."

"That applies to the Hallmans," I said. "It doesn't apply to Carl's wife. I think her mother would like to see him put away for good, but she doesn't count for much."

"I know, I mustn't let myself be unfair to the wife. She seems to be quite a decent little creature. I have to admit she stayed with it when the going was rough. She came to see Carl every week, never missed a Sunday. Which is more than you can say for a lot of them." Miss Parish cocked her head, as if she could hear a playback of herself. She flushed slowly. "Good heavens, listen to me. It's such a temptation to identify with the patients and blame the relatives for everything. It's one of our worst occupational hazards."

She sat down on the piano stool and took out a cigarette, which I lit for her. Twin lights burned deep in her eyes. I could sense her emotions burning behind her professional front, like walled atomic fires. They didn't burn for me, though.

Just to have something burning for me, I lit a cigarette of my own. Miss Parish jumped at the snap of the lighter; she had nerves, too. She turned on the stool to look up at me:

"I know I identify with my patients. Especially Carl. I can't help it."

"Isn't that doing it the hard way? If I went through the wringer every time one of my clients does—" I lost interest in the sentence, and let it drop. I had my own identification with the hunted man.

"I don't *care* about myself." Miss Parish crushed out her cigarette rather savagely, and moved to the doorway. "Carl is in serious jeopardy, isn't he?"

"It could be worse."

"It may be worse than you think. I talked to several people at the courthouse. They're raking up those other deaths in his family. He did a lot of talking, you know, at the time he was committed. Completely irrational talking. You don't take what a disturbed person says at its face value. But a lot of men in law enforcement don't understand that."

"Did the sheriff tell you about Carl's alleged confession?"

"He hinted around about it. I'm afraid he gives it a lot of weight. As if it proved anything."

"You sound as if you've heard it all before."

"Of course I have. When Carl was admitted six months ago he had himself convinced that he was the criminal of the century. He accused himself of killing both his parents."

"His mother, too?"

"I think his guilt-feelings originated with her suicide. She drowned herself several years ago."

"I knew that. But I don't understand why he'd blame himself."

"It's a typical reaction in depressed patients to blame themselves for everything bad that happens. Particularly the death of people they love. Carl was devoted to his mother, deeply dependent on her. At the same time he was trying to break away and have a life of his own. She probably killed herself for reasons that had no connection with Carl. But he saw her death as a direct result of his disloyalty to her, what he thought of as disloyalty. He felt as though his efforts to cut the umbilical cord had actually killed her. From there it was only a step to thinking that he was a murderer."

It was tempting doctrine, that Carl's guilt was compounded of words and fantasies, the stuff of childhood nightmares. It promised to solve so many problems that I was suspicious of it.

"Would a theory like that stand up in court?"

"It isn't theory, it's fact. Whether or not it was accepted as fact would depend on the human element: the judge, the jury, the quality of the expert witnesses. But there's no reason why it should ever come to court." Her eyes were watchful, ready to be angry with me.

"I'd still like to get my hands on firm evidence that he didn't do these crimes, that somebody else did. It's the only certain way to prove that his confession was a phony."

"But it definitely was. We know his mother was a suicide. His father died of natural causes, or possibly by accident. The story Carl told about that was pure fantasy, right out of the textbook."

"I haven't read the textbook."

"He said that he broke into his father's bathroom when the old man was in the tub, knocked him unconscious, and held him under water until he was dead."

"Do you know for a fact that it didn't happen that way?"

"Yes," she said. "I do. I have the word of the best possible witness, Carl himself. He knows now that he had no direct connection with his father's death. He told me that several weeks ago. He's developed remarkable insight into his guilt-feelings, and his reasons for confessing something he didn't do. He knows now that he wanted to punish himself for his father-killing fantasies. Every boy has the Oedipus fantasies, but they seldom come out so strongly, except in psychotic breakthrough.

"Carl had a breakthrough the morning he and his brother found their father in the bathtub. The night before, he'd had a serious argument with his father. Carl was very angry, murderously angry. When his father actually did die, he felt like a murderer. The guilt of his mother's death came up from the unconscious and reinforced this new guilt. His mind invented a story to explain his terrible guilt-feelings, and somehow deal with them."

"Carl told you all this?" It sounded very complicated and tenuous.

"We worked it out together," she said softly and gravely. "I don't mean to take credit to myself. Dr. Brockley directed the therapy. Carl simply happened to do his talking-out to me."

Her face was warm and bright again, with the pride a woman can take in being a woman, exerting peaceful power. It was hard to hold on to my skepticism, which seemed almost like an insult to her calm assurance.

"How can you tell the difference between true confessions and fantasies?"

"That's where training and experience come in. You get a feeling for unreality. It's partly in the tone, and partly in the content. Often you can tell by the very enormity of the fantasy, the patient's complete insistence on his guilt. You wouldn't believe the crimes I've had confessed to me. I've talked to a Jack the Ripper, a man who claimed he shot Lincoln, several who killed Christ himself. All these people feel they've done evil—we all do in some degree—and unconsciously they want to punish themselves for the worst possible crimes. As the patient gets better, and can face his actual problems, the need for punishment and the guilty fantasies disappear together. Carl's faded out that way."

"And you never make a mistake about these fantasies?"

"I don't claim that. There's no mistake about Carl's. He got over them, and that's proof positive that they were illusory."

"I hope he got over them. This morning when I talked to him, he was still hung up on his father's death. In fact, he wanted to hire me to prove that somebody else murdered his father. I guess that's some improvement over thinking he did it himself."

Miss Parish shook her head. She brushed past me and moved to the window, stood there with her thumbnail between her teeth. Her shadow on the blind was like an enlarged image of a worried child. I sensed the doubts and fears that had kept her single and turned her love toward the sick.

"He's had a setback," she said bitterly. "He should never have left the hospital so soon. He wasn't ready to face these dreadful things."

I laid my hand on one of her bowed shoulders. "Don't let it get *you* down. He's depending on people like you to help him out of it." Whether or not he's guilty, the words ran on unspoken in my head.

I looked out past the edge of the blind. The Mercury was still in the street. I could hear the squawk of its radio faintly through the glass.

"I'd do anything for Carl," Miss Parish said close to my ear. "I suppose that's no secret to you."

I didn't answer her. I was reluctant to encourage her intimacy. Miss Parish alternated between being too personal and too official. And Mildred was a long time coming down.

I went to the piano and picked out a one-finger tune. I quit when I recognized it: "Sentimental Journey." I took the conch shell and set it to my ear. Its susurrus sounded less like the sea than the labored breathing of a tiring runner. No doubt I heard what I was listening for.

Chapter 25

I SAW the reason for Mildred's delay when she appeared finally. She'd brushed her hair shining, changed to a black jersey dress which molded her figure and challenged comparison with it, changed to heels which added three inches to her height. She stood in the doorway, holding out both her hands. Her smile was forced and brilliant:

"I'm so glad to see you, Miss Parish. Forgive me for keeping you waiting. I know how precious your time must be, with all your nursing duties."

"I'm not a nurse." Miss Parish was upset. For a moment she looked quite ugly, with her black brows pulled down and her lower lip pushed out.

"I'm sorry, did I make a mistake? I thought Carl mentioned you as one of his nurses. He has mentioned you, you know."

Miss Parish rose rather awkwardly to the occasion. I gathered that the two young women had crossed swords or needles before. "It doesn't matter, dear. I know you've had a bad day."

"You're so sympathetic, Rose. Carl thinks so, too. You don't mind if I call you Rose? I've felt so close to you, through Carl."

"I *want* you to call me Rose. I'd love nothing better than for you to regard me as a big sister, somebody you can lean on."

Like other forthright people, Miss Parish got very phony when she got phony at all. I guessed that she'd come with some notion of mothering Mildred, the next best thing to mothering Mildred's husband. Clumsily, she tried to embrace the smaller woman. Mildred evaded her:

"Won't you sit down? I'll make you a cup of tea."

"Oh, no thanks."

"You must take something. You've come such a long way. Let me get you something to eat."

"Oh, no."

"Why not?" Mildred stared frankly at the other woman's body. "Are you dieting?"

"No. Perhaps I ought to." Large and outwitted and rebuffed, Miss Parish sank into a chair. Its springs creaked satirically under her weight. She tried to look small. "Perhaps, if I could have a drink?"

"I'm sorry." Mildred glanced at the bottle on the piano, and met the issue head-on. "There's nothing in the house. My mother happens to drink too much. I try to keep it unavailable. I don't always succeed, as you doubtless know. You hospital workers keep close tabs on the patients' relatives, don't you?"

"Oh, no," Miss Parish said. "We don't have the staff—"

"What a pity. But I can't complain. You've made an exception for me. I think it's marvelous of you. It makes me feel so looked-after."

"I'm sorry you feel that way. I just came by to help in any way I could."

"How thoughtful of you. I hate to disappoint you. My husband is not here."

Miss Parish was being badly mauled. Although in a way she'd asked for it, I felt sorry for her.

"About that drink," I said with faked cheerfulness. "I could use a drink, too. What do you say we surge out and find one, Rose?"

She looked up gratefully, from the detailed study she had been making of her fingernails. I noticed that they had been bitten short. Mildred said:

"Please don't rush away. I could have a bottle sent in from the liquor store. Perhaps my mother will join you. We could have a party."

"Lay off," I said to her under my breath.

She answered with her brilliant smile: "I hate to appear inhospitable."

The situation was getting nowhere except on my nerves. It was terminated abruptly by a scuffle of feet on the porch, a knock on the door. The two women followed me to the door. It was Carmichael, the sheriff's deputy. Behind him in the street, the sheriff's car was pulling away from the curb.

"What is it?" Mildred said.

"We just got a radio report from the Highway Patrol. A man answering your husband's description was sighted at the Red Barn drive-in. Sheriff Ostervelt thought you ought to be warned. Apparently he's headed in this direction."

"I'm glad if he is," Mildred said.

Carmichael gave her an astonished look. "Just the same, I'll keep guard on the house. Inside if you want."

"It isn't necessary. I'm not afraid of my husband."

"Neither am I," Miss Parish said behind her. "I know the man thoroughly. He isn't dangerous."

"A lot of people think different, ma'am."

"I know Sheriff Ostervelt thinks different. What orders did he give you, concerning the use of your gun?"

"I use my own discretion if Hallman shows. Naturally I'm not going to shoot him if I don't have to."

"You'd be wise to stick to that, Mr. Carmichael." Miss Parish's voice had regained its authority. "Mr. Hallman is a suspect, not a convict. You don't want to do something that you'll regret to the end of your days."

"She's right," I said. "Take him without gunfire if you can. He's a sick man, remember."

Carmichael's mouth set stubbornly. I'd seen that expression on his face before, in the Hallman greenhouse. "His brother Jerry is sicker. We don't want any more killings."

"That's my point exactly."

Carmichael turned away, refusing to argue further. "Anyway," he said from the steps, "I'm keeping guard on the house. Even if you don't see me, I'll be within call."

The low augh of a distant siren rose to an ee. Mildred shut the door on the sound, the voice of the treacherous night. Behind her freshly painted mask her face was haggard.

"They want to kill him, don't they?"

"Nonsense," Miss Parish said in her heartiest voice.

"I think we should try to get to him first," I said.

Mildred leaned on the door. "I wonder—it's barely possible he's trying to reach Mrs. Hutchinson's house. She lives directly across the highway from the Red Barn."

"Who on earth is Mrs. Hutchinson?" Miss Parish said.

"My sister-in-law's housekeeper. She has Zinnie's little girl with her."

"Why don't you phone Mrs. Hutchinson?"

"She has no phone, or I'd have been in touch long ago. I've been worried about Martha. Mrs. Hutchinson means well, but she's an old woman."

Miss Parish gave her a swift, dark look. "You don't seriously think there's any danger to the child?"

"I don't know."

None of us knew. On a deeper level than I'd been willing to recognize till now, I experienced fear. Fear of the treacherous darkness around us and inside of us, fear of the blind destruction that had wiped out most of a family and threatened the rest.

"We could easily check on Martha," I said, "or have the police check."

"Let's keep them out of it for now," Miss Parish said. "What's this Mrs. Hutchinson's address?"

"Fourteen Chestnut Street. It's a little white frame cottage between Elmwood and the highway." Mildred opened the door and pointed down the street. "I can easily show you."

"No. You better stay here, dear."

Rose Parish's face was dismal. She was afraid, too.

Chapter 26

M RS. HUTCHINSON'S cottage was the third of three similar houses built on narrow lots between Elmwood and the highway. Only one side of the short block was built up. The other side was vacant ground overgrown with scrub oaks. A dry creek, brimming with darkness, cut along the back of the empty lots. Beyond the continuous chain-lightning of the highway headlights, I could see the neon outline of the Red Barn, with cars clustered around it.

A softer light shone through lace curtains in Mrs. Hutchinson's front window. When I knocked on the door, a heavy shadow moved across the light. The old woman spoke through the closed door:

"Who is that?"

"Archer. We talked this morning at the Hallman ranch."

She opened the door cautiously and peered out. "What do you want?"

"Is Martha with you?"

"Sure she is. I put her to bed in my room. It looks like she's spending the night."

"Has anyone else been here?"

"The child's mother was in and out. She didn't waste much time on us, I can tell you. Mrs. Hallman has more important things on her mind than her little orphan daughter. But don't let me get started on that or I'll keep you standing on the steps all night." She glanced inquiringly at Rose Parish. With the excessive respect for privacy of her class, she had avoided noticing her till now.

"This is Miss Parish, from the state hospital."

"Pleased to meet you, I'm sure. You folks come inside, if you want. I'll ask you to be as quiet as you can. Martha isn't asleep yet. The poor child's all keyed up."

The door opened directly into the front room. The room was small and neat, warmed by rag rugs on the floor, an afghan on the couch. Embroidered mottoes on the plasterboard walls went with the character lines in the old woman's face. A piece of wool with knitting needles in it lay on the arm of a chair. She picked it up and hid it in a drawer, as if it was evidence of criminal negligence in her housekeeping.

"Sit down, if you can find a place to sit. Did you say you were from the state hospital? They offered me a job there once, but I always liked private work better."

Rose Parish sat beside me on the couch. "Are you a nurse, Mrs. Hutchinson?"

"A special nurse. I started to train for an R.N. but I never got my cap. Hutchinson wouldn't wait. Would you be an R.N., Miss?"

"I'm a psychiatric social worker. I suppose that makes me a sort of nurse. Carl Hallman was one of my patients."

"You wanted to ask me about him? Is that it? I say it's a crying shame what happened to that boy. He used to be as nice as you could want. There in that house, I watched him change right in front of my eyes. I could see his mother's trouble coming out in him like a family curse, and not one of them made a move to help him until it was too late."

"Did you know his mother?" I said.

"Know her? I nursed her for over a year. Waited on her hand and foot, day and night. I should say I did know her. She was the saddest woman you ever want to see, specially toward the end there. She got the idea in her head that nobody loved her, nobody ever *did* love her. Her husband didn't love her, her family didn't love her, even her poor dead parents didn't love her when they were alive. It became worse when Carl went away to school. He was always her special darling, and she depended on him. After he left home, she acted like there was nothing for her in life except those pills she took."

"What kind of pills?" Rose Parish said. "Barbiturates?"

"Them, or anything else she could get her hands on. She was addicted for many years. I guess she ran through every doctor in town, the old ones and then the new ones, ending up with Dr. Grantland. It isn't for me to second-guess a doctor, but I used to think those pills he let her have were her main trouble. I got up my nerve and told him so, one day toward the end. He said that he was trying to limit her, but Mrs. Hallman would be worse off without them."

"I doubt that," Rose Parish said. "He should have committed her; he might have saved her life."

"Did the question ever come up, Mrs. Hutchinson?"

"Between me and her it did, when doctor first sent me out there to look after her. I had to use *some* kind of leverage on her. She was a sad, spoiled woman, spoiled rotten all her life. She was always hiding her pills on me, and taking more than her dosage. When I bawled her out for it, she pulled out that little gun she kept under her pillow. I told her she'd have to give up those shenanigans, or the doctor would have to commit her. She said he better not. She said if he tried it on her, she'd kill herself and ruin him. As for me, I'd never get another job in this town. Oh, she could be a black devil when she was on the rampage."

Breathing heavily with remembered anger, Mrs. Hutchinson looked up at the wall above her armchair. An embroidered motto there exhorted Christian charity. It calmed her visibly. She said:

"I don't mean she was like that all the time, just when she had a spell. Most of the time she wasn't a bad sort of lady to have to deal with. I've dealt with worse. It's a pity what had to happen to her. And not only her. You young people don't read the Bible any more. I know that. There's a line from the Word keeps running in my head since all this trouble today. 'The fathers have eaten sour grapes, and the children's teeth are set on edge'."

"Right out of Freud," Rose Parish said in a knowing undertone.

I thought she was putting the cart in front of the horse, but I didn't bother arguing. The Old Testament words reverberated in my mind. I cut their echo short, and brought Mrs. Hutchinson back to the line of questioning I'd stumbled upon:

"It's funny they'd let Mrs. Hallman have a gun."

"All the ranch women have them, or used to have. It was a hangover from the old days when there were a lot of hoboes and outlaws wandering around in the west. Mrs. Hallman told me once her father sent her that gun, all the way from the old country—he was a great traveler. She took a pride in it, the way another kind of woman would take pride in a piece of jewelry. It was something like a gewgaw at that—a short-barreled little thing with a pearl handle set in filigree work. She used to spend a lot of time cleaning and polishing it. I remember the fuss she made when the Senator wanted to take it away from her."

"I'm surprised he didn't," Rose Parish said. "We don't even permit nailfiles or bottles on our closed wards."

"I know that, and I told the Senator it was a danger to her. He was a hard man to understand in some ways. He couldn't really admit to himself that there was anything the matter with her mind. It was the same with his son later. He believed that their troubles were just notions, that all they wanted was to attract some attention to themselves. He let her keep that gun in her room, and the box of shells that went with it, right up to the day of her death. You'd almost think," she added with the casual insight of the old, "you'd almost think he wanted her to do herself a harm. Or somebody else."

"Somebody else?" I said.

Mrs. Hutchinson reddened and veiled her eyes. "I didn't mean anything, I was only talking."

"You said Mrs. Hallman had that gun right up to the day of her death. Do you know that for a fact?"

"Did I say that? I didn't mean it that way."

There was a breathing silence.

"How did you mean it?"

"I wasn't trying to pin down any exact time. What I said was in a general manner of speaking."

"*Did* she have it on the day of her death?"

"I can't remember. It was a long time ago—more than three years. It doesn't matter, anyway." Her statement had the force of a question. Her gray head turned toward me, the skin of her neck stretched in diagonal folds like recalcitrant material being twisted under great pressure.

"Do you know what happened to Mrs. Hallman's gun?"

"I never was told, no. For all I know it's safe at the bottom of the ocean."

"Mrs. Hallman had it the night she drowned herself?"

"I didn't say that. I don't know."

"Did she drown herself?"

"Sure she did. But I couldn't swear to it. I didn't see her jump in." Her pale gaze was still on me, cold and watchful under slack folded lids. "What is it that's so important about her gun? Do you know where it is?"

"Don't you?"

The strain was making her irritable. "I wouldn't be asking you if I knew all about it, would I?"

"The gun is in an evidence case in the sheriff's office. It was used to shoot Jerry Hallman today. It's strange you don't know that, Mrs. Hutchinson."

"How would *I* know what they shot him with?" But the color of confusion had deepened in her face. Its vessels were purplish and congested with the hot shame of an unpracticed barefaced liar. "I didn't even hear the shot, let alone see it happen."

"There were two shots."

"That's news to me. I didn't hear either one of them. I was in the front room with Martha, and she was playing with that silver bell of her mother's. It drowned out everything."

The old woman sat in a listening attitude, screwing up her face as if she was hearing the shots now, after a long delay. I was certain that she was lying. Apart from the evidence of her face, there was at least one discrepancy in her story. I scanned back across the rush and welter of the day, trying to pin it down, but without success. Too many words had been spilled. The sense of discrepancy persisted in my mind, a gap in the known through which the darkness threatened, like sea behind a dike.

Mrs. Hutchinson shuffled her slippered feet in token flight. "Are you trying to tell me I shot him?"

"I made no such accusation. I have to make one, though. You're hiding something."

"Me hide something? Why should I do that?"

"It's the question I'm asking myself. Perhaps you're protecting a friend, or think you are."

"My friends don't get into that kind of trouble," she said angrily.

"Speaking of friends, have you known Dr. Grantland long?"

"Long enough. That doesn't mean we're friends." She corrected herself hastily: "A special nurse doesn't consider herself friends with her doctors, not if she knows her place."

"I gather he got you your job with the Hallmans."

"He recommended me."

"And he drove you into town today, shortly after the shooting."

"He wasn't doing it for me. He was doing it for *her*."

"I know that. Did he mention the shooting to you?"

"I guess he did. Yes. He mentioned it, said it was a terrible thing."

"Did he mention the gun that was used?"

She hesitated before answering. The color left her face. Otherwise she was completely immobile, concentrating on what she would say and its possible implications. "No. Martha was with us, and all. He didn't say anything about the gun."

"It still seems queer to me. Grantland saw the gun. He told me himself that he recognized it, but wasn't certain of the identification. He must have known that you were familiar with it."

"I'm no expert on guns."

"You gave me a good description of it just now. In fact, you probably knew it as well as anyone alive. But Grantland didn't say a word to you about it, ask you a single question. Or did he?"

There was another pause. "No. He didn't say a word."

"Have you seen Dr. Grantland since this afternoon?"

"What if I have?" she answered stolidly.

"Has Grantland been here tonight?"

"What if he was? Him coming here had nothing to do with me."

"Who did it have to do with? Zinnie?"

Rose Parish stirred on the couch beside me, nudging my knee with hers. She made a small coughing noise of distress. This encouraged Mrs. Hutchinson, as perhaps it was intended to. I could practically see her resistance solidifying. She sat like a monument in flowered silk:

"You're trying to make me talk myself out of a job. I'm too old to get another job. I've got too much property to qualify for the pension, and not enough to live on." After a pause, she said: "No! I'm falsifying myself. I could always get along someway. It's Martha that keeps me on the job. If it wasn't for her, I would have quit that house long ago."

"Why?"

"It's a bad-luck house, that's why. It brings bad luck to everybody who goes there. Yes, and I'd be happy to see it burn to the ground like Sodom. That may sound like a terrible thing for a Christian woman to say. No loss of life; I wouldn't wish that on them; there's been loss of life enough. I'd just like to see that house destroyed, and that family scattered forevermore."

I thought without saying it that Mrs. Hutchinson was getting her awesome wish.

"What are you leading up to?" I said. "I know the doctor and Zinnie Hallman are interested in each other. Is that the fact you're trying to keep from spilling? Or is there more?"

She weighed me in the balance of her eyes. "Just who are you, Mister?"

"I'm a private detective—"

"I know that much. Who're you detecting for? And who against?"

"Carl Hallman asked me to help him."

"Carl did? How could that be?"

I explained briefly how it could be. "He was seen in your neighborhood tonight. It's why Miss Parish and I came here to your house, to head off any possible trouble."

"You think he might try and do something to the child?"

"It occurred to us as a possibility," Rose Parish said. "I wouldn't worry about it. We probably went off half-cocked. I honestly don't believe that Carl would harm anyone."

"What about his brother?"

"I don't believe he shot his brother." She exchanged glances with me. "Neither of us believes it."

"I thought, from the paper and all, they had it pinned on him good."

"It nearly always looks like that when they're hunting a suspect," I said.

"You mean it isn't true?"

"It doesn't have to be."

"Somebody else did it?"

Her question hung unanswered in the room. An inner door at the far end was opening slowly, softly. Martha slipped in through the narrow aperture. Elfin in blue sleepers, she scampered into the middle of the room, stood and looked at us with enormous eyes.

Mrs. Hutchinson said: "Go back to bed, you minx."

"I won't. I'm not sleepy."

"Come on, I'll tuck you in."

The old woman rose ponderously and made a grab for the child, who evaded her.

"I want Mommy to tuck me in. I want my Mommy."

In the middle of her complaint, Martha stopped in front of Rose Parish. A reaching innocence, like an invisible antenna, stretched upward from her face to the woman's face, and was met by a similar reaching innocence. Rose opened her arms. Martha climbed into them.

"You're bothering the lady," Mrs. Hutchinson said.

"She's no bother, are you, honey?"

The child was quiet against her breast. We sat in silence for a bit. The tick of thought continued like a tiny stitching in my consciousness or just below it, trying to piece together the rags and bloody tatters of the day. My thoughts threatened the child, the innocent one, perhaps the only one who was perfectly innocent. It wasn't fair that her milk teeth should be set on edge.

Chapter 27

NOISES FROM outside, random voices and the scrape of boots, pulled me out of my thoughts and to the door. A guerrilla formation of men carrying rifles and shotguns went by in the street. A second, smaller group was fanning out across the vacant lots toward the creekbed, probing the tree-clotted darkness with their flashlights.

The man directing the second group wore some kind of uniform. I saw when I got close to him that he was a city police sergeant.

"What's up, Sergeant?"

"Manhunt. We got a lunatic at large in case you don't know it."

"I know it."

"If you're with the posse, you're supposed to be searching farther up the creek."

"I'm a private detective working on this case. What makes you think that Hallman's on this side of the highway?"

"The carhop at the Barn says he came through the culvert. He came up the creek from the beach, and the chances are he's following it right on up. He may be long gone by now, though. She was slow in passing the word to us."

"Where does the creekbed lead to?"

"Across town." He pointed east with his flashlight. "All the way to the mountains, if you stay with it. But he won't get that far, not with seventy riflemen tracking him."

"If he's gone off across town, why search around here?"

"We can't take chances with him. He may be lying doggo. We don't have the trained men to go through all the houses and yards, so we're concentrating on the creek." His light came up to my face for a second. "You want to pitch in and help?"

"Not right now." With seventy hunters after a single buck, conditions would be crowded. "I left my red hat home."

"Then you're taking up my time, fellow."

The sergeant moved off among the trees. I walked to the end of the block and crossed the highway, six lanes wide at this point.

The Red Barn was a many-windowed building which stood in the center of a blacktop lot on the corner. Its squat pentagonal structure was accentuated by neon tubing along the eaves and corners. Inside this brilliant red cage, a tall-hatted short-order cook kept several waitresses running between his counter and the cars in the lot. The waitresses wore red uniforms and little red caps which made them look like bellhops in skirts. The blended odors of gasoline fumes and frying grease changed in my nostrils to a foolish old hot-rod sorrow, nostalgia for other drive-ins along roads I knew in prewar places before people started dying on me.

It seemed that my life had dwindled down to a series of one-night stands in desolate places. Watch it, I said to myself; self-pity is the last refuge of little minds and aging professional hardnoses. I knew the desolation was my own. Brightness had fallen from my interior air.

A boy and a girl in a hand-painted lavender Chevrolet coupé made me feel better, for some reason. They were sitting close, like a body with two ducktailed heads, taking alternate sips of malted milk from the same straw, germ-free with love. Near them in a rusty Hudson a man in a workshirt, his dark and hefty wife, three or four children whose eyes were brilliant and bleary with drive-in-movie memories, were eating mustard-dripping hot dogs with the rapt solemnity of communicants.

Among the half-dozen other cars, one in particular interested me. It was a fairly new Plymouth two-door with Purissima *Record* lettered across the door. I walked over for a closer look.

A molded prewar Ford with a shackled rear end and too much engine came off the highway on banshee tires and pulled up beside the Plymouth. The two boys in the front seat looked me over with bold and planless eyes and forgot about me. I was a pedestrian, earth-borne. While they were waiting for a carhop, they occupied themselves with combing and rearranging their elaborate hair-structures. This process took a long time, and continued after one of the waitresses came up to the side of their car. She was a little blonde, pert-breasted in her tight uniform.

"Drive much?" she said to the boys. "I saw you come into the lot. You want to kill it before it multiplies."

"A lecture," the boy at the wheel said.

The other boy leaned toward her. "It said on the radio Gwen saw the killer."

"That's right, she's talking to the reporter now."

"Did he pull a gun on her?"

"Nothing like that. She didn't even know he *was* the killer."

"What did he *do?*" the driver said. He sounded very eager, as if he was seeking some remarkable example to emulate.

"Nothing. He was poking around in the garbage pails. When he saw her, he took off. Listen, kids, I'm busy. What'll it be?"

"You got a big George, George?" the driver asked his passenger.

"Yeah, I'm loaded. We'll have the usual, barbecued baby and double martinis. On second thought, make it a couple of cokes."

"Sure, kids, have yourselves a blast." She came around the Plymouth to me. "What can I do for you, sir?"

I realized I was hungry. "Bring me a hamburger, please."

"Deluxe, Stackburger, or Monarch? Monarchburger is the seventy-five-center. It's bigger, and you get free potatoes with it."

"Free potatoes sounds good."

"You can eat it inside if you want."

"Is Gwen inside? I want to talk to her."

"I wondered if you were plainclothes. Gwen's out behind with Gene Slovekin from the paper. He wanted to take her picture."

She indicated an open gate in the grapestake fence that surrounded the rear of the lot. There were several forty-gallon cans beside the gate. I looked into the nearest one. It was half full of a greasy tangle of food and other waste. Carl Hallman was hard-pressed.

On the other side of the gate, a footpath led along the bank of the creek. The dry bed of the creek was lined with concrete here, and narrowed down to a culvert which ran under the highway. This was high enough for a man to walk upright through it.

Slovekin and the carhop were coming back along the path toward me. She was thirtyish and plump; her body looked like a ripe tomato in her red uniform. Slovekin was carrying a camera with a flashbulb attachment. His tie was twisted, and he walked as if he was tired. I waited for them beside the gate.

"Hello, Slovekin."

"Hello, Archer. This is a mad scramble."

The carhop turned to him. "If you're finished with me, Mr. Slovekin, I got to get back to work. The manager'll be docking me, and I got a kid in school."

"I was hoping to ask you a couple of questions," I said.

"Gee, I dunno about that."

"I'll fill you in," Slovekin said, "if it doesn't take too long. Thanks, Gwen."

"You're more than welcome. Remember you promised I could have a print. I haven't had my picture taken since God made little green apples."

She touched the side of her face, delicately, hopefully, and hustled into the building on undulating hips. Slovekin deposited the camera in the back seat of his press car. We got into the front.

"Did she see Hallman enter the culvert?"

"Not actually," Slovekin said. "She made no attempt to follow him. She thought he was just a bum from the jungle on the other side of the tracks. Gwen didn't catch onto who he was until the police got here and asked some questions. They came up the creekbed from the beach, incidentally, so he couldn't have gone that way."

"What was his condition?"

"Gwen's observations aren't worth much. She's a nice girl, but not very bright. Now that she knows who he is, he was seven feet tall with horns and illuminated revolving eyeballs." Slovekin moved restlessly, turning the key in the ignition. "That's about all there is here. Can I drop you anywhere? I'm supposed to cover the movements of the sheriff's posse." His intonation satirized the phrase.

"Wear your bulletproof vest. Turning seventy hunters loose in a town is asking for double trouble."

"I agree. So does Spaulding, my editor. But we report the news, we don't make it. You got any for me, by any chance?"

"Can I talk off the record?"

"I'd rather have it on. It's getting late, and I don't mean late at night. We've never had a lynching in Purissima, but it could happen here. There's something about insanity, it frightens people, makes *them* irrational, too. Their worst aggressions start popping out."

"You sound like an expert in mob psychology," I said.

"I sort of am. It runs in the family. My father was an Austrian Jew. He got out of Vienna one jump ahead of the storm troopers. I also inherited a prejudice in favor of the underdog. So if you know something that will let Hallman off the hook, you better spill it. I can have it on the radio in ten minutes."

"He didn't do it."

"Do you know he didn't for certain?"

"Not quite. I'd stake my reputation on it, but I have to do better than that. Hallman's being used as a patsy, and a lot of planning went into it."

"Who's behind it?"

"There's more than one possibility. I can't give you any names."

"Not even off the record?"

"What would be the use? I haven't got enough to prove a case. I don't have access to the physical evidence, and I can't depend on the official interpretation of it."

"You mean it's been manipulated?"

"Psychologically speaking, anyway. There may have been some actual tampering. I don't know for sure that the gun that was found in the greenhouse fired the slugs in Jerry Hallman."

"The sheriff's men think so."

"Have they run ballistics tests?"

"Apparently. The fact that it was his mother's gun has generated a lot of heat downtown. They're going into ancient history. The rumor's running around that Hallman killed his mother, too, and possibly his father, and the family money got him off and hushed it up." He gave me a quick, sharp look. "Could there be anything in that?"

"You sound as if you're buying it yourself."

"I wouldn't say that, but I know some things it could jibe with. I went to see the Senator last Spring, just a few days before he died." He paused to organize his thoughts, and went on more slowly. "I had dug up certain facts about a certain county official whose re-election was coming up in May. Spaulding thought the Senator ought to know these facts, because he'd been supporting this certain official for a good many years. So had the paper, as a matter of fact. The paper generally went along with Senator Hallman's ideas on county government.

Spaulding didn't want to change that policy without checking with Senator Hallman. He was a big minority stockholder in the paper, and you might say the local elder statesman."

"If you're trying to say he was county boss and Ostervelt was one of his boys, why beat around the bush?"

"It wasn't quite that simple, but that's the general picture. All right, so you know." Slovekin was young and full of desire, and his tone became competitive: "What you don't know is the nature of my facts. I won't go into detail, but I was in a position to prove that Ostervelt had been taking regular payoff money from houses of prostitution. I showed Senator Hallman my affidavits. He was an old man, and he was shocked. I was afraid for a while that he might have a heart attack then and there. When he calmed down, he said he needed time to think about the problem, perhaps talk it over with Ostervelt himself. I was to come back in a week. Unfortunately, he died before the week was up."

"All very interesting. Only I don't see how it fits in with the idea that Carl killed him."

"It depends on how you look at it. Say Carl did it and Ostervelt pinned it on him, but kept the evidence to himself. It would give Ostervelt all the leverage he needed to keep the Hallman family in line. It would also explain what happened afterwards. Jerry Hallman went to a lot of trouble to quash our investigation. He also threw all his weight behind Ostervelt's re-election."

"He might have done that for any number of reasons."

"Name one."

"Say he killed his father himself, and Ostervelt knew it."

"You don't believe that," Slovekin stated.

He looked around nervously. The little blonde ankled up to the side of the car with my Monarchburger. I said, when she was out of hearing:

"This is supposed to be a progressive county. How does Ostervelt keep his hold on it?"

"He's been in office a long time, and, as you know, he's got good political backing, at least until now. He knows where the bodies are buried. You might say he's buried a couple of them himself."

"Buried them himself?"

"I was speaking more or less figuratively." Slovekin's voice had sunk to a worried whisper. "He's shot down one or two escaping prisoners—shootings that a lot of the townspeople didn't think were strictly necessary. The reason I mention it—I wouldn't want to see *you* end up with a hole in the back."

"That's a hell of a thought, when I'm eating a sandwich."

"I wish you'd take me seriously, Archer. I didn't like what happened between you this afternoon."

"Neither did I."

Slovekin leaned toward me. "Those names you have in mind that you won't give me—is Ostervelt one of them?"

"He is now. You can write it down in your little black book."

"I already have, long ago."

Chapter 28

I WAITED for the green light and walked back across the high-way. Chestnut Street was empty again, except for my car at the curb, and another car diagonally across from it near the corner of Elmwood. It hadn't been there before, or I would have noticed it.

It was a new red station wagon very like the one I had seen in the drive of the Hallman ranch-house. I went up the street and looked in at the open window on the driver's side. The key was in the ignition. The registration slip on the steering-post had Jerry Hallman's name on it.

Evidently Zinnie had come back to tuck her baby in. I glanced across the roof of the wagon toward Mrs. Hutchinson's cottage. Her light shone steadily through the lace-veiled windows. Everything seemed peaceful and as it should be. Yet a sense of disaster came down on me like a ponderous booby trap.

Perhaps I'd glimpsed and guessed the meaning of the blanket-covered shape on the floor at the rear of the wagon. I opened the back door and pulled the blanket away. So white that it seemed luminous, a woman's body lay huddled in the shadow.

I turned on the ceiling light and Zinnie jumped to my vision. Her head was twisted toward me, glaring at me open-eyed. Her grin of fear and pain had been fixed in the rictus of death. There were bloody slits in one of her breasts and in her abdomen. I touched the unwounded breast, expecting a marble coldness. The body was still warm, but unmistakably dead. I drew the blanket over it again, as if that would do any good.

Darkness flooded my mind for an instant, whirling like black water in which three bodies turned unburied. Four. I lost my Monarchburger in the gutter. Sweating cold, I looked up and down the street. Across the corner of the vacant lot, a concrete bridge carried Elmwood Street over the creekbed. Further up the creek, around a bend, I could see the moving lights of the sergeant and his men.

I could tell them what I had found, or I could keep silent. Slovekin's talk of lynching was fresh in my thought. Under it I had an urge to join the hunt, run Hallman down and kill him.

Because I distrusted that urge, I made a decision which probably cost a life. Perhaps it saved another.

I closed the door, left the wagon as it stood, and went back to Mrs. Hutchinson's house. The sight of me seemed to depress her, but she invited me in. Before I stepped inside, I pointed out the red wagon:

"Isn't that Mrs. Hallman's car?"

"I believe so. I couldn't swear to it. She drives one like it."

"Was she driving it tonight?"

The old woman hesitated. "She was in it."

"You mean someone else was driving?"

She hesitated again, but she seemed to sense my urgency.

When her words finally came, they sounded as if an inner dam had burst, releasing waves of righteous indignation:

"I've worked in big houses, with all sorts of people, and I learned long ago to hold my tongue. I've done it for the Hallmans, and I'd go on doing it, but there's a limit, and I've reached mine. When a brand-new widow goes out on the town the same night her husband was killed—"

"Was Dr. Grantland driving the car? This is important, Mrs. Hutchinson."

"You don't have to tell me that. It's a crying shame. Away they go, as gay as you please, and the devil take the hindmost. I never did think much of her, but I used to consider him a fine young doctor."

"What time were they here?"

"It was Martha's suppertime, round about six-fifteen or six-thirty. I know she spoiled the child's evening meal, running in and out like that."

"Did Grantland come in with her?"

"Yes, he came in."

"Did he say anything? Do anything?"

Her face closed up on me. She said: "It's chilly out here. Come in if you want to talk."

There was nobody else in the living-room. Rose Parish's coat lay on the couch. I could hear her behind the wall, singing a lullaby to the child.

"I'm glad for a little help with that one. I get tired," the old woman said. "Your friend seems to be a good hand with children. Does she have any of her own?"

"Miss Parish isn't married, that I know of."

"That's too bad. I was married myself for nearly forty years, but I never had one of my own either. I never had the good fortune. It was a waste of me." The wave of her indignation rose again: "You'd think that those that had would look after their own flesh and bone."

I seated myself in a chair by the window where I could watch the station wagon. Mrs. Hutchinson sat opposite me:

"Is *she* out there?"

"I want to keep an eye on her car."

"What did you mean, did Dr. Grantland say anything?"

"How did he act toward Zinnie?"

"Same as usual. Putting on the same old act, as if he wasn't interested in her, just doing his doctor's duty. As if I didn't know all about them long ago. I guess he thinks I'm old and senile, but I've got my eyes and my good ears. I've watched that woman playing him like a big stupid fish, ever since the Senator died. She's landing him, too, and he acts like he's grateful to her for slipping the gaff to him. I thought he had more sense than to go for a woman like that, just because she's come into a wad of money."

With my eye on the painted red wagon in which her body lay, I felt an obscure need to defend Zinnie:

"She didn't seem like a bad sort of woman to me."

"You talk about her like she was dead," Mrs. Hutchinson said. "Naturally you wouldn't see through her, you're a man. But I used to watch her like the flies on the wall. She came from nothing, did you know that? Mr. Jerry picked her up in a nightclub in Los Angeles, he said so in one of the arguments they had. They had a lot of arguments. She was a driving hungry woman, always hungry for something she didn't have. And when she got it, she wasn't satisfied. An unsatisfied wife is a terrible thing in this life.

"She turned against her husband after the child was born, and then she went to work to turn the child against him. She even had the brass to ask me to be a divorce-court witness for her, so's she could keep Martha. She wanted me to say that her husband treated her cruel. It would have been a lie, and I told her so. It's true they didn't get along, but he never raised a hand to her. He suffered in silence. He went to his death in silence."

"When did she ask you to testify?"

"Three-four months ago, when she thought that a divorce was what she wanted."

"So she could marry Grantland?"

"She didn't admit it outright, but that was the idea. I was surprised, surprised and ashamed for him, that he would fall for her and her shabby goods. I could have saved my feelings. They make a pair. He's no better than she is. He may be a lot worse."

"What makes you say so?"

"I *hate* to say it. I remember him when he first moved to town, an up-and-coming young doctor. There was nothing he wouldn't do for his patients. He told me once it was the great dream of his life to be a doctor. His family lost their money in the depression, and he put himself through medical school by working in a garage. He went through the college of hard knocks as well as medical college, and it taught him something. In those early days, six-eight years ago, when his patients couldn't pay him he went right on caring for them. That was before he got his big ideas."

"What happened, did he get a whiff of money?"

"More than that happened to him. Looking back, I can see that the big change in him started about three years ago. He seemed to lose interest in his medical practice. I've seen the same thing with a few other doctors, something runs down in them and something else starts up, and they go all out for the money. All of a sudden they're nothing more than pill-pushers, some of them living on their own pills."

"What happened to Dr. Grantland three years ago?"

"I don't know for sure. I can tell you it happened to more people than him, though. Something happened to me, if you want the truth."

"I do want the truth. I think you've been lying to me."

Her head jerked up as if I'd tightened a rope. She narrowed her eyes. They watched me with a faded kind of guile. I said:

"If you know something important about Alicia Hallman's death, it's your duty to bring it out."

"I've got a duty to myself, too. This thing I've kept locked up in my breast—it don't make me look good."

"You could look worse, if you let an innocent man take the blame for murder. Those men that went by in the street are after him. If you hold back until they find him and shoot him down, it's going to be too late. Too late for Carl Hallman and too late for you."

Her glance followed mine out to the street. Except for my car and Zinnie's, it was still empty. Like the street's reflection, her eyes grew dark with distant lights in them. Her mouth opened, and shut in a grim line.

"You can't sit and hold back the truth while a whole family dies off, or is killed off. You call yourself a good woman—"

"Not any more, I don't."

Mrs. Hutchinson lowered her head and looked down at her hands in her lap. On their backs the branched blue veins showed through the skin. They swelled as her fingers retracted into two clenched fists. Her voice came out half-choked, as though the moral noose had tightened on her:

"I'm a wicked woman. I did lie about that gun. Dr. Grantland brought it up on the way into town today. He brought it up again tonight when she was with the child."

"What did he say to you?"

"He said if anybody asked me about that gun, that I was to stick to my original story. Otherwise I'd be in a peck of trouble. Which I am."

"You're in less trouble than you were a minute ago. What was your original story?"

"The one he told me to tell. That she didn't have the gun the night she died. That I hadn't seen it for at least a week, or the box of shells, either."

"What happened to the shells?"

"He took them. I was to say that he took the gun and the shells away from her for her own protection."

"When did he feed you this story?"

"That very same night when he came out to the ranch."

"It was his story. Why did you buy it from him?"

"I was afraid," she said. "That night when she didn't come home and didn't come home, I was afraid she'd done herself a harm, and I'd be blamed."

"Who would blame you?"

"Everybody would. They'd say I was too old to go on nursing." The blue-veined hands opened and shut on her thighs. "I blamed myself. It was my fault. I should have stayed with her every minute, I shouldn't have let her go out. She'd had a phone call from Berkeley the evening before, something about her son, and she was upset all day. Talking about killing herself because her family deserted her and nobody loved her. She blamed it all on the Doomsters."

"The what?"

"The Doomsters. She was always talking about those Doomsters of hers. She believed her life was ruled by evil fates like, and they had killed all the love in the world the day that she was born. It was true, in a way, I guess. Nobody did love her. I was getting pretty sick of her myself. I thought if she did die it would be a relief to her and a good riddance. I took it upon myself to make that judgment which no human being has a right to do."

Her eyes seemed to focus inward, on an image in her memory. She blinked, as though the image lay under brilliant light:

"I remember the very minute I made that judgment and washed my hands of her. I walked into her room with her dinner tray, and there she was in her mink coat in front of the full-length mirror. She was loading the gun and talking to herself, about how her father abandoned her—he didn't, he just died, but she took it personally—and how her children were running out on her. She pointed the gun at herself in the mirror, and I remember thinking she ought to turn it around and put an end to herself instead of just talking about it. I didn't blame her son for running away. She was a burden on him, and on the whole family.

"I know that's no excuse for me," she added stonily. "A wicked thought is a wicked act, and it leads to wicked acts. I heard her sneak out a few minutes later, when I was making her coffee in the kitchen. I heard the car drive up and I heard it drive away. I didn't lift a finger to stop her. I just let her go, and sat there drinking coffee with the evil wish in my heart."

"Who was driving the car?"

"Sam Yogan. I didn't see him go but he was back in less than an hour. He said he dropped her off at the wharf, which was where she wanted to go. Even then, I didn't phone the police."

"Did Yogan often drive her into town?"

"She didn't go very often, but Sam did a lot of her driving for her. He's a good driver, and she liked him. He was about the only man she ever liked. Anyway, he was the only one available that night."

"Where were the rest of the family?"

"Away. The Senator and Jerry had gone to Berkeley, to try and find out where Carl was. Zinnie was staying with some friends in town here. Martha was only a few months old at the time."

"Where was Carl?"

"Nobody knew. He kind of disappeared for a while. It turned out afterwards he was in the desert all the time, over in Death Valley. At least that was his story."

"He could have been here in town?"

"He could have been, for all I know. He didn't report in to me, or anybody else for that matter. Carl didn't show up until after they found his mother in the sea."

"When did they find her?"

"Next day."

"Did Grantland come to see you before they found her?"

"Long before. He got to the ranch around midnight. I was still awake, I couldn't sleep."

"And Mrs. Hallman had left the house around dinner time?"

"Yes, around seven o'clock. She always ate at seven. That night she didn't eat, though."

"Had Grantland seen her between dinner time and midnight?"

"Not that I know of. I took it for granted he was looking for her. I never thought to ask him. I was so full of myself, and the guilt I felt. I just spilled out everything about her and the gun and me letting her go without a by-your-leave, and my wicked thoughts. Dr. Grantland said I was overexhausted, and blaming myself too much. She'd probably turn up all right. But if she didn't I was to say that I didn't know anything about any gun. That she just slipped out on me, and I took it for granted she went to town for something, maybe to see her grandchild, I didn't know what. I wasn't to mention him coming out here either. That way, they'd be more likely to believe me. Anyway, I did what Dr. Grantland said. He was a doctor. I'm only a special nurse. I don't pretend to be smart."

She let her face fall into slack and stupid folds, as if to relieve herself of responsibility. I couldn't blame her too much. She was an old woman, worn out by her ordeal of conscience, and it was getting late.

Chapter 29

ROSE PARISH came quietly into the room. She looked radiant and slightly disorganized.

"I finally got her to sleep. Goodness, it's past eleven. I didn't mean to keep you waiting so long."

"It's all right. You didn't keep me waiting."

I spent most of my working time waiting, talking and waiting. Talking to ordinary people in ordinary neighborhoods about ordinary things, waiting for truth to come up to the surface. I'd caught a glimpse of it just now, and it must have showed in my eyes.

Rose glanced from me to Mrs. Hutchinson. "Has something happened?"

"I talked his arm off, that's what happened." The old woman's face had resumed its peculiar closed look. "Thank you for helping out with the child. You ought to have some of your own to look after."

Rose flushed with pleasure, then shook her head quite sharply, as if to punish herself for the happy thought. "I'd settle for Martha any day. She's a little angel."

"Sometimes," Mrs. Hutchinson said.

A rattle in the street drew my attention back to the window. An old gray pickup had come off the highway. It slowed down as it passed the house, and stopped abreast of the station wagon. A slight, wiry figure got out of the truck on the righthand side and walked around the back of it to the wagon. I recognized Sam Yogan by his quick unhurried movements.

The truck was rattling away on Elmwood by the time I reached the wagon. Yogan was behind the wheel, trying to start it. It wouldn't start for him.

"Where are you going, Sam?"

He looked up and smiled when he saw me. "Back to the ranch. Hello."

He turned the motor over again, but it refused to catch. It sounded as though it was out of gas.

"Leave it, Sam. Get out and leave it."

His smile widened and became resistant. "No, sir. Mrs. Hall-man says take it back to the ranch."

"Did she tell you herself?"

"No, sir. Garageman phoned Juan, Juan told me."

"Garageman?"

"Yessir. He said Mrs. Hallman said to pick up the car on Chestnut Street."

"How long ago did he call?"

"Not so long. Garageman says hurry up. Juan brought me in right away."

He tried the motor again, without success. I reached across him and removed the ignition key.

"You might as well get out, Sam. The fuel line's probably cut."

He got out and started for the front of the hood. "I fix it, eh?"

"No. Come here."

I opened the back door and showed him Zinnie Hallman. I watched his face. There was nothing there but an imperturbable sorrow. If he had guilty knowledge, it was hidden beyond my reach. I didn't believe he had.

"Do you know who killed her?"

His black eyes looked up from under his corrugated forehead. "No, sir."

"It looks like whoever did it tried to blame it on you. Doesn't that make you mad?"

"No, sir."

"Don't you have any idea who it was?"

"No, sir."

"Do you remember the night old Mrs. Hallman died?"

He nodded.

"You let her off on the wharf, I believe."

"The street in front of the wharf."

"What was she doing there?"

"Said she had to meet somebody."

"Did she say who?"

"No, sir. She told me go away, don't wait. She didn't want me to see, maybe."

"Did she have her gun?"

"I dunno."

"Did she mention Dr. Grantland?"

"I don't think."

"Did Dr. Grantland ever ask you about that night?"

"No, sir."

"Or give you a story to tell?"

"No, sir." He gestured awkwardly toward the body. "We ought to tell the police."

"You're right. You go and tell them, Sam."

He nodded solemnly. I handed him the key to the wagon and showed him where to find the sergeant's party. As I was starting my own car, Rose came out of the house and got in beside me. I turned onto Elmwood, bumped over the bridge, and accelerated. The arching trees passed over us with a whoosh, like giant dark birds.

"You're in an awful hurry," she said. "Or do you always drive like this?"

"Only when I'm frustrated."

"I'm afraid I can't help you with that. Did I do something to make you angry?"

"No."

"Something *has* happened, hasn't it?"

"Something is going to. Where do you want to be dropped off?"

"I don't want to be."

"There may be trouble. I think I can promise it."

"I didn't come to Purissima with the idea of avoiding trouble. I didn't come to get killed in an auto accident, either."

The lights at the main-street intersection were flashing red. I braked to a hard stop. Rose Parish didn't go with the mood I was in. "Get out."

"I will not."

"Stop asking questions then." I turned east toward the hills.

"I will not. Is it something about Carl?"

"Yes. Now hold the thought."

It was an early-to-bed town. There was practically no traffic. A few drunks drifted and argued on the pavement in front of the bars. Two night-blooming tarts or their mothers minced purposefully toward nothing in particular. A youth on a stepladder was removing the lettering from the shabby marquee of the Mexican movie house. AMOR was the only word that was left. He started to take that down.

In the upper reaches of the main street there was no one on foot at all. The only human being in sight was the attendant of an all-night gas station. I pulled in to the curb just below Grantland's office. A light shone dimly inside, behind the glass bricks. I started to get out. Some kind of animal emerged from the shrubbery and crawled toward me onto the sidewalk.

It was a human kind of animal, a man on his hands and knees. His hands left a track of blood, black as oil drippings under my headlights. His arms gave away and he fell on his side. His face was the dirty gray of the pavement. Rica again.

Rose went to her knees beside him. She gathered his head and shoulders into her lap.

"Get him an ambulance. I think he's cut his wrists."

Rica struggled feebly in her arms. "Cut my wrists hell. You think I'm one of your psychos?"

His red hands struck at her. Blood daubed her face and smeared the front of her coat. She held him, talking softly in the voice she used for Martha:

"Poor man, you hurt yourself. How did you hurt yourself?"

"There was wire in the window-glass. I shouldn't have tried to bust it with my hands."

"Why did you want to bust it?"

"I didn't want to. He made me. He gave me a shot in the back office and said he'd be back in a minute. He never did come back. He turned the key on me."

I squatted beside him. "Grantland locked you up?"

"Yeah, and the bastard's going to pay for it." Rica's eyes swiveled toward me, heavy and occulted like ball bearings dusted with graphite. "I'm going to lock him up in San Quentin death row."

"How are you going to do that?"

"He killed an old lady, see, and I'm a witness to it. I'll stand up in any court and swear to it. You ought to've seen his office after he did it. It was a slaughterhouse, with that poor old lady lying there in the blood. And he's a dirty butcher."

"Hush now," Rose said. "Be quiet now. Take it easy."

"Don't tell him that. Do you know who she was, Tom?"

"I found out. It was old lady Hallman. He beat her to death and tossed her in the drink. And I'm the one that's gonna see him gassed for it."

"What were you doing there?"

His face became inert. "I don't remember."

Rose gave me a look of pure hatred. "I forbid you to question him. He's half out of his mind. God knows how much drug he's had, or how much blood he's lost."

"I want his story now."

"You can get it tomorrow."

"He won't be talking tomorrow. Tom, what were you doing in Grantland's office that night?"

"Nothing. I was cruising. I needed a cap, so I just dropped by to see if I could con him out of one. I heard this shot, and then this dame came out. She was dripping blood."

Tom peered at his own hands. His eyes rolled up and went blind. His head rolled loosely sideways.

I shouted in his ear: "What dame? Can you describe her?"

Rose cradled his head in her arms protectively. "We have to get him to a hospital. I believe he's had a massive overdose. Do you want him to die?"

It was the last thing I wanted. I drove back to the all-night station and asked the attendant to call an ambulance.

He was a bright-looking boy in a leather windbreaker. "Where's the accident?"

"Up the street. There's an injured man on the sidewalk in front of Dr. Grantland's office."

"It isn't Dr. Grantland?"

"No."

"I just wondered. He came in a while ago. Buys his gas from us."

The boy made the call and came out again. "They ought to be here pretty quick. Anything else I can do?"

"Did you say Dr. Grantland was here tonight?"

"Sure thing." He looked at the watch on his wrist. "Not more than thirty minutes ago. Seemed to be in a hurry."

"What did he stop for?"

"Gas. Cleaning gas, not the regular kind. He spilt something on his rug. Gravy, I think he said. It must've been a mess. He was real upset about it. The doc just got finished building himself a nice new house with wall-to-wall carpeting."

"Let's see, that's on Seaview."

"Yeah." He pointed up the street toward the ridge. "It runs

off the boulevard to the left. You'll see his name on the mailbox if you want to talk to him. Was he involved in the accident?"

"Could be."

Rose Parish was still on the sidewalk with Tom Rica in her arms. She looked up as I went by, but I didn't stop. Rose threatened something in me which I wanted to keep intact at least a little longer. As long as it would take to make Grantland pay with everything he had.

Chapter 30

HIS HOUSE stood on a terraced lot near the crest of the ridge. It was a fairly extensive layout for a bachelor, a modern redwood with wide expanses of glass and many lights inside, as though to demonstrate that its owner had nothing to hide. His Jaguar was in the slanting driveway.

I turned and stopped in the woven shadow of a pepper tree. Before I left my car, I took Maude's gun out of the dash compartment. It was a .32 caliber automatic with a full clip and an extra shell in the chamber, ready to fire. I walked down Grantland's driveway very quietly, with my hand in my heavy pocket.

The front door was slightly ajar. A rasping radio voice came from somewhere inside the house. I recognized the rhythmic monotonous clarity of police signals. Grantland had his radio tuned to the CHP dispatching station.

Under cover of the sound, I moved along the margin of the narrow light that fell across the doorstep. A man's legs and feet, toes down, were visible through the opening. My heart skipped a beat when I saw them, another beat when one of the legs moved. I kicked the door wide open and went in.

Grantland was on his knees with a red-stained cloth in his hand. There were deeper stains in the carpet which he had been scrubbing. He whirled like an animal attacked from the rear. The gun in my hand froze him in mid-action.

He opened his mouth wide as if he was going to scream at the top of his lungs. No sound came from him. He closed his mouth. The muscles dimpled along the line of his jaw. He said between his teeth:

"Get out of here."

I closed the door behind me. The hallway was full of the smell of gasoline. Beside a telephone table against the opposite wall, a gallon can stood open. Spots of undried gasoline ran the length of the hallway.

"Did she bleed a lot?" I said.

He got up slowly, watching the gun in my hand. I patted his flanks. He was unarmed. He backed against the wall and leaned there chin down, folding his arms across his chest, like a man on a cold night.

"Why did you kill her?"

"I don't know what you're talking about."

"It's a little late for that gambit. Your girl's dead. You're a dead pigeon yourself. But they can always use good hospital orderlies in the pen. Maybe you'll get some consideration if you talk."

"Who do you think you are? God?"

"I think maybe you did, Grantland. The big dream is over now. The best you have to hope for is a little consideration from a jury."

He looked down at the spotted carpet under his feet. "Why would I kill Zinnie? I loved her."

"Sure you did. You fell in love with her as soon as she got within one death of five million dollars. Only now she's one death past it, no good to you, no good to anybody."

"Do you have to grind my nose in it?" His voice was dull with the after-boredom of shock.

I felt a flicker of sympathy for him, which I repressed. "Come off it. If you didn't cut her yourself, you're covering for the ripper."

"No. I swear I'm not. I don't know who it was. I wasn't here when it happened."

"But Zinnie was?"

"Yes, she was. She was tired and ill, so I put her to bed in my room. I had an emergency patient, and had to leave the house." His face was coming to life as he talked, as though he saw an opening that he could slip through. "When I returned, she was gone. I was frantic. All I could think of was getting rid of the blood."

"Show me the bedroom."

Reluctantly, he detached himself from the support of the wall. I followed him through the door at the end of the hallway, into the lighted bedroom. The bed had been stripped. The bloody bedclothes, sheets and electric blanket, lay in the middle of the floor with a heap of women's clothes on top of them.

"What were you going to do with these? Burn them?"

"I guess so," he said with a wretched sidewise look. "There was nothing between us, you understand. My part in all this was perfectly innocent. But I knew what would happen if I didn't get rid of the traces. I'd be blamed."

"And you wanted someone else to be blamed, as usual. So you bundled her body into her station wagon and left it in the lower town, near where Carl Hallman was seen. You kept track of his movements by tuning in the police band. In case he wasn't available for the rap, you phoned the ranch and brought Zinnie's servants in, as secondary patsies."

Grantland's face took on its jaundiced look. He sat on the edge of the mattress with his head down. "You've been keeping track of my movements, have you?"

"It's time somebody did. Who was the emergency patient who called you out tonight?"

"It doesn't matter. Nobody you know."

"You're wrong again. It matters, and I've known Tom Rica for a good many years. You gave him an overdose of heroin and left him to die."

Grantland sat in silence. "I gave him what he asked for."

"Sure. You're very generous. He wanted a little death. You gave him the whole works."

Grantland began to speak rapidly, surrounding himself with a protective screen of words:

"I must have made a mistake in the dosage. I didn't know how much he was used to. He was in a bad way, and I had to give him something for temporary relief. I intended to have him moved to the hospital. I see now I shouldn't have left him without an attendant. Apparently he was worse off than I realized. These addicts are unpredictable."

"Lucky for you they are."

"Lucky?"

"Rica isn't quite dead. He was even able to do some talking before he lost consciousness."

"Don't believe him. He's a pathological liar, and he's got a grudge against me. I wouldn't provide him with drugs—"

"Wouldn't you? I thought that's what you were doing, and I've been wondering why. I've also been wondering what happened in your office three years ago."

"When?" He was hedging for time, time to build a story with escape hatches, underground passages, somewhere, anywhere to hide.

"You know when. How did Alicia Hallman die?"

He took a deep breath. "This will come as a surprise to you. Alicia died by accident. If anyone was culpable, it was her son Jerry who was. He'd made a special night appointment for her, and drove her to my office himself. She was terribly upset about something, and she wanted drugs to calm her nerves. I wouldn't prescribe any for her. She pulled a gun out of her purse and tried to shoot me with it. Jerry heard the shot. He rushed in from the waiting-room and grappled with her. She fell and struck her head on the radiator. She was mortally hurt. Jerry begged me to keep it quiet, to protect him and his mother's name and save the family from scandal. I did what I could to shield them. They were my friends as well as my patients."

He lowered his head, the serviceable martyr.

"It's a pretty good story. Are you sure it wasn't rehearsed?"

He looked up sharply. His eyes met mine for an instant. There were red fiery points in their centers. They veered away past me to the window and I glanced over my shoulder. The window framed only the half-lit sky above the city.

"Is that the story you told Carl this morning?"

"It is, as a matter of fact. Carl wanted the truth. I felt I had no right to keep it from him. It had been a load on my conscience for three years."

"I know how conscientious you are, Doctor. You got your hooks into a sick man, told him a lying story about his mother's death, gave him a gun and sicked him on his brother and turned him loose."

"It wasn't like that. He asked to see the gun. It was evidence of the truth. I suppose I'd kept it with that in mind. I brought it out of the safe and showed it to him."

"You kept it with murder in mind. You had it loaded, ready for him, didn't you?"

"That simply isn't so. Even if it were, you could never prove it. Never. He grabbed the gun and ran. I was helpless to stop him."

"Why did you lie to him about his mother's death?"

"It wasn't a lie."

"Don't contradict me, brother." I wagged the gun to remind him of it. "It wasn't Jerry who drove his mother into town. It was Sam Yogan. It wasn't Jerry who beat her to death. He was in Berkeley with his father. You wouldn't stick your neck out for Jerry, anyway. I can only think of two people you'd take that risk for—yourself, or Zinnie. Was Zinnie in your office with Alicia?"

He looked at me with flaring eyes, as if his brains were burning in his skull. "Go on. This is very interesting."

"Tom Rica saw a woman come out of there dripping blood. Was Zinnie wounded by Alicia's shot?"

"It's your story," he said.

"All right. I think it was Zinnie. She panicked and ran. You stayed behind and disposed of her mother-in-law's body. Your only motive was self-protection, but Zinnie wouldn't think of that, with the fear and guilt she had on her mind. She wouldn't stop to think that when you pushed that body into the ocean, you were converting justifiable manslaughter into murder— making a murderer out of your true love. No doubt she was grateful to you.

"Of course she wasn't your true love at the time. She wasn't rich enough yet. You wouldn't want her, or any woman, without money. Sooner or later, though, when the Senator died, Zinnie and her husband were due to come into a lot of money. But the years dragged on, and the old man's heart kept beating, and you got impatient, tired of sweating it out, living modestly on the profits from pills while other people had millions.

"The Senator needed a little help, a little send-off. You were his doctor, and you could easily have done it for him yourself, but that's not the way you operate. Better to let somebody else take the risks. Not too many risks, of course—Zinnie was going to be worth money to you. You helped her to set the psychological stage, so that Carl would be the obvious suspect. Shifting the blame onto Carl served a double purpose. It choked off any real investigation, and it got Carl and Mildred out of the picture. You wanted the Hallman money all to yourself.

"Once the Senator was gone, there was only one hurdle left between you and the money. Zinnie wanted to take it the easy way in a divorce settlement, but her child got in the way of a divorce. I imagine you did, too. You had one death to go, for the whole five million less taxes and a wife who would have to take orders the rest of her life. That death occurred today, and you've practically admitted that you set it up."

"I admitted nothing. I gave you practical proof that Carl Hallman killed his brother. The chances are he killed Zinnie, too. He could have made it across town in a stolen car."

"How long ago was Zinnie killed?"

"I'd say about four hours."

"You're a liar. Her body was warm when I found it, less than an hour ago."

"You must have been mistaken. You may not think much of me, but I am a qualified doctor. I left her before eight, and she must have died soon after. It's midnight now."

"What have you been doing since then?"

Grantland hesitated. "I couldn't move for a long time after I found her. I simply lay on the bed beside her."

"You say you found her in bed?"

"I did find her in bed."

"How did the blood get in the hall?"

"When I was carrying her out." He shuddered. "Can't you see that I'm telling you the truth? Carl must have come in and found her asleep. Perhaps he was looking for me. After all, I'm the doctor who committed him. Perhaps he killed her to get back at me. I left the door unlocked, like an idiot."

"You wouldn't have been setting her up for him? Or would you?"

"What do you think I am?"

It was a hard question. Grantland was staring down at Zinnie's clothes, his face distorted by magnetic lines of grief. I'd known murderers who killed their lovers and grieved for them. Most of them were half-hearted broken-minded men. They killed and cried and tore their prison blankets and twisted their blankets into nooses. I doubted that Grantland fitted the pattern, but it was possible.

"I think you're basically a fool," I said, "like any other man who tries to beat the ordinary human averages. I think you're a dangerous fool, because you're frightened. You proved that when you tried to silence Rica. Did you try to silence Zinnie, too, with a knife?"

"I refuse to answer such questions."

He rose jerkily and moved to the window. I stayed close to him, with the gun between us. For a moment we stood looking down the long slope of the city. Its after-midnight lights were scattered on the hillsides, like the last sparks of a firefall.

"I really loved Zinnie. I wouldn't harm her," he said.

"I admit it doesn't seem likely. You wouldn't kill the golden goose just when she was going to lay for you. Six months from now, or a year, when she'd had time to marry you and write a will in your favor, you might have started thinking of new angles."

He turned on me fiercely. "I don't have to listen to any more of this."

"That's right. You don't. I'm as sick of it as you are. Let's go, Grantland."

"I'm not going anywhere."

"Then we'll tell them to come and get you. It will be rough while it lasts, but it won't last long. You'll be signing a statement by morning."

Grantland hung back. I prodded him along the hallway to the telephone.

"You do the telephoning, Doctor."

He balked again. "Listen. There doesn't have to be any telephoning. Even if your hypothesis were correct, which it isn't, there's no real evidence against me. My hands are clean."

His eyes were still burning with fierce and unquenched light. I thought it was a light that burned from darkness, a blind arrogance masking fear and despair. Behind his several shifting masks, I caught a glimpse of the unknown dispossessed, the hungry operator who sat in Grantland's central darkness and manipulated the shadow play of his life. I struck at the shape in the darkness.

"Your hands are dirty. You don't keep your hands clean by betraying your patients and inciting them to murder. You're a dirty doctor, dirtier than any of your victims. Your hands would be cleaner if you'd taken that gun and used it on Hallman yourself. But you haven't the guts to live your own life. You want other people to do it for you, do your living, do your killing, do your dying."

He twisted and turned. His face changed like smoke and set in a new smiling mask. "You're a smart man. That hypothesis of yours, about Alicia's death—it wasn't the way it happened, but you hit fairly close in a couple of places."

"Straighten me out."

"If I do, will you let me go? All I need is a few hours to get to Mexico. I haven't committed any extraditable offense, and I have a couple of thousand—"

"Save it. You'll need it for lawyers. This is it, Grantland." I gestured with the gun in my hand. "Pick up the telephone and call the police."

His shoulders slumped. He lifted the receiver and started to dial. I ought to have distrusted his hangdog look.

He kicked sideways and upset the gasoline can. Its contents spouted across the carpet, across my feet.

"I wouldn't use that gun," he said. "You'd be setting off a bomb."

I struck at his head with the automatic. He was a millisecond ahead of me. He swung the base of the telephone by its cord and brought it down like a sledge on top of my head.

I got the message. Over and out.

Chapter 31

I CAME to crawling across the floor of a room I'd never seen. It was a long, dim room which smelled like a gas station. I was crawling toward a window at the far end, as fast as my cold and sluggish legs would push me along.

Behind me, a clipped voice was saying that Carl Hallman was still at large, and was wanted for questioning in a second murder. I looked back over my shoulder. Time and space came together, threaded by the voice from Grantland's radio. I could see the doorway into the lighted hall from which my instincts had dragged me.

There was a puff of noise beyond the doorway, a puff of color. Flames entered the room like dancers, orange-colored and whirring. I got my feet under me and my hands on a chair, carried it to the window and smashed the glass out of the frame.

Air poured in over me. The dancing flames behind me began to sing. They postured and beckoned when I looked at them, and reached for my cold wet legs, offering to warm them. My dull brain put several facts together, like a boy playing with blocks on the burning deck, and realized that my legs were gasoline-soaked.

I went over the jagged sill, fell further than I expected to, struck the earth full length and lay whooping for breath. The fire bit into my legs like a rabid fox.

I was still going on instinct. All instinct said was, Run. The fire ran with me, snapping. The providence that suffers fools and cushions drunks and tempers the wind to shorn lambs and softening hardheads rescued me from the final barbecue. I ran blind into the rim of a goldfish pond and fell down in the water. My legs Suzette sizzled and went out.

I reclined in the shallow, smelly blessed water and looked back at Grantland's house. Flames blossomed in the window I had broken and grew up to the eaves like quick yellow hollyhocks. Orange and yellow lights appeared behind other windows. Tendrils of smoke thrust delicately through the shake roof.

In no time at all, the house was a box of brilliant jumping lights. Breaking windows tinkled distinctly. Trellised vines of flame climbed along the walls. Little flame salamanders ran up the roof, leaving bright zigzag trails.

Above the central furnace roar, I heard a car engine start. Skidding in the slime at the bottom of the pool, I got to my feet and ran toward the house. The sirens were whining in the city again. It was a night of sirens.

Radiating heat kept me at a distance from the house. I waded through flowerbeds and climbed over a masonry wall. I was in time to see Grantland gun his Jaguar out of the driveway, its twin exhausts tracing parallel curves on the air.

I ran to my car. Below, the Jaguar was dropping down the hill like a bird. I could see its lights on the curves, and further down the red shrieking lights of a fire truck. Grantland had to stop to let it pass, or I'd have lost him for good.

He crossed to a boulevard running parallel with the main street, and followed it straight through town. I thought he was on his way to the highway and Mexico, until he turned left on Elmwood, and again left. When I took the second turn, into Grant Street, the Jaguar was halfway up the block with one door hanging open. Grantland was on the front porch of Mrs. Gley's house.

The rest of it happened in ten or twelve seconds, but each of the seconds was divided into marijuana fractions. Grantland shot out the lock of the door. It took three shots to do it. He pushed through into the hallway. By that time I was braking in front of the house, and could see the whole length of the hallway to the stairs. Carl Hallman came down them.

Grantland fired twice. The bullets slowed Carl to a walk. He came on staggering, as if the knife in his lifted hand was holding him up. Grantland fired again. Carl stopped in his tracks, his arms hanging loose, came on in a spraddling shuffle.

I started to run up the walk. Now Mildred was at the foot of the stairs, clinging to the newel post. Her mouth was open, and she was screaming something. The scream was punctuated by Grantland's final shot.

Carl fell in two movements, to his knees, then forehead down on the floor. Grantland aimed across him. The gun clicked twice in his hand. It held only seven shells. Mildred shuddered under imaginary bullets.

Carl rose from the floor with a Lazarus grin, bright badges of blood on his chest. His knife was lost. He looked blind. Bare-handed he threw himself at Grantland, fell short, lay prone and still in final despair.

My feet were loud on the veranda boards. I got my hands on Grantland before he could turn, circled his neck with my arm and bent him over backwards. He was slippery and strong. He bucked and twisted and broke my hold with the hammering butt of the gun.

Grantland moved away crabwise along the wall. His face was bare as bone, a wet yellow skull from which the flesh had been dissolved away. His eyes were dark and empty like the eye of the empty gun that he was still clutching.

A door opened behind me. The hallway reverberated with the roar of another gun. A bullet creased the plaster close above Grantland's head and sprinkled it with dust. It was Ostervelt, in the half-shadow under the stairs:

"Out of the way, Archer. You, Doctor, stand still, and drop it. I'll shoot to kill you this time."

Perhaps in his central darkness Grantland yearned for death. He threw the useless gun at Ostervelt, jumped across Carl's body, took off from the veranda and seemed to run in air.

Ostervelt moved to the doorway and sent three bullets after him in rapid fire, faster than any man runs. They must have been very heavy. Grantland was pushed and hustled along by their blows, until his legs were no longer under him. I think he was dead before he struck the road.

"He oughtn't to have ran," Ostervelt said. "I'm a sharp-shooter. I still don't like to kill a man. It's too damn easy to wipe one out and too damn hard to grow one." He looked down at his Colt .45 with a kind of shamed awe, and replaced it in its holster.

I liked the sheriff better for saying that, though I didn't let it run away with me. He was looking out toward the street where Grantland's body lay. People from the other houses had already begun to converge on him. Carmichael appeared from some-where and kept them off.

Ostervelt turned to me. "How in hell did you get here? You look like you swam through a swamp."

"I followed Grantland from his house. He just got finished setting fire to it."

"Was he off his rocker, too?" Ostervelt sounded ready to believe anything.

"Maybe he was in a way. His girlfriend was murdered."

"I know that. What's the rest of the story? Hallman knocked off his girl, so Grantland knocked Hallman off?"

"Something like that."

"You got another theory?"

"I'm working on one. How long have you been here?"

"Couple of hours, off and on."

"In the house?"

"Out back, mostly. I came in through the kitchen when I heard the gunfire. I just relieved Carmichael at the back. He's been keeping guard on the house for more than four hours. According to him nobody came in or went out."

"Does that mean Hallman's been in the house all this time?"

"It sure looks like it. Why?"

"Zinnie's body was warm when I found her."

"What time was that?"

"Shortly before eleven. It's a cold night for September. If she was killed before eight, you'd expect her to lose some heat."

"That's pretty thin reasoning. Anyway, she's refrigerated now. Why in hell didn't you report what you found when you found it?"

I didn't answer him. It was no time for argument. To myself, I had to admit that I was still committed to Carl Hallman. Mental case or not, I couldn't imagine a man of his courage shooting his brother in the back or cutting a defenseless woman.

Carl was still alive. His breathing was audible. Mildred was kneeling beside him in a white slip. She'd turned his head to one side and supported it on one of his limp arms. His breath bubbled and sighed.

"Better not move him any more. I'll radio for an ambulance." Ostervelt went out.

Mildred didn't seem to have heard him. I had to speak twice before she paid any attention. She looked up through the veil of hair that had fallen over her face:

"Don't look at me."

She pushed her hair back and covered the upper parts of her

breasts with her hands. Her arms and shoulders were rough with gooseflesh.

"How long has Carl been here in the house?"

"I don't know. Hours. He's been asleep in my room."

"You knew he was here?"

"Of course. I've been with him." She touched his shoulder, very lightly, like a child fingering a forbidden object. "He came to the house when you and Miss Parish were here. While I was changing my clothes. He threw a stick at my window and came up the back stairs. That's why I had to get rid of you."

"You should have taken us into your confidence."

"Not *her*. That Parish woman hates me. She's been trying to take Carl away from me."

"Nonsense," though I suspected it wasn't entirely nonsense. "You should have told us. You might have saved his life."

"He isn't going to die. They won't let him die."

She hid her face against his inert shoulder. Her mother was watching us from the curtained doorway below the stairs. Mrs. Gley looked like the wreck of dreams. She turned away, and disappeared into the back recesses of the house.

I went outside, looking for Carmichael. The street was filling up with people now. Rifles glinted among them, but there was no real menace in the crowd. Carmichael was having no trouble keeping them away from the house.

I talked to him for a minute. He confirmed the fact that he had been watching the house from various positions since eight o'clock. He couldn't be absolutely sure, but he was reasonably sure, that no one had entered or left it in that time. Our conversation was broken up by the ambulance's arrival.

I watched two orderlies roll Carl Hallman into a wire basket. He had a leg wound, at least one chest wound, and one wound in the abdomen. That was bad, but not so finally bad as it would have been in the days before antibiotics. Carl was a durable boy; he was still breathing when they carried him out.

I looked around for the knife that had dropped from his hand. It wasn't there any longer. Perhaps the sheriff had picked it up. From what I had seen of it at a distance, it was a medium-sized kitchen knife, the kind that women use for paring or chopping. It could also have been used for stabbing Zinnie, though I still didn't see how.

I FOUND Mrs. Gley in the dim, old mildew-smelling kitchen. She was barricaded behind an enamel-topped table under a hanging bulb, making a last stand against sobriety. I smelled vanilla extract when I approached her. She clutched a small brown bottle to her breast, like an only child which I was threatening to kidnap.

"Vanilla will make you sick."

"It never has yet. Do you expect a woman to face these tragedies without a drink?"

"As a matter of fact, I could use a drink myself."

"There isn't enough for me!" She remembered her manners then: "I'm sorry, I ran out of liquor way back when. You *look* as if you could use a drink."

"Forget it." I noticed a bowl of apples on the worn woodstone sink behind her. "Mind if I peel myself an apple?"

"Please do," she said very politely. "I'll get you my paring knife."

She got up and rummaged in a drawer beside the sink. "Dunno what happened to my paring knife," she muttered, and turned around with a butcher knife in her hand. "Will this do?"

"I'll just eat it in the skin."

"They say you get more vitamins."

She resumed her seat at the table. I sat across from her on a straight-backed chair, and bit into my apple. "Has Carl been in the kitchen tonight?"

"I guess he must have been. He always used to come through here and up the back stairs." She pointed towards a half-open door in the corner of the room. Behind it, bare wooden risers mounted steeply.

"Has he come in this way before?"

"I hope to tell you he has. That boy has been preying on my little girl for more years than I care to count. He cast a spell on her with his looks and his talk. I'm glad he's finally got what's coming to him. Why, when she was a little slip of a thing in

high school, he used to sneak in through my kitchen and up to
her room."

"How do you know?"

"I've got eyes in my head, haven't I? I was keeping boarders
then, and I was ashamed they'd find out about the carryings-on
in her room. I tried to reason with her time and again, but she
was under his spell. What could I do with my girl going wrong
and no man to back me up in it? When I locked her up, she ran
away, and I had to get the sheriff to bring her back. Finally she
ran away for good, went off to Berkeley and left me all alone.
Her own mother."

Her own mother set the brown bottle to her mouth and
swallowed a slug of vanilla extract. She thrust her haggard face
toward me across the table:

"But she learned her lesson, let me tell you. When a girl
gets into trouble, she finds out that she can't do without her
mother. I'd like to know where she would have been after she
lost her baby, without me to look after her. I nursed her like
a saint."

"Was this since her marriage?"

"It was not. He got her into trouble, and he wasn't man
enough to stay around and help her out of it. He couldn't stand
up to his family and face his responsibility. My girl wasn't good
enough for him and his mucky-muck folks. So look what *he*
turned out to be."

I took another bite of my apple. It tasted like ashes. I got up
and dropped the apple into the garbage container in the sink.
Mrs. Gley depressed me. Her mind veered fuzzily, like a moth
distracted by shifting lights, across the fibrous surface of the
past, never quite making contact with its meaning.

Voices floated back from the front of the house, too far
away for me to make out the words. I went into the corridor,
which darkened as I shut the door behind me. I stayed in the
shadow.

Mildred was talking to Ostervelt and two middle-aged men
in business suits. They had the indescribable unmistakable look
of harness bulls who had made it into plain clothes but would
always feel a little uncomfortable in them. One of them was
saying:

"I can't figure out what this doctor had against him. Do you have any ideas on the subject, ma'am?"

"I'm afraid not." I couldn't see Mildred's face, but she had changed to the clothes in which she'd met Rose Parish.

"Did Carl kill his sister-in-law tonight?" Ostervelt said.

"He couldn't have. Carl came directly here from the beach. He was here with me all evening. I know I did wrong in hiding him. I'm willing to take the consequences."

"It ain't legal," the second detective said, "but I hope my wife would do the same for me. Did he mention the shooting of his brother Jerry?"

"No. We've been over that. I didn't even bring the subject up. He was dog-tired when he dragged himself in. He must have run all the way from Pelican Beach. I gave him something to eat and drink, and he went right off to sleep. Frankly, gentlemen, I'm tired, too. Can't the rest of this wait till morning?"

The detectives and the sheriff looked at each other and came to a silent agreement. "Yeah, we'll let it ride for now," the first detective said. "Under the circumstances. Thanks for your co-operation, Mrs. Hallman. You have our sympathy."

Ostervelt lingered behind after they left to offer Mildred his own brand of sympathy. It took the form of a heavy pass. One of his hands held her waist. The other stroked her body from breast to thigh. She stood and endured it.

Anger stung my eyes and made me clench my fists. I hadn't been so mad since the day I took the strap away from my father. But something held me still and quiet. I'd been wearing my anger like blinders, letting it be exploited, and exploiting it for my own unacknowledged purposes. I acknowledged now that my anger against the sheriff was the expression of a deeper anger against myself. In plain terms, he was doing what I had wanted to be doing.

"Don't be so standoffish," he was saying. "You were nice to Dr. Grantland; why can't you be nice to me?"

"I don't know what you're talking about."

"Sure you do. You're not as hard to get as you pretend to be. So why play dumb with Uncle Ostie? My yen for you goes back a long ways, kid. Ever since you were a filly in high school giving your old lady a hard time. Remember?"

Her body stiffened in his hands. "How could I forget?"

Her voice was thin and sharp, but his aging lust converted it into music. He took what she said for romantic encouragement.

"I haven't forgotten, either, baby," he said, huskily. "And things are different now, now that I'm not married any more. I can make you an offer on the up-and-up."

"*I'm* still married."

"Maybe, if he lives. Even if he does live, you can get it annulled. Carl's going to be locked up for the rest of his life. I got him off easy the first time. This time he goes to the Hospital for the Criminally Insane."

"No!"

"Yes. You been doing your best to cover for him, but you know as well as I do he knocked off his brother and sister-in-law. It's time for you to cut your losses, kid, think of your own future."

"I have no future."

"I'm here to tell you you have. I can be a lot of help to you. One hand washes the other. There's no legal proof he killed his father, without me there never will be. It's a closed case. That means you can get your share of the inheritance. Your life is just beginning, baby, and I'm a part of it, built right into it."

His hands busied themselves with her. She stood quiescent, keeping her face away from his. "You always wanted me, didn't you?"

There was despair in her voice, but he heard only the words. "More than ever now. There's plenty of shots in the old locker. I'm planning to retire next year, after we settle the case and the estate. You and me, we can go anywhere we like, do anything we want."

"Is this why you shot Grantland?"

"One of the reasons. He had it coming, anyway. I'm pretty sure he masterminded Jerry's murder, if that's any comfort to you—talked Carl into doing it. But it makes a better case without Grantland in it. This way there's no danger that the Senator's death will have to be dragged in. Or the thing between you and Grantland."

Mildred lifted her face. "That was years ago, before my marriage. How did you know about it?"

"Zinnie told me this afternoon. He told Zinnie."

"He always was a rat. I'm glad you shot him."

"Sure you are. Uncle Ostie knows best."

She let him have her mouth. He seemed to devour it. She hung limp in his arms until he released her.

"I know you're tired tonight, honey. We'll leave it lay for now. Just don't do any talking, except to me. Remember we got a couple of million bucks at stake. Are you with me?"

"You know I am, Ostie." Her voice was dead.

He lifted his hand to her and went out. She wedged a newspaper between the splintered door and the doorframe. Coming back toward the stairs, her movements were awkward and mechanical, as though her body was a walking doll run by remote control. Her eyes were like blue china, without sight, and as her heels tapped up the stairs I thought of a blind person in a ruined house tapping up a staircase that ended in nothing.

In the kitchen, Mrs. Gley was subsiding lower and lower on her bones. Her chin was propped on her arms now. The brown bottle lay empty at her elbow.

"I was thinking you deserted me," she said with elocutionary carefulness. "Everybody else has."

The blind footsteps tapped across the ceiling. Mrs. Gley cocked her head like a molting red parrot. "Izzat Mildred?"

"Yes."

"She ought to go to bed. Keep up her strength. She's never been the same since she lost that child of grief."

"How long ago did she lose it?"

"Three years, more or less."

"Did she have a doctor to look after her?"

"Sure she did. It was this same Dr. Grantland, poor fellow. It's a shame what had to happen to him. He treated her real nice, never even sent her a bill. That was before she got married, of course. Long before. I told her at the time, here was her chance to break off with that Carl and make a decent connection. A rising young doctor, and all. But she never listened to me. It had to be Carl Hallman or nothing. So now it's nothing. They're both gone."

"Carl isn't dead yet."

"He might as well be. I might as well be, too. My life is nothing but disappointment and trouble. I brought my girl up to associate with nice people, marry a fine young man. But no, she had to have him. She had to marry into trouble and sickness and death." Her drunken self-pity rose in her throat like vomit. "She did it to spite me, that's what she did. She's trying to kill me with all this trouble that she brought into my house. I used to keep a nice house, but Mildred broke my spirit. She never gave me the love that a daughter owes her mother. Mooning all the time over her no-good father—you'd think *she* was the one that married him and lost him."

Her anger wouldn't come in spite of the invocation. She looked in fear at the ceiling, blinking against the light from the naked bulb. The fear in her drained parrot's eyes refused to dissolve. It deepened into terror.

"I'm not a good mother, either," she said. "I never have been any good to her. I've been a living drag on her all these years, and may God forgive me."

She slumped forward across the table, as if the entire weight of the night had fallen on her. Her harsh red hair spilled on the white tabletop. I stood and looked at her without seeing her. A pit or tunnel had opened in my mind, three years deep or long. Under white light at the bottom of it, fresh and vivid as a hallucination, I could see the red spillage where life had died and murder had been born.

I was in a stretched state of nerves where hidden things are coming clear and ordinary things are hidden. I thought of the electric blanket on the floor of Grantland's bedroom. I didn't hear Mildred's quiet feet till she was half-way down the back stairs. I met her at the foot of them.

Her whole body jerked when she saw me. She brought it under control, and tried to smile:

"I didn't know you were still here."

"I've been talking to your mother. She seems to have passed out again."

"Poor mother. Poor everybody." She shut her eyes against the sight of the kitchen and its raddled occupant. She brushed her blue-veined eyelids with the fingertips of one hand. Her other hand was hidden in the folds of her skirt. "I suppose I should put her to bed."

"I have to talk to you first."

"What on earth about? It's terribly late."

"About poor everybody. How did Grantland know that Carl was here?"

"He didn't. He couldn't have."

"I think you're telling the truth for once. He didn't know Carl was here. He came here to kill you, but Carl was in his way. By the time he got to you, the gun was empty."

She stood silent.

"Why did Grantland want to kill you, Mildred?"

She moistened her dry lips with the tip of her tongue. "I don't know."

"I think I do. The reasons he had wouldn't drive an ordinary man to murder. But Grantland was frightened as well as angry. Desperate. He had to silence you, and he wanted to get back at you. Zinnie meant more to him than money."

"What's Zinnie got to do with me?"

"You stabbed her to death with your mother's paring knife. I didn't see at first how it was possible. Zinnie's body was warm when I found her. You were here under police surveillance. The timing didn't fit, until I realized that her body was kept warm under an electric blanket in Grantland's bed. You killed her before you drove to Pelican Beach. You heard over Grantland's radio that Carl was seen there. Isn't that true?"

"Why would I do a thing like that?" she whispered.

The question wasn't entirely rhetorical. Mildred looked as if she earnestly desired an answer. Like an independent entity, her hidden fist jumped up from the folds of her skirt to supply an answer. A pointed blade projected downward from it. She drove it against her breast.

Even her final intention was divided. The knife turned in her hand, and only tore her blouse. I had it away from her before she could do more damage.

"Give it back to me. Please."

"I can't do that." I was looking at the knife. Its blade was etched with dry brown stains.

"Then kill me. Quickly. I have to die anyway. I've known it now for years."

"You have to live. They don't gas women any more."

"Not even women like me? I couldn't bear to live. Please kill me. I know you hate me."

She tore her blouse gaping and offered her breast to me in desperate seduction. It was like a virgin's, unsunned, the color of pearl.

"I'm sorry for you, Mildred."

My voice sounded strange; it had broken through into a tone that was new to me, deep as the sorrow I felt. It had nothing to do with sex, or with the possessive pity that changed to sex when the wind blew from the south. She was a human being with more grief on her young mind than it was able to bear.

Chapter 33

MRS. GLEY groaned in her sleep. Mildred ran up the stairs away from both of us. I went up after her, across a drab brown hallway, into a room where she was struggling to raise the window.

It wasn't a woman's room, or anybody's room. It was more like an unused guestroom where unwanted things were kept: old books and pictures, an old iron double bed, a decaying rug. I felt a strange proprietary embarrassment, like a pawnbroker who's lent money on somebody else's possessions, sight unseen.

The window resisted her efforts. I saw her watching me in its dark mirror. Her own reflected face was like a ghost's peering from outer darkness.

"Go away and leave me alone."

"A lot of people have. Maybe that's the trouble. Come away from the window, eh?"

She moved back into the room and stood by the bed. There was a soiled depression in the cheap chenille spread where I guessed Carl had been lying. She sat on the edge of the iron bed.

"I don't want any of your phony sympathy. People always want to be paid for it. What do you want from me? Sex? Money? Or just to see me suffer?"

I didn't know how to answer her.

"Or do you simply want to hear me say it? Listen then, I'm a murderer. I murdered four people."

She sat and looked at the faded flowers in the wallpaper. I thought that it was a place where dreams could grow rank without much competition from the actual.

"What did you want, Mildred?"

She put a name to one of the dreams. "Money. That was what set him off from everyone—the thing that made him so handsome to me, so—shining."

"Do you mean Carl?"

"Yes. Carl." Her hand moved behind her to the depression in the spread. She leaned on it. "Even tonight, when he was lying here, all dirty and stinking, I felt so happy with him. So rich. Mother used to say I talked like a whore, but I was never a whore. I never took money from him. I gave myself to him because he needed me. The books said he had to have sex. So I used to let him come up here to the room."

"What books are you talking about?"

"The books he used to read. We read them together. Carl was afraid of going homosexual. That's why I used to pretend to be excited with him. I never really was, though, with him or any man."

"How many men were there?"

"Only three," she said, "and one of them only once."

"Ostervelt?"

She made an ugly face. "I don't want to talk about him. It was different with Carl. I'd be glad for him, but then the gladness would split off from my body. I'd be in two parts, a hot part and a cold part, and the cold part would rise up like a spirit. Then I'd imagine that I was in bed with a golden man. He was putting gold in my purse, and I'd invest it and make a profit and reinvest. Then I'd feel rich and real, and the spirit would stop watching me. It was just a game I played with myself. I never told Carl about it; Carl never really knew me. Nobody ever knew me."

She spoke with the desperate pride of loneliness and lostness. Then hurried on, as though some final disaster was about to fall, and I was her one chance to be known:

"I thought if we could get married, and I was Mrs. Carl Hallman, then I'd feel rich and solid all the time. When he went away to the university I followed him. No other girl was going to get him from me. I went to business college and found a job in Oakland. I rented an apartment of my own where he could visit me. I used to make supper for him, and help him with his studies. It was almost like being married.

"Carl wanted to make it legal, too, but his parents couldn't see it, especially his mother. She couldn't see *me*. It made me mad, the way she talked about me to Carl. You'd think I was human garbage. That was when I decided to stop taking precautions.

"It took me over a year to get our baby started. I wasn't in very good health. I don't remember very much about that time. I know I went on working in the office. They even gave me a raise. But it was the nights I lived for, not so much the times with Carl—the times after he left when I would lie awake and think about the child I was going to have. I knew that he would have to be a boy. We'd call him Carl, and bring him up just right. I'd do everything for him myself, dress him and feed him his vitamins and keep him away from bad influences, such as his grandmother. Both his grandmothers.

"After Zinnie had Martha, I thought about him all the time and I became pregnant at last. I waited two months to be sure, and then I told Carl. He was frightened, he couldn't hide it. He didn't want our baby. Mainly, he was afraid of what his mother would do. She was far gone by that time, ready to do anything to have her way. When Carl first told her about me, long before, she said she'd rather kill herself than let him marry me.

"She still had him hypnotized. I have a nasty tongue, and I told him so. I told him that he was the daring young man on the umbilical cord, but it was a hangman's noose. We had a battle. He smashed my new set of dishes in the sink. I was afraid he was going to smash me, too. Perhaps that's why he ran away. I didn't see him for days, or hear from him.

"His landlady said he'd gone home. I waited as long as I could stand it before I phoned the ranch. His mother said he hadn't been there. I thought she was lying to me, trying to get rid of me. So I told her I was pregnant, and Carl would have to marry me. She called me a liar, and other things, and then she hung up on me.

"That was a little after seven o'clock on a Friday night. I'd waited for the night rates before I phoned. I sat and watched night come on. She wouldn't let Carl come back to me, ever. I could see part of the Bay from my window, and the long ramp where the cars climbed towards the Bridge, the mud flats under it, and the water like blue misery. I thought that the place for me was in the water. And I'd have done it, too. She shouldn't have stopped me."

I had been standing over her all this time. She looked up and pushed me away with her hands, not touching me. Her movements were slow and gingerly, as if any sudden gesture might upset a delicate balance, in the room or in her, and let the whole thing collapse.

I placed a straight chair by the bed and straddled it, resting my arms on the back. It gave me a queer bedside feeling, like a quack doctor, without a bedside manner:

"Who stopped you, Mildred?"

"Carl's mother did. She should have let me kill myself and be done with it. It doesn't lessen my guilt, I know that, but Alicia brought what happened on herself. She phoned me back while I was sitting there, and told me that she was sorry for what she'd said. Could I forgive her? She'd thought the whole thing over and wanted to talk to me, help me, see that I was looked after. I believed that she'd come to her senses, that my baby would bring us all together and we'd be a happy family.

"She made an appointment for me to meet her on the Purissima wharf next evening. She said she wanted to get to know me, just the two of us. I drove down Saturday, and she was waiting in the parking lot when I got there. I'd never met her face to face before. She was a big woman, wearing mink, very tall and impressive. Her eyes shone like a cat, and her voice buzzed. I think she must have been high on some kind of drug. I didn't know it then. I was so pleased that we were coming together. I was proud to have her sitting in my old clunk in a mink coat.

"But she wasn't there to do me any favors. She started out all right, very sympathetic. It was a dirty trick Carl played on me, running out like that. The worst of it was, she had her doubts that he would ever come back. Even if he did, he'd be no bargain as a husband or a father. Carl was hopelessly unstable. She was his mother, and she ought to know. It ran in the family. Her own father had died in a sanitarium, and Carl took after him.

"Even without an ancestral curse hanging over you—that was what she called it—it was a hideous world, a crime to bring children into it. She quoted a poem to me:

> 'Sleep the long sleep;
> The Doomsters heap
> Travails and teens around us here . . .'

I don't know who wrote it, but I've never been able to get those lines out of my head.

"She said it was written to an unborn child. Teens meant heartaches and troubles, and that was all any child had to look forward to in this life. The Doomsters saw to that. She talked about those Doomsters of hers as if they really existed. We were sitting looking out over the sea, and I almost thought I could see them walking up out of the black water and looming across the stars. Monsters with human faces.

"Alicia Hallman was a monster herself, and I knew it. Yet everything she said had some truth to it. There was no way to argue except from the way I felt, about my baby. It was hard to keep my feeling warm through all the talk. I didn't have sense enough to leave her, or shut my ears. I even caught myself nodding and agreeing with her, partly. Why go to all the trouble of having a child if he was going to live in grief, cut off from the stars. Or if his daddy was never coming back.

"She almost had me hypnotized with that buzzing voice of hers, like violins out of tune. I went along with her to Dr. Grantland's office. The same part of me that agreed with her knew that I was going to lose my baby there. At the last minute, when I was on the table and it was too late, I tried to stop it. I screamed and fought against him. She came into the room with that gun of hers and told me to lie down and be quiet, or she'd kill me on the spot. Dr. Grantland didn't want to go through with it. She said if he didn't she'd run him out of his practice. He put a needle in me.

"When I came back from the anesthetic, I could see her cat eyes watching me. I had only the one thought, she had killed my baby. I must have picked up a bottle. I remember smashing it over her head. Before that, she must have tried to shoot me. I heard a gun go off, I didn't see it.

"Anyway, I killed her. I don't remember driving home, but I must have. I was still drunk on pentothal; I hardly knew what I was doing. Mother put me to bed and did what she could for me, which wasn't much. I couldn't go to sleep. I couldn't understand why the police didn't come and get me. Next day, Sunday, I went back to the doctor. He frightened me, but I was even more frightened not to go.

"He was gentle with me. I was surprised how gentle. I almost loved him when he told me what he'd done for me, making it look like a suicide. They'd already recovered her body from the sea, and nobody even asked me a question about it. Carl came back on Monday. We went to the funeral together. It was a closed-coffin funeral, and I could nearly believe that the official story of suicide was true, that the rest was just a bad dream.

"Carl thought she'd drowned herself. He took it better than I expected, but it had a strange effect on him. He said he'd been in the desert for almost a week, thinking and praying for guidance. He was coming back from Death Valley when a highway patrolman stopped him and told him his family was looking for him, and why. That was on Sunday, just before sunset.

"Carl said he looked up at the Sierra, and saw an unearthly light behind it in the west toward Purissima. It streamed, like milk, from the heavens, and it made him realize that life was a precious gift which had to be justified. He saw an Indian herding sheep on the hillside, and took it for a sign. He decided then and there to study medicine and devote his life to healing, perhaps on the Indian reservations, or in Africa like Schweitzer.

"I was carried away myself. That glorious light of Carl's seemed like an answer to the darkness I'd been in since Saturday night. I told Carl I'd go along with him if he still wanted me. Carl said that he would need a worthy helpmeet, but we couldn't get married yet. He wasn't twenty-one. It was too soon after his mother's death. His father was opposed to early marriages, anyway, and we mustn't do anything to upset an old man with a heart condition. In the meantime we should live as friends, as brother and sister, to prepare ourselves for the sacrament of marriage.

"Carl was becoming more and more idealistic. He took up theology that fall, on top of his premed courses. My own little spurt of idealism, or whatever you want to call it, didn't last very long. Dr. Grantland came to see me one day that summer. He said that he was a businessman, and he understood that I was a businesswoman. He certainly hoped I was. Because if I played my cards right, with him kibitzing for me, I could be worth a lot of money with very little effort.

"Dr. Grantland had changed, too. He was very smiley and businesslike, but he didn't look like a doctor any more. He didn't talk like one—more like a ventriloquist's dummy moving his lips in time to somebody else's lines. He told me the Senator's heart and arteries were deteriorating, he was due to die before long. When he did, Carl and Jerry would divide the estate between them. If I was married to Carl, I'd be in a position to repay my friends for any help they'd given me.

"He considered us good friends, but it would sort of set the seal on our friendship if we went to bed together. He'd been told that he was very good in bed. I let him. It made no difference to me, one way or the other. I even liked being with him, in a way. He was the only one who knew about me. When I was in Purissima after that, I used to go and visit him in his office. Until I married Carl, I mean. I quit seeing Grantland then. It wouldn't have been right.

"Carl was twenty-one on the fourteenth of March, and we were married in Oakland three days later. He moved into the apartment with me, but he thought we should make up for our earlier sins by living in chastity for another year. Carl was so tense about it that I was afraid to argue with him. He was pale, and bright in the eyes. Sometimes he wouldn't talk for days at a time, and then the floodgates would open and he'd talk all night.

"He'd begun to fail in his studies, but he was full of ideas. We used to discuss reality, appearance and reality. I always thought appearance was the front you put on for people, and reality was how you really felt. Reality was death and blood and the curse. Reality was hell. Carl told me I had it all wrong, that pain and evil were only appearances. Goodness was reality, and he would prove it to me in his life. Now that he'd discovered Christian existentialism, he saw quite clearly that suffering was only a test, a fire that purified. That was the reason we couldn't sleep together. It was for the good of our souls.

"Carl had begun to lose a lot of weight. He got so nervous that spring, he couldn't sit still to work. Sometimes I'd hear him walking in the living-room all night. I thought if I could get him to come to bed with me, it would help him to get some sleep, settle him down. I had some pretty weird ideas of my own. I paraded around in floozie nightgowns, and drenched myself with perfume, and did my best to seduce him. My own husband. One night in May, I served him a candlelight dinner with wine and got him drunk enough.

"It didn't work, not for either of us. The spirit rose up from me and floated over the bed. I looked down and watched Carl using my body. And I hated him. He didn't love *me*. He didn't want to know *me*. I thought that we were both dead, and our corpses were in bed together. Zombies. Our two spirits never met.

"Carl was still in bed when I came home the next night. He hadn't been to his classes, hadn't moved all day. I thought at first he was sick, physically sick, and I called a doctor. Carl told him that the light of heaven had gone out. He had done it himself by putting out the light in his own mind. Now there was nothing in his head but darkness.

"Dr. Levin took me into the next room and told me that Carl was mentally disturbed. He should probably be committed. I telephoned Carl's father, and Dr. Levin talked to him, too. The Senator said that the idea of commitment was absurd. Carl had simply been hitting the books too hard, and what he needed was some good, hard down-to-earth work.

"Carl's father came and took him home the next day. I gave up my apartment and my job, and a few days later I followed them. I should have stayed where I was, but I wanted to be with Carl. I didn't trust his family. And I had a sneaking desire, even under the circumstances, to live on the ranch and be Mrs. Carl Hallman in Purissima. Well, I was, but it was worse than I expected. His family didn't like me. They blamed me for Carl's condition. A *good* wife would have been able to keep him healthy and wealthy and wise.

"The only person there who really liked me was Zinnie's baby. I used to play a game pretending that Martha was *my* baby. That was how I got through those two years. I'd pretend that I was alone with her in the big house. The others had all gone away, or else they'd died, and I was Martha's mother, doing for her all by myself, bringing her up just right, without any nasty influences. We did have good times, too. Sometimes I really believed that the nightmare in the doctor's office hadn't happened at all. Martha was there to prove it, my own baby, going on two.

"But Dr. Grantland was often there to remind me that it had happened. He was looking after Carl and his father, both. The Senator liked him because he didn't charge much or make expensive suggestions, such as hospitals or psychiatric treatment. Carl's father was quite a money-saver. We had margarine on the table instead of butter, and nothing but the culled oranges for our own use. I was even expected to pay board, until my money ran out. I didn't have a new dress for nearly two years. Maybe if I had, I wouldn't have killed him."

Mildred said that quietly, without any change in tone, without apparent feeling. Her face was expressionless. Only her forefinger moved on her skirted knee, tracing a small pattern: a circle and then a cross inside of the circle; as though she was trying to exorcise bad thoughts.

"I certainly wouldn't have killed him if he'd died when he was supposed to. Dr. Grantland had said a year, but the year went by, then most of another year. I wasn't the only one waiting. Jerry and Zinnie were waiting just as hard. They did their best to stir up trouble between Carl and his father, which wasn't hard to do. Carl was a little better, but still depressed and surly. He wasn't getting along with his father, and the old man kept threatening to change his will.

"One night Jerry baited Carl into a terrible argument about the Japanese people who used to own part of the valley. The Senator jumped into it, of course, as he was supposed to. Carl told him he didn't want any part of the ranch. If he ever did inherit any share of it, he'd give it back to the people who'd been sold up. I never saw the old man so angry. He said Carl was in no danger of inheriting anything. This time he meant it, too. He asked Jerry to make an appointment with his lawyer in the morning.

"I telephoned Dr. Grantland and he came out, ostensibly to see the Senator. Afterwards I talked to him outside. He took a very dim view. It wasn't that he was greedy, but he was thousands of dollars out of pocket. It was the first time he told me about the other man, this Rickey or Rica who'd been blackmailing him ever since Alicia's death. The same man who escaped with Carl last night."

"Grantland had never mentioned him to you?"

"No, he said he'd been trying to protect me. But now he was just about bled white, and something had to be done. He didn't tell me outright that I had to kill the Senator. I didn't have to be told. I didn't even have to think about it. I simply let myself forget who I was, and went through the whole thing like clockwork."

Her forefinger was active on her knee, repeating the symbol of the cross in the circle. She said, as if in answer to a question:

"You'd think I'd been planning it for years, all my life, ever since—"

She broke off, and covered the invisible device on her knee with her whole hand. She rose like a sleepwalker and went to the window. An oak tree in the backyard was outlined like a black paper cutout against the whitening sky.

"Ever since what?" I said to her still back.

"I was just remembering. When my father went away, afterwards, I used to think of funny things when I was in bed before I went to sleep. I wanted to track him down, and find him, and—"

"Kill him?"

"Oh no!" she cried. "I wanted to tell him how much we missed him and bring him back to Mother, so that we could be a happy family again. But if he wouldn't come—"

"What if he wouldn't come?"

"I don't want to talk about it. I don't remember." She struck the window where her reflection had been, not quite hard enough to break it.

Chapter 34

Dawn was coming on over the trees, like fluorescent lights in an operating room. Mildred turned away from the white agony of the light. Her outburst of feeling had passed, leaving her face smooth and her voice unshaken. Only her eyes had changed. They were heavy, and the color of ripe plums.

"It wasn't like the first time. This time I felt nothing. It's strange to kill someone and have no feeling about it. I wasn't even afraid while I was waiting for him in his bathroom closet. He always took a warm bath at night to help him sleep. I had an old ball-peen hammer I'd found on Jerry's workbench in the greenhouse. When he was in the bathtub, I slipped out of the closet and hit him on the back of the head with the hammer. I held his face under the water until the bubbles stopped.

"It only took a few seconds. I unlocked the bathroom door and locked it again on the outside and wiped the key and pushed it back under the door. Then I put the hammer where I found it, with Jerry's things. I hoped it would be taken for an accident, but if it wasn't I wanted Jerry to be blamed. It was really his fault, egging Carl on to quarrel with his father.

"But Carl was the one they blamed, as you well know. He seemed to *want* to be blamed. I think for a while he convinced himself that he had actually done it, and everyone else went along with it. The sheriff didn't even investigate."

"Was he protecting you?"

"No. If he was, he didn't know it. Jerry made some kind of a deal with him to save the county money and save the family's face. He didn't want a murder trial in his distinguished family. Neither did I. I didn't try to interfere when Jerry arranged to send Carl to the hospital. I signed the papers without a word.

"Jerry knew what he was doing. He was trained in the law, and he arranged it so that he was Carl's legal guardian. It meant that he controlled everything. I had no rights at all, as far as the family estate was concerned. The day after Carl was committed, Jerry hinted politely that I might as well move out. I believe that Jerry suspected me, but he was a cagey individual. It suited him better to blame it all on Carl, and keep his own cards face down.

634

"Dr. Grantland turned against me, too. He said he was through with me, after the mess I'd made of things. He said that he was through protecting me. For all he cared, the man he'd been paying off could go to the police and tell them all about me. And I mustn't think that I could get back at him by talking him into trouble. It would be my word against his, and I was as schitzy as hell, and he could prove it. He slapped me and ordered me out of his house. He said if I didn't like it, he'd call the police right then.

"I've spent the last six months waiting for them," she said. "Waiting for the knock on the door. Some nights I'd wish for them to come, *will* them to come, and get it over with. Some nights I wouldn't care one way or the other. Some nights—they were the worst—I'd lie burning up with cold and watch the clock and count its ticks, one by one, all night. The clock would tick like doom, louder and louder, like doomsters knocking on the door and clumping up the stairs.

"I got so I was afraid to go to sleep at night. I haven't slept for the last four nights, since I found out about Carl's friend on the ward. It was this man, Rica, the one who knew all about me. I could imagine him telling Carl. Carl would turn against me. There'd be nobody left in the world who even liked me. When they phoned me yesterday morning that Carl had escaped with him, I knew that this had to be it." She looked at me quite calmly. "You know the rest. You were here."

"I saw it from the outside."

"That's all there was, the outside. There wasn't any inside, at least for me. It was like a ritual which I made up as I went along. Every step I took had a meaning at the time, but I can't remember any of the meanings now."

"Tell me what you did, from the time that you decided to kill Jerry."

"It decided itself," she said. "I had no decision to make, no choice. Dr. Grantland phoned me at the office a little while before you got to town. It was the first I'd heard from him in six months. He said that Carl had got hold of a loaded gun. If Carl shot Jerry with it, it would solve a lot of problems. Money would be available, in case this man Rica tried to make more trouble for us. Also, Grantland would be able to use his influence with Zinnie to head off investigation of the other deaths.

I'd even have a chance at my share of the property. If Carl didn't shoot Jerry, the whole thing would blow up in our faces.

"Well, Carl had no intention of shooting anybody. I found that out when I talked to him in the orange grove. The gun he had was his mother's gun, which Dr. Grantland had given him. Carl wanted to ask Jerry some questions about it—about her death. Apparently Grantland told him that Jerry killed her.

"I didn't know for certain that Jerry suspected me, but I was afraid of what he would say to Carl. This was on top of all the other reasons I had to kill him, all the little snubs and sneers I'd had to take from him. I said I'd talk to Jerry instead, and I persuaded Carl to hand over the gun to me. If he was found armed, they might shoot him without asking questions. I told him to stay out of sight, and come here after dark if he could make it. That I would hide him.

"I hid the gun away, inside my girdle—it hurt so much I fainted, there on the lawn. When I was alone, I switched it to my bag. Later, when Jerry was alone, I went into the greenhouse and shot him twice in the back. I wiped the gun and left it there beside him. I had no more use for it."

She sighed, with the deep bone-tiredness that takes years to come to. Even the engine of her guilt was running down. But there was one more death in her cycle of killings.

And still the questions kept rising behind my teeth, always the questions, with the taste of their answers, salt as sea or tears, bitter as iron or fear, sweet-sour as folding money that has passed through many hands:

"Why did you kill Zinnie? Did you actually believe that you could get away with it, collect the money and live happily ever after?"

"I never thought of the money," she said, "or Zinnie, for that matter. I went there to see Dr. Grantland."

"You took a knife along."

"For him," she said. "I was thinking about him when I took that knife out of the drawer. Zinnie happened to be the one who was there. I killed her, I hardly know why. I felt ashamed for her, lying naked like that in his bed. It was almost like killing myself. Then I heard the radio going in the front room. It said that Carl had been seen at Pelican Beach.

"It seemed like a special message intended for me. I thought that there was hope for us yet, if only I could reach Carl. We could go away together and start a new life, in Africa or on the Indian reservations. It sounds ridiculous now, but that's what I thought on the way down to Pelican Beach. That somehow everything could be made good yet."

"So you walked in front of a truck."

"Yes. Suddenly I saw what I had done. Especially to Carl. It was my fault he was being hunted like a murderer. I was the murderer. I saw what I was, and I wanted to put an end to myself before I killed more people."

"What people are you talking about?"

Averting her face, she stared fixedly at the rumpled pillow at the head of the bed.

"Were you planning to kill Carl? Is that why you sent us away to Mrs. Hutchinson's, when he was already here?"

"No. It was Martha I was thinking about. I didn't want anything to happen to Martha."

"Who would hurt her if you didn't?"

"I was afraid I would," she said miserably. "It was one of the thoughts that came to me, that Martha had to be killed. Otherwise the whole thing made no sense."

"And Carl too? Did he have to be killed?"

"I thought I could do it," she said. "I stood over him with the knife in my hand for a long time while he was sleeping. I could say that I killed him in self-defense, and that he confessed all the murders before he died. I could get the house and the money all to myself, and pay off Dr. Grantland. Nobody else would suspect me.

"But I couldn't go through with it," she said. "I dropped the knife on the floor. I couldn't hurt Carl, or Martha. I wanted them to live. It made the whole thing meaningless, didn't it?"

"You're wrong. The fact that you didn't kill them is the only meaning left."

"What difference does it make? From the night I killed Alicia and my baby, every day I've lived has been a crime against nature. There isn't a person on the face of the earth who wouldn't hate me if they knew about me."

Her face was contorted. I thought she was trying not to cry. Then I thought she was trying to cry.

"I don't hate you, Mildred. On the contrary."

I was an ex-cop, and the words came hard. I had to say them, though, if I didn't want to be stuck for the rest of my life with the old black-and-white picture, the idea that there were just good people and bad people, and everything would be hunky-dory if the good people locked up the bad ones or wiped them out with small personalized nuclear weapons.

It was a very comforting idea, and bracing to the ego. For years I'd been using it to justify my own activities, fighting fire with fire and violence with violence, running on fool's errands while the people died: a slightly earthbound Tarzan in a slightly paranoid jungle. Landscape with figure of a hairless ape.

It was time I traded the picture in on one that included a few of the finer shades. Mildred was as guilty as a girl could be, but she wasn't the only one. An alternating current of guilt ran between her and all of us involved with her. Grantland and Rica, Ostervelt, and me. The redheaded woman who drank time under the table. The father who had deserted the household and died for it symbolically in the Senator's bathtub. Even the Hallman family, the four victims, had been in a sense the victimizers, too. The current of guilt flowed in a closed circuit if you traced it far enough.

Thinking of Alicia Hallman and her open-ended legacy of death, I was almost ready to believe in her doomsters. If they didn't exist in the actual world they rose from the depths of every man's inner sea, gentle as night dreams, with the back-breaking force of tidal waves. Perhaps they existed in the sense that men and women were their own doomsters, the secret authors of their own destruction. You had to be very careful what you dreamed.

The wave of night had passed through Mildred and left her cold and shaking. I held her in my arms for a little while. The light outside the window had turned to morning. The green tree-branches moved in it. Wind blew through the leaves.

Chapter 35

I TALKED to Rose Parish at breakfast, in the cafeteria of the local hospital. Mildred was in another part of the same building, under city police guard and under sedation. Rose and I had insisted on these things, and got our way. There would be time enough for further interrogations, statements, prosecution and defense, for all the awesome ritual of the law matching the awesome ritual of her murders.

Carl had survived a two-hour operation, and wasn't out from under the anesthetic. His prognosis was fair. Tom Rica was definitely going to live. He was resting in the men's security ward after a night of walking. I wasn't sure that Rose and the others who had helped to walk him, had done him any great favor.

Rose listened to me in silence, tearing her toast into small pieces and neglecting her eggs. The night had left bruises around her eyes, which somehow improved her looks.

"Poor girl," she said, when I finished. "What will happen to her?"

"It's a psychological question as much as a legal question. You're the psychologist."

"Not much of a one, I'm afraid."

"Don't underestimate yourself. You really called the shots last night. When I was talking to Mildred, I remembered what you said about whole families breaking down together, but putting it off onto the weakest one. The scapegoat. Carl was the one you had in mind. In a way, though, Mildred is another."

"I know. I've watched her, at the hospital, and again last night. I couldn't miss her mask, her coldness, her not-being-there. But I didn't have the courage to admit to myself that she was ill, let alone speak out about it." She bowed her head over her uneaten breakfast, maltreating a fragment of toast between her fingers. "I'm a coward and a fraud."

"I don't understand why you say that."

"I was jealous of her, that's why. I was afraid I was projecting my own wish onto her, that all I wanted was to get her out of the way."

"Because you're in love with Carl?"

"Am I so obvious?"

"Very honest, anyway."

In some incredible reserve of innocence, she found the energy to blush. "I'm a complete fake. The worst of it is, I intend to go right on being one. I don't care if he is my patient, and married to boot. I don't care if he's ill or an invalid or anything else. I don't care if I have to wait ten years for him."

Her voice vibrated through the cafeteria. Its drab utilitarian spaces were filling up with white-coated interns, orderlies, nurses. Several of them turned to look, startled by the rare vibration of passion.

Rose lowered her voice. "You won't misunderstand me. I expect to have to wait for Carl, and in the meantime I'm not forgetting his wife. I'll do everything I can for her."

"Do you think an insanity plea could be made to stick?"

"I doubt it. It depends on how sick she is. I'd guess, from what I've observed and what you tell me, that she's borderline schizophrenic. Probably she's been in-and-out for several years. This crisis may bring her completely out of it. I've seen it happen to patients, and she must have considerable ego strength to have held herself together for so long. But the crisis could push her back into very deep withdrawal. Either way, there's no way out for her. The most we can do is see that she gets decent treatment. Which I intend to do."

"You're a good woman."

She writhed under the compliment. "I wish I were. At least I used to wish it. Since I've been doing hospital work, I've pretty well got over thinking in terms of good and bad. Those categories often do more harm than—well, good. We use them to torment ourselves, and hate ourselves because we can't live up to them. Before we know it, we're turning our hatred against other people, especially the unlucky ones, the weak ones who can't fight back. We think we have to punish somebody for the human mess we're in, so we single out the scapegoats and call them evil. And Christian love and virtue go down the drain." She poked with a spoon at the cold brown dregs of coffee in her cup. "Am I making any sense, or do I just sound soft-headed?"

"Both. You sound soft-headed, and you make sense to me. I've started to think along some of the same lines."

Specifically, I was thinking about Tom Rica: the hopeful boy he had been, and the man he had become, hopeless and old in his twenties. I vaguely remembered a time in between, when hope and despair had been fighting for him, and he'd come to me for help. The rest of it was veiled in an old alcoholic haze, but I knew it was ugly.

"It's going to be a long time," Rose was saying, "before people really know that we're members of one another. I'm afraid they're going to be terribly hard on Mildred. If only there were some mitigation, or if there weren't so many. She killed so many."

"There were mitigating circumstances in the first one—the one that started her off. A judge trying it by himself would probably call it justifiable homicide. In fact, I'm not even sure she did it."

"Really?"

"You heard what Tom Rica said. He blamed that death on Grantland. Did he add anything to that in the course of the night?"

"No. I didn't press him."

"Did he do any talking at all?"

"Some." Rose wouldn't meet my eyes.

"What did he say?"

"It's all rather vague. After all, I wasn't taking notes."

"Listen, Rose. There's no point in trying to cover up for Tom, not at this late date. He's been blackmailing Grantland for years. He broke out of the hospital with the idea of converting it into a big-time operation. Carl probably convinced him that Grantland had something to do with his father's death, as well as his mother's, and that there was a lot of money involved. Tom persuaded Carl to come over the wall with him. His idea was to pile more pressure on Grantland. In case Carl couldn't boil up enough trouble by himself, Tom sent him to me."

"I know."

"Did Tom tell you?"

"If you really want to know, he told me a lot of things. Have you stopped to wonder why he picked on you?"

"We used to know each other. I guess my name stuck in his head."

"More than your name stuck. When he was a boy in high

school, you were his hero. And then you stopped being." She reached across the littered table and touched the back of my hand. "I don't mean to hurt you, Archer. Stop me if I am."

"Go ahead. I didn't know I was important to Tom." But I was lying. I knew. You always know. On the firing range, in the gym, he even used to imitate my mistakes.

"He seems to have thought of you as a kind of foster-father. Then your wife divorced you, and there were some things in the newspapers, he didn't say what they were."

"They were the usual. Or a little worse than the usual."

"I am hurting you," she said. "This sounds like an accusation, but it isn't. Tom hasn't forgotten what you did for him before your private trouble interfered. Perhaps it was unconscious on his part, but I believe he sent Carl to you in the hope that you could help him."

"Which one? Tom or Carl?"

"Both of them."

"If he thought that, how wrong he was."

"I disagree. You've done what you can. It's all that's expected of anyone. You helped to save Carl's life. I know you'll do what you can for Tom, too. It's why I wanted you to know what he said, before you talk to him."

Her approval embarrassed me. I knew how far I had fallen short. "I'd like to talk to him now."

The security ward occupied one end of a wing on the second floor. The policeman guarding the steel-sheathed door greeted Rose like an old friend, and let us through. The morning light was filtered through a heavy wire mesh screen over the single window of Tom's cubicle.

He lay like a forked stick under the sheet, his arms inert outside it. Flesh-colored tape bound his hands and wrists. Except where the beard darkened it, his face was much paler than the tape. He bared his teeth in a downward grin:

"I hear you had a rough night, Archer. You were asking for it."

"I hear you had a rougher one."

"Tell me I asked for it. Cheer me up."

"Are you feeling better?" Rose asked him.

He answered with bitter satisfaction: "I'm feeling worse. And I'm going to feel worse yet."

"You've been through the worst already," I said. "Why don't you kick it permanently?"

"It's easy to say."

"You almost had it made when you were with us," Rose said. "If I could arrange a few months in a federal hospital—"

"Save your trouble. I'd go right back on. It's my meat and drink. When I kick it there's nothing left, I know that now."

"How long have you been on heroin?"

"Five or six hundred years." He added, in a different, younger voice: "Right after I left high school. This broad I met in Vegas—" His voice sank out of hearing in his throat. He twitched restlessly, and rolled his head on the pillow, away from Rose and me and memory. "We won't go into it."

Rose moved to the door. "I'll go and see how Carl is."

I said, when the door had closed behind her: "Was it Maude who got you started on horse, Tom?"

"Naw, she's death on the stuff. She was the one that made me go to the hospital. She could have sprung me clean."

"I hear you saying it."

"It's the truth. She got my charge reduced from possession so they'd send me up for treatment."

"How could she do that?"

"She's got a lot of friends. She does them favors, they do her favors."

"Is the sheriff one of her friends?"

He changed the subject. "I was going to tell you about this kid in Vegas. She was just a kid my own age, but she was mainlining already. I met her at this alumnus party where they wanted me to play football for their college. The old boys had a lot of drinks, and we young people had some, and then they wanted me to put on a show with this kid. They kept chunking silver dollars at us when we were doing it. We collected so many silver dollars I had a hard time carrying them up to her room. I was strong in those days, too."

"I remember you were."

"Damn them!" he said in weak fury. "They made a monkey out of me. I let them do it to me, for a couple of hundred lousy silver dollars. I told them what they could do with their football scholarship. I didn't want to go to college anyway. Too much like work."

"What's the matter with work?"

"Only suckers work. And you can pin it in your hat Tom Rica is no sucker. You want to know who finally cured me of suckering for all that uplift crap? You did, and I thank you for it."

"When did all this happen?"

"Don't you kid me, you remember that day I came to your office. I thought if I could talk—but we won't go into that. You wanted no part of me. I wanted no part of you. I knew which side I was on from there on out."

He sat up in bed and bared his arm as if the marks of the needle were battle scars; which I had inflicted on him: "The day you gave me the old rush, I made up my mind I'd rather be an honest junkie than a double-talking hypocrite. When they grabbed me this last time, I was main-lining two-three times a day. And liking it," he said, in lost defiance. "If I had my life to live over, I wouldn't change a thing."

I'd begun to feel restless, and a little nauseated. The alcoholic haze was lifting from the half-forgotten afternoon when Tom had come to my office for help, and gone away without it.

"What did you come to see me about, Tom?"

He was silent for quite a while. "You really want to know?"

"Very much."

"All right, I had a problem. Matter of fact, I had a couple of problems. One of them was the heroin. I wasn't all the way gone on it yet, but I was close to gone. I figured maybe you could tell me what to do about it, where I could get treatment. Well, you told me where to go."

I sat and let it sink in. His eyes never left my face. I said, when I got my voice back:

"What was the other problem you had?"

"They were the same problem, in a way. I was getting the stuff from Grantland, all I wanted. I hear the good doctor got his last night, by the way." He tried to say it casually, but his eyes were wide with the question.

"Grantland's in the basement in a cold drawer."

"He earned it. He killed an old lady, one of his own patients. I told you that last night, didn't I? Or was it just a part of the dream I had?"

"You told me, all right, but it was just part of the dream. A girl named Mildred Hallman killed the old lady. Grantland was only an accessory after the fact."

"If he told you that, he's a liar."

"He wasn't the only one who told me that."

"They're all liars! The old lady was hurt, sure, but she was still alive when Grantland dropped her off the dock. She even tried to—" Tom put his hand over his mouth. His eyes roved round the walls and into the corners like a trapped animal's. He lay back and pulled the sheet up to his chin.

"What did she try to do, Tom? Get away?"

A darkness crossed his eyes like the shadow of a wing. "We won't talk about it."

"I think you want to."

"Not any more. I tried to tell you about her over three years ago. It's too late now. I don't see any good reason to talk myself into more trouble. How would it help *her*? She's dead and gone."

"It could help the girl who thinks she murdered her. She's in worse trouble than you are. A lot worse. And she's got a lot more guilt. You could take some of it away from her."

"Be a hero, eh? Make the home folks proud of me. The old man always wanted me to be a hero." Tom couldn't sustain his sardonic bitterness. "If I admit I was on the dock, does that make me what you call accessory?"

"It depends on what you did. They're not so likely to press it if you volunteer the information. Did you help Grantland push her in?"

"Hell no, I argued with him when I saw she was still alive. I admit I didn't argue very much. I needed a fix, and he promised me one if I'd help him."

"How did you help him?"

"I helped him carry her out of his office and put her in his car. And I drove the car. He was too jittery to drive for himself. I did argue with him, though."

"Why did he drown her, do you know?"

"He said he couldn't afford to let her live. That if it came out, what happened that night, it would knock him right out of business. I figured if it was that important, I should start a little business of my own."

"Blackmailing Grantland for drugs?"

"You'll never prove it. He's dead. And I'm not talking for the record."

"You're still alive. You'll talk."

"Am I? Will I?"

"You're a better man than you think you are. You think it's the monkey that's killing you. I say you can train the monkey, chain him up and put him in the goddam zoo where he belongs. I say it's that old lady that's been weighing you down."

His thin chest rose and fell with his breathing. He fingered it under the sheet, as if he could feel a palpable weight there.

"Christ," he said. "She floated in the water for a while. Her clothes held her up. She was trying to *swim*. That was the hell of it that I couldn't forget."

"And that's why you came to see me?"

"Yeah, but it all went down the drain with the bathwater. You wouldn't listen. I was scared to go to the law. And I got greedy, let's face it. When I bumped into Carl in the hospital, and he filled me in on the family, I got greedy as hell. He said there was five million bucks there, and Grantland was knocking them off to get his hands on it. I thought here was my big chance for real."

"You were wrong. This is your real chance now. And you're taking it."

"Come again. You lost me somewhere."

But he knew what I meant. He lay and looked up at the ceiling as if there might just possibly be sky beyond it. And stars at night. Like any man with life left in him, he wanted to find a use for himself.

"Okay, Archer. I'm willing to make a statement. What have I got to lose?" He freed his arms from the sheet, grinning derisively, and flapped them like a small boy playing airman. "Bring on the D.A. Just keep Ostervelt out of it if you can, will you? He won't like all I got to say."

"Don't worry about him. He's on his way out."

"I guess it's Maude I'm worried about." His mood swung down with a hype's lability, but not as far down as it had been. "Jesus, I'm a no-good son. When I think of the real chances I had, and the dirty trouble I stirred up for the people that treated me good. I don't want Maude to be burned."

"I think she can look after herself."

"Better than I can, eh? If you see Carl, tell him I'm sorry, will you? He treated me like a brother when I was in convulsions, spouting like a whale from every hole in my head. And I got more holes than most, don't think I don't know it. Pass the word to Archer when you see him?"

"What word?"

"Sorry." It cost him an effort to say it directly.

"Double it, Tom."

"Forget it." He was getting expansive again. "This being Old Home Week, you might as well tell the Parish broad I'm sorry for brushing *her* off. She's a pretty good broad, you know?"

"The best."

"You ever think of getting married again?"

"Not to her. She's got a waiting list."

"Too bad for you."

Tom yawned and closed his eyes. He was asleep in a minute. The guard let me out and told me how to reach the post-operative ward. On the way there, I walked through the day in the past when this story should have begun for me, but didn't.

It was a hot day in late spring, three years and a summer before. The Strip fluttered like tinsel in the heatwaves rising from the pavements. I'd had five or six Gibsons with lunch, and I was feeling sweaty and cynical. My latest attempt to effect a reconciliation with Sue had just failed. By way of compensation, I'd made a date to go to the beach with a younger blonde who had some fairly expensive connections. If she liked me well enough, she could get me a guest membership in a good beach club.

When Tom walked in, my first and final thought was to get him out. I didn't want the blonde to find him in my office, with his special haircut and his Main Street jacket, his blank smile and his sniff and the liquid pain in the holes he was using for eyes. I gave him a cheap word or two, and the walking handshake that terminates at the door.

There was more to it than that. There always is. Tom had failed me before, when he dropped out of the boys' club I was interested in. He hadn't wanted to be helped the way I wanted to help him, the way that helped me. My vanity hadn't forgiven him, for stealing his first car.

There was more to it than that. I'd been a street boy in my time, gang-fighter, thief, poolroom lawyer. It was a fact I didn't like to remember. It didn't fit in with the slick polaroid picture I had of myself as the rising young man of mystery who frequented beach clubs in the company of starlets. Who groped for a fallen brightness in private white sand, private white bodies, expensive peroxide hair.

When Tom stood in my office with the lost look on him, the years blew away like torn pieces of newspaper. I saw myself when I was a frightened junior-grade hood in Long Beach, kicking the world in the shins because it wouldn't dance for me. I brushed him off.

It isn't possible to brush people off, let alone yourself. They wait for you in time, which is also a closed circuit. Years later on a mental-hospital ward, Tom had a big colored dream and cast me for a part in it, which I was still playing out. I felt like a dog in his vomit.

I stopped and leaned on a white wall and lit a cigarette. When you looked at the whole picture, there was a certain beauty in it, or justice. But I didn't care to look at it for long. The circuit of guilty time was too much like a snake with its tail in its mouth, consuming itself. If you looked too long, there'd be nothing left of it, or you. We were all guilty. We had to learn to live with it.

Rose met me with a smile at the door of Carl's private room. She held up her right hand and brought the thumb and forefinger together in a closed circle. I smiled and nodded in response to her good news, but it took a while to penetrate to my inner ear. Where the ash-blond ghosts were twittering, and the hype dream beat with persistent violence, like colored music, trying to drown them out.

It was time I traded that in, too, on a new dream of my own. Rose Parish had hers. Her face was alive with it, her body leaned softly on it. But whatever came of her dream for better or worse belonged to her and Carl. I had no part in it, and wanted none. No Visitors, the sign on the door said.

For once in my life I had nothing and wanted nothing. Then the thought of Sue fell through me like a feather in a vacuum. My mind picked it up and ran with it and took flight. I wondered where she was, what she was doing, whether she'd aged much as she lay in ambush in time, or changed the color of her bright head.

THE GALTON CASE

For John E. Smith, bookman

Chapter 1

THE LAW offices of Wellesley and Sable were over a savings bank on the main street of Santa Teresa. Their private elevator lifted you from a bare little lobby into an atmosphere of elegant simplicity. It created the impression that after years of struggle you were rising effortlessly to your natural level, one of the chosen.

Facing the elevator, a woman with carefully dyed red hair was toying with the keyboard of an electric typewriter. A bowl full of floating begonias sat on the desk in front of her. Audubon prints picked up the colors and tossed them discreetly around the oak walls. A Harvard chair stood casually in one corner.

I sat down on it, in the interests of self-improvement, and picked up a fresh copy of the *Wall Street Journal*. Apparently this was the right thing to do. The red-headed secretary stopped typing and condescended to notice me.

"Do you wish to see anyone?"

"I have an appointment with Mr. Sable."

"Would you be Mr. Archer?"

"Yes."

She relaxed her formal manner: I wasn't one of the chosen after all. "I'm Mrs. Haines. Mr. Sable didn't come into the office today, but he asked me to give you a message when you got here. Would you mind going out to his house?"

"I guess not." I got up out of the Harvard chair. It was like being expelled.

"I realize it's a nuisance," she said sympathetically. "Do you know how to reach his place?"

"Is he still in his beach cottage?"

"No, he gave that up when he got married. They built a house in the country."

"I didn't know he was married."

"Mr. Sable's been married for nearly two years now. Very much so."

The feline note in her voice made me wonder if she was married. Though she called herself Mrs. Haines, she had the air of a woman who had lost her husband to death or divorce and was looking for a successor. She leaned toward me in sudden intimacy:

"You're the detective, aren't you?"

I acknowledged that I was.

"Is Mr. Sable hiring you personally, on his own hook? I mean, the reason I asked, he didn't say anything to me about it."

The reason for that was obvious. "Me, either," I said. "How do I get to his house?"

"It's out in Arroyo Park. Maybe I better show you on the map."

We had a brief session of map-reading. "You turn off the highway just before you get to the wye," she said, "and then you turn right here at the Arroyo Country Day School. You curve around the lake for about a half a mile, and you'll see the Sables' mailbox."

I found the mailbox twenty minutes later. It stood under an oak tree at the foot of a private road. The road climbed a wooded hill and ended at a house with many windows set under the overhang of a flat green gravel roof.

The front door opened before I got to it. A man with streaked gray hair growing low on his forehead came across the lawn to meet me. He wore the white jacket of domestic service, but even with this protective coloration he didn't fit into the expensive suburb. He carried his heavy shoulders jauntily, as if he was taking his body for a well-deserved walk.

"Looking for somebody, mister?"

"Mr. Sable sent for me."

"What for?"

"If he didn't tell you," I said, "the chances are that he doesn't want you to know."

The houseman came up closer to me and smiled. His smile was wide and raw, like a dog's grin, and meaningless, except that it meant trouble. His face was seamed with the marks of the trouble-prone. He invited violence, as certain other people invite friendship.

Gordon Sable called from the doorway: "It's all right, Peter. I'm expecting this chap." He trotted down the flagstone path and gave me his hand. "Good to see you, Lew. It's been several years, hasn't it?"

"Four."

Sable didn't look any older. The contrast of his tanned face with his wavy white hair somehow supported an illusion of youth. He had on a Madras shirt cinched in by form-fitting English flannels which called attention to his tennis-player's waistline.

"I hear you got married," I said.

"Yes. I took the plunge." His happy expression seemed a little forced. He turned to the houseman, who was standing there listening: "You'd better see if Mrs. Sable needs anything. And then come out to my study. Mr. Archer's had a long drive, and he'll be wanting a drink."

"Yaas, massuh," the houseman said broadly.

Sable pretended not to notice. He led me into the house, along a black-and-white terrazzo corridor, across an enclosed court crowded with tropical plants whose massed colors were broken up and reflected by an oval pool in the center. Our destination was a sun-filled room remote from the rest of the house and further insulated by the hundreds of books lining its walls.

Sable offered me a leather chair facing the desk and the windows. He adjusted the drapes to shut off some of the light.

"Peter should be along in a minute. I'm afraid I must apologize for his manners, or lack of them. It's hard to get the right sort of help these days."

"I have the same trouble. The squares want security, and the hipsters want a chance to push people around at fifty dollars a day. Neither of which I can give them. So I still do most of my own work."

"I'm glad to hear that." Sable sat on the edge of the desk and leaned toward me confidentially: "The matter that I'm thinking of entrusting to you is a rather delicate one. It's essential, for reasons that will emerge, that there should be no publicity. Anything you find out, if you do find anything out, you report to me. Orally. I don't want anything in writing. Is that understood?"

"You make it very clear. Is this your personal business, or for a client?"

"For a client, of course. Didn't I say so on the telephone? She's saddled me with a rather difficult assignment. Frankly, I see very little chance of satisfying her hopes."

"What does she hope for?"

Sable lifted his eyes to the bleached beams of the ceiling. "The impossible, I'm afraid. When a man's dropped out of sight for over twenty years, we have to assume that he's dead and buried. Or, at the very least, that he doesn't want to be found."

"This is a missing-persons case, then?"

"A rather hopeless one, as I've tried to tell my client. On the other hand, I can't refuse to make an attempt to carry out her wishes. She's old, and ill, and used to having her own way."

"And rich?"

Sable frowned at my levity. He specialized in estate work, and moved in circles where money was seen but not heard.

"The lady's husband left her excellently provided for." He added, to put me in my place: "You'll be well paid for your work, no matter how it turns out."

The houseman came in behind me. I knew he was there by the change in the lighting. He wore old yachting sneakers, and moved without sound.

"You took your time," Sable said.

"Martinis take time to mix."

"I didn't order Martinis."

"The Mrs. did."

"You shouldn't be serving her Martinis before lunch, or any other time."

"Tell her that."

"I intend to. At the moment I'm telling you."

"Yaas, massuh."

Sable reddened under his tan. "That dialect bit isn't funny, you know."

The houseman made no reply. His green eyes were bold and restless. He looked down at me, as if for applause.

"Quite a servant problem you have," I said, by way of supporting Sable.

"Oh, Peter means well, don't you, old boy?" As if to foreclose an answer, he looked at me with a grin pasted on over his embarrassment. "What will you drink, Lew? I'm going to have a tonic."

"That will do for me."

The houseman retreated.

"What about this disappearance?" I said.

"Perhaps disappearance isn't exactly the right word. My client's son walked out on his family deliberately. They made no attempt to follow him up or bring him back, at least not for many years."

"Why not?"

"I gather they were just as dissatisfied with him as he was with them. They disapproved of the girl he'd married. 'Disapproved' is putting it mildly, and there were other bones of contention. You can see how serious the rift was from the fact that he sacrificed his right to inherit a large estate."

"Does he have a name, or do we call him Mr. X?"

Sable looked pained. It hurt him physically to divulge information. "The family's name is Galton. The son's name is, or was, Anthony Galton. He dropped out of sight in 1936. He was twenty-two at the time, just out of Stanford."

"That's a long time ago." From where I sat, it was like a previous century.

"I told you this thing was very nearly hopeless. However, Mrs. Galton wants her son looked for. She's going to die any day herself, and she feels the need for some sort of reconciliation with the past."

"Who says she's going to die?"

"Her doctor. Dr. Howell says it could happen at any time."

The houseman loped into the room with a clinking tray. He made a show of serviceability as he passed us our gin-and-tonics. I noticed the blue anchor tattoo on the back of his hand, and wondered if he was a sailor. Nobody would mistake him for a trained servant. A half-moon of old lipstick clung to the rim of the glass he handed me.

When he went away again, I said:

"Young Galton got married before he left?"

"Indeed he did. His wife was the immediate cause of the trouble in the family. She was going to have a child."

"And all three of them dropped out of sight?"

"As if the earth had opened and swallowed them," Sable said dramatically.

"Were there any indications of foul play?"

"Not so far as I know. I wasn't associated with the Galton family at the time. I'm going to ask Mrs. Galton herself to tell you about the circumstances of her son's departure. I don't know exactly how much of it she wants aired."

"Is there more to it?"

"I believe so. Well, cheers," he said cheerlessly. He gulped his drink standing. "Before I take you to see her, I'd like some assurance that you can give us your full time for as long as necessary."

"I have no commitments. How much of an effort does she want?"

"The best you can give, naturally."

"You might do better with one of the big organizations."

"I think not. I know you, and I trust you to handle this affair with some degree of urbanity. I can't have Mrs. Galton's last days darkened by scandal. My overriding concern in this affair is the protection of the family name."

Sable's voice throbbed with emotion, but I doubted that it was related to any deep feeling he had for the Galton family. He kept looking past me or through me, anxiously, as if his real concerns lay somewhere else.

I got some hint of what they were when we were on our way out. A pretty blond woman about half his age emerged from behind a banana tree in the court. She was wearing jeans and an open-necked white shirt. She moved with a kind of clumsy stealth, like somebody stepping out of ambush.

"Hello, Gordon," she said in a brittle voice. "Fancy meeting you here."

"I live here, don't I?"

"That was supposed to be the theory."

Sable spoke carefully to her, as if he was editing his sentences in his head: "Alice, this is no time to go into all of it again. Why do you think I stayed home this morning?"

"A lot of good it did me. Where do you think you're going now?"

"Out."

"Out where?"

"You have no right to cross-examine me, you know."

"Oh yes I have a right."

She stood squarely in front of him in a deliberately ugly posture, one hip out, her breasts thrust forward under the white shirt, at the same time sharp and tender. She didn't seem to be drunk, but there was a hot moist glitter in her eyes. Her eyes were large and violet, and should have been beautiful. With dark circles under them, and heavy eyeshadow on the upper lids, they were like two spreading bruises.

"Where are you taking my husband?" she said to me.

"Mr. Sable is doing the taking. It's a business matter."

"What sort of business, eh? Whose business?"

"Certainly not yours, dear." Sable put his arm around her. "Come to your room now. Mr. Archer is a private detective working on a case for me—nothing to do with you."

"I bet not." She jerked away from him, and swung back to me. "What do you want from me? There's nothing to find out. I sit in this morgue of a house, with nobody to talk to, nothing to do. I wish I was back in Chicago. People in Chicago *like* me."

"People here like you, too." Sable was watching her patiently, waiting for her bout of emotion to wear itself out.

"People here hate me. I can't even order drinks in my own house."

"Not in the morning, and this is why."

"You don't love me at all." Her anger was dissolving into self-pity. A shift of internal pressure forced tears from her eyes. "You don't care a thing about me."

"I care very much. Which is why I hate to see you fling yourself around the landscape. Come on, dear, let's go in."

He touched her waist, and this time she didn't resist. With one arm holding her, he escorted her around the pool to a door which opened on the court. When he closed the door behind them, she was leaning heavily on him.

I found my own way out.

Chapter 2

SABLE KEPT me waiting for half an hour. From where I sat in my car, I could see Santa Teresa laid out like a contour map, distinct in the noon light. It was an old and settled city, as such things go in California. Its buildings seemed to belong to its hills, to lean with some security on the past. In contrast with them, Sable's house was a living-machine, so new it hardly existed.

When he came out, he was wearing a brown suit with a wicked little red pin stripe in it, and carrying a cordovan dispatch case. His manner had changed to match his change in costume. He was businesslike, brisk, and remote.

Following his instructions and his black Imperial, I drove into the city and across it to an older residential section. Massive traditional houses stood far back from the street, behind high masonry walls or topiary hedges.

Arroyo Park was an economic battleground where managers and professional people matched wits and incomes. The people on Mrs. Galton's street didn't know there had been a war. Their grandfathers or great-grandfathers had won it for them; death and taxes were all they had to cope with.

Sable made a signal for a left turn. I followed him between stone gateposts in which the name Galton was cut. The majestic iron gates gave a portcullis effect. A serf who was cutting the lawn with a power-mower paused to tug at his forelock as we went by. The lawn was the color of the ink they use to print the serial numbers on banknotes, and it stretched in unbroken smoothness for a couple of hundred yards. The white façade of a pre-Mizener Spanish mansion glared in the green distance.

The driveway curved around to the side of the house, and through a porte-cochere. I parked behind a Chevrolet coupé displaying a doctor's caduceus. Further back, in the shade of a great oak, two girls in shorts were playing badminton. The bird flew back and forth between them in flashing repartee. When the dark-headed girl with her back to us missed, she said:

"Oh, damn it!"

"Temper," Gordon Sable said.

She pivoted like a dancer. I saw that she wasn't a girl, but a woman with a girl's body. A slow blush spread over her face. She covered her discomfiture with an exaggerated pout which made the most of her girlishness:

"I'm off my form. Sheila *never* beats me."

"I do so!" cried the girl on the other side of the net. "I beat you three times in the last week. Today is the fourth time."

"The set isn't over yet."

"No, but I'm going to beat you." Sheila's voice had an intensity which didn't seem to go with her appearance. She was very young, no more than eighteen. She had a peaches-and-cream complexion and soft doe eyes.

The woman scooped up the bird and tossed it over the net. They went on playing, all out, as if a great deal depended on the game.

A Negro maid in a white cap let us into a reception room. Wrought-iron chandeliers hung like giant black bunches of withered grapes from the high ceiling. Ancient black furniture stood in museum arrangements around the walls under old dark pictures. The windows were narrow and deep in the thick walls, like the windows of a medieval castle.

"Is Dr. Howell with her?" Sable asked the maid.

"Yes, sir, but he ought to be leaving any time now. He's been here for quite a while."

"She didn't have an attack?"

"No, sir. It's just the doctor's regular visit."

"Would you tell him I'd like to see him before he leaves?"

"Yes, sir."

She whisked away. Sable said in a neutral tone, without looking at me: "I won't apologize for my wife. You know how women are."

"Uh-huh." I didn't really want his confidences.

If I had, he wouldn't have given them to me. "There are certain South American tribes that segregate women one week out of the month. Shut them up in a hut by themselves and let them rip. There's quite a lot to be said for the system."

"I can see that."

"Are you married, Archer?"

"I have been."

"Then you know what it's like. They want you with them all the time. I've given up yachting. I've given up golf. I've practically given up living. And still she isn't satisfied. What do you do with a woman like that?"

I'd given up offering advice. Even when people asked for it, they resented getting it. "You're the lawyer."

I strolled around the room and looked at the pictures on the walls. They were mostly ancestor-worship art: portraits of Spanish dons, ladies in hoop skirts with bare monolithic bosoms, a Civil War officer in blue, and several gentlemen in nineteenth-century suits with sour nineteenth-century pusses between their whiskers. The one I liked best depicted a group of top-hatted tycoons watching a bulldog-faced tycoon hammer a gold spike into a railroad tie. There was a buffalo in the background, looking sullen.

The maid returned with a man in Harris tweeds. Sable introduced him as Dr. Howell. He was a big man in his fifties, who carried himself with unconscious authority.

"Mr. Archer is a private investigator," Sable said. "Did Mrs. Galton mention what she has in mind?"

"Indeed she did." The doctor ran his fingers through his gray crewcut. The lines in his forehead deepened. "I thought that whole business of Tony was finished and forgotten years ago. Who persuaded her to drag it back into the light?"

"Nobody did, so far as I know. It was her own idea. How is she, Doctor?"

"As well as can be expected. Maria is in her seventies. She has a heart. She has asthma. It's an unpredictable combination."

"But there's no immediate danger?"

"I wouldn't think so. I can't say what will happen if she's subjected to shock or distress. Asthma is one of those things."

"Psychosomatic, you mean?"

"Somatopsychic, whatever you want to call it. In any case it's a disease that's affected by the emotions. Which is why I hate to see Maria getting all stirred up again about that wretched son of hers. What does she hope to gain?"

"Emotional satisfaction, I suppose. She feels she treated him badly, and wants to make up for it."

"But isn't he dead? I thought he was found to be legally dead."

"He could have been. We had an official search made some years ago. He'd already been missing for fourteen years, which is twice the time required by the law to establish presumption of death. Mrs. Galton wouldn't let me make the petition, however. I think she's always dreamed of Anthony coming back to claim his inheritance and all that. In the last few weeks it's become an obsession with her."

"I wouldn't go that far," the doctor said. "I still think some-body put a bee in her bonnet, and I can't help wondering why."

"Who do you have in mind?"

"Cassie Hildreth, perhaps. She has a lot of influence on Maria. And speaking of dreams, she had a few of her own when she was a kid. She used to follow Tony around as if he was the light of the world. Which he was far from being, as you know." Howell's smile was one-sided and saturnine.

"This is news to me. I'll talk to Miss Hildreth."

"It's pure speculation on my part, don't misunderstand me. I do think this business should be played down as much as possible."

"I've been trying to play it down. On the other hand I can't downright refuse to lift a finger."

"No, but it would be all to the good if you could just keep it going along, without any definite results, until she gets inter-ested in something different." The doctor included me in his shrewd glance. "You understand me?"

"I understand you all right," I said. "Go through the motions but don't do any real investigating. Isn't that pretty expensive therapy?"

"She can afford it, if that's what worries you. Maria has more coming in every month than she spends every year." He regarded me in silence for a moment, stroking his prow of a nose. "I don't mean you shouldn't do your job. I wouldn't ask any man to lie down on a job he's paid to do. But if you find out anything that might upset Mrs. Galton—"

Sable put in quickly: "I've already taken that up with Archer. He'll report to me. I think you know you can rely on my discretion."

"I think I know I can."

Sable's face changed subtly. His eyelids flickered as though he had been threatened with a blow, and remained heavy over his watchful eyes. For a man of his age and financial weight, he was very easily hurt.

I said to the doctor: "Did you know Anthony Galton?"

"Somewhat."

"What kind of person was he?"

Howell glanced toward the maid, who was still waiting in the doorway. She caught his look and withdrew out of sight. Howell lowered his voice:

"Tony was a sport. I mean that in the biological sense, as well as the sociological. He didn't inherit the Galton characteristics. He had utter contempt for business of any kind. Tony used to say he wanted to be a writer, but I never saw any evidence of talent. What he was really good at was boozing and fornicating. I gather he ran with a very rough crowd in San Francisco. I've always believed myself that one of them killed him for the money in his pockets and threw him in the Bay."

"Was there any indication of that sort of thing?"

"Not to my certain knowledge. But San Francisco in the thirties was a dangerous place for a boy to play around in. He must have dredged pretty deep to turn up the girl he married."

"You knew her, did you?" Sable said.

"I examined her. His mother sent her to me, and I examined her."

"Was she here in town?" I said.

"Briefly. Tony brought her home the week he married her. I don't believe he had any notion the family would accept her. It was more a case of flinging her in their faces. If that was his idea, it succeeded very well."

"What was the matter with the girl?"

"The obvious thing, and it was obvious—she was seven months' pregnant."

"And you say they'd just been married?"

"That's correct. She hooked him. I talked with her a little, and I'd wager he picked her up, hot off the streets. She was a pretty enough little thing, in spite of her big belly, but she'd had a hard life. There were scars on her thighs and buttocks. She wouldn't explain them to me, but it was evident that she'd been beaten, more than once." The cruel memory raised faint traces of scarlet on the doctor's cheekbones.

The doe-eyed girl from the badminton court appeared in the doorway behind him. Her body was like ripening fruit, only partly concealed by her sleeveless jersey and rolled shorts. She glowed with healthy beauty, but her mouth was impatient:

"Daddy? How much longer?"

The color on his cheekbones heightened when he saw her. "Roll down your pants, Sheila."

"They're not pants."

"Whatever they are, roll them down."

"Why should I?"

"Because I'm telling you to."

"You could at least tell me in private. How much longer do I have to wait?"

"I thought you were going to read to your Aunt Maria."

"Well, I'm not."

"You promised."

"You were the one who promised for me. I played badminton with Cassie, and that's my good turn for the day."

She moved away, deliberately exaggerating the swing of her hips. Howell glared at the chronometer on his wrist, as if it was the source of all his troubles. "I must be getting along. I have other calls to make."

"Can you give me the wife's description?" I said. "Or her name?"

"I don't recall her name. As for appearance, she was a little blue-eyed brunette, rather thin in spite of her condition. Mrs. Galton—no, on second thought I wouldn't ask her about the girl unless she brings the matter up herself."

The doctor turned to go, but Sable detained him: "Is it all right for Mr. Archer to question her? I mean, it won't affect her heart or bring on an asthmatic attack?"

"I can't guarantee it. If Maria insists on having an attack, there's nothing I can do to prevent it. Seriously, though, if Tony's on her mind she might as well talk about him. It's better than sitting and brooding. Good-by, Mr. Archer, nice to meet you. Good day, Sable."

Chapter 3

THE MAID took Sable and me to a sitting-room on the second floor where Mrs. Galton was waiting. The room smelled of medicine, and had a hushed hospital atmosphere. The heavy drapes were partly drawn over the windows. Mrs. Galton was resting in semi-twilight on a chaise longue, with a robe over her knees.

She was fully dressed, with something white and frilly at her withered throat; and she held her gray head ramrod straight. Her voice was reedy, but surprisingly resonant. It seemed to carry all the remaining force of her personality:

"You've kept me waiting, Gordon. It's nearly time for my lunch. I expected you before Dr. Howell came."

"I'm awfully sorry, Mrs. Galton. I was delayed at home."

"Don't apologize. I detest apologies, they're really just further demands on one's patience." She cocked a bright eye at him. "Has that wife of yours been giving you trouble again?"

"Oh, no, nothing of that sort."

"Good. You know my thoughts on the subject of divorce. On the other hand, you should have taken my advice and not married her. A man who waits until he's nearly fifty to get married should give up the idea entirely. Mr. Galton was in his late forties when we were married. As a direct consequence, I've had to endure nearly twenty years of widowhood."

"It's been hard, I know," Sable said with unction.

The maid had started out of the room. Mrs. Galton called her back: "Wait a minute. I want you to tell Miss Hildreth to bring me my lunch herself. She can bring up a sandwich and eat it with me if she likes. You tell Miss Hildreth that."

"Yes, Mrs. Galton."

The old lady waved us into chairs, one on each side of her, and turned her eye on me. It was bright and alert but somehow inhuman, like a bird's eye. It looked at me as if I belonged to an entirely different species:

"Is this the man who is going to find my prodigal son for me?"

"Yes, this is Mr. Archer."

666

"I'm going to give it a try," I said, remembering the doctor's advice. "I can't promise any definite results. Your son has been missing for a very long time."

"I'm better aware of that than you, young man. I last set eyes on Anthony on the eleventh day of October 1936. We parted in bitter anger and hatred. I've lived ever since with that anger and hatred corroding my heart. But I can't die with it inside of me. I want to see Anthony again, and talk to him. I want to forgive him. I want him to forgive me."

Deep feeling sounded in her voice. I had no doubt that the feeling was partly sincere. Still, there was something unreal about it. I suspected that she'd been playing tricks with her emotions for a long time, until none of them was quite valid.

"Forgive you?" I said.

"For treating him as I did. He was a young fool, and he made some disastrous mistakes, but none of them really justified Mr. Galton's action, and mine, in casting him off. It was a shameful action, and if it's not too late I intend to rectify it. If he still has his little wife, I'm willing to accept her. I authorize you to tell him that. I want to see my grandchild before I die."

I looked at Sable. He shook his head slightly, deprecatingly. His client was just a little out of context, but she had quick insight, at least into other people:

"I know what you're both thinking. You're thinking that Anthony is dead. If he were dead, I'd know it here." Her hand strayed over the flat silk surface of her breast. "He's my only son. He must be alive, and he must be somewhere. Nothing is lost in the universe."

Except human beings, I thought. "I'll do my best, Mrs. Galton. There are one or two things you can do to help me. Give me a list of his friends at the time of his disappearance."

"I never knew his friends."

"He must have had friends in college. Wasn't he attending Stanford?"

"He'd left there the previous spring. He didn't even wait to graduate. Anyway, none of his schoolmates knew what happened to him. His father canvassed them thoroughly at the time."

"Where was your son living after he left college?"

"In a flat in the slums of San Francisco. With that woman."

"Do you have the address?"

"I believe I may have it somewhere. I'll have Miss Hildreth look for it."

"That will be a start, anyway. When he left here with his wife, did they plan to go back to San Francisco?"

"I haven't any idea. I didn't see them before they left."

"I understood they came to visit you."

"Yes, but they didn't even stay the night."

"What might help most," I said carefully, "would be if you could tell me the exact circumstances of their visit, and their departure. Anything your son said about his plans, anything the girl said, anything you remember about her. Do you remember her name?"

"He called her Teddy. I have no idea if that was her name or not. We had very little conversation. I can't recall what was said. The atmosphere was unpleasant, and it left a bad taste in my mouth. *She* left a bad taste in my mouth. It was so evident that she was a cheap little gold-digger."

"How do you know?"

"I have eyes. I have ears." Anger had begun to whine in the undertones of her voice. "She was dressed and painted like a woman of the streets, and when she opened her mouth—well, she spoke the language of the streets. She made coarse jokes about the child in her womb, and how"—her voice faded almost out—"it got there. She had no respect for herself as a woman, no moral standards. That girl destroyed my son."

She'd forgotten all about her hope of reconciliation. The angry wheezing in the passages of her head sounded like a ghost in a ruined house. Sable was looking at her anxiously, but he held his tongue.

"Destroyed him?" I said.

"Morally, she destroyed him. She possessed him like an evil spirit. My son would never have taken the money if it hadn't been for the spell she cast on him. I know that with utter certitude."

Sable leaned forward in his chair. "What money are you referring to?"

"The money Anthony stole from his father. Haven't I told you about it, Gordon? No, I don't believe I have. I've told no one, I've always been so ashamed." She lifted her hands and dropped them in her robed lap. "But now I can forgive him for that, too."

"How much money was involved?" I said.

"I don't know exactly how much, to the penny. Several thousand dollars, anyway. Ever since the day the banks closed, Mr. Galton had had a habit of keeping a certain amount of cash for current expenses."

"Where did he keep it?"

"In his private safe, in the study. The combination was on a piece of paper pasted to the inside of his desk drawer. Anthony must have found it there, and used it to open the safe. He took everything in it, all the money, and even some of my jewels which I kept there."

"Are you sure he took it?"

"Unfortunately, yes. It disappeared at the same time he did. It's why he hid himself away, and never came back to us."

Sable's glum look deepened. Probably he was thinking the same thing I was: that several thousand dollars in cash, in the slums of San Francisco, in the depths of the depression, were a very likely passport to oblivion.

But we couldn't say it out loud. With her money, and her asthma, and her heart, Mrs. Galton was living at several removes from reality. Apparently that was how it had to be.

"Do you have a picture of your son, taken not too long before his disappearance?"

"I believe I have. I'll ask Cassie to have a look. She should be coming soon."

"In the meantime, can you give me any other information? Particularly about where your son might have gone, who or where he might have visited."

"I know nothing of his life after he left the university. He cut himself off from all decent society. He was perversely bound to sink in the social scale, to declass himself. I'm afraid my son had a *nostalgie de la boue*—a nostalgia for the gutter. He tried to cover it over with fancy talk about re-establishing contact with the earth, becoming a poet of the people, and such nonsense. His real interest was dirt for dirt's own sake. I brought him up to be pure in thought and desire, but somehow—somehow he became fascinated with the pitch that defileth. And the pitch defiled him."

Her breathing was noisy. She had begun to shake, and scratch with waxy fingers at the robe that covered her knees.

Sable leaned toward her solicitously. "You mustn't excite yourself, Mrs. Galton. It was all over long ago."

"It's not all over. I want Anthony back. I have nobody. I have nothing. He was stolen away from me."

"We'll get him back if it's humanly possible."

"Yes, I know you will, Gordon." Her mood had changed like a fitful wind. Her head inclined toward Sable's shoulder as though to rest against it. She spoke like a little girl betrayed by time and loss, by fading hair and wrinkles and the fear of death: "I'm a foolish angry old woman. You're always so good to me. Anthony will be good to me, too, won't he, when he comes? In spite of all I've said against him, he was a darling boy. He was always good to his poor mother, and he will be again."

She was chanting in a ritual of hope. If she said it often enough, it would have to come true.

"I'm sure he will, Mrs. Galton."

Sable rose and pressed her hand. I was always a little suspicious of men who put themselves out too much for rich old ladies, or even poor ones. But then it was part of his job.

"I'm hungry," she said. "I want my lunch. What's going on downstairs?"

She lunged half out of her long chair and got hold of a wired bellpush on the table beside it. She kept her finger pressed on the button until her lunch arrived. That was a tense five minutes.

Chapter 4

IT CAME on a covered platter carried by the woman I'd seen on the badminton court. She had changed her shorts for a plain linen dress which managed to conceal her figure, if not her fine brown legs. Her blue eyes were watchful.

"You kept me waiting, Cassie," the old woman said. "What on earth were you doing?"

"Preparing your food. Before that I played some badminton with Sheila Howell."

"I might have known you two would be enjoying yourselves while I sit up here starving."

"Oh come, it's not as bad as all that."

"It's not for you to say. You're not my doctor. Ask August Howell, and he'll tell you how important it is that I have my nourishment."

"I'm sorry, Aunt Maria. I thought you wouldn't want to be disturbed while you were in conference."

She stood just inside the doorway, still holding the tray like a shield in front of her. She wasn't young: close up, I could see the fortyish lines in her face and the knowledge in her blue eyes. But she held herself with adolescent awkwardness, immobilized by feelings she couldn't express.

"Well, you needn't stand there like a dummy."

Cassie moved suddenly. She set the tray on the table and uncovered the food. There was a good deal of food. Mrs. Galton began to fork salad into her mouth. The movements of her hands and jaws were rapid and mechanical. She was oblivious to the three of us watching her.

Sable and I retreated into the hallway and along it to the head of the stairs which curved in a baronial sweep down to the entrance hall. He leaned on the iron balustrade and lit a cigarette.

"Well, Lew, what do you think?"

I lit a cigarette of my own before I replied. "I think it's a waste of time and money."

"I told you that."

"But you want me to go ahead with it anyway?"

"I can't see any other way to handle it, or handle her. Mrs. Galton takes a good deal of handling."

"Can you trust her memory? She seems to be reliving the past. Sometimes old people get mixed up about what actually happened. That story about the money he stole, for example. Do you believe it?"

"I've never known her to lie. And I really doubt that she's as confused as she sounds. She likes to dramatize herself. It's the only excitement she has left."

"How old is she?"

"Seventy-three, I believe."

"That isn't so old. What about her son?"

"He'll be about forty-four, if he's still extant."

"She doesn't seem to realize that. She talks about him as if he was still a boy. How long has she been sitting in that room?"

"Ever since I've known her, anyway. Ten years. Occasionally, when she has a good day, she lets Miss Hildreth take her for a drive. It doesn't do much to bring her up to date, though. It's usually just a quick trip to the cemetery where her husband is buried. He died soon after Anthony took off. According to Mrs. Galton, that was what killed him. Miss Hildreth says he died of a coronary."

"Is Miss Hildreth a relative?"

"A distant one, second or third cousin. Cassie's known the family all her life, and lived with Mrs. Galton since before the war. I'm hoping she can give you something more definite to go on."

"I can use it."

A telephone shrilled somewhere, like a cricket in the wall. Cassie Hildreth came out of Mrs. Galton's room and moved briskly toward us:

"You're wanted on the telephone. It's Mrs. Sable."

"What does she want?"

"She didn't say, but she seems upset about something."

"She always is."

"You can take it downstairs if you like. There's an extension under the stairs."

"I know. I'll do that." Sable treated her brusquely, like a

servant. "This is Mr. Archer, by the way. He wants to ask you some questions."

"Right now?"

"If you can spare the time," I said. "Mrs. Galton thought you could give me some pictures, perhaps some information."

"Pictures of Tony?"

"If you have them."

"I keep them for Mrs. Galton. She likes to look at them when the mood is on her."

"You work for her, do you?"

"If you can call it work. I'm a paid companion."

"I call it work."

Our eyes met. Hers were dark ocean blue. Discontent flicked a fin in their depths, but she said dutifully: "She isn't so bad. She's not at her best today. It's hard on her to rake up the past like this."

"Why is she doing it?"

"She had a serious scare not long ago. Her heart almost failed. They had to put her in an oxygen tent. She wants to make amends to Tony before she dies. She treated him badly, you know."

"Badly in what way?"

"She didn't want him to live his own life, as they say. She tried to keep him all to herself, like a—a belonging. But you'd better not get me started on that."

Cassie Hildreth bit her lip. I recalled what the doctor had said about her feeling for Tony. The whole household seemed to revolve around the missing man, as if he'd left only the day before.

Quick footsteps crossed the hallway below the stairs. I leaned over the balustrade and saw Sable wrench the front door open. It slammed behind him.

"Where's he off to?"

"Probably home. That wife of his—" She hesitated, editing the end of the sentence: "She lives on emergencies. If you'd like to see those pictures, they're in my room."

Her door was next to Mrs. Galton's sitting-room. She unlocked it with a Yale key. Apart from its size and shape, its lofty ceiling, the room bore no relation to the rest of the house.

The furniture was modern. There were Paul Klee reproductions on the walls, new novels on the bookshelves. The ugly windows were masked with monks-cloth drapes. A narrow bed stood behind a woven wood screen in one corner.

Cassie Hildreth went into the closet and emerged with a sheaf of photographs in her hand.

"Show me the best likeness first."

She shuffled through them, her face intent and peaked, and handed me a posed studio portrait. Anthony Galton had been a handsome boy. I stood and let his features sink into my mind: light eyes set wide apart and arched over by intelligent brows, short straight nose, small mouth with rather full lips, a round girlish chin. The missing feature was character or personality, the meaning that should have held the features together. The only trace of this was in the one-sided smile. It seemed to say: to hell with you. Or maybe, to hell with me.

"This was his graduation picture," Cassie Hildreth said softly.

"I thought he never graduated from college."

"He didn't. This was made before he dropped out."

"Why didn't he graduate?"

"He wouldn't give his father the satisfaction. Or his mother. They forced him to study mechanical engineering, which was the last thing Tony was interested in. He stuck it out for four years, but he finally refused to take his degree in it."

"Did he flunk out?"

"Heavens, no. Tony was very bright. Some of his professors thought he was brilliant."

"But not in engineering?"

"There wasn't anything he couldn't do, if he wanted to. His real interests were literary. He wanted to be a writer."

"I take it you knew him well."

"Of course. I wasn't living with the Galtons then, but I used to visit here, often, when Tony was on vacation. He used to talk to me. He was a wonderful conversationalist."

"Describe him, will you?"

"But you've just seen his picture. And here are others."

"I'll look at them in a minute. Right now I want you to tell me about him."

"If you insist, I'll try." She closed her eyes. Her face smoothed out, as if years were being erased: "He was a lovely man. His body was finely proportioned, lean and strong. His head was beautifully balanced on his neck, and he had close fair curls." She opened her eyes. "Did you ever see the Praxiteles Hermes?"

I felt a little embarrassed, not only because I hadn't. Her description of Tony had the force of a passionate avowal. I hadn't expected anything like it. Cassie's emotion was like spontaneous combustion in an old hope chest.

"No," I said. "What color were his eyes?"

"Gray. A lovely soft gray. He had the eyes of a poet."

"I see. Were you in love with him?"

She gave me a startled look. "Surely you don't expect me to answer that."

"You just did. You say he used to talk to you. Did he ever discuss his plans for the future?"

"Just in general terms. He wanted to go away and write."

"Go away where?"

"Somewhere quiet and peaceful, I suppose."

"Out of the country?"

"I doubt it. Tony disapproved of expatriates. He always said he wanted to get *closer* to America. This was in the depression, remember. He was very strong for the rights of the working class."

"Radical?"

"I guess you'd call him that. But he wasn't a Communist, if that's what you mean. He did feel that having money cut him off from life. Tony hated social snobbery—which was one reason he was so unhappy at college. He often said he wanted to live like ordinary people, lose himself in the mass."

"It looks as if he succeeded in doing just that. Did he ever talk to you about his wife?"

"Never. I didn't even know he was married, or intended to get married." She was very self-conscious. Not knowing what to do with her face, she tried to smile. The teeth between her parted lips were like white bone showing in a wound.

As if to divert my attention from her, she thrust the other pictures into my hands. Most of them were candid shots of Tony Galton doing various things: riding a horse, sitting on a rock in swimming trunks, holding a tennis racket with a winner's fixed grin on his face. From the pictures, and from what the people said, I got the impression of a boy going through the motions.

He made the gestures of enjoyment but kept himself hidden, even from the camera. I began to have some glimmering of the psychology that made him want to lose himself.

"What did he like doing?"

"Writing. Reading and writing."

"Besides that. Tennis? Swimming?"

"Not really. Tony despised sports. He used to jeer at me for going in for them."

"What about wine and women? Dr. Howell said he was quite a playboy."

"Dr. Howell never understood him," she said. "Tony did have relations with women, and I suppose he drank, but he did it on principle."

"Is that what he told you?"

"Yes, and it's true. He was practicing Rimbaud's theory of the violation of the senses. He thought that having all sorts of remarkable experiences would make him a good poet, like Rimbaud." She saw my uncomprehending look, and added: "Arthur Rimbaud was a French poet. He and Charles Baudelaire were Tony's great idols."

"I see." We were getting off the track into territory where I felt lost. "Did you ever meet any of his women?"

"Oh, no." She seemed shocked at the idea. "He never brought any of them here."

"He brought his wife home."

"Yes, I know. I was away at school when it happened."

"When what happened?"

"The big explosion," she said. "Mr. Galton told him never to darken his door again. It was all very Victorian and heavy-father. And Tony never did darken his door again."

"Let's see, that was in October 1936. Did you ever see Tony after that?"

"Never. I was at school in the east."

"Ever hear from him?"

Her mouth started to shape the word "no," then tightened. "I had a little note from him, some time in the course of the winter. It must have been before Christmas, because I got it at school, and I didn't go back after Christmas. I think it was in the early part of December that it came."

"What did it say?"

"Nothing very definite. Simply that he was doing well, and had broken into print. He'd had a poem accepted by a little magazine in San Francisco. He sent it to me under separate cover. I've kept it, if you'd like to look at it."

She kept it in a manila envelope on the top shelf of her bookcase. The magazine was a thin little publication smudgily printed on pulp paper; its name was *Chisel*. She opened it to a middle page, and handed it to me. I read:

LUNA, by John Brown

"White her breast
As the white foam
Where the gulls rest
Yet find no home.

"Green her eyes
As the green deep
Where the tides rise
And the storms sleep.

"And fearful am I
As a mariner
When the sea and the sky
Begin to stir.

"For wild is her heart
As the sea's leaping:
She will rise and depart
While I lie sleeping."

"Did Tony Galton write this? It's signed 'John Brown.'"

"It was the name he used. Tony wouldn't use the family name. 'John Brown' had a special meaning for him, besides. He had a theory that the country was going through another civil war—a war between the rich people and the poor people. He thought of the poor people as white Negroes, and he wanted to do for them what John Brown did for the slaves. Lead them out of bondage—in the spiritual sense, of course. Tony didn't believe in violence."

"I see," I said, though it all sounded strange to me. "Where did he send this from?"

"The magazine was published in San Francisco, and Tony sent it from there."

"This was the only time you ever heard from him?"

"The only time."

"May I keep these pictures, and the magazine? I'll try to bring them back."

"If they'll help you to find Tony."

"I understand he went to live in San Francisco. Do you have his last address?"

"I had it, but there's no use going there."

"Why not?"

"Because I did, the year after he went away. It was a wretched old tenement, and it had been condemned. They were tearing it down."

"Did you make any further attempt to find him?"

"I wanted to, but I was afraid. I was only seventeen."

"Why didn't you go back to school, Cassie?"

"I didn't especially want to. Mr. Galton wasn't well, and Aunt Maria asked me to stay with her. She was the one sending me to school, so that I couldn't very well refuse."

"And you've been here ever since?"

"Yes." The word came out with pressure behind it.

As if on cue, Mrs. Galton raised her voice on the other side of the wall: "Cassie! Cassie? Are you in there? What are you doing in there?"

"I'd better go," Cassie said.

She locked the door of her sanctuary, and went, with her head down.

After twenty-odd years of that, I'd have been crawling.

Chapter 5

I MET the doctor's daughter on the stairs. She gave me a tentative smile. "Are you the detective?"

"I'm the detective. My name is Archer."

"Mine's Sheila Howell. Do you think you can find him for her?"

"I can try, Miss Howell."

"That doesn't sound too hopeful."

"It wasn't meant to."

"But you will do your best, won't you?"

"Is it important to you? You're too young to have known Anthony Galton."

"It's important to Aunt Maria." She added in a rush of feeling: "She needs somebody to love her. I try, honestly, but I just can't do it."

"Is she a relative of yours?"

"Not exactly. She's my godmother. I call her aunt because she likes me to. But I've never succeeded in feeling like a niece to her."

"I imagine she makes it hard."

"She doesn't mean to, but she simply doesn't know how to treat *people*. She's had her own way for so long." The girl colored, and compressed her lips. "I don't mean to be *critical*. You must think I'm an awful person, talking about her to a stranger like this. I really do wish her well, in spite of what Dad thinks. And if she wants me to read *Pendennis* to her, I will."

"Good for you. I was on my way to make a phone call. Is there a telephone handy?"

She showed me the telephone under the stairs. It was an ancient wall telephone which nobody had ever bothered to change for a modern one. The Santa Teresa directory lay on a table under it. I looked up Sable's number.

He was a long time answering. Finally, I heard the receiver being lifted at the other end of the line. After another wait, I heard his voice. I hardly recognized it. It had a blurred quality, almost as if Sable had been crying:

679

"This is Gordon Sable."

"Archer speaking. You took off before we could make definite arrangements. On a case like this I need an advance, and expense money, at least three hundred."

There was a click, and then a whirring on the wire. Someone was dialing. A woman's voice said: "Operator! I want the police."

"Get off the line," Sable said.

"I'm calling the police." It was his wife's voice, shrill with hysteria.

"I've already called them. Now get off the line. It's in use."

A receiver was fumbled into place. I said: "You still there, Sable?"

"Yes. There's been an accident, as you must have gathered." He paused. I could hear his breathing.

"To Mrs. Sable?"

"No, though she's badly upset. My houseman, Peter, has been stabbed. I'm afraid he's dead."

"Who stabbed him?"

"It isn't clear. I can't get much out of my wife. Apparently some goon came to the door. When Peter opened it, he was knifed."

"You want me to come out?"

"If you think it will do any good. Peter is past help."

"I'll be there in a few minutes."

But it took me longer than that. The Arroyo Park suburb was new to me. I took a wrong turning and got lost in its system of winding roads. The roads all looked alike, with flat-roofed houses, white and gray and adobe, scattered along the terraced hillsides.

I went around in circles for a while, and came out on top of the wrong hill. The road dwindled into a pair of ruts in a field where nothing stood but a water tower. I turned, and stopped to get my bearings.

On a hilltop a mile or more to my left, I could make out a flat pale green roof which looked like the Arizona gravel roof of Sable's house. On my right, far below, a narrow asphalt road ran like a dark stream along the floor of the valley. Between the road and a clump of scrub oaks an orange rag of flame came and went. Black smoke trickled up from it into the still blue air. When I moved I caught a flash of sunlight on metal. It was a car, nose down in the ditch, and burning.

I drove down the long grade and turned right along the asphalt road. A fire siren was ululating in the distance. The smoke above the burning car was twisting higher and spreading like a slow stain over the trees. Watching it, I almost ran down a man.

He was walking toward me with his head bent, as if in meditation, a thick young man with shoulders like a bull. I honked at him and applied the brakes. He came on doggedly. One of his arms swung slack, dripping red from the fingers. The other arm was cradled in the front of his sharp flannel jacket.

He came up to the door on my side and leaned against it. "Can you gimme a lift?" Oily black curls tumbled over his hot black eyes. The bright blood on his mouth gave him an obscene look, like a painted girl.

"Smash up your car?"

He grunted.

"Come around to the other side if you can make it."

"Negative. This side."

I caught the glint of larceny in his eyes, and something worse. I reached for my car keys. He was ahead of me. The short blue gun in his right hand peered at the corner of the open window:

"Leave the keys where they are. Open the door and get out."

Curlyhead talked and acted like a pro, or at least a gifted amateur with a vocation. I opened the door and got out.

He waved me away from the car. "Start walking."

I hesitated, weighing my chances of taking him.

He used his gun to point toward the city. "Get going, Bud. You don't want a calldown with me."

I started walking. The engine of my car roared behind me. I got off the road. But Curlyhead turned in a driveway, and drove off in the other direction, away from the sirens.

The fire was out when I got to it. The county firemen were coiling their hose, replacing it on the side of the long red truck. I went up to the cab and asked the man at the wheel:

"Do you have two-way radio?"

"What's it to you?"

"My car was stolen. I think the character who took it was driving the one in the ditch there. The Highway Patrol should be notified."

"Give me the details, I'll shoot them in."

I gave him the license number and description of my car, and a thumbnail sketch of Curlyhead. He started feeding them into his mike. I climbed down the bank to look at the car I'd traded mine in on. It was a black Jaguar sedan, about five years old. It had slewed off the road, gouging deep tracks in the dirt, and crumpled its nose against a boulder. One of the front tires had blown out. The windshield was starred, and the finish blistered by fire. Both doors were sprung.

I made a note of the license number, and moved up closer to look at the steering-post. The registration was missing. I got in and opened the dash compartment. It was clean.

In the road above, another car shrieked to a halt. Two sheriff's men got out on opposite sides and came down the bank in a double cloud of dust. They had guns in their hands, nononsense looks on their brown faces.

"This your car?" the first one snapped at me.

"No."

I started to tell him what had happened to mine, but he didn't want to hear about it:

"Out of there! Keep your hands in sight, shoulder-high."

I got out, feeling that all this had happened before. The first deputy held his gun on me while the second deputy shook me down. He was very thorough. He even investigated the fuzz in my pockets. I commented on this.

"This is no joke. What's your name?"

The firemen had begun to gather around us. I was angry and sweating. I opened my mouth and put both feet in, all the way up to the knee.

"I'm Captain Nemo," I said. "I just came ashore from a hostile submarine. Curiously enough, we fuel our subs with seaweed. The hull itself is formed from highly compressed seaweed. So take me to your wisest man. There is no time to be lost."

"He's a hophead," the first deputy said. "I kind of figured the slasher was a hophead. You heard me say so, Barney."

"Yeah." Barney was reading the contents of my wallet. "He's got a driver's license made out to somebody name of Archer,

West Hollywood. And a statewide private-eye ducat, same name. But it's probably a phony."

"It's no phony." Vaudeville had got me nowhere except into deeper trouble. "My name is Archer. I'm a private investigator, employed by Mr. Sable, the lawyer."

"Sable, he says." The deputies exchanged significant looks. "Give him his wallet, Barney."

Barney held it out to me. I reached for it. The cuffs clinked snug on my wrist.

"Other wrist now," he said in a soothing voice. I was a hophead. "Let's have the other wrist now."

I hesitated. But rough stuff not only wouldn't work. It would put me in the wrong. I wanted them to be in the wrong, falling on their faces with foolishness.

I surrendered the other wrist without a struggle. Looking down at my trapped hands, I saw the dab of blood on one of my fingers.

"Let's go," the first deputy said. He dropped my wallet in the side pocket of my jacket.

They herded me up the bank and into the back of their car. The driver of the fire truck leaned from his cab:

"Keep a close eye on him, fellows. He's a cool customer. He gave me a story about his car getting stolen, took me in completely."

"Not us," the first deputy said. "We're trained to spot these phonies, the way you're trained to put out fires. Don't let anybody else near the Jag. Leave a guard on it, eh? I'll send a man as soon as we can spare one."

"What did he do?"

"Knifed a man."

"Jesus, and I thought he was a citizen."

The first deputy climbed into the back seat beside me. "I got to warn you anything you say can be used against you. Why did you do it?"

"Do what?"

"Cut Peter Culligan."

"I didn't cut him."

"You got blood on your hand. Where did it come from?"

"Probably the Jaguar."

"Your car, you mean?"

"It isn't my car."

"The hell it isn't. I got a witness saw you drive away from the scene of the crime."

"I wasn't in it. The man who was in it just stole my car."

"Don't give me that. You can fool a fireman with it. I'm a cop."

"Was it woman trouble?" Barney said over his shoulder. "If it was a woman, we can understand it. Crime of passion, and all. Shucks," he added lightly, "it wouldn't even be second-degree, probably. You could be out in two-three years. Couldn't he, Conger?"

"Sure," Conger said. "You might as well tell us the truth now, get it over with."

I was getting bored with the game. "It wasn't a woman. It was seaweed. I'm a seaweed-fancier from way back. I like to sprinkle a little of it on my food."

"What's that got to do with Culligan?"

Barney said from the front seat: "He sounds to me like he's all hopped up."

Conger leaned across me. "Are you?"

"Am I what?"

"All hopped up?"

"Yeah. I chew seaweed, then I orbit. Take me to the nearest launching pad."

Conger looked at me pityingly. I was a hophead. The pity was gradually displaced by doubt. He had begun to grasp that he was being ragged. Very suddenly, his face turned dusky red under the tan. He balled his right fist on his knee. I could see the packed muscles tighten under the shoulder of his blouse. I pulled in my chin and got ready to roll with the punch. But he didn't hit me.

Under the circumstances, this made him a good cop. I almost began to like him, in spite of the handcuffs. I said:

"As I told you before, my name is Archer. I'm a licensed private detective, retired sergeant from the Long Beach P.D. The California Penal Code has a section on false arrest. Do you think you better take the jewelry off?"

Barney said from the front seat: "A poolroom lawyer, eh?"

Conger didn't say anything. He sat in pained silence for what seemed a long time. The effort of thought did unexpected things to his heavy face. It seemed to alarm him, like a loud noise in the night.

The car left the county road and climbed Sable's hill. A second sheriff's car stood in front of the glass house. Sable climbed out, followed by a heavy-set man in mufti.

Sable looked pale and shaken. "You took your time about getting here." Then he saw the handcuffs on my wrists. "For heaven's sake!"

The heavy-set man stepped past him, and yanked the car door open. "What's the trouble here?"

Conger's confusion deepened. "No trouble, Sheriff. We picked up a suspect, claims he's a private cop working for Mr. Sable."

The sheriff turned to Sable. "This your man?"

"Of course."

Conger was already removing the handcuffs, unobtrusively, as if perhaps I wouldn't notice they'd ever been on my wrists. The back of Barney's neck reddened. He didn't turn around, even when I stepped out of the car.

The Sheriff gave me his hand. He had a calm and weathered face in which quick bright eyes moved with restless energy. "I'm Trask. I won't apologize. We all make mistakes. Some of us more than others, eh, Conger?"

Conger didn't reply. I said: "Now that we've had our fun, maybe you'd like to get on the radio with the description of my car and the man that took it."

"What man are we talking about?" Trask said.

I told him, and added: "If you don't mind my saying so, Sheriff, it might be a good idea for you to check with the Highway Patrol yourself. Our friend took off in the direction of San Francisco, but he may have circled back."

"I'll put out the word."

Trask started toward his radio car. I held him for a minute: "One other thing. That Jaguar ought to be checked by an expert. It may be just another stolen car—"

"Yeah, let's hope it isn't."

Chapter 6

THE DEAD man was lying where he had fallen, on a patch of blood-filmed grass, about ten feet from Sable's front door. The lower part of his white jacket was red-stained. His upturned face was gray and impervious-looking, like the stone faces on tombs.

A Sheriff's identification man was taking pictures of him with a tripod camera. He was a white-haired officer with a long inquisitive nose. I waited until he moved his camera to get another angle:

"Mind if I have a look at him?"

"Long as you don't touch him. I'll be through here in a minute."

When he had finished his work, I leaned over the body for a closer look. There was a single deep wound in the abdomen. The right hand had cuts across the palm and inside the curled fingers. The knife that had done the damage, a bloody five-inch switch-blade, lay on the grass in the angle between the torso and the outstretched right arm.

I took hold of the hand: it was still warm and limp: and turned it over. The skin on the tattooed knuckles was torn, probably by teeth.

"He put up quite a struggle," I said.

The identification officer hunkered down beside me. "Yeah. Be careful with those fingernails. There's some kind of debris under 'em, might be human skin. You notice the tattoo marks?"

"I'd have to be blind to miss them."

"I mean these." He took the hand away from me, and pointed out four dots arranged in a tiny rectangle between the first and second fingers. "Gang mark. He had it covered up later with a standard tattoo. A lot of old gang members do that. I see them on people we vag."

"What kind of gang?"

"I don't know. This is a Sac or Frisco gang. I'm no expert on the northern California insignia. I wonder if Lawyer Sable knew he had an old gang member working for him."

"We could ask him."

The front door was standing open. I walked in and found Sable in the front sitting-room. He raised a limp arm, and waved me into a chair:

"Sit down, Archer. I'm sorry about what happened. I can't imagine what they thought they were pulling."

"Eager-beavering. Forget it. We got off to a poor start, but the local boys seem to know what they're doing."

"I hope so," he said, not very hopefully.

"What do you know about your late houseman?"

"Not a great deal, I'm afraid. He only worked for me for a few months. I hired him originally to look after my yacht. He lived aboard the yacht until I sold it. Then he moved up here. He had no place to go, and he didn't ask for much. Peter wasn't very competent indoors, as you may have noticed. But it's hard for us to get help out in the country, and he was an obliging soul, so I let him stay on."

"What sort of a background did he have?"

"I gathered he was pretty much of a floater. He mentioned various jobs he'd held: marine cook, longshoreman, house-painter."

"How did you hire him? Through an employment agency?"

"No. I picked him up on the dock. I think he'd just come off a fishing-boat, a Monterey seiner. I was polishing brass, varnishing deck, and so on, and he offered to help me for a dollar an hour. He did a good day's work, so I took him on. He never failed to do a good day's work."

A cleft of pain, like a knife-cut, had appeared between Sable's eyebrows. I guessed that he had been fond of the dead man. I hesitated to ask my next question:

"Would you know if Culligan had a criminal record?"

The cleft in his brow deepened. "Good Lord, no. I trusted him with my boat and my house. What makes you ask such a question?"

"Two things mainly. He had a tattoo mark on his hand, four little black dots at the edge of the blue tattoo. Gangsters and drug addicts wear that kind of mark. Also, this has the look of a gang killing. The man who took my car is almost certainly the killer, and he has the earmarks of a pro."

Sable looked down at the polished terrazzo as if at any moment it might break up under his feet. "You think Peter Culligan was involved with criminals?"

"Involved is putting it mildly. He's dead."

"I realize that," he said rather shrilly.

"Did he seem nervous lately? Afraid of anything?"

"If he was, I never noticed. He didn't talk about himself."

"Did he have any visitors, before this last one?"

"Never. At least, not to my knowledge. He was a solitary person."

"Could he have been using your place and his job here as a sort of hide-out?"

"I don't know. It's hard to say."

An engine started up in front of the house. Sable rose and moved to the glass wall, parting the drapes. I looked out over his shoulder. A black panel truck rolled away from the house and started down the hill.

"Come to think of it," Sable said, "he certainly kept out of sight. He wouldn't chauffeur for me, said he'd had bad luck with cars. But he may have wanted to avoid going to town. He never went to town."

"He's on his way there now," I said. "How many people knew he was out here?"

"Just my wife and I. And you, of course. I can't think offhand of anyone else."

"Have you had visitors from out of town?"

"Not in the last few months. Alice has been having her ups and downs. It's one reason I took Peter on out here. We'd lost our housekeeper, and I didn't like to leave Alice by herself all day."

"How is Mrs. Sable now?"

"Not so good, I'm afraid."

"Did she see it happen?"

"I don't believe so. But she heard the sounds of the struggle, and saw the car drive away. That was when she phoned me. When I got here, she was sitting on the doorstep in a half daze. I don't know what it will do to her emotional state."

"Any chance of my talking to her?"

"Not now, please. I've already spoken to Dr. Howell, and he told me to give her sedation. The Sheriff has agreed not to question her for the present. There's a limit to what the human mind can endure."

Sable might have been talking about himself. His shoulders drooped as he turned from the window. In the harsh sunlight his face was a grainy white, and puffy like boiled rice. In murder cases, there are usually more victims than one.

Sable must have read the look on my face. "This is an unsettling thing to me, too. It can't conceivably relate to Alice and me. And yet it does, very deeply. Peter was a member of the household. I believe he was quite devoted to us, and he died in our front yard. That really brings it home."

"What?"

"*Timor mortis*," he said. "The fear of death."

"You say Culligan was a member of your household. I take it he slept in."

"Yes, of course."

"I'd like to have a look at his room."

He took me across the court and through a utility room to a back bedroom. The room was furnished with a single bed, a chest of drawers, a chair, and a reading-lamp.

"I'll just look in on Alice," Sable said, and left me.

I went through Peter Culligan's meager effects. The closet contained a pair of Levi's, a couple of workshirts, boots, and a cheap blue suit which had been bought at a San Francisco department store. There was a Tanforan pari-mutuel stub in the outside breast pocket of the suit coat. A dirty comb and a safety razor lay on top of the chest of drawers. The drawers were practically empty: a couple of white shirts, a greasy blue tie, a T-shirt and a pair of floral shorts, socks and handkerchiefs, and a cardboard box containing a hundred shells for a .38-caliber automatic. Not quite a hundred: the box wasn't full. No gun.

Culligan's suitcase was under the bed. It was a limp old canvas affair, held together with straps, which looked as if it had been kicked around every bus station between Seattle and San Diego. I unstrapped it. The lock was broken, and it fell open. Its contents emitted a whiff of tobacco, sea water, sweat, and the subtler indescribable odor of masculine loneliness.

It contained a gray flannel shirt, a rough blue turtle-neck sweater, and other heavier work clothes. A broad-bladed fisherman's knife had fish scales still clinging like faded sequins to the cork handle. A crumpled greenish tuxedo jacket was preserved as a memento from some more sophisticated past.

A union card issued in San Francisco in 1941 indicated that Culligan had been a paid-up active member of the defunct Marine Cooks' Union. And there was a letter, addressed to Mr. Peter Culligan, General Delivery, Reno, Nevada. Culligan hadn't been a loner all his life. The letter was written on pink notepaper in an unformed hand. It said:

Dear Pete,

Dear is not the word after all I suffered from you, which is all over now and I'm going to keep it that way. I hope you realize. Just so you do I'll spell it out, you never realized a fact in your life until you got hit over the head with it. So here goes, no I don't love you anymore. Looking back now I don't see how I ever did love you, I was "infatuated." When I think of all you made me suffer, the jobs you lost and the fights and the drinking and all. You certainly didn't love me, so don't try to "kid" me. No I'm not crying over "spilt milk." I had only myself to blame for staying with you. You gave me fair warning plenty of times. What kind of person you were. I must say you have your "guts" writing to me. I don't know how you got hold of my address. Probably from one of your crooked cop friends, but they don't scare me.

I am happily married to a wonderful man. He knows that I was married before. But he does not know about "us." If you have any decency, stay away from me and don't write any more letters. I'm warning you, don't make trouble for me. I could make trouble for you, double trouble. Remember L. Bay.

Wishing you all success in your new life (I hope youre making as much money as you claim),

                                        Marian

   Mrs. Ronald S. Matheson (and bear it in mind). Me come back to you? Don't ever give it another thought.

Ronald is a very successful business exec! I wouldn't rub it in, only you really put me through the "wringer" and you know it. No hard feelings on my part, just leave me alone, please.

The letter had no return address, but it was postmarked San Mateo, Calif. The date was indecipherable.

I put everything back and closed the suitcase and kicked it under the bed.

I went out into the court. In a room on the other side of it, a woman or an animal was moaning. Sable must have been watching for me. The sound became louder as he opened a sliding glass door, and was shut off as he closed it. He came toward me, his face tinged green by the reflected light from the foliage:

"Find anything significant?"

"He kept shells for an automatic in his drawer. I didn't come across the automatic."

"I didn't know Peter had a gun."

"Maybe he had, and sold it. Or it's possible the killer took it away from him."

"Anything else?"

"I have a tentative lead to his ex-wife, if you want me to explore his background."

"Why not leave it to the police? Trask is very competent, and an old friend of mine into the bargain. I wouldn't feel justified in taking you off the Galton case."

"The Galton case doesn't seem so very urgent."

"Possibly not. Still, I think you should stay with it for the present. Was Cassie Hildreth any help?"

"Some. I can't think of much more to be done around here. I was planning to drive to San Francisco."

"You can take a plane. I wrote you a check for two hundred dollars, and I'll give you a hundred in cash." He handed me the check and the money. "If you need any more, don't hesitate to call on me."

"I won't, but I'm afraid it's money down the drain."

Sable shrugged. He had worse problems. The moaning behind the glass door was louder, rising in peaks of sound which pierced my eardrums.

Chapter 7

I HATE coincidences. Aboard the plane, I spent a fruitless hour trying to work out possible connections between Maria Galton's loss of her son and Peter Culligan's loss of life. I had a delayed gestalt after I'd given up on the subject.

I was flipping through the smudged pages of *Chisel*, the little magazine that Cassie Hildreth had given me. Somebody named Chad Bolling was listed on the masthead as editor and publisher. He also had a poem in the magazine, "Elegy on the Death of Bix Beiderbecke." It said that the inconsolable cornet would pipe Eurydice out of Boss Pluto's smoke-filled basement. I liked it better than the poem about Luna.

I reread Anthony Galton's poem, wondering if Luna was his wife. Then the gestalt clicked. There was a town named Luna Bay on the coast south of San Francisco. From where I sat, a few thousand feet above the Peninsula, I could practically spit on it. And Culligan's ex-wife had referred to an "L. Bay" in her letter to him.

When the plane let down at International Airport, I headed for a telephone booth. The woman had signed herself Mrs. Ronald S. Matheson; the envelope had been postmarked in San Mateo.

I hardly expected a hit on such a random shot, after an indefinite lapse of time. But the name was in the directory: Ronald S. Matheson, 780 Sherwood Drive, Redwood City. I dialed the Emerson number.

I couldn't tell if it was a girl or a boy who answered. It was a child, pre-pubic: "Hello?"

"Is Mrs. Matheson there?"

"Just a minute, please. Mummy, you're wanted on the phone."

The child's voice trailed off, and a woman's took its place. It was cool and smooth and careful:

"Marian Matheson speaking. Who is calling, please?"

"My name is Archer. You've never heard of me."

"That's right, I haven't."

"Ever hear of a man named Culligan?"

692

There was a long pause. "Come again? I didn't catch the name."

"Culligan," I said. "Peter Culligan."

"What about him?"

"Did you ever know him?"

"Maybe I did, a long time ago. So what? Maybe I didn't."

"Let's not play games, Mrs. Matheson. I have some information, if you're interested."

"I'm not. Not if you're talking for Pete Culligan." Her voice had become harsher and deeper. "I don't care anything about him, as long as he leaves me alone. You can tell him that for me."

"I can't, though."

"Why not?"

"Because he's dead."

"Dead?" Her voice was a leaden echo.

"I'm investigating his murder." I'd just decided I was. "I'd like to talk to you about the circumstances."

"I don't see why. I had nothing to do with it. I didn't even know it happened."

"I'm aware of that. It's one reason I called."

"Who killed him?"

"I'll tell you when I see you."

"Who says you're seeing me?"

I waited.

"Where are you now?" she said.

"At the San Francisco Airport."

"I guess I can come there, if it has to be. I don't want you coming to the house. My husband—"

"I understand that. It's good of you to come at all. I'll be in the coffee shop."

"Are you in uniform?"

"Not at the moment." Or for the last ten years, but let her go on thinking I was law. "I'm wearing a gray suit. You won't miss me. I'll be sitting beside the windows close to the entrance."

"I'll be there in fifteen minutes. Did you say Archer?"

"Yes. Archer."

It took her twenty-five. I passed the time watching the big planes circling in, dragging their late-afternoon shadows along the runways.

A woman in a dark cloth coat came in, paused at the doorway, and looked around the huge room. Her eye lighted on me. She came toward my table, clutching her shiny leather purse as if it was a token of respectability. I got up to meet her:

"Mrs. Matheson?"

She nodded, and sat down hurriedly, as if she was afraid of being conspicuous. She was an ordinary-looking woman, decently dressed, who would never see forty again. There were flecks of gray in her carefully waved black hair, like little shards of iron.

She had once been handsome in a strong-boned way. Maybe she still was, under favorable lighting and circumstances. Her black eyes were her best feature, but they were hard with tension:

"I didn't want to come. But here I am."

"Will you have some coffee?"

"No, thanks. Let's have the bad news. I'll take it straight."

I gave it to her straight, leaving out nothing important. She began to twist the wedding ring on her finger, round and round.

"Poor guy," she said when I finished. "Why did they do it to him, do you know?"

"I was hoping you could help me answer that."

"You say you're not a policeman?"

"No. I'm a private investigator."

"I don't see why you come to me. We haven't been married for fifteen years. I haven't even seen him for ten. He wanted to come back to me, I guess he finally got tired of bucketing around. But I wasn't having any. I'm happily married to a good man—"

"When was the last time you heard from Culligan?"

"About a year ago. He wrote me a letter from Reno, claimed he'd struck it rich, that he could give me anything I wanted if I'd come back. Pete was always a dreamer. The first while after we were married, I used to believe in his dreams. But they all went blooey, one after another. I caught onto him so many years ago it isn't funny. I'm not laughing, notice."

"What kind of dreams did he dream?"

"Great big ones, the kind that never come off. Like he was going to open a chain of restaurants where food of all nations would be served. He'd hire the best chefs in the country, French, Chinese, Armenian, and so on. At which time he was a short-order cook on lower Market. Then there was the time he worked out a new system to beat the ponies. He took every cent we possessed to try it out. He even hocked my furniture. It took me all that winter to work it off." Her voice had the driving energy of old anger that had found an outlet. "That was Pete's idea of a honeymoon, me working and him playing the ponies."

"How did you get hooked up with him?"

"I was a dreamer, too, I guess you'd say. I thought I could straighten him out, make a man of him. That all he needed was the love of a good woman. I wasn't a good woman, and I don't pretend to be. But I was better than he was."

"Where did you meet?"

"In the San Francisco Hospital where I was working. I was a nurse's aide, and Pete was in the ward with a broken nose and a couple of broken ribs. He got beaten up in a gang fight."

"A gang fight?"

"That's all I know. Pete just said it was some rumble on the docks. I should have taken warning, but after he got out of the hospital I went on seeing him. He was young and good-looking, and like I said I thought he had the makings of a man. So I married him—the big mistake of my life, and I've made some doozies."

"How long ago was that?"

"Nineteen-thirty-six. That dates me, doesn't it? But I was only twenty-one at the time." She paused, and raised her eyes to my face. "I don't know why I'm telling you all this. I've never told a living soul in my life. Why don't you stop me?"

"I'm hoping you'll tell me something that will help. Did your husband go in for gambling?"

"Please don't call him that. I married Pete Culligan, but he was no husband to me." She lifted her head. "I have a real husband now. Incidentally, he'll be expecting me back to make his dinner." She leaned forward in her chair and started to get up.

"Can't you give me a few minutes more, Mrs. Matheson? I've told you all I know about Peter—"

She laughed shortly. "If I told you all *I* know, it would take all night. Okay, a few more minutes, if you promise me there won't be any publicity. My husband and me have a position to keep up. I'm a member of the PTA, the League of Women Voters."

"There won't be any publicity. Was he a gambler?"

"As much as he could afford to be. But he was always small-time."

"This money he said he made in Reno—did he tell you how he made it?"

"Not a word. But I don't think it was gambling. He was never that lucky."

"Do you still have his letter?"

"Certainly not. I burned it, the same day I got it."

"Why?"

"Because I didn't want it around the house. I felt like it was dirt tracked into the house."

"Was Culligan a crook, or a hustler?"

"Depends what you mean by that." Her eyes were wary.

"Did he break the law?"

"I guess everybody does from time to time."

"Was he ever arrested?"

"Yeah. Mostly for drunk and disorderly, nothing serious."

"Did he carry a gun?"

"Not when I was with him. I wouldn't let him."

"But the issue came up?"

"I didn't say that." She was becoming evasive. "I meant I wouldn't let him even if he wanted to."

"Did he own a gun?"

"I wouldn't know," she said.

I'd almost lost her. She wasn't talking frankly or willingly any more. So I threw her the question I didn't expect her to answer, hoping to gather something from her reaction to it:

"You mentioned an L. Bay in your letter to Culligan. What happened there?"

Her lips were pushed out stiff and pale, as if they were made of bone. The dark eyes seemed to shrink in her head:

"I don't know what makes you ask that." The tip of her tongue moved along her upper lip, and she tried again: "What was that about a bay in my letter? I don't remember any bay in my letter."

"I do, Mrs. Matheson." I quoted: "'I could make trouble for you, double trouble. Remember L. Bay.'"

"If I said that, I don't know what I meant."

"There's a place called Luna Bay about twenty-five or thirty miles from here."

"Is there?" she said stupidly.

"You know it. What did Pete Culligan do there?"

"I don't remember. It must have been some dirty trick he played on me." She was a poor liar, as most honest people are. "Does it matter?"

"It seems to matter to you. Did you and Pete live in Luna Bay?"

"I guess you could call it living. I had a job there, doing practical nursing."

"When?"

"Way back when. I don't remember what year."

"Who were you working for?"

"Some people. I don't remember their name." She leaned toward me urgently, her eyes pointed like flints. "You have that letter with you?"

"I left it where I found it, in Culligan's suitcase in the house where he worked. Why?"

"I want it back. I wrote it, and it belongs to me."

"You may have to take that up with the police. It's probably in their hands by now."

"Will they be coming here?" She looked behind her, and all around the crowded restaurant, as if she expected to find a policeman bearing down on her.

"It depends on how soon they catch the killer. They may have him already, in which case they won't bother with secondary leads. Do you have any idea who it was, Mrs. Matheson?"

"How could I? I haven't seen Pete in ten years, I told you."

"What happened in Luna Bay?"

"Change the record, can't you? If anything happened, which I can't remember, it was strictly between me and Pete. Nothing to do with anybody else, understand?"

Her voice and looks were altering under pressure. She seemed to have broken through into a lower stratum of experience and a coarser personality. And she knew it. She pulled her purse toward her and held on to it with both hands. It was a good purse, beautifully cut from genuine lizard. In contrast with it, her hands were rough, their knuckles swollen and cracked by years of work.

She raised her eyes to mine. I caught the red reflection of fear in their centers. She was afraid of me, and she was afraid to leave me.

"Mrs. Matheson, Peter Culligan was murdered today—"

"You expect me to go into mourning?"

"I expect you to give me any information that might have a bearing on his death."

"I already did. You can leave me alone, understand? You're not getting me mixed up in no murder. Any murder."

"Did you ever hear of a man named Anthony Galton?"

"No."

"John Brown?"

"No."

I could see the bitter forces of her will gathering in her face. She exerted them, and got up, and walked away from me and her fear.

Chapter 8

I WENT back to the telephone booths and looked up the name Chad Bolling in the Bay Area directories. I didn't expect to find it, after more than twenty years, but I was still running in luck. Bolling had a Telegraph Hill address. I immured myself in one of the booths and called him.

A woman's voice answered: "This is the Bolling residence."

"Is Mr. Bolling available?"

"Available for what?" she said abruptly.

"It has to do with magazine publication of a poem. The name is Archer," I added, trying to sound like a wealthy editor.

"I see." She softened her tone. "I don't know where Chad is at the moment. And I'm afraid he won't be home for dinner. I do know he'll be at The Listening Ear later this evening."

"The Listening Ear?"

"It's a new night club. Chad's giving a reading there tonight. If you're interested in poetry, you owe it to yourself to catch it."

"What time does he go on?"

"I think ten."

I rented a car and drove it up Bayshore to the city, where I parked it under Union Square. Above the lighted towers of the hotels, twilight had thickened into darkness. A damp chill had risen from the sea; I could feel it through my clothes. Even the colored lights around the square had a chilly look.

I bought a pint of whisky to ward off the chill and checked in at the Salisbury, a small side-street hotel where I usually stayed in San Francisco. The desk clerk was new to me. Desk clerks are always moving up or down. This one was old and on his way down; his sallow face drooped in the pull of gravity. He handed me my key reluctantly:

"No luggage, sir?"

I showed him my bottle in its paper bag. He didn't smile.

"My car was stolen."

"That's too bad." His eyes were sharp and incredulous behind fussy little pince-nez. "I'm afraid I'll have to ask you to pay in advance."

"All right." I gave him the five dollars and asked for a receipt.

The bellhop who took me up in the old open ironwork elevator had been taking me up in the same elevator for nearly twenty years. We shook hands. His was crumpled by arthritis.

"How are you, Coney?"

"Fine, Mr. Archer, fine. I'm taking a new pill, phenylbuta-something. It's doing wonders for me."

He stepped out and did a little soft-shoe step to prove it. He'd once been half of a brother act that played the Orpheum circuit. He danced me down the corridor to the door of my room.

"What brings you up to the City?" he said when we were inside. To San Franciscans, there's only one city.

"I flew up for a little entertainment."

"I thought Hollywood was the world's center of entertainment."

"I'm looking for something different," I said. "Have you heard of a new club called The Listening Ear?"

"Yeah, but you wouldn't like it." He shook his white head. "I hope you didn't come all the way up here for *that*."

"What's the matter with it?"

"It's a culture cave. One of these bistros where guys read poems to music. It ain't your speed at all."

"My taste is becoming more elevated."

His grin showed all his remaining teeth. "Don't kid an old man, eh?"

"Ever hear of Chad Bolling?"

"Sure. He promotes a lot of publicity for himself." Coney looked at me anxiously. "You really going in for the poetry kick, Mr. Archer? With music?"

"I have long yearned for the finer things."

Such as a good French dinner at a price I could pay. I took a taxi to the Ritz Poodle Dog, and had a good French dinner. When I finished eating, it was nearly ten o'clock.

The Listening Ear was full of dark blue light and pale blue music. A combo made up of piano, bass fiddle, trumpet, and drums was playing something advanced. I didn't have my slide rule with me, but the four musicians seemed to understand each other. From time to time they smiled and nodded like space jockeys passing in the night.

The man at the piano seemed to be the head technician. He

smiled more distantly than the others, and when the melody had been done to death, he took the applause with more exquisite remoteness. Then he bent over his keyboard again like a mad scientist.

The tight-hipped waitress who brought my whisky-and-water was interchangeable with nightclub girls anywhere. Even her parts looked interchangeable. But the audience was different from other nightclub crowds. Most of them were young people with serious expressions on their faces. A high proportion of the girls had short straight hair through which they ran their fingers from time to time. Many of the boys had longer hair than the girls, but they didn't run their fingers through it so much. They stroked their beards instead.

Another tune failed to survive the operation, and then the lights went up. A frail-looking middle-aged man in a dark suit sidled through the blue curtains at the rear of the room. The pianist extended his hand and assisted him onto the bandstand. The audience applauded. The frail-looking man, by way of a bow, allowed his chin to subside on the big black bow tie which blossomed on his shirt front. The applause rose to a crescendo.

"I give you Mr. Chad Bolling," the pianist said. "Master of all the arts, singer of songs to be sung, painter of pictures, hepcat, man of letters. Mr. Chad Bolling."

The clapping went on for a while. The poet lifted his hand as if in benediction, and there was silence.

"Thank you, friends," he said. "With the support of my brilliant young friend Fingers Donahue, I wish to bring to you tonight, if my larynx will permit, my latest poem." His mouth twisted sideways as if in self-mockery. "It ain't chopped liver."

He paused. The instruments began to murmur behind him. Bolling took a roll of manuscript out of his inside breast pocket and unrolled it under the light.

"'Death Is Tabu,'" he said, and began to chant in a hoarse carrying voice that reminded me of a carnival spieler. He said that at the end of the night he sat in wino alley where the angels drink canned heat, and that he heard a beat. It seemed a girl came to the mouth of the alley and asked him what he was doing in death valley. "'Death is the ultimate crutch,' she said," he said. She asked him to come home with her to bed.

He said that sex was the ultimate crutch, but he turned out to be wrong. It seemed he heard a gong. She fled like a ghost, and he was lost, at the end of the end of the night.

While the drummer and the bass fiddler made shock waves on the roof, Bolling raised his voice and began to belt it out. About how he followed her up and down and around and underground, up Russian Hill and Nob Hill and Telegraph Hill and across the Bay Bridge and back by way of the Oakland ferry. So he found the sphinx on Market Street cadging drinks and they got tight and danced on the golden asphalt of delight.

Eventually she fell upon her bed. "I'm star-transfixed," she said. He drank the canned hell of her lips, and it went on like that for quite a while, while the music tittered and moaned. She finally succeeded in convincing him that death was the ultimate crutch, whatever that meant. She knew, because it happened she was dead. "Good night, mister," she said, or he said she said. "Good night, sister," he said.

The audience waited to make sure that Bolling was finished, then burst into a surge of clapping, interspersed with *bravo*s and *ole*'s. Bolling stood with pursed lips and absorbed it like a little boy sucking soda pop through a straw. While the lower part of his face seemed to be enjoying itself, his eyes were puzzled. His mouth stretched in a clownish grin:

"Thanks, cats. I'm glad you dig me. Now dig this."

He read a poem about the seven blind staggers of the soul, and one about the beardless wonders on the psycho wards who were going to be the *gurus* of the new truth. At this point I switched off my hearing aid, and waited for it to be over. It took a long time. After the reading there were books to be autographed, questions to be answered, drinks to be drunk.

It was nearly midnight when Bolling left a tableful of admirers and made for the door. I got up to follow him. A large girl with a very hungry face cut in front of me. She attached herself to Bolling's arm and began to talk into his ear, bending over because she was taller than he was.

He shook his head. "Sorry, kiddie, I'm a married man. Also I'm old enough to be your father."

"What are years?" she said. "A woman's wisdom is ageless."

"Let's see you prove it, honey."

He shook her loose. Tragically clutching the front of her baggy black sweater, she said: "I'm not pretty, am I?"

"You're beautiful, honey. The Greek navy could use you for launching ships. Take it up with them, why don't you?"

He reached up and patted her on the head and went out. I caught up with him on the sidewalk as he was hailing a taxi.

"Mr. Bolling, do you have a minute?"

"It depends on what you want."

"I want to buy you a drink, ask you a few questions."

"I've had a drink. Several, in fact. It's late. I'm beat. Write me a letter, why don't you?"

"I can't write."

He brightened a little. "You mean to tell me you're not an unrecognized literary genius? I thought everybody was."

"I'm a detective. I'm looking for a man. You may have known him at one time."

His taxi had turned in the street and pulled into the curb. He signaled the driver to wait:

"What's his name?"

"John Brown."

"Oh sure, I knew him well at Harpers Ferry. I'm older than I look." His empty clowning continued automatically while he sized me up.

"In 1936 you printed a poem of his in a magazine called *Chisel*."

"I'm sorry you brought that up. What a lousy name for a magazine. No wonder it folded."

"The name of the poem was 'Luna.'"

"I'm afraid I don't remember it. A lot of words have flowed under the bridge. I did know a John Brown back in the thirties. Whatever happened to John?"

"That's what I'm trying to find out."

"Okay, buy me a drink. But not at the Ear, eh? I get tired of the shaves and the shave-nots."

Bolling dismissed his taxi. We walked about sixty feet to the next bar. A pair of old girls on the two front stools flapped their eyelashes at us as we went in. There was nobody else in the place but a comatose bartender. He roused himself long enough to pour us a couple of drinks.

We sat down in one of the booths, and I showed Bolling my pictures of Tony Galton. "Do you recognize him?"

"I think so. We corresponded for a while, but I only met him once or twice. Twice. He called on us when we were living in Sausalito. And then one Sunday when I was driving down the coast by Luna Bay, I returned the visit."

"Were they living at Luna Bay?"

"A few miles this side of it, in an old place on the ocean. I had the very devil of a time finding it, in spite of the directions Brown had given me. I remember now, he asked me not to tell anyone else where he was living. I was the only one who knew. I don't know why he singled me out, except that he was keen to have me visit his home, and see his son. He may have had some sort of father feeling about me, though I wasn't much older than he was."

"He had a son?"

"Yes, they had a baby. He'd just been born, and he wasn't much bigger than my thumb. Little John was the apple of his father's eye. They were quite a touching little family."

Bolling's voice was gentle. Away from the crowd and the music he showed a different personality. Like other performers, he had a public face and a private one. Each of them was slightly phony, but the private face suited him better.

"You met the wife, did you?"

"Certainly. She was sitting on the front porch when I got there, nursing the baby. She had lovely white breasts, and she didn't in the least mind exposing them. It made quite a picture, there on the bluff above the sea. I tried to get a poem out of her, but it didn't come off. I never really got to know her."

"What sort of a girl was she?"

"Very attractive, I'd say, in the visual sense. She didn't have too much to say for herself. As a matter of fact, she massacred the English language. I suppose she had the fascination of ignorance for Brown. I've seen other young writers and artists fall for girls like that. I've been guilty of it myself, when I was in my pre-Freudian period." He added wryly: "That means before I got analyzed."

"Do you remember her name?"

"Mrs. Brown's name?" He shook his head. "Sorry. In the

poem I botched I called her Stella Maris, star of the sea. But that doesn't help you, does it?"

"Can you tell me when you were there? It must have been toward the end of the year 1936."

"Yes. It was around Christmas, just before Christmas—I took along some bauble for the child. Young Brown was very pleased that I did." Bolling pulled at his chin, lengthening his face. "It's queer I never heard from him after that."

"Did you ever try to get in touch with him?"

"No, I didn't. He may have felt I'd brushed him off. Perhaps I did, without intending to. The woods were full of young writers; it was hard to keep track of them all. I was doing valid work in those days, and a lot of them came to me. Frankly, I've hardly thought of Brown from that day to this. Is he still living on the coast?"

"I don't know. What was he doing in Luna Bay, did he tell you?"

"He was trying to write a novel. He didn't seem to have a job, and I can't imagine what they were living on. They couldn't have been completely destitute, either. They had a nurse to look after the mother and child."

"A nurse?"

"I suppose she was what you'd call a practical nurse. One of those young women who take charge," he added vaguely.

"Do you recall anything about her?"

"She had remarkable eyes, I remember. Sharp black eyes which kept watching me. I don't think she approved of the literary life."

"Did you talk to her at all?"

"I may have. I have a distinct impression of her, that she was the only sensible person in the house. Brown and his wife seemed to be living in Cloud-Cuckoo-Land."

"How do you mean?"

"They were out of touch with the ordinary run of life. I don't mean that as a criticism. I've been out of touch enough in my own life, God knows. I still am." He gave me his clown grin. "You can't make a Hamlet without breaking egos. But let's not talk about me."

"Getting back to the nurse, do you think you can remember her name?"

"I know perfectly well I can't."

"Would you recognize it if I said it?"

"That I doubt. But try me."

"Marian Culligan," I said. "C-u-l-l-i-g-a-n."

"It rings no bell with me. Sorry."

Bolling finished his drink and looked around the bar as if he expected something to happen. I guessed that most of the things that can happen to a man had already happened to him. He changed expressions like rubber masks, but between the masks I could see dismay in his face.

"We might as well have another drink," he said. "This one will be on me. I'm loaded. I just made a hundred smackers at the Ear." Even his commercialism sounded phony.

While I lit a fire under the bartender, Bolling studied the photographs I'd left on the table:

"That's John all right. A nice boy, and perhaps a talented one, but out of this world. All the way out of this world. Where did he get the money for horses and tennis?"

"From his family. They're heavily loaded."

"Good Lord, don't tell me he's the missing heir. Is that why you're making a search for him?"

"That's why."

"They waited long enough."

"You can say that again. Can you tell me how to get to the house the Browns were living in when you visited them?"

"I'm afraid not. I might be able to *show* you, though."

"When?"

"Tomorrow morning if you like."

"That's good of you."

"Not at all. I *liked* John Brown. Besides, I haven't been to Luna Bay for years. Eons. Maybe I'll rediscover my lost youth."

"Maybe." But I didn't think it likely.

Neither did he.

Chapter 9

IN THE morning I picked up Bolling at his Telegraph Hill apartment. It was one of those sparkling days that make up for all the fog in San Francisco. An onshore wind had swept the air clear and tessellated the blue surface of the Bay. A white ship cutting a white furrow was headed out toward the Golden Gate. White gulls hung above her on the air.

Bolling looked at all this with a fishy eye. He was frowsy and gray and shivering with hangover. He crawled into the back seat and snored all the way to our destination. It was a dingy, formless town sprawling along the coast highway. Its low buildings were dwarfed by the hills rising behind it, the broad sea spreading out in front.

I stopped beside a filling-station where the inland road met Highway 1, and told Bolling to wake up.

"Wha' for?" he mumbled from the depths of sleep. "Wha' happen?"

"Nothing yet. Where do we go from here?"

He groaned and sat up and looked around. The glare from the ocean made his eyes water. He shaded them with his hand. "Where are we?"

"Luna Bay."

"It doesn't look the same," he complained. "I'm not sure whether I can find the place or not. Anyway, we turn north here. Just drive along slowly, and I'll try to spot the road."

Almost two miles north of Luna Bay, the highway cut inland across the base of a promontory. On the far side of the promontory, a new-looking asphalt road turned off toward the sea. A billboard stood at the intersection: "Marvista Manor. Three bedrooms and rumpus room. Tile bathrooms. Built-in kitchens. All utilities in. See our model home."

Bolling tapped my shoulder. "This is the place, I think."

I backed up and made a left turn. The road ran straight for several hundred yards up a gentle slope. We passed a rectangle of bare adobe as big as a football field, where earth-movers were working. A wooden sign at the roadside explained their activity: "Site of the Marvista Shopping Center."

From the crest of the slope we looked down over the roof-tops of a hundred or more houses. They stood along the hillside on raw earth terraces which were only just beginning to sprout grass. Driving along the winding street between them, I could see that most of the houses were occupied. There were curtains at the windows, children playing in the yards, clothes drying on the lines. The houses were painted different colors, which only seemed to emphasize their sameness.

The street unwound itself at the foot of the slope, paralleling the edge of the bluffs. I stopped the car and turned to look at Bolling.

"I'm sorry," he said. "It's changed so much, I can't be certain this is the place. There were some clapboard bungalows, five or six of them, scattered along the bluff. The Browns lived in one of them, if memory serves me."

We got out and walked toward the edge of the bluff. A couple of hundred feet below, the sea wrinkled like blue metal against its base, and burst in periodic white explosions. A mile to the south, under the shelter of the promontory, a cove of quiet water lay in a brown rind of beach.

Bolling pointed toward the cove. "This has to be the place. I remember Brown telling me that inlet was used as a harbor by rum-runners in the old Prohibition days. There used to be an old hotel on the bluff above it. You could see it from the Browns' front porch. Their bungalow must have stood quite near here."

"They probably tore it down when they put in the road. It wouldn't have done me much good to see it, anyway. I was hoping I'd run across a neighbor who remembered the Browns."

"I suppose you could canvass the tradesmen in Luna Bay."

"I could."

"Oh well, it's nice to get out in the country."

Bolling wandered off along the edge of the bluff. Suddenly he said: "Whee!" in a high voice like a gull's screak. He began to flap his arms.

I ran toward him. "What's the matter?"

"Whee!" he said again, and let out a childish laugh. "I was just imagining that I was a bird."

"How did you like it?"

"Very much." He flapped his arms some more. "I can fly! I breast the windy currents of the sky. I soar like Icarus toward the sun. The wax melts. I fall from a great height into the sea. Mother Thalassa."

"Mother who?"

"Thalassa, the sea, the Homeric sea. We could build another Athens. I used to think we could do it in San Francisco, build a new city of man on the great hills. A city measured with forgiveness. Oh, well."

His mood sank again. I pulled him away from the edge. He was so unpredictable I thought he might take a flying leap into space, and I was beginning to like him.

"Speaking of mothers," I said, "if John Brown's wife had just had a baby, she must have been going to a doctor. Did they happen to mention where the baby was born?"

"Yes. Right in their house. The nearest hospital is in Redwood City, and Brown didn't want to take his wife there. The chances are she had a local doctor."

"Let's hope he's still around."

I drove back through the housing-tract until I saw a young woman walking a pram. She shied like a filly when I pulled up beside her. In the daytime the tract was reserved for women and children; unknown men in cars were probably kidnappers. I got out and approached her, smiling as innocuously as I could.

"I'm looking for a doctor."

"Oh. Is somebody sick?"

"My friend's wife is going to have a baby. They're thinking of moving into Marvista Manor, and they thought they'd better check on the medical situation."

"Dr. Meyers is very good," she said. "I go to him myself."

"In Luna Bay?"

"That's right."

"How long has he practiced there?"

"I wouldn't know. We just moved out from Richmond month before last."

"How old is Dr. Meyers?"

"Thirty, thirty-five, I dunno."

"Too young," I said.

"If your friend will feel safer with an older man, I think there is one in town. I don't remember his name, though. Personally I like a young doctor, they know all the latest wonder drugs and all."

Wonder drugs. I thanked her, and drove back to Luna Bay in search of a drugstore. The proprietor gave me a rundown on the three local doctors. A Dr. George Dineen was the only one who had practiced there in the thirties. He was an elderly man on the verge of retirement. I'd probably find him in his office if he wasn't out on a call. It was only a couple of blocks from the drugstore.

I left Bolling drinking coffee at the fountain, and walked to the doctor's office. It occupied the front rooms of a rambling house with green shingle walls which stood on a dusty side street. A woman of about sixty answered the door. She had blue-white hair and a look on her face you don't see too often any more, the look of a woman who hasn't been disappointed:

"Yes, young man?"

"I'd like to see the doctor."

"His office hours are in the afternoon. They don't start till one-thirty."

"I don't want to see him as a patient."

"If you're a pharmaceutical salesman, you'd better wait till after lunch. Dr. Dineen doesn't like his mornings to be disturbed."

"I'm only in town for the morning. I'm investigating a disappearance. He may be able to help me to find a missing man."

She had a very responsive face, in spite of its slack lines of age. Her eyes imagined what it would be like to lose a loved one. "Well, that's different. Come in, Mr.—"

"Archer. I'm a private detective."

"My husband is in the garden. I'll bring him in."

She left me in the doctor's office. Several diplomas hung on the wall above the old oak desk. The earliest stated that Dr. Dineen had graduated from the University of Ohio Medical School in 1914. The room itself was like a preserve of prewar time. The cracked leather furniture had been molded by use into comfortable human shapes. A set of old chessmen laid out on a board stood like miniature armies stalled in the sunlight that fell slanting from the window.

The doctor came in and shook hands with me. He was a tall high-shouldered old man. His eyes were noncommittal under shaggy gray brows which hung like bird's-nests on the cliff of his face. He lowered himself into the chair behind his desk. His head was partly bald; a few strands of hair lay lankly across the top of his scalp.

"You mentioned a missing person to my wife. One of my patients, perhaps?"

"Perhaps. His name was John Brown. In 1936 he and his wife lived a few miles up the coast where the Marvista tract is now."

"I remember them very well," the doctor said. "Their son was in this office not so very long ago, sitting where you're sitting."

"Their son?"

"John, Junior. You may know him. He's looking for his father, too."

"No," I said, "I don't know him. But I'd certainly like to."

"I daresay that could be arranged." Dr. Dineen's deep voice rumbled to a stop. He looked at me intently, as if he was getting ready to make a diagnosis. "First, I'd want to know the reasons for your interest in the family."

"I was hired to make a search for the father, the senior John Brown."

"Has your search had any results?"

"Not until now. You say this boy who came to see you is looking for his father?"

"That is correct."

"What brought him to you?"

"He has the ordinary filial emotions. If his father is alive, he wants to be with him. If his father is dead, he wants to know."

"I mean what brought him here to your office specifically? Had you known him before?"

"I brought him into the world. In my profession, that constitutes the best possible introduction."

"Are you sure it's the same boy?"

"I have no reason to doubt it." The doctor looked at me with some distaste, as if I'd criticized some work he'd done with his hands. "Before we go any further, Mr. Archer, you can oblige me with a fuller response to my question. You haven't told me who hired you."

"Sorry, I can't do that. I've been asked to keep my client's identity confidential."

"No doubt you have. I've been keeping such matters confidential for the past forty years."

"And you won't talk unless I do, is that it?"

The doctor raised his hand and brushed the thought away from his face, like an annoying insect. "I suggested no bargain. I simply want to know who I'm dealing with. There may be grave matters involved."

"There are."

"I think you ought to elucidate that remark."

"I can't."

We faced each other in a stretching silence. His eyes were steady, and bright with the hostility of a proud old man. I was afraid of losing him entirely, just as the case seemed to be breaking open. While I didn't doubt his integrity, I had my own integrity to think of, too. I'd promised Gordon Sable and Mrs. Galton to name no names.

Dr. Dineen produced a pipe, and began to pack its charred bowl with tobacco from an oilskin pouch. "We seem to have reached a stalemate. Do you play chess, Mr. Archer?"

"Not as well as you do, probably. I've never studied the book."

"I would have thought you had." He finished packing his pipe, and lit it with a kitchen match. The blue smoke swirled in the hollow shafts of sunlight from the window. "We're wasting both our times. I suggest you make a move."

"I thought this was a stalemate."

"New game." A flicker of interest showed in his eyes for the first time. "Tell me about yourself. Why would a man of your sort spend his life doing the kind of work you do? Do you make much money?"

"Enough to live on. I don't do it for the money, though. I do it because I want to."

"Isn't it dirty work, Mr. Archer?"

"It depends on who's doing it, like doctoring or anything else. I try to keep it clean."

"Do you succeed?"

"Not entirely. I've made some bad mistakes about people. Some of them assume that a private detective is automatically crooked, and they act accordingly, as you're doing now."

The old man emitted a grunt which sounded like a seal's bark. "I can't act blindly in a matter of this importance."

"Neither can I. I don't know what makes it important to you—"

"I'll tell you," he said shortly. "Human lives are involved. A boy's love for his parents is involved. I try to handle these things with the care they deserve."

"I appreciate that. You seem to have a special interest in John Brown, Junior."

"I do have. The young fellow's had a rough time of it. I don't want him hurt unnecessarily."

"It's not my intention to hurt him. If the boy is actually John Brown's son, you'd be doing him a favor by leading me to him."

"You're going to have to prove that to me. I'll be frank to say I've had one or two experiences with private detectives in my time. One of them had to do with the blackmailing of a patient of mine—a young girl who had a child out of wedlock. I don't mean that reflects on you, but it makes a man leery."

"All right. I'll put my position hypothetically. Let's say I'd been hired to find the heir to several million dollars."

"I've heard that one before. You'll have to invent a better gambit than that."

"I didn't invent it. It happens to be the truth."

"Prove it."

"That will be easy to do when the time comes. Right now, I'd say the burden of proof is on this boy. Can he prove his identity?"

"The question never came up. As a matter of fact, the proof of his identity is on his face. I knew whose son he was as soon as he stepped in here. His resemblance to his father is striking."

"How long ago did he turn up?"

"About a month. I've seen him since."

"As a patient?"

"As a friend," Dineen said.

"Why did he come to you in the first place?"

"My name is on his birth certificate. Now hold your horses, young man. Give me a chance to think." The doctor smoked in silence for a while. "Do you seriously tell me that this boy is heir to a fortune?"

"He will be, if his father is dead. His grandmother is still living. She has the money."

"But you won't divulge her name?"

"Not without her permission. I suppose I could call her long distance. But I'd rather have a chance to talk to the boy first."

The doctor hesitated. He held his right hand poised in the air, then struck the desk-top with the flat of it. "I'll take a chance on you, though I may regret it later."

"You won't if I can help it. Where can I find him?"

"We'll come to that."

"What did he have to say about his origins?"

"It would be more appropriate if you got that from him. I'm willing to tell you what I know about his father and mother from my own direct observation. And this has more relevance than you may think." He paused. "What precisely did this anonymous client of yours hire you to do?"

"Find John Brown, Senior," I said.

"I take it that isn't his real name."

"That's right, it isn't."

"I'm not surprised," Dineen said. "At the time I knew him, I did some speculating about him. It occurred to me he might be a remittance man—one of those ne'er-do-wells whose families paid them to stay away from home. I remember when his wife was delivered, Brown paid me with a hundred-dollar-bill. It didn't seem to suit with their scale of living. And there were other things, his wife's jewels, for example—diamonds and rubies in ornate gold settings. One day she came in here like a walking jewelry store.

"I warned her not to wear them. They were living out in the country, near the old Inn, and it was fairly raw territory in those days. Also, people were poor. A lot of them used to pay me for my services in fish. I had so much fish during the Depression I've never eaten it since. No matter. A public display of jewels was an incitement to robbery. I told the young lady so, and she left off wearing them, at least when I saw her."

"Did you see her often?"

"Four or five times, I'd say. Once or twice before the boy was born, and several times afterwards. She was a healthy enough wench, no complications. The main thing I did for her was to instruct her in the care of an infant. Nothing in her background had prepared her for motherhood."

"Did she talk about her background?"

"She didn't have to. It had left marks on her body, for one thing. She'd been beaten half to death with a belt buckle."

"Not by her husband?"

"Hardly. There had been other men in her life, as the phrase goes. I gathered that she'd been on her own from an early age. She was one of the wandering children of the thirties—quite a different sort from her husband."

"How old was she?"

"I think nineteen or twenty, perhaps older. She looked older. Her experiences hadn't hardened her, but as I said they left her unprepared for motherhood. Even after she was back on her feet, she needed a nurse to help her care for the child. Actually, she was a child herself in emotional development."

"Do you remember the nurse's name?"

"Let me see. I believe she was a Mrs. Kerrigan."

"Or Culligan?"

"Culligan, that was it. She was a good young woman, fairly well trained. I believe she took off at the same time the Brown family did."

"The Brown family took off?"

"They skipped, without a good-by or a thank-you to anybody. Or so it appeared at the time."

"When was this?"

"A very few weeks after the child was born. It was close to Christmas Day of 1936, I think a day or two after. I remember it so distinctly because I've gone into it since with the sheriff's men."

"Recently?"

"Within the last five months. To make a long story short, when they were clearing the land for the Marvista tract, a set of bones were unearthed. The local deputy asked me to look them over to see what I could learn from them. I did so. They were human bones, which had probably belonged to a man of medium height, in his early twenties.

"It's not unlikely, in my opinion, that they are John Brown's bones. They were found buried under the house he lived in. The house was torn down to make way for the new road. Unfortunately, we had no means of making a positive identification. The skull was missing, which ruled out the possibility of dental evidence."

"It rules in the possibility of murder."

Dineen nodded gravely. "There's rather more than a possibility of murder. One of the cervical vertebrae had been cut through by a heavy instrument. I'd say John Brown, if that is who he is, was decapitated with an ax."

Chapter 10

B EFORE I left Dr. Dineen, he gave me a note of introduction to the deputy in charge of the local sheriff's office, written on a prescription blank; and the address of the gas station where John Brown, Jr., worked. I walked back to the drugstore in a hurry. Bolling was still at the fountain, with a grilled cheese sandwich in his left hand and a pencil in his right. He was simultaneously munching the sandwich and scribbling in a notebook.

"Sorry to keep you waiting—"

"Excuse me, I'm writing a poem."

He went on scribbling. I ate an impatient sandwich while he finished, and dragged him out to the car:

"I want to show you somebody; I'll explain who he is later." I started the car and turned south on the highway. "What's your poem about?"

"The city of man. I'm making a break-through into the affirmative. It's going to be good—the first good poem I've written in years."

He went on telling me about it, in language which I didn't understand. I found the place I was looking for on the southern outskirts of the town. It was a small independent station with three pumps, one attendant. The attendant was a young man in white drill coveralls. He was busy gassing a pickup truck whose bed was piled with brown fishermen's nets. I pulled in behind it and watched him.

There was no doubt that he looked like Anthony Galton. He had the same light eyes set wide apart, the same straight nose and full mouth. Only his hair was different; it was dark and straight.

Bolling was leaning forward in the seat. "For Christ's sake! Is it Brown? It can't be Brown. He's almost as old as I am."

"He had a son, remember."

"Is this the son?"

"I think so. Do you remember the color of the baby's hair?"

"It was dark, what there was of it. Like his mother's."

Bolling started to get out of the car.

"Wait a minute," I said. "Don't tell him who you are."

"I want to ask him about his father."

"He doesn't know where his father is. Besides, there's a question of identity. I want to see what he says without any prompting."

Bolling gave me a frustrated look, but he stayed in the car. The driver of the pickup paid for his gas and rattled away. I pulled up even with the pumps, and got out for a better look at the boy.

He appeared to be about twenty-one or -two. He was very good-looking, as his putative father had been. His smile was engaging.

"What can I do for you, sir?"

"Fill her up. It'll only take a couple of gallons. I stopped because I want you to check the oil."

"I'll be glad to, sir."

He seemed like a willing boy. He filled the tank, and wiped the windshield spotless. But when he lifted the hood to check the oil, he couldn't find the dip-stick. I showed him where it was.

"Been working here long?"

He looked embarrassed. "Two weeks. I haven't caught on to all the new cars yet."

"Think nothing of it." I looked across the highway at the windswept shore where the long combers were crashing. "This is nice country. I wouldn't mind settling out here."

"Are you from San Francisco?"

"My friend is." I indicated Bolling, who was still in the car, sulking. "I came up from Santa Teresa last night."

He didn't react to the name.

"Who owns the beach property across the highway, do you know?"

"I'm sorry, I wouldn't know. My boss probably would, though."

"Where is he?"

"Mr. Turnell has gone to lunch. He should be back pretty soon, if you want to talk to him."

"How soon?"

He glanced at the cheap watch on his wrist. "Fifteen or twenty minutes. His lunch-hour is from eleven to twelve. It's twenty to twelve now."

"I might as well wait for him. I'm in no hurry."

Bolling was in visible pain by this time. He made a conspiratorial gesture, beckoning me to the car.

"Is it Brown's son?" he said in a stage whisper.

"Could be."

"Why don't you ask him?"

"I'm waiting for him to tell me. Take it easy, Mr. Bolling."

"May I talk to him?"

"I'd just as soon you didn't. This is a ticklish business."

"I don't see why it should be. Either he is or he isn't."

The boy came up behind me. "Is something the matter, sir? Anything more I can do?"

"Nothing on both counts. The service was fine."

"Thank you."

His teeth showed bright in his tanned face. His smile was strained, though. He seemed to sense the tension in me and Bolling. I said as genially as I knew how:

"Are you from these parts?"

"I could say I was, I guess. I was born a few miles from here."

"But you're not a local boy."

"That's true. How can you tell?"

"Accent. I'd say you were raised in the middle west."

"I was." He seemed pleased by my interest. "I just came out from Michigan this year."

"Have you had any higher education?"

"College, you mean? As a matter of fact I have. Why do you ask?"

"I was thinking you could do better for yourself than jockeying a gas pump."

"I hope to," he said, with a look of aspiration. "I regard this work as temporary."

"What kind of work would you like to do?"

He hesitated, flushing under his tan. "I'm interested in acting. I know that sounds ridiculous. Half the people who come to California probably want to be actors."

"Is that why you came to California?"

"It was one of the reasons."

"This is a way-stop to Hollywood for you, then?"

"I guess you could say that." His face was closing up. Too many questions were making him suspicious.

"Ever been to Hollywood?"

"No. I haven't."

"Had any acting experience?"

"I have as a student."

"Where?"

"At the University of Michigan."

I had what I wanted: a way to check his background, if he was telling the truth; if he was lying, a way to prove that he was lying. Universities kept full dossiers on their students.

"The reason I'm asking you all these questions," I said, "is this. I have an office on Sunset Boulevard in Hollywood. I'm interested in talent, and I was struck by your appearance."

He brightened up considerably. "Are you an agent?"

"No, but I know a lot of agents." I wanted to avoid the lie direct, on general principles, so I brought Bolling into the conversation: "My friend here is a well-known writer. Mr. Chad Bolling. You may have heard of him."

Bolling was confused. He was a sensitive man, and my underhanded approach to the boy troubled him. He leaned out of the car to shake hands:

"Pleased to meet you."

"I'm very glad to meet you, sir. My name is John Brown, by the way. Are you in the picture business?"

"No."

Bolling was tongue-tied by the things he wanted to say and wasn't supposed to. The boy looked from Bolling to me, wondering what he had done to spoil the occasion. Bolling took pity on him. With a defiant look at me, he said:

"Did you say your name was John Brown? I knew a John Brown once, in Luna Bay."

"That was my father's name. You must have known my father."

"I believe I did." Bolling climbed out of the car. "I met you when you were a very small baby."

I watched John Brown. He flushed up warmly. His gray eyes shone with pleasure, and then were moist with deeper feelings. I had to remind myself that he was a self-admitted actor.

He pumped Bolling's hand a second time. "Imagine your knowing my father! How long is it since you've seen him?"

"Twenty-two years—a long time."

"Then you don't know where he is now?"

"I'm afraid not, John. He dropped out of sight, you know, quite soon after you were born."

The boy's face stiffened. "And Mother?" His voice cracked on the word.

"Same story," I said. "Don't you remember either of your parents?"

He answered reluctantly: "I remember my mother. She left me in an orphanage in Ohio when I was four. She promised to come back for me, but she never did come back. I spent nearly twelve years in that institution, waiting for her to come back." His face was dark with emotion. "Then I realized she must be dead. I ran away."

"Where was it?" I said. "What town?"

"Crystal Springs, a little place near Cleveland."

"And you say you ran away from there?"

"Yes, when I was sixteen. I went to Ann Arbor, Michigan, to get an education. A man named Lindsay took me in. He didn't adopt me, but he let me use his name. I went to school under the name of John Lindsay."

"Why the name change?"

"I didn't want to use my own name. I had good reason."

"Are you sure it wasn't the other way around? Are you sure John Lindsay wasn't your real name, and you took the name of Brown later?"

"Why would I do that?"

"Somebody hired you, maybe."

He flushed up darkly. "Who are you?"

"A private detective."

"If you're a detective, what was all that bushwa about Hollywood and Sunset Boulevard?"

"I have my office on Sunset Boulevard."

"But what you said was deliberately misleading."

"Don't worry about me so much. I needed some information, and I got it."

"You could have asked me directly. I have nothing to hide."

"That remains to be seen."

Bolling stepped between us, sputtering at me in sudden anger: "Leave the boy alone now. He's obviously genuine. He even has his father's voice. Your implications are an insult."

I didn't argue with him. In fact, I was ready to believe he was right. The boy stepped back away from us as if we'd threatened his life. His eyes had turned the color of slate, and there were white rims on his nostrils:

"What is this, anyway?"

"Don't get excited," I said.

"I'm not excited." He was trembling all over. "You come here and ask me a bunch of questions and tell me you knew my father. Naturally I want to know what it means."

Bolling moved toward him and laid an impulsive hand on his arm. "It could mean a great deal to you, John. Your father belonged to a wealthy family."

The boy brushed him off. He was young for his age in some ways. "I don't care about that. I want to see my father."

"Why is it so important?" Bolling said.

"I never had a father." His working face was naked to the light. Tears ran down his cheeks. He shook them off angrily.

I bought him, and made a down payment: "I've asked enough questions for now, John. Have you talked to the local police, by the way?"

"Yes, I have. And I know what you're getting at. They have a box of bones at the sheriff's station. Some of them claim that they're my father's bones, but I don't believe it. Neither does Deputy Mungan."

"Do you want to come down there with me now?"

"I can't," he said. "I can't close up the station. Mr. Turnell expects me to stay on the job."

"What time do you get off?"

"About seven-thirty, week nights."

"Where can I get in touch with you tonight?"

"I live in a boardinghouse about a mile from here. Mrs. Gorgello's." He gave me the address.

"Aren't you going to tell him who his father was?" Bolling said.

"I will when it's been proved. Let's go, Bolling."

He climbed into the car reluctantly.

Chapter 11

THE SHERIFF'S substation was a stucco shoebox of a building across the street from a sad-looking country hotel. Bolling said he would stay in the car, on the grounds that skeletons frightened him:

"It even horrifies me to think that I contain one. Unlike Webster in Mr. Eliot's poem, I like to remain oblivious to the skull beneath the skin."

I never knew whether Bolling was kidding me.

Deputy Mungan was a very large man, half a head taller than I was, with a face like unfinished sculpture. I gave him my name and occupation, and Dineen's note of introduction. When he'd read it, he reached across the counter that divided his little office, and broke all the bones in my hand:

"Any friend of Doc Dineen's is a friend of mine. Come on in around behind and tell me your business."

I went on in around behind and sat in the chair he placed for me at the end of his desk:

"It has to do with some bones that were found out in the Marvista tract. I understand you've made a tentative identification."

"I wouldn't go so far as to say that. Doc Dineen thinks it was a man he knew—fellow by the name of John Brown. It fits in with the location of the body, all right. But we haven't been able to nail it down. The trouble is, no such man was ever reported missing in these parts. We haven't been able to turn up any local antecedents. Naturally we're still working on it."

Mungan's broad face was serious. He talked like a trained cop, and his eyes were sharp as tacks. I said: "We may be able to help each other to clarify the issue."

"Any help you can give me will be welcome. This has been dragging on for five months now, more like six." He threw out a quick hooked question: "You represent his family, maybe?"

"I represent a family. They asked me not to use their name. And there's still a question whether they are the dead man's family. Was there any physical evidence found with the bones? A watch, or a ring? Shoes? Clothing?"

"Nothing. Not even a stitch of clothing."

"I suppose it could rot away completely in twenty-two years. What about buttons?"

"No buttons. Our theory is he was buried the way he came into the world."

"But without a head."

Mungan nodded gravely. "Doc Dineen filled you in, eh? I've been thinking about that head myself. A young fellow came in here a few weeks ago, claimed to be John Brown's son."

"Don't you think he is?"

"He acted like it. He got pretty upset when I showed him the bones. Unfortunately, he didn't know any more about his father than I do. Which is nil, absolutely nil. We know this John Brown lived out on the old Bluff Road for a couple of months in 1936, and that's the sum-total of it. On top of that, the boy doesn't believe these are his father's bones. And he could just be right. I've been doing some thinking, as I said.

"This business about the head, now. We assumed when the body was first turned up, that he was killed by having his head cut off." Mungan made a snicking sound between tongue and palate, and sheared the air with the edge of his huge hand. "Maybe he was. Or maybe the head was chopped off after death, to remove identification. You know how much we depend on teeth and fillings. Back in the thirties, before we developed our modern lab techniques, teeth and fillings were the main thing we had to go on.

"If my hypothesis is right, the killer was a pro. And that fits in with certain other facts. In the twenties and thirties, the Bluff Road area was a stamping ground for hoods. It was until quite recently, as a matter of fact. In those days it was a real hotbed. A lot of the liquor that kept San Francisco going during Prohibition came in by sea and was funneled through Luna Bay. They brought in other things than liquor—drugs, for instance, and women from Mexico and Panama. You ever hear of the Red Horse Inn?"

"No."

"It stood on the coast about a mile south of where we found the skeleton. They tore it down a couple of years ago, after we put the stopper on it. That was a place with a history. It used to be a resort hotel for well-heeled people from the City and the Peninsula. The rum-runners took it over in the twenties. They converted it into a three-way operation: liquor warehouse in the basement, bars and gaming on the first floor, women upstairs. The reason I know so much about it, I had my first drink there back about 1930. And my first woman."

"You don't look that old."

"I was sixteen at the time. I think that's one of the reasons I went into law enforcement. I wanted to put bastards like Lempi out of circulation. Lempi was the boss hood who ran the place in the twenties. I knew him personally, but the law got to him before I grew up to his size. They got him for income tax in 1932, he died on the Rock a few years later. Some of his guns were sent up at the same time.

"I knew those boys, see, and this is the point I'm coming to. I knew what they were capable of doing. They killed for pay, and they killed because they enjoyed it. They bragged in public that nobody could touch them. It took a federal indictment to cool Lempi. Meantime a number of people lost their lives. Our Mr. Bones could be one of them."

"But you say Lempi and his boys were cleaned out in '32. Our man was killed in '36."

"We don't know that. We jumped to that conclusion on the basis of what Doc Dineen said, but we've got no concrete evidence to go on. The Doc himself admits that given the chemistry of that particular soil, he can't pinpoint time of burial closer than five years either way. Mr. Bones could have been knocked off as early as 1931. I say *could* have."

"Or as late as 1941?" I said.

"That's right. You see how little we have to go on."

"Do I get to take a look at what you have?"

"Why not?"

Mungan went into a back room and returned lugging a metal box about the size of a hope chest. He set it on top of his desk, unlocked it, lifted the lid. Its contents were jumbled like kindling. Only the vertebrae had been articulated with wire, and lay coiled on the heap like the skeleton of a snake. Mungan showed me where the neck bone had been severed by a cutting instrument.

The larger bones had been labeled: left femur, left fibula, and so on. Mungan picked out a heavy bone about a foot long; it was marked "right humerus."

"This is the bone of the upper arm," he said in a lecturer's tone. "Come along on over to the window here. I want to show you something."

He held the bone to the light. Close to one knobbed end, I made out a thin line filled and surrounded by deposits of calcium.

"A break?" I said.

"I hope in more senses than one. It's a mended fracture, the only unusual thing in the entire skeleton. Dineen says it was probably set by a trained hand, a doctor. If we could find the doctor that set it, it would answer some of our questions. So if you've got any ideas . . ." Mungan let his voice trail off, but his eyes stayed hard on my face.

"I'll do some telephoning."

"You can use my phone."

"A pay phone would suit me better."

"If you say so. There's one across the street, in the hotel."

I found the telephone booth at the rear of the dingy hotel lobby, and placed a call to Santa Teresa. Sable's secretary put him on the line.

"Archer speaking, the one-man dragnet," I said. "I'm in Luna Bay."

"You're where?"

"Luna Bay. It's a small town on the coast south of San Francisco. I have a couple of items for you: a dead man's bones, and a live boy. Let's start with the bones."

"Bones?"

"Bones. They were dug up by accident about six months ago, and they're in the sheriff's substation here. They're unidentified, but the chances are better than even that they belong to the man I'm looking for. The chances are also better than even that he was murdered twenty-two years ago."

The line was silent.

"Did you get that, Sable? He was probably murdered."

"I heard you. But you say the remains haven't been identified."

"That's where you can help me, if you will. You better write this down. There's a fracture in the right humerus, close to the elbow. It was evidently set by a doctor. I want you to check on whether Tony Galton ever had a broken right arm. If so, who was the doctor that looked after it? It may have been Howell, in which case there's no sweat. I'll call you back in fifteen minutes."

"Wait. You mentioned a boy. What's he got to do with all this?"

"That remains to be seen. He thinks he's the dead man's son."

"Tony's son?"

"Yes, but he isn't sure about it. He came here from Michigan in the hope of finding out who his father was."

"Do you think he's Tony's son?"

"I wouldn't bet my life savings on it. I wouldn't bet against it, either. He bears a strong resemblance to Tony. On the other hand, his story is weak."

"What story does he tell?"

"It's pretty long and complicated for the telephone. He was brought up in an orphanage, he says, went to college under an assumed name, came out here a month ago to find out who he really is. I don't say it couldn't have happened the way he says, but it needs to be proved out."

"What kind of a boy is he?"

"Intelligent, well spoken, fairly well mannered. If he's a con artist, he's smooth for his age."

"How old is he?"

"Twenty-two."

"You work very quickly," he said.

"I was lucky. What about your end? Has Trask got anything on my car?"

"Yes. It was found abandoned in San Luis Obispo."

"Wrecked?"

"Out of gas. It's in perfectly good shape, I saw it myself. Trask has it impounded in the county garage."

"What about the man who stole it?"

"Nothing definite. He probably took another car in San Luis. One disappeared late yesterday afternoon. Incidentally, Trask tells me that the Jaguar, the murder car, as he calls it, was another stolen car."

"Who was the owner?"

"I have no idea. The Sheriff is having the engine number traced."

I hung up, and spent the better part of fifteen minutes thinking about Marian Culligan Matheson and her respectable life in Redwood City which I was going to have to invade again. Then I called Sable back. The line was busy. I tried again in ten minutes, and got him.

"I've been talking to Dr. Howell," he said. "Tony broke his right arm when he was in prep school. Howell didn't set the break himself, but he knows the doctor who did. In any case, it was a fractured humerus."

"See if they can turn up the X-ray, will you? They don't usually keep X-ray pictures this long, but it's worth trying. It's the only means I can think of for making a positive identification."

"What about teeth?"

"Everything above the neck is missing."

It took Sable a moment to grasp this. Then he said: "Good Lord!" After another pause: "Perhaps I should drop everything and come up there. What do you think?"

"It might be a good idea. It would give you a chance to interview the boy."

"I believe I'll do that. Where is he now?"

"Working. He works at a gas station in town. How long will it take you to get here?"

"I'll be there between eight and nine."

"Meet me at the sheriff's substation at nine. In the meantime, is it all right if I take the local deputy into my confidence? He's a good man."

"I'd just as soon you didn't."

"You can't handle murder without publicity."

"I'm aware of that," Sable said acidly. "But then we don't know for certain that the victim was Tony, do we?"

Before I could give him any further argument, Sable hung up.

Chapter 12

I PHONED the Santa Teresa courthouse. After some palaver, I got Sheriff Trask himself on the other end of the line. He sounded harried:

"What is it?"

"Gordon Sable just told me you traced the murder car in the Culligan case."

"A fat lot of good it did us. It was stolen in San Francisco night before last. The thief changed the license plates."

"Who owns it?"

"San Francisco man. I'm thinking of sending somebody up to talk to him. Far as I can make out, he didn't report the theft."

"That doesn't sound so good. I'm near San Francisco now, in Luna Bay. Do you want me to look him up?"

"I'd be obliged. I can't really spare anybody. His name is Roy Lemberg. He lives at a hotel called the Sussex Arms."

An hour later, I drove into the garage under Union Square. Bolling said good-by to me at the entrance:

"Good luck with your case."

"Good luck with your poem. And thanks."

The Sussex Arms was another side-street hotel like the one I had spent the night in. It was several blocks closer to Market Street, and several degrees more dilapidated. The desk clerk had large sorrowful eyes and a very flexible manner, as if he had been run through all the wringers of circumstance.

He said Mr. Lemberg was probably at work.

"Where does he work?"

"He's supposed to be a car salesman."

"Supposed to be?"

"I don't think he's doing so good. He's just on commission with a secondhand dealer. The reason I know, he tried to sell *me* a car." He snickered, as if he possessed the secret of a more advanced type of transportation.

"Has Lemberg lived here long?"

"A few weeks, more or less. This wouldn't happen to be a police matter?"

"I want to see him on personal business."

"Maybe Mrs. Lemberg is up in the room. She usually is."

"Try her, will you? My name is Archer. I'm interested in buying their car."

He went to the switchboard and relayed the message. "Mrs. Lemberg says come right on up. It's three-eleven. You can take the elevator."

The elevator jerked me up to the third floor. At the end of the dust-colored hallway, a blonde in a pink robe gleamed like a mirage. Closer up, her luster was dimmer. She had darkness at the roots of her hair, and a slightly desperate smile.

She waited until I was practically standing on her feet; then she yawned and stretched elastically. She had wine and sleep on her breath. But her figure was very good, lush-breasted and narrow-waisted. I wondered if it was for sale or simply on exhibition by the owner.

"Mrs. Lemberg?"

"Yeah. What's all this about the Jag? Somebody phones this morning and he tells them it was stole. And now you want to buy it."

"Was the car stolen?"

"That was just some of Roy's malarkey. He's full of it. You serious about buying?"

"Only if he has clear title," I said fussily.

My show of reluctance made her eager, as it was intended to. "Come in, we'll talk about it. The Jag is in his name, but I'm the one that makes the money decisions."

I followed her into the little room. At the chinks in the drawn blinds, daylight peered like a spy. She turned on a lamp and waved her hand vaguely toward a chair. A man's shirt hung on the back of it. A half-empty half-gallon jug of muscatel stood on the floor beside it.

"Siddown, excuse the mess. With all the outside work I do, I don't get time to houseclean."

"What do you do?"

"I model. Go ahead, siddown. That shirt is ready for the laundry, anyway."

I sat down against the shirt. She flung herself on the bed, her body falling automatically into a cheesecake pose:

"Were you thinking of paying cash?"

"If I buy."

"We sure could use a chunk of ready cash. What price did you have in mind? I'm warning you, I won't let it go too cheap. That's my chief recreation in life, driving out in the country. The trees and everything." Her own words seemed to bewilder her. "Not that he takes me out in it. I hardly ever see the car any more. That brother of his monopolizes it. Roy's so soft, he don't stick up for his rights the way he should. Like the other night."

"What happened the other night?"

"Just more of the same. Tommy comes up full of the usual. He's got another one of these big job opportunities that never pan out. All he needs is a car, see, and he'll be making a fortune in no time. So Roy lends him the car, just like that. Tommy could talk the fillings right out of his teeth."

"How long ago was this?"

"Night before last, I think. I lose count of the nights and days."

"I didn't know Roy had a brother," I prompted her.

"Yeah, he's got a brother." Her voice was flat. "Roy's all fixed up with a brother, till death doth us part. We'd still be in Nevada, living the life of O'Reilly, if it wasn't for that punk."

"How so?"

"I'm talking too much." But bad luck had dulled her brains, bad wine had loosened her tongue: "The Adult Authority said they'd give him a parole if he had somebody willing to be responsible. So back we move to California, to make a home for Tommy."

I thought: This is a home? She caught my look:

"We didn't always live here. We made a down payment on a real nice little place in Daly City. But Roy started drinking again, we couldn't hold onto it." She turned over onto her stomach, supporting her chin on her hand. Her china-blue eyes looked fractured in the light. "Not that I blame him," she added more softly. "That brother of his would drive a saint to drink. Roy never hurt nobody in his life. Except me, and you expect that from any man."

I was touched by her asphalt innocence. The long curve of her hip and thigh, the rich flesh of her bosom, were like the disguise of a frightened adolescent.

"What was Tommy in for?"

"He beat up a guy and took his wallet. The wallet had three bucks in it, and Tommy was in for six months."

"That works out to fifty cents a month. Tommy must be quite a mastermind."

"Yeah, to hear him tell it. It was supposed to be longer, but I guess he's good when he's in, with somebody watching him. It's just when he gets out." She cocked her head sideways, and her bright hair fell across her hand. "I don't know why I'm telling you all this. In my experience, the guys do most of the talking. I guess you have a talkable-attable face."

"You're welcome to the use of it."

"Sanctuary mucho. But you came here to buy a car. I was almost forgetting. I worry so much, I forget things." Her gaze slid down from my face to the muscatel jug. "I had a few drinkies, too, if the truth be knownst." She drew a lock of hair across her eyes and looked at me through it.

Her kittenish mood was depressing. I said: "When can I have a look at the Jaguar?"

"Any time, I guess. Maybe you better talk to Roy."

"Where can I find him?"

"Don't ask me. Tell you the truth, I don't even know if Tommy brought it back yet."

"Why did Roy say the car was stolen?"

"I dunno. I was half asleep when he left. I didn't ask him."

The thought of sleep made her yawn. She dropped her head and lay still. Traffic went by in the street like a hostile army. Then footsteps came down the corridor and paused outside the door. A man spoke softly through it:

"You busy, Fran?"

She raised herself on her arms like a fighter hearing a far-off count. "Is that you, hon?"

"Yeah. You busy?"

"Not so's you'd notice. Come ahead in."

He flung the door open, saw me, and hung back like an interloper. "Excuse me."

His dark eyes were quick and uncertain. He was still in his early thirties, but he had a look about him, intangible and definite as an odor. The look of a man who has lost his grip and is sliding. His suit was sharply pressed, but it hadn't been cleaned for too long. The very plumpness of his face gave it a lardlike inertness, as if it had stopped reacting to everything but crises.

His face interested me. Unless I was getting hipped on family resemblances, he was an older softer version of the boy who'd stolen my car. This one's dark curls were thinner and limper. And the violence of the younger man was petulance in him. He said to his wife:

"You told me you weren't busy."

"I'm not. I'm only resting." She rolled over and sat up. "This gentleman wants to buy the Jaguar."

"It's not for sale." Lemberg closed the door behind him. "Who told you it was?"

"Grapevine."

"What else did you hear?"

He was quick on the uptake. I couldn't hope to con him for long, so I struck at his vulnerable spot:

"Your brother's in trouble."

His gaze went to my shoulder, my hands, my mouth, and then my eyes. I think in his extremity he would have liked to hit me. But I could have broken him in half, and he must have known it. Still, anger or frustration made him foolish:

"Did Schwartz send you to tell me this?"

"Who?"

"You needn't play dumb. Otto Schwartz." He gargled the words. "If he sent you, you can take a message back for me. Tell him to take a running jump in the Truckee River and do us all a favor."

I got up. Instinctively, one of Lemberg's arms rose to guard his face. The gesture told a lot about him and his background.

"Your brother's in very bad trouble. So are you. He drove down south to do a murder yesterday. You provided the car."

"I didn't know whah—" His jaw hung open, and then clicked shut. "Who are you?"

"A friend of the family. Show me where Tommy is."

"But I don't know. He isn't in his room. He never came back." The woman said: "Are you from the Adult Authority?"

"No."

"Who are you?" Lemberg repeated. "What do you want?"

"Your brother, Tommy."

"I don't know where Tommy is. I swear."

"What's Otto Schwartz got to do with you and Tommy?"

"I don't know."

"You brought up his name. Did Schwartz give Tommy a contract to murder Culligan?"

"Who?" the woman said. "Who did you say got murdered?"

"Peter Culligan. Know him?"

"No," Lemberg answered for her. "We don't know him."

I advanced on him: "You're lying, Lemberg. You better let down your back hair, tell me all about it. Tommy isn't the only one in trouble. You're accessory to any crime he did."

He backed away until the backs of his legs were touching the bed. He looked down at his wife as if she was his only source of comfort. She was looking at me:

"What did you say Tommy did?"

"He committed a murder."

"For gosh sake." She swung her legs down and stood up facing her husband. "And you lent him the car?"

"I had to. It was his car. It was only in my name."

"Because he was on parole?" I said.

He didn't answer me.

The woman took hold of his arm and shook it. "Tell the man where he is."

"I don't know where he is." Lemberg turned to me: "And that's the honest truth."

"What about Schwartz?"

"Tommy used to work for him, when we lived in Reno. They were always asking him to come back to work."

"Doing what?"

"Any dirty thing they could dream up."

"Including murder?"

"Tommy never did a murder."

"Before this one, you mean."

"I'll believe it when I hear it from him."

The woman groaned. "Don't be an idiot all your life. What did he ever do for you, Roy?"

"He's my brother."

"Do you expect to hear from him?" I said.

"I hope so."

"If you do, will you let me know?"

"Sure I will," he lied.

I went down in the elevator and laid a ten-dollar bill on the counter in front of the room clerk. He raised a languid eyebrow:

"What's this for? You want to check in?"

"Not today, thanks. It's your certificate of membership in the junior G-men society. Tomorrow you get your intermediate certificate."

"Another ten?"

"You catch on fast."

"What do I have to do for it?"

"Keep track of Lemberg's visitors, if he has any. And any telephone calls, especially long-distance calls."

"Can do." His hand moved quickly, flicking the bill out of sight. "What about *her* visitors?"

"Does she have many?"

"They come and go."

"She pay you to let them come and go?"

"That's between me and her. Are you a cop?"

"Not me," I said, as if his question was an insult. "Just keep the best track you can. If it works out, I may give you a bonus."

"If what works out?"

"Developments. Also I'll mention you in my memoirs."

"That will be just ducky."

"What's your name?"

"Jerry Farnsworth."

"Will you be on duty in the morning?"

"What time in the morning?"

"Any time."

"For a bonus I can be."

"An extra five," I said, and went outside.

There was a magazine shop on the opposite corner. I crossed to it, bought a *Saturday Review*, and punched a hole in the cover. For an hour or more, I watched the front of the Sussex Arms, trusting that Lemberg wouldn't penetrate my literate disguise.

But Lemberg didn't come out.

Chapter 13

IT WAS past five when I got to Redwood City. The commuting trains were running south every few minutes. The commuters in their uniforms, hat on head, briefcase in hand, newspaper under arm, marched wearily toward their waiting cars. The cop on traffic duty at the station corner told me how to get to Sherwood Drive.

It was in a junior-executive residential section, several cuts above the Marvista tract. The houses were set further apart, and differed from each other in architectural detail. Flowers bloomed competitively in the yards.

A bicycle lay on the grass in front of the Matheson house. A small boy answered my knock. He had black eyes like his mother's, and short brown hair which stuck up all over his head like visible excitement.

"I was doing pushups," he said, breathing hard. "You want my daddy? He ain't, I mean, he isn't home from the city yet."

"Is your mother home?"

"She went to the station to get him. They ought to be back in about eleven minutes. That's how old I am."

"Eleven minutes?"

"Eleven *years*. I had my birthday last week. You want to see me do some pushups?"

"All right."

"Come in, I'll show you."

I followed him into a living-room which was dominated by a large brick fireplace with a raised hearth. Everything in the room was so new and clean, the furniture so carefully placed around it, that it seemed forbidding. The boy flung himself down in the middle of the green broadloom carpet:

"Watch me."

He did a series of pushups, until his arms collapsed under him. He got up panting like a dog on a hot day:

"Now that I got the knack, I can do pushups all night if I want to."

"You wouldn't want to wear yourself out."

"Shucks, I'm strong. Mr. Steele says I'm very strong for my age, it's just my co-ordination. Here, feel my muscle."

He pulled up the sleeve of his jersey, flexed his biceps, and produced an egg-sized lump. I palpated this:

"It's hard."

"That's from doing pushups. You think I'm big for my age, or just average?"

"A pretty fair size, I'd say."

"As big as you when you were eleven?"

"Just about."

"How big are you now?"

"Six feet or so."

"How much do you weigh?"

"About one-ninety."

"Did you ever play football?"

"Some, in high school."

"Do you think, will I ever get to be a football player?" he said wistfully.

"I don't see why not."

"That's my ambition, to be a football player."

He darted out of the room and was back in no time with a football which he threw at me from the doorway.

"Y. A. Tittle," he said.

I caught the ball and said: "Hugh McElhenny."

This struck him as very funny. He laughed until he fell down. Being in position, he did a few pushups.

"Stop it. You're making me tired."

"I never get tired," he bragged exhaustedly. "When I get through doing pushups, I'm going to take a run around the block."

"Don't tell me. It wears me out."

A car turned into the driveway. The boy struggled to his feet:

"That's Mummy and Daddy now. I'll tell them you're here, Mr. Steele."

"My name is Archer. Who's Mr. Steele?"

"My coach in the Little League. I got you mixed up with him, I guess."

It didn't bother him, but it bothered me. It was a declaration of trust, and I didn't know what I was going to have to do to his mother.

She came in alone. Her face hardened and thinned when she saw me:

"What do you want? What are you doing with my son's football?"

"Holding it. He threw it to me. I'm holding it."

"We were making like Forty-niners," the boy said. But the laughter had gone out of him.

"Leave my son alone, you hear me?" She turned on the boy: "James, your father is in the garage. You can help him bring in the groceries. And take that football with you."

"Here." I tossed him the ball. He carried it out as if it was made of iron. The door closed behind him. "He's a likely boy."

"A lot you care, coming here to badger me. I talked to the police this morning. I don't have to talk to you."

"I think you want to, though."

"I can't. My husband—he doesn't know."

"What doesn't he know?"

"Please." She moved toward me rapidly, heavily, almost as though she was falling, and grasped my arm. "Ron will be coming in any minute. You won't force me to talk in front of him?"

"Send him away."

"How can I? He wants his dinner."

"You need something from the store."

"But we just came from the store."

"Think of something else."

Her eyes narrowed to two black glittering slits. "Damn you. You come in here disrupting my life. What did I do to bring this down on me?"

"That's the question that needs answering, Mrs. Matheson."

"Won't you go away and come back later?"

"I have other things to do later. Let's get this over with."

"I only wish I could."

The back door opened. She pulled away from me. Her face smoothed out and became inert, like the face of someone dying.

"Sit down," she said. "You might as well sit down."

I sat on the edge of an overstuffed chesterfield covered with hard shiny green brocade. Footsteps crossed the kitchen, and paper rustled. A man raised his voice:

"Marian, where are you?"

"I'm in here," she said tightly.

Her husband appeared in the doorway. Matheson was a thin small man in a gray suit who looked about five years younger than his wife. He stared at me through his glasses with the belligerence of his size. It was his wife he spoke to:

"I didn't know you had a visitor."

"Mr. Archer is Sally Archer's husband. You've heard me speak of Sally Archer, Ron." In spite of his uncomprehending look, she rushed on: "I promised to send her a cake for the church supper, and I forgot to bake it. What am I going to do?"

"You'll have to skip it."

"I can't. She's depending on me. Ron, would you go downtown and bring me a cake for Mr. Archer to take to Sally? Please?"

"Now?" he said with disgust.

"It's for tonight. Sally's waiting for it."

"Let her wait."

"But I can't. You wouldn't want it to get around that I didn't do my share."

He turned out his hands in resignation. "How big a cake does it have to be?"

"The two-dollar size will do. Chocolate. You know the bakery at the shopping center."

"But that's way over on the other side of town."

"It's got to be good, Ron. You don't want to shame me in front of my friends."

Some of her real feeling was caught in the words. His eyes jabbed at me and returned to her face, searching it:

"Listen, Marian, what's the trouble? Are you okay?"

"Certainly I'm okay." She produced a smile. "Now run along like a good boy and bring me that cake. You can take Jimmy with you, and I'll have supper ready when you get back."

Matheson went out, slamming the door behind him in protest. I heard his car engine start, and sat down again:

"You've got him well trained."

"Please leave my husband out of this. He doesn't deserve trouble."

"Does he know the police were here?"

"No, but the neighbors will tell him. And then I'll have to do some more lying. I hate this lying."

"Stop lying."

"And let him know I'm mixed up in a murder? That would be just great."

"Which murder are you talking about?"

She opened her mouth. Her hand flew up to cover it. She forced her hand down to her side and stood very still, like a sentinel guarding her hearth.

"Culligan's?" I said. "Or the murder of John Brown?"

The name struck her like a blow in the mouth. She was too shaken to speak for a minute. Then she gathered her forces and straightened up and said:

"I don't know any John Brown."

"You said you hated lying, but you're doing it. You worked for him in the winter of 1936, looking after his wife and baby."

She was silent. I brought out one of my pictures of Anthony Galton and thrust it up to her face:

"Don't you recognize him?"

She nodded resignedly. "I recognize him. It's Mr. Brown."

"And you worked for him, didn't you?"

"So what? Working for a person is no crime."

"Murder is the crime we're talking about. Who killed him, Marian? Was it Culligan?"

"Who says anybody killed him? He pulled up stakes and went away. The whole family did."

"Brown didn't go very far, just a foot or two underground. They dug him up last spring, all but his head. His head was missing. Who cut it off, Marian?"

The ugliness rose like smoke in the room, spreading to its far corners, fouling the light at the window. The ugliness entered the woman and stained her eyes. Her lips moved, trying to find the words that would exorcise it. I said:

"I'll make a bargain with you, and keep it if I can. I don't want to hurt your boy. I've got nothing against you or your husband. I suspect you're material witness to a murder. Maybe the law would call it accessory—"

"No." She shook her head jerkily. "I had nothing to do with it."

"Maybe not. I'm not interested in pinning anything on you. If you'll tell me the whole truth as you know it, I'll do my best to keep you out of it. But it has to be the whole truth, and I have to have it now. A lot depends on it."

"How could a lot depend, after all these years?"

"Why did Culligan die, after all these years? I think that the two deaths are connected. I also think that you can tell me how."

Her deeper, cruder personality rose to the surface. "What do you think I am, a crystal ball?"

"Stop fooling around," I said sharply. "We only have a few minutes. If you won't talk to me alone, you can talk in front of your husband."

"What if I refuse to talk at all?"

"You'll be having another visit from the cops. It'll start here and end up at the courthouse. And everybody west of the Rockies will have a chance to read all about it in the papers. Now talk."

"I need a minute to think."

"You've had it. Who murdered Brown?"

"I didn't know he was murdered, not for sure. Culligan wouldn't let me go back to the house after that night. He said the Browns moved on, bag and baggage. He even tried to give me money he said they left for me."

"Where did he get it?"

After a silence, she blurted: "He stole it from them."

"Did he murder Brown?"

"Not Culligan. He wouldn't have the nerve."

"Who did?"

"There was another man. It must have been him."

"What was his name?"

"I don't know."

"What did he look like?"

"I hardly remember. I only saw him the once, and it was at night."

Her story was turning vague, and it made me suspicious. "Are you sure the other man existed?"

"Of course he did."

"Prove it."

"He was a jailbird," she said. "He escaped from San Quentin. He used to belong to the same gang Culligan did."

"What gang is that?"

"I wouldn't know. It broke up long before I married Culligan. He never talked about his gang days. I wasn't interested."

"Let's get back to this man who broke out of 'Q.' He must have had a name. Culligan must have called him something."

"I don't remember what."

"Try harder."

She looked toward the window. Her face was drawn in the tarnished light.

"Shoulders. I think it was Shoulders."

"No last name?"

"Not that I remember. I don't think Culligan ever told me his last name."

"What did he look like?"

"He was a big man, dark-haired. I never really saw him, not in the light."

"What makes you think he murdered Brown?"

She answered in a low voice, to keep her house from hearing: "I heard them arguing that night, in the middle of the night. They were sitting out in my car arguing about money. The other man—Shoulders—said that he'd knock off Pete, too, if he didn't get his way. I heard him say it. The walls of the shack we lived in were paper thin. This Shoulders had a kind of shrill voice, and it cut through the walls like a knife. He wanted all the money for himself, and most of the jewels.

"Pete said it wasn't fair, that he was the finger man and should have an equal split. He needed money, too, and God knows that he did. He always needed money. He said that a couple of hot rubies were no good to him. That was how I guessed what happened. Little Mrs. Brown had these big red jewels, I always thought they were glass. But they were rubies."

"What happened to the rubies?"

"The other man took them, he must of. Culligan settled for part of the money, I guess. At least he was flush for a while."

"Did you ever ask him why?"

"No. I was afraid."

"Afraid of Culligan?"

"Not him so much." She tried to go on, but the words stuck in her throat. She plucked at the skin of her throat as if to dislodge them. "I was afraid of the truth, afraid he'd tell me. I didn't want to believe what happened, I guess. That argument I heard outside our house—I tried to pretend to myself it was all a dream. I was in love with Culligan in those days. I couldn't face my own part in it."

"You mean the fact that you didn't take your suspicions to the police?"

"That would have been bad enough, but I did worse. I was the one responsible for the whole thing. I've lived with it on my conscience for over twenty years. It was all my fault for not keeping my loud mouth shut." She gave me an up-from-under look, her eyes burning with pain: "Maybe I ought to be keeping it shut now."

"How were you responsible?"

She hung her head still lower. Her eyes sank out of sight under her black brows. "I told Culligan about the money," she said. "Mr. Brown kept it in a steel box in his room. I saw it when he paid me. There must have been thousands of dollars. And I had to go and mention it to my hus—to Culligan. I would have done better to go and cut my tongue out instead." She raised her head, slowly, as if she was balancing a weight. "So there you have it."

"Did Brown ever tell you where *he* got the money?"

"Not really. He made a joke about it—said he stole it. But he wasn't the type."

"What type was he?"

"Mr. Brown was a gentleman, at least he started out to be a gentleman. Until he married that wife of his. I don't know what he saw in her outside of a pretty face. She didn't know from nothing, if you ask me. But he knew plenty, he could talk your head off."

She gasped. The enormity of the image struck her. "God! They cut his head off?" She wasn't asking me. She was asking the dark memories flooding up from the basement of her life.

"Before death or after, we don't know which. You say you never went back to the house?"

"I never did. We went back to San Francisco."

"Do you know what happened to the rest of the family, the wife and son?"

She shook her head. "I tried not to think about them. What did happen to them?"

"I'm not sure, but I think they went east. The indications are they got away safe, at any rate."

"Thank God for that." She tried to smile, and failed. Her eyes were still intent on the guilty memory. She looked at the walls of her living-room as if they were transparent. "I guess you wonder what kind of a woman I am, that I could run out on a patient like that. Don't think it didn't bother me. I almost went out of my mind for a while that winter. I used to wake up in the middle of the night and listen to Culligan's breathing and wish it would stop. But I stuck to him for five more years after that. Then I divorced him."

"And now he's stopped breathing."

"What do you mean by that?"

"You could have hired a gun to knock him off. He was threatening to make trouble for you. You have a lot to lose." I didn't believe it, but I wanted to see what she would make of it.

Her two hands went to her breasts and grasped them cruelly. "Me? You think I'd do that?"

"To keep your husband and son, you would. Did you?"

"No. For God's sake, no."

"That's good."

"Why do you say that?" Her eyes were dull with the sickness of the past.

"Because I want you to keep what you have."

"Don't do me any favors."

"I'm going to, though. I'm going to keep you out of the Culligan case. As for the information you've given me, I'm going to use it for private reference only. It would be easier for me if I didn't—"

"So you want to be paid for your trouble, is that it?"

"Yes, but not in money. I want your confidence, and any other information you can give me."

"But there isn't any more. That's all there is."

"What happened to Shoulders?"

"I don't know. He must of got away. I never heard of him again."

"Culligan never mentioned him?"

"No. Honest."

"And you never brought the subject up?"

"No. I was too much of a coward."

A car entered the driveway. She started, and went to the window. The light outside was turning dusky gray. In the yard across the street, red roses burned like coals. She rubbed her eyes with her knuckles, as if she wanted to wipe out all her past experiences, live innocent in an innocent world.

The little boy burst through the door. Matheson came at his heels, balancing a cake box in his hands.

"Well, I got the darn thing." He thrust it into my hands. "That takes care of the church supper."

"Thanks."

"Don't mention it," he said brusquely, and turned to his wife: "Is supper ready? I'm starved."

She stood on the far side of the room, cut off from him by the ugliness. "I didn't make supper."

"You didn't make it? What is this? You said you'd have it ready when I got home."

Hidden forces dragged at her face, widening her mouth, drawing deep lines between her eyes. Suddenly her eyes were blind with tears. The tears ran in the furrows of her face. Sobbing, she sat on the edge of the hearth like an urchin on a curb.

"Marian? What's the matter? What's the trouble, kiddie?"

"I'm not a good wife to you."

Matheson went across the room to her. He sat on the hearth beside her and took her in his arms. She buried her face in his neck.

The boy started toward them, and then turned back to me. "Why is Mother crying?"

"People cry."

"I don't cry," he said.

Chapter 14

I DROVE back across the ridge toward the last fading light in the sky. On the road that wound down to Luna Bay I passed an old man with a burlap bag on his back. He was one of the old-time hoboes who follow the sun like migratory birds. But the birds fly, and the men walk. The birds mate and nest; the old men have no nests. They pace out their lives along the roadsides.

I stopped and backed up and gave him the cake.

"Thank you very kindly." His mouth was a rent in shaggy fur. He put the cake in his bag. It was a cheap gift, so I gave him a dollar to go with it. "Do you want a ride into town?"

"No, thank you very kindly. I'd smell up your car."

He walked away from me with a long, slow, swinging purposeless stride, lost in a dream of timeless space. When I passed him, he didn't raise his bearded head. He was like a moving piece of countryside on the edge of my headlight beam.

I had fish and chips at a greasy spoon and went to the sheriff's substation. It was eight by the clock on the wall above Mungan's desk. He looked up from his paperwork:

"Where you been? The Brown kid's been looking for you."

"I want to see him. Do you know where he went?"

"Over to Doc Dineen's house. They're pretty good friends. He told me that the doc is teaching him how to play chess. That game was always a little over my head. Give me a hand of poker any time."

I went around the end of the counter and complied with his request, in a way:

"I've been doing some asking around. A couple of things came up that ought to interest you. You say you knew some of the hoods in these parts, back in the early thirties. Does the name Culligan mean anything to you?"

"Yeah. Happy Culligan, they called him. He was in the Red Horse mob."

"Who were his friends?"

"Let's see." Mungan stroked his massive chin. "There was Rossi, Shoulders Nelson, Lefty Dearborn—all of them Lempi's guns. Culligan was more the operator type, but he liked to hang around with the guns."

"What about Shoulders Nelson?"

"He was about the hardest limb in the bunch. Even his buddies were afraid of him." A trace of his boyhood admiration showed in Mungan's eyes. "I saw him beat Culligan to a pulp one night. They both wanted the same girl."

"What girl?"

"One of the girls upstairs at the Red Horse. I didn't know her name. Nelson shacked up with her for a while, I heard."

"What did Nelson look like?"

"He was a big man, almost as big as me. The women went for him, he must have been good-looking to them. I never thought so, though. He was a mean-looking bastard, with a long sad face and mean eyes. Him and Rossi and Dearborn got sent up the same time as Lempi."

"To Alcatraz?"

"Lempi went there, when the Government took it over. But the others took the fall on a larceny charge. Highjacking. The three of them went to San Quentin."

"What happened to them after that?"

"I didn't keep any track of them. I wasn't in law enforcement at the time. Where is all this supposed to be leading?"

"Shoulders Nelson may be the killer you want," I said. "Would your Redwood City office have a dossier on him?"

"I doubt that. He hasn't been heard of around here in more than twenty-five years. It was a state case, anyway."

"Then Sacramento should have it. You could have Redwood City teletype them."

Mungan spread his hands on the desk-top and stood up, wagging his big head slowly from side to side. "If all you got is a hunch, you can't use official channels to test it out for you."

"I thought we were co-operating."

"I am. You're not. I've been doing the talking, you've been doing the listening. And this has been going on for quite some time."

"I told you Nelson's probably our killer. That's a fairly big mouthful."

"By itself, it doesn't do anything for me."

"It could if you let it. Try querying Sacramento."

"What's your source of information?"

"I can't tell you."

"Like that, eh?"

"I'm afraid so."

Mungan looked down at me in a disappointed way. Not surprised, just disappointed. We had had the beginning of a beautiful friendship, but I had proved unworthy.

"I hope you know what you're doing."

"I hope I do. You think about this Nelson angle. It's worth going into. You could earn yourself some very nice publicity."

"I don't give a damn about publicity."

"Good for you."

"And you can go to hell."

I didn't blame him for blowing off. It's tough to live with a case for half a year and then watch it elope with a casual pickup.

But I couldn't afford to leave him feeling sore. I didn't even want to. I went outside the counter and sat down on a wooden bench against the wall. Mungan resumed his place at his desk and avoided looking at me. I sat there like a penitent while the minute hand of the clock took little pouncing bites of eternity.

At eight-thirty-five Mungan got up and made an elaborate show of discovering me:

"You still here?"

"I'm waiting for a friend—a lawyer from down south. He said he'd be here by nine o'clock."

"What for? To help you to pick my brains?"

"I don't know why you're browned off, Mungan. This is a big case, bigger than you realize. It's going to take more than one of us to handle it."

"What makes it so big?"

"The people involved, the money, and the names. At this end we have the Red Horse gang, or what's left of it; at the other end, one of the richest and oldest families in California. It's their lawyer I'm expecting, a man named Sable."

"So what? I get down on my knees? I give everybody an even shake, treat 'em all alike."

"Mr. Sable may be able to identify those bones of yours."

Mungan couldn't repress his interest. "He the one you talked to on the phone?"

"He's the one."

"You're working on this case for him?"

"He hired me. And he may be bringing some medical data that will help us identify the remains."

Mungan went back to his paperwork. After a few minutes, he said casually:

"If you're working for a lawyer, it lets you off the hook. It gives you the same rights of privacy a lawyer has. You probably wouldn't know that, but I've made quite a study of the law."

"It's news to me," I lied.

He said magnanimously: "People in general, even law officers, they don't know all the fine points of the law."

His pride and his integrity were satisfied. He called the county courthouse and asked them to get a rundown on Nelson from Sacramento.

Gordon Sable walked in at five minutes to nine. He had on a brown topcoat and a brown Homburg, and a pair of yellow pigskin driving gloves. The lids of his gray eyes were slightly inflamed. His mouth was drawn down at the corners, and lines of weariness ran from them to the wings of his nose.

"You made a quick trip," I said.

"Too quick to suit me. I didn't get away until nearly three o'clock."

He looked around the small office as if he doubted that the trip had been worth making. Mungan rose expectantly.

"Mr. Sable, Deputy Mungan."

The two men shook hands, each of them appraising the other.

"Glad to meet you," Mungan said. "Mr. Archer tells me you've got some medical information about this—these remains we turned up last spring."

"That may be." Sable glanced sideways at me. "How much more detail did you go into?"

"Just that, and the fact that the family is important. We're not going to be able to keep them anonymous from here on in."

"I realize that," he snapped. "But let's get the identification established first, if we can. Before I left, I talked to the doctor who set the broken arm. He did have X-ray pictures taken, but unfortunately they don't survive. He has his written record, however, and he gave me the—ah—specifications of the fracture." Sable produced a folded piece of paper from an inner pocket. "It was a clean break in the right humerus, two inches above the joint. The boy sustained it falling off a horse."

Mungan said: "It figures."

Sable turned to him. "May we see the exhibit in question?"

Mungan went into the back room.

"Where's the boy?" Sable said in an undertone.

"At a friend's house, playing chess. I'll take you to him when we finish here."

"Tony was a chess-player. Do you really think he's Tony's son?"

"I don't know. I'm waiting to have my mind made up for me."

"By the evidence of the bones?"

"Partly. I've got hold of another piece of evidence that fits in. Brown has been identified from one of Tony Galton's pictures."

"You didn't tell me that before."

"I didn't know it before."

"Who's your witness?"

"A woman named Matheson in Redwood City. She's Culligan's ex-wife and Galton's ex-nurse. I've made a commitment to keep her name out of the police case."

"Is that wise?" Sable's voice was sharp and unpleasant.

"Wise or not, it's the way it is."

We were close to quarreling. Mungan came back into the room and cut it short. The bones rattled in his evidence box. He hoisted it onto the counter and raised the lid. Sable looked down at John Brown's leavings. His face was grave.

Mungan picked out the arm bone and laid it on the counter. He went to his desk and came back with a steel foot-rule. The break was exactly two inches from the end.

Sable was breathing quickly. He spoke in repressed excitement: "It looks very much as if we've found Tony Galton. Why is the skull missing? What was done to him?"

Mungan told him what he knew. On the way to the Dineen house I told Sable the rest of it.

"I have to congratulate you, Archer. You certainly get results."

"They fell into my lap. It's one of the things that made me suspicious. Too many coincidences came together—the Culligan murder, the Brown-Galton murder, the Brown-Galton boy turning up, if that's who he is. I can't help feeling that the whole business may have been planned to come out this way. There are mobsters involved, remember. Those boys look a long way ahead sometimes, and they're willing to wait for their payoff."

"Payoff?"

"The Galton money. I think the Culligan killing was a gang killing. I think it was no accident that Culligan came to work for you three months ago. Your house was a perfect hide-out for him, and a place where he could watch developments in the Galton family."

"For what possible purpose?"

"My thinking hasn't got that far," I said. "But I'm reasonably certain that Culligan didn't go there on his own."

"Who sent him?"

"That's the question." After a pause, I said: "How is Mrs. Sable, by the way?"

"Not good. I had to put her in a nursing home. I couldn't leave her by herself at home."

"I suppose it's the Culligan killing that got her down?"

"The doctors seem to think it's what triggered her breakdown. But she's had emotional trouble before."

"What sort of emotional trouble?"

"I'd just as soon not go into it," he said bleakly.

Chapter 15

D<small>R. DINEEN</small> came to the door in an ancient smoking-jacket made of red velvet which reminded me of the plush in old railway coaches. His wrinkled face was set in a frown of concentration. He looked at me impatiently:

"What is it?"

"I think we've identified your skeleton."

"Really? How?"

"Through the mended break in the arm bone. Dr. Dineen, this is Mr. Sable. Mr. Sable's an attorney representing the dead man's family."

"Who were his family?"

Sable answered: "His true name was Anthony Galton. His mother is Mrs. Henry Galton of Santa Teresa."

"You don't say. I used to see her name on the society pages. She cut quite a swathe at one time."

"I suppose she did," Sable said. "She's an old woman now."

"We all grow older, don't we? But come in, gentlemen."

He stood back to let us enter. I turned to him in the hallway:

"Is John Brown with you?"

"He is, yes. I believe he was trying to locate you earlier in the evening. At the moment he's in my office studying the chessboard. Much good may it do him. I propose to beat him in six more moves."

"Can you give us a minute, Doctor, by ourselves?"

"If it's important, and I gather it is."

He steered us into a dining-room furnished in beautiful old mahogany. Light from a yellowing crystal chandelier fell on the dark wood and on the sterling tea set which stood in geometrical order on the tall buffet. The room recalled the feeling I'd had that morning, that the doctor's house was an enclave of the solid past.

He sat at the head of the table and placed us on either side of him. Sable leaned forward across the corner of the table. The events of the day and the one before it had honed his profile sharp:

"Will you give me your opinion of the young man's moral character?"

"I entertain him in my house. That ought to answer your question."

"You consider him a friend?"

"I do, yes. I don't make a practice of entertaining casual strangers. At my age you can't afford to waste your time on second-rate people."

"Does that imply that he's a first-rate person?"

"It would seem to." The doctor's smile was slow, and almost indistinguishable from his frown. "At least he has the makings. You don't ask much more from a boy of twenty-two."

"How long have you known him?"

"All his life, if you count our initial introduction. Mr. Archer may have told you that I brought him into the world."

"Are you certain this is the same boy that you brought into the world?"

"I have no reason to doubt it."

"Would you swear to it, Doctor?"

"If necessary."

"It may be necessary. The question of his identity is a highly important one. A very great deal of money is involved."

The old man smiled, or frowned. "Forgive me if I'm not overly impressed. Money is only money, after all. I don't believe John is particularly hungry for money. As a matter of fact, this development will be quite a blow to him. He came here in the hope of finding his father, alive."

"If he qualifies for a fortune," Sable said, "it ought to be some comfort to him. Were his parents legally married, do you know?"

"It happens that I can answer that question, in the affirmative. John has been making some inquiries. He discovered just last week that a John Brown and a Theodora Gavin were married in Benicia, by civil ceremony, in September 1936. That seems to make him legitimate, by a narrow margin."

Sable sat in silence for a minute. He looked at Dineen like a prosecutor trying to weigh the credibility of a witness.

"Well," the old man said. "Are you satisfied? I don't wish to appear inhospitable, but I'm an early riser, and it happens to be my bedtime."

"There are one or two other things, if you'll bear with me, Doctor. I'm wondering, for instance, just how you happen to be so close to the boy's affairs."

"I choose to be," Dineen said abruptly.

"Why?"

The doctor looked at Sable with faint dislike. "My motives are no concern of yours, Counselor. The young man knocked on my door a month ago, looking for some trace of his family. Naturally I did my best to help him. He has a moral right to the protection and support of his family."

"If he can prove that he's a member of it."

"There seems to be no question of that. I think you're being unnecessarily hard on him, and I see no reason why you should continue in that vein. Certainly there's no indication that he's an impostor. He has his birth certificate, which proves the facts of his birth. My name is on it as attending physician. It's why he came to me in the first place."

"Birth certificates are easy to get," I said. "You can write in, pay your money, and take your choice."

"I suppose you can, if you're a cheat and a scoundrel. I resent the implication that this boy is."

"Please don't." Sable moderated his tone. "As Mrs. Galton's attorney, it's my duty to be skeptical of these claims."

"John has been making no claims."

"Perhaps not yet. He will. And very important interests are involved, human as well as financial. Mrs. Galton is in uncertain health. I don't intend to present her with a situation that's likely to blow up in her face."

"I don't believe that's the case here. You asked me for my opinion, and now you have it. But no human situation is entirely predictable, is it?" The old man leaned forward to get up. His bald scalp gleamed like polished stone in the light from the chandelier. "You'll be wanting to talk to John, I suppose. I'll tell him you're here."

He left the room and came back with the boy. John was wearing flannel slacks and a gray sweater over an open-necked shirt. He looked like the recent college graduate that he was supposed to be, but he wasn't at ease in the situation. His eyes shifted from my face to Sable's. Dineen stood beside him in an almost protective posture.

"This is Mr. Sable," he said in a neutral tone. "Mr. Sable is an attorney from Santa Teresa, and he's very much interested in you."

Sable stepped forward and gave him a brisk handshake. "I'm glad to meet you."

"Glad to meet you." His gray eyes matched Sable's in watchfulness. "I understand you know who my father is."

"Was, John," I said. "We've identified those bones at the station, pretty definitely. They belonged to a man named Anthony Galton. The indications are that he was your father."

"But my father's name was John Brown."

"He used that name. It started out as a pen name, apparently." I looked at the lawyer beside me. "We can take it for granted, can't we, that Galton and Brown were the same man, and that he was murdered in 1936?"

"It appears so." Sable laid a restraining hand on my arm. "I wish you'd let me handle this. There are legal questions involved."

He turned to the boy, who looked as if he hadn't absorbed the fact of his father's death. The doctor laid an arm across his shoulders:

"I'm sorry about this, John. I know how much it means to you."

"It's funny, it doesn't seem to mean a thing. I never knew my father. It's simply words, about a stranger."

"I'd like to talk to you in private," Sable said. "Where can we do that?"

"In my room, I suppose. What are we going to talk about?"

"You."

He lived in a workingmen's boardinghouse on the other side of town. It was a ramshackle frame house standing among others which had known better days. The landlady intercepted us at the front door. She was a large-breasted Portuguese woman with rings in her ears and spice on her breath. Something in the boy's face made her say:

"Whatsamatter, Johnny? You in trouble?"

"Nothing like that, Mrs. Gorgello," he said with forced lightness. "These men are friends of mine. Is it all right if I take them up to my room?"

"It's your room, you pay rent. I cleaned it up today for you, real nice. Come right in, gentlemen," she said royally.

Not so royally, she jostled the boy as he passed her in the doorway. "Lift up the long face, Johnny. You look like judgment day."

His room was a small bare cubicle on the second floor at the rear. I guessed that it had been a servant's room in the days when the house was a private residence. Torn places and stains among the faded roses of the wallpaper hinted at a long history of decline.

The room was furnished with an iron cot covered by an army blanket, a stained pine chest of drawers topped by a clouded mirror, a teetery wardrobe, a kitchen chair standing beside a table. In spite of the books on the table, something about the room reminded me of the dead man Culligan. Perhaps it was the smell, compound of hidden dirt and damp and old grim masculine odors.

My mind skipped to Mrs. Galton's grandiose estate. It would be quite a leap from this place to that. I wondered if the boy was going to make it.

He was standing by the single window, looking at us with a sort of defiance. This was his room, his bearing seemed to say, and we could take it or leave it. He lifted the kitchen chair and turned it away from the table:

"Sit down if you like. One of you can sit on the bed."

"I'd just as soon stand, thanks," Sable said. "I had a long drive up here, and I'm going to have to drive back tonight."

The boy said stiffly: "I'm sorry to put you to all this trouble."

"Nonsense. This is my job, and there's nothing personal about it. Now I understand you have your birth certificate with you. May I have a look at it?"

"Certainly."

He pulled out the top drawer of the chest of drawers and produced a folded document. Sable put on horn-rimmed spectacles to read it. I read it over his shoulder. It stated that John Brown, Jr., had been born on Bluff Road in San Mateo County on December 2, 1936; father, John Brown; mother, Theodora Gavin Brown; attending physician, Dr. George T. Dineen.

Sable glanced up, snatching off his glasses like a politician:

"You realize this document means nothing in itself? Anyone can apply for a birth certificate, any birth certificate."

"This one happens to be mine, sir."

"I notice it was issued only last March. Where were you in March?"

"I was still in Ann Arbor. I lived there for over five years."

"Going to the University all that time?" I asked.

"Most of it. I attended high school for a year and a half, then I shifted over to the University. I graduated this spring." He paused, and caught with his teeth at his full lower lip. "I suppose you'll be checking all this, so I might as well explain that I didn't go to school under my own name."

"Why? Didn't you know your own name?"

"Of course I did. I always have. If you want me to go into the circumstances, I will."

"I think that's very much to be desiderated," Sable said.

The boy picked up one of the books from the table. Its title was *Dramas of Modernism*. He opened it to the flyleaf and showed us the name "John Lindsay" written in ink there.

"That was the name I used, John Lindsay. The Christian name was my own, of course. The surname belonged to Mr. Lindsay, the man who took me into his home."

"He lived in Ann Arbor?" Sable said.

"Yes, at 1028 Hill Street." The boy's tone was faintly sardonic. "I lived there with him for several years. His full name was Mr. Gabriel R. Lindsay. He was a teacher and counselor at the high school."

"Isn't it rather odd that you used his name?"

"I didn't think so, under the circumstances. The circumstances were odd—that's putting it mildly—and Mr. Lindsay was the one who took a real interest in my case."

"Your case?"

The boy smiled wryly. "I was a case, all right. I've come a long way in five years, thanks to Mr. Lindsay. I was a mess when I showed up at that high school—a mess in more ways than one. I'd been two days on the road, and I didn't have decent clothes, or anything. Naturally they wouldn't let me in. I didn't have a school record, and I wouldn't tell them my name."

"Why not?"

"I was mortally scared that they'd drag me back to Ohio and put me in training-school. They did that to some of the boys who ran away from the orphanage. Besides, the superintendent didn't like me."

"The superintendent of the orphanage?"

"Yes. His name was Mr. Merriweather."

"What was the name of the orphanage?"

"Crystal Springs. It's near Cleveland. They didn't call it an orphanage. They called it a Home. Which didn't make it any more homelike."

"You say your mother put you there?" I said.

"When I was four."

"Do you remember your mother?"

"Of course. I remember her face, especially. She was very pale and thin, with blue eyes. I think she must have been sick. She had a bad cough. Her voice was husky, very low and soft. I remember the last thing she ever said to me: 'Your daddy's name was John Brown, too, and you were born in California.' I didn't know what or where California was, but I held on to the word. You can see why I had to come here, finally." His voice seemed to have the resonance of his life behind it.

Sable was unimpressed by his emotion. "Where did she say that to you?"

"In the superintendent's office, when she left me there. She promised to come back for me, but she never did. I don't know what happened to her."

"But you remember her words from the age of four?"

"I was bright for my age," he answered matter-of-factly. "I'm bright, and I'm not ashamed of it. It stood me in good stead when I was trying to get into the high school in Ann Arbor."

"Why did you pick Ann Arbor?"

"I heard it was a good place to get an education. The teachers in the Home were a couple of ignorant bullies. I wanted an education more than anything. Mr. Lindsay gave me an aptitude test, and he decided that I deserved an education, even if I didn't have any transcript. He put up quite a battle for me, getting me into the high school. And then he had to fight the welfare people. They wanted to put me in Juvenile, or find a foster-home for me. Mr. Lindsay convinced them that his home would do, even if he didn't have a wife. He was a widower."

"He sounds like a good man," I said.

"He was the best, and I ought to know. I lived with him for nearly four years. I looked after the furnace, mowed the lawn in the summer, worked around the house to pay for my board and room. But board and room was the least of what he gave me. I was a little bum when he took me in. He made a decent person out of me."

He paused, and his eyes looked past us, thousands of miles. Then they focused on me:

"I had no right today, to tell you that I never had a father. Gabe Lindsay was a father to me."

"I'd like to meet him," I said.

"So that you can check up on me?"

"Not necessarily. Don't take all this so hard, John. As Mr. Sable said, there's nothing personal about it. It's our business to get the facts."

"It's too late to get them from Mr. Lindsay. Mr. Lindsay died the winter before last. He was good to me right up to the end, and past it. He left me enough money to finish my studies."

"How much did he leave you?" Sable said.

"Two thousand dollars. I still have a little of it left."

"What did he die of?"

"Pneumonia. He died in the University Hospital in Ann Arbor. I was with him when he died. You can check that. Next question."

His irony was young and vulnerable. It failed to mask his feeling. I thought if his feeling was artificial, he didn't need the Galton money: he could make his fortune as an actor.

"What motivated you to come here to Luna Bay?" Sable said. "It couldn't have been pure coincidence."

"Who said it was?" Under the pressure of cross-questioning, the boy's poise was breaking down. "I had a right to come here. I was born here, wasn't I?"

"Were you?"

"You just saw my birth certificate."

"How did you get hold of it?"

"I wrote to Sacramento. Is there anything wrong with that? I gave them my birthdate, and they were able to tell me where I was born."

"Why the sudden interest in where you were born?"

"It wasn't a sudden interest. Ask any orphan how important it is to him. The only sudden part of it was my bright idea of writing to Sacramento. It hadn't occurred to me before."

"How did you know your birthdate?"

"My mother must have told the orphanage people. They always gave me a birthday present on December second." He grinned wryly. "Winter underwear."

Sable smiled, too, in spite of himself. He waved his hand in front of his face, as if to dissipate the tension in the room: "Are you satisfied, Archer?"

"I am for now. We've all had a long day. Why don't you lay over for the night?"

"I can't. I have an important probate coming up at ten tomorrow morning. Before that, I have to talk to the Judge in his chambers." He turned suddenly to the boy: "Do you drive a car?"

"I don't have one of my own, but I can drive."

"How would you like to drive me to Santa Teresa? Now."

"To stay?"

"If it works out. I think it will. Your grandmother will be eager to see you."

"But Mr. Turnell's counting on me at the station."

"He can get himself another boy," I said. "You better go, John. You're due for a big change, and this is the beginning of it."

"I'll give you ten minutes to pack," Sable said.

The boy seemed dazed for a minute. He looked around the walls of the mean little room as if he hated to leave it. Perhaps he was afraid to make the big leap.

"Come on," Sable said. "Snap into it."

John shook himself out of his apathy, and dragged an old leather suitcase from the wardrobe. We stood and watched him pack his meager belongings: a suit, a few shirts and socks, shaving gear, a dozen books, his precious birth certificate.

I wondered if we were doing him a favor. The Galton household had hot and cold running money piped in from an inexhaustible reservoir. But money was never free. Like any other commodity, it had to be paid for.

Chapter 16

I SAT up late in my motel room, making notes on John Brown's story. It wasn't a likely story, on the face of it. His apparent sincerity made it plausible; that, and the fact that it could easily be checked. Some time in the course of the interview I'd made a moral bet with myself that John Brown was telling the truth. John Galton, that is.

In the morning I mailed my notes to my office in Hollywood. Then I paid a visit to the sheriff's substation. A young deputy with a crewcut was sitting at Mungan's desk.

"Yessir?"

"Is Deputy Mungan anywhere around?"

"Sorry, he's off duty. If you're Mr. Archer, he left a message for you."

He took a long envelope out of a drawer and handed it across the counter. It contained a hurried note written on yellow scratch-pad paper:

> R.C. phoned me some dope on Fred Nelson. Record goes back to S.F. docks in twenties. Assault with intent, nolle-prossed. Lempi gang enforcer 1928 on. Arrested suspicion murder 1930, habeas-corpused. Convicted grand theft 1932, sentenced "Q." Attempted escape 1933, extended sentence. Escaped December 1936, never apprehended.
>
> Mungan.

I walked across the street to the hotel and phoned Roy Lemberg's hotel, the Sussex Arms. The desk clerk answered:

"Sussex Arms. Mr. Farnsworth speaking."

"This is Archer. Is Lemberg there?"

"Who did you say it was?"

"Archer. I gave you ten dollars yesterday. Is Lemberg there?"

"Mr. and Mrs. Lemberg both checked out."

"When?"

"Yesterday aft, right after you left."

"Why didn't I see them go?"

761

"Maybe because they went out the back way. They didn't even leave a forwarding address. But Lemberg made a long-distance call before they took off. A call to Reno."

"Who did he call in Reno?"

"Car-dealer name of Generous Joe. Lemberg used to work for him, I think."

"And that's all there is?"

"That's all," Farnsworth said. "I hope it's what you want."

I drove across country to International Airport, turned in my rented car, and caught a plane to Reno. By noon I was parking another rented car in front of Generous Joe's lot.

A huge billboard depicted a smiling Santa Claus type scattering silver dollars. The lot had a kiosk on one corner, and a row of late-model cars fronting for half an acre of clunks. A big corrugated metal shed with a Cars Painted sign on the wall stood at the rear of the lot.

An eager young man with a rawhide tie cantered out of the kiosk almost before I'd brought my car to a halt. He patted and stroked the fender:

"Nice. Very nice. Beautiful condition, clean inside and out. Depending on your equity, you can trade up and still carry cash away."

"They'd put me in jail. I just rented this crate."

He gulped, performed a mental back somersault, and landed on his feet: "So why pay rent? On our terms, you can *own* a car for less money."

"You wouldn't be Generous Joe?"

"Mr. Culotti's in the back. You want to talk to him?"

I said I did. He waved me toward the shed, and yelled: "Hey, Mr. Culotti, customer!"

A gray-haired man came out, looking cheaply gala in an ice-cream suit. His face was swarthy and pitted like an Epstein bronze, and its two halves didn't quite match. When I got closer to him, I saw that one of his brown eyes was made of glass. He looked permanently startled.

"Mr. Culotti?"

"That's me." He smiled a money smile. "What can I do for you?" A trace of Mediterranean accent added feminine endings to some of his words.

"A man named Lemberg called you yesterday."

"That's right, he used to work for me, wanted his old job back. Nix." A gesture of his spread hand swept Lemberg into the dust-bin.

"Is he back in Reno? I'm trying to locate him."

Culotti picked at his nose and looked wise, in a startled way. He smiled expansively, and put a fatherly arm around my back. "Come in, we'll talk."

He propelled me toward the door. Hissing sounds came from the shed, and the sweet anesthetic odor of sprayed paint. Culotti opened the door and stepped back. A goggled man with a paint-gun turned from his work on a blue car.

I was trying to recognize him, when Culotti's shoulder caught me like a trunk-bumper in the small of the back. I staggered toward the goggled man. The paint-gun hissed in his hands.

A blue cloud stung my eyes. In the burning blue darkness, I recalled that the room clerk Farnsworth hadn't asked me for more money. Then I felt the sap's soft explosion against the back of my head. I glissaded down blue slopes of pain to a hole which opened for me.

Later there was talking.

"Better wash out his eyes," the first gravedigger said. "We don't want to blind him."

"Let him go blind," the second gravedigger said. "Teach him a lesson. I got a hook in the eye."

"Did it teach you a lesson, Blind-eye? Do what I tell you."

I heard Culotti breathe like a bull. He spat, but made no answer. My hands were tied behind me. My face was on cement. I tried to blink. My eyelids were stuck tight.

The fear of blindness is the worst fear there is. It crawled on my face and entered my mouth. I wanted to beg them to save my eyes. A persistent bright speck behind my eyes stared me down and shamed me into continued silence.

Liquid gurgled in a can.

"Not with gasoline, greaseball."

"Don't call me that."

"Why not? You're a blind-eye greaseball, hamburger that used to be a muscle." This voice was light and featureless, without feeling, almost without meaning. "You got any olive oil?"

"At home, plenty."

"Go and get it. I'll keep store."

My consciousness must have lapsed. Oil ran on my face like tears. I thought of a friend named Angelo who made his own oil from the olives he grew on his hillside in the Valley. The Mafia had killed his father.

A face came into blurred focus, Culotti's face, hanging slack-mouthed over me. I twisted from my side onto my back, and lashed at him with both feet. One heel caught him under the chin, and he went down. Something bounced and rolled on the floor. Then he stood one-eyed over me, bleeding at the mouth. He stamped my head back down into earthy darkness.

It was a bad afternoon. Quite suddenly it was a bad evening. Somebody had awakened me with his snoring. I listened to the snoring for a while. It stopped when I held my breath and started again when I let my breath out. For a long time I missed the significance of this.

There were too many other interesting things to do and think about. The staring speck was back again in the center of my mind. It moved, and my hands moved with it. They felt my face. It bored me. Ruins always bored me.

I was lying in a room. The room had walls. There was a window in one of the walls. Snow-capped mountains rose against a yellow sky which darkened to green, then blue. Twilight hung like blue smoke in the room.

I sat up; springs creaked under me. A man I hadn't noticed moved away from the wall he'd been leaning on. I dropped my feet to the floor and turned to face him, slowly and carefully, so as not to lose my balance.

He was a thick young man with shiny black curls tumbling over his forehead. One of his arms was in a sling. The other arm had a gun at the end of it. His hot eyes and the cold eye of the gun triangulated my breastbone.

"Hello, Tommy," I tried to say. It came out: "Huddo, Tawy."

My mouth contained ropes of blood. I tried to spit them out. That started a chain-reaction which flung me back on the bed retching and cawing. Tommy Lemberg stood and watched me.

He said when I was still: "Mr. Schwartz is waiting to talk to you. You want to clean up a little?"

"Wheh do I do dat?" I said in my inimitable patois.

"There's a bathroom down the hall. Think you can walk?"

"I can walk."

But I had to lean on the wall to reach the bathroom. Tommy Lemberg stood and watched me wash my face and gargle. I tried to avoid looking into the mirror over the sink. I looked, though, finally, when I was drying my face. One of my front teeth was broken off short. My nose resembled a boiled potato.

All of this made me angry. I moved on Tommy. He stepped back into the doorway. I lost my footing and fell to my knees, took the barrel of his gun in the nape of my neck. Pain went through me so large and dull it scared me. I got up, supporting myself on the sink.

Tommy was grinning in an excited way. "Don't *do* things like that. I don't want to hurt you."

"Or Culligan, either, I bet." I was talking better now, but my eyes weren't focusing properly.

"Culligan? Who he? I never heard of any Culligan."

"And you've never been in Santa Teresa?"

"Where's that?"

He ushered me to the end of the corridor and down a flight of steps into a big dim room. In its picture windows, the mountains now stood black against the darkening sky. I recognized the mountains west of Reno. Tommy turned on lights which blotted them out. He moved around the room as if he was at home there.

I suppose it was the living-room of Otto Schwartz's house, but it was more like the lobby of a hotel or the recreation room of an institution. The furniture stood around in impersonal groupings, covered with plastic so that nothing could harm it. An antique bar and a wall of bottles took up one whole end. A jukebox, an electric player piano, a roulette layout, and several slot machines stood against the rear wall.

"You might as well sit down." Tommy waved his gun at a chair.

I sat down and closed my eyes, which still weren't focusing. Everything I looked at had a double outline. I was afraid of concussion. I was having a lot of fears.

Tommy turned on the player piano. It started to tinkle out a tune about a little Spanish town. Tommy did a few dance steps to it, facing me and holding the gun in his hand. He didn't seem to know what to do with himself.

I concentrated on wishing that he would put his gun away and give me some kind of chance at him. He never would, though. He loved holding the gun. He held it different ways, posturing in front of his reflection in the window. I began to draft a mental letter to my congressman advocating legislation prohibiting the manufacture of guns except for military purposes.

Mr. J. Edgar Hoover entered the room at this point. He must have been able to read minds, because he said that he approved of my plan and intended to present it to the President. I felt my forehead. It was hot and dry, like a heating-pad. Mr. Hoover faded away. The player piano went on hammering out the same tune: music to be delirious by.

The man who came in next radiated chill from green glacial eyes. He had a cruel nose and under it the kind of mouth that smiles by stretching horizontally. He must have been nearly sixty but he had a well-sustained tan and a lean quick body. He wore a light fedora and a topcoat.

So did the man who moved a step behind him and towered half a foot over him. This one had the flat impervious eyes, the battered face and pathological nervelessness of an old-fashioned western torpedo. When his boss paused in front of me, he stood to one side in canine watchfulness. Tommy moved up beside him, like an apprentice.

"You're quite a mess." Schwartz's voice was chilly, too, and very soft, expecting to be listened to. "I'm Otto Schwartz, in case you don't know. I got no time to waste on two-bit private eyes. I got other things on my mind."

"What kind of things have you got on it? Murder?"

He tightened up. Instead of hitting me, he took off his hat and threw it to Tommy. His head was completely bald. He put his hands in his coat pockets and leaned back on his heels and looked down the curve of his nose at me:

"I was giving you the benefit, that you got in over your head without knowing. What's going to happen, you go on like this, talk about murder, crazy stuff like that?" He wagged his head solemnly from side to side. "Lake Tahoe is very deep. You could take a long dive, no Aqualung, concrete on the legs."

"You could sit in a hot seat, no cushion, electrodes on the bald head."

The big man took a step toward me, watching Schwartz with a doggy eye, and lunged around with his big shoulders. Schwartz surprised me by laughing, rather tinnily:

"You are a brave young man. I like you. I wish you no harm. What do you suggest? A little money, and that's that?"

"A little murder. Murder everybody. Then you can be the bigshot of the world."

"I am a bigshot, don't ever doubt it." His mouth pursed suddenly and curiously, like a wrinkled old wound: "I take insults from nobody! And nobody steals from me."

"Did Culligan steal from you? Is that why you ordered him killed?"

Schwartz looked down at me some more. His eyes had dark centers. I thought of the depths of Tahoe, and poor drowned Archer with concrete on his legs. I was in a susceptible mood, and fighting it. Tommy Lemberg spoke up:

"Can I say something, Mr. Schwartz? I didn't knock the guy off. The cops got it wrong. He must of fell down on the knife and stabbed himself."

"Yah! Moron!" Schwartz turned his contained fury on Tommy: "Go tell that to the cops. Just leave me out of it, please."

"They wouldn't believe me," he said in a misunderstood whine. "They'd pin it on me, just because I tried to defend myself. I was the one got shot. He pulled a gun on me."

"Shut up! Shut up!" Schwartz spread one hand on top of his head and pulled at imaginary hair. "Why is there no intelligence left in the world? All morons!"

"The intelligent ones wouldn't touch your rackets with a ten-foot pole."

"I heard enough out of you."

He jerked his head at the big man, who started to take off his coat:

"Want me to work him over, Mr. Schwartz?"

It was the light and meaningless voice that had argued with Culotti. It lifted me out of my chair. Because Schwartz was handy, I hit him in the stomach. He jackknifed, and went down gasping. It doesn't take much to make me happy, and that gave me a happy feeling which lasted through the first three or four minutes of the beating.

Then the big man's face began to appear in red snatches. When the light in the room failed entirely, the bright staring speck in my mind took over for a while. Schwartz's voice kept making tinny little jokes:

"Just promise to forget it, that will be that."

"All you gotta do, give me your word. I'm a man of my word, you're another."

"Back to L.A., that's all you gotta do. No questions asked, no harm done."

The bright speck stood like a nail in my brain. It wouldn't let me let go of the room. I cursed it, but it wouldn't go away. It wrote little luminous remarks on the red pounding darkness: This is it. You take a stand.

Then it was a light surging away from me like the light of a ship. I swam for it, but it rose away, hung in the dark heaven still as a star. I let go of the pounding room, and swung from it up and over the black mountains.

Chapter 17

I CAME to early next morning in the accident ward of the Reno hospital. When I had learned to talk with a packed nose and a wired jaw, a couple of detectives asked me who took my wallet. I didn't bother disturbing their assumption that I was a mugging victim.

Anything I told them about Schwartz would be wasted words. Besides, I needed Schwartz. The thought of him got me through the first bad days, when I doubted from time to time that I would be very active in the future. Everything was still fuzzy at the edges. I got very tired of fuzzy nurses and earnest young fuzzy doctors asking me how my head felt.

By the fourth day, though, my vision was clear enough to read some of yesterday's newspapers which the voluntary aides brought around for the ward patients. There was hardware in the sky, and dissension on earth. A special dispatch in the back pages told how a real-life fairy-tale had reached its happy ending when the long-lost John Galton was restored to the bosom of his grandmother, the railroad and oil widow. In the accompanying photograph, John himself was wearing a new-looking sports jacket and a world-is-my-oyster grin.

This spurred me on. By the end of the first week, I was starting to get around. One morning after my Cream of Wheat I sneaked out to the nurses' station and put in a collect call to Santa Teresa. I had time to tell Gordon Sable where I was, before the head nurse caught me and marched me back to the ward.

Sable arrived while I was eating my Gerber's-baby-food dinner. He waved a checkbook. Before I knew it I was in a private room with a bottle of Old Forester which Sable had brought me. I sat up late with him, drinking highballs through a glass tube and talking through my remaining teeth like a gangster in very early sound.

"You're going to need a crown on that tooth," Sable said comfortingly. "Also, plastic surgery on the nose. Do you have any hospital insurance?"

"No."

"I'm afraid I can't commit Mrs. Galton." Then he took another look at me, and his manner softened: "Well, yes, I think I can. I think I can persuade her to underwrite the expense, even though you did exceed your instructions."

"That's mighty white of you and her." But the words didn't come out ironic. It had been a bad eight days. "Doesn't she give a good goddam about who murdered her son? And what about Culligan?"

"The police are working on both cases, don't worry."

"They're the same case. The cops are sitting on their tails. Schwartz put the fix in."

Sable shook his head. "You're way off in left field, Lew."

"The hell I am. Tommy Lemberg's his boy. Have they arrested Tommy?"

"He dropped out of sight. Don't let it ride you. You're a willing man, but you can't take on responsibility for all the trouble in the world. Not in your present condition, anyway."

"I'll be on my feet in another week. Sooner." The whisky in the bottle was falling like a barometer. I was full of stormy optimism. "Give me another week after that and I'll break the case wide open for you."

"I hope so, Lew. But don't take too much on yourself. You've been hurt, and naturally your feelings are a bit exaggerated."

He was sitting directly under the light, but his face was getting fuzzy. I leaned out of bed and grabbed his shoulder. "Listen, Sable, I can't prove it, but I can feel it. That Galton boy is a phony, part of a big conspiracy, with the Organization behind it."

"I think you're wrong. I've spent hours on his story. It checks out. And Mrs. Galton is quite happy, for the first time in many years."

"I'm not."

He rose, and pushed me gently back against the pillows. I was still as weak as a cat. "You've talked enough for one night. Let it rest, and don't worry, eh? Mrs. Galton will take care of everything, and if she doesn't want to, I'll make her. You've earned her gratitude. We're all sorry this had to happen."

He shook my hand and started for the door.

"Flying back tonight?" I asked him.

"I have to. My wife's in bad shape. Take it easy, now, you'll hear from me. And I'll leave some money for you at the desk."

Chapter 18

I SPRUNG myself out of the hospital three days later, and assembled myself aboard a plane for San Francisco. From International Airport I took a cab to the Sussex Arms Hotel.

The room clerk, Farnsworth, was sitting behind the counter at the rear of the dim little lobby, looking as if he hadn't moved in two weeks. He was reading a muscle magazine, and he didn't look up until I was close enough to see the yellows of his eyes. Even then he didn't recognize me right away: the bandages on my face made an effective mask.

"You wish a room, sir?"

"No. I came to see you."

"Me?" His eyebrows jumped, and then came down in a frown of concentration.

"I owe you something."

The color left his face. "No. No, you don't. That's all right."

"The other ten and the bonus. That makes fifteen I owe you. Excuse the delay. I got held up."

"That's too bad." He craned his neck around and looked behind him. There was nothing there but the switchboard, staring like a wall of empty eyes.

"Don't let it bother you, Farnsworth. It wasn't your fault. Was it?"

"No." He swallowed several times. "It wasn't my fault."

I stood and smiled at him with the visible parts of my face.

"What happened?" he said after a while.

"It's a long sad story. You wouldn't be interested."

I took the creaking new wallet out of my hip pocket and laid a five and a ten on the counter between us. He sat and looked at the money.

"Take it," I said.

He didn't move.

"Go ahead, don't be bashful. The money belongs to you."

"Well. Thanks."

Slowly and reluctantly, he reached out for the bills. I caught his wrist in my left hand, and held it. He jerked convulsively, reached under the counter and came up with a gun in his left hand:

"Turn me loose."

"Not a chance."

"I'll shoot!" But the gun was wavering.

I reached for his gun wrist, and twisted it until the gun dropped on the counter between us. It was a .32 revolver, a little nickel-plated suicide gun. I let go of Farnsworth and picked it up and pointed it at the knot of his tie. Without moving, he seemed to draw away from it. His eyes got closer together.

"Please. I couldn't help it."

"What couldn't you help?"

"I had orders to give you that contact in Reno."

"Who gave you the orders?"

"Roy Lemberg. It wasn't my fault."

"Lemberg doesn't give orders to anybody. He's the kind that takes them."

"Sure, he passed the word, that's what I meant."

"Who gave him the word?"

"Some gambler in Nevada, name of Schwartz." Farnsworth wet his mauve lips with his tongue. "Listen, you don't want to ruin me. I make a little book, lay off the heavy bets. If I don't do like the money boys say, I'm out of business. So have a heart, mister."

"If you level with me. Does Lemberg work for Schwartz?"

"His brother does. Not him."

"Where are the Lembergs now?"

"I wouldn't know about the brother. Roy took off like I said, him and his wife both. Put the gun down, mister. Jeeze. I got a nervous stomach."

"You'll have a perforated ulcer if you don't talk. Where did the Lembergs go?"

"Los Angeles, I think."

"Where in Los Angeles?"

"I dunno." He spread his hands. They had a tremor running through them, like dry twigs in a wind. "Honest."

"You know, Farnsworth," I said in my menacing new lockjaw voice, "I'll give you five seconds to tell me."

He looked around at the switchboard again, as if it was an instrument of execution, and swallowed audibly. "All right, I'll tell you. They're at a motor court on Bayshore, down by

Moffett Field. The Triton Motor Court. At least, that's where they said they were going. Now will you put down the gun, mister?"

Before the rhythm of his fear ran down, I said: "Do you know a man named Peter Culligan?"

"Yeah. He roomed here for a while, over a year ago."

"What did he do for a living?"

"He was a horseplayer."

"That's a living?"

"I guess he hacked a little, too. Put the gun down, eh? I told you what you wanted to know."

"Where did Culligan go from here?"

"I heard he got a job in Reno."

"Working for Schwartz?"

"Could be. He told me once he used to be a stickman."

I dropped the gun in my jacket pocket.

"Hey," he said. "That's my gun. I bought it myself."

"You're better off without it."

Looking back from the door, I saw that Farnsworth was half-way between the counter and the switchboard. He stopped in mid-motion. I went back across the lobby:

"If it turns out you're lying, or if you tip off the Lembergs, I'll come back for you. Is that clear?"

A kind of moral wriggle moved up his body from his waist to his fish-belly face. "Yeah. Sure. Okay."

This time I didn't look back. I walked up to Union Square, where I made a reservation on an afternoon flight to L.A. Then I rented a car and drove down Bayshore past the airport.

The hangars of Moffett Field loomed up through the smog like gray leviathans. The Triton Motor Court stood in a waste-land of shacks on the edge of the flight pattern. Its buildings were a fading salmon pink. Its only visible attraction was the $3.00 Double sign. Jets snored like flies in the sky.

I parked on the cinder driveway beside the chicken-coop office. The woman who ran it wore a string of fake pearls dirt-ied by her neck. She said that Mr. and Mrs. Lemberg weren't registered there.

"They may be going under their maiden name." I described them.

"Sounds like the girl in seven, maybe. She don't want to be disturbed, not in the daytime."

"She won't mind. I have no designs on her."

She bridled. "Who said you had? What kind of a place do you think this is, anyway?"

It was a tough question to answer. I said: "What name is she going under?"

"You from the cops? I don't want trouble with the cops."

"I was in an accident. She may be able to help me find the driver."

"That's different." The woman probably didn't believe me, but she chose to act as if she did. "They registered under the name Hamburg, Mr. and Mrs. Rex Hamburg."

"Is her husband with her?"

"Not for the last week. Maybe it's just as well," she added cryptically.

I knocked on the weathered door under the rusted iron seven. Footsteps dragged across the floor behind it. Fran Lemberg blinked in the light. Her eyes were puffed. The roots of her hair were darker. Her robe was taking on a grimy patina.

She stopped blinking when she recognized me.

"Go away."

"I'm coming in for a minute. You don't want trouble."

She looked past me, and I followed her look. The woman with the dirty pearls was watching us from the window of the office.

"All right, come in."

She let me come in past her, and slammed the door on day-light. The room smelled of wine and smoke, stale orange-peel and a woman's sleep, and a perfume I didn't recognize, Original Sin perhaps. When my eyes became night-adapted, I saw the confusion on the floor and the furniture: clothes and looped stockings and shoes and empty bottles, ashes and papers, the congealed remains of hamburgers and french fries.

She sat in a defensive posture on the edge of the unmade bed. I cleared a space for myself on the chair.

"What happened to you?" she said.

"I had a run-in with some of Tommy's playmates. Your hus-band set me up for the fall."

"Roy did?"

"Don't kid me, you were with him at the time. I thought he was a straight joe trying to help his brother, but he's just another errandboy for mobsters."

"No. He isn't."

"Is that what he told you?"

"I lived with him nearly ten years, I ought to know. He worked one time for a crooked car-dealer in Nevada. When Roy found out about the crookedness, he quit. That's the kind of guy he is."

"If you mean Generous Joe, that hardly qualifies Roy as a boy scout."

"I didn't say he was. He's just a guy trying to get through life."

"Some of us make it harder for the others."

"You can't blame Roy for trying to protect himself. He's wanted for accessory in a murder. But it isn't fair. You can't blame him for what Tommy did."

"You're a loyal wife," I said. "But where is it getting you?"

"Who says I want to get any place?"

"There are better places than this."

"You're telling me. I've lived in some of them."

"How long has Roy been gone?"

"Nearly two weeks, I guess. I don't keep track of the time. It goes faster that way."

"How old are you, Fran?"

"None of your business." After a pause she added: "A hundred and twenty-eight."

"Is Roy coming back?"

"He says he is. But he always sides with his brother when the chips are down." Emotion flooded up in her eyes, but drained away again. "I guess I can't blame him. This time the chips are really down."

"Tommy's staying in Nevada," I said, trying to find the wedge that would open her up.

"Tommy's in Nevada?"

"I saw him there. Schwartz is looking after him. And Roy, too, probably."

"I don't believe you. Roy said they were leaving the country."

"The state, maybe. Isn't that what he said, that they were leaving the state?"

"The country," she repeated stubbornly. "That's why they couldn't take me along."

"They were stringing you. They just don't want a woman in the way. So here you sit in a rundown crib on Bayshore. Hustling for hamburgers, while the boys are living high on the hog in Nevada."

"You're a liar!" she cried. "They're in Canada!"

"Don't let them kid you."

"Roy is going to send for me as soon as he can swing it."

"You've heard from him, then."

"Yeah, I've heard from him." Her loose mouth tightened, too late to hold back the words. "Okay, so you got it out of me. That's all you're going to get out of me." She folded her arms across her half-naked breasts, and looked at me grimly: "Why don't you beat it? You got nothing on me, you never will have."

"As soon as you show me Roy's letter."

"There was no letter. I got the message by word of mouth."

"Who brought it?

"A guy."

"What guy?"

"Just a guy. Roy told him to look me up."

"He sent him from Nevada, probably."

"He did not. The guy drove a haulaway out from Detroit. He talked to Roy in Detroit."

"Is that where Roy and Tommy crossed the border?"

"I guess so."

"Where were they headed?"

"I don't know, and I wouldn't tell you if I did know."

I sat on the bed beside her. "Listen to me, Fran. You want your husband back, don't you?"

"Not in a convict suit, or on a slab."

"It doesn't have to be that way. Tommy's the one we're after. If Roy will turn him over to us, he'll be taking a long step out of trouble. Can you get that message to Roy from me?"

"Maybe if he phones me or something. All I can do is wait."

"You must have some idea where they went."

"Yeah, they said something about this town in Ontario near Windsor. Tommy was the one that knew about it."

"What's the name of the place?"

"They didn't say."

CHAPTER 18777

"Was Tommy ever in Canada before?"

"No, but Pete Culligan—"

She covered the lower part of her face with her hand and looked at me over it. Fear and distress hardened her eyes, but not for long. Her feelings were too diffuse to sustain themselves.

I said: "Tommy did know Culligan, then?"

She nodded.

"Did he have a personal reason for killing Culligan?"

"Not that I know of. Him and Pete were palsy-walsy."

"When did you see them together?"

"Last winter in Frisco. Tommy was gonna jump parole until Roy talked him out of it, and Pete told him about this place in Canada. It's sort of an irony of fate like, now Tommy's hiding out there for knocking Pete off."

"Did Tommy admit to you that he killed Culligan?"

"No, to hear him tell it he's innocent as an unborn babe. Roy even believes him."

"But you don't?"

"I swore off believing Tommy the day after I met him. But we won't go into that."

"Where is this hideout in Canada?"

"I don't know." Her voice was taking on an edge of hysteria. "Why don't you go away and leave me alone?"

"Will you contact me if you hear from them?"

"Maybe I will, maybe I won't."

"How are you fixed for money?"

"I'm loaded," she said. "What do you think? I park in this crib because I like the homey atmosphere."

I dropped a ten in her lap as I went out. Before my plane took off for Los Angeles, I had time to phone Sheriff Trask. I filled him in, with emphasis on Culligan's probable connection with Schwartz. In the rational light of day, I didn't want Schwartz all to myself.

Chapter 19

IN THE morning, after a session with my dentist, I opened up my office on Sunset Boulevard. The mailbox was stuffed with envelopes, mostly bills and circulars. There were two envelopes mailed from Santa Teresa in the past few days.

The first one I opened contained a check for a thousand dollars and a short letter from Gordon Sable typed on the letterhead of his firm. Sad as was the fact of Anthony Galton's death, his client and he both felt that the over-all outcome was better than could have been hoped for. He hoped and trusted that I was back in harness, and none the worse for wear, and would I forward my medical bills as I received them.

The other letter was a carefully hand-written note from John Galton:

Dear Mr. Archer—

Just a brief note to thank you for your labours on my behalf. My father's death is a painful blow to all of us here. There is tragedy in the situation, which I have to learn to face up to. But there is also opportunity, for me. I hope to prove myself worthy of my patrimony.

Mr. Sable told me how you "fell among thieves." I hope that you are well again, and Grandmother joins me in this wish. For what it's worth, I did persuade Grandmother to send you an additional check in token of appreciation. She joins me in inviting you to visit us when you can make the trip up this way.

I myself would like very much to talk to you.

Respectfully yours,
John Galton.

It seemed to be pure gratitude undiluted by commercialism, until I reflected that he was taking credit for the check Sable had sent me. His letter stirred up the suspicions that had been latent in my mind since I'd talked to Sable in the hospital. Whatever John was, he was a bright boy and a fast worker. I wondered what he wanted from me.

After going through the rest of my mail, I called my answering-service. The girl at the switchboard expressed surprise that I was still in the land of the living, and told me that a Dr. Howell had been trying to reach me. I called the Santa Teresa number he'd left.

A girl's voice answered: "Dr. Howell's residence."

"This is Lew Archer. Miss Howell?" The temporary crown I'd just acquired that morning pushed out against my upper lip, and made me lisp.

"Yes, Mr. Archer."

"Your father has been trying to get in touch with me."

"Oh. He's just leaving for the hospital. I'll see if I can catch him."

After a pause, Howell's precise voice came over the line: "I'm glad to hear from you, Archer. You may recall that we met briefly at Mrs. Galton's house. I'd like to buy you a lunch."

"Lunch will be fine. What time and place do you have in mind?"

"The time is up to you—the sooner the better. The Santa Teresa Country Club would be the most convenient place for me."

"It's a long way for me to come for lunch."

"I had a little more than lunch in mind." He lowered his voice as though he suspected eavesdroppers. "I'd like to engage your services, if you're free."

"To do what?"

"I'd much prefer to discuss that in person. Would today be possible for you?"

"Yes. I'll be at the Country Club at one."

"You can't drive it in three hours, man."

"I'll take the noon plane."

"Oh, fine."

I heard the click as he hung up, and then a second click. Someone had been listening on an extension. I found out who it was when I got off the plane at Santa Teresa. A young girl with doe eyes and honey-colored hair was waiting for me at the barrier.

"Remember me? I'm Sheila Howell. I thought I'd pick you up."

"That was a nice thought."

"Not really. I have an ulterior motive."

She smiled charmingly. I followed her through the sunlit terminal to her car. It was a convertible with the top down.

Sheila turned to me as she slid behind the wheel: "I might as well be frank about it. I overheard what was said, and I wanted to talk to you about John before Dad does. Dad is a well-meaning person, but he's been a widower for ten years, and he has certain blind spots. He doesn't understand the modern world."

"But you do?"

She colored slightly, like a peach in the sun. "I understand it better than Dad does. I've studied social science at college, and people just don't go around any more telling other people who to be interested in. That sort of thing is as dead as the proverbial dodo. Deader." She nodded her small head, once, with emphasis.

"First-year social science?"

The color in her cheeks deepened. Her eyes were candid, the color of the sky. "How did you know? Anyway, I'm a sophomore now." As if this made all the difference between adolescence and maturity.

"I'm a mind reader. You're interested in John Galton."

Her pure gaze didn't waver. "I love John. I think he loves me."

"Is that what you wanted to say to me?"

"No." She was suddenly flustered. "I didn't mean to say it. But it's true." Her eyes darkened. "The things that Dad believes aren't true, though. He's just a typical patriarch type, full of prejudices against the boy I happen to like. He believes the most awful things against John, or pretends to."

"What things, Sheila?"

"I wouldn't even repeat them, so there. Anyway, you'll be hearing them from him. I know what Dad wants you to do, you see. He let the cat out of the bag last night."

"What does he want me to do?"

"Please," she said, "don't talk to me as if I were a child. I know that tone so well, and I'm so tired of it. Dad uses it on me all the time. He doesn't realize I'm practically grown up. I'm going to be nineteen on my next birthday."

"Wow," I said softly.

"All right, go ahead and patronize me. Maybe I'm not mature. I'm mature enough to know good people from bad people."

"We all make mistakes about people, no matter how ancient we are."

"But I couldn't be mistaken about John. He's the nicest boy I ever met in my life."

I said: "I like him, too."

"I'm so glad." Her hand touched my arm, like a bird alighting and then taking off again: "John likes you, or I wouldn't be taking you into our confidence."

"You wouldn't be planning on getting married?"

"Not just yet," she said, as if this was a very conservative approach. "John has a lot of things he wants to do first, and of course I couldn't go against Father's wishes."

"What things does John want to do?"

She answered vaguely: "He wants to make something of himself. He's very ambitious. And of course the one big thing in his life is finding out who killed his father. It's all he thinks about."

"Has he done anything about it?"

"Not yet, but I know he has plans. He doesn't tell me all he has on his mind. I probably wouldn't understand, anyway. He's much more intelligent than I am."

"I'm glad you realize that. It's a good thing to bear in mind."

"What do you mean?" she said in a small voice. But she knew what I meant: "It isn't true, what Father says, that John is an impostor. It can't be true!"

"What makes you so sure?"

"I know it here." Her hand touched her breast, ever so lightly. "He couldn't be lying to me. And Cassie says he's the image of his dad. So does Aunt Maria."

"Does John ever talk about his past to you?"

She regarded me with deepening distrust. "Now you sound just like Father again. You mustn't ask me questions about John. It wouldn't be fair to John."

"Give yourself some thought, too," I said. "I know it doesn't seem likely, but if he is an impostor, you could be letting yourself in for a lot of pain and trouble."

"I don't even care if he is!" she cried, and burst into tears.

A young man in airline coveralls came out of the terminal and glared at me. I was making a pretty girl cry, and there ought to be a law. I assumed a very legal expression. He went back inside again.

My plane took off with a roar. The roar diminished to a cicada humming in the northern sky. Sheila's tears passed like a summer shower. She started the engine and drove me into town, very efficiently, like a chauffeur who happened to be a deaf-mute.

John was a very fast worker.

Chapter 20

BEFORE SHE deposited me in the main lounge of the club-house, Sheila apologized for her emotional outburst, as she called it, and said something inarticulate about not telling Daddy. I said that no apology was necessary, and that I wouldn't.

The windows of the lounge overlooked the golf course. The players were a shifting confetti of color on the greens and fairways. I watched them until Howell came in at five minutes after one.

He shook my hand vigorously. "Good to see you, Archer. I hope you don't mind eating right away. I have to meet a committee shortly after two."

He led me into a huge dining-room. Most of the tables were roped off and empty. We took one by a window which looked out across a walled swimming-pool enclosure where young people were romping and splashing. The waiter deferred to Howell as if he was a member of the stewardship committee.

Since I knew nothing about the man, I asked him the first question that occurred to me: "What kind of a committee are you meeting?"

"Aren't all committees alike? They spend hours making up their collective mind to do something which any one of their members could accomplish in half the time. I'm thinking of setting up a committee to work for the abolition of committees." His smile was a rapid flash. "As a matter of fact, it's a Heart Association committee. We're laying plans for a fund campaign, and I happen to be chairman. Will you have something to drink? I'm going to have a Gibson."

"That will do for me."

He ordered two Gibsons from the hovering waiter. "As a medical man, I feel it's my duty to perpetuate the little saving vices. It's probably safer to overdrink than it is to overeat. What will you have to eat?"

I consulted the menu.

"If you like sea food," he said executively, "the lobster

Newberg is easy to chew. Gordon Sable told me about your little accident. How's the jaw?"

"Mending, thanks."

"What precisely was the trouble about, if you don't object to the question?"

"It's a long story, which boils down to something like this: Anthony Galton was killed for his money by a criminal named Nelson who had just escaped from prison. Your original guess was very close to the truth. But there's more to the case. I believe Tony Galton's murder and Pete Culligan's murder are related."

Howell leaned forward across the table, his short gray hair bristling. "How related?"

"That's the problem I was trying to solve when I got my jaw broken. Let me ask you a question, Doctor. What's your impression of John Galton?"

"I was going to ask you the same question. Since you got to it first, I'll take first turn in answering. The boy *seems* open and aboveboard. He's certainly intelligent, and I suppose prepossessing if you like obvious charm. His grand—Mrs. Galton seems to be charmed with him."

"She doesn't question his identity?"

"Not in the slightest, she hasn't from the beginning. For Maria, the boy is practically the reincarnation of her son Tony. Her companion, Miss Hildreth, feels very much the same way. I have to admit myself that the resemblance is striking. But such things can be arranged, when a great deal of money is involved. I suppose there's no man alive who doesn't have a double somewhere in the world."

"You're suggesting that he was searched out and hired?"

"Hasn't the possibility occurred to you?"

"Yes, it has. I think it should be explored."

"I'm glad to hear you say that. I'll be frank with you. It occurred to me when the boy turned up here, that you might be a part of the conspiracy. But Gordon Sable vouches for you absolutely, and I've had other inquiries made." His gray eyes probed mine. "In addition to which, you have the marks of honesty on your face."

"It's the hard way to prove you're honest."

Howell smiled slightly, looking out over the pool. His daughter, Sheila, had appeared at the poolside in a bathing-suit. She was beautifully made, but the fact seemed to give her no pleasure. She sat by herself, with a pale closed look, undergoing the growing pains of womanhood. Howell's glance rested on her briefly, and a curious woodenness possessed his face.

The waiter brought our drinks, and we ordered lunch. When the waiter was out of hearing, Howell said:

"It's the boy's story that bothers me. I understand you were the first to hear it. What do you think about it?"

"Sable and I gave him quite a going-over. He took it well, and his story stood up. I made notes on it the same night. I've gone over the notes since I talked to you this morning, and couldn't find any self-contradictions."

"The story may have been carefully prepared. Remember that the stakes are very high. You may be interested to know that Maria is planning to change her will in his favor."

"Already?"

"Already. She may already have done. Gordon wouldn't agree to it, so she called in another attorney to draw up a will. Maria's half out of her mind—she's pent up her generous feelings for so long, that she's intoxicated with them."

"Is she incompetent?"

"By no means," he said hastily. "I don't mean to overstate the case. And I concede her perfect right to do what she wants to do with her own money. On the other hand, we can't let her be defrauded by a—confidence man."

"How much money is involved?"

He raised his eyes over my head as if he could see a mountain of gold in the distance. "I couldn't estimate. Something like the national debt of a medium-sized European country. I know Henry left her oil property that brings in a weekly income in the thousands. And she has hundreds of thousands in securities."

"Where does it all go if it doesn't go to the boy?"

Howell smiled mirthlessly. "I'm not supposed to know that. It happens that I do, but I'm certainly not supposed to tell."

"You've been frank with me," I said. "I'll be frank with you. I'm wondering if you have an interest in the estate."

He scratched at his jaw, violently, but gave no other sign of discomposure. "I have, yes, in several senses. Mrs. Galton named me executor in her original will. I assure you personal considerations are not influencing my judgment. I think I know my own motives well enough to say that."

It's a lucky man who does, I thought. I said: "Apart from the amount of money involved, what exactly is bothering you?"

"The young man's story. As he tells it, it doesn't really start till age sixteen. There's no way to go beyond that to his origins, whatever they may be. I tried, and came up against a stone wall."

"I'm afraid I don't follow you. The way John tells it, he was in an orphanage until he ran away at the age of sixteen. The Crystal Springs Home, in Ohio."

"I've been in touch with a man I know in Cleveland—chap I went to medical school with. The Crystal Springs Home burned to the ground three years ago."

"That doesn't make John a liar. He says he left there five and a half years ago."

"It doesn't make him a liar, no. But if he is, it leaves us with no way to prove that he is. The records of the Home were completely destroyed in the fire. The staff was scattered."

"The superintendent should be traceable. What was his name—Merriweather?"

"Merriweather died in the fire of a heart attack. All of this suggests the possibility—I'd say probability—that John provided himself with a story *ex post facto*. Or was provided with one. He or his backers looked around for a foolproof background to equip him with—one that was uncheckable. Crystal Springs was it—a large institution which no longer existed, which had no surviving records. Who knows if John Brown ever spent a day there?"

"You've been doing a lot of thinking about this."

"I have, and I haven't told you all of it. There's the question of his speech, for instance. He represents himself as an American, born and raised in the United States."

"You're not suggesting he's a foreigner?"

"I am, though. National differences in speech have always interested me, and it happens I've spent some time in central Canada. Have you ever listened to a Canadian pronounce the word 'about'?"

"If I did, I never noticed. 'About'?"

"You say aba-oot, more or less. A Canadian pronounces the word more like 'aboat.' And that's the way John Brown pronounces it."

"Are you certain?"

"Of course I'm certain."

"About the theory, I mean?"

"It isn't a theory. It's a fact. I've taken it up with specialists in the subject."

"In the last two weeks?"

"In the last two days," he said. "I hadn't meant to bring this up, but my daughter, Sheila is—ah—interested in the boy. If he's a criminal, as I suspect—" Howell broke off, almost choking on the words.

Both our glances wandered to the poolside. Sheila was still alone, sitting on the edge and paddling her feet in the water. She turned to look toward the entrance twice while I watched her. Her neck and body were stiff with expectancy.

The waiter brought our food, and we ate in silence for a few minutes. Our end of the dining-room was slowly filling up with people in sports clothes. Slice and sand-trap seemed to be the passwords. Dr. Howell glanced around independently from time to time, as if to let the golfers know that he resented their intrusion on his privacy.

"What do you intend to do, Doctor?"

"I propose to employ you myself. I understand that Gordon has terminated your services."

"So far as I know. Have you taken it up with him?"

"Naturally I have. He's just as keen as I am that there should be further investigation. Unfortunately Maria won't hear of it, and as her attorney he can't very well proceed on his own. I can."

"Have you discussed it with Mrs. Galton?"

"I've tried to." Howell grimaced. "She won't listen to a word against the blessed youth. It's frustrating, to say the least, but I can understand why she has to believe in him. The fact of her son Anthony's death came as a great shock to her. She had to hold on to something, and there was Anthony's putative son, ready and willing. Perhaps it was planned that way. At any rate, she's clinging to the boy as if her life depended on it."

"What will the consequences be if we prove he's crooked?"

"Naturally we'll put him in prison where he belongs."

"I mean the consequences to Mrs. Galton's health. You told me yourself that any great shock might kill her."

"That's true, I did."

"Aren't you concerned about that?"

His face slowly reddened, in blotches. "Of course I'm concerned. But there are ethical priorities in life. We can't sit still for a criminal conspiracy, merely because the victim has diseases. The longer we permit it to go on, the worse it will be in the long run for Maria."

"You're probably right. Anyway, her health is your responsibility. I'm willing to undertake the investigation. When do I begin?"

"Now."

"I'll probably have to go to Michigan, for a start. That will cost money."

"I understand that. How much?"

"Five hundred."

Howell didn't blink. He produced a checkbook and a fountain pen. While he was making out the check, he said:

"It might be a good idea if you talked to the boy first. That is, if you can do it without arousing suspicion."

"I think I can do that. I got an invitation from him this morning."

"An invitation?"

"A written invitation to visit the Galton house."

"He's making very free with Mrs. Galton's property. Do you happen to have the document with you?"

I handed him the letter. He studied it with growing signs of excitement. "I was right, by God!"

"What do you mean?"

"The dirty little hypocrite is a Canadian. Look here." He put the letter on the table between us, and speared at it with his forefinger. "He spells the word 'labor' l, a, b, o, u, r. It's the British spelling, still current in Canada. He isn't even American. He's an impostor."

"It's going to take more than this to prove it."

"I realize that. Get busy, man."

"If you don't mind, I'll finish my lunch first."

Howell didn't hear me. He was looking out of the window again, half out of his seat.

A dark-headed youth in a tan sport shirt was talking to Sheila Howell at the poolside. He turned his head slightly. I recognized John Galton. He patted the shoulder of her terrycloth robe familiarly. Sheila smiled up full into his face.

Howell's light chair fell over backwards. He was out of the room before I could stop him. From the front door of the clubhouse, I saw him striding across the lawn toward the entrance of the swimming-pool enclosure.

John and Sheila came out hand-in-hand. They were so intent on each other that they didn't see Howell until he was on top of them. He thrust himself between them, shaking the boy by the arm. His voice was an ugly tearing rent in the quietness:

"Get out of here, do you hear me? You're not a member of this club."

John pulled away and faced him, white and rigid. "Sheila invited me."

"I dis-invite you." The back of Howell's neck was carbuncle red.

Sheila touched his arm. "Please, Daddy, don't make a scene. There's nothing to be gained."

John was encouraged to say: "My grandmother won't like this, Doctor."

"She will when she knows the facts." But the threat had taken the wind out of Howell's sails. He wasn't as loud as he had been.

"Please," Sheila repeated. "John's done no harm to anyone."

"Don't you understand, Sheila, I'm trying to protect you?"

"From what?"

"From corruption."

"That's silly, Dad. To hear you talk, you'd think John was a criminal."

The boy's head tilted suddenly, as if the word had struck a nerve in his neck. "Don't argue with him, Sheila. I oughtn't to've come here."

He turned on his heel and walked head down toward the parking-lot. Sheila went in the other direction. Molded in terrycloth, her body had a massiveness and mystery that hadn't struck me before. Her father stood and watched her until she entered the enclosure. She seemed to be moving heavily and fatally out of his control.

I went back to the dining-room and let Howell find me there. He came in pale and slack-faced, as if he'd had a serious loss of blood. His daughter was in the pool now, swimming its length back and forth with slow and powerful strokes. Her feet churned a steady white wake behind her.

She was still swimming when we left. Howell drove me to the courthouse. He scowled up at the barred windows of the county jail:

"Put him behind bars, that's all I ask."

Chapter 21

SHERIFF TRASK was in his office. Its walls were hung with testimonials from civic organizations and service clubs; recruiting certificates from Army, Navy, and Air Force; and a number of pictures of the Sheriff himself taken with the Governor and other notables. Trask's actual face was less genial than the face in the photographs.

"Trouble?" I said.

"Sit down. You're the trouble. You stir up a storm, and then you drop out of the picture. The trouble with you private investigators is irresponsibility."

"That's a rough word, Sheriff." I fingered the broken bones in my face, thoughtfully and tenderly.

"Yeah, I know you got yourself hurt, and I'm sorry. But what can I do about it? Otto Schwartz is outside my jurisdiction."

"Murder raps cross state lines, or haven't you heard."

"Yeah, and I also heard at the same time that you can't extradite without a case. Without some kind of evidence, I can't even get to Schwartz to question him. And you want to know why I have no evidence?"

"Let me guess. Me again."

"It isn't funny, Archer. I was depending on you for some discretion. Why did you have to go and spill your guts to Roy Lemberg? Scare my witnesses clear out of the damn country?"

"I got overeager, and made a mistake. I wasn't the only one."

"What is that supposed to mean?"

"You told me Lemberg's car had been stolen."

"That's what switched license plates usually mean." Trask sat and thought about this for a minute, pushing out his lower lip. "Okay. We made mistakes. I made a medium-sized dilly and you made a peacheroo. So you took a beating for it. We won't sit around and cry. Where do we go from here?"

"It's your case, Sheriff. I'm just your patient helper."

He leaned toward me, heavy-shouldered and earnest. "You really mean to help? Or have you got an angle?"

"I mean to help, that's my angle."

"We'll see. Are you still working for Sable—for Mrs. Galton, that is?"

"Not at the moment."

"Who's bankrolling you, Dr. Howell?"

"News travels fast."

"Heck, I knew it before you did. Howell came around asking me to check your record with L.A. You seem to have some good friends down south. If you ever conned any old ladies, you never got caught."

"Young ones are more my meat."

Trask brushed aside the badinage with an impatient gesture. "I assume you're being hired to go into the boy's background. Howell wanted me to. Naturally I told him I couldn't move without some indication that law's been broken. You got any such indication?"

"Not yet."

"Neither have I. I talked to the boy, and he's as smooth as silk. He doesn't even make any definite claims. He merely says that people tell him he's his father's son, so it's probably so."

"Do you think he's been coached, Sheriff?"

"I don't know. He may be quarterbacking his own plays. When he came in to see me, it had nothing to do on the face of it with establishing his identity. He wanted information about his father's murder, if this John Brown was his father."

"Hasn't that been proved?"

"As close as it ever will be. There's still room for doubt, in my opinion. But what I started to say, he came in here to tell *me* what to do. He wanted more action on that old killing. I told him it was up to the San Mateo people, so what did he do? He made a trip up there to build a fire under the San Mateo sheriff."

"It's barely possible he's serious."

"Either that, or he's a psychologist. That kind of behavior doesn't go with consciousness of guilt."

"The Syndicate hires good lawyers."

Trask pondered this, his eyes withdrawing under the ledges of his brows. "You think it's a Syndicate job, eh? A big conspiracy?"

"With a big payoff, in the millions. Howell tells me Mrs. Galton's rewriting her will, leaving everything to the boy. I think her house should be watched."

"You honestly believe they'd try to knock her off?"

"They kill people for peanuts. What wouldn't they do to get hold of the Galton property?"

"Don't let your imagination run away. It won't happen, not in Santa Teresa County."

"It started to happen two weeks ago, when Culligan got it. That has all the marks of a gang killing, and in your territory."

"Don't rub it in. That case isn't finished yet."

"It's the same case," I said. "The Brown killing and the Culligan killing and the Galton impersonation, if it is one, all hang together."

"That's easy to say. How do we prove it?"

"Through the boy. I'm taking off for Michigan tonight. Howell thinks his accent originated in central Canada. That ties in with the Lembergs. Apparently they crossed the border into Canada from Detroit, and were headed for an address Culligan gave them. If you could trace Culligan that far back—"

"We're working on it." Trask smiled, rather forbiddingly. "Your Reno lead was a good one, Archer. I talked long distance last night to a friend in Reno, captain of detectives. He called me back just before lunch. Culligan was working for Schwartz about a year ago."

"Doing what?"

"Steerer for his casino. Another interesting thing: Culligan was arrested in Detroit five-six years ago. The FBI has a rap sheet on him."

"What was this particular rap?"

"An old larceny charge. It seems he left the country to evade it, got nabbed as soon as he showed his face on American soil, spent the next couple of years in Southern Michigan pen."

"What was the date of his arrest in Detroit?"

"I don't remember exactly. It was about five-and-a-half years ago. I could look it up, if it matters."

"It matters."

"What's on your mind?"

"John Galton turned up in Ann Arbor five-and-a-half years ago. Ann Arbor is practically a suburb of Detroit. I'm asking myself if he crossed the Canadian border with Culligan."

Trask whistled softly, and flicked on the switch of his squawk-box:

"Conger, bring me the Culligan records. Yeah, I'm in my office."

I remembered Conger's hard brown face. He didn't remember me at first, then did a double take:

"Long time no see."

I quipped lamely: "How's the handcuff business?"

"Clicking."

Trask rustled the papers Conger had brought, and frowned impatiently. When he looked up his eyes were crackling bright:

"A little over five-and-a-half years. Culligan got picked up in Detroit January 7. Does that fit with your date?"

"I haven't pinned it down yet, but I will."

I rose to go. Trask's parting handshake was warm. "If you run into anything, call me collect, anytime day or night. And keep the hard nose out of the chopper."

"That's my aspiration."

"By the way, your car's in the county garage. I can release it to you if you want."

"Save it for me. And take care of the old lady, eh?"

The Sheriff was giving Conger orders to that effect before I reached the door.

Chapter 22

I CASHED Howell's check at his bank just before it closed for business at three. The teller directed me to a travel agency where I made a plane reservation from Los Angeles to Detroit. The connecting plane didn't leave Santa Teresa for nearly three hours.

I walked the few blocks to Sable's office. The private elevator let me out into the oak-paneled anteroom.

Mrs. Haines looked up from her work, and raised her hand to smooth her dyed red hair. She said in maternal dismay:

"Why, Mr. Archer, you were *badly* injured. Mr. Sable *told* me you'd been hurt, but I had no idea—"

"Stop it. You're making me feel sorry for myself."

"What's the matter with feeling sorry for yourself? I do it all the time. It bucks me up no end."

"You're a woman."

She dipped her bright head as if I'd paid her a compliment. "What's the difference?"

"You don't want me to spell it out."

She tittered, not unpleasantly, and tried to blush, but her experienced face resisted the attempt. "Some other time, perhaps. What can I do for you now?"

"Is Mr. Sable in?"

"I'm sorry, he isn't back from lunch."

"It's three-thirty."

"I know. I don't expect he'll be in again today. He'll be sorry he missed you. The poor man's schedule has been all broken up, ever since that trouble at his house."

"The murder, you mean?"

"That, and other things. His wife isn't well."

"So I understand. Gordon told me she had a breakdown."

"Oh, did he tell you that? He doesn't do much talking about it to anyone. He's awfully sensitive on the subject." She made a confidential gesture, raising her red-tipped hand vertically beside her mouth. "Just between you and me, this isn't the first time he's had trouble with her."

"When was the other time?"

"Times, in the plural. She came here one night in March when we were doing income tax, and accused me of trying to steal her husband. I could have told her a thing or two, but of course I couldn't say a word in front of Mr. Sable. I tell you, he's a living saint, what he's taken from that woman, and he goes right on looking after her."

"What did she do to him?"

Color dabbed her cheekbones. She was slightly drunk with malice. "Plenty. Last summer she took off and went rampaging around the country spending his good money like water. Spending it on other men, too, can you imagine? He finally tracked her down in Reno, where she was *living* with another man."

"Reno?"

"Reno," she repeated flatly. "She probably intended to divorce him or something, but she gave up on the idea. She'd have been doing him a favor, if you ask me. But the poor man talked her into coming back with him. He seems to be infatuated with her." Her voice was disconsolate. After a moment's thought, she said: "I oughtn't to be telling you all this. Ought I?"

"I knew she had a history of trouble. Gordon told me himself that he had to put her in a nursing home."

"That's right, he's probably there with her now. He generally goes over to eat lunch with her, and most of the time he stays the rest of the day. Wasted devotion, I call it. If you ask me, that's one marriage doomed to failure. I did a horoscope on it, and you never saw such antagonism in the stars."

Not only in the stars.

"Where is the nursing home she's in, Mrs. Haines?"

"It's Dr. Trenchard's, on Light Street. But I wouldn't go there, if that's what you're thinking of. Mr. Sable doesn't like to be disturbed when he's visiting Mrs. Sable."

"I'll take my chances. And I won't mention that I've been here. Okay?"

"I guess so," she said dubiously. "It's over on the west side, 235 Light Street."

I took a cab across town. The driver looked me over curiously as I got out. Perhaps he was trying to figure out if I was a patient or just a visitor.

"You want me to wait?"

"I think so. If I don't come out, you know what that will mean."

I left him having a delayed reaction. The "home" was a long stucco building set far back from the street on its own acre. Nothing indicated its specialness, except for the high wire fence which surrounded the patio at the side.

A man and a woman were sitting in a blue canvas swing behind the fence. Their backs were to me, but I recognized Sable's white head. The woman's blond head rested on his shoulder.

I resisted the impulse to call out to them. I climbed the long veranda, which was out of sight of the patio, and pressed the bellpush beside the front door. The door was unlocked and opened by a nurse in white, without a cap. She was unexpectedly young and pretty.

"Yes, sir?"

"I'd like to speak to Mr. Sable."

"And who shall I say is calling?"

"Lew Archer."

She left me in a living-room or lounge whose furniture was covered with bright chintz. Two old ladies in shawls were watching a baseball game on television. A young man with a beard squatted on his heels in a corner, watching the opposite corner of the ceiling. His lips were moving.

One of the half-curtained windows looked out across the sun-filled patio. I saw the young nurse cross to the blue swing, and Sable's face come up as if from sleep. He disengaged himself from his wife. Her body relaxed into an awkward position. Blue-shadowed by the canvas shade of the swing, her face had the open-eyed blankness of a doll's.

Sable dragged his shadow across the imitation flagstone. He looked small, oddly diminished, under the sky's blue height. The impression persisted when he entered the lounge. Age had fallen on him. He needed a haircut, and his tie was pulled to one side. The look he gave me was red-eyed; his voice was cranky.

"What brings you here, anyway?"

"I wanted to see you. I don't have much time in town."

"Well. You see me." He lifted his arms from his sides, and dropped them.

The old ladies, who had greeted him with smiles and nods, reacted like frightened children to his bitterness. One of them hitched her shawl high around her neck and slunk out of the room. The other stretched her hand out toward Sable as if she wanted to comfort him. She remained frozen in that position while she went on watching the ball game. The bearded man watched the corner of the ceiling.

"How is Mrs. Sable?"

"Not well." He frowned, and drew me out into the corridor. "As a matter of fact, she's threatened with melancholia. Dr. Trenchard tells me she's had a similar illness before—before I married her. The shock she suffered two weeks ago stirred up the old trouble. Good Lord, was that only two weeks ago?"

I risked asking: "What sort of background does she have?"

"Alice was a model in Chicago, and she's been married before. She lost a child, and her first husband treated her badly. I've tried to make it up to her. With damn poor success."

His voice sank toward despair.

"I take it she's having therapy."

"Of course. Dr. Trenchard is one of the best psychiatrists on the coast. If she gets any worse, he's going to try shock treatment." He leaned on the wall, looking down at nothing in particular. His red eyes seemed to be burning.

"You should go home and get some sleep."

"I haven't been sleeping much lately. It's easy to say, sleep. But you can't will yourself to sleep. Besides, Alice needs me with her. She's much calmer when I'm around." He shook himself, and straightened. "But you didn't come here to discuss my woes with me."

"That's true, I didn't. I came to thank you for the check, and to ask you a couple of questions."

"You earned the money. I'll answer the questions if I can."

"Dr. Howell has hired me to investigate John Galton's background. Since you brought me into the case, I'd like to have your go-ahead."

"Of course. You have it, as far as I'm concerned. I can't speak for Mrs. Galton."

"I understand that. Howell tells me she's sold on the boy. Howell himself is convinced that he's a phoney."

"We've discussed it. There seems to be some sort of romance between John and Howell's daughter."

"Does Howell have any other special motive?"

"For doing what?"

"Investigating John, trying to prevent Mrs. Galton from changing her will."

Sable looked at me with some of his old sharpness. "That's a good question. Under the present will, Howell stands to benefit in several ways. He himself is executor, and due to inherit a substantial sum, I really mustn't say how much. His daughter, Sheila, is in for another substantial sum, very substantial. And after various other bequests have been met, the bulk of the estate goes to various charities, one of which is the Heart Association. Henry Galton died of cardiovascular trouble. Howell is an officer of the Heart Association. All of which makes him a highly interested party."

"And highly interesting. Has the will been changed yet?"

"I can't say. I told Mrs. Galton I couldn't conscientiously draw up a new will for her, under the circumstances. She said she'd get someone else. Whether she has or not, I can't say."

"Then you're not sold on the boy, either."

"I was. I no longer know what to think. Frankly, I haven't been giving the matter much thought." He moved impatiently, and made a misstep to one side, his shoulder thudding against the wall. "If you don't mind, I think I'll get back to my wife."

The young nurse let me out.

I looked back through the wire fence. Mrs. Sable remained in the same position on the swing. Her husband joined her in the blue shadow. He raised her inert head and insinuated his shoulder behind it. They sat like a very old couple waiting for the afternoon shadows to lengthen and merge into night.

Chapter 23

T HE CAB-DRIVER stopped at the curb opposite the gates of the Galton estate. He hung one arm over the back of the seat and gave me a quizzical look:

"No offense, Mister, but you want the front entrance or the service entrance?"

"The front entrance."

"Okay. I just didn't want to make a mistake."

He let me off under the porte-cochere. I paid him, and told him not to wait. The Negro maid let me into the reception hall, and left me to cool my heels among the ancestors.

I moved over to one of the tall, narrow windows. It looked out across the front lawn, where the late afternoon sunlight lay serenely. I got some sense of the guarded peace that walled estates like this had once provided. In the modern world the walls were more like prison walls, or the wire fence around a nursing-home garden. When it came right down to it, I preferred the service entrance. The people in the kitchen usually had more fun.

Quick footsteps descended the stairs, and Cassie Hildreth came into the room. She had on a skirt and a sweater which emphasized her figure. She looked more feminine in other, subtler, ways. Something had happened to change her style.

She gave me her hand. "It's good to see you, Mr. Archer. Sit down. Mrs. Galton will be down in a minute."

"Under her own power?"

"Yes, isn't it remarkable? She's becoming much more active than she was. John takes her out for a drive nearly every day."

"That's nice of him."

"He actually seems to enjoy it. They hit it off from the start."

"He's the one I really came to see. Is he around?"

"I haven't seen him since lunch. Probably he's out in his car somewhere."

"His car?"

"Aunt Maria bought him a cute little Thunderbird. John's crazy about it. He's like a child with a new toy. He told me he's never had a car of his own before."

"I guess he has a lot of things he never had before."

"Yes. I'm so happy for him."

"You're a generous woman."

"Not really. I've a lot to be thankful for. Now that John's come home, I wouldn't trade my life for any other. It may sound like a strange thing to say, but life is suddenly just as it was in the old days—before the war, before Tony died. Everything seems to have fallen into harmony."

She sounded as if she had transferred her lifelong crush from Tony to John Galton. A dream possessed her face. I wanted to warn her not to bank too heavily on it. Everything could fall into chaos again.

Mrs. Galton was fussing on the stairs. Cassie went to the door to meet her. The old lady had on a black tailored suit with something white at her throat. Her hair was marcelled in hard gray corrugations which resembled galvanized iron. She extended her bony hand:

"I'm most pleased to see you. I've been wanting to express my personal appreciation to you. You've made my house a happier one."

"Your check was a very nice expression," I said.

"The laborer is worthy of his hire." Perhaps she sensed that that wasn't the most tactful way to put it, because she added: "Won't you stay for tea? My grandson will want to see you. I expect him back for tea. He should be here now."

The querulous note was still in her voice. I wondered how much of her happiness was real, how much sheer will to believe that something good could happen to a poor old rich lady. She lowered herself into a chair, exaggerating the difficulty of her movements. Cassie began to look anxious.

"I think he's at the country club, Aunt Maria."

"With Sheila?"

"I think so," Cassie said.

"Is he still seeing a lot of her?"

"Just about every day."

"We'll have to put a stop to that. He's much too young to think of taking an interest in any one girl. Sheila is a dear sweet child, of course, but we can't have her monopolizing John. I have other plans for him."

"What plans," I said, "if you don't mind my asking?"

"I'm thinking of sending John to Europe in the fall. He needs broadening, and he's very much interested in the modern drama. If the interest persists, and deepens, I'll build him a repertory theater here in Santa Teresa. John has great talent, you know. The Galton distinction comes out in a different form in each generation."

As if to demonstrate this proposition, a red Thunderbird convertible careened up the long driveway. A door slammed. John came in. His face was flushed and sullen. He stood inside the doorway and pushed his fists deep in his jacket pockets, his head thrust forward in a peering attitude.

"Well!" he said. "Here we all are. The three fates, Clotho, Lachesis, and Mr. Archer."

"That isn't funny, John," Cassie said in a voice of warning.

"I think it's funny. Very, very funny."

He came toward us, weaving slightly, exaggerating the movements of his shoulders. I went to meet him:

"Hello, John."

"Get away from me. I know why you're here."

"Tell me."

"I'll tell you all right."

He threw a wild fist in my direction, staggering off balance. I moved in close, turned him with his back to me, took hold of his jacket collar with both hands and pulled it halfway down his arms. He sputtered words at me which smelled like the exhalations from a still. But I could feel the lethal force vibrating through him.

"Straighten up and quiet down," I said.

"I'll knock your block off."

"First you'll have to load yourself up with something solider than whisky."

Mrs. Galton breathed at my shoulder. "Has he been drinking?"

John answered her himself, in a kind of small-boy defiance: "Yes I have been drinking. And I've been thinking. Thinking and drinking. I say it's a lousy setup."

"What?" she said. "What's happened?"

"A lot of things have happened. Tell this man to turn me loose."

"Let him go," Mrs. Galton said commandingly.

"Do you think he's ready?"

"Damn you, let me go."

He made a violent lunge, and tore loose from the arms of his jacket. He whirled and faced me with his fists up:

"Come on and fight. I'm not afraid of you."

"This is hardly the time and place."

I tossed his jacket to him. He caught and held it, looking down at it stupidly. Cassie stepped between us. She took the jacket and helped him on with it. He submitted almost meekly to her hands.

"You need some black coffee, John. Let me get you some black coffee."

"I don't want coffee, I'm not drunk."

"But you've been drinking." Mrs. Galton's voice rose almost an octave and stayed there on a querulous monotone: "Your *father* started drinking young, you mustn't let it happen all over again. Please, you must promise me."

The old lady hung on John's arm, making anxious noises, while Cassie tried to soothe her. John's head swung around, his eyes on me:

"Get that man out of here! He's spying for Dr. Howell."

Mrs. Galton turned on me, the bony structure of her face pushing out through the seamed flesh:

"I trust my grandson is mistaken about you. I know Dr. Howell is incapable of committing disloyal acts behind my back."

"Don't be too sure of that," John said. "He doesn't want me seeing Sheila. There's nothing he wouldn't do to break it up."

"I'm asking you, Mr. Archer. Did Dr. Howell hire you?"

"I'll have to ask you to take it up with Howell."

"It is true, then?"

"I can't answer that, Mrs. Galton."

"In that case please leave my house. You entered it under false pretenses. If you trespass again, I'll have you prosecuted. I've a good mind to go to the authorities as it is."

"No, don't do that," John said. "We can handle it, Grandma."

He seemed to be sobering rapidly. Cassie chimed in:

"You mustn't get so excited about nothing. You know what Dr. Howell—"

"Don't mention his name in my presence. To be betrayed by an old and trusted friend—well, that's what it is to have money.

They think they have a right to it simply because it's there. I see now what August Howell has been up to, insinuating himself and his chit of a daughter into my life. Well, he's not getting a cent of my money. I've seen to that."

"Please calm down, Aunt Maria."

Cassie tried to lead her back to her chair. Mrs. Galton wouldn't budge. She called hoarsely in my direction:

"You can go and tell August Howell he's overreached himself. He won't get a cent of my money, not a cent. It's going to my own kith and kin. And tell him to keep that daughter of his from flinging herself at my grandson. I have other plans for him."

The breath rustled and moaned in her head. She closed her eyes; her face was like a death mask. She tottered and almost fell. John held her around the shoulders.

"Get out," he said to me. "My grandmother is a sick woman. Can't you see what you're doing to her?"

"Somebody's doing it to her."

"Are you going to get out, or do I call the police?"

"You'd better go," Cassie said. "Mrs. Galton has a heart condition."

Mrs. Galton's hand went to her heart automatically. Her head fell loosely onto John's shoulder. He stroked her gray hair. It was a very touching scene.

I wondered as I went out how many more scenes like that the old lady's heart would stand. The question kept me awake on the night plane to Chicago.

Chapter 24

I PUT in two days of legwork in Ann Arbor, where I repre-sented myself as a personnel investigator for a firm with over-seas contracts. John's account of his high school and college life checked out in detail. I established one interesting additional detail: He had enrolled in the high school under the name of John Lindsay five-and-a-half years before, on January 9. Peter Culligan had been arrested in Detroit, forty miles away, on January 7 of the same year. Apparently it had taken the boy just two days to find a new protector in Gabriel Lindsay.

I talked to friends of Lindsay's, mostly high-school teachers. They remembered John as a likely boy, though he had been, as one of them said: "A tough little egg to start with." They understood that Lindsay had taken him off the streets.

Gabriel Lindsay had gone in for helping young people in trouble. He was an older man who had lost a son in the war, and his wife soon after the war. He died himself in the University Hospital in February of the previous year, of pneumonia.

His doctor remembered John's constant attendance at his bedside. The copy of his will on file in the Washtenaw County courthouse left two thousand dollars to "my quasi-foster-son, known as John Lindsay, for the furtherance of his education." There were no other specific bequests in Lindsay's will; which probably meant it was all the money he had.

John had graduated from the University in June, as a Speech major, with honors. His counselor in the Dean's office said that he had been a student without any overt problems; not exactly popular perhaps: he seemed to have no close friends. On the other hand, he had been active in campus theatrical produc-tions, and moderately successful as an actor in his senior year.

His address at the time of his graduation had been a rooming-house on Catherine Street, over behind the Graduate School. The landlady's name was Mrs. Haskell. Maybe she could help me.

Mrs. Haskell lived on the first floor of an old three-story gin-gerbread mansion. I guessed from the bundles of mail on the table inside the door that the rest of her house was given over to roomers. She led me along the polished parquetry hallway into a half-blinded parlor. It was a cool oasis in the heat of the Michigan July.

Somewhere over our heads, a typewriter pecked at the silence. The echo of a southern drawl twanged like a mandolin in Mrs. Haskell's voice:

"Do sit down and tell me how John is. And how is he doing in his position?" Mrs. Haskell clasped her hands enthusiastically on her flowered print bosom. The curled bangs on her forehead shook like silent bells.

"He hasn't started with us yet, Mrs. Haskell. The purpose of my investigation is to clear him for a confidential assignment."

"Does that mean the other thing has fallen through?"

"What other thing is that?"

"The acting thing. You may not know it, but John Lindsay's a very fine actor. One of the most talented boys I've ever had in my house. I never missed an appearance of his at the Lydia Mendelssohn. In *Hobson's Choice* last winter, he was rich."

"I bet he was. And you say he had acting offers?"

"I don't know about offers in the plural, but he had one very good one. Some big producer wanted to give him a personal contract and train him professionally. The last I heard, John had accepted it. But I guess he changed his mind, if he's going with your firm. Security."

"It's interesting about his acting," I said. "We like our employees to be well-rounded people. Do you remember the producer's name?"

"I'm afraid I never knew it."

"Where did he come from?"

"I don't know. John was very secretive about his private affairs. He didn't even leave a forwarding address when he left in June. All I really know about this is what Miss Reichler told me after he left."

"Miss Reichler?"

"His friend. I don't mean she was his girlfriend exactly. Maybe she thought so, but he didn't. I warned him not to get mixed up with a rich young lady like her, riding around in her Cadillacs and her convertibles. My boys come and go, but I try to keep them from overstepping themselves. Miss Reichler is several years older than John." Her lips moved over his name with a kind of maternal greed. The mandolin twang was becoming more pronounced.

"He sounds like the kind of young man we need. Socially mobile, attractive to the ladies."

"Oh, he was always that. I don't mean he's girl-crazy. He paid the girls no mind, unless they forced themselves on his attention. Ada Reichler practically beat a path to his door. She used to drive up in her Cadillac every second or third day. Her father's a big man in Detroit. Auto parts."

"Good," I said. "A high-level business connection."

Mrs. Haskell sniffed. "Don't count too much on that one. Miss Reichler was sore as a boil when John left without even saying good-by. She was really let down. I tried to explain to her that a young man just starting out in the world couldn't carry any excess baggage. Then she got mad at me, for some god-forsaken reason. She slam-banged into her car and ground those old Cadillac gears to a pulp."

"How long did they know each other?"

"As long as he was with me, at least a year. I guess she had her nice qualities, or he wouldn't have stuck with her so long. She's pretty enough, if you like that slinky type."

"Do you have her address? I'd like to talk to her."

"She might tell you a lot of lies. You know: 'Hell hath no fury like a woman scorned.'"

"I can discount anything like that."

"See that you do. John's a fine young man, and your people will be lucky if he decides to go with them. Her father's name is Ben, I think, Ben Reichler. They live over in the section by the river."

I drove on winding roads through a semi-wooded area. Eventually I found the Reichlers' mailbox. Their driveway ran between rows of maples to a low brick house with a sweeping roof. It looked small from a distance, and massive when I got up close to it. I began to understand how John could have made the leap from Mrs. Gorgello's boardinghouse to the Galton house. He'd been training for it.

A man in overalls with a spraygun in his hands climbed up the granite steps of a sunken garden.

"The folks aren't home," he said. "They're never home in July."

"Where can I find them?"

"If it's business, Mr. Reichler's in his office in the Reichler Building three-four days a week."

"Miss Ada Reichler's the one I want."

"Far as I know, she's in Kingsville with her mother. Kingsville, Canada. They have a place up there. You a friend of Miss Ada's?"

"Friend of a friend," I said.

It was early evening when I drove into Kingsville. The heat hadn't let up, and my shirt was sticking to my back. The lake lay below the town like a blue haze in which white sails hung upright by their tips.

The Reichlers' summer place was on the lakeshore. Green terraces descended from the house to a private dock and boathouse. The house itself was a big old lodge whose brown shingled sides were shaggy with ivy. The Reichlers weren't camping out, though. The maid who answered the door wore a fresh starched uniform, complete with cap. She told me that Mrs. Reichler was resting and Miss Ada was out in one of the boats. She was expected back at any time, if I cared to wait.

I waited on the dock, which was plastered with No Trespassing signs. A faint breeze had begun to stir, and the sailboats were leaning shoreward. Mild little land-locked waves lapped at the pilings. A motorboat went by like a bird shaking out wings of white water. Its wash rocked the dock. The boat turned and came in, slowing down. A girl with dark hair and dark glasses was at the wheel. She pointed a finger at her brown chest, and cocked her head questioningly.

"You want me?"

I nodded, and she brought the boat in. I caught the line she threw and helped her onto the dock. Her body was lean and supple in black Capris and a halter. Her face, when she took off her glasses, was lean and intense.

"Who are you?"

I had already decided to discard my role. "My name is Archer. I'm a private detective from California."

"You came all this way to see me?"

"Yes."

"Why on earth?"

"Because you knew John Lindsay."

Her face opened up, ready for anything, wonderful or otherwise.

"John sent you here?"

"Not exactly."

"Is he in some kind of trouble?"

I didn't answer her. She jerked at my arm like a child wanting attention.

"Tell me, is John in trouble? Don't be afraid, I can take it."

"I don't know whether he is or not, Miss Reichler. What makes you jump to the conclusion that he is?"

"Nothing, I don't mean that." Her speech was staccato. "You said that you're a detective. Doesn't that indicate trouble?"

"Say he is in trouble. What then?"

"I'd want to help him, naturally. Why are we talking in riddles?"

I liked her rapid, definite personality, and guessed that honesty went along with it:

"I don't like riddles any more than you do. I'll make a bargain with you, Miss Reichler. I'll tell you my end of the story if you'll tell me yours."

"What is this, true confession hour?"

"I'm serious, and I'm willing to do my talking first. If you're interested in John's situation—"

"Situation is a nice neutral word."

"That's why I used it. Is it a bargain?"

"All right." She gave me her hand on it, as a man would have. "I warn you in advance, though, I won't tell you anything against him. I don't *know* anything against him, except that he treated me—well, I was asking for it." She lifted her high thin shoulders, shrugging off the past. "We can talk in the garden, if you like."

We climbed the terraces to a walled garden in the shadow of the house. It was crowded with the colors and odors of flowers. She placed me in a canvas chair facing hers. I told her where John was and what he was doing.

Her eyes were soft and black, lit tremulously from within. Their expression followed all the movements of my story. She said when I'd finished:

"It sounds like one of Grimm's fairy tales. The goatherd turns out to be the prince in disguise. Or like Œdipus. John had an Œdipus theory of his own, that Œdipus killed his father because he banished him from the kingdom. I thought it was very clever." Her voice was brittle. She was marking time.

"John's a clever boy," I said. "And you're a clever girl, and you knew him well. Do you believe he's who he claims to be?"

"Do you?" When I failed to answer, she said: "So he has a girl in California, already." Her hands lay open on her slender thighs. She hugged them between her thighs.

"The girl's father hired me. He thinks John is a fraud."

"And you do, too?"

"I don't like to think it, but I'm afraid I do. There are some indications that his whole story was invented to fit the occasion."

"To inherit money?"

"That's the general idea. I've been talking to his landlady in Ann Arbor, Mrs. Haskell."

"I know her," the girl said shortly.

"Do you know anything about this offer John had from a producer?"

"Yes, he mentioned it to me. It was one of these personal contracts that movie producers give to promising young actors. This man saw him in *Hobson's Choice*."

"When?"

"Last February."

"Did you meet the man?"

"I never did. John said he flew back to the coast. He didn't want to discuss it after that."

"Did he mention any names before he dried up?"

"Not that I recall. Do you think John was lying about him, that it wasn't an acting job he was offered?"

"That could be. Or it could be John was sucked in. The conspirators made their approach as movie producers or agents, and later told him what was required of him."

"Why would John fall in with their plans? He's not a criminal."

"The Galton estate is worth millions. He stands to inherit all of it, any day. Even a small percentage of it would make him a rich man."

"But he never cared about money, at least not the kind you inherit. He could have married me: Barkis was willing. My father's money was one of the reasons he didn't. At least that's what he said. The real reason, I guess, was that he didn't love me. Does he love her?"

"My client's daughter? I couldn't say for sure. Maybe he doesn't love anybody."

"You're very honest, Mr. Archer. I gave you an opening, but you didn't try to use her on me as a wedge. You could have said that he was crazy about her, thus fanning the fires of jealousy." She winced at her own self-mockery.

"I try to be honest with honest people."

She gave me a flashing look. "That's intended to put me on the spot."

"Yes."

She turned her head and looked out over the lake as if she could see all the way to California. The last sails were converging toward shore, away from the darkness falling like soot along the horizon. As light drained from the sky, it seemed to gather more intensely on the water.

"What will they do to him if they find out he's an impostor?"

"Put him in jail."

"For how long?"

"It's hard to say. It'll be easier on him if we get it over with soon. He hasn't made any big claims yet, or taken any big money."

"You really mean, really and truly, that I'd be doing him a favor by puncturing his story?"

"That's my honest opinion. If it's all a pack of lies, we'll find out sooner or later. The sooner the better."

She hesitated. Her profile was stark. One cord in her neck stood out under the skin. "You say that he claims that he was brought up in an orphanage in Ohio."

"Crystal Springs, Ohio. Did he ever mention the place to you?"

She shook her head in a quick short arc. I said:

"There are some indications that he was raised here in Canada."

"What indications?"

"Speech. Spelling."

She rose suddenly, walked to the end of the garden, stooped to pick a snapdragon, threw it away with a spurning gesture.

She came back toward me and stood with her face half-averted. She said in a rough dry voice:

"Just don't tell him I was the one that told you. I couldn't bear to have him hate me, even if I never see him again. The poor damn silly fool was born and raised right here in Ontario. His real name is Theodore Fredericks, and his mother runs a boardinghouse in Pitt, not more than sixty miles from here."

I stood up, forcing her to look at me. "How do you know, Miss Reichler?"

"I talked to Mrs. Fredericks. It wasn't a very fortunate meeting. It didn't do anything for either of us. I should never have gone there."

"Did he take you to meet his mother?"

"Hardly. I went to see her myself a couple of weeks ago, after John left Ann Arbor. When I didn't hear from him I got it into my head that perhaps he'd gone home to Pitt."

"How did you learn about his home in Pitt? Did he tell you?"

"Yes, but I don't believe he intended to. It happened on the spur of the moment, when he was spending a week-end here with us. It was the only time he ever came to visit us here in Kingsville, and it was a bad time for me—the worst. I hate to think of it."

"Why?"

"If you have to know, he turned me down. We went for a drive on Sunday morning. I did the driving, of course. He'd never touch the wheel of my car. That's the way he was with me, so proud, and I had no pride at all with him. I got carried away by the flowers and the bees, or something, and I asked him to marry me. He gave me a flat refusal.

"He must have seen how hurt I was, because he asked me to drive him to Pitt. We weren't too far from there, and he wanted to show me something. When we got there he made me drive down a street that runs along by the river on the edge of the Negro section. It was a dreadful neighborhood, filthy children of all colors playing in the mud, and slatternly women screaming at them. We stopped across from an old red brick house where some men in their undershirts were sitting on the front steps passing around a wine jug.

"John asked me to take a good look, because he said he belonged there. He said he'd grown up in that neighborhood, in that red house. A woman came out on the porch to call the men in for dinner. She had a voice like a kazoo, and she was a hideous fat pig of a woman. John said that she was his mother.

"I didn't believe him. I thought he was hoaxing me, putting me to some kind of silly test. It was a test, in a way, but not in the way I imagined. He wanted to be *known*, I think. He wanted me to accept him as he actually was. But by the time I understood that, it was too late. He'd gone into one of his deep freezes." She touched her mournful mouth with the tips of her long fingers.

"When did this happen?"

"Last spring. It must have been early in March, there was still some snow on the ground."

"Did you see John after that?"

"A few times, but it wasn't any good. I think he regretted telling me about himself. In fact I know he did. That Sunday in Pitt was the end of any real communication between us. There were so many things we couldn't talk about, finally we couldn't talk at all. The last time I saw him was humiliating, for him, and for me, too. He asked me not to mention what he'd said about his origins, if anyone ever brought it up."

"Who did he expect to bring it up? The police?"

"The immigration authorities. Apparently there was something irregular about his entry into the United States. That fitted in with what his mother told me afterwards. He'd run away with one of her boarders when he was sixteen, and apparently crossed over into the States."

"Did she give you the boarder's name?"

"No. I'm surprised Mrs. Fredericks told me as much as she did. You know how the lower classes are, suspicious. But I gave her a little money, and that loosened her up." Her tone was contemptuous, and she must have overheard herself: "I know, I'm just what John said I was, a dollar snob. Well, I had my comeuppance. There I was prowling around the Pitt slums on a hot summer day like a lady dog in season. And I might as well have stayed at home. His mother hadn't laid eyes on him for over five years, and she never expected to see him again, she said. I realized that I'd lost him, for good."

"He was easy to lose," I said, "and no great loss."

She looked at me like an enemy. "You don't know him. John's

a fine person at heart, fine and deep. I was the one who failed in our relationship. If I'd been able to understand him that Sunday, say the right thing and hold him, he mightn't have gone into this fraudulent life. I'm the one who wasn't good for anything."

She screwed up her face like a monkey and tugged at her hair, making herself look ugly.

"I'm just a hag."

"Be quiet."

She looked at me incredulously, one hand flat against her temple. "Who do you think you're talking to?"

"Ada Reichler. You're worth five of him."

"I'm not. I'm no good. I betrayed him. Nobody could love me. *No*body could."

"I told you to be quiet." I'd never been angrier in my life.

"Don't you dare speak to me like that. Don't you dare!"

Her eyes were as bright and heavy as mercury. She ran blind to the end of the garden, knelt at the edge of the grass, and buried her face in flowers.

Her back was long and beautiful. I waited until she was still, and lifted her to her feet. She turned toward me.

The last light faded from the flowers and from the lake. Night came on warm and moist. The grass was wet.

Chapter 25

THE TOWN of Pitt was dark except for occasional street lights and the fainter lights that fell from the heavily starred sky. Driving along the street Ada Reichler had named, I could see the moving river down between the houses. When I got out of the car, I could smell the river. A chanting chorus of frogs made the summer night pulsate at its edges.

On the second floor of the old red house, a bleary light outlined a window. The boards of the veranda groaned under my weight. I knocked on the alligatored door. A card offering "Rooms for Rent" was stuck inside the window beside the door.

A light went on over my head. Moths swirled up around it like unseasonable snow. An old man peered out, cocking his narrow gray head at me out of a permanent stoop.

"Something you want?" His voice was a husky whisper.

"I'd like to speak to Mrs. Fredericks, the landlady."

"I'm Mr. Fredericks. If it's a room you want, I can rent you a room just as good as she can."

"Do you rent by the night?"

"Sure, I got a nice front room you can have. It'll cost you—let's see." He stroked the bristles along the edge of his jaw, making a rasping noise. His dull eyes looked me over with stupid cunning. "Two dollars?"

"I'd like to see the room first."

"If you say so. Try not to make too much noise, eh? The old woman—Mrs. Fredericks is in bed."

He must have been just about to go himself. His shirt was open so that I could have counted his ribs, and his broad striped suspenders were hanging down. I followed him up the stairs. He moved with elaborate secrecy, and turned at the top to set a hushing finger to his lips. The light from the hall below cast his hunched condor shadow on the wall.

A woman's voice rose from the back of the house: "What are you creeping around for?"

"Didn't want to disturb the boarders," he said in his carrying whisper.

"The boarders aren't in yet, and you know it. Is somebody with you?"

"Nope. Just me and my shadow."

He smiled a yellow-toothed smile at me, as if he expected me to share the joke.

"Come to bed then," she called.

"In a minute."

He tiptoed to the front of the hallway, beckoned me through an open door, and closed the door quietly behind me. For a moment we were alone in the dark, like conspirators. I could hear his emotional breathing.

Then he reached up to pull on a light. It swung on its cord, throwing lariats of shadow up to the high ceiling, and shifting gleam and gloom on the room's contents. These included a bureau, a washstand with pitcher and bowl, and a bed which had taken the impress of many bodies. The furnishings reminded me of the room John Brown had had in Luna Bay.

John Brown? John Nobody.

I looked at the old man's face. It was hard to imagine what quirk of his genes had produced the boy. If Fredericks had ever possessed good looks, time had washed them out. His face was patchily furred leather, stretched on gaunt bones, held in place by black nailhead eyes.

"The room all right?" he said uneasily.

I glanced at the flowered paper on the walls. Faded morning-glories climbed brown lattices to the watermarked ceiling. I didn't think I could sleep in a room with morning-glories crawling up the walls all night.

"If it's bugs you're worried about," he said, "we had the place fumigated last spring."

"Oh. Good."

"I'll let in some fresh air." He opened the window and sidled back to me. "Pay me cash in advance, and I can let you have it for a dollar and a half."

I had no intention of staying the night, but I decided to let him have the money. I took out my wallet and gave him two ones. His hand trembled as he took them:

"I got no change."

"Keep it. Mr. Fredericks, you have a son."

He gave me a long slow cautious look. "What if I have?"

"A boy named Theodore."

"He's no boy. He'll be grown up now."

"How long is it since you've seen him?"

"I dunno. Four-five years, maybe longer. He ran away when he was sixteen. It's a tough thing to have to say about your own boy, but it was good riddance of bad rubbish."

"Why do you say that?"

"Because it's the truth. You acquainted with Theo?"

"Slightly."

"Is he in trouble again? Is that why you're here?"

Before I could answer, the door of the room flew open. A short stout woman in a flannelette nightgown brushed past me and advanced on Fredericks: "What you think you're doing, renting a room behind my back?"

"I didn't."

But the money was still in his hand. He tried to crumple it in his fist and hide it. She grabbed for it:

"Give me my money."

He hugged his valuable fist against his washboard chest. "It's just as much my money as it is yours."

"Aw no it isn't. I work myself to the bone keeping our heads above water. And what do you do? Drink it up as fast as I can make it."

"I ain't had a drink for a week."

"You're a liar." She stamped her bare foot. Her body shook under the nightgown, and her gray braids swung like cables down her back. "You were drinking wine last night with the boys in the downstairs bedroom."

"That was free," he said virtuously. "And you got no call to talk to me like this in front of a stranger."

She turned to me for the first time. "Excuse us, mister. It's no fault of yours, but he can't handle money." She added unnecessarily: "He drinks."

While her eyes were off him, Fredericks made for the door. She intercepted him. He struggled feebly in her embrace. Her upper arms were as thick as hams. She pried open his bony fist and pushed the crumpled bills down between her breasts. He watched the money go as though it represented his hope of heaven:

"Just give me fifty cents. Fifty cents won't break you."

"Not one red cent," she said. "If you think I'm going to help you get the d.t.'s again, you got another think coming."

"All I want is one drink."

"Sure, and then another and another. Until you feel the rats crawling up under your clothes, and I got to nurse you out of it again."

"There's all different kinds of rats. A woman that won't give her lawful husband four bits to settle his stomach is the worst kind of rat there is."

"Take that back."

She moved on him, arms akimbo. He backed into the hallway:

"All right, I take it back. But I'll get a drink, don't worry. I got good friends in this town, they know my worth."

"Sure they do. They feed you stinking rotgut across the river, and then they come to me asking for money. Don't you set foot outside this house tonight."

"You're not going to order me around, treat me like a has-been. It ain't my fault I can't work, with a hole in my belly. It ain't my fault I can't sleep without a drink to ease the pain."

"Scat," she said. "Go to bed, old man."

He shambled away, trailing his slack suspenders. The fat woman turned to me.

"I apologize for my husband. He's never been the same since his accident."

"What happened to him?"

"He got hurt bad." Her answer seemed deliberately vague. Under folds of fat, her face showed traces of her son's stubborn intelligence. She changed the subject: "I notice you paid with American money. You from the States?"

"I just drove over from Detroit."

"You live in Detroit? I never been over there, but I hear it's an interesting place."

"It probably is. I was just passing through on my way from California."

"What brings you all the way from California?"

"A man named Peter Culligan was murdered there several weeks ago. Culligan was stabbed to death."

"Stabbed to death?"

I nodded. Her head moved slightly in unison with mine.

Without shifting her eyes from my face, she moved around me and sat on the edge of the bed.

"You know him, don't you, Mrs. Fredericks?"

"He boarded with me for a while, years ago. He had this very room."

"What was he doing in Canada?"

"Don't ask me. I don't ask my boarders where their money comes from. Mostly he sat in this room and studied his racing sheets." She looked up shrewdly from under frowning brows. "Would you be a policeman?"

"I'm working with the police. Are you sure you don't know why Culligan came here?"

"I guess it was just a place like any other. He was a loner and a drifter—I get quite a few of them. He probably covered a lot of territory in his time." She looked up at the shadows on the ceiling. The light was still now, and the shadows were concentric, spreading out like ripples on a pool. "Listen, mister, who stabbed him?"

"A young hoodlum."

"My boy? Was it my boy that done it? Is that why you come to me?"

"I think your son is involved."

"I knew it." Her cheeks shuddered. "He took a knife to his father before he was out of high school. He would of killed him, too. Now he really is a murderer." She pressed her clenched hands deep into her bosom; it swelled around her fists like rising dough. "I didn't have enough trouble in my life. I had to give birth to a murderer."

"I don't know about that, Mrs. Fredericks. He committed fraud. I doubt that he committed murder." Even as I said it, I was wondering if he had been within striking distance of Culligan, and if he had an alibi for that day. "Do you have a picture of your son?"

"I have when he was in high school. He ran away before he graduated."

"May I have a look at the picture, Mrs. Fredericks? It's barely possible we're talking about two different people."

But any hope of this died a quick death. The boy in the snapshot she brought was the same one, six years younger. He stood on a riverbank, his back to the water, smiling with conscious charm into the camera.

I gave the picture back to Mrs. Fredericks. She held it up to the light and studied it as if she could re-create the past from its single image.

"Theo was a good-looking boy," she said wistfully. "He was doing so good in school and all, until he started getting those ideas of his."

"What kind of ideas did he have?"

"Crazy ideas, like he was the son of an English lord, and the gypsies stole him away when he was a baby. When he was just a little tyke, he used to call himself Percival Fitzroy, like in a book. That was always his way—he thought he was too good for his own people. I worried about where all that daydreaming was going to land him."

"He's still dreaming," I said. "Right now he's representing himself as the grandson of a wealthy woman in Southern California. Do you know anything about that?"

"I never hear from him. How would I know about it?"

"Apparently Culligan put him up to it. I understand he ran away from here with Culligan."

"Yeah. The dirty scamp talked him into it, turned him against his own father."

"And you say he knifed his father?"

"That very same day." Her eyes widened and glazed. "He stabbed him with a butcher knife, gave him an awful wound. Fredericks was on his back for weeks. He's never got back on his feet entirely. Neither have I, to think my own boy would do a thing like that."

"What was the trouble about, Mrs. Fredericks?"

"Wildness and willfulness," she said. "He wanted to leave home and make his own way in the world. That Culligan encouraged him. He pretended to have Theo's welfare at heart and I know what you're thinking, that Theo did right to run away from home with his old man a bum and the kind of boarders I get. But the proof of the pudding is in the eating. Look at how Theo turned out."

"I have been, Mrs. Fredericks."

"I knew he was headed for a bad end," she said. "He didn't

show natural feelings. He never wrote home once since he left. Where has he been all these years?"

"Going to college."

"To college? He went to college?"

"Your son's an ambitious boy."

"Oh, he always had an ambition, if that's what you want to call it. Is that what he learned in college, how to cheat people?"

"He learned that someplace else."

Perhaps in this room, I thought, where Culligan spun his fantasies and laid a long-shot bet on an accidental resemblance to a dead man. The room had Culligan's taint on it.

The woman stirred uncomfortably, as if I'd made a subtle accusation:

"I don't claim we were good parents to him. He wanted more than we could give him. He always had a dream of himself, like."

Her face moved sluggishly, trying to find the shape of truth and feeling. She leaned back on her arms and let her gaze rest on the swollen slopes of her body, great sagging breasts, distended belly from which a son had struggled headfirst into the light. Over her bowed head, insects swung in eccentric orbits around the hanging bulb, tempting hot death.

She managed to find some hope in the situation: "At least he didn't murder anybody, eh?"

"No."

"Who was it that knifed Culligan? You said it was a young hoodlum."

"His name is Tommy Lemberg. Tommy and his brother Roy are supposed to be hiding out in Ontario—"

"Hamburg, did you say?"

"They may be using that name. Do you know Roy and Tommy?"

"I hope to tell you. They been renting the downstairs room for the last two weeks. They told me their name was Hamburg. How was I to know they were hiding out?"

Chapter 26

I WAITED for the Lembergs on the dark porch. They came home after midnight, walking a bit unsteadily down the street. My parked car attracted their attention, and they crossed the street to look it over. I went down the front steps and across the street after them.

They turned, so close together that they resembled a single amorphous body with two white startled faces. Tommy started toward me, a wide lopsided shape. His arm was still in a white sling under his jacket.

Roy lifted his head with a kind of hopeless alertness. "Come back here, kid."

"The hell. It's old man trouble himself." He walked up to me busily, and spat in the dust at my feet.

"Take it easy, Tommy." Roy came up behind him. "Talk to him."

"Sure I'll talk to him." He said to me: "Didn't you get enough from Mr. Schwartz? You came all this way looking for more?"

Without giving the matter any advance thought, I set myself on my heels and hit him with all my force on the point of the jaw. He went down and stayed. His brother knelt beside him, making small shocked noises which resolved themselves into words:

"You had no right to hit him. He wanted to talk to you."

"I heard him."

"He's been drinking, and he was scared. He was just putting on a big bluff."

"Put away the violin. It doesn't go with a knifing rap."

"Tommy never knifed anybody."

"That's right, he was framed. Culligan framed him by falling down and stabbing himself. Tommy was just an innocent bystander."

"I don't claim he was innocent. Schwartz sent him there to throw his weight around. But nobody figured he was going to run into Culligan, let alone Culligan with a knife and a gun. He got shot taking the gun away from Culligan. Then he knocked

Culligan out, and that's the whole thing as far as Tommy's concerned."

"At which point the Apaches came out of the hills."

"I thought maybe you'd be interested in the truth," Roy said in a shaking voice. "But your thinking is the same as all the others. Once a fellow takes a fall, he's got no human rights."

"Sure, I'm unfair to organized crime."

The wisecrack sounded faintly tinny, even to me. Roy made a disgusted sound in his throat. Tommy groaned as if in response. His eyes were still turned up, veined white between half-closed lids. Roy inserted one arm under his brother's head and lifted it.

Peering down at the dim face, unconscious and innocent-looking, I had a pang of doubt. I knew my bitterness wasn't all for Tommy Lemberg. When I hit him I was lashing out at the other boy, too, reacting to a world of treacherous little hustlers that wouldn't let a man believe in it.

I scraped together a nickel's worth of something, faith or gullibility, and invested it:

"Lemberg, do you believe this yarn your brother told you?"

"Yes."

"Are you willing to put it to the test?"

"I don't understand you." But his white face slanted up fearfully. "If you're talking about him going back to California, no. They'd put him in the gas chamber."

"Not if his story is true. He could do a lot to back it up by coming back with me voluntarily."

"He can't. He's been in jail. He has a record."

"That record of his means a lot to you, doesn't it? More than it does to other people, maybe."

"I don't dig you."

"Why don't you dissolve the brother act? Commit yourself where there's some future. Your wife could do with a piece of you. She's in a bad way, Lemberg."

He didn't answer me. He held his brother's head possessively against his shoulder. In the light of the stars they seemed like twins, mirror images of each other. Roy looked at Tommy in a puzzled way, as if he couldn't tell which was the real man and which was the reflection. Or which was the possessor and which was the possessed.

Footfalls thudded in the dust behind me. It was Mrs. Fredericks, wearing a bathrobe and carrying a pan of water.

"Here," was all she said.

She handed me the pan and went back into the house. She wanted no part of the trouble in the street. Her house was well supplied with trouble.

I sprinkled some water on Tommy's face. He snorted and sat up blinking. "Who hit me?" Then he saw me, and remembered: "You sucker-punched me. You sucker-punched a cripple."

He tried to get up. Roy held him down with both hands on his shoulders:

"You had it coming, you know that. I've been talking to Mr. Archer. He'll listen to what you have to say."

"I'm willing to listen to the truth," I said. "Anything else is a waste of time."

With his brother's help, Tommy got onto his feet. "Go ahead," Roy prompted him. "Tell him. And no more kid stuff."

"The whole truth, remember," I said, "including the Schwartz angle."

"Yeah. Yeah." Tommy was still dazed. "Schwartz was the one hired me in the first place. He sent one of his boys to look me up, promised me a hundred bucks to put a little fear into this certain party."

"A little death, you mean?"

He shook his head violently. "Nothing like that, just a little working over."

"What did Schwartz have against Culligan?"

"Culligan wasn't the one. He wasn't supposed to be there, see. He got in the picture by mistake."

"I told you that," Roy said.

"Be quiet. Let Tommy do the talking."

"Yeah, sure," Tommy said. "It was this beast that I was supposed to put on a little show for. I wasn't supposed to hurt her, nothing like that, just put the fear of God in her so she'd cough up what she owed Schwartz. It was like a collection agency, y'unnerstan'? Legit."

"What was her name?"

"Alice Sable. They sent me because I knew what she looked like. Last summer in Reno she used to run around with Pete Culligan. But he wasn't supposed to be there at her house, for

God sake. The way they told it to me, she was alone by herself out there all day. When Culligan came marching out, armed up to the teeth, you could of knocked me over with a 'dozer.

"I moved in on him, very fast, very fast reflexes I got, talking all the time. Got hold of the gun but it went off, the slug plowed up my arm, same time he dropped the gun. I picked it up. By that time he had his knife out. What could I do? He was going to gut me. I slammed him on the noggin with the gun and chilled him. Then I beat it."

"Did you see Alice Sable?"

"Yeah, she came surging out and yelled at me. I was starting the Jag, and I couldn't hear what she said over the engine. I didn't stop or turn around. Hell, I didn't want to rough up no beast, anyway."

"Did you pick up Culligan's knife before you left, and cut him with it?"

"No sir. What would I do that for? Man, I was hurt. I wanted out."

"What was Culligan doing when you left?"

"Laying there." He glanced at his brother. "Lying there."

"Who coached you to say that?"

"Nobody did."

"That's true," Roy said. "It's just the way he told it to me. You've got to believe him."

"I'm not the important one. The man he has to convince is Sheriff Trask of Santa Teresa County. And planes are taking off for there all the time."

"Aw, no." Tommy's gaze swiveled frantically from me to Roy. "They'll throw the book at me if I go back."

"Sooner or later you have to go back. You can come along peaceably now, or you can force extradition proceedings and make the trip in handcuffs and leg-chains. Which way do you want it, hard or easy?"

For once in his young life, Tommy Lemberg did something the easy way.

Chapter 27

I PHONED Sheriff Trask long distance. He agreed to wire me transportation authorization for the Lemberg brothers. I picked it up at Willow Run, and the three of us got aboard an early plane. Trask had an official car waiting to meet the connecting plane when it landed in Santa Teresa.

Before noon we were in the interrogation room in the Santa Teresa courthouse. Roy and Tommy made statements, which were recorded by a court reporter on steno and tape-machine. Tommy seemed to be awed by the big room with its barred windows, the Sheriff's quiet power, the weight of the law which both man and building represented. There were no discrepancies in the part of his statement I heard.

Trask motioned me out before Tommy was finished. I followed him down the corridor to his office. He took off his coat and opened the neck of his shirt. Blotches of sweat spread from his armpits. He filled a paper cup with water from a cooler, drained the cup, and crushed it in his fist.

"If we buy this," he said at last, "it puts us back at the beginning. You buy it, don't you, Archer?"

"I've taken an option on it. Naturally I think it should be investigated. But that can wait. Have you questioned Theo Fredericks about the Culligan killing?"

"No."

"Is Fredericks doing any talking at all?"

"Not to me he isn't."

"But you picked him up last night?"

Trask's face had a raw red look. I thought at first that he was on the verge of a heart attack. Then I realized that he was painfully embarrassed. He turned his back on me, walked over to the wall, and stood looking at a photograph of himself shaking hands with the Governor.

"Somebody tipped him off," he said. "He flew the coop five minutes before I got there." He turned to face me: "The worst part of it is, he took Sheila Howell with him."

"By force?"

"You kidding? She was probably the one who tipped him off. I made the mistake of phoning Dr. Howell before I moved on the little rat. In any case, she went along with him willingly—walked out of her father's house and drove away with him in the middle of the night. Howell's been on my back ever since."

"Howell's very fond of his daughter."

"Yeah, I know how he feels, I have a daughter of my own. I was afraid for a while that he was going to take off after her with a shotgun, and I mean literally. Howell's a trapshooter, one of the best in the county. But I got him calmed down. He's in the communications room, waiting to hear some word of them."

"They're traveling by car?"

"The one Mrs. Galton bought for him."

"A red Thunderbird should be easy to spot."

"You'd think so. But they've been gone over eight hours without a trace. They may be in Mexico by now. Or they may be cuddled up in an L.A. motel under one of his aliases." Trask scowled at the image. "Why do so many nice young girls go for the dangerous ones?"

The question didn't expect an answer, and that was just as well. I hadn't any.

Trask sat down heavily behind his desk. "Just how dangerous is he? When we talked on the telephone last night, you mentioned a knifing he did before he left Canada."

"He stabbed his father. Apparently he meant to kill him. The old man is no saint, either. In fact, the Fredericks' boarding-house is a regular thieves' kitchen. Peter Culligan was staying there at the time of the knifing. The boy ran away with him."

Trask took up a pencil and broke it in half, abstractedly, dropping the pieces on his blotter. "How do we know the Fredericks boy didn't murder Culligan? He had a motive: Culligan was in a position to call his bluff and tell the world who he really was. And M.O. figures, with his knifing record."

"We've been thinking the same thing, Sheriff. There's even a strong likelihood that Culligan was his partner in the conspiracy. That would give him a powerful motive to silence Culligan. We've been assuming that Fredericks was in Luna Bay that day. But has his alibi ever been checked?"

"There's no time like the present."

Trask picked up his phone and asked the switchboard to put through a call to the San Mateo County sheriff's office in Redwood City.

"I can think of one other possibility," I said. "Alice Sable was involved with Culligan last year in Reno, and maybe since. Remember how she reacted to his death. We put it down to nervous shock, but it could have been something worse."

"You're not suggesting that she killed him?"

"As a hypothesis."

Trask shook his head impatiently. "Even putting it hypothetically, it's pretty hard to swallow about a lady like her."

"What kind of a lady is she? Do you know her?"

"I've met her, that's about all. But hell, Gordon Sable's one of the top lawyers in the city."

The politician latent in every elected official was rising to the surface and blurring Trask's hard, clear attitudes. I said:

"That doesn't put his wife above suspicion. Have you questioned her?"

"No." Trask became explanatory, as though he felt that he had missed a move: "I haven't been able to get to her. Sable was opposed, and the head-shrinkers backed him up. They say she shouldn't be questioned on painful subjects. She's been borderline psychotic since the killing, and any more pressure might push her over the edge."

"Howell's her personal doctor, isn't he?"

"He is. As a matter of fact, I tried to get to her through Howell. He was dead set against it, and as long as it looked like an open-and-shut case, I didn't press the point."

"Howell should be ready to change his mind. Did you say he's somewhere around the courthouse?"

"Yeah, he's down in Communications. But wait a minute, Archer." Trask rose and came around the desk. "This is a touchy business, and you don't want to hang too much weight on the Lemberg brothers' story. They're not disinterested witnesses."

"They don't know enough to invent the story, either."

"Schwartz and his lawyers do."

"Are we back on the Schwartz kick again?"

"You were the one that got me on it in the first place. You were convinced that the Culligan killing was a gang killing."

"I was wrong."

"Maybe. We'll let the facts decide when they all come out. But if you were wrong, you could be wrong again." Trask punched me in the stomach in a friendly way. "How about that, Archer?"

His telephone chirped, and he lifted the receiver. I couldn't make out the words that came scratchily over the wire, but I saw their effect on Trask. His body stiffened, and his face seemed to grow larger.

"I'll use my Aero Squadron," he said finally, "and I ought to be there in two hours. But don't sit around waiting for me." He slammed down the receiver and reached for the coat draped over the back of his chair.

"They made the red Thunderbird," he said. "Fredericks abandoned it in San Mateo. They were just going to put the word on the teletype when they got my call."

"Where in San Mateo?"

"Parking-lot of the S.P. station. Fredericks and the girl probably took a train into San Francisco."

"Are you flying up?"

"Yeah, I've had a volunteer pilot standing by all morning. Ride along with us if you want. He has a four-passenger Beechcraft."

"Thanks, I've had enough flying to last me for a while. You didn't ask them to check Fredericks's alibi."

"I forgot," Trask said lightly. "I'll take it up with Fredericks personally."

He seemed glad to be leaving Alice Sable in my lap.

Chapter 28

THE COMMUNICATIONS center of the courthouse was a windowless room on the basement level, full of the chatter and whine of short-wave radio signals. Dr. Howell was sitting with his head down in front of a quiet teletype machine. He raised his head abruptly when I spoke to him. His face was gray in the white overhead light:

"So here you are. While you've been junketing around the country at my expense, she's gone away with him. Do you understand what that means?"

His voice rose out of control. The two deputies monitoring the radios looked at him and then at each other. One of them said: "If you two gentlemen want to talk in private, this is no place to do it."

"Come outside," I said to Howell: "You're not accomplishing anything here. They'll be picked up soon, don't worry."

He sat in inert silence. I wanted to get him away from the teletype machine before the message from San Mateo hit it. It would send him off to the Bay area, and I had a use for him here:

"Doctor, is Alice Sable still under your care?"

He looked up questioningly. "Yes."

"Is she still in the nursing home?"

"Yes. I should try to get out there today." He brushed his forehead with his fingertips. "I've been neglecting my patients, I'm afraid."

"Come out there with me now."

"What on earth for?"

"Mrs. Sable may be able to help us terminate this case, and help us reach your daughter."

He rose, but stood irresolute beside the teletype machine. Sheila's defection had robbed him of his force. I took hold of his elbow and steered him out into the basement corridor. Once moving, he went ahead of me up the iron stairs into the hot white noon.

His Chevrolet was in the county parking-lot. He turned to me as he started the engine:

"How can Mrs. Sable help us to find Sheila?"

"I'm not certain she can. But she was involved with Culligan, the Fredericks boy's probable partner in the conspiracy. She may know more about Theo Fredericks than anyone else does."

"She never said a word about him to me."

"Has she been talking to you about the case?"

He said after some hesitation: "Not being a practicing psychiatrist, I haven't encouraged that line of discussion with her. The matter has come up, however. Unavoidably so, since it's part and parcel of her mental condition."

"Can you be more specific?"

"I prefer not to. You know the ethics of my profession. The doctor-patient relationship is sacrosanct."

"So is human life. Don't forget a man was murdered. We have evidence that Mrs. Sable knew Culligan before he came to Santa Teresa. She was also a witness to his death. Anything she has to say about it may be very significant."

"Not if her memory of the event is delusional."

"Does she have delusions on the subject?"

"She has indeed. Her account doesn't agree with the actual event as we know it. I've gone into this with Trask, and there's no doubt whatever that a thug named Lemberg stabbed the man."

"There's a good deal of doubt," I said. "The Sheriff just took a statement from Lemberg. A Reno gambler sent Lemberg to collect money from Alice Sable, and maybe rough her up a bit. Culligan got in the way. Lemberg knocked him out, was shot in the process, left him unconscious on the ground. He claims that somebody else did the knifing after he left."

Howell's face underwent a curious change. His eyes became harder and brighter. He wasn't looking at me, or at anything external. The lines around his eyes and at the corners of his mouth curved and deepened, as if he was being forced to look against his will at something horrible.

"But Trask said Lemberg was undeniably guilty."

"Trask was wrong. We all were."

"Do you honestly mean to say that Alice Sable has been speaking the truth all along?"

"I don't know what she's been saying, Doctor. You do."

"But Trenchard and the other psychiatrists were convinced that her self-accusations were fantasies. They had me convinced."

"What does she accuse herself of? Does she blame herself for Culligan's death?"

Howell sat over the wheel in silence. He had been shaken, and wide open, for a few minutes. Now his personality closed up again:

"You have no right to cross-examine me about the intimate affairs of one of my patients."

"I'm afraid I have to, Doctor. If Alice Sable murdered Culligan, there's no way you can cover up for her. I'm surprised you want to. You're not only breaking the law, you're violating the ethics you set such store by."

"I'll be the judge of my own ethics," he said in a strained voice.

He sat and wrestled with his unstated problem. His gaze was inward and glaring. Sweat-drops studded his forehead. I got some sense of the empathy he felt for his patient. Even his daughter was forgotten.

"She has confessed the murder to you, Doctor?"

Slowly his eyes remembered me again. "What did you say?"

"Has Mrs. Sable confessed Culligan's murder?"

"I'm going to ask you not to question me further."

Abruptly, he released the emergency brake. I kept quiet all the way to the nursing home, hoping my patience might earn me an interview with Alice Sable herself.

A gray-haired nurse unlocked the front door, and smiled with special intensity at Howell. "Good morning, Doctor. We're a little late this morning."

"I'm having to skip my regular calls today. I do want to see Mrs. Sable."

"I'm sorry, Doctor, she's already gone."

"Gone where, for heaven's sake?"

"Mr. Sable took her home this morning, didn't you know? He said it was all right with you."

"It certainly is not. You don't release disturbed patients without specific orders from a doctor. Haven't you learned that yet, nurse?"

Before she could answer, Howell turned on his heel and started back to his car. I had to run to catch him.

"The man's a fool!" he cried above the roar of the engine. "He can't be permitted to take a chance like this with his wife's safety. She's dangerous to herself and other people."

I said when we were underway: "Was she dangerous to Culligan, Doctor?"

His answer was a sigh which seemed to rise from the center of his body. The outskirts of Santa Teresa gave place to open country. The hills of Arroyo Park rose ahead of us. With his eyes on the green hills, Howell said:

"The poor wretch of a woman told me that she killed him. And I didn't have sense enough to believe her. Somehow her story didn't ring true to me. I was convinced that it was fantasy masking the actual event."

"Is that why you wouldn't let Trask talk to her?"

"Yes. The present state of the law being what it is, a doctor has a duty to protect his patients, especially the semi-psychotic ones. We can't run off to the police with every sick delusion they come up with. But in this case," he added reluctantly, "it seems I was mistaken."

"You're not sure."

"I'm no longer sure about anything."

"Exactly what did she say to you?"

"She heard the sounds of a struggle, two men fighting and calling each other names. A gun went off. She was terrified, of course, but she forced herself to go to the front door. Culligan was lying on the lawn. The other man was just driving away in the Jaguar. When he was out of sight, she went out to Culligan. Her intention was to help him, she said, but she saw his knife in the grass. She picked it up and—used it."

We had reached the foot of Sable's hill. Howell wrestled his car up the climbing curves. The tires shuddered and screeched like lost souls under punishment.

Chapter 29

SABLE MUST have heard the car, and been waiting behind the door for Howell's knock. He opened the door at once. His bloodshot eyes began to water in the strong sunlight, and he sneezed.

"Where is your wife?" Howell said.

"In her own room, where she belongs. There was so much noise and confusion in the nursing home—"

"I want to see her."

"I don't think so, Doctor. I understand you've been grilling her about the unfortunate crime that occurred on our premises. It's been most disturbing to Alice. You told me yourself that she shouldn't be forced to talk about it."

"She brought up the subject of her own accord. I demand to be allowed to see her."

"Demand, Doctor? How can you do that? I should make it clear, I suppose, that I'm terminating your services as of now. I intend to hire a new crew of doctors, and find a place where Alice can rest in peace."

The phrase set up whispering echoes which Howell's voice cut through:

"You don't hire doctors, Sable, and you don't fire them."

"Your law is rusty. Perhaps you should hire a lawyer. You're certainly going to need one if you try to force your way into my house." Sable's voice was controlled, but queerly atonal.

"I have a duty to my patient. You had no right to remove her from nursing care."

"From your third-degree methods, you mean? Let me remind you, if you need reminding, that anything Alice has said to you is privileged. I employed you and the others in my capacity as her lawyer in order to have your assistance in determining certain facts. Is that clear? If you communicate these facts or alleged facts to anyone, official or unofficial, I'll sue you for criminal libel."

"You're talking doubletalk," I said. "You won't be suing anybody."

"Won't I, though? You're in roughly the same position as Dr. Howell. I employed you to make a certain investigation, and ordered you to communicate the results orally to me. Any further communication is a breach of contract. Try it out, and by God I'll have your license."

I didn't know if he was legally right. I didn't care. When he started to swing the door shut, I set my foot against it:

"We're coming in, Sable."

"I think not," his queer new voice said.

He reached behind the door and stepped back with a gun in his hands. It was a long, heavy gun, a deer rifle with a telescopic sight. He raised it deliberately. I looked directly into the muzzle, at the clean, glinting spiral of the rifling.

Sable curled his finger on the trigger, and cuddled the polished stock against his cheek. His face had a fine glaze on it, like porcelain. I realized that he was ready to kill me.

"Put it down," Howell said.

He moved ahead of me into the doorway, taking my place in the line of fire:

"Put it down, Gordon. You're not yourself, you're feeling upset, you're terribly worried about Alice. But we're your friends, we're Alice's friends, too. We want to help you both."

"I have no friends," Sable said. "I know why you're here, why you want to talk to Alice. And I'm not going to let you."

"Don't be silly, Gordon. You can't look after a sick woman by yourself. I know you don't care about your personal safety, but you have to consider Alice's safety. She needs looking after, Gordon. So put it down now, let me in to see her."

"Get back. I'll shoot."

Sable's voice was a high sharp yell. His wife must have heard it. From deep inside the house, she cried out in answer:

"No!"

Sable blinked against the light. He looked like a sleepwalker waking up on the verge of a precipice. Behind him his wife's crying went on, punctuated by resounding blows and then a crash of glass.

Caught between impossible pressures, Sable half-turned toward the noise. The rifle swung sideways with his movement. I went in past Howell and got one hand on the gun-barrel and the other on the knot of Sable's tie. I heaved. Man and rifle came apart.

Sable thudded against the wall and almost fell. He was breathing hard. His hair was in his eyes. He bore a strange resemblance to an old woman peering out through the fringes of a matted white wig.

I opened the breech of the rifle. While I was unloading it, running feet slapped the pavement of the inner court. Alice Sable appeared at the end of the hallway. Her light hair was ruffled and her nightgown was twisted around her slender body. Blood ran down over her naked foot from a cut in her leg.

"I hurt myself on the window," she said in a small voice. "I cut myself on the glass."

"Did you have to break it?" Sable made an abrupt, threatening movement toward her. Then he remembered us, and sweetened his tone: "Go back to your room, dear. You don't want to run around half-dressed in front of visitors."

"Dr. Howell isn't a visitor. You came to fix it where I hurt myself, didn't you?"

She moved uncertainly toward the doctor. He went to meet her with his hands out. "Of course I did. Come back to your room with me and we'll fix it now."

"But I don't want to go back in there. I hate it in there, it depresses me. Peter used to visit me in there."

"Be quiet!" Sable said.

She moved behind the doctor, making her body small as if to claim a child's irresponsibility. From the protection of Howell's shoulder, she peered sadly at her husband:

"Be quiet is all you say to me. Be quiet, hush it up. But what's the use, Gordon? Everybody knows about me and Peter. Dr. Howell knows. I made a clean breast of it to him." Her hand went to her breast, and fingered the rosebuds embroidered on her nightgown. Her heavy gaze swung to me. "This man knows about me, too, I can see it in his face."

"Did you kill him, Mrs. Sable?"

"Don't answer," Sable said.

"But I want to confess. I'll feel better then, won't I?" Her smile was bright and agonized. It faded, leaving its lines in her face and her teeth bare: "I did kill him. The fellow in the black car knocked him out, and I went out and stabbed him."

Her hand jerked downward from her breast, clenched on an imaginary knife. Her husband watched her like a poker-player.

"Why did you do it?" I said.

"I don't know. I guess I just got sick of him. Now it's time for me to take my punishment. I killed, and I deserve to die."

The tragic words had an unreal quality. She spoke them like a life-size puppet activated by strings and used by a voice that didn't belong to her. Only her eyes were her own, and they contained a persistent stunned innocence.

"I deserve to die," she repeated. "Don't I, Gordon?"

He flushed up darkly. "Leave me out of this."

"But you said—"

"I said nothing of the sort."

"You're lying, Gordon," she chided him. Perhaps there was an undertone of malice in her voice. "You told me after all my crimes that I deserved to die. And you were right. I lost your good money gambling and went with another man and now on top of it all I'm a murderer."

Sable appealed to Howell: "Can't we put an end to this? My wife is ill and hurt. It's inconceivable that you should let her be questioned. This man isn't even a policeman—"

"I'll take the responsibility for what I do," I said. "Mrs. Sable, do you remember stabbing Peter Culligan?"

She raised one hand to her forehead, pushing back her hair as if it got in the way of her thoughts. "I don't remember exactly, but I must have."

"Why do you say you must have, if you don't remember?"

"Gordon saw me."

I looked at Sable. He wouldn't look at me. He stood against the wall, trying to merge with the wall.

"Gordon wasn't here," I said. "He was at Mrs. Galton's house when you telephoned."

"But he came. He came right over. Peter was lying there on the grass for a long time. He was making a funny noise, it sounded like snoring. I unbuttoned the top of his shirt to help him breathe."

"You remember all this, but you don't remember stabbing him?"

"I must have blanked out on that part. I'm always blanking out on things, ask Gordon."

"I'm asking you, Mrs. Sable."

"Let me think. I remember, I slid my hand down under his shirt, to see if his heart was beating properly. I could feel it there thumping and jumping. You'd think it was a little animal trying to get out. The hair on his chest was scratchy, like wire."

Sable made a noise in his throat.

"What did you do then?" I said.

"I—nothing. I just sat for a while and looked at him and his poor old beat-up face. I put my arms around him and tried to coax him awake. But he went on snoring at me. He was still snoring when Gordon got there. Gordon was angry, catching me with him like that. I ran into the house. But I watched from the window."

Suddenly her face was incandescent. "I didn't kill him. It wasn't me out there. It was Gordon, and I watched him from the window. He picked up Peter's knife and pushed it into his stomach." Her clenched hand repeated its downward gesture, striking her own soft abdomen. "The blood spurted out and ran red on the grass. It was all red and green."

Sable thrust his head forward. The rest of his body, even his arms and hands, remained stuck to the wall:

"You can't believe her. She's hallucinating again."

His wife seemed not to hear him. Perhaps she was tuned to a higher frequency, singing like salvation in her head. Tears streamed from her eyes:

"I didn't kill him."

"Hush now." Howell quieted her face against his shoulder.

"This is the truth, isn't it?" I said.

"It must be. I'm certain of it. Those self-accusations of hers were fantasy after all. This account is much more circumstantial. I'd say she's taken a long step toward reality."

"She's crazier than she ever was," Sable said. "If you think you can use this against me, you're crazier than she is. Don't forget I'm a lawyer—"

"Is that what you are—a lawyer?" Howell turned his back on Sable and spoke to his wife: "Come on, Alice, we'll put a bandage on that cut and you can get some clothes on. Then we'll take a little ride, back to the nice place with the other ladies."

"It isn't a nice place," she said.

Howell smiled down at her. "That's the spirit. Keep saying what you really think and know, and we'll get you out of there to stay. But not for a while yet, eh?"

"Not for a while yet."

Holding her with one arm, Howell stretched out his other hand to Sable. "The key to your wife's room. You won't be needing it."

Sable produced a flat brass key which Howell accepted from him without a word. The doctor walked Alice Sable down the hallway toward the court.

Chapter 30

GORDON SABLE watched them go with something approaching relief. The bright expectancy had left his eyes. He had had it.

"I wouldn't have done it," he said, "if I'd known what I know now. There are factors you don't foresee—the factor of human change, for example. You think you can handle anything, that you can go on forever. But your strength wears away under pressure. A few days, or a few weeks, and everything looks different. Nothing seems worth struggling for. It all goes blah." He made a loose bumbling sound with his lips: "All gone to bloody blah. So here we are."

"Why did you kill him?"

"You heard her. When I got back here she was crying and moaning over him, trying to wake him up with kisses. It made me sick to death."

"Don't tell me it was a sudden crime of passion. You must have known about them long before."

"I don't deny that." Sable shifted his stance, as if to prepare himself for a shift in his story. "Culligan picked her up in Reno last summer. She went there to divorce me, but she ended up on a gambling spree with Culligan egging her on. No doubt he collected commissions on the money she lost. She lost a great deal, all the ready money I could raise. When it was gone, and her credit was exhausted, he let her share his apartment for a while. I had to go there and beg her to come home with me. She didn't want to come. I had to pay him to send her away."

I didn't doubt the truth of what he was saying. No man would invent such a story against himself. It was Sable who didn't seem to believe his own words. They fell weightlessly from his mouth, like a memorized report of an accident he didn't understand, which had happened to people in a foreign country:

"I never felt quite the same about myself after that. Neither of us did. We lived in this house I'd built for her as if there were always a glass partition between us. We could see each other, but we couldn't really speak. We had to act out our feelings like clowns, or apes in separate cages. Alice's gestures became queerer, and no doubt mine did, too. The things we acted out got uglier. She would throw herself on the floor and strike herself with her fist until her face was bruised and swollen. And I would laugh at her and call her names.

"We did such things to each other," he said. "I think we were both glad, in a strange way, when Culligan turned up here in the course of the winter. Anthony Galton's bones had been unearthed, and Culligan had read about it in the papers. He knew who they belonged to, and came to me with the information."

"How did he happen to pick you?"

"It's a good question. I've often asked myself that good question. Alice had told him that I was Mrs. Galton's lawyer, of course. It may have been the source of his interest in her. He knew that her gambling losses had put me in financial straits. He needed expert help with the plan he had; he wasn't clever enough to execute it alone. He was just clever enough to realize that I was infinitely cleverer."

And he knew other things about you, I thought. You were a loveless man who could be bent and finally twisted.

"How did Schwartz get in on the deal?"

"Otto Schwartz? He wasn't in on it." Sable seemed offended by the notion. "His only connection with it was the fact that Alice owed him sixty thousand dollars. Schwartz had been pressing for payment, and it finally reached the point where he was threatening both of us with a beating. I had to raise money somehow. I was desperate. I didn't know which way to turn."

"Leave out the drama, Sable. You didn't go into this conspiracy on the spur of the moment. You've been working on it for months."

"I'm not denying that. There was a lot of work to be done. Culligan's idea didn't look too promising at first. He'd been carrying it around ever since he ran into the Fredericks boy in Canada five or six years ago. He'd known Anthony Galton in Luna Bay, and was struck by the boy's resemblance to him. He even brought Fredericks into the States in the hope of cashing in on the resemblance in some way. But he ran into trouble with the law, and lost track of the boy. He believed that if I'd stake him, he could find him again.

"Culligan did find him, as you know, going to school in Ann Arbor. I went east myself in February, and saw him in one of the student plays. He was a fairly good actor, with a nice air of sincerity about him. I decided when I talked to him that he could carry the thing off if anyone could. I introduced myself as a Hollywood producer interested in his talent. Once he was hooked on that, and had taken money from me, he wasn't too hard to talk around to the other.

"I prepared his story for him, of course. It required considerable thought. The most difficult problem was how to lead investigation of his actual Canadian background into a blind alley. The Crystal Springs orphanage was my inspiration. But I realized that the success of the imposture depended primarily on him. If he did succeed in bringing it off, he would be entitled to the lion's share. I was modest in my own demands. He simply gave me an option to buy, at a nominal price, a certain amount of producing oil property."

I watched him, trying to understand how a man with so much foresight could have ended where Sable was. Something had cut off the use of his mind from constructive purposes. Perhaps it was the shallow pride which he seemed to take in his schemes, even at this late date.

"They talk about the crime of the century," he said. "This would have been the greatest of all—a multi-million-dollar enterprise with no actual harm done to anyone. The boy was simply to let himself be discovered, and let the facts speak for themselves."

"The facts?" I said sharply.

"The apparent facts, if you like. I'm not a philosopher. We lawyers don't deal in ultimate realities. Who knows what they are? We deal in appearances. There was very little manipulation of the facts in this case, no actual falsification of documents. True, the boy had to tell one or two little lies about his childhood and his parents. What did a few little lies matter? They made Mrs. Galton just as happy as if he was her real grandson. And if she chose to leave him her money, that was her affair."

"Has she made a new will?"

"I believe so. I had no part in it. I advised her to get another lawyer."

"Wasn't that taking a chance?"

"Not if you know Maria Galton as I know her. Her reactions are so consistently contrary that you can depend on them. I got her to make a new will by urging her not to. I got her interested in looking for Tony by telling her it was hopeless. I persuaded her to hire you by opposing the whole idea of a detective."

"Why me?"

"Schwartz was prodding me, and I had to get the ball rolling. I couldn't take the chance of finding the boy for myself. I had to have someone to do it for me, someone I could trust. I thought, too, if we could get past you, we could get past anyone. And if we failed to get past you, I thought you'd be—more flexible, shall we say?"

"Crooked, shall we say?"

Sable winced at the word. Words meant more to him than the facts they stood for.

A door opened at the end of the corridor, and Alice Sable and Dr. Howell came toward us. She hung on the doctor's arm, dressed and freshly groomed and empty-faced under her makeup. He was carrying a white leather suitcase in his free hand.

"Sable has made a full confession," I said to Howell. "Phone the Sheriff's office, will you?"

"I already have. They ought to be here shortly. I'm taking Mrs. Sable back where she'll be properly attended to." He added in an undertone: "I hope this will be a turning-point for her."

"I hope so, too," Sable said. "Honestly I do."

Howell made no response. Sable tried again:

"Good-by, Alice. I really do wish you well, you know."

Her neck stiffened, but she didn't look at him. She went out leaning on Howell. Her brushed hair shone like gold in the sunlight. Fool's gold. I felt a twinge of sympathy for Sable. He hadn't been able to carry her weight. In the stretching gap between his weakness and her need, Culligan had driven a wedge, and the whole structure had fallen.

Sable was a subtle man, and he must have noticed some change in my expression:

"You surprise me, Lew. I didn't expect you to bear down so hard. You have a reputation for tempering the wind to the shorn lamb."

"Stabbing Culligan to death wasn't exactly a lamblike gesture."

"I had to kill him. You don't seem to understand."

"On account of your wife?"

"My wife was only the beginning. He kept moving in on me. He wasn't content to share my wife and my house. He was very hungry, always wanting more. I finally saw that he wanted it all to himself. Everything." His voice trembled with indignation. "After all my contributions, all my risks, he was planning to shut me out."

"How could he?"

"Through the boy. He had something on Theo Fredericks. I never learned what it was, I couldn't get it out of either of them. But Culligan said that it was enough to ruin my whole plan. It was his plan, too, of course, but he was irresponsible enough to wreck it unless he got his way."

"So you killed him."

"The chance offered itself, and I took it. It wasn't premeditated."

"No jury will believe that, after what you did to your wife. It looks as premeditated as hell. You waited for your chance to knock off a defenseless man, and then tried to push the guilt onto a sick woman."

"She asked for it," he said coldly. "She wanted to believe that she killed him. She was half-convinced before I talked to her, she felt so guilty about her affair with him. I only did what any man would do under the circumstances. She'd seen me stab him. I had to do something to purge her mind of the memory."

"Is that what you've been doing on your long visits, pounding guilt into her mind?"

He struck the wall with the flat of his hand. "She was the cause of the trouble. She brought him into our life. She deserved to suffer for it. Why should I do all the suffering?"

"You don't have to. Spread it around a little. Tell me how to get to the Fredericks boy."

He glanced at me from the corners of his eyes. "I'd want a quid pro quo." The legal phrase seemed to encourage him. He went on in quickening tempo until he was almost chattering: "As a matter of fact, he should take the blame for most of this frightful mess. If it will help to clear up the matter, I'm willing to turn state's evidence. Alice can't be made to testify against me. You don't even know that what she said was true. How do you know her story is true? I may be simply covering up for her." His voice was rising like a manic hope.

"How do you know you're alive, Sable? I want your partner. He was in San Mateo this morning. Where is he headed for?"

"I haven't the faintest idea."

"When did you see him last?"

"I don't know why I should co-operate with you if you won't co-operate with me."

I still had his empty rifle in my hands. I reversed it and raised it like a club. I was angry enough to use it if I had to.

"This is why."

He pulled his head back so sharply it rapped the wall. "You can't use third-degree methods on me. It isn't legal."

"Stop blowing bubbles, Sable. Was Fredericks here last night?"

"Yes. He wanted me to cash a check for him. I gave him all the cash I had in the house. It amounted to over two hundred dollars."

"What did he want it for?"

"He didn't tell me. Actually, he wasn't making too much sense. He talked as if the strain had been too much for him."

"What did he say?"

"I can't reproduce it verbatim. I was upset myself. He asked me a lot of questions, which I wasn't able to answer, about Anthony Galton and what happened to him. The imposture must have gone to his head; he seemed to have himself convinced that he actually was Galton's son."

"Was Sheila Howell with him?"

"Yes, she was present, and I see what you mean. He may have been talking for her benefit. If it was an act, she was certainly taken in by it. But as I said, he seemed to be taken in by it himself. He became very excited, and threatened me with force unless I told him who murdered Galton. I didn't know what to tell him. I finally thought of the name of that woman in Redwood City—the Galtons' former nurse."

"Mrs. Matheson?"

"Yes. I had to tell him something, get rid of him somehow."

A patrol car whined up the hill and stopped in front of the house. Conger and another deputy climbed out. Sable was going to have a hard time getting rid of them.

Chapter 31

THEY DROPPED me at the airport, and I got aboard a plane. It was the same two-engine bucket, on the same flight, that had taken me north three weeks ago. Even the stewardess was the same. Somehow she looked younger and more innocent. Time had stood still for her while it had been rushing me along into premature middle age.

She comforted me with Chiclets and coffee in paper cups. And there was the blessed Bay again, and the salt flats.

The Matheson house was closed up tight, with the drapes pulled over the windows, as if there was sickness inside. I asked my cab-driver to wait and knocked on the front door. Marian Matheson answered it herself.

She had been living on my time-schedule, and growing old rapidly. There was more gray in her hair, more bone in her face. But the process of change had softened her. Even her voice was gentler:

"I've been sort of expecting you. I had another visitor this morning."

"John Galton?"

"Yes. John Galton—the little boy I looked after in Luna Bay. It was quite an experience meeting him after all these years. And his girl, too. He brought his girl along." She hesitated, then opened the door wider. "Come in if you want."

She took me into the darkened living-room and placed me in a chair.

"What did they come to you for, Mrs. Matheson?"

"The same thing you did. Information."

"What about?"

"That night. I thought he had a right to know the truth, so I told him all I told you, about Culligan and Shoulders." Her answer was vague; perhaps she was trying to keep the memory vague in her mind.

"What was his reaction?"

"He was very interested. Naturally. He really pricked up his ears when I told him about the rubies."

"Did he explain his interest in the rubies?"

"He didn't explain anything. He got up and left in a hurry, and they rocketed off in that little red car of his. They didn't even wait to drink the coffee I was brewing."

"Were they friendly?"

"To me, you mean? Very friendly. The girl was lovely to me. She confided they were going to get married as soon as her young man worked his way out of the darkness."

"What did she mean by the darkness?"

"I don't know, that was just the phrase she used." But she squinted at the sunlight filtering through the drapes, like someone who understood what darkness meant. "He seemed to be very concerned about his father's death."

"Did he say what he was going to do next, or where he was going?"

"No. He did ask me how to get to the airport—if there were buses running. It seemed kind of funny, him asking about buses when he had a brand-new sports car standing out front."

"He's evading arrest, Mrs. Matheson. He knew his car would be spotted right away if he parked it at the airport."

"Who wants to arrest him?"

"I do, for one. He isn't Galton's son, or Brown's son. He's an impostor."

"How can that be? Why, he's the spitting image of his father."

"Appearances can be deceiving, and you're not the first one to be taken in by his appearance. His real name is Theo Fredericks. He's a small-time crook from Canada with a record of violence."

Her hand went to her mouth. "From Canada, did you say?"

"Yes. His parents run a boardinghouse in Pitt, Ontario."

"But that's where they're going, Ontario. I heard him say to her, when I was out in the kitchen, that there were no direct flights to Ontario. That was just before they took off from here."

"What time were they here?"

"It was early in the morning, just past eight. They were waiting out front when I got back from driving Ron to the station."

I looked at my watch. It was nearly five. They had had almost nine hours. With the right connections, they could be in Canada by now.

And with the right connections, I could be there in another eight or nine hours.

Mrs. Matheson followed me to the door. "Is this trouble going to go on forever?"

"We're coming to the end of it," I said. "I'm sorry I couldn't keep you out of it after all."

"It's all right. I've talked it out with Ron. Whatever comes up—if I have to testify in court or anything—we can handle it together. My husband is a very good man."

"He has a good wife."

"No." She shook the compliment off her fingers. "But I love him and the boy, and that's something. I'm glad it all came out between me and Ron. It's a big load off my heart." She smiled gravely. "I hope it works out some way for that young girl. It's hard to believe that her boy is a criminal. But I know how these things can be in life."

She looked up at the sun.

On the way to International Airport my taxi passed the Redwood City courthouse. I thought of stopping and getting in touch with Trask. Then I decided not to. It was my case, and I wanted to end it.

Perhaps I had a glimmering of the truth.

Chapter 32

I DROVE my rented car into Pitt at three o'clock, the darkest hour of the night. But there were lights in the red house on the riverbank. Mrs. Fredericks came to the door fully dressed in rusty black. Her heavy face set stubbornly when she saw me.

"You got no call coming here again. What do you think you're after? I didn't know those Hamburg fellows were wanted by the police."

"They're not the only ones. Has your son been here?"

"Theo?" Her eyes and mouth sought obtusely for an answer. "He hasn't come near me for years."

A husky whisper rose from the shadows behind her. "Don't believe her, mister." Her husband came forward, supporting himself with one hand against the wall. He looked and sounded very drunk: "She'd lie her false heart out for him."

"Hold your tongue, old man."

Dark anger filled her eyes like a seepage of ink: I'd seen the same thing happen to her son. She turned on Fredericks, and he backed away. His face looked porous and moist like a deliquescent substance. His clothes were covered with dust.

"Have you seen him, Mr. Fredericks?"

"No. Lucky for him I was out, or I'd of shown him what's what." His hatchet profile chopped the air. "She saw him, though."

"Where is he, Mrs. Fredericks?"

Her husband answered for her: "She told me they went to check in at the hotel, him and the girl both."

Some obscure feeling, guilt or resentment, made the woman say: "They didn't have to go to the hotel. I offered them the use of my house. I guess it isn't good enough for mucky-mucks like her."

"Is the girl all right?"

"I guess so. Theo's the one that's got me worried. What did he want to come here for, after all these years? I can't figure him out."

"He always did have crazy ideas," Fredericks said. "But he's crazy like a fox, see. Watch him close when you go to nab him. He talks smooth, but he's a real snake-in-the-grass."

"Where is this hotel?"

"Downtown. The Pitt Hotel—you can't miss it. Just keep us out of it, eh? He'll try to drag us into his trouble, but I'm a respectable man—"

His wife cried: "Shut up, you. I want to see him again if you don't."

I left them locked in the combat which seemed the normal condition of their nights.

The hotel was a three-story red brick building with one lighted window on the second floor corner. One other light was burning in the lobby. I punched the hand-bell on the desk. A middle-aged little man in a green eyeshade came yawning out of a dark room behind it.

"You're up early," he said.

"I'm up late. Can you rent me a room?"

"Sure can. I got more vacancies than you can shake a stick at. With or without bath?"

"With."

"That will be three dollars." He opened the heavy leather-cornered register, and pushed it across the desk. "Sign on the line."

I signed. The registration above my signature was: Mr. and Mrs. John Galton, Detroit, Michigan.

"I see you have some other Americans staying here."

"Yeah. Nice young couple, checked in late last night. I believe they're honeymooners, probably on their way to Niagara Falls. Anyway, I put them in the bridal chamber."

"Corner room on the second floor?"

He gave me a sharp dry look. "You wouldn't want to disturb them, mister."

"No, I thought I'd say hello to them in the morning."

"Better make it late in the morning." He took a key from a hook and dropped it on the desk. "I'm putting you in two-ten, at the other end. I'll show you up if you want."

"Thanks, I can find it by myself."

I climbed the stairs that rose from the rear of the lobby. My legs were heavy. In the room, I took my .32 automatic out of my overnight bag and inserted one of the clips I had brought for it. The carpet in the dim corridor was threadbare, but it was thick enough to silence my footsteps.

There was still light in the corner room, spilling over through the open transom. A sleeper's heavy breathing came over, too, a long sighing choked off and then repeated. I tried the door. It was locked.

Sheila Howell spoke clearly from the darkness: "Who is that?" I waited. She spoke again:

"John. Wake up."

"What is it?" His voice sounded nearer than hers.

"Somebody's trying to get in."

I heard the creak of bed springs, the pad of his feet. The brass doorknob rotated.

He jerked the door open, stepped out with his right fist cocked, saw me and started to swing, saw the gun and froze. He was naked to the waist. His muscles stood out under his pale skin.

"Easy, boy. Raise your hands."

"This nonsense isn't necessary. Put the gun down."

"I'm giving the orders. Clasp your hands and turn around, walk slowly into the room."

He moved reluctantly, like stone forced into motion. When he turned, I saw the white scars down his back, hundreds of them, like fading cuneiform cuts.

Sheila was standing beside the rumpled bed. She had on a man's shirt which was too big for her. The shirt and the lipstick smudged on her mouth gave her a dissolute air.

"When did you two have time to get married?"

"We didn't. Not yet." A blush mounted like fire from her neck to her cheekbones. "This isn't what you think. John shared my room because I asked him to. I was frightened. And he slept across the foot of the bed, so there."

He made a quelling gesture with his raised hands. "Don't tell him anything. He's on your father's side. Anything we say he'll twist against us."

"I'm not the twister, Theo."

He turned on me, so suddenly I almost shot him. "Don't call me by that name."

"It belongs to you, doesn't it?"

"My name is John Galton."

"Come off it. Your partner, Sable, made a full confession to me yesterday afternoon."

"Sable is not my partner. He never was."

"Sable tells a different story, and he tells it very well. Don't get the idea that he's covering up for you. He'll be turning state's witness on the conspiracy charge to help him with the murder charge."

"Are you trying to tell me that Sable murdered Culligan?"

"It's hardly news to you, is it? You sat on the information while we were wasting weeks on a bum lead."

The girl stepped between us. "Please. You don't understand the situation. John had his suspicions of Mr. Sable, it's true, but he wasn't in any position to go to the police with them. He was under suspicion himself. Won't you put that awful gun away, Mr. Archer? Give John a chance to explain?"

Her blind faith in him made me angry. "His name isn't John. He's Theo Fredericks, a local boy who left Pitt some years ago after knifing his father."

"The Fredericks person is not his father."

"I have his mother's word for it."

"She's lying," the boy said.

"Everybody's lying but you, eh? Sable says you're a phony, and he ought to know."

"I let him think it. The fact is, when Sable first approached me I didn't know who I was. I went into the deal he offered me partly in the hope of finding out."

"Money had nothing to do with it?"

"There's more than money to a man's inheritance. Above everything else, I wanted to be sure of my identity."

"And now you are?"

"Now I am. I'm Anthony Galton's son."

"When did this fortunate revelation strike you?"

"You don't want a serious answer, but I'll give you one anyway. It grew on me gradually. I think it began when Gabe Lindsay saw something in me I didn't know was there. And then Dr. Dineen recognized me as my father's son. When my grandmother accepted me, too, I thought it must be true. I didn't know it was true until these last few days."

"What happened in the last few days?"

"Sheila believed me. I told her everything, my whole life, and she believed me."

He glanced at her, almost shyly. She reached for his hand. I began to feel like an intruder in their room. Perhaps he sensed this shift in the moral balance, because he began to talk about himself in a deeper, quieter tone:

"Actually, it goes back much further. I suspected the truth about myself, or part of it, when I was a little kid. Nelson Fredericks never treated me as if I belonged to him. He used to beat me with a belt-buckle. He never gave me a kind word. I knew he couldn't possibly be my father."

"A lot of boys feel like that about their real fathers."

Sheila moved closer to him, in a tender protective movement, pressing his hand unconsciously to her breast. "Please let him tell his story. I know it sounds wild, but it's only as wild as life. John's telling you the honest truth, so far as he knows it."

"Assuming that he is, how far does he know it? Some very earnest people have fantastic ideas about who they are and what they've got coming to them."

I expected him to flare up again. He surprised me by saying: "I know, it's what I was scared of, that I was hipped on the subject. I really used to be hipped when I was a boy. I imagined I was the prince in the poorhouse, and so on. My mother encouraged me. She used to dress me up in velvet suits and tell me I was different from the other kids.

"Even before that, though, long before, she had a story that she used to tell me. She was a young woman then. I remember her face was thin, and her hair hadn't turned gray. I was only a toddler, and I used to think it was a fairy-tale. I realize now it was a story about myself. She wanted me to know about myself, but she was afraid to come right out with it.

"She said that I was a king's son, and we used to live in a palace in the sun. But the young king died and the bogeyman stole us away to the caves of ice where nothing was nice. She made a sort of rhyme of it. And she showed me a gold ring with a little red stone set in it that the king had left her for a remembrance."

He gave me a curious questioning look. Our eyes met solidly for the first time. I think the reality formed between us then.

"A ruby?" I said.

"It must have been. I talked to a woman named Matheson yesterday in Redwood City. You know her, don't you, and you've heard her story? It made sense of some of the things that had puzzled me, and it confirmed what Culligan told me long before. He said that my stepfather was an ex-convict whose real name was Fred Nelson. He had taken my mother out of a place called the Red Horse Inn and made her his—lover. She married my father after Nelson was sent to prison. But he escaped, and found them, and murdered my father." His voice had sunk almost out of hearing.

"When did Culligan tell you this?"

"The day I ran away with him. He'd just had a fight with Fredericks about his board bill. I listened to it from the cellar stairs. They were always fighting. Fredericks was older than Culligan, but he gave him an awful lacing, worse than usual, and left him unconscious on the kitchen floor. I poured water on Culligan's face and brought him to. It was then he told me that Fredericks killed my father. I got a butcher knife out of the drawer, and hid it upstairs in my room. When Fredericks tried to lock me in, I stabbed him in the guts.

"I thought I'd killed him. By the time I saw a newspaper and found out that I hadn't, I was across the border. I rode through the Detroit tunnel under the burlaps in an empty truck-trailer. The border police didn't find me, but they caught Culligan. I didn't see him again until last winter. Then he claimed that he'd been lying to me. He said that Fredericks had nothing to do with my father's death, that he'd simply blamed Fredericks to get back at him, through me.

"You can see why I decided to play along with Culligan and his scheme. I didn't know which of his stories was true, or if the truth was something else again. I even suspected that Culligan had killed my father himself. How else would he know about the murder?"

"He was involved in it," I said. "It's why he changed his story when he wanted to use you again. It's also the reason he couldn't admit to other people, even Sable, that he knew who you were."

"How was he involved?"

How wasn't he? I thought. His life ran through the case like a dirty piece of cord. He had marked Anthony Galton for the ax and Anthony Galton's murderer for the knife. He had helped a half-sane woman to lose her money, then sold her husband a half-sane dream of wealth. Which brought him to the ironic day when his half-realities came together in a final reality, and Gordon Sable killed him to preserve a lie.

"I don't understand," John said. "What did Culligan have to do with my father's death?"

"Apparently he was the finger man. Have you talked to your mother about the circumstances of the killing? She was probably a witness."

"She was more than that." The words almost strangled him.

Sheila turned to him anxiously. "John?" she said. "Johnny?"

He made no response to her. His gaze was dark and inward:

"Even last night she was lying to me, trying to pretend that I was Fredericks's son, that I never had another father. She's stolen half my life away already. Isn't she satisfied?"

"You haven't seen Fredericks?"

"Fredericks has gone away, she wouldn't tell me where. But I'll find him."

"He can't be far. He was at home an hour ago."

"Damn you! Why didn't you say so?"

"I just did. I'm wondering now if I made a mistake."

John got the message. He didn't speak again until we were a few blocks from his mother's house. Then he turned in the seat and said across Sheila:

"Don't worry about me. There's been enough death and violence. I don't want any more of it."

Along the riverside street the rooftops thrust their dark angles up against a whitening sky. I watched the boy as he got out of the car. His face was pinched and pale as a revenant's. Sheila held his arm, slowing his abrupt movements.

I knocked on the front door. After a long minute, the door was unlocked from the inside. Mrs. Fredericks peered out at us.

"Yes? What now?"

John brushed past me, and faced her on the threshold:

"Where is he?"

"He went away."

"You're a liar. You've lied to me all your life." His voice broke, and then resumed on a different, higher note. "You knew he killed my father, you probably helped him. I know you helped him to hush it up. You left the country with him, changed your name when he did."

"I'm not denying that much," she said levelly.

His whole body heaved as if in nausea. He called her an ugly name. In spite of his promise to me, he was on the thin edge of violence. I laid one hand on his shoulder, heavily:

"Don't be too hard on your mother. Even the law admits mitigation, when a woman is dominated or threatened by a man."

"But that isn't the case. She's still trying to protect him."

"Am I?" the woman said. "Protect him from what?"

"From punishment for murder."

She shook her head solemnly. "It's too late for that, son. Fredericks has took his punishment. He said he would rather have digger get him than go back behind walls. Fredericks hung himself, and I didn't try to argue him out of doing it."

We found him in a back room on the second floor. He was on an old brass bed, in a half-sitting position. A piece of heavy electrical cord was tied to the head of the bed and wrapped several times around his neck. The free end of the cord was clenched in his right hand. There was no doubt that he had been his own executioner.

"Get Sheila out of here," I said to John.

She stood close to him. "I'm all right. I'm not afraid."

Mrs. Fredericks came into the doorway, heavy and panting. She looked at her son with her head up:

"This is the end of it. I told him it was him or you, and which it was going to be. I couldn't go on lying for him, and let you get arrested instead of him."

He faced her, still the accuser. "Why did you lie for so long? You stayed with him after he killed my father."

"You got no call to judge me for doing that. It was to save your life that I married him. I saw him cut off your daddy's head with an ax, fill it with stones, and chunk it in the sea. He said that if I ever told a living soul, that he would kill you, too. You were just a tiny baby, but that wouldn't of stopped him. He held up the bloody ax over your crib and made me swear to marry him and keep my lips shut forever. Which I have done until now."

"Did you have to spend the rest of your life with him?"

"That was my choice," she said. "For sixteen years I stood between you and him. Then you ran away and left me alone with him. I had nobody else left in my life excepting him. Do you understand what it's like to have nobody at all, son?"

He tried to speak, to rise to the word, but the gorgon past held him frozen.

"All I ever wanted in my life," she said, "was a husband and a family and a place I could call my own."

Sheila made an impulsive movement toward her. "You have us."

"Aw, no. You don't want me in your life. We might as well be honest about it. The less you see of me, the better you'll like it. Too much water flowed under the bridge. I don't blame my son for hating me."

"I don't hate you," John said. "I'm sorry for you, Mother. And I'm sorry for what I said."

"You and who else is sorry?" she said roughly. "You and who else?"

He put his arm around her, awkwardly, trying to comfort her. But she was past comforting, perhaps beyond sorrow, too. Whatever she felt was masked by unfeeling layers of flesh. The stiff black silk she was wearing curved over her breast like armor.

"Don't bother about me. Just take good care of your girl."

Somewhere outside, a single bird raised its voice for a few notes, then fell into abashed silence. I went to the window. The river was white. The trees and buildings on its banks were resuming their colors and shapes. A light went on in one of the other houses. As if at this human signal, the bird raised its voice again.

Sheila said: "Listen."

John turned his head to listen. Even the dead man seemed to be listening.

OTHER WRITINGS

Letter to Alfred A. Knopf

2136 Cliff Drive
Santa Barbara, Calif.
August 28, 1952

Dear Alfred:

Thank you for your letter, and for the generous contract which I signed the other day. *The Convenient Corpse* seems to me to be a fairly good title, except that it may be a little too flip for the book and so far as relevance is concerned, "The Inconvenient Corpse" would probably be more suitable. What do you think of "The Guilty Ones," which I like better? Is it too lugubrious? If *The Convenient Corpse* seems best to you, I have no objections to its use.

I'll bear in mind the criticism of my work which you passed on to me, as I write the new book. I'm afraid I can't promise anything very definite, because I'm a good enough writer to be under the necessity of calling the shots as I see them. As you know from your own unmatched experience with writers, even a moderately good writer fails to follow his own lights at the risk of losing his personal vision and his capacity for growth. I realize that forcing any particular preordained approach on me is the furthest thing from your mind—I remember your saying in Bel Air that you didn't think I was the kind of writer who should be told what to write—but I'm not at all sure that that would be true of Pocket Books. Their suggestion that an expert might write the book, or revise it, startled me a little. It might work for a book, but it can't work for a writer. So many Hollywood and magazine writers lose their morale quickly and their talent eventually, because they permit their standards to be displaced outside of their own judgment. Personal judgment however imperfect and a sense of freedom however illusory are the source of creative energy. So I feel I must do any rewriting that has to be done.

Do you think the book needs rewriting? It's already had a lot. While I'm perfectly willing to rewrite places where the action drags or characters fade out—just show me the places—and to concede that any of my books is improvable, I think that perhaps a main difficulty arises from Pocket Books' assumption that this is a hardboiled novel, which it is not, and more specifically that this is an imitation of Chandler which fails for some reason to come off. I must confess I was pleased with the characterization—the characters are more human than in anything I've done, closer to life—and more than pleased with the plot. Plot is important to me. I try to make my plots carry meaning, and this meaning such as it is determines and controls the movement of the story. I know I have a tendency to subordinate individual scenes to the overall intention, to make the book the unit of effect. Perhaps this needs some correction, without going to the opposite extreme. This opposite extreme is represented by Chandler, one of my masters with whose theory and practice I am in growing disagreement. For him any old plot will do—most of his plots depend on the tired and essentially meaningless device of blackmail—and he has stated that a good plot is one that makes for good scenes. So far from taking him as the last word and model in my field, which Pocket Books thinks I should do, it would seem—I am interested in doing things in the mystery which Chandler didn't do, and probably couldn't.

His subject is the evilness of evil, his most characteristic achievement the short vivid scene of conflict between (conventional) evil and (what he takes to be) good. With all due respect for the power of these scenes and the remarkable intensity of his vision, I can't accept Chandler's vision of good and evil. It is conventional to the point of occasional old-maidishness, anti-human to the point of frequent sadism (Chandler hates all women and most men, reserving only lovable oldsters, boys and Marlowe for his affection), and the mind behind it, for all its enviable imaginative force, is uncultivated and second-rate. At least it strikes my mind that way. I owe a lot to Chandler (and more to Hammett), but it would be simple self-stultification for me to take him as the last word in the mystery. My literary range greatly exceeds his, and my approach to writing will not wear out so fast.

My subject is something like this: human error, and the ambivalence of motive. My interest is the exploration of lives. If my stories lack a powerful contrast between good and evil, as

Pocket Books points out, it isn't mere inadvertence. I don't see things that way, and haven't since *Blue City*. Even in *Blue City*, you may recall, the victim of the murder and the father of the "hero" was also the source of corruption in the city. Because my theme is exploration, I employ a more open and I think subtler set of values than is usual; its background is sociological and psychological rather than theological. I chose the hardboiled convention in the first place because it seemed to offer both a market, and a structure with which almost anything could be done, a technique both difficult and free, adapted to my subject matter, and a field in which I might hope to combine the "popular" and the "sensitive" hero, and forge a style combining flexibility, literacy and depth with the solidity and eloquence of the American-colorful-colloquial. These have been my literary aims; my hope is to write "popular" novels which will not be inferior to "serious" novels. I have barely started.

In spite of the Spillane phenomenon which has nothing much to do with the mystery but which probably has unsettled paperback publishers' notions of what a mystery is, I think the future of the mystery is in the hands of a few good writers like myself. The old-line hardboiled novel with its many guns and fornications and fisticuffs has been ruined by its practitioners, including the later Chandler. Spillane pulled the plug. I have no intention of plunging after it down the drain. My new book, though it is an offspring or variant of the hardboiled form, is a stage in my emergence from that form and a conscious step towards the popular novel I envisage. That very tone to which Pocket Books objects, and which I have tried to make literate without being forbidding, human without being smeary, and let us face it adult, is what distinguishes it from the run-of-the-gin-mill mystery. It isn't as if I were out on a limb by myself. The critics and my colleagues know what I am doing. Some of my fellow mystery-writers, and they are the real experts, think that my last two books are the best that have ever been done in the tradition that Hammett started. While I don't think myself that I possess Hammett's genius—and that's a hard thing for me to admit—I do think the talent I have is flexible and durable. My rather disproportionate (for a fiction writer) training in literary history and criticism which tended to make me a slow and diffident starter also operates to keep me going and I think improving. I do know I can write a sample of the ordinary hardboiled mystery with my eyes closed. But preferring as I do to keep my eyes open, I've spent several years developing it into a form of my own, which nobody can imitate. When the tough school dies its inevitable death I expect to be going strong, twenty or thirty books from now. As I see it, my hope of real success as a writer, both artistic and commercial, resides in developing my own point of view and narrative approach to the limit. If I overvalue my point of view and the work I do from it, that is the defect of the virtue of believing in what I am doing. I believe in the present book, though it's not by any means as good a book as I am sure I can write.

I agree with Pocket Books that *The Convenient Corpse* is lacking in some of the more obvious forms of excitement. The murders are few and offstage: the plot required them to be. There are no gangsters, and not much use of the overused device of the man coming through a doorway with a gun. The main villains are a trapped housewife and an old psychoneurotic, whom I try to present in the penumbra of their entire lives, so far as the pace permits. Compared with Chandler's brilliant phantasmagoria, this world is a little pale. But so is the real world, with which I would rather have my world compared than with Chandler's world. I don't quite see the point of the Chandler comparison, since this is not an imitation of Chandler. I like it better than a Chandler book, and think I can point out various ways in which it is superior to a Chandler book. If the characters are less striking, they are more lifelike, and the reader gets to know them better. There is none, or very little, of Chandler's glamour-stricken phoniness. None of my scenes, so far as I'm competent to judge, have been written before, and some of them have depth and moral excitement. None of my characters are familiar. They are freshly conceived from a point of view which rejects the black and white classification. The writing itself is fresh, and the imagery more integral to the narrative with every book I write. The plot makes sense, and could actually have happened. I could go on for pages. I already have.

I'm interested in creating moral excitement, which I think will be the successor to physical excitement. The success of a radio and television program like *Dragnet* tends to confirm the thought, and the related one that the popular audience is working its way gradually through a delayed adolescence. All this, which may strike you as an exaggerated and even swell-headed response to a just criticism, doesn't mean that I'm not eager to give my books every possible saleable quality consistent with the overall quality I'm aiming at. If anyone in your office or Pocket Books' has ideas on how to give this story more power or speed or vividness, I'll go to work on them and it. I did feel, however, that there was something to be said counter to the criticism you quoted, and to the assumption that I'm an unconsciously unsuccessful disciple of the Chandler school. I've written some descriptive copy, as you suggested, which I enclose and which may help to clarify my idea of the book. (My typist accidentally got the dedication onto the same page.) Make whatever use of it you like.

The gout seems to be licked, and we're getting ready to go up into the Sierra for a short vacation. I see by your *New Yorker* letter that you were out in Aspen last month. Thank you, by the way, for the kind mention of *Ivory Grin*.

Sincerely,

Ken

The Writer As Detective Hero

A PRODUCER who last year was toying with the idea of making a television series featuring my private detective Lew Archer asked me over lunch at Perino's if Archer was based on any actual person. "Yes," I said. "Myself." He gave me a semi-pitying Hollywood look. I tried to explain that while I had known some excellent detectives and watched them work, Archer was created from the inside out. I wasn't Archer, exactly, but Archer was me.

The conversation went downhill from there, as if I had made a damaging admission. But I believe most detective-story writers would give the same answer. A close paternal or fraternal relationship between writer and detective is a marked peculiarity of the form. Throughout its history, from Poe to Chandler and beyond, the detective hero has represented his creator and carried his values into action in society.

Poe, who invented the modern detective story, and his detective Dupin, are good examples. Poe's was a first-rate but guilt-haunted mind painfully at odds with the realities of pre-Civil-War America. Dupin is a declassed aristocrat, as Poe's heroes tend to be, an obvious equivalent for the artist-intellectual who has lost his place in society and his foothold in tradition. Dupin has no social life, only one friend. He is set apart from other people by his superiority of mind.

In his creation of Dupin, Poe was surely compensating for his failure to become what his extraordinary mental powers seemed to fit him for. He had dreamed of an intellectual hierarchy governing the cultural life of the nation, himself at its head. Dupin's outwitting of an unscrupulous politician in "The Purloined Letter," his "solution" of an actual New York case in "Marie Roget," his repeated trumping of the cards held by the Prefect of Police, are Poe's vicarious demonstrations of superiority to an indifferent society and its officials.

Of course Poe's detective stories gave the writer, and give the reader, something deeper than such obvious satisfactions. He devised them as a means of exorcising or controlling guilt and horror. The late William Carlos Williams, in a profound essay, related Poe's sense of guilt and horror to the terrible aware-ness of a hyper-conscious man standing naked and shivering on a new continent. The guilt was doubled by Poe's anguished insight into the unconscious mind. It had to be controlled by some rational pattern, and the detective story, "the tale of ratio-cination," provided such a pattern.

The tale of the bloody murders in the Rue Morgue, Poe's first detective story (1841), is a very hymn to analytic reason intended, as Poe wrote later, "to depict some very remarkable features in the mental character of my friend, the Chevalier C. Auguste Dupin." Dupin clearly represents the reason, which was Poe's mainstay against the nightmare forces of the mind. These latter are acted out by the murderous ape: "Gnashing its teeth, and flashing fire from its eyes, it flew upon the body of the girl and embedded its fearful talons in her throat, retaining its grasp until she expired."

Dupin's reason masters the ape and explains the inexplicable—the wrecked apartment behind the locked door, the corpse of a young woman thrust up the chimney—but not without leav-ing a residue of horror. The nightmare can't quite be explained away, and persists in the teeth of reason. An unstable balance between reason and more primitive human qualities is charac-teristic of the detective story. For both writer and reader it is an imaginative arena where such conflicts can be worked out safely, under artistic controls.

The first detective story has other archetypal features, par-ticularly in the way it is told. The "I" who narrates it is not the detective Dupin. The splitting of the protagonist into a narrator and a detective has certain advantages: it helps to eliminate the inessential, and to postpone the solution. More important, the author can present his self-hero, the detective, without undue embarrassment, and can handle dangerous emotional material at two or more removes from himself, as Poe does in "Rue Morgue."

The disadvantages of the split protagonist emerge more clearly in the saga of Dupin's successor Sherlock Holmes. One projection of the author, the narrator, is made to assume a pos-ture of rather blind admiration before another projection of the author, the detective hero, and the reader is invited to share Dr. Watson's adoration of the great man. An element of narcissistic fantasy, impatient with the limits of the self, seems to be built into this traditional form of the detective story.

I'm not forgetting that Holmes' *modus operandi* was based on that of an actual man, Conan Doyle's friend and teacher, Dr. Joseph Bell. Although his "science" usually boils down to careful observation, which was Dr. Bell's forte, Holmes is very much the scientific criminologist. This hero of scientism may be in fact the dominant culture hero of our technological society.

Though Holmes is a physical scientist specializing in chemistry and anatomy, and Dupin went in for literary and psychological analysis, Holmes can easily be recognized as Dupin's direct descendant. His most conspicuous feature, his ability to read thoughts on the basis of associative clues, is a direct borrowing from Dupin. And like Dupin, he is a projection of the author, who at the time of Holmes' creation was a not very busy young doctor. According to his son Adrian, Conan Doyle admitted when he was dying: "If anyone is Sherlock Holmes, then I confess it is myself."

Holmes had other ancestors and collateral relations which reinforce the idea that he was a portrait of the artist as a great detective. His drugs, his secrecy and solitude, his moods of depression (which he shared with Dupin) are earmarks of the Romantic rebel then and now. Behind Holmes lurk the figures of nineteenth-century poets, Byron certainly, probably Baudelaire, who translated Poe and pressed Poe's guilty knowledge to new limits. I once made a case for the theory (and Anthony Boucher didn't disagree) that much of the modern development of the detective story stems from Baudelaire, his "dandyism" and his vision of the city as inferno. Conan Doyle's London, which influenced Eliot's "Wasteland," has something of this quality.

But Holmes' Romantic excesses aren't central to his character. His Baudelairean spleen and drug addiction are merely the idiosyncrasies of genius. Holmes is given the best of both worlds, and remains an English gentleman, accepted on the highest social levels. Permeating the thought and language of Conan Doyle's stories is an air of blithe satisfaction with a social system based on privilege.

This obvious characteristic is worth mentioning because it was frozen into one branch of the form. Nostalgia for a privileged society accounts for one of the prime attractions of the traditional English detective story and its innumerable American counterparts. Neither wars nor the dissolution of governments and societies interrupt that long weekend in the country house which is often, with more or less unconscious symbolism, cut off by a failure in communications from the outside world.

The contemporary world is the special province of the American hardboiled detective story. Dashiell Hammett, Raymond Chandler, and the other writers for *Black Mask* who developed it, were in conscious reaction against the Anglo-American school which, in the work of S. S. Van Dine for example, had lost contact with contemporary life and language. Chandler's dedication, to the editor of *Black Mask*, of a collection of his early stories (1944), describes the kind of fiction they had been trying to supplant: "For Joseph Thompson Shaw with affection and respect, and in memory of the time when we were trying to get murder away from the upper classes, the weekend house party and the vicar's rose-garden, and back to the people who are really good at it." While Chandler's novels swarm with plutocrats as well as criminals, and even with what pass in Southern California for aristocrats, the *Black Mask* revolution was a real one. From it emerged a new kind of detective hero, the classless, restless man of American democracy, who spoke the language of the street.

Hammett, who created the most powerful of these new heroes in Sam Spade, had been a private detective and knew the corrupt inner workings of American cities. But Sam Spade was a less obvious projection of Hammett than detective heroes usually are of their authors. Hammett had got his early romanticism under strict ironic control. He could see Spade from outside, without affection, perhaps with some bleak compassion. In this as in other respects Spade marks a sharp break with the Holmes tradition. He possesses the virtues and follows the code of a frontier male. Thrust for his sins into the urban inferno, he pits his courage and cunning against its denizens, plays for the highest stakes available, love and money, and loses nearly everything in the end. His lover is guilty of murder; his narrow, bitter code forces Spade to turn her over to the police. The Maltese falcon has been stripped of jewels.

Perhaps the stakes and implied losses are higher than I have suggested. The worthless falcon may symbolize a lost tradition, the great cultures of the Mediterranean past which have become inaccessible to Spade and his generation. Perhaps the bird stands for the Holy Ghost itself, or for its absence.

The ferocious intensity of the work, the rigorous spelling-out of Sam Spade's deprivation of his full human heritage, seem to me to make his story tragedy, if there is such a thing as dead-pan tragedy. Hammett was the first American writer to use the detective-story for the purposes of a major novelist, to present a vision, blazing if disenchanted, of our lives. Sam Spade was the product and reflection of a mind which was not at home in Zion, or in Zenith.

Chandler's vision is disenchanted, too, but in spite of its hallucinated brilliance of detail it lacks the tragic unity of Hammett's. In his essay on "The Simple Art of Murder," an excitingly written piece of not very illuminating criticism, Chandler offers a prescription for the detective hero which suggests a central weakness in his vision:

> In everything that can be called art there is a quality of redemption. . . . But down these mean streets a man must go who is not himself mean, who is neither tarnished nor afraid. . . . The detective in this kind of story must be such a man. He is the hero, he is everything. . . . He must be the best man in his world and a good enough man for any world.

While there may be "a quality of redemption" in a good novel, it belongs to the whole work and is not the private property of one of the characters. No hero of serious fiction could act within a moral straitjacket requiring him to be consistently virtuous and unafraid. Sam Spade was submerged and struggling in tragic life. The detective-as-redeemer is a backward step in the direction of sentimental romance, and an over-simplified world of good guys and bad guys. The people of Chandler's early novels, though they include chivalrous gangsters and gangsters' molls with hearts of gold, are divided into two groups by an angry puritanical morality. The goats are usually separated from the sheep by sexual promiscuity or perversion. Such a strong and overt moralistic bias actually interferes with the broader moral effects a novelist aims at.

Fortunately in the writing of his books Chandler toned down his Watsonian enthusiasm for his detective's moral superiority. The detective Marlowe, who tells his own stories in the first person, and sometimes admits to being afraid, has a self-deflating wit which takes the curse off his knight-errantry:

> I wasn't wearing a gun . . . I doubted if it would do me any good. The big man would probably take it away from me and eat it. (*Farewell, My Lovely*, 1940)

The Chandler-Marlowe prose is a highly charged blend of laconic wit and imagistic poetry set to breakneck rhythms. Its strong colloquial vein reaffirms the fact that the *Black Mask* revolution was a revolution in language as well as subject matter. It is worth noticing that H. L. Mencken, the great lexicographer of our vernacular, was an early editor of *Black Mask*. His protegé James M. Cain once said that his discovery of the western roughneck made it possible for him to write fiction. Marlowe and his predecessors performed a similar function for Chandler, whose English education put a special edge on his passion for our new language, and a special edge on his feelings against privilege. Socially mobile and essentially classless (he went to college but has a working-class bias), Marlowe liberated his author's imagination into an overheard democratic prose which is one of the most effective narrative instruments in our recent literature.

Under the obligatory "tough" surface of the writing, Marlowe is interestingly different from the standard hardboiled hero who came out of *Black Mask*. Chandler's novels focus in his hero's sensibility, and could almost be described as novels of sensibility. Their constant theme is big-city loneliness, and the wry pain of a sensitive man coping with the roughest elements of a corrupt society.

It is Marlowe's doubleness that makes him interesting: the hard-boiled mask half-concealing Chandler's poetic and satiric mind. Part of our pleasure derives from the interplay between the mind of Chandler and the voice of Marlowe. The recognized difference between them is part of the dynamics of the narrative, setting up bipolar tensions in the prose. The marvellous opening paragraph of *The Big Sleep* (1939) will illustrate some of this:

> It was about eleven o'clock in the morning, mid October, with the sun not shining and a look of hard wet rain in the clearness of the foothills. I was wearing my powder-blue suit, with dark blue shirt, tie and display handkerchief, black brogues, black wool socks with dark blue clocks on them. I was neat, clean, shaved and sober, and I didn't care who knew it. I was everything the well-dressed private detective ought to be. I was calling on four million dollars.

Marlowe is making fun of himself, and of Chandler in the rôle of brash young detective. There is pathos, too, in the idea that a man who can write like a fallen angel should be a mere private eye; and Socratic irony. The gifted writer conceals himself behind Marlowe's cheerful mindlessness. At the same time the retiring, middle-aged, scholarly author acquires a durable mask, forever 38, which allows him to face the dangers of society high and low.

Chandler's conception of Marlowe, and his relationship with his character, deepened as his mind penetrated the romantic fantasy, and the overbright self-consciousness, that limited his vision. At the end of *The Long Goodbye* (1953) there is a significant confrontation between Marlowe and a friend who had betrayed him and apparently gone homosexual. In place of the righteous anger which Marlowe would have indulged in in one of the earlier novels he now feels grief and disquiet, as if the confrontation might be with a part of himself.

The friend, the ex-friend, tries to explain his moral breakdown: "I was in the commandos, bud. They don't take you if you're just a piece of fluff. I got badly hurt and it wasn't any fun with those Nazi doctors. It did something to me." This is all we are told. At the roaring heart of Chandler's maze there is a horror which even at the end of his least evasive novel remains unspeakable. Whatever its hidden meaning, this scene was written by a man of tender and romantic sensibility who had been injured. Chandler used Marlowe to shield while half-expressing his sensibility, and to act out the mild paranoia which often goes with this kind of sensibility and its private hurts, and which seems to be virtually endemic among contemporary writers.

I can make this judgment with some assurance because it applies with a vengeance to some of my earlier books, particularly *Blue City* (1947). A decade later, in *The Doomsters*, I made my detective Archer criticize himself as "a slightly earthbound Tarzan in a slightly paranoid jungle." This novel marked a fairly clean break with the Chandler tradition, which it had taken me some years to digest, and freed me to make my own approach to the crimes and sorrows of life.

I learned a great deal from Chandler—any writer can—but there had always been basic differences between us. One was in our attitude to plot. Chandler described a good plot as one that made for good scenes, as if the parts were greater than the whole. I see plot as a vehicle of meaning. It should be as complex as contemporary life, but balanced enough to say true things about it. The surprise with which a detective novel concludes should set up tragic vibrations which run backward through the entire structure. Which means that the structure must be single, and *intended*.

Another difference between Chandler and me is in our use of language. My narrator Archer's wider and less rigidly stylized range of expression, at least in more recent novels, is related to a central difference between him and Marlowe. Marlowe's voice is limited by his rôle as the hardboiled hero. He must speak within his limits as a character, and these limits are quite narrowly conceived. Chandler tried to relax them in *The Long Goodbye*, but he was old and the language failed to respond. He was trapped like the late Hemingway in an unnecessarily limiting idea of self, hero, and language.

I could never write of Archer: "He is the hero, he is everything." It is true that his actions carry the story, his comments on it reflect my attitudes (but deeper attitudes remain implicit), and Archer or a narrator like him is indispensable to the kind of books I write. But he is not their emotional center. And in spite of what I said at the beginning, Archer has developed away from his early status as a fantasy projection of myself and my personal needs. Cool, I think, is the word for our mature relationship. Archer himself has what New Englanders call "weaned affections."

An author's heavy emotional investment in a narrator-hero can get in the way of the story and blur its meanings, as some of Chandler's books demonstrate. A less encumbered narrator permits greater flexibility, and fidelity to the intricate truths of life. I don't have to celebrate Archer's physical or sexual prowess, or work at making him consistently funny and charming. He can be self-forgetful, almost transparent at times, and concentrate as good detectives (and good writers) do, on the people whose problems he is investigating. These other people are for me the main thing: they are often more intimately related to me and my life than Lew Archer is. He is the obvious self-projection which holds the eye (my eye as well as the reader's) while more secret selves creep out of the woodwork behind the locked door. Remember how the reassuring presence of Dupin permitted Poe's mind to face the nightmare of the homicidal ape and the two dead women.

Archer is a hero who sometimes verges on being an anti-hero. While he is a man of action, his actions are largely directed to putting together the stories of other people's lives and discovering their significance. He is less a doer than a questioner, a consciousness in which the meanings of other lives emerge. This gradually developed conception of the detective hero as the mind of the novel is not wholly new, but it is probably my main contribution to this special branch of fiction. Some such refinement of the conception of the detective hero was needed to bring this kind of novel closer to the purpose and range of the mainstream novel.

It may be that internal realism, a quality of mind, is one of the most convincing attributes a character can have. Policemen and lawyers have surprised me with the opinion that Archer is quite true to life. The two best private detectives I personally know resemble him in their internal qualities: their intelligent humaneness, an interest in other people transcending their interest in themselves, and a toughness of mind which enables them to face human weaknesses, including their own, with open eyes. Both of them dearly love to tell a story.

1965

Archer in Hollywood

THE WAR had a great deal to do with my becoming a professional writer. It plucked me out of graduate school, gave me a rough, short course in American geography and society, and sent me back to my native California. It provided me with the subject matter for my first two books, which were spy novels. In a way it gave me matter for all my books. Crime, as *The Moving Target* seems to imply, is often war continued by other means.

My Navy discharge papers (March, 1946) said hopefully that my first choice for civilian employment was "freelance writer in California." We lived that year in a four-room stucco house on Bath Street in Santa Barbara. It had orange trees in the back yard but no central heating. My wife and I used to sit and write in our overcoats. It was a lucky, slightly chilly year and by the end of it I had written two books, *Blue City* and *The Three Roads*, which Alfred Knopf liked well enough to publish.

The next year wasn't so lucky. I felt it was now my duty to write an autobiographical novel about my depressing childhood in Canada. I tried, and got badly bogged down in sloppy feelings and groping prose. I began to doubt my vocation as a writer and my mind turned back toward the comparative safety of graduate school.

I was in trouble, and Lew Archer got me out of it. I resembled one of his clients in needing a character to front for me. Like many other writers—the most extreme example is a man I knew who wrote fiction from the point of view of his pet turtle—I couldn't work directly with my own experiences and feelings. A narrator had to be interposed, like protective lead, between me and the radioactive material.

Raymond Chandler had recently shown, in a brilliant series of novels, how a private detective could be used to block off overpersonal excitements while getting on with the story. Archer in his early days, though he was named for Sam Spade's partner, was patterned on Chandler's Marlowe. Chandler's Anglo-American background and my Canadian-American one gave our detectives a common quality: the fresh suspicious eye of a semi-outsider who is fascinated but not completely taken in by the customs of the natives.

We shared, for related reasons, a powerful interest in the American colloquial language. Democracy is as much a language as it is a place. If a man has suffered (as we both had) under a society of privilege, the American vernacular can serve him as a kind of passport to freedom and equality. Marlowe and Archer can go anywhere, at least once, and talk to anybody. Their rough-and-ready brand of democracy is still peculiarly rampant on this side of the Sierra Nevada.

If California is a state of mind, Hollywood is where you take its temperature. There is a peculiar sense in which this city existing mainly on film and tape is our national capital, alas, and not just the capital of California. It's the place where our children learn how and what to dream and where everything happens just before, or just after, it happens to us.

American novelists have a lover's quarrel with Hollywood. We have grown accustomed to losing it. Our finest novelist Scott Fitzgerald felt in his uncertain last years that the art of film was the master art that had superseded the novel. The hero of his last, unfinished novel was a movie producer.

My lover's quarrel with Hollywood began at the age of seven when, on successive Saturday afternoons in my uncle's theater, I formed a precocious attachment to Pearl White. The quarrel and the attachment have since taken more devious forms. One thing that strikes me, over and above a recurrent fascination with Hollywood, is my use of film techniques. *The Moving Target* in particular is a story clearly aspiring to be a movie. It was no accident that when Warner Brothers made it into one last year they were able to follow the story virtually scene by scene.

I remember how I labored over those scenes, striking them out in heat and then reworking them over and over for more than a year. I was no longer writing at home. My sister-in-law Dorothy Schlagel had an apartment nearby on Sola Street. It was vacant all day while Dorothy was at work, and I wrote there.

By 1950, when I wrote *The Way Some People Die*, Dorothy had moved to a house on the far side of town and I rode over every morning on a motor scooter. The labor I'd put into forming a style in *Target* had begun to pay off. Rummaging through old papers the other day, I found the opening paragraph of *Way* written out in a spiral notebook, for the first and final time, just as it was to be printed.

Some of my colleagues—Mike Avallone is one—think that *Way* is the best of my twenty books. I hope it isn't. If it were it would mean I'd been over the hill for sixteen or seventeen years, which is the unthinkable dread of every writer past the age of forty.

The Barbarous Coast was written when I was forty. Though I've always been a slow developer, by that time I was getting myself and my form under more personal control. It was my largest book so far, in both social range and moral complexity. In it I was learning to get rid of the protective wall between my mind and the perilous stuff of my own life.

I'm not and never was George Wall, the angry young Canadian lost in Hollywood. But I once lived, as George did, on Spadina Avenue in Toronto. Like the three young divers in the story, I was a tower diver before my bones got brittle. And I once went to a party not wholly unlike the long party in the book.

We writers, as we work our way deeper into our craft, learn to drop more and more personal clues. Like burglars who secretly wish to be caught, we leave our fingerprints on the broken locks, our voiceprints in the bugged rooms, our footprints in the wet concrete and the blowing sand.

1967

Writing The Galton Case

for Donald Davie

DETECTIVE STORY writers are often asked why we devote our talents to working in a mere popular convention. One answer is that there may be more to our use of the convention than meets the eye. I tried to show in an earlier piece how the literary detective has provided writers since Poe with a disguise, a kind of welder's mask enabling us to handle dangerously hot material.

One night in his fifth year when we were alone in my house, my grandson Jimmie staged a performance which demonstrated the uses of disguise. His main idea seemed to be to express and discharge his guilts and fears, particularly his overriding fear that his absent parents might punish his (imperceptible) moral imperfections by never coming back to him. Perhaps he had overheard and been alarmed by the name of the movie they were attending, *Divorce American Style*.

Jimmie's stage was the raised hearth in the kitchen, his only prop a towel. He climbed up on the hearth and hid himself behind the back of an armchair. "Grandpa, what do you see?"

"Nothing."

He put the towel in view. "What do you see now?"

"Your towel."

He withdrew the towel. There was a silence. "What am I doing with my towel?"

I guessed that he was doing something "wrong," and that he wanted me to suspend judgment. "You're chewing it," I said boldly.

"No. But I have it in my mouth."

My easy acceptance of his wickedness encouraged him to enact it before my eyes. His head popped up. He was completely hooded with the towel, like a miniature inductee into the Ku Klux Klan.

"I'm a monster," he announced.

Then he threw off the towel, laughing. I sat and watched him for a time while the hooded monster and the laughing boy took alternate possession of the stage. Finally, soothed and purged by his simple but powerful art, Jimmie lay down on the cushioned hearth and went to sleep.

His little show speaks for itself, and needs no Aristotle. But let me point out some connections between his monodrama and my detective fiction. Both draw directly on life and feed back into it. Both are something the artist does for his own sake. But they need an audience to fulfill even their private function, let alone their public ones. Disguise is the imaginative device which permits the work to be both private and public, to half-divulge the writer's crucial secrets while deepening the whole community's sense of its own mysterious life.

I was forty-two when I wrote *The Galton Case*. It had taken me a dozen years and as many books to learn to tell highly personal stories in terms of the convention I had chosen. In the winter of 1957–1958 I was as ready as I would ever be to cope in fiction with some of the more complicated facts of my experience.

Central among these was the fact that I was born in California, in 1915, and was thus an American citizen; but I was raised in Canada by Canadian relatives. After attending university in Canada, I taught high school there for two years. In 1941, in one of the decisive moves of my life, I came back to the United States with my wife and young daughter, and started work on a doctorate in English at the University of Michigan.

It was a legitimate move, but the crossing of the border failed to dispel my dual citizen's sense of illegitimacy, and probably deepened it. This feeling was somewhat relieved by a couple of years in the American Navy. After the war I closed a physical circle, if not an emotional one, by settling in California, in Santa Barbara. At the same time I took up my lifelong tenancy in the bare muffled room of the professional writer where I am sitting now, with my back to the window, writing longhand in a Spiral notebook.

After ten years this writing routine was broken by circumstances which my later books more than adequately suggest. My wife and I lived in the San Francisco area for a year, and then came back to Santa Barbara. We rented a house on a cliff overlooking the sea and lived in it for a winter and a summer.

The Pacific had always lapped like blue eternity at the far edge of my life. The tides of that winter brought in old memories, some of which had drifted for forty years. In 1919, I remembered, my sea-captain father took me on a brief voyage and showed me a shining oceanic world from which I had felt exiled ever since, even during my sea duty in the Navy.

Exile and half-recovery and partial return had been the themes of at least two earlier books, *Blue City* and *The Three Roads* (which got its title from *Oedipus Tyrannus*). I wrote them in 1946, the year I left the Navy and came back to California after my long absence. These novels borrowed some strength from my return to my native state but they missed the uniquely personal heart of the matter—matter which I will call Oedipal, in memory of that Theban who was exiled more than once.

In the red Spiral notebook where I set down my first notes for *The Galton Case*, Oedipus made an appropriately early appearance. His ancient name was surrounded by a profusion of ideas and images which I can see in retrospect were sketching out the groundwork for the novel. A crude early description of its protagonist turns up in two lines of verse about a tragicomic track meet:

> A burst of speed! Half angel and half ape,
> The youthful winner strangles on the tape.

Two lines from another abortive poem—

> Birds in the morning, scattered atomies:
> The voice is one, the voice is not my own.—

were to supply an important detail to the closing page of the completed novel. The morning birds appear there as reminders of a world which encloses and outlasts the merely human.

A third and final example of these multitudinous early notes is one for an unwritten story—"'The Fortieth Year' (downgrade reversed by an act of will)"—which recalls my then recent age and condition and suggests another character in the novel, the poet Chad Bolling. This middle-aged San Francisco poet is at the same time an object of parody and my spokesman for the possibilities of California life. Bolling's involvement in the Galton case takes him back to a sea cliff which he had visited as a young man, and he recovers some of a young man's high spirits:

He flapped his arms some more. "I can fly! I breast the windy currents of the sky. I soar like Icarus toward the sun. The wax melts. I fall from a great height into the sea. Mother Thalassa."

"Mother who?"

"Thalassa, the sea, the Homeric sea. We could build another Athens. I used to think we could do it in San Francisco, build a new city of man on the great hills. A city measured with forgiveness. Oh, well."

Not long after this outburst, Bolling sits down to write his best poem in years, as he says. While I am not a true poet, I am content to have Bolling represent me here. He shows the kite-flying exuberance of a man beginning a lucky piece of work, and speaks unashamedly for the epic impulse which almost all writers of fiction try to serve in some degree.

It was a complex business, getting ready to write even this moderately ambitious novel. Dozens of ideas were going through my mind in search of an organizing principle. The central idea which was to magnetize the others and set them in narrative order was a variation on the Oedipus story. It appears in the red notebook briefly and abruptly, without preparation: "Oedipus angry vs. parents for sending him away into a foreign country."

This simplification of the traditional Oedipus stories, Sopho-clean or Freudian, provides Oedipus with a conscious reason for turning against his father and suggests that the latter's death was probably not unintended. It rereads the myth through the lens of my own experience, and in this it is characteristic of my plots. Many of them are founded on ideas which question or invert or criticize received ideas and which could, if brevity were my forte, be expressed in aphorisms.

Neither plots nor characters can be borrowed, even from Freud or Sophocles. Like the moving chart of an encephalo-graph, the plot of a novel follows the curve of the mind's inten-tion. The central character, and many of the other characters, are in varying degrees versions of the author. Flaubert said that he was Madame Bovary, William Styron that he became Nat Turner. The character holding the pen has to wrestle and con-spire with the one taking shape on paper, extracting a vision of the self from internal darkness—a self dying into fiction as it comes to birth.

My mind had been haunted for years by an imaginary boy whom I recognized as the darker side of my own remembered boyhood. By his sixteenth year he had lived in fifty houses and committed the sin of poverty in each of them. I couldn't think of him without anger and guilt.

This boy became the central figure of *The Galton Case*. His nature and the nature of his story are suggested by some early titles set down in the red notebook: "A Matter of Identity," "The Castle and the Poorhouse," "The Impostor." He is, to put it briefly and rather inexactly, a false claimant, a poorhouse graduate trying to lie his way into the castle.

"The Castle and the Poorhouse," old-fashioned and melodramatic as the phrase is, accurately reflects the vision of the world which my adult imagination inherited from my childhood. It was a world profoundly divided, between the rich and the poor, the upright and the downcast, the sheep and the goats. We goats knew the moral pain inflicted not so much by poverty as by the doctrine, still current, that poverty is always deserved.

In the first winters of the Depression in Ontario, skilled factory workers were willing to put in a full week on piecework for as little as five dollars. The year I left high school, 1932, I was glad to work on a farm for my board alone. Healthy as that year of farm life was, it was a year of waiting without much hope. I shared with many others the dilemma of finding myself to be at the same time two radically different kinds of people, a pauper and a member of the middle class. The dilemma was deepened by my fear that I'd never make it to college, and by my feeling of exile, which my mother had cultivated by teaching me from early childhood that California was my birthplace and natural home.

Such personal dilemmas tend to solidify along traditional philosophic lines. In a puritanical society the poor and fatherless, suffering the quiet punishments of despair, may see themselves as permanently and justifiably damned for crimes they can't remember having committed.

The Platonic split between more worthy and less worthy substances, idea and matter, spirit and flesh, widens under pressure. The crude pseudo-Darwinian dualism of my own phrase, "half angel and half ape," suggests an image of man not only divided but at war.

The Galton Case was an attempt to mend such gross divisions on the imaginative level. It tried to bring the Monster and the Laughing Boy into unity or congruence at least, and build a bridge, or a tunnel, between the poorhouse and the castle.

The castle is represented by the Galton family's Southern California estate, described as if it was literally a medieval demesne: "The majestic iron gates gave a portcullis effect. A serf who was cutting the lawn with a power-mower paused to tug at his forelock as we went by." The old widow who presides over this estate had quarreled with her son Anthony some twenty years ago, and Anthony had walked out and disappeared. Now Mrs. Galton has begun to dream of a reconciliation with her son. Through her attorney she hires the detective Lew Archer to look for him.

My earliest note on Anthony Galton will give an idea of his place in the story. A very young man and a poet, Anthony deliberately declassed himself in an effort, the note says, "to put together 'the castle and the poorhouse.' He changed his name [to John Brown] and became a workingman. . . . Married under his pseudonym, to the common law wife of a man in jail," he was murdered when the other man got out.

About one-third of the way through the novel, the detective Archer is shown an incomplete set of human bones which prove to be Anthony Galton's. At the same time and the same place—not many miles up the coast from the Northern California town where I was born—Archer finds or is found by a boy who represents himself as Anthony's son and calls himself John Brown. The rest of the novel is concerned with this boy and his identity.

Perhaps I have encouraged the reader to identify this boy with me. If so, I must qualify that notion. The connections between a writer and his fiction, which are turning out to be my present subject, are everything but simple. My nature is probably better represented by the whole book than by any one of its characters. At the same time John Brown, Jr.'s life is a version of my early life: the former could not have existed without the latter.

The extent of this symbiosis can be seen in the two false starts I made on the novel, more clearly than in the finished product, where personal concerns were continually reshaped by over-riding artistic needs. The most striking fact about these early versions is that they begin the story approximately where the completed novel ends it. Both Version One and Version Two, as I'll call them, are narrated by a boy who recalls aspects of my Canadian boyhood. The other characters including the father and mother are imaginary, as they are in the published novel.

In Version One the narrator's name is Tom. He lives on the poorer side of London, Ontario (where I attended university and in a sense graduated from the "poorhouse" of my child-hood). Tom has finished high school but has no prospects. At the moment he is playing semi-pro pool.

He is challenged to a game by an American named Dawson who wears an expensive suit with a red pin-stripe in it. Tom wins easily and sees, when Dawson pays, that his wallet is "thick with money—American money, which always seems a little bit like stage money to me." From the standpoint of a poor Cana-dian boy, the United States and its riches seem unreal.

Tom has a taste for unreality. He had done some acting in high school, he tells Dawson.

> "Did you enjoy acting?"
> Did I? It was the only time I ever felt alive, when I could forget myself and the hole I lived in, and turn into an imaginary character. "I liked it, yeah."

Tom is not speaking for me here. I don't like acting. But it is probably not a coincidence that the American, Dawson, is a Ph.D. trained, as I was trained at the University of Toronto, "in the evaluation of intelligence."

Dawson is testing the boy's memory and acting ability and talking vaguely about hiring him, as Version One died in mid-sentence on its thirteenth page. This version suffered from lack of adequate planning, and from the associated difficulty of tell-ing the boy's complicated story in his own simple person. Nei-ther structure nor style was complex enough to let me discover my largely undiscovered purposes.

But immediately I made a second stab at having the boy narrate his own story. His name is Willie now, and he lives in Toronto, almost as if he was following in my footsteps. He has an appointment with an American, now named Mr. Sablacan, who is waiting for him at the Royal York Hotel.

Willie never gets there. All of Version Two takes place in his home, in the early morning. This rather roughly written six-page scene breaks the ground for my book and introduces some of its underlying themes: the hostility between father and son, for instance, here brought to an extreme pitch:

> The old man was sitting at the kitchen table when I went down. He looked like a ghost with a two-day beard. The whole room stank of wine, and he was holding a partly empty bottle propped up between his crotch.
> . . . I kept one eye on him while I made breakfast. . . . He wouldn't throw the bottle as long as it had wine in it. After that, you never knew.

The shades of Huck Finn and his father are pretty well dispelled, I think, when the boy's mother comes down. She approaches her drunken husband "with that silly adoring look on her face, as if he was God Almighty giving her a break just by letting her live. 'You've been working and thinking all night,' she said. 'Your poor head needs a rest. I'll fix you a nice cup of tea . . .'"

Later, she stops an argument between the father and the boy by silencing the father.

> He sat in his chair and looked down into his bottle. You'd think from the expression on his face that it was a telescope which let him see all the way down to hell. All of a sudden his face went slack. He went to sleep in his chair. The old lady took the bottle away from him as if he was a baby . . .
> . . . I sat and ate my breakfast in silence. With the old man propped up opposite me, eyes closed and mouth open, it was a little like eating with a dead man at the table.

My story had begun to feed on its Oedipal roots, both mythical and psychological. Relieved by the mother of his crotch-held bottle, the father has undergone symbolic death. The short scene ends with the boy's determination to get away not only from his father but from his mother:

She'd go on feeding me until I choked. She'd be pouring me cups of tea until I drowned in the stuff. She'd give me loving encouragement until I suffocated.

Version Two was a good deal more than a false start. Swarming with spontaneous symbolism, it laid out one whole side, the sinister side, of the binocular vision of my book. In fact it laid it out so completely that it left me, like Willie, nowhere to go but away. I couldn't begin the novel with the infernal vision on which part of its weight would finally rest; the novel must converge on that gradually. But by writing my last scene first, in effect, and facing its Medusa images—poverty and family failure and hostility—my imagination freed itself to plan the novel without succumbing to the more obvious evasions.

Even so, as I was trying to finish the first draft, I got morally tired and lost my grip on my subject, ending the book with a dying fall in Nevada. My friend John Mersereau read this draft—entitled, appropriately, "The Enormous Detour"—and reminded me that a book like mine could not succeed as a novel unless it succeeded in its own terms as a detective novel. For my ending I went back to Version Two, which contains the dramatic essence of the final confrontations. Willie's scene with his parents served me well, leading me into the heart of my subject not just once but again.

A second break-through at the beginning, more technical and less obviously important, came with my decision to use the detective Archer as the narrator. This may seem a small matter, but it was not. The decision on narrative point-of-view is a key one for any novelist. It determines shape and tone, and even the class of detail that can be used. With this decision I made up my mind that the convention of the detective novel, in which I had been working for fifteen years, would be able to contain the materials of my most ambitious and personal work so far. I doubt that my book could have been written in any other form.

Miss Brigid Brophy has alleged against the detective story that it cannot be taken seriously because it fails to risk the author's ego and is therefore mere fantasy. It is true as I have noted that writers since Poe have used detectives like Dupin as a sort of rational strong point from which they can observe and report on a violent no-man's-land. Unfortunately this violent world is not always fantastic, although it may reflect psychological elements. Miss Brophy's argument disregards the fact that the detective and his story can become means of knowing oneself and saying the unsayable. You can never hit a distant target by aiming at it directly.

In any case I have to plead not guilty to unearned security of the ego. As I write a book, as I wrote *The Galton Case*, my ego is dispersed through several characters, including usually some of the undesirable ones, and I am involved with them to the limit of my imaginative strength. In modern fiction the narrator is not always the protagonist or hero, nor is the protagonist always single. Certainly my narrator Archer is not the main object of my interest, nor the character with whose fate I am most concerned. He is a deliberately narrowed version of the writing self, so narrow that when he turns sideways he almost disappears. Yet his semi-transparent presence places the story at one remove from the author and lets it, as we say (through sweat and tears), write itself.

I remember the rush of invention that occurred when the emotional and imaginative urges, the things *The Galton Case* was to be about, were released by Willie's scene with his parents, and channeled by my decision to write the book from Archer's point of view. The details came unbidden in a benign avalanche which in two or three days filled the rest of the red notebook. The people and the places weren't all final, but they were definite enough to let me begin the wild masonry of laying detail on detail to make a structure. (Naturally many of the details came in already organized gestalts: people in relationship, events in narrative order.)

Detective novels differ from some other kinds of novel, in having to have a rather hard structure built in logical coherence. But the structure will fail to satisfy the mind, writer's or reader's, unless the logic of imagination, tempered by feelings and rooted in the unconscious, is tied to it, often subverting it. The plans for a detective novel in the making are less like blueprints than like travel notes set down as you once revisited a city. The city had changed since you saw it last. It keeps changing around you. Some of the people you knew there have changed their names. Some of them wear disguises.

Take for example Dr. Dawson who lost a game of pool to Tom in Version One and became, in Version Two, a Mr. Sablacan waiting for Willie at the Royal York. In my final notes and in the novel itself he has become Gordon Sable, identifiable with his earlier personae by his name and by the fact that, like Dr. Dawson, he wears a suit with a wicked red pin-stripe in it. His occupation has changed, and his function in the novel has expanded. Gordon Sable is the attorney who hires Lew Archer on Mrs. Galton's behalf to look for her lost son Anthony.

Archer and Gordon Sable know each other. The nature of their relationship is hinted at by a small incident on the first page of the novel. A line of it will illustrate some of the implications of style, which could be described as structure on a small scale. Archer sits down on a Harvard chair in Gordon Sable's office, and then gets up. "It was like being expelled."

In a world of rich and poor, educated and disadvantaged, Archer's dry little joke places him on the side of the underdog. It suggests that he is the kind of man who would sympathize with the boy impostor waiting in the wings. And of course it speaks for the author—my own application for a graduate fellowship at Harvard was turned down thirty years ago—so that like nearly everything in fiction the joke has a private side which partly accounts for its having been made. The University of Michigan gave me a graduate fellowship in 1941, by the way, and my debt to Ann Arbor is duly if strangely acknowledged in the course of John Brown, Jr.'s story.

Detective stories are told backward, as well as forward, and full revelation of the characters and their lives' meanings is deferred until the end, or near the end. But even deeper structural considerations require the main dynamic elements of a story to be laid in early. For this and other reasons, such as the further weight and dimension imparted by repetition, it is sometimes a good idea to let a character and his story divide. One part or aspect of him can perform an early function in the story which foreshadows the function of his later persona, without revealing too much of it.

John Brown, Jr., as I've already said, doesn't enter the story until it is one-third told. I decided, though hardly on the fully conscious level, to provide John with a stand-in or alter ego to pull his weight in the early part of the narrative. When I invented this other boy, and named him Tom Lemberg, I had totally forgotten that Tom was the name of the boy in Version One who beat Dr. Dawson at pool. But here he is in the novel: an earlier stage in the development of my boy impostor. A specimen of fiction, like a biological specimen, seems to recapitulate the lower stages of its evolution. I suspect Tom had to be brought in to validate my novel, proving that I had touched in order all the bases between life and fiction. At any rate the book comes alive when Archer and Tom Lemberg, two widely distinct versions of the author, confront each other in Chapter Five.

This confrontation with Tom of course prefigures Archer's confrontation with the boy impostor John. Tom serves an even more important purpose at the beginning of the book, when he is held responsible for the murder of Peter Culligan. The structure of the story sufficiently identifies Culligan with the wino father, so that Culligan's death parallels and anticipates the final catastrophe. Like the repeated exile of Oedipus, the crucial events of my novel seem to happen at least twice. And like a young Oedipus, Tom is a "son" who appears to kill a "father," thus setting the whole story in circular motion.

I have told a little too much of that story for comfort, and a little too much of my own story. One final connection between the private story and the public one should suffice. When Archer opens the dead Culligan's suitcase, "Its contents emitted a whiff of tobacco, sea water, sweat, and the subtler indescribable odor of masculine loneliness." These were the smells, as I remembered and imagined them, of the pipe-smoking sea-captain who left my mother and me when I was about the age that grandson Jimmie was when he became a monster in my poor castle, and then a laughing boy, and fell asleep.

1969

Down These Streets a Mean Man Must Go

I ONCE compared the detective story to a welder's mask which enables both writer and reader to handle dangerously hot materials. For even at its least realistic crime fiction reminds us of real things. The world is a treacherous place, it says, where a man must learn to watch his step and guard his rights. It is a difficult place to know; still, both the natural and the human worlds are subject to certain laws which we can understand rationally and make predictions by. Traditional detective fiction offers us the assurance that in spite of all its horrors—the speckled band in Conan Doyle, the dead girl thrust up the chimney in Poe's *Rue Morgue*—the world makes sense and can be understood.

Poe lived out in his short brilliant career the last days of the age of reason and the descent into the maelstrom of the unconscious, where everything revolved at a new angle. It was with a kind of desperation—a desperation we continue to feel—that he held on to rational explanations. The murdered girl in the chimney, Dupin assures us, was only the victim of an animal. But in spite of this explanation the story leaves a residue of horror. The forces of terror and reason remain in unresolved conflict.

In the following century that conflict became the central feature of the detective story. Explaining fears which can't quite be explained away, transforming nightmares into day-mares, it helped to quiet the nerves and satisfy the minds of countless readers.

Poe's master Coleridge had written of the Gothic romance, the precursor of the modern detective story:

"As far, therefore, as the story is concerned, the praise which a romance can claim, is simply that of having given pleasure during its perusal. . . . To this praise, however, our author has not entitled himself. The sufferings which he describes are so frightful and intolerable, that we break with abruptness from the delusion and indignantly suspect the man of a species of brutality. . . . Let him work *physical* wonders only, and we will be content to dream with him for a while; but the first *moral* miracle which he attempts, he disgusts and awakens us . . . how beings like ourselves would feel and act . . . our own feelings sufficiently instruct us; and we instantly reject the clumsy fiction that does not harmonize with them."

This is as you may recognize from a review of Lewis's *The Monk* written by Coleridge in 1796, the year that he began to compose *The Ancient Mariner*. It is worth quoting not just for its associations but because it can remind us that the Gothic tradition goes back at least as far as the eighteenth century, and its basic rule hasn't changed radically since. The moral life of the characters is the essence of the story, authenticated by the moral life of the reader.

It was not just as a critic that Coleridge was interested in Gothic romance. *The Ancient Mariner* was touched by it, and the unfinished *Christabel* might almost be described as a Gothic novel in verse. Perhaps I am old enough to confess publicly what forty years ago was my secret ambition. When I was a young would-be poet going to school at the University of Western Ontario, I planned to finish *Christabel* and made an attempt which fortunately doesn't survive, indeed it was stillborn. With the shocking realization of my limitations, my ambition split into two divergent parts which I have spent most of my life trying to put together again. I migrated to Ann Arbor and wrote a dissertation on the psychological backgrounds of Coleridge's criticism. At the same time I followed my wife's example and began to write mystery stories.

For a long time I was made to feel by my friends and colleagues that these two departments of my mental life, the scholarly and the popular, were rather schizophrenically at odds with each other. Most of my best friends are fiction writers and scholars—most of my enemies, too. The writers viewed my interest in scholarship with suspicion not untinged with superstitious awe. The scholars—with significant exceptions like Marshall McLuhan and Hugh Kenner—considered my fiction writing a form of prostitution out of which they tried to wrestle my soul. But I persisted in my intellectual deviance, trying to stretch my legs to match Chandler's markings, telling myself that down these streets a mean man must go.

It may be timely—I may not have another chance—to offer for the record some further autobiographical fragments and a few conclusions. The connections between the work and the life—other men's as well as my own—have always interested me. It becomes more and more evident that novels, popular or otherwise, are built like Robinson Crusoe's cabin out of the flotsam of the author's past and his makeshift present. A man's fiction, no matter how remote it may seem to be from the realistic or the autobiographical, is very much the record of his particular life. Gradually it may tend to become a substitute for the life, a shadow of the life clinging to the original so closely that (as in Malcolm Lowry's *Under the Volcano*) it becomes hard to tell which is fiction and which is confession.

As a writer grows older more and more of his energy goes to sustain the shadow. He seems to live primarily in order to go on writing, secondarily in order to have something to write about. This double *modus vivendi* is like that of an aging husband and wife each of whom knows what the other is going to say, and it often issues in stretching silences. Then we turn back in memory to the past, where the crucial events and conversations of our lives repeat themselves forever in the hope of being understood and perhaps forgiven.

I was born near San Francisco in 1915. My father and his father were both Scots-Canadian newspaper editors. There are writers and painters in my mother's family. My father left my mother when I was four. To me he ultimately bequeathed his copy of *Walden* and a life insurance policy for two thousand dollars which in Canada, in the thirties, was exactly enough to see me through four years of University.

Before I reached University, looking for something to become in my father's absence, I had become a writer. I think most fiction writers must suffer some degree of alienation, a suppression of the conative by the cognitive which stands like a reflecting window between them and the actual world of satisfactions. We wish to reach and remake that world symbolically, sometimes out of anger and revenge, sometimes out of a humane desire to reclaim it.

When I was eleven I discovered *Oliver Twist* and read that novel with such intense absorption that my mother feared for my health. She took the book away and sent me outside to play hockey. The scene was Kitchener, Ontario, a main source of talent for the National Hockey League. I fell on the ice and got my face cut by the skate of my friend Wilbert Hiller, who not many years later was playing for the New York Rangers. Thus I acquired my wound.

I seem to have got the makings of my bow at the Kitchener Public Library. The librarian, B. Mabel Dunham, was a novelist whose books are still alive though she is not. At least one of her novels was about the migration of the Pennsylvania Dutch to Canada in the nineteenth century. My mother's people, like Miss Dunham's were Pennsylvania Dutch; I must be the only American crime novelist who got his early ethical training in a Canadian Mennonite Sunday School. I believe that Mabel Dunham's living example, combined with the books both English and American with which she stocked the public library, permitted me to think of becoming a writer. By my middle teens I was a practising crime writer, and my high school classmate and future wife Margaret had begun to write in the Gothic vein, too. I have often wondered why. Perhaps we both felt that with the suppression of the personal and emotional life which afflicted Canada, particularly in those depression years, expressions of the angry self had to come out in devious ways.

What were we angry about? I think it may have been our sense of being provincial in a double sense, in relation to both Great Britain and the United States. My own feeling of distance from the center was deepened by the fact that I had been born in California and was an American citizen by birth. *Civis Romanus sum*.

Popular fiction is not generally thought of as autobiographical—it is considered less a person than a thing—and it is true that the popular conventions offer an apparent escape from both the author's and the reader's lives. But in a deeper sense they can offer the writer a mask for autobiography—a fencer's mask to deflect the cold steel of reality as he struggles with his own Falstaffian shadows. The convention provides means of disguising the authorial self, but that self reappears on other levels in the forms of other characters, and as the Hamlet's cloud on which the whole thing is projected.

I can think of few more complex critical enterprises than disentangling the mind and life of a first-person detective story writer from the mask of his detective-narrator. The assumption of the mask is as public as vaudeville but as intensely private as a lyric poem. It is like taking an alias, the alias John Doe or Richard Roe; and it constitutes among other things an act of identification with the people one is writing for. Sam Spade is both Hammett and Hammett's audience, a Janus figure representing a city.

Hammett's books were not in the thirties to be found on the open shelves of the Kitchener Public Library. Neither were the novels of Hemingway, Faulkner, or Flaubert: as I recorded in my own early novel *Blue City*, these masters were kept in a locked cupboard for posterity. But one day in 1930 or 1931 I found *The Maltese Falcon* on the shelf of a lending library in a Kitchener tobacco shop, and I read a good part of it on the spot. It wasn't escape reading. As I stood there absorbing Hammett's novel, the slot machines at the back of the shop were clanking and whirring, and in the billiard room upstairs the perpetual poker game was being played. Like iron filings magnetized by the book in my hands, the secret meanings of the city began to organize themselves around me like a second city.

For the first time that I can remember I was consciously experiencing in my own sensibility the direct meeting of art and contemporary actuality—an experience that popular art at its best exists to provide—and beginning to find a language and a shape for that experience. It was a long time before I got it into writing, even crudely: *Blue City* was written fifteen years later. And it was much later still, long after I had made my way back to California and realized that the work of writers like Hammett and Chandler was as much my heritage as anyone's, that I wrote a detective novel called *The Galton Case*, about the reclamation of a California birthright. I was forty or so, and it was getting very late. I made an all-out effort to bend the bow that Hammett and Chandler, and Mabel Dunham, had strung for me, and to hit the difficult target of my own life.

Most popular writers seem to begin, as I did, by imitating their predecessors. There is a convention to be learned. It keeps the forms of the art alive for both the writer and his readers, endowing both with a common stock of structural shapes and formal possibilities. A popular work like Mrs. Radcliffe's *Mysteries of Udolpho*, which incidentally Coleridge gave a better review than he gave Monk Lewis's book, prepares the ground for a *Northanger Abbey*, possibly even for a *Christabel*. The story line of Coleridge's unfinished poem, if not its subtle content, had its sources in several popular modes, including the Gothic tales of terror and the ballads, as well as in the terrible dreams that shook Coleridge nightly.

I believe that popular culture is not and need not be at odds with high culture, any more than the rhythms of walking are at odds with the dance. Popular writers learn what they can from the masters; and even the masters may depend on the rather sophisticated audience and the vocabulary of shapes and symbols which popular fiction provides. Without the traditional Gothic novel and its safety net of readers, even Henry James could not have achieved the wire-walking assurance with which he wrote *The Turn of the Screw*. The work which T.S. Eliot considered the next step taken after James by the Anglo-American novel, *The Great Gatsby*, has obvious connections with American crime fiction and the revolution effected in that fiction during the twenties. The skeleton of Fitzgerald's great work, if not its nervous system, is that of a mystery novel.

A functioning popular literature appears to be very useful if not essential to the growth of a higher literature. Chandler's debt to Fitzgerald suggests that the reverse is also true. There is a two-way connection between the very greatest work and the anonymous imaginings of a people.

I don't intend to suggest that popular literature is primarily a matrix for higher forms. Popular fiction, popular art in general, is the very air a civilization breathes. (Air itself is 80 percent nitrogen.) Popular art is the form in which a culture comes to be known by most of its members. It is the carrier and guardian of the spoken language. A book which can be read by everyone, a convention which is widely used and understood in all its variations, holds a civilization together as nothing else can.

It reaffirms our values as they change, and dramatizes the conflicts of those values. It absorbs and domesticates the spoken language, placing it in meaningful context with traditional language, forming new linguistic synapses in the brain and body of the culture. It describes new modes of behavior, new versions of human character, new shades and varieties of good and evil, and implicitly criticizes them. It holds us still and contemplative for a moment, caught like potential shoplifters who see their own furtive images in a scanning mirror, and wonder if the store detective is looking.

1977

Chronology

1915   Born Kenneth Millar, December 13, in Los Gatos, California, the only child of Anna Moyer Millar and John Macdonald Millar. (Mother was born in Walkerton, Ontario, Canada, in 1875, lived in Chicago, and worked as a hospital nurse in Winnipeg until typhoid fever caught from a patient ended her career; father was born in 1873 in southern Ontario, mined for silver in Nevada, and edited and managed newspapers in frontier and mining towns in British Columbia and Alberta. Parents married in Calgary, Alberta, in 1909.) Kenneth's birth commemorated by father's Scots-dialect poem, printed in the *Los Gatos Mail*.

1916–1918   Family moves to Vancouver, British Columbia. Father works as harbor boat pilot. Millar visits studio of artist John Innes with his father, who had helped guide Innes on a pack-train journey across two provinces in 1899.

1918–1922   Parents quarrel over father's lack of ambition, religion (mother is a Christian Scientist, father a freethinking atheist). Father abandons mother and child, who travel by train to Kitchener, Ontario, and live at first with her widowed mother, then in furnished rooms. Millar's mother, too weak to work, sometimes begs on street for food. She takes Millar to an orphanage and fills out forms for his admission. Rescued by Rob Millar, a married male cousin of his father's, Millar goes to live in Wiarton, Ontario, for two years without his mother. Listens to popular music on radio, reads mystery serials in newspaper, sees silent movie adventure serials at Wonderland Theatre, does well in school.

1923–1926   Sudden death of Wiarton "aunt" Elizabeth Millar prompts return to Kitchener in 1923, to grandmother's house and mother's care. Parents attempt unsuccessfully to reconcile. Millar moves with mother from one rooming house to another; alone, stays at different times with one or another of mother's sisters. Attends Kitchener public school. Escapes into constant reading: Edgar Wallace,

Edgar Rice Burroughs. At ten, discovers Dickens's *Oliver Twist*, a life-changing event.

1927–1928   Thanks to father's sister Margaret, lives for two years in Winnipeg, Manitoba (with summers in Kitchener); attends St. John's College School, an Anglican prep academy. Studies Latin, French, English, geography, math, algebra, geometry, physics, religion; British, Canadian, and general history; competes in gym, hockey, and team equestrian events. Aunt Margaret supervises string of beauty parlors; Uncle Ed, sometime dentist and chiropractor, keeps heavy handgun in his Packard's glove box, and Millar later in life concludes that he was involved in a criminal racket. Father visits Winnipeg en route to the West; offers to take Millar, who declines to go. Millar has fistfights, homosexual episodes with classmates; steals; gets drunk; but works hard at school, winning honors. Decides to be a writer and works on poems and stories.

1929–1930   Finishes first in school form, mid-1929, but is forced to leave Winnipeg, supposedly due to aunt's stock market losses. Takes train from Kitchener to Medicine Hat, Alberta, and lives with mother's sister Laura's family for a year; then goes back to grandmother's Kitchener house, now home also to mother, bachelor Uncle Edwin, widowed Aunt Adeline. Enrolls for eleventh grade at Kitchener-Waterloo Collegiate Institute (KCI), gets after-school job as stock boy and delivery boy at "groceteria."

1931   Receives encouragement on his poetry from mother's cousin Sheldon Brubacher, a university-educated high school teacher. Makes a "second home" of Kitchener public library, whose head librarian, B. Mabel Dunham, is a published historical novelist. Decides that the best publisher on the continent is Alfred A. Knopf and reads every Knopf book he finds. Scours Kitchener for back issues of H. L. Mencken–edited *The American Mercury*. Befriends other male students who write and forms a group to discuss works by Aristotle and the pre-Socratics. Becomes acquainted with mother's brother Stanley Moyer, Toronto painter and occasional writer. Admires from afar classmate Margaret Sturm, daughter of Kitchener mayor. As literary editor of high school annual, accepts for publication his own and Margaret Sturm's first printed stories.

In rental library at McCallum's tobacco shop and pool hall, reads a recently published Dashiell Hammett novel (probably *The Glass Key*, although in later years Millar sometimes identified it as *The Maltese Falcon*) and finds it a mirror of his own urban experience: "As I stood there absorbing Hammett's novel . . . the secret meanings of the city began to organize themselves around me like a second city." Discovers that this Knopf book, along with other controversial fiction, is kept out of public sight in Kitchener library; breaks into public library at night, steals popular novels he deems false to truth, and throws them down a manhole into the Kitchener sewer. Shoplifts, steals money from cloakrooms and lockers; is caught and punished but not turned in to police, and renounces criminal and moral wrongdoing.

1932   Graduates high school. Works for room and board on Snyder farm; stays up late reading Schopenhauer and Kierkegaard.

1933   Father dies at age fifty-nine, leaving $2,212 insurance money that mother gives Millar to finance education. Enters Waterloo College; writes for *College Cord* newspaper, heads thirty-six-member class.

1934–1935   Transfers to University of Western Ontario (London, Ontario). Reconciles with mother, with whom he has not lived for three years, and invites her to live with him in London apartment. Joins wrestling and swimming teams; acts in plays by Shakespeare and Noël Coward.

1936   Mother dies of a brain tumor in January at age sixty. Millar takes year off from college, travels by bicycle in Ireland, Scotland, England, and France; stays eight weeks in Nazi Munich.

1937   Re-enters University of Western Ontario, where his best friends are Robert Ford, future poet and diplomat, and Donald Pearce, future scholar and professor. Co-edits university literary magazine with Ford. Keeps company with Margaret Sturm, who has dropped out of University of Toronto and also wants to be a writer.

1938   Graduates university with honors in June; marries Margaret Sturm the next day. Attends Ontario College of Education, where he will earn high school teaching credential.

1939			Daughter Linda born on June 18. Millar's first professional
			work—poems, reviews, stories—published in *Toronto Sat-
			urday Night*. Moves with family to Kitchener, where he
			will teach for two years at his former high school, KCI.
			Academically mentors female student June Callwood,
			who later becomes a highly regarded Ontario journalist,
			broadcaster, and social activist.

1940			Attends graduate classes at University of Michigan during
			summer. Margaret develops enthusiasm for mysteries;
			Millar encourages and edits her first mystery novel, *The
			Invisible Worm*.

1941–42		Accepts fellowship at University of Michigan and moves
			with family to Ann Arbor. Studies with W. H. Auden
			(whom he later describes as "a remarkable kind of saint")
			and Cleanth Brooks; befriends fellow graduate students
			and future poets Robert Hayden and Chad Walsh. *The
			Invisible Worm* by Margaret Millar published by Double-
			day, Doran in June 1941. The Millars befriend H. C. Bran-
			son, another Ann Arbor detective story writer. Margaret
			publishes two more mystery novels in 1942. With help
			of novelist Faith Baldwin (one of her readers), Margaret
			signs with Harold Ober Agency; her fourth novel (*Wall
			of Eyes*) is accepted by Random House.

1943–44		Millar completes courses for doctorate but continues to
			work on dissertation on Samuel Taylor Coleridge. Work-
			ing two hours a night in campus office, Millar in a month
			writes his first novel, *The Dark Tunnel*, a spy thriller
			concerning Nazi infiltration of a midwestern university,
			which Ober sells to Dodd, Mead. (*Wall of Eyes* published
			in September 1943.) Millar secures commission in Naval
			Reserve, studies at Princeton and Harvard to be a naval
			communications officer; plans to be full-time writer after
			war service. Travels with Margaret and Linda by train to
			Southern California. Joins crew of escort carrier USS *Shi-
			pley Bay* for Pacific runs. Begins a second thriller, *Trouble
			Follows Me*, aboard ship. *The Dark Tunnel* is published in
			September.

1945			Margaret's sixth book, *The Iron Gates*, is published to rave
			reviews; movie rights are bought by Warner Brothers for
			$15,000, with which she buys them a house in Santa Bar-
			bara, California. She begins working at Warners on the

screenplay of her novel at $750 per week. Millar serves on *Shipley Bay* during Battle of Okinawa, May–June. On leave, visits Warners, meets Faulkner and other writers on August 14, 1945 (V-J Day). On his next leave, in San Francisco, he meets Anthony Boucher (William A. P. White), influential mystery critic, who suggests that both Millars enter the first *Ellery Queen's Mystery Magazine* short story contest. Aboard *Shipley Bay*, Millar writes two stories featuring Los Angeles private detective Joe Rogers for the competition, one of which ("Find the Woman") wins the $300 fourth prize.

1946   In April joins family in Santa Barbara house, 2124 Bath Street. Gives himself a year to prove he can make a living as a novelist. *Trouble Follows Me* published by Dodd, Mead in September. Writes *Blue City*, a Hammett-inspired hard-boiled crime novel, in a month; it is bought by Alfred A. Knopf. Begins a thriller about amnesia, *The Three Roads*.

1947   *Blue City* is published in August to mixed reviews. Attempts autobiographical novel ("Winter Solstice") but gets bogged down. Resurrects Joe Rogers, private eye character from *Ellery Queen* contest stories, and renames him Lew Archer for novel eventually titled *The Moving Target*.

1948   *The Three Roads* is published by Knopf, receiving reasonably good reviews. Expecting quick sale of his new novel to Knopf, drives alone to Ann Arbor to resume work on PhD, in hopes that an eventual teaching post in California will allow time and money to craft mainstream fiction. Knopf is unhappy with the Archer novel, calling it "ordinary, average, fair-to-middling run-of-the-mill stuff," and balks at publishing it, until Millar suggests using pseudonym "John Macdonald" (from his father's first and middle names). Meets Knopf for the first time in November when publisher visits Ann Arbor. Finishes draft of dissertation and returns to West Coast.

1949   *The Moving Target* published in March. It receives an enthusiastic review from Anthony Boucher in *The New York Times Book Review*. (Raymond Chandler, reading the book on advice of critic James Sandoe, claims in a letter that its prose displays "the stylistic misuse of language" typical of "literary eunuchs.") When New York writer

John D. MacDonald complains that Millar's pseudonym is causing confusion between the two writers, Millar agrees to modify it to John Ross Macdonald, which he will maintain for the next six books.

1950   In February, as guest of Random House publisher Bennett Cerf, the Millars attend party given by Darryl F. Zanuck in Palm Springs; guests include many well-known Hollywood figures. Millar researches Southern California society by joining Coral Casino Beach Club (across from Santa Barbara Biltmore Hotel). With Margaret, regularly attends trials at the Santa Barbara courthouse. Forms friendship with Hugh Kenner, Canadian-born literary scholar teaching at UCSB. Second Archer novel, *The Drowning Pool*, is published in July.

1951   Returns to Michigan in the summer for a successful defense of his dissertation (receives PhD the following year). Summoned by daughter Linda's school to discuss her "maladjustment." Publishes *The Way Some People Die* in July; Boucher hails it as "the best novel in the tough tradition . . . since [Chandler's] *Farewell, My Lovely* . . . and possibly since [Hammett's] *The Maltese Falcon*." Suffering work stress and family strain, Millar attempts suicide (possibly by defenestration); refuses professional treatment. He rejects Alfred Knopf's suggestion that he insert more danger and action into new Archer manuscript; meets with Knopf at Hotel Bel-Air in September. Eases family situation by moving in October to larger house with ocean view at 2136 Cliff Drive.

1952   *The Ivory Grin* published; Margaret in the same year publishes *Rose's Last Summer* and *Vanish in an Instant*. "Between us," Millar writes Hollywood agent H. N. Swanson, "we've had about the best critical receptions of the year in the mystery field." Writes *Meet Me at the Morgue*, non-Archer book featuring probation officer Howard Cross. Suffers from gout and is confined to a wheelchair for weeks. For paperback edition, Pocket Books suggests a rewrite of *Meet Me at the Morgue* to hew closer to fictional model of Raymond Chandler; Millar responds with impassioned letter to Knopf: "With all due respect . . . I can't accept Chandler's vision of good and evil. It is conventional to the point of occasional old-maidishness, anti-human to the point of frequent sadism

. . . and the mind behind it, for all its enviable imaginative force, is uncultivated and second-rate." (See page 861 of this volume.)

1953   In July delivers lecture on the detective story as part of University of Michigan symposium on popular arts; praises Dashiell Hammett (whose works have been banned from U.S. libraries abroad due to author's politics), asserting that *The Maltese Falcon* "has astonishing imaginative energy after more than twenty years. I believe it can still express contemporary truth and comes close to tragedy." Dropped by paperback house Pocket Books, he is quickly signed by Bantam. *Wilson Library Bulletin* breaks "secret" of Millar being Macdonald in December. In [London] *Times Literary Supplement* an unsigned review by Julian Symons compares Macdonald favorably with Raymond Chandler.

1954   For fiction research, spends early weeks of January with psychiatric social worker Stanley Tenny, visiting juvenile halls and state hospitals; attends Civil Service Commission hearings on firing of veteran police detective. Cofounds bimonthly writers' luncheon attended by other Santa Barbara authors: Paul Ellerbe, Willard Temple, John Mersereau, William Campbell Gault, Al Stump. *Find a Victim*, the fifth Archer novel, is published in August to lackluster reviews. Bantam collects Millar's short stories as *The Name Is Archer*, which proves highly successful. Cowrites two scripts with Margaret for *City Detective* television series (starring Rod Cameron). Helps Margaret revise structure and ending of her novel *Beast in View*.

1955   During trip east in the spring, buys used Ford sedan in Saline, Michigan, for Linda, who will soon turn sixteen, as a reward for good grades and in hope of easing her social progress in high school. Thanks in part to good French sales, enjoys best year yet as freelance author, grossing $14,500.

1956   Daughter Linda involved in fatal hit-and-run accident on February 23, killing a thirteen-year-old pedestrian on a rain-slick street. She is arraigned on two felony counts; after suffering a breakdown, she is admitted to Dani Rest Home and subsequently to the state mental hospital in

Camarillo, where she remains for three months. Front-page newspaper stories identify her parents as successful authors. *Beast in View* wins Mystery Writers of America's Edgar Award as best novel of 1955. Testifying before superior court grand jury, Millar refuses (on his lawyer's advice) to discuss Linda's statements to him about the accident, even under threat of being cited for contempt. *The Barbarous Coast*, sixth Archer novel (the first to be published as by "Ross Macdonald"), is published in June and gets his best reviews so far. In August, juvenile court no-jury trial finds Linda guilty and sentences her to ten years' probation. Family moves to Menlo Park, California, late in the year; Linda enrolls in public high school there. Millar begins psychiatric treatment with Menlo Park analyst. Becomes client of Ober agent Dorothy Olding, who also handles J. D. Salinger. Starts writing *The Doomsters*, an Archer novel drawing on insights gained from analysis; calls it his "diary of psychic progress." (Later remarks: "The real change in [Archer], I think, occurred in *The Doomsters*; he became a man who was not so much trying to find the criminal as understand him. He became more of a representative of man rather than just a detective who finds things out.")

1957   Sends *The Doomsters* to his agent in May, calling it "the culminating book (though not the last) in the Archer series." Margaret is elected president of the Mystery Writers of America. Linda does well in Menlo Park high school and enrolls at UC Davis, near Sacramento. Millars move back to Santa Barbara in August, leasing a house at 1843 Camino de la Luz on Santa Barbara mesa. He sails often on rented boat with old Michigan friend Donald Pearce and writer Robert Easton. Teaches adult education writing class; students include future novelist Herb Harker and Noel Young, later founder of Capra Press.

1958   *The Doomsters* published in February to mixed reviews, and sales are disappointing. Forms friendships with visiting UCSB lecturers, English poet Donald Davie and Canadian cultural critic Marshall McLuhan. Has satisfying meeting in July with Alfred Knopf at Beverly Hills Brown Derby; is visited in September by Oscar Dystel and Saul David of Bantam Books, who say Macdonald is now Bantam's best-selling mystery writer. (Other Bantam authors at this time include Rex Stout, Georges Simenon, Eric Ambler, and Margaret Millar.) As near-neighbor Davie works on translation of Polish poem about a search for a lost father, Millar writes Archer novel with similar themes, drawing on his own personal history, *The Galton Case*, which he will later refer to as "my first really good book." He submits it to Knopf in May under the working title *The Enormous Detour*. Begins publishing book reviews, mostly under Kenneth Millar byline, in the *San Francisco Chronicle* weekend section; some fifty appear over the next two years. Meets professor-author Richard Lid, who will become a close friend. The Millars move in December to a new home at 840 Chelham Way.

1959   Adaptation of "Find the Woman" is broadcast on CBS live television series *Pursuit*, starring Michael Rennie as detective "Joe Rogers." *The Galton Case* is published in March to good reviews, but sales are again disappointing. Linda, in May, after a Saturday trip to a casino in Stateline, Nevada, fails to return to UC Davis dorm; an all-points bulletin is issued for her as a probation violator. Millar hires Reno husband-wife team of private detectives; flies to Los Angeles when Linda is suspected of being there. Nearly sleepless, he makes numerous press, radio, and television appeals: the case of the mystery writer's missing daughter is covered by newspapers from coast to coast and in Europe. Linda is found in Reno after eight days and is admitted to UCLA Medical Center for psychiatric treatment; Millar is hospitalized for two weeks for severe hypertension, kidney stones, and heart damage. Completes a non-Archer novel with a lawyer hero, *The Ferguson Affair*.

1960   Begins a new Archer novel. *The Ferguson Affair* is published in July and sells well; movie rights are sold for $16,500, although no film results. In New York, the Millars give joint interviews with newspaper book pages (one of which inspires a *New Yorker* sketch by S. J. Perelman). *Cosmopolitan* buys condensation rights to *The Wycherly Woman*, the new Archer novel.

1961   Revises dissertation "Coleridge and The Inward Eye" in hopes of publication, but in spite of positive recommendations by top scholars, it is rejected by several university presses, deterred apparently because Millar is a mystery writer. *The Wycherly Woman* is published in May. Works on tenth Archer novel, *The Zebra-Striped Hearse*, traveling to Lake Tahoe and Ajijic, Mexico, for research. Linda marries engineering student in September. Millar instigates exercise regimen, swimming a daily half-mile. Margaret's new interest in bird-watching inspires his own involvement.

1962   Submits manuscript of *The Zebra-Striped Hearse* in May; condensation rights are sold to *Cosmopolitan*. Posthumous collection *Raymond Chandler Speaking* published, making public Chandler's private criticisms of Macdonald's writing. With Margaret, makes birding trips to Yellowstone, Teton Park, and other locations.

1963   *The Zebra-Striped Hearse* published in January; it is nominated for an Edgar award for Best Novel. In an interview for a feature article in *Los Angeles* magazine, Millar remarks: "My main theme, I really think, is the possibility of communication between men and women, and the tragedy that occurs when that communication breaks down. Failure of communication is built right into the form of the detective novel." Becomes grandfather in April with birth of Linda's son James. Forms friendships with mystery novelist Dennis Lynds (who writes as "Michael Collins") and poet Henri ("Hank") Coulette. With Margaret, helps found Santa Barbara chapter of the Audubon Society.

1964   Publishes eleventh Archer novel, *The Chill*, in March. It wins British Crime Writers Association's Silver Dagger Award. Helps lead fight to save the endangered California condor by effectively protesting construction of a proposed road near Los Padres National Forest; meets critic Brooks Atkinson, who helps publicize the issue. In March, Millar declares in speech in Santa Barbara: "Some few things are so rare and ancient and valuable that they can't be improved by development, so fragile that they can't be carelessly exposed. Let us leave the condor alone." Completes new Archer novel *The Far Side of the Dollar*. With Margaret, travels to Alberta and British Columbia in the spring for bird-watching. Sells film rights option to first Archer book, *The Moving Target*, for $12,500. In September, stands on roof and waters down house, two nights in a row, as Coyote Fire burns neighboring homes.

1965   Twelfth Archer novel, *The Far Side of the Dollar*, appears in January. In essay "The Writer as Detective Hero," published in *Show*, Millar declares independence from Chandler school of detective fiction ("Chandler described a good plot as one that made for good scenes . . . I see plot as a vehicle of meaning"). Receives growing critical acclaim; Walter Hogan in *San Francisco Chronicle* calls him "an important American novelist." Elected president of Mystery Writers of America. Goes to New York in April for annual dinner; meets and becomes friends with English writer Julian Symons. Production begins on Warner Brothers movie based on *The Moving Target*, with screenplay by William Goldman and directed by Jack Smight, starring Paul Newman, with supporting cast including Lauren Bacall, Robert Wagner, and Julie Harris. Hoping to make a series of Lew Archer films with Newman, Warners wants to acquire long-term rights to Archer; Millar insists on adequate compensation ($50,000); studio refuses, instead choosing to change name of Archer (and movie) to *Harper*. Using ten years' savings, Millars put down payment on $90,000 hilltop home at 4420 Via Esperanza, Hope Ranch Park, and move in September. Margaret, author now of nineteen published books, is named one of twelve Women of the Year by *The Los Angeles Times*.

1966   *Black Money* is published in January and becomes best seller. *Harper* opens in April and is a hit (opens in England in June as *The Moving Target*). *The Far Side of the Dollar* wins English Crime Writers Association's Gold Dagger Award. Warner Brothers pays $50,000 for film rights to *The Chill*. Millar works on *The Hunters*, script for a possible television series; resigns from project in June.

1967   Warner Brothers drops *The Chill* after Paul Newman expresses dissatisfaction with the script. Millar completes new Archer novel *The Instant Enemy* in June. A feature article on Millar appears in *The Los Angeles Times* in December. With Margaret participates in protests against the Vietnam War.

1968   *The Instant Enemy* published to strong reviews. Declines an invitation to work on a script for Alfred Hitchcock. Longtime critical supporter Anthony Boucher dies in April. At a San Francisco meeting of Mystery Writers of America, Millar delivers talk "A Preface to *The Galton Case*." (See page 878 in this volume.) In September completes new Archer novel *The Goodbye Look*.

1969   In January, underwater oil well off Santa Barbara shore blows out, polluting water and coastline, endangering birdlife. Both Millars are in the forefront of environmental protest, which leads to establishment of annual Earth Day. *The Goodbye Look*, fifteenth Archer novel, published in May. *The New York Times Book Review* runs a front-page notice by William Goldman calling the Macdonald books "the finest series of detective novels ever written by an American," supplemented by a John Leonard interview with Millar; the book becomes a *New York Times* best seller, staying on the list for fourteen weeks.

1970   Antiwar protests near UCSB in February lead to burning of Isla Vista branch of Bank of America, and one student is killed; Millar joins forty-six-member self-appointed Citizens Commission on Civil Disorders in hopes of airing issues and calming city. Faithfully attends trial of eleven young people indicted in the bank burning. In a *New York Times Book Review* interview in April, Mississippi author Eudora Welty reveals she is a longtime Ross Macdonald fan. He writes her a letter, and a long correspondence and friendship ensue. Completes *The Underground Man*, sixteenth Archer novel. Arthur Kaye directs and produces short educational film "Ross Macdonald: In the First Person." Sam Peckinpah signs to direct *The Chill*, but once again the project falls apart. On November 5, daughter Linda dies in her sleep at age thirty-one. "She was a valiant girl," he writes a friend, "one of the great moral forces in my life and after Margaret my dearest love." Linda's widower and their seven-year-old son become frequent weekend visitors to Hope Ranch.

1971   *New York Times Book Review* assigns Eudora Welty *The Underground Man*; her front-page celebratory review appears on February 14: "*The Underground Man* is written so close to the nerve of today as to expose most of the apprehensions we live with." (Millar tells Knopf: "I'm overwhelmed by her generosity.") Raymond Sokolov interviews Millar for *Newsweek* magazine, which makes Ross Macdonald its cover subject for the March 22 issue. *The Underground Man* soars near the top of all major fiction best seller lists. On a New York visit in May, Millar unexpectedly meets Welty at the Algonquin and she accompanies him to a party in his honor at Alfred Knopf's apartment on West 55th Street; afterward, they go for dinner, walk around town until past midnight, and promise to keep in touch. Producer Martin Ransohoff buys film rights to *The Underground Man* and six other Macdonald books for $1.35 million. The Millars travel to Europe in October, visiting France, Switzerland, and England (where publisher William Collins hosts lunch for them with leading London crime fiction reviewers).

1972   *The Goodbye Look* is serialized in Russian literary review *Znamya*; Macdonald said to be first American detective novelist translated in Russia since Hammett. New York filmmaker Craig Gilbert, after reading *The Underground Man*, enlists Millar's help in finding a California household as subject for PBS documentary series *An American Family*; Millar introduces him to *Santa Barbara News-Press* staffers, who steer him to the Louds of Montecito. Receives Outstanding Achievement Award for alumni of University of Michigan in November.

1973   *Sleeping Beauty*, seventeenth Lew Archer novel, published in May, with dedication to Eudora Welty; reviews are mixed but the book is Millar's third best seller in a row. Travels to Jackson, Mississippi, for six-day Welty celebration, sponsored by Mississippi Arts Festival. Others attending include Welty's longtime agent Diarmuid Russell and novelist Reynolds Price, to whom Millar declares his love for Welty. Popular Culture Association awards Macdonald its first Merit Award in December at Chicago's Palmer House.

1974   Edits anthology *Great Stories of Suspense* (1974). A TV movie of *The Underground Man*, directed by Paul Wendkos and starring Peter Graves as Archer, with Judith Anderson and Jack Klugman in supporting roles, is broadcast in May. Mystery Writers of America votes him the Grandmaster Award. He visits New York to attend MWA dinner; is photographed by Jill Krementz, meets and likes her companion (later husband), novelist Kurt Vonnegut.

1975   Television series *Archer* starring Brian Keith premieres on NBC in January; reviews are poor and the show is canceled after two episodes. Millar travels to Toronto in April to publicize and attract financial backing for Canadian film of *The Three Roads* (the film, starring Michael Sarrazin and Susan Clark, is released in 1981 as *Double Negative*). Attends Mystery Writers of America annual dinner, where he presents Grandmaster Award to Eric Ambler. Participates in Santa Barbara Writers Conference, at which Eudora Welty is a featured guest. Film of *The Drowning Pool*, starring Paul Newman and directed by Stuart Rosenberg, is released during the summer. Struggles with memory problems and other mental difficulties while writing *The Blue Hammer* (eighteenth and final Archer novel).

1976   Goes to New York in April; guest-teaches session of graduate nonfiction workshop at Columbia taught by Frank MacShane, who has just published a biography of Raymond Chandler. Takes part in National Book Critics Circle panel with MacShane, Nona Balakian, Anatole Broyard, Wilfred Sheed, Hortense Calisher, and others. Margaret joins him in Ontario for family visits. Meets young *Toronto Star* writer Linwood Barclay, later a successful novelist, whom he has mentored by mail since Barclay was a teenager. Eudora Welty again travels from Mississippi to take part in Santa Barbara Writers Conference. *The Blue Hammer* published in June. Millar participates in summer-long series of interviews with Paul Nelson for projected *Rolling Stone* magazine piece, but his stipulation that any published article exclude mention of Linda's troubles hamstrings Nelson's efforts. Through Nelson, meets singer-songwriter Warren Zevon, who reveres Millar's writing. Travels alone to Europe; trip is marred by news of recent death in London of Julian Symons's daughter. Meets again with his English publisher Sir William Collins, who dies two days later. In Zurich, meets his (and Margaret's) German publisher Daniel Keel. Voyages on to Venice before returning to Santa Barbara by way of New York.

1977   Otto Penzler collects all the Archer short stories in *Lew Archer: Private Investigator*, published by his newly established Mysterious Press. Is subject of half-hour documentary directed by Richard Moore for 1977 PBS series *The Originals: The Writer in America*. Margaret has successful operation for lung cancer. Eudora Welty participates for a third time in Santa Barbara Writers Conference. Millar finds writing increasingly difficult. Begins psychiatric sessions with Santa Barbara analyst in hopes of resolving memory problems. Works on screenplay for a proposed film of *The Instant Enemy* (the project ultimately falls through).

1978   Goes to New York in March for Second International Congress of Crime Writers. Often seems vague in thought and manner. Margaret, having published two new novels in quick succession after six-year temporary retirement, suffers macular degeneration and is declared legally blind. With special optical equipment, she begins work on another book. Welty publishes *The Eye of the Story: Selected Essays and Reviews*—a volume Millar encouraged her to assemble—and dedicates it: "To Kenneth Millar."

1979   Millar has increasing trouble with everyday tasks. In December, signs contract with Knopf for novel due December 1981.

1980   Warren Zevon dedicates his album *Bad Luck in Dancing School* to Millar. Journalists who see Millar are alarmed by his deteriorating state. He asks bookseller friend Ralph Sipper to inform correspondents he can no longer answer letters.

1981   Diagnosed with Alzheimer's disease. *Self-Portrait: Ceaselessly Into the Past*, a collection of short pieces by Millar, is published by Capra Press with a foreword by Welty.

1982   Early in the year, Margaret makes his condition public in interview with *The Los Angeles Times*. At the third annual *Los Angeles Times* Book Prizes in November, Millar receives Robert Kirsch Award for a distinguished body of work; Margaret accepts the prize in his absence. Welty visits Millar in Santa Barbara, communicates with him better than most others. In December, he is moved into Cliff View Terrace, a private rest home.

1983   In June, suffers a "cerebrovascular accident" and is admitted to Cottage Hospital, then transferred to Pinecrest facility, where he dies on July 11.

Note on the Texts

This volume contains the Ross Macdonald novels *The Way Some People Die* (1951), *The Barbarous Coast* (1956), *The Doomsters* (1958), and *The Galton Case* (1959), along with a selection of writings in which Macdonald (born Kenneth Millar) comments on his approach to crime writing and on the origin of some of the works published here.

The Way Some People Die was Millar's seventh novel (the first four were published under his birth name) and the third to feature as protagonist the private investigator Lew Archer. The first of the Archer novels, *The Moving Target* (1949), had been published under the pseudonym John Macdonald; when this elicited a protest from the already established crime writer John D. MacDonald, Millar agreed to change his byline to John Ross Macdonald, a pseudonym that was retained for his next six books. *The Way Some People Die* was described by Millar during its composition as "a more human book than either of the others, more original, not so slick, and a truer picture of our very messed-up society." It was published in July 1951 by Alfred A. Knopf, the publisher of all the author's novels, beginning with *Blue City* in 1947. In May 1953 it was published in the United Kingdom by Cassell & Co. Ltd.

With *The Barbarous Coast*, the sixth Lew Archer novel, Millar assumed the pseudonym Ross Macdonald, which he retained for all subsequent works. The novel was originally submitted to Knopf under the title *The Dying Animal*, and it was under this title that it appeared in a condensed version in *Cosmopolitan* (March 1956). *The Barbarous Coast* was published in June 1956. An English edition was published by Cassell in 1957.

The Doomsters was begun in the autumn of 1956, using as its point of departure an unpublished novelette about Lew Archer, "The Angry Man." Upon its completion in May 1957, Millar sent it to his agent Ivan von Auw with a letter in which he described it as "the culminating book (though not the last) in the Archer series." *The Doomsters* was published by Knopf in February 1958. Cassell issued an English edition in October of the same year.

His next novel, *The Galton Case*, drew on Millar's personal history: "In the winter of 1957–1958 I was as ready as I would ever be to cope in fiction with some of the more complicated facts of my existence." The book, which was originally submitted to Knopf under the title *The Enormous Detour*, was regarded by Millar as a turning point in his work. It was published by Knopf in March 1959. An English edition by Cassell appeared in January 1960.

The texts used here are those of the novels' first editions.

The following are the sources for the additional writings included in this volume:

"Letter to Alfred A. Knopf, August 28, 1952": Typescript, The Harry Ransom Center, The University of Texas at Austin. An alternate draft of this letter was published as "Farewell, Chandler" in Ralph B. Sipper, ed., *Inward Journey* (New York: The Mysterious Press, 1984).

"The Writer as Detective Hero": Originally published in *Show*, January 1965. The text printed here is from Ross Macdonald, *On Crime Writing* (Santa Barbara: Capra Press, 1973).

"Preface to *Archer in Hollywood*": Originally published in *Archer in Hollywood* (New York: Alfred A. Knopf, 1967), an omnibus containing *The Moving Target*, *The Way Some People Die*, and *The Barbarous Coast*. The text printed here is from Ross Macdonald, *Self-Portrait: Ceaselessly into the Past* (Santa Barbara: Capra Press, 1981).

"Writing *The Galton Case*": Originally published as "A Preface to *The Galton Case*" in *Afterwords: Novelists on Their Novels*, ed. Thomas McCormack (New York: Harper & Row, 1968). The text printed here is from Ross Macdonald, *On Crime Writing*.

"Down These Streets a Mean Man Must Go": Originally published in *Antaeus*, Spring/Summer 1977. The text printed here is from Ross Macdonald, *Self-Portrait: Ceaselessly into the Past*.

This volume presents the texts of the original printings chosen for inclusion here, but it does not attempt to reproduce nontextual features of their typographic design. The texts are presented without change, except for the correction of typographical errors. Spelling, punctuation, and capitalization are often expressive features and are not altered, even when inconsistent or irregular. The following is a list of typographical errors corrected, cited by page and line number: 8.11, 'The; 9.12, You've; 9.37, but it; 34.13, old fashioned; 56.39, woudn't; 60.31, adress-book; 166.21, He eyelids; 182.27, indentification."; 183.27 (and *passim*), Guiseppe; 193.11, McCucheon; 260.22, *Salambô*; 334.2, itself . . . ."; 364.29, winoes; 392.4, pro's.; 401.20, Maffia; 429.22, a part; 438.20, about?; 490.13, crumped; 493.14, proprietory; 493.30, filagree; 501.19, reason.; 514.23, you've; 523.19, somebody's; 553.27, Mrs; 557.31, our her; 605.3, usual So; 605.5, seen You; 629.3–4, guidace.; 643.28, aluminus; 689.21, Levis,; 692.33, Marion; 703.21, Harper's; 727.40, Marion; 745.21, mater?; 764.4, Maffia; 871.6, superoriity.; 880.7, *Tryannus*).; 891.33, MacLuhan; 895.2, possibily.

Notes

In the notes below, the reference numbers denote page and line of this volume (the line count includes headings). No note is made for material included in standard desk-reference books. Biblical quotations are keyed to the King James Version. Quotations from Shakespeare are keyed to *The Riverside Shakespeare*, ed. G. Blakemore Evans (Boston: Houghton Mifflin, 1974). For references to other studies and further information than is included in the Chronology, see Tom Nolan, *Ross Macdonald: A Biography* (New York: Scribner, 1999); Ross Macdonald, *Self-Portrait: Ceaselessly into the Past* (Santa Barbara: Capra Press, 1981); Ralph B. Sipper, ed., *Inward Journey: Ross Macdonald* (New York: The Mysterious Press, 1987); Matthew J. Bruccoli, *Ross Macdonald/Kenneth Millar: A Descriptive Bibliography* (Pittsburgh: University of Pittsburgh Press, 1983).

THE WAY SOME PEOPLE DIE

7.31　Swedenborg] Emmanuel Swedenborg (1688–1772), Swedish scientist and theologian whose accounts of mystical visions in such works as *Heaven and Hell* (1758) and *Divine Love and Wisdom* (1763) influenced William Blake, Ralph Waldo Emerson, and others.

8.6　the Black Dahlia] Nickname bestowed on Massachusetts-born Elizabeth Short (1924–1947), whose dismembered corpse was found in a Los Angeles lot in January 1947. The murder remained unsolved.

13.33　the G.I.] The Servicemen's Readjustment Act of 1944, or G.I. Bill, provided, among other benefits, payment of tuition costs and living expenses for returning veterans attending college.

22.1　Ben Hur perfume] Popular scent manufactured by Jergens, inspired by the 1880 novel *Ben-Hur: A Tale of the Christ* by General Lew Wallace (1827–1905) and its subsequent stage and film adaptations. Macdonald would say that Lew Archer's first name derived from the author of *Ben-Hur*.

29.2　Musso's] Musso & Frank Grill, which bills itself as "the oldest restaurant in Hollywood" (established 1919), a literary as well as culinary landmark. Patronized by many authors employed by or involved with movie studios (including William Faulkner, Dashiell Hammett, Lillian Hellman, F. Scott Fitzgerald, Ernest Hemingway, John O'Hara, Dorothy Parker, and Raymond Chandler), Musso's appears or is mentioned in several other well-known Los Angeles novels, including Chandler's *The Long Goodbye*, Budd Schulberg's *What Makes Sammy Run?*, and Nathanael West's *The Day of the Locust*.

34.22   Channel Island boar's-head] Some of the eight Channel Islands off the Southern California coast were home to huntable wild boar.

34.23   Mauve Age] The American 1890s, so called in Thomas Beer's study *The Mauve Decade* (1926).

37.3   Ciro's] West Hollywood nightspot patronized by celebrities. At 8433 Sunset Boulevard, it was a few doors west, on the unincorporated Sunset Strip, of Lew Archer's office at 8411½.

37.3   Westmore's] The House of Westmore beauty salon, on Sunset Boulevard, founded in 1935 by the Westmore family of Hollywood studio makeup artists.

39.3–4   a miniature Wilshire] Wilshire, a long east-west Los Angeles boulevard, was the site of such upscale department stores as Bullock's, and home of the "Miracle Mile."

39.10–11   most unkindest cut of all] See *Julius Caesar*, III.ii.183.

39.24   Hopalong Cassidy] Western hero created in 1904 by Clarence E. Mulford (1883–1956) and played in films and on television by William Boyd (1895–1972).

45.11   PBY] Consolidated PBY Catalina, amphibious aircraft widely used in World War II.

52.33   Monel metal] Corrosion-resistant nickel-copper alloy.

59.10–11   *Daily Variety* and *Hollywood Reporter*] Entertainment business trade papers.

59.12   Thorne Smith] Author (1892–1934) of humorous novels, including *Topper* (1926), *The Night Life of the Gods* (1931), and *Topper Takes a Trip* (1932).

59.12   Erskine Caldwell] Georgia-born author (1903–1987) of earthy fiction, including *Tobacco Road* (1932) and *God's Little Acre* (1933).

59.12–13   Joseph Moncure March] Poet and screenwriter (1899–1977) best known for his book-length narrative poems *The Wild Party* (1928) and *The Set-Up* (1928).

59.13   *The Lost Weekend*] Novel (1944) about alcoholism by Charles Jackson (1903–1968); filmed in 1945 by director Billy Wilder (1906–2002).

59.14   *Sonnets from the Portuguese*] Sequence of poems (1850) by Elizabeth Barrett Browning (1806–1861). The line quoted is from Sonnet 14.

59.18   Murphy bed] A hinged bed that folds up to be stored behind a wall.

62.15   a stone-faced building on Sunset] This unnamed facility would seem to be CBS's Columbia Square complex, from which were broadcast, in 1951, such radio programs as *The Adventures of Philip Marlowe*.

66.10–11   Miranda Sampson] Miranda appears in the first Archer novel, *The Moving Target* (1949).

68.3   lakhs of rupees] In India and elsewhere, the equivalent of thousands of dollars.

77.37   Lochinvar] Chivalrous hero of Walter Scott's narrative poem *Marmion* (1808).

79.25   Gretna Green] Village in southern Scotland, famous as a marriage site for eloping couples.

86.10   Willie Hoppe] American billiards champion (1887–1959), winner of fifty-one world titles between 1906 and 1952.

100.32   *bracero*] Hispanic manual laborer, "guest worker" from Mexico.

104.7   Achilles was fighting Hector] Achilles slays Hector in single-handed combat in Book 22 of *The Iliad*.

104.7–8   Jacob was wrestling with the angel] See Genesis 32:22–31.

113.8   a merman like the poem] See "The Forsaken Merman" (1849) by Matthew Arnold (1822–1888).

131.22   Hearthstone of the Death Squad] Police inspector who was featured on the radio series *Mystery Theatre* beginning in 1949; the show was retitled *Inspector Hearthstone of the Death Squad* before going off the air in 1952.

135.5   *The Rover Boys*] Boarding school (later college) students featured in a long-running series of popular novels, 1899–1926.

137.2–3   seven sleepers of Ephesus] In Christian lore, a group of persecuted Christian youths imprisoned by the Romans in a tomb, where they slept for some 150 years, emerging to find their city converted to Christianity.

141.19–20   *Dolce far niente*] Italian: Pleasant idleness.

150.16–24   *Moonlight and Roses . . . Stormy Weather*] "Moonlight and Roses" (1921), song adapted from Edwin Lemare's *Andantino in D-flat* (1888) with lyrics by Ben Black and Charles Daniels; "Stardust" (1927), composition by Hoagy Carmichael with lyrics added later by Mitchell Parish; "Blue Moon" (1934), song by Richard Rodgers and Lorenz Hart; "Happy Days Are Here Again" (1929), song by Milton Ager and Jack Yellen; "Stormy Weather" (1933), song by Harold Arlen and Ted Koehler.

166.23   you're rocking my dreamboat] The pop song "Someone's Rocking My Dreamboat," written by Leon and Otis Rene and Emerson Scott, was a hit in the early 1940s for several recording artists, including Artie Shaw with vocalist Paula Kelly.

170.8   the husks that the swine did eat] See Luke 15:16.

170.29   Dwight Troy] Troy ran afoul of Archer in *The Moving Target*.

203.11   Tehachapi] California Correctional Institution, located near Tehachapi in Southern California.

THE BARBAROUS COAST

215.1   *Stanley Tenny*] Psychiatric social worker with whom Millar visited juvenile halls and state hospitals (including Camarillo: see note 305.5) in the early weeks of 1954.

223.5   Neutraesque] In the style of Vienna-born Southern California architect Richard Neutra (1892–1970).

225.12   Joshua Severn] In *The Way Some People Die*, radio producer encountered by Archer.

226.29   Calpurnia] Julius Caesar's third wife. In Plutarch's *Life of Caesar*, he is said to have stated that "Caesar's wife ought to be above suspicion" when divorcing his second wife Pompeia for her involvement in a scandal.

230.8   Southern California Blue Book] Social register.

238.27   "The life you save may be your own."] Highway safety slogan.

248.22   San Berdoo] San Bernardino.

250.19   muscadoodle] Muscatel.

251.2   *bracero*] See note 100.32.

253.16   *Grand battement, s'il vous plaît. Non, non*, grand *battement*.] The teacher is calling for an extreme ballet movement in which the dancer lifts one leg very high from the floor.

254.25   *Pas trop*.] French: Not too much.

256.3   *apache*] Member of one of the violent Parisian gangs of the Belle Époque; they were noted for their characteristic attire and style of dancing.

260.22   *Salammbô*] Historical novel (1862) by Gustave Flaubert (1821–1880).

261.5   Brando] Marlon Brando (1924–2004), stage and screen actor.

276.22   Ninety-nine and forty-four one-hundredths] Allusion to the Ivory Soap slogan "99 and 44/100ths % pure."

285.8   Mizener Spanish] California-born architect Addison Mizner (1872–1933) popularized Mediterranean Revival and Spanish Colonial Revival styles in south Florida and Southern California.

288.30   Sunset Limited] Southern Pacific Railroad train running from New Orleans to Los Angeles.

289.5   Forest Lawn] Cemetery in Glendale, California.

289.5   Elysian fields] In Greek mythology, afterlife abode of those blessed by the gods.

305.5   Camarillo] Camarillo State Mental Hospital, which closed in 1997.

305.24   Siegel] Benjamin "Bugsy" Siegel (1906–1947), gangster who was a founder of Murder Inc. and a principal developer of the Las Vegas Strip. He was shot dead in Beverly Hills.

305.24–25   Kefauver hearings] Senator Estes Kefauver (1903–1963) chaired a committee investigating organized crime, 1950–51; the hearings were televised and attracted a wide audience.

306.8   St. John's Hospital] Located in Santa Monica, near Westwood.

311.23–24   Atmos clock] Swiss-manufactured mechanical clock drawing energy from atmospheric changes, thus needing no winding.

312.21   the Miracle Mile] A section of Wilshire Boulevard.

313.1   Jack Dempsey] Boxer (1895–1983) who was World Heavyweight Champion, 1919–1926.

323.1   *galère*] French: galley. The line echoes a passage in Molière's *Les Fourberies de Scapin* (1671): *"Mais que diable est-il allé faire dans cette galère?"* (But what the devil was he doing in that galley?")

325.31   Matho] In Flaubert's *Salammbô*, the leader of the rebellious mercenaries, who is tortured and executed at the novel's conclusion.

335.9   "Someone to Watch Over Me"] Song (1926) by George and Ira Gershwin.

340.32–33   *mens sana in corpore sano*] Latin: a sound mind in a sound body.

355.11   Lethe] In Greek mythology, a river in Hades whose waters, when drunk, erase memory.

358.34–35   Man of distinction] "Men of distinction" was a catchphrase used in advertisements for Lord Calvert Whiskey.

361.20   Cuchulain the Hound of Ulster] Hero in Irish mythology.

401.2   Anastasia] Albert Anastasia (1902–1957), mob boss associated with Murder Inc. and the Gambino crime family; he was assassinated in the barbershop of the Park Sheraton Hotel in New York.

401.9–10   Lepke . . . Game Boy Miller . . . Lefty Clark . . . Trans America] Louis "Lepke" Buchalter (1897–1944), hit man and head of Murder Inc.; Samuel "Game Boy" Miller, gambling racketeer in Cleveland; Harry "Lefty" Clark, associate of Florida mobster Santo Trafficante Jr.; Trans America, illegal wire service operated in California by Bugsy Siegel (see note 305.24).

402.11   Camarillo] See note 305.5.

408.10   Augean stables] In Greek mythology, the fifth labor of Hercules was to clean the stables of Augeas, king of Elis, which he accomplished by diverting two rivers.

THE DOOMSTERS

501.15   white *bouclé* oblong] Low backless sofa covered in nubby yarn fabric.

520.5   Keystone cop] One of the comically inept policemen featured in silent comedies produced by Mack Sennett for Keystone Film Company, 1912–17.

527.25–26   LaGuardia . . . a beaut] In 1941, New York mayor Fiorello LaGuardia (1882–1947), acknowledging that a judge he opposed was his own appointee, remarked: "When I make a mistake, it's a beaut."

541.33   Somebody down here hates me.] *Somebody Up There Likes Me*, the autobiography of boxer Rocky Graziano, was a best seller in 1955, and was adapted a year later into a film starring Paul Newman.

544.31–32   Every day . . . badder and badder] The self-motivational phrase "Every day, in every way, I'm getting better and better" was popularized by French inspirational psychologist Émile Coué (1857–1926).

548.1   green stamps] Trading stamps dispensed with purchases at gas stations, supermarkets, and other stores and redeemable for catalog merchandise.

556.16   "The deep tangled wildwood,"] See Samuel Woodworth's popular poem "The Bucket" (or "The Old Oaken Bucket"), published in 1818: "How dear to this heart are the scenes of my childhood, / When fond recollection presents them to view: / The orchard, the meadow, the deep-tangled wildwood, / And ev'ry loved spot which my infancy knew."

556.34   Simon Legree] Cruel slave owner in Harriet Beecher Stowe's *Uncle Tom's Cabin* (1852).

570.2   "Sentimental Journey."] Popular song (1944) by Les Brown, Ben Homer, and Bud Green.

577.23–24   'The fathers have eaten . . . set on edge.'] See Ezekiel 18:2.

611.27   See Laurence Sterne, *A Sentimental Journey* (1768): "God tempers the wind . . . to the shorn lamb." The notion is proverbial.

627.29–31   'Sleep the long sleep . . . around us here . . .'] See Thomas Hardy's "To an Unborn Pauper Child" (1901), stanza 1: "Breathe not, hid Heart; cease silently, / And though thy birth-hour beckons thee, / Sleep the long sleep: / The Doomsters heap / Travails and teens around us here, / And Time-wraiths turn our songsingings to fear."

629.13   in Africa like Schweitzer] Albert Schweitzer (1875–1965), theologian and musician, founded a hospital in West Africa, in what is now Gabon, in 1913.

647.21   Sue] Archer's ex-wife.

THE GALTON CASE

651.1 *John E. Smith*] Santa Barbara city librarian; later, founding librarian at University of California at Irvine, and creator there of the Kenneth and Margaret Millar Collections of books and manuscripts.

653.10–11 Audubon prints] Reproductions from *The Birds of America* (1827–38) by John James Audubon (1785–1851).

653.12 Harvard chair] Wooden armchair modeled on nineteenth-century design originally made for Harvard's Freshman Dining Hall.

660.29 pre-Mizener] See note 285.8.

674.1 Paul Klee] German-Swiss painter (1879–1940).

675.3 Praxiteles Hermes] Statue of the god Hermes and the infant Dionysos, discovered at the Temple of Hera at Olympia, Greece, in 1877, and attributed by some to the fourth century BCE sculptor Praxiteles.

676.15–16 Rimbaud's theory . . . the senses] In a May 15, 1871, letter to Paul Demeny, Arthur Rimbaud (1854–1891) wrote: "The poet makes himself a *seer* by an immense, long, deliberate *derangement* of all the senses."

676.19 Charles Baudelaire] French poet (1821–1867).

677.9 John Brown] Abolitionist (1800–1859), executed after his failed insurrectionist attack on the federal armory at Harpers Ferry, Virginia.

679.26 *Pendennis*] *The History of Pendennis* (1848–50), novel by William Makepeace Thackeray (1811–1863), concerning a young man trying to find his place in the world.

682.33 Captain Nemo] Fictional submarine commander in Jules Verne's *Twenty Thousand Leagues under the Sea* (1870), filmed by Walt Disney in 1954.

689.23 Tanforan] Racetrack at San Bruno, California, 1899–1964.

692.5 gestalt] German: shape or form; a central term in gestalt psychology.

692.10 Bix Beiderbecke] Jazz cornet player, pianist, and composer (1903–1931).

692.11 Eurydice] In Greek mythology, the musician Orpheus descends to the underworld realm of Pluto in a vain attempt to bring back his wife, Eurydice, from the dead.

699.14 The Listening Ear] Allusion to the hungry i, one of San Francisco's hippest nightclubs at the time.

700.8 the Orpheum circuit] Chain of vaudeville and later movie theaters, 1886–1927.

703.3–4 The Greek navy . . . launching ships.] See Christopher Marlowe, *The Tragical History of Doctor Faustus* (1604): "Was this the face that launch'd a thousand ships?"

723.6–8   Webster ... beneath the skin."] See T. S. Eliot's "Whispers of Immortality" (1919), stanza 1: "Webster was much possessed by death / And saw the skull beneath the skin; / And breastless creatures under ground / Leaned backward with a lipless grin."

735.31   *Saturday Review*] Weekly magazine devoted to literature and culture.

737.23–24   Y. A. Tittle ... Hugh McElhenny.] Tittle (b. 1926), football star who played for the New York Giants and other teams; McElhenny (b. 1928), football running back who played for the New York Giants, the Detroit Lions, and other teams.

757.15   *Dramas of Modernism*] *Dramas of Modernism and Their Forerunners* (1933), edited by Montrose J. Moses, textbook anthology including such plays as Chekhov's *The Cherry Orchard*, Maugham's *The Circle*, and O'Neill's *Desire Under the Elms*.

762.32–33   Epstein bronze] The work of American-born English sculptor Sir Jacob Epstein (1880–1959) was known for its rough-hewn quality.

765.37–38   a tune about a little Spanish town] "In a Little Spanish Town" (1926), song by Mabel Wayne, Sam Lewis, and Joe Young, popularized by Paul Whiteman.

778.21   "fell among thieves."] See Luke 10:30.

801.22   The laborer is worthy of his hire.] See Timothy 5:18.

806.18   *Hobson's Choice*] Play (1915) by Harold Brighouse (1882–1958).

810.38   Barkis was willing.] In Charles Dickens's *David Copperfield* (1850), Mr. Barkis indicates his wish to marry Peggotty with the message "Barkis is willing."

843.39–40   tempering ... shorn lamb.] See note 611.27.

OTHER WRITINGS

861.7   *The Convenient Corpse*] The author's original title for the book in question, a non-Archer novel with a probation officer protagonist, was "Message from Hell." Pocket Books suggested "The Convenient Corpse." The book was published by Knopf in 1953 as *Meet Me at the Morgue* (and in England, in 1954, as *Experience with Evil*.)

862.5   Chandler] Crime novelist Raymond Chandler (1888–1959).

862.34   Hammett] Crime novelist Dashiell Hammett (1894–1961).

863.2   *Blue City*] The novel was published under the name Kenneth Millar by Alfred A. Knopf in 1947.

863.17   Spillane] Mickey Spillane (1918–2006), crime novelist whose novels, which sold many millions of copies, include *I, the Jury* (1947), *My Gun Is Quick* (1950), and *Vengeance Is Mine!* (1950).

864.16–17 overused device . . . with a gun.] In his essay "The Simple Art of Murder" (1950), Raymond Chandler wrote: "When in doubt have a man come through a door with a gun in his hand."

864.39 *Dragnet*] The police procedural series *Dragnet*, starring Jack Webb as Sergeant Joe Friday, ran on radio from 1949 to 1957, and on television from 1951 to 1959. It was later revived, 1967–70, and also served as the basis for three feature films.

867.1 William Carlos Williams . . . profound essay] "Edgar Allan Poe," in *In the American Grain* (1925).

868.28–29 Anthony Boucher] Editor and fiction writer (1911–1968) who was a prolific reviewer of crime fiction and an early supporter of Macdonald's work.

869.12 *Black Mask*] Pulp magazine (1920–1951), originally edited by H. L. Mencken and George Jean Nathan. Under the editorship of Joseph Thompson Shaw, 1926–36, it published the work of Dashiell Hammett, Raymond Chandler, Paul Cain, Frederick Nebel, Raoul Whitfield, and other notable crime writers of the hard-boiled school.

869.14 S. S. Van Dine] Pseudonym of Willard Huntington Wright (1888–1939), author of a series of detective novels featuring Philo Vance, beginning with *The Benson Murder Case* (1926).

870.15 Zenith] Fictional midwestern city, the setting for *Babbitt* (1922) and other novels by Sinclair Lewis (1885–1951).

871.17–18 H. L. Mencken . . . vernacular] Mencken (1880–1956), journalist and editor, was a founding co-editor of *Black Mask*, but sold his interest in the magazine after the first eight issues. His pioneering study *The American Language: An Inquiry into the Development of English in the United States* was published in 1919; Mencken subsequently revised and expanded it, and issued two lengthy supplements.

871.19 James M. Cain] Novelist (1892–1977), author of *The Postman Always Rings Twice* (1934), *Mildred Pierce* (1941), and other works.

876.25 Pearl White] Movie actress (1889–1938) who starred in the serial *The Perils of Pauline* (1914).

876.30 when Warner Brothers made it into one] *Harper* (1966), directed by Jack Smight and starring Paul Newman, Lauren Bacall, and Julie Harris.

877.4 Mike Avallone] Michael Avallone (1924–1999), prolific writer of crime novels and other genre fiction.

878.2 Donald Davie] English poet and critic (1922–1995).

878.17 *Divorce American Style*] Film (1967) directed by Bud Yorkin and written by Norman Lear, starring Dick Van Dyke and Debbie Reynolds.

880.6–7   *The Three Roads . . . Oedipus Tyrannus*] In his 1948 novel, Macdonald quotes this passage from Sophocles' drama: "For now I am discovered vile, and of the vile. O ye three roads, and thou concealed dell, and oaken copse, and narrow outlet of three ways, which drank my own blood."

881.36–37   Flaubert . . . Madame Bovary] In a 1909 biography by René Descharnes, Gustave Flaubert was reported to have said of the protagonist of his 1856 novel: "*Madame Bovary, c'est moi!*"

881.37–38   William Styron . . . Nat Turner] Styron's novel *The Confessions of Nat Turner* was published in 1967.

886.35   Brigid Brophy] British novelist and critic (1929–1995). Her essay "Detective Fiction: A Modern Myth of Violence?" was published in *The Hudson Review* (Spring 1965).

891.4–5   Lewis's *The Monk*] *The Monk: A Romance* (1796), Gothic novel by Matthew Gregory Lewis (1775–1818).

891.6–14   *The Ancient Mariner . . . Christabel*] The long narrative poem "The Rime of the Ancient Mariner" by Samuel Taylor Coleridge (1772–1834) was published in the first edition of *Lyrical Ballads* (1798); the first part of the unfinished "Christabel" appeared in 1816.

891.32–33   Marshall McLuhan and Hugh Kenner] McLuhan (1911–1980), Canadian philosopher, author of *Understanding Media* (1964); Kenner (1923–2003), Canadian literary critic, author of *The Pound Era* (1971) and other studies. Both were friends of Macdonald.

893.25–26   *Civis Romanus sum.*] Latin: I am a citizen of Rome.

894.38–39   Mrs. Radcliffe's *Mysteries of Udolpho*] Four-volume novel (1794) by Ann Radcliffe (1764–1823).

895.2   *Northanger Abbey*] Catherine Morland, the protagonist of Jane Austen's novel (published posthumously in 1817), is deeply influenced by her reading of *Mysteries of Udolpho*.

*This book is set in 10 point ITC Galliard, a
face designed for digital composition by Matthew Carter
and based on the sixteenth-century face Granjon. The paper
is acid-free lightweight opaque and meets the requirements for
permanence of the American National Standards Institute.
The binding material is Brillianta, a woven rayon cloth
made by Van Heek–Scholco Textielfabrieken, Holland.
Composition by Publishers' Design and Production Services, Inc.
Printing and binding by Edwards Brothers Malloy, Ann Arbor.
Designed by Bruce Campbell.*

THE LIBRARY OF AMERICA SERIES

The Library of America fosters appreciation and pride in America's literary heritage by publishing, and keeping permanently in print, authoritative editions of America's best and most significant writing. An independent nonprofit organization, it was founded in 1979 with seed funding from the National Endowment for the Humanities and the Ford Foundation.

To subscribe to the series or to order individual copies, please visit www.loa.org or call (800) 964-5778.